BY BLOOD
WE LIVE

Other Anthologies by John Joseph Adams

Federations
Seeds of Change
The Living Dead
Wastelands: Stories of the Apocalypse

Forthcoming Anthologies

Brave New Worlds
The Improbable Adventures of Sherlock Holmes
The Living Dead 2
The Mad Scientist's Guide to World Domination
The Way of the Wizard

BY BLOOD
WE LIVE

edited by John Joseph Adams

NIGHT SHADE BOOKS
SAN FRANCISCO

First Edition

ISBN 978-1-59780-156-0

Night Shade Books
Please visit us on the web at
http://www.nightshadebooks.com

CONTENTS

INTRODUCTION

by John Joseph Adams

How do we define the vampire? Are they barely animated corpses, of a horrific visage, killing indiscriminately? Or are they suave, charismatic symbols of sexual repression in the Victorian era? Do they die in sunlight, or does it only make them itch a little, or, God forbid, sparkle? Do crosses and holy symbols work at repelling them, or is that just a superstition from the old times? Are they born, or made by other vampires? And anyway, are these vampires created through scientific means, such as genetic research or a virus, or are they the magical kind? Can they transform into bats? Or are they stuck in the appearance they had when they were turned? Are we talking the traditional Eastern European vampire, or something more exotic, like the Tagalog mandurugo, a pretty girl during the day, and a winged, mosquito-like monstrosity by night? Do they even drink blood, or are they some kind of psychic vampire, more directly attacking the life-force of their victims?

Vampire stories come from our myths, but their origins are quite diverse. Stories of the dead thirsting for human life have existed for thousands of years, although the most common version we speak of in popular culture originated in eighteenth-century Eastern Europe. Why is the notion of the dead risen to prey on the living such an omnipresent myth across so many cultures?

Perhaps the myth of the vampire comes from a little bit of projection on the part of the living. We have a hard time imagining our existence after death, and it may be easier to imagine a life that goes on somehow. But what kind of life would a corpse live? Our ancestors were intimately familiar with decomposition, even if they didn't precisely understand it. If I were dead, I know I would have a certain fixation for living things. And perhaps I might, finding death an unagreeable state, attempt to steal from the living some essence that defines the barrier between the living and death. Blood stands in for the notion of life easily enough. Now I just have to get that essence inside of me somehow, hmm… slurp.

Or perhaps there's a darker, more insidious reason for the pervasiveness of the vampire story. Is there some kernel of universal truth behind all these stories? Many of the tales included here will offer their own explanations for the stories and myths. Because if there's one thing we love almost as much as vampires themselves, it's exploring their true natures. With the wealth of material accumulated on the nasty bloodsuckers, no two authors approach the vampire myth in quite the same way. The commonality of the vampire's story means their tales can take place in any time and in any place. The backdrop changes, and the details too, but always, underneath it all, there is blood. All draw from those dark, fearful histories, but provide their own fresh take, each like a rare blood type, to be sought by connoisseurs such as yourself.

Hear again one of our oldest and most well-known fairy tales from a new, darker perspective in Neil Gaiman's "Snow, Glass, Apples." And just who is the mysterious Tribute in Elizabeth Bear's "House of the Rising Sun"? He seems so familiar... Visit the Philippines in Gabriela Lee's "Hunger," and see the world from the eyes of a creature of decidedly non-European origin. If that is not exotic enough for your tastes, then travel into the future and beyond with Ken Macleod's "Undead Again."

Is your thirst still not satisfied? Hunt through these pages for stories by authors such as Stephen King, Joe Hill, Kelley Armstrong, Lilith Saintcrow, Carrie Vaughn, Harry Turtledove, and many more. There is a feast here to be had. Drink deeply.

SNOW, GLASS, APPLES

by Neil Gaiman

Neil Gaiman is the bestselling author of *American Gods, Coraline,* and *Anansi Boys,* among many other novels. His most recent novel, *The Graveyard Book,* won the prestigious Newbery Medal, given to great works of children's literature. In addition to his novel-writing, Gaiman is also the writer of the popular *Sandman* comic book series, and has done work in television and film.

The story of Snow White is best known from the 1937 Disney animated feature, which is about seven lovable dwarfs with names like Happy and Bashful. Gaiman's take on that tale is new, but in a way it's also old. For long ago, before Disney Disneyfied it, the story of Snow White was told to children—children who would almost certainly die before reaching adulthood, and whose parents couldn't afford to be so delicate about the cruelties of the world. It was a tale in which a woman's feet are shoved into burning hot iron shoes so that she is forced to dance until she falls down dead.

This story harkens back to that earlier, darker tradition… and then takes it a few steps farther. Mutilation, pedophilia, necrophilia. This definitely isn't Disney.

I do not know what manner of thing she is. None of us do. She killed her mother in the birthing, but that's never enough to account for it.

They call me wise, but I am far from wise, for all that I foresaw fragments of it, frozen moments caught in pools of water or in the cold glass of my mirror. If I were wise I would not have tried to change what I saw. If I were wise I would have killed myself before ever I encountered her, before ever I caught him.

Wise, and a witch, or so they said, and I'd seen his face in my dreams and in reflections for all my life: sixteen years of dreaming of him before he reined his horse by the bridge that morning, and asked my name. He helped me onto his high horse and we rode together to my little cottage, my face buried in the gold of his hair. He asked for the best of what I had; a king's right, it was.

His beard was red-bronze in the morning light, and I knew him, not as a king, for I knew nothing of kings then, but as my love. He took all he wanted from me, the right of kings, but he returned to me on the following day, and on the night after that: his beard so red, his hair so gold, his eyes the blue of a summer sky, his skin tanned the gentle brown of ripe wheat.

His daughter was only a child: no more than five years of age when I came to the palace. A portrait of her dead mother hung in the princess's tower room; a tall woman, hair the colour of dark wood, eyes nut-brown. She was of a different blood to her pale daughter.

The girl would not eat with us.

I do not know where in the palace she ate.

I had my own chambers. My husband the king, he had his own rooms also. When he wanted me he would send for me, and I would go to him, and pleasure him, and take my pleasure with him.

One night, several months after I was brought to the palace, she came to my rooms. She was six. I was embroidering by lamplight, squinting my eyes against the lamp's smoke and fitful illumination. When I looked up, she was there.

"Princess?"

She said nothing. Her eyes were black as coal, black as her hair; her lips were redder than blood. She looked up at me and smiled. Her teeth seemed sharp, even then, in the lamplight.

"What are you doing away from your room?"

"I'm hungry," she said, like any child.

It was winter, when fresh food is a dream of warmth and sunlight; but I had strings of whole apples, cored and dried, hanging from the beams of my chamber, and I pulled an apple down for her.

"Here."

Autumn is the time of drying, of preserving, a time of picking apples, of rendering the goose fat. Winter is the time of hunger, of snow, and of death; and it is the time of the midwinter feast, when we rub the goose-fat into the skin of a whole pig, stuffed with that autumn's apples, then we roast it or spit it, and we prepare to feast upon the crackling.

She took the dried apple from me and began to chew it with her sharp yellow teeth.

"Is it good?"

She nodded. I had always been scared of the little princess, but at that moment I warmed to her and, with my fingers, gently, I stroked her cheek. She looked at me and smiled—she smiled but rarely—then she sank her teeth into the base of my thumb, the Mound of Venus, and she drew blood.

I began to shriek, from pain and from surprise; but she looked at me and I fell silent.

The little princess fastened her mouth to my hand and licked and sucked and drank. When she was finished, she left my chamber. Beneath my gaze the cut that she had made began to close, to scab, and to heal. The next day it was an old scar: I might have cut my hand with a pocket-knife in my childhood.

I had been frozen by her, owned and dominated. That scared me, more than the blood she had fed on. After that night I locked my chamber door at dusk, barring it with an oaken pole, and I had the smith forge iron bars, which he placed across my windows.

My husband, my love, my king, sent for me less and less, and when I came to him he was dizzy, listless, confused. He could no longer make love as a man makes love; and he would not permit me to pleasure him with my mouth: the one time I tried, he started, violently, and began to weep. I pulled my mouth away and held him tightly, until the sobbing had stopped, and he slept, like a child.

I ran my fingers across his skin as he slept. It was covered in a multitude of ancient scars. But I could recall no scars from the days of our courtship, save one, on his side, where a boar had gored him when he was a youth.

Soon he was a shadow of the man I had met and loved by the bridge. His bones showed, blue and white, beneath his skin. I was with him at the last: his hands were cold as stone, his eyes milky-blue, his hair and beard faded and lustreless and limp. He died unshriven, his skin nipped and pocked from head to toe with tiny, old scars.

He weighed near to nothing. The ground was frozen hard, and we could dig no grave for him, so we made a cairn of rocks and stones above his body, as a memorial only, for there was little enough of him left to protect from the hunger of the beasts and the birds.

So I was queen.

And I was foolish, and young—eighteen summers had come and gone since first I saw daylight—and I did not do what I would do, now.

If it were today, I would have her heart cut out, true. But then I would have her head and arms and legs cut off. I would have them disembowel her. And then I would watch, in the town square, as the hangman heated the fire to white-heat with bellows, watch unblinking as he consigned each part of her to the fire. I would have archers around the square, who would shoot any bird or animal who came close to the flames, any raven or dog or hawk or rat. And I would not close my eyes until the princess was ash, and a gentle wind could scatter her like snow.

I did not do this thing, and we pay for our mistakes.

They say I was fooled; that it was not her heart. That it was the heart of an animal—a stag, perhaps, or a boar. They say that, and they are wrong.

And some say (but it is her lie, not mine) that I was given the heart, and that I ate it. Lies and half-truths fall like snow, covering the things that I remember, the things I saw. A landscape, unrecognisable after a snowfall; that is what she has made of my life.

There were scars on my love, her father's thighs, and on his ballock-pouch, and on his male member, when he died.

I did not go with them. They took her in the day, while she slept, and was at her weakest. They took her to the heart of the forest, and there they opened her blouse, and they cut out her heart, and they left her dead, in a gully, for the forest to swallow.

The forest is a dark place, the border to many kingdoms; no one would be foolish enough to claim jurisdiction over it. Outlaws live in the forest. Robbers live in the forest, and so do wolves. You can ride through the forest for a dozen days and never see a soul; but there are eyes upon you the entire time.

They brought me her heart. I know it was hers—no sow's heart or doe's would have continued to beat and pulse after it had been cut out, as that one did.

I took it to my chamber.

I did not eat it: I hung it from the beams above my bed, placed it on a length of twine that I strung with rowan-berries, orange-red as a robin's breast; and with bulbs of garlic.

Outside, the snow fell, covering the footprints of my huntsmen, covering her tiny body in the forest where it lay.

I had the smith remove the iron bars from my windows, and I would spend some time in my room each afternoon through the short winter days, gazing out over the forest, until darkness fell.

There were, as I have already stated, people in the forest. They would come out, some of them, for the Spring Fair: a greedy, feral, dangerous people; some were stunted—dwarfs and midgets and hunchbacks; others had the huge teeth and vacant gazes of idiots; some had fingers like flippers or crab-claws. They would creep out of the forest each year for the Spring Fair, held when the snows had melted.

As a young lass I had worked at the fair, and they had scared me then, the forest folk. I told fortunes for the fairgoers, scrying in a pool of still water; and, later, when I was older, in a disc of polished glass, its back all silvered—a gift from a merchant whose straying horse I had seen in a pool of ink.

The stallholders at the fair were afraid of the forest folk; they would nail their wares to the bare boards of their stalls—slabs of gingerbread or leather belts were nailed with great iron nails to the wood. If their wares were not nailed, they said, the forest folk would take them, and run away, chewing on the stolen gingerbread, flailing about them with the belts.

The forest folk had money, though: a coin here, another there, sometimes stained green by time or the earth, the face on the coin unknown to even the oldest of us. Also they had things to trade, and thus the fair continued, serving the outcasts and the dwarfs, serving the robbers (if they were circumspect) who preyed on the rare travellers from lands beyond the forest, or on gypsies, or on the deer. (This was robbery in the eyes of the law. The deer were the queen's.)

The years passed by slowly, and my people claimed that I ruled them with wisdom. The heart still hung above by bed, pulsing gently in the night. If there were any who mourned the child, I saw no evidence: she was a thing of terror, back then, and they believed themselves well rid of her.

Spring Fair followed Spring Fair: five of them, each sadder, poorer, shoddier than the one before. Fewer of the forest folk came out of the forest to buy. Those who did seemed subdued and listless. The stallholders stopped nailing their wares to the boards of their stalls. And by the fifth year but a handful of folk came from the forest—a fearful huddle of little hairy men, and no one else.

The Lord of the Fair, and his page, came to me when the fair was done. I had known him slightly, before I was queen.

"I do not come to you as my queen," he said.

I said nothing. I listened.

"I come to you because you are wise," he continued. "When you were a child you found a strayed foal by staring into a pool of ink; when you were a maiden you found a lost infant who had wandered far from her mother, by staring into that mirror of yours. You know secrets and you can seek out things hidden. My queen," he asked, "what is taking the forest folk? Next year there will be no Spring Fair. The travellers from other kingdoms have grown scarce and few, the folk of the forest are almost gone. Another year like the last, and we shall all starve."

I commanded my maidservant to bring me my looking-glass. It was a simple thing, a silver-backed glass disc, which I kept wrapped in a doe-skin, in a chest, in my chamber.

They brought it to me, then, and I gazed into it:

She was twelve and she was no longer a little child. Her skin was still pale, her eyes and hair coal-black, her lips as red as blood. She wore the clothes she had worn when she left the castle for the last time—the blouse, the skirt—although they were much let-out, much mended. Over them she wore a leather cloak, and instead of boots she had leather bags, tied with thongs, over her tiny feet.

She was standing in the forest, beside a tree.

As I watched, in the eye of my mind, I saw her edge and step and flitter and pad from tree to tree, like an animal: a bat or a wolf. She was following someone.

He was a monk. He wore sackcloth, and his feet were bare, and scabbed and hard. His beard and tonsure were of a length, overgrown, unshaven.

She watched him from behind the trees. Eventually he paused for the night, and began to make a fire, laying twigs down, breaking up a robin's nest as kindling. He had a tinder-box in his robe, and he knocked the flint against the steel until the sparks caught the tinder and the fire flamed. There had been two eggs in the nest he had found, and these he ate, raw. They cannot have been much of a meal for so big a man.

He sat there in the firelight, and she came out from her hiding place. She crouched down on the other side of the fire, and stared at him. He grinned, as if it were a long time since he had seen another human, and beckoned her over to him.

She stood up and walked around the fire, and waited, an arm's-length away. He pulled in his robe until he found a coin—a tiny, copper penny—and tossed it to her. She caught it, and nodded, and went to him. He pulled at the rope around his waist, and his robe swung open. His body was as hairy as a bear's. She pushed him back onto the moss. One hand crept, spider-like, through the tangle of hair, until it closed on his manhood; the other hand traced a circle on his left nipple. He closed his eyes, and fumbled one huge hand under her skirt. She lowered her mouth to the nipple she had been teasing, her smooth skin white on the furry brown body of him.

She sank her teeth deep into his breast. His eyes opened, then they closed again, and she drank.

She straddled him, and she fed. As she did so a thin blackish liquid began to dribble from between her legs...

"Do you know what is keeping the travellers from our town? What is happening to the forest people?" asked the Head of the Fair.

I covered the mirror in doe-skin, and told him that I would personally take it upon myself to make the forest safe once more.

I had to, although she terrified me. I was the queen.

A foolish woman would have gone then into the forest and tried to capture the creature; but I had been foolish once and had no wish to be so a second time.

I spent time with old books, for I could read a little. I spent time with the gypsy women (who passed through our country across the mountains to the south, rather than cross the forest to the north and the west).

I prepared myself, and obtained those things I would need, and when the first snows began to fall, then I was ready.

Naked, I was, and alone in the highest tower of the palace, a place open to the sky. The winds chilled my body; goose-pimples crept across my arms and thighs and breasts. I carried a silver basin, and a basket in which I had placed a silver knife, a silver pin, some tongs, a grey robe and three green apples.

I put them down and stood there, unclothed, on the tower, humble before the night sky and the wind. Had any man seen me standing there, I would have had his eyes; but there was no-one to spy. Clouds scudded across the sky, hiding and uncovering the waning moon.

I took the silver knife, and slashed my left arm—once, twice, three times. The blood dripped into the basin, scarlet seeming black in the moonlight.

I added the powder from the vial that hung around my neck. It was a brown dust, made of dried herbs and the skin of a particular toad, and from certain other things. It thickened the blood, while preventing it from clotting.

I took the three apples, one by one, and pricked their skins gently with my silver pin. Then I placed the apples in the silver bowl, and let them sit there while the first tiny flakes of snow of the year fell slowly onto my skin, and onto the apples, and onto the blood.

When dawn began to brighten the sky I covered myself with the grey cloak, and took the red apples from the silver bowl, one by one, lifting each into my basket with silver tongs, taking care not to touch it. There was nothing left of my blood or of the brown powder in the silver bowl, save nothing save a black residue, like a verdigris, on the inside.

I buried the bowl in the earth. Then I cast a glamour on the apples (as once, years before, by a bridge, I had cast a glamour on myself), that they were, beyond any doubt, the most wonderful apples in the world; and the crimson blush of their skins was the warm colour of fresh blood.

I pulled the hood of my cloak low over my face, and I took ribbons and pretty hair ornaments with me, placed them above the apples in the reed basket, and I walked alone into the forest, until I came to her dwelling: a high, sandstone cliff, laced with deep caves going back a way into the rock wall.

There were trees and boulders around the cliff-face, and I walked quietly and gently from tree to tree, without disturbing a twig or a fallen leaf. Eventually I found my place to hide, and I waited, and I watched.

After some hours a clutch of dwarfs crawled out of the cave-front—ugly, misshapen, hairy little men, the old inhabitants of this country. You saw them seldom now.

They vanished into the wood, and none of them spied me, though one of them stopped to piss against the rock I hid behind.

I waited. No more came out.

I went to the cave entrance and hallooed into it, in a cracked old voice.

The scar on my Mound of Venus throbbed and pulsed as she came towards me, out of the darkness, naked and alone.

She was thirteen years of age, my stepdaughter, and nothing marred the perfect whiteness of her skin save for the livid scar on her left breast, where her heart had been cut from her long since.

The insides of her thighs were stained with wet black filth.

She peered at me, hidden, as I was, in my cloak. She looked at me hungrily. "Ribbons, goodwife," I croaked. "Pretty ribbons for your hair…"

She smiled and beckoned to me. A tug; the scar on my hand was pulling me towards her. I did what I had planned to do, but I did it more readily than I had planned: I dropped my basket, and screeched like the bloodless old pedlar woman I was pretending to be, and I ran.

My grey cloak was the colour of the forest, and I was fast; she did not catch me.

I made my way back to the palace.

I did not see it. Let us imagine though, the girl returning, frustrated and hungry, to her cave, and finding my fallen basket on the ground.

What did she do?

I like to think she played first with the ribbons, twined them into her raven hair, looped them around her pale neck or her tiny waist.

And then, curious, she moved the cloth to see what else was in the basket; and she saw the red, red apples.

They smelled like fresh apples, of course; and they also smelled of blood. And she was hungry. I imagine her picking up an apple, pressing it against her cheek, feeling the cold smoothness of it against her skin.

And she opened her mouth and bit deep into it…

By the time I reached my chambers, the heart that hung from the roof-beam, with the apples and hams and the dried sausages, had ceased to beat. It hung there, quietly, without motion or life, and I felt safe once more.

That winter the snows were high and deep, and were late melting. We were all hungry come the spring.

The Spring Fair was slightly improved that year. The forest folk were few, but they were there, and there were travellers from the lands beyond the forest.

I saw the little hairy men of the forest-cave buying and bargaining for pieces of glass, and lumps of crystal and of quartz-rock. They paid for the glass with silver coins—the spoils of my stepdaughter's depredations, I had no doubt. When it got about what they were buying, townsfolk rushed back to their homes, came back with their lucky crystals, and, in a few cases, with whole sheets of glass.

I thought, briefly, about having them killed, but I did not. As long as the heart hung, silent and immobile and cold, from the beam of my chamber, I was safe, and so were the folk of the forest, and, thus, eventually, the folk of the town.

My twenty-fifth year came, and my stepdaughter had eaten the poisoned fruit two winters back, when the prince came to my palace. He was tall, very tall, with cold green eyes and the swarthy skin of those from beyond the mountains.

He rode with a small retinue: large enough to defend him, small enough that another monarch—myself, for instance—would not view him as a potential threat.

I was practical: I thought of the alliance of our lands, thought of the Kingdom running from the forests all the way south to the sea; I thought of my golden-haired bearded love, dead these eight years; and, in the night, I went to the prince's room.

I am no innocent, although my late husband, who was once my king, was truly my first lover, no matter what they say.

At first the prince seemed excited. He bade me remove my shift, and made me stand in front of the opened window, far from the fire, until my skin was chilled stone-cold. Then he asked me to lie upon my back, with my hands folded across my breasts, my eyes wide open—but staring only at the beams above. He told me not to move, and to breathe as little as possible. He implored me to say nothing. He spread my legs apart.

It was then that he entered me.

As he began to thrust inside me, I felt my hips raise, felt myself begin to match him, grind for grind, push for push. I moaned. I could not help myself.

His manhood slid out of me. I reached out and touched it, a tiny, slippery thing.

"Please," he said, softly. "You must neither move, nor speak. Just lie there on the stones, so cold and so fair."

I tried, but he had lost whatever force it was that had made him virile; and, some short while later, I left the prince's room, his curses and tears still resounding in my ears.

He left early the next morning, with all his men, and they rode off into the forest.

I imagine his loins, now, as he rode, a knot of frustration at the base of his manhood. I imagine his pale lips pressed so tightly together. Then I imagine his little troupe riding through the forest, finally coming upon the glass-and-crystal cairn of my stepdaughter. So pale. So cold. Naked, beneath the glass, and little more than a girl, and dead.

In my fancy, I can almost feel the sudden hardness of his manhood inside his britches, envision the lust that took him then, the prayers he muttered beneath his breath in thanks for his good fortune. I imagine him negotiating with the little hairy men—offering them gold and spices for the lovely corpse under the crystal mound.

Did they take his gold willingly? Or did they look up to see his men on their horses, with their sharp swords and their spears, and realize they had no alternative?

I do not know. I was not there; I was not scrying. I can only imagine...

Hands, pulling off the lumps of glass and quartz from her cold body. Hands, gently caressing her cold cheek, moving her cold arm, rejoicing to find the corpse still fresh and pliable.

Did he take her there, in front of them all? Or did he have her carried to a secluded nook before he mounted her?

I cannot say.

Did he shake the apple from her throat? Or did her eyes slowly open as he pounded into her cold body; did her mouth open, those red lips part, those sharp yellow teeth close on his swarthy neck, as the blood, which is the life, trickled down her throat, washing down and away the lump of apple, my own, my poison?

I imagine; I do not know.

This I do know: I was woken in the night by her heart pulsing and beating once more. Salt blood dripped onto my face from above. I sat up. My hand burned and pounded as if I had hit the base of my thumb with a rock.

There was a hammering on the door. I felt afraid, but I am a queen, and I would not show fear. I opened the door.

First his men walked in to my chamber, and stood around me, with their sharp swords, and their long spears.

Then he came in; and he spat in my face.

Finally, she walked into my chamber, as she had when I was first a queen, and she was a child of six. She had not changed. Not really.

She pulled down the twine on which her heart was hanging. She pulled off the dried rowan-berries, one by one; pulled off the garlic bulb—now a dried thing, after all these years; then she took up her own, her pumping heart—a small thing, no larger than that of a nanny-goat or a she-bear—as it brimmed and pumped its blood into her hand.

Her fingernails must have been as sharp as glass: she opened her breast with them, running them over the purple scar. Her chest gaped, suddenly, open and bloodless. She licked her heart, once, as the blood ran over her hands, and she pushed the heart deep into her breast.

I saw her do it. I saw her close the flesh of her breast once more. I saw the purple scar begin to fade.

Her prince looked briefly concerned, but he put his arm around her nonetheless, and they stood, side by side, and they waited.

And she stayed cold, and the bloom of death remained on her lips, and his lust was not diminished in any way.

They told me they would marry, and the kingdoms would indeed be joined. They told me that I would be with them on their wedding day.

It is starting to get hot in here.

They have told the people bad things about me; a little truth to add savour to the dish, but mixed with many lies.

I was bound and kept in a tiny stone cell beneath the palace, and I remained there through the autumn. Today they fetched me out of the cell; they stripped the rags from me, and washed the filth from me, and then they shaved my head and my loins, and they rubbed my skin with goose grease.

The snow was falling as they carried me—two men at each hand, two men at each leg—utterly exposed, and spread-eagled and cold, through the midwinter crowds; and brought me to this kiln.

My stepdaughter stood there with her prince. She watched me, in my indignity, but she said nothing.

As they thrust me inside, jeering and chaffing as they did so, I saw one snowflake land upon her white cheek, and remain there without melting.

They closed the kiln-door behind me. It is getting hotter in here, and outside they are singing and cheering and banging on the sides of the kiln.

She was not laughing, or jeering, or talking. She did not sneer at me or turn away. She looked at me, though; and for a moment I saw myself reflected in her eyes.

I will not scream. I will not give them that satisfaction. They will have my body, but my soul and my story are my own, and will die with me.

The goose-grease begins to melt and glisten upon my skin. I shall make no sound at all. I shall think no more on this.

I shall think instead of the snowflake on her cheek.

I think of her hair as black as coal, her lips as red as blood, her skin, snow-white.

THE MASTER OF RAMPLING GATE

by Anne Rice

Anne Rice is the bestselling author of dozens of novels, including the books in the immensely popular Vampire Chronicles series, which began with *Interview with the Vampire*. Recently, she's turned her hand from writing about the undead, to writing about someone who died and came back to life—Jesus Christ—in her Christ the Lord series: *Out of Egypt* and *The Road to Cana*. Other notable books include *The Witching Hour* and the others in the Mayfair Witches series.

This story is the only piece of short fiction Rice has published in her career. It first appeared in *Redbook Magazine* in 1984, and demonstrates all the characteristics of her best work, and the best of vampire fiction.

In some houses, the walls bleed. There is a miasma of doom. Those who spend the night in such a house (only ever on a bet) flee screaming or are found dead the next morning. One wonders how such flashy and obstreperous houses avoid getting themselves burned to the ground by a mob of local citizens. But here is an entirely different sort of house. This house is beautiful, serene. Here everyone is smiling. So take off your coat and have a drink. Sit by the fire. Stay a while.

Rampling Gate: It was so real to us in those old pictures, rising like a fairytale castle out of its own dark wood. A wilderness of gables and chimneys between those two immense towers, grey stone walls mantled in ivy, mullioned windows reflecting the drifting clouds.

But why had Father never gone there? Why had he never taken us? And why on his deathbed, in those grim months after Mother's passing, did he tell my brother, Richard, that Rampling Gate must be torn down stone by stone? Rampling Gate that had always belonged to Ramplings, Rampling Gate which had stood for over four hundred years.

We were in awe of the task that lay before us, and painfully confused. Richard had just finished four years at Oxford. Two whirlwind social seasons in London had proven me something of a shy success. I still preferred scribbling poems and stories in the quiet of my room to dancing the night away, but I'd kept that a good secret, and though we were not spoilt children, we had enjoyed the best of everything our parents could give. But now the carefree years were ended. We had to be careful and wise.

And our hearts ached as, sitting together in Father's book-lined study, we looked at the old pictures of Rampling Gate before the small coal fire. "Destroy it, Richard, as soon as I am gone," Father had said.

"I just don't understand it, Julie," Richard confessed, as he filled the little crystal glass in my hand with sherry. "It's the genuine article, that old place, a real four-teenth-century manor house in excellent repair. A Mrs. Blessington, born and reared in the village of Rampling, has apparently managed it all these years. She was there when Uncle Baxter died, and he was the last Rampling to live under that roof."

"Do you remember," I asked, "the year that Father took all these pictures down and put them away?"

"I shall never forget that." Richard said. "How could I? It was so peculiar, and so unlike Father, too." He sat back, drawing slowly on his pipe. "There had been that bizarre incident in Victoria Station, when he had seen that young man."

"Yes, exactly," I said, snuggling back into the velvet chair and looking into the tiny dancing flames in the grate. "You remember how upset Father was?"

Yet it was a simple incident. In fact nothing really happened at all. We couldn't have been more than six and eight at the time and we had gone to the station with Father to say farewell to friends. Through the window of a train Father saw a young man who startled and upset him. I could remember the face clearly to this day. Remarkably handsome, with a narrow nose and well-drawn eyebrows, and a mop of lustrous brown hair. The large black eyes had regarded Father with the saddest expression as Father had drawn us back and hurried us away.

"And the argument that night, between Father and Mother," Richard said thought-fully. "I remember that we listened on the landing and we were so afraid."

"And Father said *he* wasn't content to be master of Rampling Gate anymore; *he* had come to London and revealed himself. An unspeakable horror, that is what he called it, that *he* should be so bold."

"Yes, exactly, and when Mother tried to quiet him, when she suggested that he was imagining things, he went into a perfect rage."

"But who could it have been, the master of Rampling Gate, if Father wasn't the master? Uncle Baxter was long dead by then."

"I just don't know what to make of it," Richard murmured. "And there's nothing in Father's papers to explain any of it at all." He examined the most recent of the pictures, a lovely tinted engraving that showed the house perfectly reflected in the azure water of its lake. "But I tell you, the worst part of it, Julie," he said shaking his head, "is that we've never even seen the house ourselves."

I glanced at him and our eyes met in a moment of confusion that quickly passed to something else. I leant forward:

"He did not say we couldn't go there, did he, Richard?" I demanded. "That we couldn't visit the house before it was destroyed."

"No, of course he didn't!" Richard said. The smile broke over his face easily. "After all, don't we owe it to the others, Julie? Uncle Baxter who spent the last of his fortune restoring the house, even this old Mrs. Blessington that has kept it all these years?"

"And what about the village itself?" I added quickly. "What will it mean to these people to see Rampling Gate destroyed? Of course we must go and see the place ourselves."

"Then it's settled. I'll write to Mrs. Blessington immediately. I'll tell her we're coming and that we can not say how long we will stay."

"Oh, Richard, that would be too marvelous!" I couldn't keep from hugging him, though it flustered him and he pulled on his pipe just exactly the way Father would have done. "Make it at least a fortnight," I said. "I want so to know the place, especially if…"

But it was too sad to think of Father's admonition. And much more fun to think of the journey itself. I'd pack my manuscripts, for who knew, maybe in that melancholy and exquisite setting I'd find exactly the inspiration I required. It was almost a wicked exhilaration I felt, breaking the gloom that had hung over us since the day that Father was laid to rest.

"It is the right thing to do, isn't it, Richard?" I asked uncertainly, a little disconcerted by how much I wanted to go. There was some illicit pleasure in it, going to Rampling Gate at last.

"'Unspeakable horror,'" I repeated Father's words with a little grimace. What did it all mean? I thought again of the strange, almost exquisite young man I'd glimpsed in that railway carriage, gazing at us all with that wistful expression on his lean face. He had worn a black greatcoat with a red woollen cravat, and I could remember how pale he had been against that dash of red. Like bone china his complexion had been. Strange to remember it so vividly, even to the tilt of his head, and that long luxuriant brown hair. But he had been a blaze against that window. And I realized now that, in those few remarkable moments, he had created for me an ideal of masculine beauty which I had never questioned since. But Father had been so angry in those moments… I felt an unmistakable pang of guilt.

"Of course it's the right thing, Julie," Richard answered. He at the desk, already writing the letters, and I was at a loss to understand the full measure of my thoughts.

It was late afternoon when the wretched old trap carried us up the gentle slope from the little railway station, and we had at last our first real look at that magnificent house. I think I was holding my breath. The sky had paled to a deep rose hue beyond a bank of softly gilded clouds, and the last rays of the sun struck the uppermost panes of the leaded windows and filled them with solid gold.

"Oh, but it's too majestic," I whispered, "too like a great cathedral, and to think that it belongs to us." Richard gave me the smallest kiss on the cheek. I felt mad suddenly and eager somehow to be laid waste by it, through fear or enchantment I could not say, perhaps a sublime mingling of both.

I wanted with all my heart to jump down and draw near on foot, letting those towers grow larger and larger above me, but our old horse had picked up speed. And the little line of stiff starched servants had broken to come forward, the old withered housekeeper with her arms out, the men to take down the boxes and the trunks.

Richard and I were spirited into the great hall by the tiny, nimble figure of Mrs. Blessington, our footfalls echoing loudly on the marble tile, our eyes dazzled by the dusty shafts of light that fell on the long oak table and its heavily carved chairs, the sombre, heavy tapestries that stirred ever so slightly against the soaring walls.

"It is an enchanted place," I cried, unable to contain myself. "Oh, Richard, we are home!" Mrs. Blessington laughed gaily, her dry hand closing tightly on mine.

Her small blue eyes regarded me with the most curiously vacant expression despite her smile. "Ramplings at Rampling Gate again, I can not tell you what a joyful day this is for me. And yes, my dear," she said as if reading my mind that very second, "I am and have been for many years, quite blind. But if you spy a thing out of place in this house, you're to tell me at once, for it would be the exception, I assure you, and not the rule." And such warmth emanated from her wrinkled little face that I adored her at once.

We found our bedchambers, the very finest in the house, well aired with snow-white linen and fires blazing cozily to dry out the damp that never left the thick walls. The small diamond pane windows opened on a glorious view of the water and the oaks that enclosed it and the few scattered lights that marked the village beyond.

That night, we laughed like children as we supped at the great oak table, our candles giving only a feeble light. And afterwards, it was a fierce battle of pocket billiards in the game room which had been Uncle Baxter's last renovation, and a little too much brandy, I fear.

It was just before I went to bed that I asked Mrs. Blessington if there had been anyone in this house since Uncle Baxter died. That had been the year 1838, almost fifty years ago, and she was already housekeeper then.

"No, my dear," she said quickly, fluffing the feather pillows. "Your father came that year as you know, but he stayed for no more than a month or two and then went on home."

"There was never a young man after that…" I pushed, but in truth I had little appetite for anything to disturb the happiness I felt. How I loved the Spartan cleanliness of this bedchamber, the stone walls bare of paper or ornament, the high luster of the walnut-paneled bed.

"A young man?" She gave an easy, almost hearty laugh as with unerring certainty of her surroundings, she lifted the poker and stirred the fire. "What a strange thing for you to ask."

I sat silent for a moment looking in the mirror, as I took the last of the pins from my hair. It fell down heavy and warm around my shoulders. It felt good, like a cloak under which I could hide. But she turned as if sensing some uneasiness in me, and drew near.

"Why do you say a young man, Miss?" she asked. Slowly, tentatively, her fingers examined the long tresses that lay over my shoulders. She took the brush from my hands.

I felt perfectly foolish telling her the story, but I managed a simplified version, somehow, our meeting unexpectedly a devilishly handsome young man whom my father in anger had later called the master of Rampling Gate.

"Handsome, was he?" she asked as she brushed out the tangles in my hair gently. It seemed she hung upon every word as I described him again.

"There were no intruders in this house, then, Mrs. Blessington?" I asked. "No mysteries to be solved…"

She gave the sweetest laugh.

"Oh, no, darling, this house is the safest place in the world," she said quickly. "It is a happy house. No intruder would dare to trouble Rampling Gate!"

Nothing, in fact, troubled the serenity of the days that followed. The smoke and noise of London, and our father's dying words, became a dream. What was real were our long walks together through the overgrown gardens, our trips in the little skiff to and fro across the lake. We had tea under the hot glass of the empty conservatory. And early evening found us on our way upstairs with the best of the books from Uncle Baxter's library to read by candlelight in the privacy of our rooms.

And all our discreet inquiries in the village met with more or less the same reply: the villagers loved the house and carried no old or disquieting tales. Repeatedly, in fact, we were told that Rampling was the most contented hamlet in all England, that no one dared—Mrs. Blessington's very words—to make trouble here.

"It's our guardian angel, that old house," said the old woman at the bookshop where Richard stopped for the London papers. "Was there ever the town of Rampling without the house called Rampling Gate?"

How were we going to tell them of Father's edict? How were we going to remind ourselves? But we spoke not one word about the proposed disaster, and Richard wrote to his firm to say that we should not be back in London till Fall.

He was finding a wealth of classical material in the old volumes that had belonged to Uncle Baxter, and I had set up my writing in the little study that opened off the library which I had all to myself.

Never had I known such peace and quiet. It seemed the atmosphere of Rampling Gate permeated my simplest written descriptions and wove its way richly into the plots and characters I created. The Monday after our arrival I had finished my first short story and went off to the village on foot to boldly post it to the editors of *Blackwood's Magazine*.

It was a glorious morning, and I took my time as I came back on foot.

What had disturbed our father so about this lovely corner of England, I wondered? What had so darkened his last hours that he laid upon this spot his curse?

My heart opened to this unearthly stillness, to an undeniable grandeur that caused me utterly to forget myself. There were times here when I felt I was a disembodied intellect drifting through a fathomless silence, up and down garden paths and stone corridors that had witnessed too much to take cognizance of one small and fragile young woman who in random moments actually talked aloud to the suits of armour around her, to the broken statues in the garden, the fountain cherubs who had not had water to pour from their conches for years and years.

But was there in this loveliness some malignant force that was eluding us still, some untold story to explain all? Unspeakable horror... In my mind's eye I saw that young man, and the strangest sensation crept over me, that some enrichment of the picture had taken place in my memory or imagination in the recent past. Perhaps in a dream I had re-invented him, given a ruddy glow to his lips and his cheeks. Perhaps in my re-creation for Mrs. Blessington, I had allowed him to raise his hand to that red cravat and had seen the fingers long and delicate and suggestive of a musician's hand.

It was all very much on my mind when I entered the house again, soundlessly, and saw Richard in his favorite leather wing chair by the fire.

The air was warm coming through the open garden doors, and yet the blaze was cheerful, made the vast room with its towering shelves of leatherbound volumes appear inviting and almost small.

"Sit down," Richard said gravely, scarcely giving me a glance. "I want to read you something right now." He held a long narrow ledger in his hands. "This was Uncle Baxter's," he said, "and at first I thought it was only an account book he kept during the renovations, but I've found some actual diary entries made in the last weeks of his life. They're hasty, almost indecipherable, but I've managed to make them out."

"Well, do read them to me," I said, but I felt a little tug of fear. I didn't want to know anything terrible about this place. If we could have remained here forever... but that was out of the question, to be sure.

"Now listen to this," Richard said, turning the page carefully. "'Fifth of May, 1838: He is here, I am sure of it. He is come back again.' And several days later: 'He thinks this is his house, he does, and he would drink my wine and smoke my cigars if only he could. He reads my books and my papers and I will not stand for it. I have given orders that everything is to be locked.' And finally, the last entry written the morning before he died: 'Weary, weary, unto death and he is no small cause of my weariness. Last night I beheld him with my own eyes. He stood in this very room. He moves and speaks exactly as a mortal man, and dares tell me his secrets, and he a demon wretch with the face of a seraph and I a mere mortal, how am I to bear with him!'"

"Good Lord," I whispered slowly. I rose from the chair where I had settled, and standing behind him, read the page for myself. It was the scrawl, the writing, the very last notation in the book. I knew that Uncle Baxter's heart had given out. He had not died by violence, but peacefully enough in this very room with his prayer book in his hand.

"Could it be the very same person Father spoke of that night?" Richard asked.

In spite of the sun pouring through the open doors, I experienced a violent chill.

For the first time I felt wary of this house, wary of our boldness in coming here, heedful of our father's words.

"But that was years before, Richard…" I said. "And what could this mean, this talk of a supernatural being! Surely the man was mad! It was no spirit I saw in that railway carriage!"

I sank down into the chair opposite and tried to quiet the beating of my heart.

"Julie," Richard said gently, shutting the ledger. "Mrs. Blessington has lived here contentedly for years. There are six servants asleep every night in the north wing. Surely there is nothing to all of this."

"It isn't very much fun, though, is it?" I said timidly, "Not at all like swapping ghost stories the way we used to do, and peopling the dark with imaginary beings, and laughing at friends at school who were afraid."

"All my life," he said, his eyes fixing me steadily, "I've heard tales of spooks and spirits, some imagined, some supposedly true, and almost invariably there is some mention of the house in question feeling haunted, of having an atmosphere to it that fills one with foreboding, some sense of menace or alarm…"

"Yes, I know, and there is no such poisonous atmosphere here at all."

"On the contrary, I've never been more at ease in my life." He shoved his hand into his pocket to extract the inevitable match to light his pipe which had gone out. "As a matter of fact, Julie, I don't know how in the world I'm going to comply with Father's last wish to tear down this place."

I nodded sympathetically. The very same thing had been on my mind since we'd arrived. Even now, I felt so comfortable, natural, quite safe.

I was wishing suddenly, irrationally, that he had not found the entries in Uncle Baxter's book.

"I should talk to Mrs. Blessington again!" I said almost crossly, "I mean quite seriously…"

"But I have, Julie," he said. "I asked her about it all this morning when I first made the discovery, and she only laughed. She swears she's never seen anything unusual here, and that there's no one left alive in the village who can tell tales of this place. She said again how glad she was that we'd come home to Rampling Gate. I don't think she has an inkling we mean to destroy the house. Oh, it would destroy her heart if she did."

"Never seen anything unusual?" I asked. "That is what she said? But what strange words for her to use, Richard, when she can not see at all."

But he had not heard me. He had laid the ledger aside and risen slowly, almost sluggishly, and he was wandering out of the double doors into the little garden and was looking over the high hedge at the oaks that bent their heavy elbowed limbs almost to the surface of the lake. There wasn't a sound at this early hour of the day, save the soft rustle of the leaves in the moving air, the cry now and then of a distant bird.

"Maybe it's gone, Julie," Richard said, over his shoulder, his voice carrying clearly in the quiet, "if it was ever here. Maybe there is nothing any longer to frighten anyone at all. You don't suppose you could endure the winter in this house, do you? I suppose you'd want to be in London again by then." He seemed quite small against the towering trees, the sky broken into small gleaming fragments by the canopy of foliage that gently filtered the light.

Rampling Gate had him. And I understood perfectly, because it also had me. I could very well endure the winter here, no matter how bleak or cold. I never wanted to go home.

And the immediacy of the mystery only dimmed my sense of everything and every place else.

After a long moment, I rose and went out into the garden, and placed my hand gently on Richard's arm.

"I know this much, Julie," he said just as if we had been talking to each other all the while. "I swore to Father that I would do as he asked, and it is tearing me apart. Either way, it will be on my conscience forever, obliterating this house or going against my own father and the charge he laid down to me with his dying breath."

"We must seek help, Richard. The advice of our lawyers, the advice of Father's clergymen. You must write to them and explain the whole thing. Father was feverish when he gave the order. If we could lay it out before them, they would help us decide."

It was three o'clock when I opened my eyes. But I had been awake for a long time. I had heard the dim chimes of the clock below hour by hour. And I felt not fear lying here alone in the dark but something else. Some vague and relentless agitation, some sense of emptiness and need that caused me finally to rise from my bed. What was required to dissolve this tension, I wondered. I stared at the simplest things in the shadows. The little arras that hung over the fireplace with its slim princes and princesses lost in fading fiber and thread. The portrait of an Elizabethan ancestor gazing with one almond-shaped eye from his small frame.

What was this house, really? Merely a place or a state of mind? What was it doing to my soul? Why didn't the entries in Uncle Baxter's book send us flying back to London? Why had we stayed so late in the great hall together after supper, speaking not a single word?

I felt overwhelmed suddenly, and yet shut out of some great and dazzling secret, and wasn't that the very word that Uncle Baxter had used?

Conscious only of an unbearable restlessness, I pulled on my woollen wrapper, buttoning the lace collar and tying the sash. And putting on my slippers, I went out into the hall.

The moon fell full on the oak stairway, and on the deeply recessed door to Richard's room. On tiptoe I approached and, peering in, saw the bed was empty, the covers completely undisturbed.

So he was off on his own tonight the same as I. Oh, if only he had come to me, asked me to go with him.

I turned and made my way soundlessly down the long stairs.

The great hall gaped like a cavern before me, the moonlight here and there touching upon a pair of crossed swords, or a mounted shield. But far beyond the great hall, in the alcove just outside the library, I saw unmistakably a flickering light. And a breeze moved briskly through the room, carrying with it the sound and the scent of a wood fire.

I shuddered with relief. Richard was there. We could talk. Or perhaps we could go exploring together, guarding our fragile candle flames behind cupped fingers as we went from room to room? A sense of well-being pervaded me and quieted me, and yet the dark distance between us seemed endless, and I was desperate to cross it, hurrying suddenly past the long supper table with its massive candlesticks, and finally into the alcove before the library doors.

Yes, Richard was there. He sat with his eyes closed, dozing against the inside of the leather wing chair, the breeze from the garden blowing the fragile flames of the candles on the stone mantel and on the table at his side.

I was about to go to him, about to shut the doors, and kiss him gently and ask did he not want to go up to bed, when quite abruptly I saw in the corner of my eye that there was someone else in the room.

In the far left corner at the desk stood another figure, looking down at the clutter of Richard's papers, his pale hands resting on the wood.

I knew that it could not be so. I knew that I must be dreaming, that nothing in this room, least of all this figure, could be real. For it was the same young man I had seen fifteen years ago in the railway carriage and not a single aspect of that taut young face had been changed. There was the very same hair, thick and lustrous and only carelessly combed as it hung to the thick collar of his black coat, and the skin so pale it was almost luminous in the shadows, and those dark eyes looking up suddenly and fixing me with the most curious expression as I almost screamed.

We stared at one another across the dark vista of that room, I stranded in the doorway, he visibly and undeniably shaken that I had caught him unawares. My heart stopped.

And in a split second he moved towards me, closed the gap between us, towering over me, those slender white fingers gently closing on my arms.

"Julie!" he whispered, in a voice so low it seemed my own thoughts speaking to me. But this was no dream. He was real. He was holding to me and the scream had broken loose from me, deafening, uncontrollable and echoing from the four walls.

I saw Richard rising from the chair. I was alone. Clutching to the door frame, I staggered forward, and then again in a moment of perfect clarity I saw the young intruder, saw him standing in the garden, looking back over his shoulder, and then he was gone.

I could not stop screaming. I could not stop even as Richard held me and pleaded with me, and sat me down in the chair.

And I was still crying when Mrs. Blessington finally came.

She got a glass of cordial for me at once, as Richard begged me once more to tell what I had seen.

"But you know who it was!" I said to Richard almost hysterically. "It was he, the young man from the train. Only he wore a frockcoat years out of fashion and his silk tie was open at his throat. Richard, he was reading your papers, turning them over, reading them in the pitch dark."

"All right," Richard said, gesturing with his hand up for calm. "He was standing at the desk. And there was no light there so you could not see him well."

"Richard, it was he! Don't you understand? He touched me, he held my arms." I looked imploringly to Mrs. Blessington who was shaking her head, her little eyes like blue beads in the light. "He called me Julie," I whispered. "He knows my name!"

I rose, snatching up the candle, and all but pushing Richard out of the way went to the desk. "Oh, dear God," I said, "Don't you see what's happened? It's your letters to Dr. Partridge, and Mrs. Sellers, about tearing down the house!"

Mrs. Blessington gave a little cry and put her hand to her cheek. She looked like a withered child in her nightcap as she collapsed into the straight-backed chair by the door.

"Surely you don't believe it was the same man, Julie, after all these years…"

"But he had not changed, Richard, not in the smallest detail. There is no mistake, Richard, it was he, I tell you, the very same."

"Oh, dear, dear…" Mrs. Blessington whispered, "What will he do if you try to tear it down? What will he do now?"

"What will who do?" Richard asked carefully, narrowing his eyes. He took the candle from me and approached her. I was staring at her, only half realizing what I had heard.

"So you know who he is!" I whispered.

"Julie, stop it!" Richard said.

But her face had tightened, gone blank and her eyes had become distant and small.

"You knew he was here!" I insisted. "You must tell us at once!"

With an effort she climbed to her feet. "There is nothing in this house to hurt *you*," she said, "nor any of us." She turned, spurning Richard as he tried to help her, and wandered into the dark hallway alone. "You've no need of me here any longer," she said softly, "and if you should tear down this house built by your forefathers, then you should do it without need of me."

"Oh, but we don't mean to do it, Mrs. Blessington!" I insisted. But she was making her way through the gallery back towards the north wing. "Go after her, Richard. You heard what she said. She knows who he is."

"I've had quite enough of this tonight," Richard said almost angrily. "Both of us should go up to bed. By the light of day we will dissect this entire matter and search this house. Now come."

"But he should be told, shouldn't he?" I demanded.

"Told what? Of whom do you speak!"

"Told that we will not tear down this house!" I said clearly, loudly, listening to the echo of my own voice.

The next day was indeed the most trying since we had come. It took the better part of the morning to convince Mrs. Blessington that we had no intention of tearing down Rampling Gate. Richard posted his letters and resolved that we should do nothing until help came.

And together we commenced a search of the house. But darkness found us only half finished, having covered the south tower and the south wing, and the main portion of the house itself. There remained still the north tower, in a dreadful state of disrepair, and some rooms beneath the ground which in former times might have served as dungeons and were now sealed off. And there were closets and private stairways everywhere that we had scarce looked into, and at times we lost all track of where precisely we had been.

But it was also quite clear by supper time that Richard was in a state of strain and exasperation, and that he did not believe that I had seen anyone in the study at all.

He was further convinced that Uncle Baxter had been mad before he died, or else his ravings were a code for some mundane happening that had him extraordinarily overwrought.

But I knew what I had seen. And as the day progressed, I became ever more quiet and withdrawn. A silence had fallen between me and Mrs. Blessington. And I understood only too well the anger I'd heard in my father's voice on that long ago night when we had come home from Victoria Station and my mother had accused him of imagining things.

Yet what obsessed me more than anything else was the gentle countenance of the mysterious man I had glimpsed, the dark, almost innocent, eyes that had fixed on me for one moment before I had screamed.

"Strange that Mrs. Blessington is not afraid of him," I said in a low distracted voice, no longer caring if Richard heard me. "And that no one here seems in fear of him at all…" The strangest fancies were coming to me. The careless words of the villagers were running through my head. "You would be wise to do one very important thing before you retire," I said. "Leave out in writing a note to the effect that you do not intend to tear down the house."

"Julie, you have created an impossible dilemma," Richard demanded. "You insist we reassure this apparition that the house will not be destroyed, when in fact you verify the existence of the very creature that drove our father to say what he did."

"Oh, I wish I had never come here!" I burst out suddenly.

"Then we should go, both of us, and decide this matter at home."

"No, that's just it. I could never go without knowing… 'his secrets'… 'the demon wretch.' I could never go on living without knowing now!"

Anger must be an excellent antidote to fear, for surely something worked to alleviate my natural alarm. I did not undress that night, nor even take off my shoes, but rather sat in that dark hollow bedroom gazing at the small square of diamond-paned window until I heard all of the house fall quiet. Richard's door at last closed. There came those distant echoing booms that meant other bolts had been put in place.

And when the grandfather clock in the great hall chimed the hour of eleven, Rampling Gate was as usual fast asleep.

I listened for my brother's step in the hall. And when I did not hear him stir from his room, I wondered at it, that curiosity would not impel him to come to me, to say that we must go together to discover the truth.

It was just as well. I did not want him to be with me. And I felt a dark exultation as I imagined myself going out of the room and down the stairs as I had the night before. I should wait one more hour, however, to be certain. I should let the night reach its pitch. Twelve, the witching hour. My heart was beating too fast at the thought of it, and dreamily I recollected the face I had seen, the voice that had said my name.

Ah, why did it seem in retrospect so intimate, that we had known each other, spoken together, that it was someone I recognized in the pit of my soul?

"What is your name?" I believe I whispered aloud. And then a spasm of fear startled me. Would I have the courage to go in search of him, to open the door to him? Was I losing my mind? Closing my eyes, I rested my head against the high back of the damask chair.

What was more empty than this rural night? What was more sweet?

I opened my eyes. I had been half dreaming or talking to myself, trying to explain to Father why it was necessary that we comprehend the reason ourselves. And I realized, quite fully realized—I think before I was even awake—that *he* was standing by the bed.

The door was open. And he was standing there, dressed exactly as he had been the night before, and his dark eyes were riveted on me with that same obvious curiosity, his mouth just a little slack like that of a school boy, and he was holding to the bedpost almost idly with his right hand. Why, he was lost in contemplating me. He did not seem to know that I was looking at him.

But when I sat forward, he raised his finger as if to quiet me, and gave a little nod of his head.

"Ah, it is you!" I whispered.

"Yes," he said in the softest, most unobtrusive voice.

But we had been talking to each other, hadn't we, I had been asking him questions, no, telling him things. And I felt suddenly I was losing my equilibrium or slipping back into a dream.

No. Rather I had all but caught the fragment of some dream from the past. That rush of atmosphere that can engulf one at any moment of the day following when something evokes the universe that absorbed one utterly in sleep. I mean I heard our voices for an instant, almost in argument, and I saw Father in his top hat and black overcoat rushing alone through the streets of the West End, peering into one door after another, and then, rising from the marble-top table in the dim smoky music hall you… your face.

"Yes…"

Go back, Julie! It was Father's voice.

"… to penetrate the soul of it," I insisted, picking up the lost thread. But did my lips move? "To understand what it is that frightened him, enraged him. He said, 'Tear it down!'"

"… you must never, never, can't do that." His face was stricken, like that of a schoolboy about to cry.

"No, absolutely, we don't want to, either of us, you know it… and you are not a spirit!" I looked at his mud-spattered boots, the faintest smear of dust on that perfect white cheek.

"A spirit?" he asked almost mournfully, almost bitterly. "Would that I were."

Mesmerized I watched him come towards me and the room darkened, and I felt his cool silken hands on my face. I had risen. I was standing before him, and I looked up into his eyes.

I heard my own heartbeat. I heard it as I had the night before, right at the moment I had screamed. Dear God, I was talking to him! He was in my room and I was talking to him! And I was in his arms.

"Real, absolutely real!" I whispered, and a low zinging sensation coursed through me so that I had to steady myself against the bed.

He was peering at me as if trying to comprehend something terribly important to him, and he didn't respond. His lips did have a ruddy look to them, a soft look for all his handsomeness, as if he had never been kissed. And a slight dizziness had come over me, a slight confusion in which I was not at all sure that he was even there.

"Oh, but I am," he said softly. I felt his breath against my cheek, and it was almost sweet. "I am here, and you are with me, Julie…"

"Yes…"

My eyes were closing. Uncle Baxter sat hunched over his desk and I could hear the furious scratch of his pen. "Demon wretch!" he said to the night air coming in the open doors.

"No!" I said. Father turned in the door of the music hall and cried my name.

"Love me, Julie," came that voice in my ear. I felt his lips against my neck. "Only a little kiss, Julie, no harm…" And the core of my being, that secret place where all desires and all commandments are nurtured, opened to him without a struggle or a sound. I would have fallen if he had not held me. My arms closed about him, my hands slipping into the soft silken mass of his hair.

I was floating, and there was as there had always been at Rampling Gate an endless peace. It was Rampling Gate I felt around me, it was that timeless and impenetrable soul that had opened itself at last… A power within me of enormous ken… To see as a god sees, and take the depth of things as nimbly as the outward eyes can size and shape pervade… Yes, I whispered aloud, those words from Keats, those words… To cease upon the midnight without pain…

No. In a violent instant we had parted, he drawing back as surely as I.

I went reeling across the bedroom floor and caught hold of the frame of the window, and rested my forehead against the stone wall.

For a long moment I stood with my eyes closed. There was a tingling pain in my throat that was almost pleasurable where his lips had touched me, a delicious throbbing that would not stop.

Then I turned, and I saw all the room clearly, the bed, the fireplace, the chair. And he stood still exactly as I'd left him and there was the most appalling distress in his face.

"What have they done to me?" he whispered. "Have they played the cruelest trick of all?"

"Something of menace, unspeakable menace," I whispered.

"Something ancient, Julie, something that defies understanding, something that can and will go on."

"But why, what are you?" I touched that pulsing pain with the tips of my fingers and, looking down at them, gasped. "And you suffer so, and you are so seemingly innocent, and it is as if you can love!"

His face was rent as if by a violent conflict within. And he turned to go. With my whole will, I stood fast not to follow him, not to beg him to turn back. But he did turn, bewildered, struggling and then bent upon his purpose as he reached for my hand. "Come with me," he said.

He drew me to him ever so gently, and slipping his arm around me guided me to the door.

Through the long upstairs corridor we passed hurriedly, and through a small wooden doorway to a screw stairs that I had never seen before.

I soon realized we were ascending the north tower of the house, the ruined portion of the structure that Richard and I had not investigated before.

Through one tiny window after another I saw the gently rolling landscape moving out from the forest that surrounded us, and the small cluster of dim lights that marked the village of Rampling and the pale streak of white that was the London road.

Up and up we climbed until we had reached the topmost chamber, and this he opened with an iron key. He held back the door for me to enter and I found myself in a spacious room whose high narrow windows contained no glass. A flood of moonlight revealed the most curious mixture of furnishings and objects, the clutter that suggests an attic and a sort of den. There was a writing table, a great shelf of books, soft leather chairs and scores of old yellowed and curling maps and framed pictures affixed to the walls. Candles were everywhere stuck in the bare stone niches or to the tables and the shelves. Here and there a barrel served as a table, right alongside the finest old Elizabethan chair. Wax had dripped over everything, it seemed, and in the very midst of the clutter lay rumpled copies of the most recent papers, the *Mercure de Paris,* the London *Times.*

There was no place for sleeping in this room.

And when I thought of that, where he must lie when he went to rest, a shudder passed over me and I felt, quite vividly, his lips touching my throat again, and I felt the sudden urge to cry.

But he was holding me in his arms, he was kissing my cheeks and my lips again ever so softly, and then he guided me to a chair. He lighted the candles about us one by one.

I shuddered, my eyes watering slightly in the light. I saw more unusual objects: telescopes and magnifying glasses and a violin in its open case, and a handful of gleaming and exquisitely shaped sea shells. There were jewels lying about, and a black silk top hat and a walking stick, and a bouquet of withered flowers, dry as straw, and daguerreotypes and tintypes in their little velvet cases, and opened books.

But I was too distracted now by the sight of him in the light, the gloss of his large black eyes, and the gleam of his hair. Not even in the railway station had I seen him so clearly as I did now amid the radiance of the candles. He broke my heart.

And yet he looked at me as though I were the feast for his eyes, and he said my name again and I felt the blood rush to my face. But there seemed a great break suddenly in the passage of time. I had been thinking, yes, what are you, how long have you existed... And I felt dizzy again.

I realized that I had risen and I was standing beside him at the window and he was turning me to look down and the countryside below had unaccountably changed. The lights of Rampling had been subtracted from the darkness that lay like a vapor over the land. A great wood, far older and denser than the forest of Rampling Gate, shrouded the hills, and I was afraid suddenly, as if I were slipping into a maelstrom from which I could never, of my own will, return.

There was that sense of us talking together, talking and talking in low agitated voices and I was saying that I should not give in.

"Bear witness, that is all I ask of you..."

And there was in me some dim certainty that by knowledge alone I should be fatally changed. It was the reading of a forbidden book, the chanting of a forbidden charm.

"No, only what was," he whispered.

And then even the shape of the land itself eluded me. And the very room had lost its substance, as if a soundless wind of terrific force had entered this place and was blowing it apart.

We were riding in a carriage through the night. We had long long ago left the tower, and it was late afternoon and the sky was the color of blood. And we rode into a forest whose trees were so high and so thick that scarcely any sun at all broke through to the soft leafstrewn ground.

We had no time to linger in this magical place. We had come to the open country, to the small patches of tilled earth that surrounded the ancient village of Knorwood with its gabled roofs and its tiny crooked streets. We saw the walls of the monastery of Knorwood and the little church with the bell chiming Vespers under the lowering sky. A great bustling life resided in Knorwood, a thousand hearts beat in Knorwood, a thousand voices gave forth their common prayer.

But far beyond the village on the rise above the forest stood the rounded tower of a truly ancient castle, and to that ruined castle, no more than a shell of itself anymore, as darkness fell in earnest, we rode. Through its empty chambers we roamed, impetuous children, the horse and the road quite forgotten, and to the Lord of the Castle, a gaunt and white-skinned creature standing before the roaring fire of the roofless hall, we came. He turned and fixed us with his narrow and glittering eyes. A dead thing he was, I understood, but he carried within himself a priceless magic. And my young companion, my innocent young man passed by me into the Lord's arms. I saw the kiss. I saw the young man grow pale and struggle to turn away. It was as I had done this very night, beyond this dream, in my own bedchamber; and from the Lord he retreated, clutching to the sharp pain in his throat.

I understood. I knew. But the castle was dissolving as surely as anything in this dream might dissolve, and we were in some damp and close place.

The stench was unbearable to me, it was that most terrible of all stenches, the stench of death. And I heard my steps on the cobblestones and I reached to steady myself against the wall. The tiny square was deserted; the doors and windows gaped open to the vagrant wind. Up one side and down the other of the crooked street I saw the marks on the houses. And I knew what the marks meant. The Black Death had come to the village of Knorwood. The Black Death had laid it waste. And in a moment of suffocating horror I realized that no one, not a single person, was left alive.

But this was not quite right. There was someone walking in fits and starts up the narrow alleyway. Staggering he was, almost falling, as he pushed in one door after another, and at last came to a hot, stinking place where a child screamed on the floor. Mother and Father lay dead in the bed. And the great fat cat of the household, unharmed, played with the screaming infant, whose eyes bulged from its tiny sunken face.

"Stop it," I heard myself gasp. I knew that I was holding my head with both hands. "Stop it, stop it please!" I was screaming and my screams would surely pierce the vision and this small crude little room should collapse around me, and I should rouse the household of Rampling Gate to me, but I did not. The young man turned and stared at me, and in the close stinking room, I could not see his face.

But I knew it was he, my companion, and I could smell his fever and his sickness, and the stink of the dying infant, and see the sleek, gleaming body of the cat as it pawed at the child's outstretched hand.

"Stop it, you've lost control of it!" I screamed surely with all my strength, but the infant screamed louder. "Make it stop!"

"I cannot…" he whispered. "It goes on forever! It will never stop!"

And with a great piercing shriek I kicked at the cat and sent it flying out of the filthy room, overturning the milk pail as it went, jetting like a witch's familiar over the stones.

Blanched and feverish, the sweat soaking his crude jerkin, my companion took me by the hand. He forced me back out of the house and away from the crying child and into the street.

Death in the parlour, death in the bedroom, death in the cloister, death before the high altar, death in the open fields. It seemed the Judgment of God that a thousand souls had died in the village of Knorwood—I was sobbing, begging to be released—it seemed the very end of Creation itself.

And at last night came down over the dead village and he was alive still, stumbling up the slopes, through the forest, towards that rounded tower where the Lord stood with his hand on the stone frame of the broken window waiting for him to come.

"Don't go!" I begged him. I ran alongside him crying, but he didn't hear. Try as I might, I could not affect these things.

The Lord stood over him smiling almost sadly as he watched him fall, watched the chest heave with its last breaths. Finally the lips moved, calling out for salvation when it was damnation the Lord offered, when it was damnation that the Lord would give.

"Yes, damned then, but living, breathing!" the young man cried, rising in a last spasmodic movement. And the Lord, who had remained still until that instant, bent to drink.

The kiss again, the lethal kiss, the blood drawn out of the dying body, and then the Lord lifting the heavy head of the young man to take the blood back again from the body of the Lord himself.

I was screaming again, *Do not, do not drink.* He turned and looked at me. His face was now so perfectly the visage of death that I couldn't believe there was animation left in him, yet he asked: What would you do? Would you go back to Knorwood, would you open those doors one after another, would you ring the bell in the empty church, and if you did would the dead rise?

He didn't wait for my answer. And I had none now to give. He had turned again to the Lord who waited for him, locked his innocent mouth to that vein that pulsed with every semblance of life beneath the Lord's cold and translucent flesh. And the blood jetted into the young body, vanquishing in one great burst the fever and the sickness that had wracked it, driving it out with the mortal life.

He stood now in the hall of the Lord alone. Immortality was his and the blood thirst he would need to sustain it, and that thirst I could feel with my whole soul. He stared at the broken walls around him, at the fire licking the blackened stones of the giant fireplace, at the night sky over the broken roof, throwing out its endless net of stars.

And each and every thing was transfigured in his vision, and in my vision—the vision he gave now to me—to the exquisite essence of itself. A wordless and eternal voice spoke from the starry veil of heaven, it sang in the wind that rushed through the broken timbers; it sighed in the flames that ate the sooted stones of the hearth.

It was the fathomless rhythm of the universe that played beneath every surface, as the last living creature—that tiny child—feel silent in the village below.

A soft wind sifted and scattered the soil from the new-turned furrows in the empty fields. The rain fell from the black and endless sky.

Years and years passed. And all that had been Knorwood melted into the very earth. The forest sent out its silent sentinels, and mighty trunks rose where there had been huts and houses, where there had been monastery walls.

Finally nothing of Knorwood remained: not the little cemetery, not the little church, not even the name of Knorwood lived still in the world. And it seemed the horror beyond all horrors that no one anymore should know of a thousand souls who had lived and died in that small and insignificant village, that not any-where in the great archives in which all history is recorded should a mention of that town remain.

Yet one being remained who knew, one being who had witnessed, and stood now looking down upon the very spot where his mortal life had ended, he who had scrambled up on his hands and knees from the pit of Hell that had been that disaster; it was the young man who stood beside me, the master of Rampling Gate.

And all through the walls of his old house were the stones of the ruined castle, and all through the ceilings and floors the branches of those ancient trees.

What was solid and majestic here, and safe within the minds of those who slept tonight in the village of Rampling, was only the most fragile citadel against horror, the house to which he clung now.

A great sorrow swept over me. Somewhere in the drift of images I had relin-quished myself, lost all sense of the point in space from which I saw. And in a great rush of lights and noise I was enlivened now and made whole as I had been when we rode together through the forest, only it was into the world of now, this hour, that we passed. We were flying it seemed through the rural darkness along the railway towards the London where the nighttime city burst like an enormous bubble in a shower of laughter, and motion, and glaring light. He was walking with me under the gas lamps, his face all but shimmering with that same dark innocence, that same irresistible warmth. And it seemed we were holding tight to one another in the very midst of a crowd. And the crowd was a living thing, a writhing thing, and everywhere there came a dark rich aroma from it, the aroma of fresh blood. Women in white fur and gentlemen in opera capes swept into the brightly lighted doors of the theatre; the blare of the music hall inundated us, then faded away. Only a thin soprano voice was left, singing a high, plaintive song. I was in his arms, and his lips were covering mine, and there came that dull zing-ing sensation again, that great uncontrollable opening within myself. Thirst, and the promise of satiation measured only by the intensity of that thirst. Up stairs we fled together, into high-ceilinged bedrooms papered in red damask where the loveliest women reclined on brass bedsteads, and the aroma was so strong now I could not bear it, and before me they offered themselves, they opened their arms. "Drink," he whispered, yes, drink. And I felt the warmth filling me, charging me, blurring my vision, until we broke again, free and light and invisible it seemed as we moved over the rooftops and down again through rain-drenched streets. But the rain did not touch us; the falling snow did not chill us; we had within ourselves a great and indissoluble heat. And together in the carriage, we talked to each other in low, exuberant rushes of language; we were lovers; we were constant; we were immortal. We were as enduring as Rampling Gate.

I tried to speak; I tried to end the spell. I felt his arms around me and I knew we were in the tower room together, and some terrible miscalculation had been made.

"Do not leave me," he whispered. "Don't you understand what I am offering you; I have told you everything; and all the rest is but the weariness, the fever and the fret, those old words from the poem. Kiss me, Julie, open to me. Against your will I will not take you…" Again I heard my own scream. My hands were on his cool white skin, his lips were gentle yet hungry, his eyes yielding and ever young. Father turned in the rain-drenched London street and cried out: "Julie!" I saw Richard lost in the crowd as if searching for some one, his hat shadowing his dark eyes, his face haggard, old. Old!

I moved away. I was free. And I was crying softly and we were in this strange and cluttered tower room. He stood against the backdrop of the window, against the distant drift of pale clouds. The candle-light glimmered in his eyes. Immense and sad and wise they seemed, and oh, yes, innocent as I have said again and again. "I revealed myself to them," he said. "Yes, I told my secret. In rage or bitterness, I know not which, I made them my dark co-conspirators and always I won. They could not move against me, and neither will you. But they would triumph still. For they torment me now with their fairest flower. Don't turn away from me, Julie. You are mine, Julie, as Rampling Gate is mine. Let me gather the flower to my heart."

Nights of argument. But finally Richard had come round. He would sign over to me his share of Rampling Gate, and I should absolutely refuse to allow the place torn down. There would be nothing he could do then to obey Father's command. I had given him the legal impediment he needed, and of course I should leave the house to him and his children. It should always be in Rampling hands.

A clever solution, it seemed to me, as Father had not told *me* to destroy the place, and I had no scruples in the matter now at all.

And what remained was for him to take me to the little train station and see me off for London, and not worry about me going home to Mayfair on my own.

"You stay here as long as you wish, and do not worry," I said. I felt more tenderly towards him than I could ever express. "You knew as soon as you set foot in the place that Father was all wrong. Uncle Baxter put it in his mind, undoubtedly, and Mrs. Blessington has always been right. There is nothing to harm there, Richard. Stay, and work or study as you please."

The great black engine was roaring past us, the carriages slowing to a stop. "Must go now, darling, kiss me," I said.

"But what came over you, Julie, what convinced you so quickly…"

"We've been through all, Richard," I said. "What matters is that we are all happy, my dear." And we held each other close.

I waved until I couldn't see him anymore. The flickering lamps of the town were lost in the deep lavender light of the early evening, and the dark hulk of Rampling Gate appeared for one uncertain moment like the ghost of itself on the nearby rise.

I sat back and closed my eyes. Then I opened them slowly, savouring this moment for which I had waited too long.

He was smiling, seated there as he had been all along, in the far corner of the leather seat opposite, and now he rose with a swift, almost delicate movement and sat beside me and enfolded me in his arms.

"It's five hours to London," he whispered in my ear.

"I can wait," I said, feeling the thirst like a fever as I held tight to him, feeling his lips against my eyelids and my hair. "I want to hunt the London streets tonight," I confessed, a little shyly, but I saw only approbation in his eyes.

"Beautiful Julie, my Julie..." he whispered.

"You'll love the house in Mayfair," I said.

"Yes..." he said.

"And when Richard finally tires of Rampling Gate, we shall go home."

UNDER ST. PETER'S

by Harry Turtledove

Harry Turtledove—who is often referred to as the "master of alternate history"—is the Hugo Award-winning author of more than 80 novels and 100 short stories. His most recent novels are *The Man with the Iron Heart, After the Downfall, Give Me Back My Legions!,* and *Hitler's War.* In addition to his SF, fantasy, and alternate history works, he's also published several straight historical novels under the name H. N. Turteltaub. Turtledove obtained a Ph.D. in Byzantine history from UCLA in 1977.

Turtledove says that part of the appeal of vampire fiction is that we humans like to think we're at the top of the food chain. "But what if we're not?" he said. "Vampire stories also often involve immortality—as this one does—and sex—which this one doesn't—and both of those are abiding themes to which vampires give a different slant."

This story takes place in St. Peter's Basilica in Vatican City—one of Christianity's holiest sites—and tells the tale of the vampire living underneath it. It's a difficult story to talk about without giving away the good parts. Let it suffice to say that it's oh-so blasphemous. Say three Hail Marys and an Our Father after reading.

Incense in the air, even down here behind the doors. Frankincense and myrrh, the scents he remembered from days gone by, days when he could face the sun. Somber Latin chants. He recognized them even now, though the chanters didn't pronounce Latin the way the legionaries had back in those bright days.

And the hunger. Always the hunger.

Would he finally feed? It had been a long time, such a very long time. He could hardly remember the last time he'd had to wait so long.

He wouldn't die of starvation. He couldn't die of starvation. His laughter sent wild echoes chasing one another in his chamber. No, he couldn't very well die, not when he was already dead. But he could wish himself extinguished. He could, and he did, every waking moment—and every moment, from now to forever or the sun's next kiss, was a waking moment.

Much good wishing did him.

He waited, and he remembered. What else did he have to do? Nothing. They made sure of it. His memory since his death and resurrection was perfect. He could bring back any day, any instant, with absolute clarity, absolute accuracy.

Much good that did him, too.

He preferred recalling the days before, the days when he was only a man. (Was he ever only a man? He knew how many would say no. Maybe they were right, but he remembered himself as man and man alone. But his memories of those days blurred and shifted—as a man's would—so he might have been wrong. Maybe he was something else, something different, right from the start.)

He'd packed a lot into thirty-odd years. Refugee, carpenter, reformer, rebel… convict. He could still hear the thud of the hammer that drove in the spikes. He could still hear his own screams as those spikes pierced him. He'd never thought, down deep in his heart, that it would come to that—which only just went to show how much he knew.

He'd never thought, down deep in his heart, that it would come to this, either. Which, again, just went to show how much he knew.

If he were everything people said he was, would he have let it come to this? He could examine that portion of his—not of his life, no, but of his existence, with the perfect recall so very distant from mortality. He could examine it, and he had, time and again. Try as he would, he couldn't see anything he might have done differently.

And even if he did see something like that, it was much too late to matter now.

"Habemus papam!"

When you heard the Latin acclamation, when you knew it was for you… Was there any feeling to match that, any in all the world? People said a new Orthodox Patriarch once fell over dead with joy at learning he was chosen. That had never happened on this trunk of the tree that split in 1054, but seeing how it might wasn't hard. A lifetime of hopes, of dreams, of work, of prayer, of patience… and then, at last, you had to try to fill the Fisherman's sandals.

They will remember me forever, was the first thought that went through his mind. For a man who, by the nature of his office, had better not have children, it was the only kind of immortality he would ever get. A cardinal could run things behind the scenes for years, could be the greatest power in the oldest continually functioning institution in the world—and, five minutes after he was dead, even the scholars in the Curia would have trouble coming up with his name.

But once you heard "Habemus papam!"…

He would have to deal with Italians for the rest of his life. He would have to smell garlic for the rest of his life. Part of him had wanted to retire when his friend, his patron, passed at last: to go back north of the Alps, to rusticate.

That was only part of him, though. The rest… He had been running things behind the scenes for years. Getting his chance to come out and do it in the open, to be noted for it, to be noticed for it, was sweet. And his fellow cardinals hadn't waited long before they chose him, either. What greater honor was there than the approval of your own? More than anyone else, they understood what this meant. Some of them wanted it, too. Most of them wanted it, no doubt, but most of the ones who did also understood they had no chance of gaining it.

Coming out of the shadows, becoming the public face of the Church, wasn't easy for a man who'd spent so long in the background. But he'd shown what he could do when he was chosen to eulogize his predecessor. He wrote the farewell in his own tongue, then translated it into Italian. That wasn't the churchly lingua franca Latin had been, but still, no one who wasn't fluent in it could reasonably hope to occupy Peter's seat.

If he spoke slowly, if he showed Italian wasn't his native tongue—well, so what? It gave translators around the world the chance to stay up with him. And delivering the eulogy meant people around the world saw him and learned who he was. When the College of Cardinals convened to deliberate, that had to be in the back of some minds.

He wouldn't have a reign to match the one that had gone before, not unless he lived well past the century mark. But Achilles said glory mattered more than length of days. And John XXIII showed you didn't need a long reign to make your mark.

Vatican II cleared away centuries of deadwood from the Church. Even the Latin of the Mass went. Well, there was reason behind that. Who spoke Latin nowadays? This wasn't the Roman Empire any more, even if cardinals' vestments came straight out of Byzantine court regalia.

But change always spawned a cry for more change. Female priests? Married priests? Homosexuality? Contraception? Abortion? When? Ever? The world shouted for all those things. The world, though, was a weather vane, turning now this way, now that, changeable as the breeze. The Church was supposed to stand for what was right… whatever that turned out to be.

If changes come, they'll come because of me. If they don't, that will also be because of me, the new Holy Father thought. Which way more than a billion people go depends on me.

Why anyone would want a job like this made him scratch his head. That he wanted it himself, or that most of him did… was true, no matter how strange it seemed. So much to decide, to do. So little time.

A tavern in the late afternoon. They were all worried. Even the publican was worried; he hadn't looked for such a big crowd so late in the day. They were all eating and drinking and talking. They showed no signs of getting up and leaving. If they kept hanging around, he would have to light the lamps, and olive oil wasn't cheap.

But they kept digging their right hands into the bowl of chickpeas and mashed garlic he'd set out, and eating more bread, and calling for wine. One of them had already drunk himself into quite a state.

Looking back from down here, understanding why was easy. Hindsight was always easy. Foresight? They'd called it prophecy in those days. Had he had the gift? His human memory wasn't sure. But then, his human memory wasn't sure about a lot of things. That was what made trying to trace the different threads twisting through the fabric so eternally fascinating.

He wished he hadn't used that word, even to himself. He kept hoping it wasn't so. He'd been down here a long, long, long time, but not forever. He wouldn't stay down here forever, either. He couldn't.

Could he?

He was so hungry.

The tavern. He'd been looking back at the tavern again. He wasn't hungry then. He'd eaten his fill, and he'd drunk plenty of wine, wine red as blood.

What did wine taste like? He remembered it was sweet, and he remembered it could mount to your head… almost the way any food did these days. But the taste? The taste, now, was a memory of a memory of a memory—and thus so blurred, it was no memory at all. He'd lost the taste of wine, just as he'd lost the tastes of bread and chickpeas. Garlic, though, garlic he still knew.

He remembered the sensation of chewing, of reducing the resistive mass in his mouth—whatever it tasted like—to something that easily went down the throat. He almost smiled, there in the darkness. He hadn't needed to worry about that in a while.

Where was he? So easy to let your thoughts wander down here. What else did they have to do? Oh, yes. The tavern. The wine. The feel of the cup in his hands. The smell of the stuff wafting upwards, nearly as intoxicating as… But if his thoughts wandered there, they wouldn't come back. He was so hungry.

The tavern, then. The wine. The cup. The last cup. He remembered saying, "And I tell you, I won't drink from the fruit of the vine any more till that day when I drink it anew with you in my father's kingdom."

They'd nodded. He wasn't sure how much attention they paid, or whether they even took him seriously. How long could anybody go without drinking wine? What would you use instead? Water? Milk? You were asking for a flux of the bowels if you did.

But he'd kept that promise. He'd kept it longer than he dreamt he would, longer than he dreamt he could. He was still keeping it now, after all these years.

Soon, though, soon, he would have something else to drink.

If you paid attention to the television, you would think he was the first Pope ever installed. His predecessor had had a long reign, so long that none of the reporters remembered the last succession. For them, it was as if nothing that came before this moment really happened. One innocent—an American, of course—even remarked, "The new Pope is named after a previous one."

He was not a mirthful man, but he had to laugh at that. What did the fool think the Roman numeral after his name stood for? He wasn't named after just one previous Pope. He was named after fifteen!

One of these days, he would have to try to figure out what to do about the United Sates. So many people there thought they could stay good Catholics while turning their backs on any teachings they didn't happen to like. If they did that, how were they any different from Protestants? How could he tell them they couldn't do that without turning them into Protestants? Well, he didn't have to decide right away, Deo gratias.

So much had happened, this first day of his new reign. If this wasn't enough to overwhelm a man, nothing ever would be. Pretty soon, he thought, he would get around to actually being Pope. Pretty soon, yes, but not quite yet.

As if to prove as much, a tubby little Italian—not even a priest but a deacon— came up to him and waited to be noticed. The new Pope had seen the fellow around for as long as he could remember. Actually, he didn't really remember seeing him around—the deacon was about as nondescript as any man ever born. But the odor of strong, garlicky sausages always clung to him.

When it became obvious the man wouldn't go away, the Pope sighed a small, discreet sigh. "What is it, Giuseppe?"

"Please to excuse me, Holy Father, but there's one more thing each new Keeper of the Keys has to do," the deacon said.

"Ah?" Now the Pope made a small, interested noise. "I thought I knew all the rituals." He was, in fact, sure he knew all the rituals—or he had been sure, till this moment.

But Deacon Giuseppe shook his head. He seemed most certain, and most self-assured. "No, sir. Only the Popes know—the Popes and the men of the Order of the Pipistrelle."

"The what?" The new Pope had also been sure he was acquainted with all the orders, religious and honorary and both commingled, in Vatican City.

"The Order of the Pipistrelle," Giuseppe repeated patiently. "We are small, and we are quiet, but we are the oldest order in this place. We go... back to the very beginning of things, close enough." Pride rang in his voice.

"Is that so?" The Pope carefully held his tone neutral. Any order with a foundation date the least bit uncertain claimed to be much older than anyone outside its ranks would have wanted to believe. Even so, he'd never heard of an order with pretensions like that. Back to the beginning of things? "I suppose you came here with Peter?"

"That's right, your Holiness. We handled his baggage." Deacon Giuseppe spoke altogether without irony. He either believed what he was saying or could have gone on the stage with his acting.

"Did my friend, my predecessor, do... whatever this is?" the Pope asked.

"Yes, sir, he did. And all the others before him. If you don't do this, you aren't really the Pope. You don't really understand what being the Pope means."

Freemasonry. We have a freemasonry of our own. Who would have thought that? Freemasonry, of course, wasn't nearly so old as its members claimed, either. But that was—or might be—beside the point. "All right," the Pope said. "This must be complete, whatever it is."

Deacon Giuseppe raised his right hand in what wasn't a formal salute but certainly suggested one. "Grazie, Holy Father. Mille grazie," he said. "I knew you were a… thorough man." He nodded, seeming pleased he'd found the right word. And it was the right word; the Pope also nodded, acknowledging its justice.

Deacon Giuseppe took his elbow and steered him down the long nave of St. Peter's, away from the Papal altar and toward the main entrance. Past the haloed statue of St. Peter and the altar of St. Jerome they went, past the Chapel of the Sacrament and, on the Pope's right, the tombs of Innocent VIII and Pius X.

Not far from the main entrance, a red porphyry disk was set into the floor, marking the spot where, in the Old St. Peter's that preceded Bernini's magnificent building, Charlemagne was crowned Roman Emperor. Now, to the Pope's surprise, crimson silk draperies surrounded the disk, discreetly walling it off from view.

Another surprise: "I've never seen these draperies before."

"They belong to the Order," Deacon Giuseppe said, as if that explained everything. To him, it must have. But he had to see it didn't explain everything to his companion, for he added, "We don't use them very often. Will you step through with me?"

The Pope did. Once inside the blood-red billowing silk, he got surprised yet again. "I didn't know that disk came up."

"You weren't supposed to, Holy Father," Deacon Giuseppe said. "You'd think we'd do this over in the Sacred Grotto. It would make more sense, what with the Popes' tombs there—even Peter's, they say. Maybe it was like that years and years ago, but it hasn't been for a long, long time. Here we do it, and here it'll stay. Amen." He crossed himself.

"There's… a stairway going down," the Pope said. How many more amazements did the Vatican hold?

"Yes. That's where we're going. You first, Holy Father," Giuseppe said. "Be careful. It's narrow, and there's no bannister."

Air. Fresh air. Even through doors closed and locked and warded against him, he sensed it. His nostrils twitched. He knew what fresh air meant, sure as a hungry dog knew a bell meant it was time to salivate. When he was a man, he'd lived out in the fresh air. He'd taken it for granted. He'd lived in it. And, much too soon, he'd died in it.

Crucifixion was a Roman punishment, not a Jewish one. Jews killed even animals as mercifully as they could. When they had to kill men, the sword or the axe got it over with fast. The Romans wanted criminals to suffer, and be seen to suffer. They thought that resulted in fewer criminals. The number of men they crucified made the argument seem dubious, but they didn't care.

As for the suffering… They were right about that. The pain was the worst thing he'd ever known. It unmanned him so that he cried out on the cross. Then he swooned, swooned so deeply the watching soldiers and people thought he was dead.

He dimly remembered them taking him down from the cross—pulling out the spikes that nailed him to it was a fresh torment. And one more followed it, for one of the Roman soldiers bit him then, hard enough to tear his flesh open but not hard enough, evidently, to force a sound past his dry throat and parched lips.

How the rest of the Romans laughed! That was the last purely human memory he had, of their mirth at their friend's savagery. When he woke to memory again, he was... changed.

No. There was one thing more. They'd called the biter Dacicus. At the time, it didn't mean anything to a man almost dead. But he never forgot it even though it was meaningless, so maybe—probably—the change in him had begun that soon. When he did think about it again, for a while he believed it was only a name.

Then he learned better. Dacicus meant the Dacian, the man from Dacia. Not one more human in ten thousand, these days, could tell you where Dacia lay—had lain. But its borders matched those of what they called Romania these days, or near enough. And people told stories about Romania... He had no way to know how many of those stories were true. Some, like sliding under doors, surely weren't, or he would have. Considering what had happened to him, though, he had no reason to doubt others.

And now he smelled fresh air. Soon, very soon...

"How long has this been here?" the Pope asked. "I never dreamt anything like this lay under St. Peter's!" The stone spiral stairway certainly seemed ancient. Deacon Giuseppe lit it, however, not with a flickering olive-oil lamp but with a large, powerful flashlight that he pulled from one of the large, deep pockets of his black vestments.

"Your Holiness, as far as I know, it's been here since Peter's day," Giuseppe answered seriously. "I told you before: the Order of the Pipistrelle is in charge of what Peter brought in his baggage."

"And that was?" the Pope asked, a trifle impatiently.

"I don't want to talk about it now. You'll see soon enough. But I'm a keeper of the keys, too." Metal jingled as the deacon pulled a key ring from a pocket. The Pope stopped and looked back over his shoulder. Giuseppe obligingly shone the flashlight beam on the keys. They were as ordinary, as modern, as boring, as the flashlight itself. The Pope had hoped for massive, ancient ones, rusty or green with verdigris. No such luck.

At the bottom of the stairway, a short corridor led to a formidable steel door. The Pope's slippers scuffed through the dust of ages. Motes he kicked up danced in the flashlight beam. "Who last came here?" he asked in a low voice.

"Why, your blessed predecessor, your Holiness," Deacon Giuseppe replied. "Oh, and mine, of course." He opened the door with the key, which worked smoothly. As he held it for the Pope, he went on, "This used to be wood—well, naturally. That's what they had in the old days. They replaced it after the last war. Better safe than sorry, you know."

"Safe from what? Sorry because of what?" As the Pope asked the questions, the door swung behind the deacon and him with what sounded like a most definitive and final click. A large and fancy crucifix was mounted on the inner surface. Another such door, seemingly identical, lay a short distance ahead.

"With Peter's baggage, of course," Giuseppe answered.

"Will you stop playing games with me?" The Pope was a proud and touchy man.

"I'm not!" The deacon crossed himself again. "Before God, your Holiness, I'm not!" He seemed at least as touchy, and at least as proud, as the Pope himself. And then, out of the same pocket from which he'd taken the flashlight, he produced a long, phallic chunk of sausage and bit off a good-sized chunk. The odors of pepper and garlic assailed the Pope's nostrils.

And the incongruity assailed his strong sense of fitness even more. He knocked the sausage out of Giuseppe's hand and into the dust. "Stop that!" he cried.

To his amazement, the Italian picked up the sausage, brushed off most of whatever clung to it, and went on eating. The Pope's gorge rose. "Meaning no disrespect, Holy Father," Giuseppe mumbled with his mouth full, "but I need this. It's part of the ritual. God will strike me dead if I lie."

Not, *May God strike me dead if I lie.* The deacon said, *God will strike me dead.* The Pope, relentlessly precise, noted the distinction. He pointed to the door ahead. "What is on the other side of that?" he asked, a sudden and startling quaver in his voice.

"An empty chamber," Deacon Giuseppe replied.

"And beyond that? Something, I hope."

"Think on the Last Supper, Holy Father," the deacon answered, which didn't help.

He thought of his last supper, which didn't help. Not now, not with his raging hunger. It was too long ago. They were out there. He could hear them out there, talking in that language that wasn't Latin but sounded a little like it. He could see the dancing light under the door. Any light at all stung his eyes, but he didn't mind. And he could smell them. Man's flesh was the most delicious odor in the world, but when he smelled it up close it was always mingled with the other smell, the hateful smell.

His keepers knew their business, all right. Even without garlic, the cross on the farthest door would have held him captive here—had held him captive here. He'd tasted the irony of that, times uncounted.

"This is my blood," he'd said. "This is my flesh." Irony there, too. Oh, yes. Now—soon—he hoped to taste something sweeter than irony.

Where would he have been without Dacicus? Not here—he was sure of that, anyhow. He supposed his body would have stayed in the tomb where they laid it, and his spirit would have soared up to the heavens where it belonged. Did he even have a spirit any more? Or was he all body, all hunger, all appetite? He didn't know. He didn't much care, either. It had been too long.

Dacicus must have been new when he bit him, new or stubborn in believing he remained a man. After being bitten, rolling away the stone was easy. Going about with his friends was easy, too—for a little while. But then the sun began to pain him, and then the hunger began. Taking refuge in the daytime began to feel natural. So did slaking the hunger… when he could.

Soon now. Soon!

"Why the Last Supper?" the Pope demanded.

"Because we reenact it—in a manner of speaking—down here," Deacon Giuseppe replied. "This is the mystery of the Order of the Pipistrelle. Even the Orthodox, even the Copts, would be jealous if they knew. They have relics of the Son. We have… the Son."

The Pope stared at him. "Our Lord's body lies here?" he whispered hoarsely. "His body? He was not taken up as we preach? He was—a man?" Was that the mystery at—or rather, here below—the heart of the Church? The mystery being that there was no mystery, that since the days of the Roman Empire prelates had lived a lie?

His stern faith stumbled. No, his friend, his predecessor, would never have told him about this. It would have been too cruel.

But the little round sausage-munching deacon shook his head. "It's not so simple, your Holiness. I'll show you."

He had another key on the ring. He used it to unlock the last door, and he shone the flashlight into the chamber beyond.

Light! A spear of light! It stabbed into his eyes, stabbed straight through his eyes and into his brain! How long had he gone without? As long as he'd gone without food. But sustenance he cherished, he craved, he yearned for. Light was the pain that accompanied it, the pain he couldn't avoid or evade.

He got used to it, moment by agonizing moment. So long here in the silent dark, he had to remember how to see. Yes, there was the black-robed one, the untouchable, inedible one, the stinker, who carried his light-thrower like a sword. What had happened to torches and oil lamps? Like the last several of his predecessors, this black-robe had one of these unnatural things instead.

Well, I am an unnatural thing myself these days, he thought, and his lips skinned back from his teeth in a smile both wryly amused and hungry, so very hungry.

Now the Pope crossed himself, violently. "Who is this?" he gasped. "What… is this?"

But even as he gasped, he found himself fearing he knew the answer. The short, scrawny young man impaled on the flashlight beam looked alarmingly like so many Byzantine images of the Second Person of the Trinity: shaggy dark brown hair and beard, long oval face, long nose. The wounds to his hands and feet, and the one in his side, looked fresh, even if they were bloodless. And there was another wound, a small one, on his neck. None of the art showed that one; none of the texts spoke of it. Seeing it made the Pope think of films he'd watched as a boy. And when he did…

His hand shaped the sign of the cross once more. It had no effect on the young-looking man who stood there blinking. He hadn't thought it would, not really.

"No!" he said. "It cannot be! It must not be!"

He noticed one thing more. Even when Deacon Giuseppe shone the flashlight full in the young-looking man's face, the pupils did not contract. Did not… Could not? With each passing second, it seemed more likely.

Deacon Giuseppe's somber nod told him it wasn't just likely—it was true. "Well, Holy Father, now you know," said the Deacon from the Order of the Pipistrelle. "Behold the Son of Man. Behold the Resurrection. Behold the greatest secret of the Church."

"But… why? How?" Not even the Pope, as organized and coherent as any man now living, could speak clearly in the presence of—that.

"Once—that—happened to him, he couldn't stand the sun after a while." Deacon Giuseppe told the tale as if it had been told many times before. And so, no doubt, it had. "When Peter came to Rome, he came, too, in the saint's baggage—under the sign of the cross, of course, to make sure nothing… untoward happened. He's been here ever since. We keep him. We take care of him."

"Great God!" The Pope tried to make sense of his whirling thoughts. "No wonder you told me to think of the Last Supper." He forced some iron into his spine. A long-dead Feldwebel who'd drilled him during the last round of global madness would have been proud of how well his lessons stuck. "All right. I've seen him. God help me, I have. Take me up to the light again."

"Not quite yet, your Holiness," the deacon replied. "We finish the ritual first."

"Eh?"

"We finish the ritual," Deacon Giuseppe repeated with sad patience. "Seeing him does not suffice. It is his first supper in a very long time, your predecessor being so young when he was chosen. Remember the text: your blood is his wine, your flesh his bread."

He said something else, in a language that wasn't Italian. The Pope, a formidable scholar, recognized it as Aramaic. He even understood it: "Supper's ready!"

The last meal had been juicier. That was his first thought. But he wasn't complaining, not after so long. He drank and drank: his own communion with the world of the living. He would have drunk the life right out of him if not for the black-robed one.

"Be careful!" that one urged, still speaking the only language he really knew well. "Remember what happened time before last!"

He remembered. He'd got greedy. He'd drunk too much. The man died not long after coming down here to meet him. Then he'd fed again—twice in such a little while! They didn't let him do anything like that the next time, however much he wanted to. And that one lasted and lasted—lasted so long, he began to fear he'd made the man into one like himself.

He hadn't done that very often. He wondered whether Dacicus intended to do that with him—to him. He never had the chance to ask. Did Dacicus still wander the world, not alive any more but still quick? One of these centuries, if Dacicus did, they might meet again. You never could tell.

When he didn't let go fast enough, the black-robed one breathed full in his face. That horrible, poisonous stink made him back away in a hurry.

He hadn't got enough. It could never be enough, not if he drank the world dry. But it was ever so much better than nothing. Before he fed, he was empty. He couldn't end, barring stake, sunlight, or perhaps a surfeit of garlic, but he could wish he would. He could—and he had.

No more. Fresh vitality flowed through him. He wasn't happy—he didn't think he could be happy—but he felt as lively as a dead thing could.

"My God!" the new Pope said, not in Aramaic, not in Latin, not even in Italian. His hand went to the wound on his neck. The bleeding had already stopped. He shuddered. He didn't know what he'd expected when Deacon Giuseppe took him down below St. Peter's, but not this. Never this.

"Are you all right, your Holiness?" Real concern rode the deacon's voice.

"I—think so." And the Pope had to think about it before he answered, too.

"Good." Deacon Giuseppe held out a hand. Automatically, the Pope clasped it, and, in so doing, felt how cold his own flesh had gone. The round little nondescript Italian went on, "Can't let him have too much. We did that not so long ago, and it didn't work out well."

The new Pope understood him altogether too well. Then he touched the wound again, a fresh horror filling him. Yes, he remembered the films too well. "Am I going to turn into... one of those?" He pointed toward the central figure of his faith, who was licking blood off his lips with a tongue that seemed longer and more prehensile than a mere man's had any business being.

"We don't think so," Giuseppe said matter-of-factly. "Just to be sure, though, the papal undertaker drives a thin ash spike through the heart after each passing. We don't talk about that to the press. One of the traditions of the Order of the Pipistrelle is that when the sixth ecumenical council anathematized Pope Honorius, back thirteen hundred years ago, it wasn't for his doctrine, but because...."

"Is... Honorius out there, too? Or under here somewhere?"

"No. He was dealt with a long time ago." Deacon Giuseppe made pounding motions.

"I see." The Pope wondered if he could talk to... talk to the Son of God. Or the son of someone, anyhow. Did he have Aramaic enough for that? Or possibly Hebrew? How the Rabbi of Rome would laugh—or cry—if he knew! "Does every Pope do this? Endure this?"

"Every single one," Giuseppe said proudly. "What better way to connect to the beginning of things? Here is the beginning of things. He was risen, you know, Holy Father. How much does why really matter?"

For a lot of the world, why would matter enormously. The Muslims... The Protestants... The Orthodox... His head began to hurt, although the wound didn't. Maybe talking with... him wasn't such a good idea after all. How much do I really want to know?

"When we go back up, I have a lot of praying to do," the Pope said. Would all the prayer in the world free him from the feel of teeth in his throat? And what could he tell his confessor? The truth? The priest would think he'd gone mad—or, worse, wouldn't think so and would start the scandal. A lie? But wasn't inadequate confession of sin a sin in and of itself? The headache got worse.

Deacon Giuseppe might have read his thoughts. "You have a dispensation against speaking of this, your Holiness. It dates from the fourth century, and it may be the oldest document in the Vatican Library. It's not like the Donation of Constantine, either—there's no doubt it's genuine."

"Deo gratias!" the Pope said again.

"Shall we go, then?" the deacon asked.

"One moment." The Pope flogged his memory and found enough Aramaic for the question he had to ask: "Are you the Son of God?"

The sharp-toothed mouth twisted in a—reminiscent?—smile. "You say it," came the reply.

Well, he told Pilate the same thing, even if the question was a bit different, the Pope thought as he left the little chamber and Deacon Giuseppe meticulously closed and locked doors behind them. And, when the Pope was on the stairs going back up to the warmth and blessed light of St. Peter's, one more question occurred to him. How many Popes had heard that same answer?

How many of them had asked that same question? He'd heard it in Aramaic, in Greek, in Latin, and in the language Latin had turned into. He always said the same thing, and he always said it in Aramaic.

"You say it," he murmured to himself, there alone in the comfortable darkness again. Was he really? How could he know? But if they thought he was, then he was—for them. Wasn't that the only thing that counted?

That Roman had washed his hands of finding absolute truth. He was a brute, but not a stupid brute.

And this new one was old, and likely wouldn't last long. Pretty soon, he would feed again. And if he had to try to answer that question one more time afterwards... then he did, that was all.

CHILD OF AN ANCIENT CITY

by Tad Williams

Tad Williams is the bestselling author of the Memory, Sorrow & Thorn series, the Otherland series, and the Shadowmarch series. He has also written several other novels, such as *Tailchaser's Song*, *The War of the Flowers*, and *The Dragons of Ordinary Farm*, which was co-written with his wife, Deborah Beale. His short fiction has appeared in such venues as *Weird Tales*, *The Magazine of Fantasy & Science Fiction*, and in the anthologies *Legends* and *Legends II*. A collection of his short work, *Rite*, was released in 2006. He has also written for D.C. Comics, first with the miniseries *The Next*, and then doing a stint on *Aquaman*.

This story, which first appeared in *Weird Tales*, puts an Islamic spin on the traditional vampire tale (the roots of which, of course, are Christian). Set in the lands north of Baghdad, during the reign of Caliph Harun al-Rashid (late eighth century), a group of merchants encounter a strange creature in the desert, and soon find themselves unwilling Scheherazades to the bloodthirsty beast.

Merciful Allah! I am as a calf, fatted for slaughter!" Masrur al-Adan roared with laughter and crashed his goblet down on the polished wood table—once, twice, thrice. A trail of crescent-shaped dents followed his hand. "I can scarce move for gorging."

The fire was banked, and shadows walked the walls. Masrur's table—for he was master here—stood scatter-spread with the bones of small fowl.

Masrur leaned forward and squinted across the table. "A calf," he said. "Fatted." He belched absently and wiped his mouth with wine-stained sleeve.

Ibn Fahad broke off a thin, cold smile. "We have indeed wreaked massacre on the race of pigeons, old friend." His slim hand swept above the littered table-top. "We have also put the elite guard of your wine cellars to flight. And, as usual, I thank you for your hospitality. But do you not sometimes wonder if there is more to life than growing fat in the service of the Caliph?"

"Hah!" Masrur goggled his eyes. "Doing the Caliph's bidding has made me wealthy. I have made *myself fat*." He smiled. The other guests laughed and whispered.

Abu Jamir, a fatter man in an equally stained robe, toppled a small tower erected

45

from the bones of squab. "The night is young, good Masrur!" he cried. "Have someone fetch up more wine and let us hear some stories!"

"Baba!" Masrur bellowed. "Come here, you old dog!"

Within three breaths an old servant stood in the doorway, looking to his sportive master with apprehension.

"Bring us the rest of the wine, Baba—or have you drunk it all?" Baba pulled at his grizzled chin. "Ah… ah, but *you* drank it, Master. You and Master Ibn Fahad took the last four jars with you when you went to shoot arrows at the weathercock."

"Just as I suspected," Masrur nodded. "Well, get on across the bazaar to Abu Jamir's place, wake up his manservant, and bring back several jugs. The good Jamir says we must have it now."

Baba disappeared. The chagrined Abu Jamir was cheerfully back-thumped by the other guests.

"A story, a story!" someone shouted. "A tale!"

"Oh, yes, a tale of your travels, Master Masrur!" This was young Hassan, sinfully drunk. No one minded. His eyes were bright, and he was full of innocent stupidity. "Someone said you have traveled to the green lands of the north."

"The north… ?" Masrur grumbled, waving his hand as though confronted with something unclean, "No, lad, no… that I cannot give to you." His face clouded and he slumped back on his cushions; his tarbooshed head swayed.

Ibn Fahad knew Masrur like he knew his horses—indeed, Masrur was the only human that could claim so much of Ibn Fahad's attention. He had seen his old comrade drink twice this quantity and still dance like a dervish on the walls of Baghdad, but he thought he could guess the reason for this sudden incapacity.

"Oh, Masrur, please!" Hassan had not given up; he was as unshakeable as a young falcon with its first prey beneath its talons. "Tell us of the north. Tell us of the infidels!"

"A good Moslem should not show such interest in unbelievers." Abu Jamir sniffed piously, shaking the last drops from a wine jug. "If Masrur does not wish to tell a tale, let him be."

"Hah!" snorted the host, recovering somewhat. "You only seek to stall me, Jamir, so that my throat shall not be so dry when your wine arrives. No, I have no fear of speaking of unbelievers: Allah would not have given them a place in the world for their own if they had not *some* use. Rather it is… certain other things that happened which make me hesitate." He gazed kindly on young Hassan, who in the depths of his drunkenness looked about to cry. "Do not despair, eggling. Perhaps it would do me good to unfold this story. I have kept the details long inside." He emptied the dregs of another jar into his cup. "I still feel it so strongly, though—bitter, bitter times. Why don't *you* tell the story, my good friend?" he said over his shoulder to Ibn Fahad. "You played as much a part as did I."

"No," Ibn Fahad replied. Drunken puppy Hassan emitted a strangled cry of despair.

"But why, old comrade?" Masrur asked, pivoting his bulk to stare in amazement. "Did the experience so chill even *your* heart?"

Ibn Fahad glowered. "Because I know better. As soon as I start you will interrupt, adding details here, magnifying there, then saying: 'No, no, I cannot speak of it! Continue, old friend!' Before I have taken another breath you will interrupt me again. You *know* you will wind up doing all the talking, Masrur. Why do you not start from the beginning and save me my breath?"

All laughed but Masrur, who put on a look of wounded solicitousness. "Of course, old friend," he murmured. "I had no idea that you harbored such grievances. Of course I shall tell the tale." A broad wink was offered to the table. "No sacrifice is too great for a friendship such as ours. Poke up the fire, will you, Baba? Ah, he's gone. Hassan, will you be so kind?"

When the youth was again seated Masrur took a swallow, stroked his beard, and began.

In those days [Masrur said], I myself was but a lowly soldier in the service of Harun al-Rashid, may Allah grant him health. I was young, strong, a man who loved wine more than he should—but what soldier does not?—and a good deal more trim and comely than you see me today.

My troop received a commission to accompany a caravan going north, bound for the land of the Armenites beyond the Caucassian Mountains. A certain prince of that people had sent a great store of gifts as tribute to the Caliph, inviting him to open a route for trade between his principality and our caliphate. Harun al-Rashid, wisest of wise men that he is, did not exactly make the camels groan beneath the weight of the gifts that he sent in return; but he sent several courtiers, including the under-vizier Walid al-Salameh, to speak for him and to assure this Armenite prince that rich rewards would follow when the route over the Caucassians was opened for good.

We left Baghdad in grand style, pennants flying, the shields of the soldiers flashing like golden dinars, and the Caliph's gifts bundled onto the backs of a gang of evil, contrary donkeys.

We followed the banks of the faithful Tigris, resting several days at Mosul, then continued through the eastern edge of Anatolia. Already as we mounted northward the land was beginning to change, the clean sands giving way to rocky hills and scrub. The weather was colder, and the skies gray, as though Allah's face was turned away from that country, but the men were not unhappy to be out from under the desert sun. Our pace was good; there was not a hint of danger except the occasional wolf howling at night beyond the circles of the campfires. Before two months had passed we had reached the foothills of the Caucassians—what is called the steppe country.

For those of you who have not strayed far from our Baghdad, I should tell you that the northern lands are like nothing you have seen. The trees there grow so close together you could not throw a stone five paces without striking one. The land itself seems always dark—the trees mask the sun before the afternoon is properly finished—and the ground is damp. But, in truth, the novelty of it fades quickly, and before long it seems that the smell of decay is always with you. We caravaneers had been over eight weeks a-traveling, and the bite of homesickness was strong, but we contented ourselves with the thought of the accommodations that would be ours when we reached the palace of the prince, laden as we were with our Caliph's good wishes—and the tangible proof thereof.

We had just crossed the high mountain passes and begun our journey down when disaster struck.

We were encamped one night in a box canyon, a thousand steep feet below the summit of the tall Caucassian peaks. The fires were not much but glowing coals, and nearly all the camp was asleep except for two men standing sentry. I was wrapped in my bedroll, dreaming of how I would spend my earnings, when a terrible shriek awakened me. Sitting groggily upright, I was promptly knocked down by some bulky thing tumbling onto me. A moment's horrified examination showed that it was one of the sentries, throat pierced with an arrow, eyes bulging with his final surprise. Suddenly there was a chorus of howls from the hillside above. All I could think of was wolves, that the wolves were coming down on us; in my witless state I could make no sense of the arrow at all.

Even as the others sprang up around me the camp was suddenly filled with leaping, whooping shadows. Another arrow hissed past my face in the darkness, and then something crashed against my bare head, filling the nighttime with a great splash of light that illuminated nothing. I fell back, insensible.

I could not tell how long I had journeyed in that deeper darkness when I was finally roused by a sharp boot prodding at my ribcage.

I looked up at a tall, cruel figure, cast by the cloud-curtained morning sun in bold silhouette. As my sight became accustomed I saw a knife-thin face, dark-browed and fierce, with mustachios long as a Tartar herdsman's. I felt sure that whoever had struck me had returned to finish the job, and I struggled weakly to pull my dagger from my sash. This terrifying figure merely lifted one of his pointy boots and trod delicately on my wrist, saying in perfect Arabic: "Wonders of Allah, this is the dirtiest man I have ever seen."

It was Ibn Fahad, of course. The caravan had been of good size, and he had been riding with the Armenite and the under-vizier—not back with the hoi polloi—so we had never spoken. Now you see how we first truly met: me on my back, covered with mud, blood, and spit; and Ibn Fahad standing over me like a rich man examining carrots in the bazaar. Infamy!

Ibn Fahad had been blessed with what I would come later to know as his usual luck. When the bandits—who must have been following us for some days—came down upon us in the night, Ibn Fahad had been voiding his bladder some way downslope. Running back at the sound of the first cries, he had sent more than a few mountain bandits down to Hell courtesy of his swift sword, but they were too many. He pulled together a small group of survivors from the main party and they fought their way free, then fled along the mountain in the darkness listening to the screams echoing behind them, cursing their small numbers and ignorance of the country.

Coming back in the light of day to scavenge for supplies, as well as ascertain the nature of our attackers, Ibn Fahad had found me—a fact he has never allowed me to forget, and for which *I* have never allowed *him* to evade responsibility.

While my wounds and bandit-spites were doctored, Ibn Fahad introduced me to the few survivors of our once-great caravan.

One was Susri al-Din—a cheerful lad, fresh-faced and smooth-cheeked as young Hassan here, dressed in the robes of a rich merchant's son. The soldiers who had survived rather liked him, and called him "Fawn," to tease him for his wide-eyed good looks. There was a skinny wretch of a chief-clerk named Abdallah, purse-mouthed and iron-eyed, and an indecently plump young mullah, who had just left the *madrasa* and was getting a rather rude introduction to life outside the seminary. Ruad, the mullah, looked as though he would prefer to be drinking and laughing with the soldiers—besides myself and Ibn Fahad there were four or five more of these—while Abdallah the prim-faced clerk looked as though *he* should be the one who never lifted his head out of the Koran. Well, in a way that was true, since for a man like Abdallah the balance book *is* the Holy Book, may Allah forgive such blasphemy.

There was one other, notable for the extreme richness of his robes, the extreme whiteness of his beard, and the vast weight of his personal jewelry—Walid al-Salameh, the under-vizier to His Eminence the Caliph Harun al-Rashid. Walid was the most important man of the whole party. He was also, surprisingly, not a bad fellow at all.

So there we found ourselves, the wrack of the Caliph's embassy, with no hope but to try and find our way back home through a strange, hostile land.

The upper reaches of the Caucassians are a cold and godless place. The fog is thick and wet; it crawls in of the morning, leaves briefly at the time the sun is high, then comes creeping back long before sunset. We had been sodden as well-diggers from the moment we had stepped into the foothills. A treacherous place, those mountains: home of bear and wolf, covered in forest so thick that in places the sun was lost completely. Since we had no guide—indeed, it was several days before we saw any sign of inhabitants whatsoever—we wandered unsteered, losing half as much ground as we gained for walking in circles.

At last we were forced to admit our need for a trained local eye. In the middle slopes the trees grew so thick that fixing our direction was impossible for hours at a time. We were divining the location of Mecca by general discussion, and—blasphemy again—we probably spent as much time praying toward Aleppo as to Mecca. It seemed a choice between possible discovery and certain doom.

We came down by night and took a young man out of an isolated shepherd's hovel, as quietly as ex-brigands like ourselves (or at least like many of us, Ibn Fahad. My apologies!) could. The family did not wake, the dog did not bark; we were two leagues away before sunrise, I'm sure.

I felt sorry in a way for the young peasant-lout we'd kidnapped. He was a nice fellow, although fearfully stupid—I wonder if we are now an old, dull story with which he bores his children? In any case, once this young rustic—whose name as far as I could tell was unpronounceable by civilized tongues—realized that we were not ghosts or Jinni, and were *not* going to kill him on the spot, he calmed down and was quite useful. We began to make real progress, reaching the peak of the nearest ridge in two days.

There was a slight feeling of celebration in the air that night, our first in days under the open skies. The soldiers cursed the lack of strong drink, but spirits were good nonetheless—even Ibn Fahad pried loose a smile.

As the under-vizier Walid told a humorous story, I looked about the camp. There were but two grim faces: the clerk Abdallah—which was to be expected, since he seemed a patently sour old devil—and the stolen peasant-boy. I walked over to him.

"Ho, young one," I said, "why do you look so downcast? Have you not realized that we are good-hearted, Godfearing men, and will not harm you?" He did not even raise his chin, which rested on his knees, shepherd-style, but he turned his eyes up to mine.

"It is not those things," he said in his awkward Arabic. "It is not you soldiers but… this place."

"Gloomy mountains they are indeed," I agreed, "but you have lived here all your young life. Why should it bother you?"

"Not this place. We never come here—it is unholy. The vampyr walks these peaks."

"*Vampyr?*" said I. "And what peasant-devil is that?"

He would say no more; I left him to his brooding and walked back to the fire.

The men all had a good laugh over the vampyr, making jesting guesses as to what type of beast it might be, but Ruad, the young mullah, waved his hands urgently.

"I have heard of such afreets," he said. "They are not to be laughed at by such a godless lot as yourselves."

He said this as a sort of scolding joke, but he wore a strange look on his round face; we listened with interest as he continued.

"The vampyr is a restless spirit. It is neither alive nor dead, and Shaitan possesses its soul utterly. It sleeps in a sepulcher by day, and when the moon rises it goes out to feed upon travelers, to drink their blood."

Some of the men again laughed loudly, but this time it rang false as a brass-merchant's smile.

"I have heard of these from one of our foreign visitors," said the under-vizier Walid quietly. "He told me of a plague of these vampyr in a village near Smyrna. All the inhabitants fled, and the village is still uninhabited today."

This reminded someone else (myself, perhaps) of a tale about an afreet with teeth growing on both sides of his head. Others followed with their own demon stories. The talk went on late into the night, and no one left the campfire until it had completely burned out.

By noon the next day we had left the heights and were passing back down into the dark, tree-blanketed ravines. When we stopped that night we were once more hidden from the stars, out of sight of Allah and the sky.

I remember waking up in the foredawn hours. My beard was wet with dew, and I was damnably tangled up in my cloak. A great, dark shape stood over me. I must confess to making a bit of a squawking noise.

"It's me," the shape hissed—it was Rifakh, one of the other soldiers.

"You gave me a turn."

Rifakh chuckled. "Thought I was that vampyr, eh? Sorry. Just stepping out for a piss." He stepped over me, and I heard him trampling the underbrush. I slipped back into sleep.

The sun was just barely over the horizon when I was again awakened, this time by Ibn Fahad tugging at my arm. I grumbled at him to leave me alone, but he had a grip on me like an alms-beggar.

"Rifakh's gone," he said. "Wake up. Have you seen him?"

"He walked on me in the middle of the night, on his way to go moisten a tree," I said. "He probably fell in the darkness and hit his head on something—have you looked?"

"Several times," Ibn Fahad responded. "All around the camp. No sign of him. Did he say anything to you?"

"Nothing interesting. Perhaps he has met the sister of our shepherd-boy, and is making the two-backed beast."

Ibn Fahad made a sour face at my crudity. "Perhaps not. Perhaps he has met some *other* beast."

"Don't worry," I said. "If he hasn't fallen down somewhere close by, he'll be back."

But he did not come back. When the rest of the men arose we had another long search, with no result. At noon we decided, reluctantly, to go on our way, hoping that if he had strayed somewhere he could catch up with us.

We hiked down into the valley, going farther and farther into the trees. There was no sign of Rifakh, although from time to time we stopped and shouted in case he was searching for us. We felt there was small risk of discovery, for that dark valley was as empty as a pauper's purse, but nevertheless, after a while the sound of our voices echoing back through the damp glades became unpleasant. We continued on in silence.

Twilight comes early in the bosom of the mountains; by midafternoon it was already becoming dark. Young Fawn—the name had stuck, against the youth's protests—who of all of us was the most disturbed by the disappearance of Rifakh, stopped the company suddenly, shouting: "Look there!"

We straightaway turned to see where he was pointing, but the thick trees and shadows revealed nothing.

"I saw a shape!" the young one said. "It was just a short way back, following us. Perhaps it is the missing soldier."

Naturally the men ran back to look, but though we scoured the bushes we could find no trace of anyone. We decided that the failing light had played Fawn a trick—that he had seen a hind or some such.

Two other times he called out that he saw a shape. The last time one of the other soldiers glimpsed it too: a dark, man-like form, moving rapidly beneath the trees a bow-shot away. Close inspection still yielded no evidence, and as the group trod wearily back to the path again Walid the under-vizier turned to Fawn with a hard, flat look.

"Perhaps it would be better, young master, if you talked no more of shadow-shapes."

"But I saw it!" the boy cried. "That soldier Mohammad saw it too!"

"I have no doubt of that," answered Walid al-Salameh, "but think on this: we have gone several times to see what it might be, and have found no sign of any living man. Perhaps our Rifakh is dead; perhaps he fell into a stream and drowned, or hit his head upon a rock. His spirit may be following us because it does not wish to stay in this unfamiliar place. That does not mean we want to go and find it."

"But…" the other began.

"Enough!" spat the chief-clerk Abdallah. "You heard the under-vizier, young prankster. We shall have no more talk of your godless spirits. You will straightaway leave off telling such things!"

"Your concern is appreciated, Abdallah," Walid said coldly, "but I do not require your help in this matter." The vizier strode away.

I was almost glad the clerk had added his voice, because such ideas would not keep the journey in good order… but like the under-vizier I, too, had been rubbed and grated by the clerk's highhandedness. I am sure others felt the same, for no more was said on the subject all evening.

Allah, though, always has the last word—and who are *we* to try to understand His ways? We bedded down a very quiet camp that night, the idea of poor Rifakh's lost soul hanging unspoken in the air.

From a thin, unpleasant sleep I woke to find the camp in chaos. "It's Mohammad, the soldier!" Fawn was crying. "He's been killed! He's dead!"

It was true. The mullah Ruad, first up in the morning, had found the man's blanket empty, then found his body a few short yards out of the clearing.

"His throat has been slashed out," said Ibn Fahad.

It looked like a wild beast had been at him. The ground beneath was dark with blood, and his eyes were wide open.

Above the cursing of the soldiers and the murmured holy words of the mullah, who looked quite green of face, I heard another sound. The young shepherd-lad, grimly silent all the day before, was rocking back and forth on the ground by the remains of the cook-fire, moaning.

"Vampyr…" he wept, "…vampyr, the vampyr…"

All the companions were, of course, completely unmanned by these events. While we buried Mohammad in a hastily dug grave, those assembled darted glances over their shoulders into the forest vegetation. Even Ruad, as he spoke the words of the holy Koran, had trouble keeping his eyes down. Ibn Fahad and I agreed between ourselves to maintain that Mohammad had fallen prey to a wolf or some other beast, but our fellow travelers found it hard even to pretend agreement. Only the under-vizier and the clerk Abdallah seemed to have their wits fully about them, and Abdallah made no secret of his contempt for the others. We set out again at once.

Our company was somber that day—and no wonder. No one wished to speak of the obvious, nor did they have much stomach for talk of lighter things—it was a silent file of men that moved through the mountain fastnesses.

As the shadows of evening began to roll down, the dark shape was with us again, flitting along just in sight, disappearing for a while only to return, bobbing along behind us like a jackdaw. My skin was crawling—as you may well believe—though I tried to hide it.

We set camp, building a large fire and moving near to it, and had a sullen, close-cramped supper. Ibn Fahad, Abdallah, the under-vizier, and I were still speaking of the follower only as some beast. Abdallah may even have believed it—not from ordinary foolishness, but because he was the type of man who was unwilling to believe there might be anything he himself could not compass.

As we took turns standing guard the young mullah led the far-from-sleepy men in prayer. The voices rose up with the smoke, neither seeming to be of much substance against the wind of those old, cold mountains.

I sidled over to the shepherd-lad. He'd become, if anything, more close-mouthed since the discovery of the morning.

"This 'vampyr' you spoke of…" I said quietly. "What do your people do to protect themselves from it?"

He looked up at me with a sad smile.

"Lock the doors."

I stared across at the other men—young Fawn with clenched mouth and furrowed brow; the mullah Ruad, eyes closed, plump cheeks awash with sweat as he prayed; Ibn Fahad gazing coolly outward, ever outward—and then I returned the boy's sad smile.

"No doors to lock, no windows to bar," I said. "What else?"

"There is an herb we hang about our houses…" he said, and fumbled for the word in our unfamiliar language. After a moment he gave up. "It does not matter. We have none. None grows here."

I leaned forward, putting my face next to his face. "For the love of God, boy, what else?"—*I* knew it was not a beast of the Earth. *I knew.* I had seen that fluttering shadow.

"Well…" he mumbled, turning his face away, "… they say, some men do, that you can tell stories…."

"What!" I thought he had gone mad.

"This is what my grandfather says. The vampyr will stop to hear the story you tell—if it is a good one—and if you continue it until daylight he must return to the… place of the dead."

There was a sudden shriek. I leaped to my feet, fumbling for my knife… but it was only Ruad, who had put his foot against a hot coal. I sank down again, heart hammering.

"Stories?" I asked.

"I have only heard so," he said, struggling for the right phrases. "We try to keep them farther away than that—they must come close to hear a man talking."

Later, after the fire had gone down, we placed sentries and went to our blankets. I lay a long while thinking of what the Armenite boy had said before I slept.

A hideous screeching sound woke me. It was not yet dawn, and this time no one had burned himself on a glowing ember.

One of the two soldiers who had been standing picket lay on the forest floor, blood gouting from a great wound on the side of his head. In the torchlight it looked as though his skull had been smashed with a heavy cudgel. The other sentry was gone, but there was a terrible thrashing in the underbrush beyond the camp, and screams that would have sounded like an animal in a cruel trap but for the half-formed words that bubbled up from time to time.

We crouched, huddled, staring like startled rabbits. The screaming began to die away. Suddenly Ruad started up, heavy and clumsy getting to his feet. I saw tears in his eyes. "We... we must not leave our fellow to s-s-suffer so!" he cried, and looked around at all of us. I don't think anyone could hold his eye except the clerk Abdallah. I could not.

"Be silent, fool!" the clerk said, heedless of blasphemy. "It is a wild beast. It is for these cowardly soldiers to attend to, not a man of God!"

The young mullah stared at him for a moment, and a change came over his face. The tears were still wet on his cheeks, but I saw his jaw firm and his shoulders square."

"No," he said. "We cannot leave him to Shaitan's servant. If you will not go to him, I will." He rolled up the scroll he had been nervously fingering and kissed it. A shaft of moonlight played across the gold letters.

I tried to grab his arm as he went past me, but he shook me off with surprising strength, then moved toward the brush, where the screeching had died down to a low, broken moaning.

"Come back, you idiot!" Abdallah shrieked at him. "This is foolishness! Come back!"

The young holy man looked back over his shoulder, darting a look at Abdallah I could not easily describe, then turned around and continued forward, holding the parchment scroll before him as if it were a candle against the dark night.

"*There is no God but Allah!*" I heard him cry, "*and Mohammad is His prophet!*" Then he was gone.

After a long moment of silence there came the sound of the holy words of the Koran, chanted in an unsteady voice. We could hear the mullah making his ungraceful way out through the thicket. I was not the only one who held his breath.

Next there was crashing, and branches snapping, as though some huge beast was leaping through the brush; the mullah's chanting became a howl. Men cursed helplessly. Before the cry had faded, though, another scream came—numbingly loud, the rage of a powerful animal, full of shock and surprise. It had words in it, although not in any tongue I had ever heard before... or since.

Another great thrashing, and then nothing but silence. We lit another fire and sat sleepless until dawn.

In the morning, despite my urgings, the company went to look for trace of the sentry and the young priest. They found them both.

It made a grim picture, let me tell you, my friends. They hung upside down from the branches of a great tree. Their necks were torn, and they were white as chalk: all the blood had been drawn from them. We dragged the two stone-cold husks back to the camp-circle, and shortly thereafter buried them commonly with the other sentry, who had not survived his head wound.

One curious thing there was: on the ground beneath the hanging head of the young priest lay the remains of his holy scroll. It was scorched to black ash, and crumbled at my touch.

"So it *was* a cry of pain we heard," said Ibn Fahad over my shoulder. "The devil-beast can be hurt, it appears."

"Hurt, but not made to give over," I observed. "And no other holy writings remain, nor any hands so holy to wield them, or mouth to speak them." I looked pointedly over at Abdallah, who was giving unwanted instructions to the two remaining soldiers on how to spade the funeral dirt. I half-hoped one of them would take it on himself to brain the old meddler.

"True," grunted Ibn Fahad. "Well, I have my doubts on how cold steel will fare, also."

"As do I. But it could be there is yet a way we may save ourselves. The shepherd-boy told me of it. I will explain when we stop at mid-day."

"I will be waiting eagerly," said Ibn Fahad, favoring me with his half-smile. "I am glad to see someone else is thinking and planning beside myself. But perhaps you should tell us your plan on the march. Our daylight hours are becoming precious as blood, now. As a matter of fact, I think from now on we shall have to do without burial services."

Well, there we were in a very nasty fix. As we walked I explained my plan to the group; they listened silently, downcast, like men condemned to death—not an unreasonable attitude, in all truth.

"Now, here's the thing," I told them. "If this young lout's idea of tale-telling will work, we shall have to spend our nights yarning away. We may have to begin taking stops for sleeping in the daylight. Every moment walking, then, is precious—we must keep the pace up or we will die in these damned, haunted mountains. Also, while you walk, think of stories. From what the lad says we may have another ten days or a fortnight to go until we escape this country. We shall soon run out of things to tell about unless you dig deep into your memories."

There was grumbling, but it was too dispirited a group to offer much protest.

"Be silent, unless you have a better idea," said Ibn Fahad. "Masrur is quite cor-rect—although, if what I suspect is true, it may be the first time in his life he finds himself in that position." He threw me a wicked grin, and one of the soldiers snickered. It was a good sound to hear.

We had a short mid-day rest—most of us got at least an hour's sleep on the rocky ground—and then we walked on until the beginning of twilight. We were in the bottom of a long, thickly forested ravine, where we promptly built a large fire to keep away some of the darkness of the valley floor. Ah, but fire is a good friend!

Gathered around the blaze, the men cooked strips of venison on the ends of green sticks. We passed the waterskin and wished it was more—not for the first time.

"Now then," I said, "I'll go first, for at home I was the one called upon most often to tell tales, and I have a good fund of them. Some of you may sleep, but not all—there should always be two or three awake in case the teller falters or forgets. We cannot know if this will keep the creature at bay, but we should take no chances."

So I began, telling first the story of The Four Clever Brothers. It was early, and no one was ready to sleep; all listened attentively as I spun it out, adding details here, stretching a description there.

When it ended I was applauded, and straight away began telling the story of the carpet merchant Salim and his unfaithful wife. That was perhaps not a good choice—it is a story about a vengeful djinn, and about death; but I went on none-theless, finished it, then told two more.

As I was finishing the fourth story, about a brave orphan who finds a cave of jewels, I glimpsed a strange thing.

The fire was beginning to die down, and as I looked out over the flames I saw movement in the forest. The under-vizier Walid was directly across from me, and beyond his once-splendid robes a dark shape lurked. It came no closer than the edge of the trees, staying just out of the fire's flickering light. I lost my voice for a moment then and stuttered, but quickly caught up the thread and finished. No one had noticed, I was sure.

I asked for the waterskin and motioned for Walid al-Salameh to continue. He took up with a tale of the rivalry beyond two wealthy houses in his native Isfahan. One or two of the others wrapped themselves tightly in their cloaks and lay down, staring up as they listened, watching the sparks rise into the darkness.

I pulled my hood down low on my brow to shield my gaze, and squinted out past Walid's shoulder. The dark shape had moved a little nearer now to the lap-ping glow of the campfire.

It was man-shaped, that I could see fairly well, though it clung close to the trunk of a tree at clearing's edge. Its face was in darkness; two ember-red eyes unblink-ingly reflected the firelight. It seemed clothed in rags, but that could have been a trick of the shadows.

Huddled in the darkness a stone-throw away, it was listening.

I turned my head slowly across the circle. Most eyes were on the under-vizier;

Fawn had curtained his in sleep. But Ibn Fahad, too, was staring out into the darkness. I suppose he felt my gaze, for he turned to me and nodded slightly: he had seen it too.

We went on until dawn, the men taking turns sleeping as one of the others told stories—mostly tales they had heard as children, occasionally of an adventure that had befallen them. Ibn Fahad and I said nothing of the dark shape that watched. Somewhere in the hour before dawn it disappeared.

It was a sleepy group that took to the trail that day, but we had all lived through the night. This alone put the men in better spirits, and we covered much ground.

That night we again sat around the fire. I told the story of The Gazelle King, and The Enchanted Peacock, and The Little Man with No Name, each of them longer and more complicated than the one before. Everyone except the clerk Abdallah contributed something—Abdallah and the shepherd-boy, that is. The chief-clerk said repeatedly that he had never wasted his time on foolishness such as learning stories. We were understandably reluctant to press our self-preservation into such unwilling hands.

The Armenite boy, our guide, sat quietly all the evening and listened to the men yarning away in a tongue that was not his own. When the moon had risen through the treetops, the shadow returned and stood silently outside the clearing. I saw the peasant lad look up. He saw it, I know, but like Ibn Fahad and I, he held his silence.

The next day brought us two catastrophes. As we were striking camp in the morning, happily no fewer than when we had set down the night before, the local lad took the waterskins down to the river that threaded the bottom of the ravine. When a long hour had passed and he had not returned, we went fearfully down to look for him.

He was gone. All but one of the waterskins lay on the streambank. He had filled them first.

The men were panicky. "The vampyr has taken him!" they cried.

"What does that foul creature need with a waterskin?" pointed out al-Salameh.

"He's right," I said. "No, I'm afraid our young friend has merely jumped ship, so to speak. I suppose he thinks his chances of getting back are better if he is alone."

I wondered… I *still* wonder… if he made it back. He was not a bad fellow: witness the fact that he took only one waterbag, and left us the rest.

Thus, we found ourselves once more without a guide. Fortunately, I had discussed with him the general direction, and he had told Ibn Fahad and myself of the larger landmarks… but it was nevertheless with sunken hearts that we proceeded.

Later that day, in the early afternoon, the second blow fell.

We were coming up out of the valley, climbing diagonally along the steep side of the ravine. The damned Caucassian fogs had slimed the rocks and turned the ground soggy; the footing was treacherous.

Achmed, the older of the remaining pike-men, had been walking poorly all day.

He had bad joints, anyway, he said; and the cold nights had been making them worse.

We had stopped to rest on an outcropping of rock that jutted from the valley wall; and Achmed, the last in line, was just catching up to us when he slipped. He fell heavily onto his side and slid several feet down the muddy slope.

Ibn Fahad jumped up to look for a rope, but before he could get one from the bottom of his pack the other soldier—named Bekir, if memory serves—clambered down the grade to help his comrade.

He got a grip on Achmed's tunic, and was just turning around to catch Ibn Fahad's rope when the leg of the older man buckled beneath him and he fell backward. Bekir, caught off his balance, pitched back as well, his hand caught in the neck of Achmed's tunic, and the two of them rolled end over end down the slope. Before anyone could so much as cry out they had both disappeared over the edge, like a wine jug rolling off a table-top. Just that sudden.

To fall such a distance certainly killed them.

We could not find the bodies, of course… could not even climb back down the ravine to look. Ibn Fahad's remark about burials had taken on a terrible, ironic truth. We could but press on, now a party of five—myself, Ibn Fahad, the under-vizier Walid, Abdallah the clerk, and young Fawn. I doubt that there was a single one of our number who did not wonder which of us would next meet death in that lonesome place.

Ah, by Allah most high, I have never been so sick of the sound of my own voice as I was by the time nine more nights had passed. Ibn Fahad, I know, would say that I have never understood how sick *everyone* becomes of the sound of my voice—am I correct, old friend? But I *was* tired of it, tired of talking all night, tired of rack-ing my brain for stories, tired of listening to the cracked voices of Walid and Ibn Fahad, tired to sickness of the damp, gray, oppressive mountains.

All were now aware of the haunting shade that stood outside our fire at night, waiting and listening. Young Fawn, in particular, could hardly hold up his turn at tale-telling, so much did his voice tremble.

Abdallah grew steadily colder and colder, congealing like rendered fat. The thing which followed was no respecter of his cynicism or his mathematics, and would not be banished for all the scorn he could muster. The skinny chief-clerk did not turn out to us, though, to support the story-circle, but sat silently and walked apart. Despite our terrible mutual danger he avoided our company as much as possible.

The tenth night after the loss of Achmed and Bekir we were running out of tales. We had been ground down by our circumstances, and were ourselves become nearly as shadowy as that which we feared.

Walid al-Salameh was droning on about some ancient bit of minor intrigue in the court of the Emperor Darius of Persia. Ibn Fahad leaned toward me, lowering his voice so that neither Abdallah or Fawn—whose expression was one of complete and hopeless despair—could hear.

"Did you notice," he whispered, "that our guest has made no appearance to-night?"

"It has not escaped me," I said. "I hardly think it a good sign, however. If our talk no longer interests the creature, how long can it be until its thoughts return to our other uses?"

"I fear you're right," he responded, and gave a scratchy, painful chuckle. "There's a good three or four more days walking, and hard walking at that, until we reach the bottom of these mountains and come *once more onto the plain*, at *which* point we might hope the devil-beast would leave us."

"Ibn Fahad," I said, shaking my head as I looked across at Fawn's drawn, pale face, "I fear we shall not manage…"

As if to point up the truth of my fears, Walid here stopped his speech, coughing violently. I gave him to drink of the waterskin, but when he had finished he did not begin anew; he only sat looking darkly, as one lost, out to the forest.

"Good vizier," I asked, "can you continue?"

He said nothing, and I quickly spoke in his place, trying to pick up the threads of a tale I had not been attending to. Walid leaned back, exhausted and breathing raggedly. Abdallah clucked his tongue in disgust. If I had not been fearfully occupied, I would have struck the clerk.

Just as I was beginning to find my way, inventing a continuation of the vizier's Darian political meanderings, there came a shock that passed through all of us like a cold wind, and a new shadow appeared at the edge of the clearing. The vampyr had joined us.

Walid moaned and sat up, huddling by the fire. I faltered for a moment but went on. The candle-flame eyes regarded us unblinkingly, and the shadow shook for a moment as if folding great wings.

Suddenly Fawn leaped to his feet, swaying unsteadily. I lost the strands of the story completely and stared up at him in amazement.

"Creature!" he screamed. "Hell-spawn! Why do you torment us in this way? Why, why, why?"

Ibn Fahad reached up to pull him down, but the young man danced away like a shying horse. His mouth hung open and his eyes were starting from their dark-rimmed sockets.

"You great beast!" he continued to shriek. "Why do you toy with us? Why do you not just kill me—kill us *all*, set us free from this terrible, terrible…"

And with that he walked *forward*—away from the fire, toward the thing that crouched at forest's edge.

"End this now!" Fawn shouted, and fell to his knees only a few strides from the smoldering red eyes, sobbing like a child.

"Stupid boy, get back!" I cried. Before I could get up to pull him back—and I would have, I swear by Allah's name—there was a great rushing noise, and the black shape was gone, the lamps of its stare extinguished. Then, as we pulled the shuddering youth back to the campfire, something rustled in the trees. On the opposite side of the campfire one of the near branches suddenly bobbed beneath the weight of a strange new fruit—a black fruit with red-lit eyes. It made an awful croaking noise.

In our shock it was a few moments before we realized that the deep, rasping sound was speech—and the words were Arabic!

"…It… was… you…" it said, "…who chose… to play the game this way…"

Almost strangest of all, I would swear that this thing had never spoken our language before, never even heard it until we had wandered lost into the mountains. Something of its halting inflections, its strange hesitations, made me guess it had learned our speech from listening all these nights to our campfire stories.

"Demon!" shrilled Abdallah. "What manner of creature are you?!"

"You know… very well what kind of… thing I am, man. You may none of you know *how,* or *why*… but by now, you know *what* I am."

"Why… why do you torment us so?!" shouted Fawn, writhing in Ibn Fahad's strong grasp.

"Why does the… serpent kill… a rabbit? The serpent does not… hate. It kills to live, as do I… as do you."

Abdallah lurched forward a step. "We do not slaughter our fellow men like this, devil-spawn!"

"C-c-clerk!" the black shape hissed, and dropped down from the tree. "C-close your foolish mouth! You push me too far!" It bobbed, as if agitated. "The curse of human ways! Even now you provoke me more than you should, you huffing… insect! *Enough!*"

The vampyr seemed to leap upward, and with a great rattling of leaves he scuttled away along the limb of a tall tree. I was fumbling for my sword, but before I could find it the creature spoke again from his high perch.

"The young one asked me why I 'toy' with you. I do not. If I do not kill, I will suffer. More than I suffer already.

"Despite what this clerk says, though, I am not a creature without… without feelings as men have them. Less and less do I wish to destroy you.

"For the first time in a great age I have listened to the sound of human voices that were not screams of fear. I have approached a circle of men without the barking of dogs, and have listened to them talk.

"It has almost been like being a man again."

"And this is how you show your pleasure?" the under-vizier Walid asked, teeth chattering. "By k-k-killing us?"

"I am what I am," said the beast. "… But for all that, you have inspired a certain desire for companionship. It puts me in mind of things that I can barely remember.

"I propose that we make a… bargain," said the vampyr. "A… wager?"

I had found my sword, and Ibn Fahad had drawn his as well, but we both knew we could not kill a thing like this—a red-eyed demon that could leap five cubits in the air and had learned to speak our language in a fortnight.

"No bargains with Shaitan!" spat the clerk Abdallah.

"What do you mean?" I demanded, inwardly marveling that such an unlikely dialogue should ever take place on the earth. "Pay no attention to the…" I curled my lip, "… holy man." Abdallah shot me a venomous glance.

"Hear me, then," the creature said, and in the deep recesses of the tree seemed once more to unfold and stretch great wings. "Hear me. I must kill to live, and my nature is such that I cannot choose to die. That is the way of things.

"I offer you now, however, the chance to win safe passage out of my domain, these hills. We shall have a contest, a wager if you like; if you best me you shall go freely, and I shall turn once more to the musty, slow-blooded peasants of the local valleys."

Ibn Fahad laughed bitterly. "What, are we to fight you then? So be it!"

"I would snap your spine like a dry branch," croaked the black shape. "No, you have held me these many nights telling stories; it is story-telling that will win you safe passage. We will have a contest, one that will suit my whims: we shall relate the saddest of all stories. That is my demand. You may tell three, I will tell only one. If you can best me with any or all, you shall go unhindered by me."

"And if we lose?" I cried. "And who shall judge?"

"You may judge," it said, and the deep, thick voice took on a tone of grim amusement. "If you can look into my eyes and tell me that you have bested *my* sad tale… why, then I shall believe you.

"If you lose," it said, "then one of your number shall come to me, and pay the price of your defeat. Those are my terms, otherwise I shall hunt you down one at a time—for in truth, your present tale-telling has begun to lose my interest."

Ibn Fahad darted a worried look in my direction. Fawn and the others stared at the demon-shape in mute terror and astonishment.

"We shall… we shall give you our decision at sunset tomorrow," I said. "We must be allowed to think and talk."

"As you wish," said the vampyr. "But if you accept my challenge, the game must begin then. After all, we have only a few more days to spend together." And at this the terrible creature laughed, a sound like the bark being pulled from the trunk of a rotted tree. Then the shadow was gone.

In the end we had to accede to the creature's wager, of course. We knew he was not wrong in his assessment of us—we were just wagging our beards over the nightly campfire, no longer even listening to our own tales. Whatever magic had held the vampyr at bay had drained out like meal from a torn sack.

I racked my poor brains all afternoon for stories of sadness, but could think of nothing that seemed to fit, that seemed significant enough for the vital purpose at hand. I had been doing most of the talking for several nights running, and had exhausted virtually every story I had ever heard—and I was never much good at making them up, as Ibn Fahad will attest. Yes, go ahead and smile, old comrade.

Actually, it was Ibn Fahad who volunteered the first tale. I asked him what it was, but he would not tell me. "Let me save what potency it may have," he said. The under-vizier Walid also had something he deemed suitable, I was racking my brain fruitlessly for a third time when young Fawn piped up that he would tell a tale himself. I looked him over, rosy cheeks and long-lashed eyes, and asked him what he could possibly know of sadness. Even as I spoke I realized my cruelty, standing as we all did in the shadow of death or worse; but it was too late to take it back.

Fawn did not flinch. He was folding his cloak as he sat cross-ankled on the ground, folding and unfolding it. He looked up and said: "I shall tell a sad story about love. All the saddest stories are about love."

These young shavetails, I thought—although I was not ten years his senior—*a sad story about love.* But I could not think of better, and was forced to give in.

We walked as fast and far as we could that day, as if hoping that somehow, against all reason, we should find ourselves out of the gloomy, mist-sodden hills. But when twilight came the vast bulk of the mountains still hung above us. We made camp on the porch of a great standing rock, as though protection at our backs would avail us of something if the night went badly.

The fire had only just taken hold, and the sun had dipped below the rim of the hills a moment before, when a cold wind made the branches of the trees whip back and forth. We knew without speaking, without looking at one another, that the creature had come.

"Have you made your decision?" The harsh voice from the trees sounded strange, as if its owner was trying to speak lightly, carelessly—but I only heard death in those cold syllables.

"We have," said Ibn Fahad, drawing himself up out of his involuntary half-crouch to stand erect. "We will accept your wager. Do you wish to begin?"

"Oh, no…" the thing said, and made a flapping noise. "That would take all of the… suspense from the contest, would it not? No, I insist that you begin."

"I am first, then," Ibn Fahad said, looking around our circle for confirmation. The dark shape moved abruptly toward us. Before we could scatter the vampyr stopped, a few short steps away.

"Do not fear," it grated. Close to one's ear the voice was even odder and more strained. "I have come nearer to hear the story and see the teller—for surely that is part of any tale—but I shall move no farther. Begin."

Everybody but myself stared into the fire, hugging their knees, keeping their eyes averted from the bundle of darkness that sat at our shoulders. I had the fire between myself and the creature, and felt safer than if I had sat like Walid and Abdallah, with nothing between the beast and my back but cold ground.

The vampyr sat hunched, as if imitating our posture, its eyes hooded so that only a flicker of scarlet light, like a half-buried brand, showed through the slit. It was black, this manlike thing—not black as a Negro, mind you, but black as burnt steel, black as the mouth of a cave. It bore the aspect of someone dead of the plague. Rags wrapped it, mouldering, filthy bits of cloth, rotten as old bread… but the curve of its back spoke of terrible life—a great black cricket poised to jump.

IBN FAHAD'S STORY

Many years ago [he began], I traveled for a good time in Egypt. I was indigent, then, and journeyed wherever the prospect of payment for a sword arm beckoned.

I found myself at last in the household guard of a rich merchant in Alexandria.

I was happy enough there; and I enjoyed walking in the busy streets, so unlike the village in which I was born.

One summer evening I found myself walking down an unfamiliar street. It emptied out into a little square that sat below the front of an old mosque. The square was full of people, merchants and fishwives, a juggler or two, but most of the crowd was drawn up to the facade of the mosque, pressed in close together.

At first, as I strolled across the square, I thought prayers were about to begin, but it was still some time until sunset. I wondered if perhaps some notable *imam* was speaking from the mosque steps, but as I approached I could see that all the assembly were staring upward, craning their necks back as if the sun itself, on its way to its western mooring, had become snagged on one of the minarets.

But instead of the sun, what stood on the onion-shaped dome was the silhouette of a man, who seemed to be staring out toward the horizon.

"Who is that?" I asked a man near me.

"It is Ha'arud al-Emwiya, the Sufi," the man told me, never lowering his eyes from the tower above.

"Is he caught up there?" I demanded. "Will he not fall?"

"Watch," was all the man said. I did.

A moment later, much to my horror, the small dark figure of Ha'arud the Sufi seemed to go rigid, then toppled from the minaret's rim like a stone. I gasped in shock, and so did a few others around me, but the rest of the crowd only stood in hushed attention.

Then an incredible thing happened. The tumbling holy man spread his arms out from his shoulders, like a bird's wings, and his downward fall became a swooping glide. He bottomed out high above the crowd, then sped upward, riding the wind like a leaf, spinning, somersaulting, stopping at last to drift to the ground as gently as a bit of eiderdown. Meanwhile, all the assembly was chanting "God is great! God is great!" When the Sufi had touched the earth with his bare feet the people surrounded him, touching his rough woolen garments and crying out his name. He said nothing, only stood and smiled, and before too long the people began to wander away, talking amongst themselves.

"But this is truly marvelous!" I said to the man who stood by me.

"Before every holy day he flies," the man said, and shrugged. "I am surprised this is the first time you have heard of Ha'arud al-Emwiya."

I was determined to speak to this amazing man, and as the crowd dispersed I approached and asked if I might buy him a glass of tea. Close up he had a look of seamed roguishness that seemed surprising placed against the great favor in which Allah must have held him. He smilingly agreed, and accompanied me to a tea shop close by in the Street of Weavers.

"How is it, if you will pardon my forwardness, that you of all holy men are so gifted?"

He looked up from the tea cupped in his palms and grinned. He had only two teeth. "Balance," he said.

I was surprised. "A cat has balance," I responded, "but they nevertheless must wait for the pigeons to land."

"I refer to a different sort of balance," he said. "The balance between Allah and Shaitan, which, as you know, Allah the All-Knowing has created as an equilibrium of exquisite delicacy."

"Explain please, master." I called for wine, but Ha'arud refused any himself.

"In all things care must be exercised," he explained. "Thus it is too with my flying. Many men holier than I are as earthbound as stones. Many other men have lived so poorly as to shame the Devil himself, yet they cannot take to the air, either. Only I, if I may be excused what sounds self-satisfied, have discovered perfect balance. Thus, each year before the holy days I tot up my score carefully, committing small peccadilloes or acts of faith as needed until the balance is exactly, exactly balanced. Thus, when I jump from the mosque, neither Allah nor the Arch-Enemy has claim on my soul, and they bear me up until a later date, at which time the issue shall be clearer." He smiled again and drained his tea.

"You are… a sort of chessboard on which God and the Devil contend?" I asked, perplexed.

"A flying chessboard, yes."

We talked for a long while, as the shadows grew long across the Street of the Weavers, but the Sufi Ha'arud adhered stubbornly to his explanation. I must have seemed disbelieving, for he finally proposed that we ascend to the top of the mosque so he could demonstrate.

I was more than a little drunk, and he, imbibing only tea, was filled nonetheless with a strange gleefulness. We made our way up the many winding stairs and climbed out onto the narrow ledge that circled the minaret like a crown. The cool night air, and the thousands of winking lights of Alexandria far below, sobered me rapidly. "I suddenly find all your precepts very sound," I said. "Let us go down."

But Ha'arud would have none of it, and proceeded to step lightly off the edge of the dome. He hovered, like a bumblebee, a hundred feet above the dusty street. "Balance," he said with great satisfaction.

"But," I asked, "is the good deed of giving me this demonstration enough to offset the pride with which you exhibit your skill?" I was cold and wanted to get down, and hoped to shorten the exhibition.

Instead, hearing my question, Ha'arud screwed up his face as though it was something he had not given thought to. A moment later, with a shriek of surprise, he plummeted down out of my sight to smash on the mosque's stone steps, as dead as dead.

Ibn Fahad, having lost himself in remembering the story, poked at the campfire. "Thus, the problem with matters of delicate balance," he said, and shook his head.

The whispering rustle of our dark visitor brought us sharply back. "Interesting," the creature rasped. "Sad, yes. Sad enough? We shall see. Who is the next of your number?"

A cold chill, like fever, swept over me at those calm words.

"I… I am next…" said Fawn, voice taut as a bowstring. "Shall I begin?"

The vampyr said nothing, only bobbed the black lump of his head. The youth cleared his throat and began.

FAWN'S STORY

There was once… [Fawn began, and hesitated, then started again.] There was once a young prince named Zufik, the second son of a great sultan. Seeing no prospects for himself in his father's kingdom, he went out into the wild world to search for his fortune. He traveled through many lands, and saw many strange things, and heard tell of others stranger still.

In one place he was told of a nearby sultanate, the ruler of which had a beautiful daughter, his only child and the very apple of his eye.

Now this country had been plagued for several years by a terrible beast, a great white leopard of a kind never seen before. So fearsome it was that it had killed hunters set to trap it, yet was it also so cunning that it had stolen babies from their very cradles as the mothers lay sleeping. The people of the sultanate were all in fear; and the sultan, whose best warriors had tried and failed to kill the beast, was driven to despair. Finally, at the end of his wits, he had it proclaimed in the market place that the man who could destroy the white leopard would be gifted with the sultan's daughter Rassoril, and with her the throne of the sultanate after the old man was gone.

Young Zufik heard how the best young men of the country, and others from countries beyond, one after the other had met their deaths beneath the claws of the leopard, or… or… in its jaws….

[Here I saw the boy falter, as if the vision of flashing teeth he was conjuring had suddenly reminded him of our predicament. Walid the under-vizier reached out and patted the lad's shoulder with great gentleness, until he was calm enough to resume.]

So… [He swallowed.] So young Prince Zufik took himself into that country, and soon was announced at the sultan's court.

The ruler was a tired old man, the fires in his sunken eyes long quenched. Much of the power seemed to have been handed over to a pale, narrow-faced youth named Sifaz, who was the princess's cousin. As Zufik announced his purpose, as so many had done before him, Sifaz's eyes flashed.

"You will no doubt meet the end all the others have, but you are welcome to the attempt—and the prize, should you win."

Then for the first time Zufik saw the Princess Rassoril, and in an instant his heart was overthrown.

She had hair as black and shiny as polished jet, and a face upon which Allah himself must have looked in satisfaction, thinking: "Here is the summit of My art." Her delicate hands were like tiny doves as they nested in her lap, and a man could fall into her brown eyes and drown without hope of rescue—which is what Zufik did, and he was not wrong when he thought he saw Rassoril return his ardent gaze.

Sifaz saw, too, and his thin mouth turned in something like a smile, and he narrowed his yellow eyes. "Take this princeling to his room, that he may sleep now and wake with the moon. The leopard's cry was heard around the palace's walls last night."

Indeed, when Zufik woke in the evening darkness, it was to hear the choking cry of the leopard beneath his very window. As he looked out, buckling on his scabbard, it was to see a white shape slipping in and out of the shadows in the garden below. He took also his dagger in his hand and leaped over the threshold.

He had barely touched ground when, with a terrible snarl, the leopard bounded out of the obscurity of the hedged garden wall and came to a stop before him. It was huge—bigger than any leopard Zufik had seen or heard of—and its pelt gleamed like ivory. It leaped, claws flashing, and he could barely throw himself down in time as the beast passed over him like a cloud, touching him only with its hot breath. It turned and leaped again as the palace dogs set up a terrible barking, and this time its talons raked his chest, knocking him tumbling. Blood started from his shirt, spouting so fiercely that he could scarcely draw himself to his feet. He was caught with his back against the garden wall; the leopard slowly moved toward him, yellow eyes like tallow lamps burning in the niches of Hell.

Suddenly there was a crashing at the far end of the garden: the dogs had broken down their stall and were even now speeding through the trees. The leopard hesitated—Zufik could almost see it thinking—and then, with a last snarl, it leaped onto the wall and disappeared into the night.

Zufik was taken, his wounds bound, and he was put into his bed. The princess Rassoril, who had truly lost her heart to him, wept bitterly at his side, begging him to go back to his father's land and to give up the fatal challenge. But Zufik, weak as he was, would no more think of yielding than he would of theft or treason, and refused, saying he would hunt the beast again the following night. Sifaz grinned and led the princess away. Zufik thought he heard the pale cousin whistling as he went.

In the dark before dawn Zufik, who could not sleep owing to the pain of his injury, heard his door quietly open. He was astonished to see the princess come in, gesturing him to silence. When the door was closed she threw herself down at his side and covered his hand and cheek with kisses, proclaiming her love for him and begging him again to go. He admitted his love for her, but reminded her that his honor would not permit him to stop short of his goal, even should he die in the trying.

Rassoril, seeing that there was no changing the young prince's mind, then took from her robe a black arrow tipped in silver, fletched with the tail feathers of a falcon. "Then take this," she said. "This leopard is a magic beast, and you will never kill it otherwise. Only silver will pierce its heart. Take the arrow and you may fulfill your oath." So saying, she slipped out of his room.

The next night Zufik again heard the leopard's voice in the garden below, but this time he took also his bow and arrow when he went to meet it. At first he was loath to use it, since it seemed somehow unmanly; but when the beast had again given him injury and he had struck three sword blows in turn without effect, he at last nocked the silver-pointed shaft on his bowstring and, as the beast charged him once more, let fly. The black arrow struck to the leopard's heart; the creature gave a hideous cry and again leaped the fence, this time leaving a trail of its mortal blood behind it.

When morning came Zufik went to the sultan for men, so that they could follow the track of blood to the beast's lair and prove its death. The sultan was displeased when his vizier, the princess's pale cousin, did not answer his summons. As they were all going down into the garden, though, there came a great cry from the sleeping rooms upstairs, a cry like a soul in mortal agony. With fear in their hearts Zufik, the sultan, and all the men rushed upstairs. There they found the missing Sifaz.

The pale man lifted a shaking, red-smeared finger to point at Zufik, as all the company stared in horror. "*He* has done it—the foreigner!" Sifaz shouted.

In Sifaz's arms lay the body of the Princess Rassoril, a black arrow standing from her breast.

After Fawn finished there was a long silence. The boy, his own courage perhaps stirred by his story, seemed to sit straighter.

"Ah…" the vampyr said at last, "love and its prices—that is the message? Or is it perhaps the effect of silver on the supernatural? Fear not, I am bound by no such conventions, and fear neither silver, steel, nor any other metal." The creature made a huffing, scraping sound that might have been a laugh. I marveled anew, even as I felt the skein of my life fraying, that it had so quickly gained such command of our unfamiliar tongue.

"Well…" it said slowly. "Sad. But… sad enough? Again, *that* is the important question. Who is your last… contestant?"

Now my heart truly went cold within me, and I sat as though I had swallowed a stone. Walid al-Salameh spoke up.

"I am," he said, and took a deep breath. "I am."

THE VIZIER'S STORY

This is a true story—or so I was told. It happened in my grandfather's time, and he had it from someone who knew those involved. He told it to me as a cautionary tale.

There once was an old caliph, a man of rare gifts and good fortune. He ruled a small country, but a wealthy one—a country upon which all the gifts of Allah had been showered in grand measure. He had the finest heir a man could have, dutiful and yet courageous, beloved by the people almost as extravagantly as the caliph himself. He had many other fine sons, and two hundred beautiful wives, and an army of fighting men the envy of his neighbors. His treasury was stacked roofbeam-high with gold and gemstones and blocks of fragrant sandalwood, crisscrossed with ivories and bolts of the finest cloth. His palace was built around a spring of fragrant, clear water; and everyone said that they must be the very Waters of Life, so fortunate and well-loved this caliph was. His only sadness was that age had robbed his sight from him, leaving him blind, but hard as this was, it was a small price to pay for Allah's beneficence.

One day the caliph was walking in his garden, smelling the exquisite fragrance of the blossoming orange trees. His son the prince, unaware of his father's presence, was also in the garden, speaking with his mother, the caliph's first and chiefest wife.

"He is terribly old," the wife said. "I cannot stand even to touch him anymore. It is a horror to me."

"You are right, mother," the son replied, as the caliph hid behind the trees and listened, shocked. "I am sickened by watching him sitting all day, drooling into his bowl, or staggering sightless through the palace. But what are we to do?"

"I have thought on it long and hard," the caliph's wife replied. "We owe it to ourselves and those close to us to kill him."

"Kill him?" the son replied. "Well, it is hard for me, but I suppose you are right. I still feel some love for him, though—may we at least do it quickly, so that he shall not feel pain at the end?"

"Very well. But do it soon—tonight, even. If I must feel his foul breath upon me one more night I will die myself."

"Tonight, then," the son agreed, and the two walked away, leaving the blind caliph shaking with rage and terror behind the orange trees. He could not see what sat on the garden path behind them, the object of their discussion: the wife's old lap-dog, a scrofulous creature of extreme age.

Thus the caliph went to his vizier, the only one he was sure he could trust in a world of suddenly traitorous sons and wives, and bade him to have the pair arrested and quickly beheaded. The vizier was shocked, and asked the reason why, but the caliph only said he had unassailable proof that they intended to murder him and take his throne. He bade the vizier go and do the deed.

The vizier did as he was directed, seizing the son and his mother quickly and quietly, then giving them over to the headsman after tormenting them for confessions and the names of confederates, neither of which were forthcoming.

Sadly, the vizier went to the caliph and told him it was done, and the old man was satisfied. But soon, inevitably, word of what had happened spread, and the brothers of the heir began to murmur among themselves about their father's deed. Many thought him mad, since the dead pair's devotion to the caliph was common knowledge.

Word of this dissension reached the caliph himself, and he began to fear for his life, terrified that his other sons meant to emulate their treasonous brother. He called the vizier to him and demanded the arrest of these sons, and their beheading. The vizier argued in vain, risking his own life, but the caliph would not be swayed; at last the vizier went away, returning a week later a battered, shaken man.

"It is done, O Prince," he said. "All your sons are dead."

The caliph had only a short while in which to feel safe before the extreme wrath of the wives over the slaughter of their children reached his ears. "Destroy them, too!" the blind caliph insisted.

Again the vizier went away, soon to return.

"It is done, O Prince," he reported. "Your wives have been beheaded."

Soon the courtiers were crying murder, and the caliph sent his vizier to see them dealt with as well.

"It is done, O Prince," he assured the caliph. But the ruler now feared the angry townspeople, so he commanded his vizier to take the army and slaughter them. The vizier argued feebly, then went away.

"It is done, O Prince," the caliph was told a month later. But now the caliph realized that with his heirs and wives gone, and the important men of the court dead, it was the soldiers themselves who were a threat to his power. He commanded his vizier to sow lies amongst them, causing them to fall out and slay each other, then locked himself in his room to safely outlast the conflict. After a month and a half the vizier knocked upon his door.

"It is done, O Prince."

For a moment the caliph was satisfied. All his enemies were dead, and he himself was locked in: no one could murder him, or steal his treasure, or usurp his throne. The only person yet alive who even knew where the caliph hid was... his vizier.

Blind, he groped about for the key with which he had locked himself in. Better first to remove the risk that someone might trick him into coming out. He pushed the key out beneath the door and told the vizier to throw it away somewhere it might never be found. When the vizier returned he called him close to the locked portal that bounded his small world of darkness and safety.

"Vizier," the caliph said through the keyhole, "I command you to go and kill yourself, for you are the last one living who is a threat to me."

"*Kill* myself, my prince?" the vizier asked, dumbfounded. "Kill *myself*?"

"Correct," the caliph said. "Now go and do it. That is my command."

There was a long silence. At last the vizier said: "Very well." After that there was silence.

For a long time the caliph sat in his blindness and exulted, for everyone he distrusted was gone. His faithful vizier had carried out all his orders, and now had killed himself....

A sudden, horrible thought came to him then: What if the vizier had *not* done what he had told him to do? What if instead he had made compact with the caliph's enemies, and was only reporting false details when he told of their deaths? *How was the caliph to know?* He almost swooned with fright and anxiousness at the realization.

At last he worked up the courage to feel his way across the locked room to the door. He put his ear to the keyhole and listened. He heard nothing but silence. He took a breath and then put his mouth to the hole.

"Vizier?" he called in a shaky voice. "Have you done what I commanded? Have you killed yourself?"

"It is done, O Prince," came the reply.

Finishing his story, which was fully as dreadful as it was sad, the under-vizier Walid lowered his head as if ashamed or exhausted. We waited tensely for our guest to speak; at the same time I am sure we all vainly hoped there would be no more speaking, that the creature would simply vanish, like a frightening dream that flees the sun.

"Rather than discuss the merits of your sad tales," the black, tattered shadow said at last—confirming that there would be no waking from *this* dream—"rather than argue the game with only one set of moves completed, perhaps it is now time for me to speak. The night is still youthful, and my tale is not long, but I wish to give you a fair time to render judgment."

As he spoke the creature's eyes bloomed scarlet like unfolding roses. The mist curled up from the ground beyond the fire-circle, wrapping the vampyr in a cloak of writhing fogs, a rotted black egg in a bag of silken mesh.

"… May I begin?" it asked… but no one could say a word. "Very well…."

THE VAMPYR'S STORY

The tale *I* will tell is of a child, a child born of an ancient city on the banks of a river. So long ago this was that not only has the city itself long gone to dust, but the later cities built atop its ruins, tiny towns and great walled fortresses of stone, all these too have gone beneath the mill-wheels of time—rendered, like their predecessor, into the finest of particles to blow in the wind, silting the timeless river's banks.

This child lived in a mud hut thatched with straw, and played with his fellows in the shallows of the sluggish brown river while his mother washed the family's clothes and gossiped with her neighbors.

Even *this* ancient city was built upon the bones of earlier cities, and it was into the collapsed remnants of one—a great, tumbled mass of shattered sandstone—that the child and his friends sometimes went. And it was to these ruins that the child, when he was a little older… almost the age of your young, romantic companion… took a pretty, doe-eyed girl.

It was to be his first time beyond the veil—his initiation into the mysteries of women. His heart beat rapidly; the girl walked ahead of him, her slender brown body tiger-striped with light and shade as she walked among the broken pillars. Then she saw something, and screamed. The child came running.

The girl was nearly mad, weeping and pointing. He stopped in amazement, staring at the black, shrivelled thing that lay on the ground—a twisted something that might have been a man once, wizened and black as a piece of leather dropped into the cookfire. Then the thing opened its eyes.

The girl ran, choking—but he did not, seeing that the black thing could not move. The twitching of its mouth seemed that of someone trying to speak; he thought he heard a faint voice asking for help, begging for him to do something. He leaned down to the near-silent hiss, and the thing squirmed and bit him, fastening its sharp teeth like barbed fishhooks in the muscle of his leg. The man-child screamed, helpless, and felt his blood running out into the horrible sucking mouth of the thing. Fetid saliva crept into the wounds and coursed hotly through his body, even as he struggled against his writhing attacker. The poison climbed through him, and it seemed he could feel his own heart flutter and die within his chest, delicate and hopeless as a broken bird. With final, desperate strength the child pulled free. The black thing, mouth gaping, curled on itself and shuddered, like a beetle on a hot stone. A moment later it had crumbled into ashes and oily flakes.

But it had caught me long enough to destroy me—for of course I was that child—to force its foul fluids into me, leeching my humanity and replacing it with the hideous, unwanted wine of immortality. My child's heart became an icy fist.

Thus was I made what I am, at the hands of a dying vampyr—which had been a creature like I am now. Worn down at last by the passing of millennia, it had chosen a host to receive its hideous malady, then died—as I shall do someday, no doubt, in the grip of some terrible, blind, insect-like urge... but not soon. Not today.

So that child, which had been in all ways like other children—loved by its family, loving in turn noise and games and sweetmeats—became a dark thing sickened by the burning light of the sun.

Driven into the damp shadows beneath stones and the dusty gloom of abandoned places, then driven out again beneath the moon by an unshakeable, irresistable hunger, I fed first on my family—my uncomprehending mother wept to see her child returned, standing by her moonlit pallet—then on the others of my city. Not last, or least painful of my feedings was on the dark-haired girl who had run when I stayed behind. I slashed other throats, too, and lapped up warm, sea-salty blood while the trapped child inside me cried without a sound. It was as though I stood behind a screen, unable to leave or interfere as terrible crimes were committed before me....

And thus the years have passed: sand grains, deposited along the riverbank, uncountable in their succession. Every one has contained a seeming infinitude of killings, each one terrible despite their numbing similarity. Only the blood of mankind will properly feed me, and a hundred generations have known terror of me.

Strong as I am, virtually immortal, unkillable as far as I know or can tell—blades pass through me like smoke; fire, water, poison, none affect me—still the light of the sun causes a pain to me so excruciating that you with only mortal lives, whose pain at least eventually ends in death, cannot possibly comprehend it. Thus, kingdoms of men have risen and fallen to ashes since I last saw daylight. Think only on that for a moment, if you seek sad stories! I must be in darkness when the sun rises, so as I range in search of prey my accommodations are shared with toads and slugs, bats, and blindworms.

People can be nothing to me anymore but food. I know of none other like myself, save the dying creature who spawned me. The smell of my own corruption is in my nostrils always.

So there is all of *my* tale. I cannot die until my time is come, and who can know when that is? Until then I will be alone, alone as no mere man can ever be, alone with my wretchedness and evil and self-disgust until the world collapses and is born anew....

The vampyr rose now, towering up like a black sail billowing in the wind, spreading its vast arms or wings on either side, as if to sweep us before it. "How do your stories compare to this?" it cried; the harshness of its speech seemed somehow muted, even as it grew louder and louder. "Whose is the saddest story, then?" There was pain in that hideous voice that tore at even my fast-pounding heart. "Whose is saddest? Tell me! It is time to *judge…*"

And in that moment, of all the moments when lying could save my life… I could not lie. I turned my face away from the quivering black shadow, that thing of rags and red eyes. None of the others around the campfire spoke—even Abdallah the clerk only sat hugging his knees, teeth chattering, eyes bulging with fear.

"…I thought so," the thing said at last. "I thought so." Night wind tossed the treelimbs above our heads, and it seemed as though beyond them stood only ultimate darkness—no sky, no stars, nothing but unending emptiness.

"Very well," the vampyr said at last. "Your silence speaks all. I have won." There was not the slightest note of triumph in its voice. "Give me my prize, and then I may let the rest of you flee my mountains." The dark shape withdrew a little way.

We all of us turned to look at one another, and it was just as well that the night veiled our faces. I started to speak, but Ibn Fahad interrupted me, his voice a tortured rasp.

"Let there be no talk of volunteering. We will draw lots; that is the only way." Quickly he cut a thin branch into five pieces, one of them shorter than the rest, and cupped them in a closed hand.

"Pick," he said. "I will keep the last."

As a part of me wondered what madness it was that had left us wagering on story-telling and drawing lots for our lives, we each took a length from Ibn Fahad's fist. I kept my hand closed while the others selected, not wanting to hurry Allah toward his revelation of my fate. When all had selected we extended our hands and opened them, palms up.

Fawn had selected the short stick.

Strangely, there was no sign of his awful fortune on his face: he showed no signs of grief—indeed, he did not even respond to our helpless words and prayers, only stood up and slowly walked toward the huddled black shape at the far edge of the clearing. The vampyr rose to meet him.

"No!" came a sudden cry, and to our complete surprise the clerk Abdallah leaped to his feet and went pelting across the open space, throwing himself between the youth and the looming shadow. "He is too young!" Abdallah shouted, sounding truly anguished. "Do not do this horrible thing! Take me instead!"

Ibn Fahad, the vizier, and I could only sit, struck dumb by this unexpected behavior, but the creature moved swiftly as a viper, smacking Abdallah to the ground with one flicking gesture.

"You are indeed mad, you short-lived men!" the vampyr hissed. "This one would do nothing to save himself—not once did I hear his voice raised in tale-telling—yet now he would throw himself into the jaws of death for this other! Mad!" The monster left Abdallah choking on the ground and turned to silent Fawn. "Come, you. I have won the contest, and you are the prize. I am… sorry… it must be this way…." A great swath of darkness enveloped the youth, drawing him in. "Come," the vampyr said, "think of the better world you go to—that is what you believe, is it not? Well, soon you shall—"

The creature broke off.

"Why do you look so strangely, man-child?" the thing said at last, its voice troubled. "You cry, but I see no fear. Why? Are you not afraid of dying?"

Fawn answered; his tones were oddly distracted. "Have you really lived so long? And alone, always alone?"

"I told you. I have no reason to lie. Do you think to put me off with your strange questions?"

"Ah, how could the good God be so unmerciful!?" The words were made of sighs. The dark shape that embraced him stiffened.

"Do you cry for *me? For me?*"

"How can I help?" the boy said. "Even Allah must weep for you... for such a pitiful thing, lost in the lonely darkness..."

For a moment the night air seemed to pulse. Then, with a wrenching gasp, the creature flung the youth backward so that he stumbled and fell before us, landing atop the groaning Abdallah.

"*Go!*" the vampyr shrieked, and its voice cracked and boomed like thunder. "Get you gone from my mountains! *Go!*"

Amazed, we pulled Fawn and the chief-clerk to their feet and went stumbling down the hillside, branches lashing at our faces and hands, expecting any moment to hear the rush of wings and feel cold breath on our necks.

"Build your houses well, little men!" a voice howled like the wild wind behind us. "My life is long... and someday I may regret letting you go!"

We ran and ran, until it seemed the life would flee our bodies, until our lungs burned and our feet blistered... and until the topmost sliver of the sun peered over the eastern summits....

Masrur al-Adan allowed the tale's ending to hang in silence for a span of thirty heartbeats, then pushed his chair away from the table.

"We escaped the mountains the next day," he said. "Within a season we were back in Baghdad, the only survivors of the caravan to the Armenites."

"Aaaahh... !" breathed young Hassan, a long drawn-out sound full of wonder and apprehension. "What a marvelous, terrifying adventure! I would *never* have survived it, myself. How frightening! And did the... the creature... did he *really* say he might come back someday?"

Masrur solemnly nodded his large head. "Upon my soul. Am I not right, Ibn Fahad, my old comrade?"

Ibn Fahad yielded a thin smile, seemingly of affirmation.

"Yes," Masrur continued, "those words chill me to this very day. Many is the night I have sat in this room, looking at that door—" He pointed. "—wondering if someday it may open to show me that terrible, misshapen black thing, come back from Hell to make good on our wager."

"Merciful Allah!" Hassan gasped.

Abu Jamir leaned across the table as the other guests whispered excitedly. He wore a look of annoyance. "Good Hassan," he snapped, "kindly calm yourself. We are all grateful to our host Masrur for entertaining us, but it is an insult to sensible, Godly men to suggest that at any moment some blood-drinking afreet may knock down the door and carry us—"

The door leaped open with a crash, revealing a hideous, twisted shape looming in the entrance, red-splattered and trembling. The shrieking of Masrur's guests filled the room.

"Master... ?" the dark silhouette quavered. Baba held a wine jar balanced on one shoulder. The other had broken at his feet, splashing Abu Jamir's prize stock everywhere. "Master," he began again, "I am afraid I have dropped one."

Masrur looked down at Abu Jamir, who lay pitched full-length on the floor, insensible.

"Ah, well, that's all right, Baba." Masrur smiled, twirling his black mustache. "We won't have to make the wine go so far as I thought—it seems my story-telling has put some of our guests to sleep."

LIFEBLOOD

by Michael A. Burstein

Michael A. Burstein is a ten-time finalist for the Hugo Award and the winner of the 1996 John W. Campbell Award for best new writer. His fiction frequently appears in *Analog Science Fiction & Fact* magazine, and much of his short work was recently collected in *I Remember the Future*, from Apex Publications.

"Lifeblood" takes the vampire mythos out of its usual Christian context and adds Judaism to the equation. "I've always been interested in the question of how someone who doesn't use the cross as a religious symbol would turn a vampire," Burstein said. "I was interested in the specific question of how a Jewish person might turn a vampire. Could he or she use a cross? Would a Jewish symbol have any sort of power?"

Although Burstein originally wrote the story just to play with the concept of Jews vs. vampires, the story ended up being a cautionary tale about the dangers of assimilation. "A lot of debate takes place among the Jewish people, especially American Jews, about assimilating into the overall culture," he said. "Without my realizing it, 'Lifeblood' turned out to display my own biases in the debate."

Lincoln Kliman burst into the synagogue, causing the cantor at the front of the room to halt his chanting momentarily. Lincoln panted, catching his breath, and the congregants turned to look at him. He knew his disheveled appearance would not endear him to them, and he noticed one or two of the congregants scowling.

The cantor resumed his Hebrew chant, and Lincoln took a moment to study the synagogue. It wasn't a synagogue really, just a small room where these particular Jews gathered to pray. There were three rows of folding chairs set up, mostly empty of people, which gave the room an aura of despair, at least for Lincoln. He was used to much more elaborate synagogues, but then again, he hadn't been in one for over fifteen years.

He counted the number of congregants. Ten men, exactly the minimum number of Jews required for a minyan. Technically, Lincoln's presence made the number eleven.

He approached a man sitting alone in the back row, bent over and murmuring

75

to himself.

"Pardon me," he said, "but—"

The man looked up from his *siddur*, his prayer book, and waved his hand to quiet Lincoln. "Shush," he said. "Put on a *yarmulka*."

Lincoln nodded and went to the back of the room to don a skullcap, another thing he hadn't done in a very long time. He sat down next to the man and said, as quietly as he could, "I must speak with the cantor. It's important."

The man glared at him. "You must wait. We're about to do the *Alenu*; the service will be over soon." His tone was accusatory, as if he was questioning Lincoln's right to show up at the end of a service.

Lincoln wondered that himself, but felt better when he realized that he still remembered to stand and bow at the appropriate times. He didn't pray, though. The man next to him offered his *siddur*, but Lincoln shook his head; he couldn't read Hebrew anymore even well enough to pronounce the words, let alone understand them.

True to the man's word, the service ended in a few minutes. The congregants began folding the chairs and stacking them up next to the wall. Lincoln muttered, "Excuse me," to his row companion, and darted to the front of the room. The cantor was just removing his *tallis*, his prayer shawl, when Lincoln approached. He was an old man, slightly stooped, with a pair of round glasses on his face.

Despite the fact that Lincoln had interrupted him before, the cantor smiled as he folded his *tallis*. "Good shabbes," he said. He spoke with a slight Hungarian accent.

Lincoln repeated the phrase; it echoed oddly in his ears. "Good shabbes, Cantor—?"

"Erno Gross. How may I help you?"

Lincoln's eyes darted around the room. Two congregants were opening boxes of little pastries and setting them out on a table, and speaking in a language Lincoln didn't recognize. Another man hummed, and poured small cups of red wine out of a dark bottle. Lincoln almost shuddered at that, but controlled himself.

"Cantor, where is your rabbi? I need to speak with him."

The cantor sighed. "Unfortunately, we have no rabbi. Rabbi Weinberg, a dear friend of mine, was the last rabbi to serve this congregation. We are a small group, and so can't offer a new rabbi enough of an incentive to join us on a permanent basis. Not that one is needed for a service, you must know."

Lincoln felt embarrassed. "Actually, I didn't know. But if you have no rabbi, then all hope is lost. The others—" He shook his head.

"Perhaps all is not lost," said the cantor. He put his hand on Lincoln's shoulder. "Perhaps I can help you, Mister—?"

"Kliman, with a long 'i.' Lincoln Kliman."

"Lincoln. An odd name, for a Jew."

Lincoln shrugged. "My father was a historian, studied American history." He was used to explaining it.

"Very well, Mr. Kliman. How can I help you?"

"Not here. Can we go talk alone some—"

Lincoln was interrupted by shouts of "Erno!" The cantor said, "Excuse me a moment; I must make *kiddush*." He gave Lincoln an odd look. "Unless you would rather do the honors?"

Lincoln felt his face flush. "Uh, no thank you, Cantor, I really would rather not."

The cantor nodded. "At least take a cup of wine."

Lincoln assented, and tried not to look uncomfortable as the cantor began chanting kiddush and the others joined in. The only words he remembered was the last part of the blessing over wine, *borai p'ri hagafen*, and after the cantor sang it, Lincoln chorused "Amen" with the rest of the congregation.

The wine tasted sweet going down his throat.

Lincoln walked over to a small bookcase afterwards, studying the titles as the cantor circulated among the congregation. One by one, the elderly men put on their coats and left the room, until finally, the cantor came over to Lincoln.

"I believe you wanted to talk with me alone?" he said.

"Yes. Thank you."

"What can I do for you, Mr. Kliman?"

Lincoln looked into the cantor's eyes. "There is a boy. My son. He's very sick."

"Sick? Shouldn't you be fetching a doctor, and not a rabbi? Unless…" The cantor looked grim.

"It's not that kind of illness, not physical."

"Spiritual?"

Lincoln thought for a moment. "Cantor, may I ask you a question?"

"Certainly."

"Have you studied *Kaba*—*Kaba*—Jewish mysticism?"

"*Kabala*. Why do you ask?"

"You believe in God, right?" Lincoln blurted.

The cantor looked shocked. "An impudent question, Mr. Kliman, but yes, of course I believe in God. I devoted my life to helping the Jewish people practice our religion." There was a chastising tone in his voice; Lincoln noticed that he slightly stressed the word "our."

"I didn't mean to question your faith, Cantor," Lincoln said. "I just don't want you to think I'm crazy. I needed to know that you can accept the possibility of something out there that you have no direct evidence for, something—something mystical."

"As a Jew," the cantor said, "I have all the evidence I need for God in seeing the wonders of the Earth each and every day. I rise from bed with praise of Him on my lips and I go to sleep the same way. That does not necessarily mean that I will believe in anything at all, Mr. Kliman."

"I'm sorry, I didn't mean to offend you. It's just that—well, I needed to find a religious man, a religious leader, and I didn't feel comfortable going to a Catholic priest. I thought a rabbi could help as well."

"Help with what, Mr. Kliman? You barge in here, claim to be worried about your son, and then question my faith. What do you need my help with?"

Lincoln looked down at his shoes for a moment and wrung his hands. "I'll have to trust you. My son's been bitten, and I need you to lift the curse."

"Bitten? By a dog? Better to see a doctor."

"No, not a dog. Cantor, my son Joseph has been bitten three times by a vampire. And unless I can find a cure by sundown tonight, he's going to turn into one himself."

An hour later, Lincoln and the cantor arrived at Lincoln's apartment building. It would have taken only ten minutes if they had driven, but the cantor would not ride on the Sabbath, and so Lincoln left his car parked at the synagogue. Although it was early spring, the weather was cold and overcast, and Lincoln had to bundle himself up in his thin jacket as best as he could while they walked.

When they got to his building, the cantor also refused to take the elevator up to Lincoln's ninth floor apartment, so they slowly climbed the stairs.

The cantor had been decidedly uncommunicative during the walk over, but as they ascended he began to ask Lincoln about the boy.

"Tell me exactly what it is you think happened."

"You don't believe me, do you?"

The cantor shrugged. "That remains to be seen. But I will tell you this much: I find what you describe hard to believe."

Lincoln sighed. "Well, you've trusted me this far, at least. I appreciate that. The others refused to even listen to me."

"The others?"

Lincoln felt his cheeks redden. "Yours wasn't the first synagogue I went to, Cantor. I tried a Reform temple and a Conservative synagogue first, but neither of the rabbis believed me. They wouldn't help."

The cantor nodded, stopped at a landing to catch his breath. "The boy," he prodded.

"Yes. The boy. Joseph is a pretty good kid, does well in school and all that, but recently has been acting very independent. He's just turned twelve; you know what that means."

The cantor shook his head. "Go on."

"Anyway, it started when Joseph came home very late from school three weeks ago. It's only a few blocks away, and I've let him run around the neighborhood before. I mean, I grew up in New York as well, and I never got in serious trouble. But this time he didn't call."

"Don't you meet him after school to bring him home?"

"I can't. I work."

"What about the boy's mother?"

Lincoln looked away from the cantor. "Gone, these past five years."

"Oh. I am sorry, Mr. Kliman."

"Thanks. It's been hard, raising Joseph on my own. Anyway, he finally did come home that night, well after sundown, and he looked terrible. His color was bad, and he looked sick to his stomach. I thought it was food poisoning, as he smelled like he'd been to a fast food place. You know, that cheeseburger smell."

The cantor glared at him. "No, I do not know."

Lincoln felt embarrassed again. "Right. Well, anyway, he practically passed out when he came in the door, and I rushed him to the doctor."

"Nu? What did he find?"

"Anemia. Loss of blood. That and two tiny pinpricks on Joseph's neck."

"Hm. Did he say anything about that?"

"No. He gave Joseph a shot of something, chastised him and me over drug use, and that was all. Only thing is, he didn't find drugs in Joseph's system.

"Joseph refused to answer my questions about where he was that night, and the next day he acted like he had forgotten the whole thing. His color had returned, though, and he ate a big breakfast, so I let him go to school. The next day he came home on time, and I thought that would be the end of it."

"I presume it was not."

"Well, it was for about a week. Then the same thing happened. He came home late, looking very sick, and he almost passed out before I could get him to bed."

The cantor's eyebrows shot up. "You didn't bring him to the doctor this time?"

Lincoln shook his head. "No, I didn't. I know what you're thinking, but after that first time, I didn't want the doctor to chastise *me* again."

"And did you send Joseph to school again the next day?"

"No, because it was Saturday. A week ago today."

"That makes two bites."

"The third one was last night. Same pattern, only this time Joseph told me the full story. Apparently the vampire—"

"Yes?" the cantor prodded.

Lincoln whispered. "I'd rather not say. Let's just say that she promised to show Joseph a good time, and being the adolescent that he is…"

"I understand. You need not elaborate."

They had reached the door to Lincoln's apartment, and Lincoln let them in. The room was dark. Lincoln turned on the light and then pulled his hand back from the switch. "Sorry. I forgot, no lights on shabbat, right?"

"No using electricity," replied the cantor. "But you can leave lights on from the day before. Where is the boy?"

"This way." Lincoln showed the cantor through the living room to a small bedroom. They entered and closed the door behind them. It was dark inside. A small figure writhed under the blankets of the bed.

"I'm not going to turn the lights on in here. Joseph asked me not to. He says it hurts his eyes."

The boy moaned from under the blankets. "Dad? Is that you?"

"Yes, Joseph, and I've brought help."

Joseph coughed. "I'm so sorry, Dad. I don't know what got into me. Lily promised so much pleasure, but this is all pain."

"It's okay, son." To the cantor he said, "Please look at him. You'll see that I didn't lie to you. Then maybe you can tell me what to do."

The cantor approached the bed, and slowly removed the sheets. All he could make out was the outline of a shivering child.

"Joseph, I will need light to see you. May I open the shades?"

"Yes," the boy replied weakly, "but please be quick." He moaned again.

The cantor pulled up a window shade, allowing sunlight to fall upon Joseph, who screamed. "It hurts! It hurts! It's too hot! Make it stop!"

"Quiet, Joseph," Lincoln said. "It'll only be for a second." He opened the window, and a breeze drifted in. "There, that will cool you off."

The cantor turned back to Joseph, who quieted down but was clearly in great pain. The boy's face was pale, but his lips were a bright red and there was a reddish tinge in his eyes. The cantor cupped the boy's chin in his hand and pulled open his mouth.

His canine teeth were half an inch long, and glowing brightly in a sickening mixture of orange, red, and white.

He jerked his hand away and the boy's head fell to the pillow. "Dear Lord. You were right."

A few minutes later, Lincoln and the cantor sat across from each other in the living room, where they could talk. Joseph had passed out again, and Lincoln had restored the bedroom to darkness for his son's comfort.

"I find it difficult to believe that a Jew could be turned into a vampire, even if he were bitten by one. Possession by a *dybbuk*, perhaps, but not transformation into a vampire. Vampires are not part of the Jewish *Kabala*. They are part of Christian lore, not Jewish. They should only be able to affect Christians."

"Perhaps," said Lincoln slowly, "it's because Joseph has not yet been Bar Mitzvahed. He won't turn thirteen until next year."

The cantor looked startled. "That doesn't make sense at all. One does not become Jewish when one is Bar Mitzvah. You are Jewish at birth, and you join the covenant at the age of eight days."

Lincoln's eyes lit up. "Cantor, can't you do it anyway?"

"Do what?"

"Bar Mitzvah the boy? So he'll be an adult? Maybe that's the key to saving him!"

The cantor gave Lincoln a hard stare. "Mr. Kliman, you seem to be under the impression that a Bar Mitzvah ceremony is a magical ritual that will establish the boy as Jewish and render him immune to the vampirism. Bar Mitzvah is not a ceremony; it happens to a Jewish boy at the age of thirteen even if no ceremony occurs. All it means is that the Jew becomes responsible for his own actions in the eyes of God. It is akin to turning eighteen, and becoming an adult in the eyes of the law."

"Cantor Gross." Lincoln leaned forward. He felt tears on the side of his face. "Joseph is my only son, my only family. He is all that I have left. I beg of you, would you please do this? You don't know that it *isn't* the thing to do. It may save him."

The cantor looked deep into Lincoln's eyes. "There is nothing logical in your request, but I must agree. I don't know that it won't work."

He stood up. "Let me return to the synagogue and get a *siddur* and *chumash*."

"*Chumash?*" Lincoln asked.

"The Torah, Mr. Kliman, with all the passages we recite aloud on shabbat as the year progresses. Surely you know what the Torah is."

"Yes," Lincoln said quietly.

"Very well," the cantor said as he headed towards the door. "I shall return soon, and with God's help, we shall teach the boy to fight the curse of the dead with the ancient songs of life."

"Repeat after me, Joseph: *Baruch atah…*"

"*Baruch atah*," the boy said weakly.

"No," said the cantor. "Sing it. As I am."

"Why do I have to sing? It hurts so much."

"It is a Hasidic custom, Joseph. It will help you concentrate your thoughts to the spiritual task at hand. Listen again…"

Lincoln closed the door of the bedroom behind him and sat down to read. The song of the cantor filtered out through the closed door, haunting and lilting. It was a chant that went up and down in pitch, but always seemed to hover around the same notes. Its effects were so hypnotic, that Lincoln forwent his book, closed his eyes, and leaned back to contemplate the past.

He remembered his own Bar Mitzvah ceremony, and the agony that led up to it for almost half a year. Every Wednesday afternoon he had gone to the cantor's office to learn his Torah portion, the verses of the Torah that he would be expected to sing on the Saturday morning of the ceremony. Lincoln's voice was not good, and its cracking had embarrassed him.

Finally, the day arrived. He had stood in front of a large synagogue filled with his parents' friends, and a few of his own. He was called to the Torah, and trembling with nervousness, somehow he had managed to get through it.

The very next week his parents pulled him out of Hebrew School. They had never been particularly religious anyway. Lincoln's Bar Mitzvah had been solely a social thing, and once it was over, they had felt no need for Lincoln to continue his Jewish studies.

Perhaps they had been mistaken.

Lincoln blinked, and realized that he was back in his apartment. He was surprised to see that many hours had passed. The cantor's music had been so powerful that it had felt to Lincoln as if he had actually been sent back in time to relive his own Bar Mitzvah. He strained to hear the final words of song coming from his son's bedroom.

"*…nosain hatora-ah.*" Was that his son's voice, sounding so strong?

A minute later, the cantor opened the door and approached Lincoln. He had a sad look on his face. "It did not work. I helped the boy sing today's *parsha*, with the appropriate blessings before and after, but it did not work."

He sat down across from Lincoln and said, "I did not think it would."

"But your music—your singing—so beautiful."

The cantor nodded. "Thank you. But it takes more than beautiful singing to ward off a curse."

He leaned back, removed his glasses, and rubbed the bridge of his nose. "I still do not understand how this is possible, Mr. Kliman, how a Jew could be turned into a vampire. Nothing in our history, in our legends, would account for it. A Jew simply cannot become a vampire."

Lincoln coughed and cleared his throat. "Ummm."

The cantor peered at him. "What is it, Mr. Kliman? Was there something you did not tell me?"

"Well…" Lincoln shifted in his seat. "Cantor, I didn't want to admit this before, but…" He trailed off.

"But what? How can I help the boy if you don't tell me what I need to know?"

"Joseph's not Jewish," he blurted out.

There was a moment of silence. "You are Jewish, are you not?" the cantor asked.

"Yes," Lincoln whispered.

"Then his mother—"

"She wasn't."

The cantor sighed. "*Oy*. You know that by Jewish law, the boy follows the religion of the mother. What was she?"

Lincoln shrugged. "I don't know. Christian of some sort, I guess. We were both agnostic when we met, and I never really bothered to find out, since we never celebrated any holidays anyway."

"You lied to me, Mr. Kliman. You said your son was Jewish."

"I know. I'm sorry. But like I said, I would never have felt comfortable asking a priest or a reverend for help. I may not practice my religion much, Cantor, but I would never—"

The cantor interrupted. "A thought occurs to me. Was the boy ever circumcised?"

"Well, yes. By a doctor in the hospital when—"

The cantor leaped out of his seat, startling Lincoln. "That may be it." He marched towards the bedroom door.

"What may be it?" Lincoln asked.

The cantor stopped short and turned back to Lincoln. "The boy may yet be saved. The vampirism is affecting him because technically, he is not Jewish. And yet, he has your Jewish blood within him. So I shall make the vampire think he is Jewish."

"You mean—"

"I mean that I shall convert him."

Lincoln sputtered. "But—but—I thought conversion was something that took study, and time!"

The cantor gave him an odd look. "You know little of the ways of your own people, and yet you are familiar with the conversion ceremony?"

"Um—it's a long story. My wife wasn't Jewish, but my parents wanted her to convert."

The cantor nodded. "A familiar pattern. The parents who never teach their child about Judaism, and are surprised when he chooses to marry outside the tribe. At any rate, you are correct. A real conversion requires the person converting to study Judaism, and present his or her knowledge to a *Bes Din*, a court of three rabbis. A man must undergo circumcision, or if he is already circumcised, a tiny drop of blood is sufficient. Then he must be brought to the *mikvah*, the ritual pool, to be immersed and to make a blessing that declares his decision to become Jewish. And none of this can be done on shabbes.

"But time here is of the essence, Mr. Kliman, as the boy's life is in danger, and God is not without mercy. There is a principle called *pikuach nefesh*, which states that saving a life overrides all else. Indeed, the Talmud states that he who saves a life, it is as if he has saved the entire world. I will teach the boy the proper blessings, perform the proper rituals. I am sure that once the boy is saved, you will take steps to ensure that his conversion remains valid. Otherwise the vampirism may return."

Lincoln nodded weakly. "If you save Joseph, I will do anything. He's all I have."

The cantor nodded back and opened the door to Joseph's bedroom. Just before entering, he said, "Ironic, isn't it?"

"What?"

"The vampire has been drawing blood to doom the boy. Now I shall draw blood to save him."

Lincoln couldn't stand the sight of blood, but he had to know what was going on. So after a few minutes of pacing around the apartment and saying what prayers he could recall, he entered Joseph's bedroom.

The cantor sat on the bed next to Joseph, holding his hand and cradling his head. Joseph was crying, but his color seemed better. Joseph was singing something, along with the cantor, that Lincoln did not recognize. The cantor stopped when he saw Lincoln.

"Good, Joseph, very good," he said to the boy. "Keep singing."

He stood up and walked over to Lincoln. "The boy has a way to go, but I believe it is working. I have him reciting the Psalms."

"How much longer?" Lincoln asked.

"I am not sure. But he is getting better."

"Yes, but—Cantor, have you had a chance to look out the window?"

The cantor turned to the window; it was dark outside. "Shabbes is over. I must recite *Havdalah*."

"That's not exactly what I meant. Are you sure Joseph will be cured? According to legend, since he's been bitten three times and sundown has now come—"

The cantor smiled. "Fear not, Mr. Kliman. Your son should be fine. I don't think there is anything more you need to—"

A loud bang at the window startled the three of them, and Lincoln looked up. For a moment he thought he saw a bat, but then smoke swirled around it and into the room, blocking his vision.

"Oh God. Oh no oh no oh no..."

The smoke curled around the window, and coalesced into a pretty woman with long blonde hair falling over her shoulders. She wore a white V-neck sweater, cut low enough to display her cleavage, and a pair of tight blue jeans. She smelled of sweet perfume. She looked around the room, her red eyes peering out over a pair of dark sunglasses.

Lincoln shouted, "Go away! We haven't invited you in!"

"Ah, but the boy has, and I have come for the boy," said the vampire. She smiled, displaying two prominent canine teeth. "He is mine."

"You can't have him!" shouted Lincoln. He rushed at the vampire, who laughed and turned to smoke just as Lincoln got to where she had been standing. Lincoln lost his balance and almost fell out the window, but the cantor grabbed him.

The vampire re-formed at the bed. "Hello, Joseph." She reached her hand out to Joseph's head; Joseph recoiled, a look of horror upon his face.

"Keep her away!" Joseph shouted.

"Why, Joseph! Is that the way to treat your good friend Lily?" She cupped his chin and stared into his eyes. "Are you ready to come with me? To become one of us?"

The cantor walked over to the bed and spoke directly into the vampire's ear. "You are too late," he intoned. "The boy is lost to you. I have ensured it. Depart."

The vampire laughed. "Do you think I have not dealt with these last minute conversions before? I look into the boy and I see the soul of an agnostic. He has no belief in the God of the Jews. I have encountered many of his type before, brought up unprotected from my magic. He is mine for the taking."

"Why do you want *him*?" Lincoln asked. "Why can't you leave him alone?"

She grinned at Lincoln, showing her long canine teeth. He shuddered. "Because he is so easy to take, so defenseless. As are so many of your sons." She turned away, bent over the boy, and began to kiss him all over his face.

"Come, Joseph," she crooned. "Forget this religious nonsense. Your dad didn't let it stop him from marrying out of the faith; why should it stop you? Your friends are waiting for you, Joseph. It is time to join us."

Lincoln felt a chill at the back of his neck, and he turned around to look back at the window. There were definitely figures out there, dark silhouettes hovering outside, waiting for Joseph to join them.

Entranced by his fear of what lay outside, he barely heard Joseph's next words. "Yes, Lily, it is time to join our friends." He began to lift himself out of the bed.

"No!" shouted the cantor. "Joseph, don't listen to her! What about all you have gone through today?"

Joseph snarled. "You don't understand! Lily and her friends have shown me so much of the world I never knew. We've gone out and had so much fun, every night! I want to live in her world!"

Lincoln broke out of his trance. "No!" he screamed, and rushed at the vampire. She changed into a bat this time, and Lincoln stopped short. The transformation was too frightening.

"Lincoln!" shouted the cantor. "Grab her!"

Lincoln broke out of his trance of fear and lunged at the bat, which flew away from him to the other side of the room.

"Now!" the cantor shouted, and jumped to Joseph's side. "Joseph, you must sing. You must sing the ancient melodies that will protect you from this evil creature, or you will become like her. You must sing of your faith, your belief, in the Lord.

"Sing, Joseph. Sing with me."

The cantor began to sing, in sepulchral tones. "*Mizmor l'David*. Repeat it, Joseph!"

"No, I—"

He grabbed Joseph by the shoulders and shook him. "Come to your senses! Her world offers you nothing but corruption! You shall lose everything that defines who you are, Joseph. Your background, your ancestors—you will never see your father again."

"My father," he said weakly. "I love my father."

"Then sing! *Mizmor l'David*."

"*Mizmor l'David*," Joseph sang, in a faint imitation of the cantor's voice.

"Louder, Joseph! Listen to the tune. *Hashem ro'i lo echsar. Bin'ot Desheh yarbitzaini al me minuchos yinahalayni.*"

Joseph repeated the song, more strongly this time.

The bat turned back into a woman. "No," she whispered. "Stop!"

Lincoln blinked his eyes in surprise. As Joseph and the cantor sang, the room started to glow with a faint, yellow light. It was a soft, comforting glow, like that of the afternoon sun in a perfect blue sky.

"No," said the vampire, much more weakly. "Stop, Joseph. If I ever meant anything to you, stop." She crouched down and covered her eyes with her arm.

Noticing this, Lincoln realized that the light had distracted him. He turned his attention back to the song, and discovered with surprise that he now understood the Hebrew words. He knew what they meant, translating them instantly as they were sung.

"*Gam ki aylech b'gai tsalmavet lo eir'eh ra ki atah imadi*," Joseph sang.

Though I walk through the valley of the shadow of death, I fear no evil, for You are with me.

"*Shivt'cha umishantecha haymah y'nachamuni.*"

Thy rod and Thy staff, they comfort me.

The glow became brighter, emanating from all around, but as they finished singing it started to gather around the forms of Joseph and the cantor. The light became so bright and hot that Lincoln followed the vampire's lead and shielded his eyes.

Then Lincoln heard the song change. Without any prompting from the cantor, Joseph began singing another psalm. He listened carefully.

"*Omar ladoshem machsee umtsudati, elokai evtach bo, kee hu yahtseel'cha meepach yakoosh, midever havot.*"

I say of the Lord, my refuge and stronghold, my God in whom I trust, that He will save you from the fowler's trap, from the destructive plague.

Lincoln opened his eyes and looked over his arm. Was the light starting to move towards the vampire?

"*Lo teera meepachad lailah…*" You need not fear the terror by night…

The light began to coalesce around the vampire. She screamed. "Joseph! No!"

"*…meedever ba'ofel yahaloch.*" The plague that stalks in the darkness.

The light surrounded her completely, so brightly that her form was completely covered. Her screams became softer, muffled.

Joseph stopped singing. "Begone," the cantor and he said in unison.

Lincoln heard one more loud scream, and the light flared up, forcing him to cover his eyes again. When the light faded from beyond his arm, he looked up again, and noticed three things in succession. First, he saw Joseph, lying on his bed asleep, with all the normal color back in his face. Second, he saw the cantor holding up in front of him a silver *Magen David*, a Star of David.

Finally, he looked to where the vampire had last stood. All that was left of her was a pile of black dust, and a pair of sunglasses.

"Perhaps she was sent to test you, Mr. Kliman, perhaps not. I would not even guess."

It was Monday afternoon, two days later, and Lincoln had stopped by the synagogue to thank the cantor once again.

"At any rate, Cantor, it was your music that saved my son. And your Star of David. I owe you my eternal gratitude."

Cantor Gross shook his head slightly and smiled. "It was not merely my music, Mr. Kliman, but what my music represented, where it came from. As for the star of David, it has absolutely no religious significance at all. But I counted on the vampire not knowing that, and I was right. In short, I think your gratitude is well meant, but misplaced."

"Yes. Well. Cantor, I need to get back home now. I want to check on Joseph."

Lincoln turned to go, but the cantor gripped him by the arm. "Mr. Kliman, remember what we went through a few nights ago. What Joseph went through. Do not take his pseudo-conversion lightly and assume that he is now safe. The vampirism may still return."

"What do you suggest?" Lincoln asked softly.

The cantor looked him directly in the eye. "Start bringing the boy to synagogue. If you are not comfortable with this place, then bring him to one easier for you to accept. But do bring him to one. Let him build up an understanding, an appreciation of his background, his culture, his religion."

Lincoln pulled his arm away. "I'll consider it," he said, and to his surprise realized that he was speaking sincerely.

The cantor nodded. "It would be best for the boy to develop his own beliefs, his own defenses. Remember, Mr. Kliman, religion protects us from the many vampires of the world."

Lincoln nodded and walked out. It was a cold day, and he sneezed when he got outside. He reached into his coat pocket and found the *yarmulka* that he had been told to wear when he first entered the synagogue. He had forgotten to return it.

He looked back at the synagogue for a moment, then returned the *yarmulka* to his pocket and walked home. Perhaps he would find use for it soon.

ENDLESS NIGHT

by Barbara Roden

Barbara Roden, along with her husband Christopher Roden, is the proprietor of Ash-Tree Press. Together, they are also the editors of several anthologies, including *Acquainted with the Night*, which won the World Fantasy Award. Barbara is also the editor of *All Hallows*, the journal of the Ghost Story Society. Her first collection of short stories, *Northwest Passages*, will be published by Prime Books in October.

This story, which first appeared in *Exotic Gothic 2*, is about an expedition to Antarctica in the Golden Age of South Polar exploration: the days of Shackleton, Amundsen, Scott, and Mawson. However, when the expedition has to replace a crew member at the last moment, it becomes apparent his replacement has his own reasons for wanting to go to a continent where there's no daylight for months on end.

The story asks: How would you feel in such an isolated setting, if you became convinced there was someone present who wasn't supposed to be there? And how would you feel if, in order to ensure the survival of yourself and everyone else, you had to do something which goes against all your values and beliefs?

"Thank you so much for speaking with me. And for these journals, which have never seen the light of day. I'm honoured that you'd entrust them to me."

"That's quite all right." Emily Edwards smiled; a delighted smile, like a child surveying an unexpected and particularly wonderful present. "I don't receive very many visitors; and old people do like speaking about the past. No"—she held up a hand to stop him—"I *am* old; not elderly, not 'getting on,' nor any of the other euphemisms people use these days. When one has passed one's centenary, 'old' is the only word which applies."

"Well, your stories were fascinating, Miss Edwards. As I said, there are so few people alive now who remember these men."

Another smile, gentle this time. "One of the unfortunate things about living to my age is that all the people one knew in any meaningful or intimate way have died; there is no one left with whom I can share these things. Perhaps that is why I have so enjoyed this talk. It brings them all back to me. Sir Ernest; such a charismatic man, even when he was obviously in ill-health and worried about money. I used to thrill to his stories; to hear him talk of that desperate crossing of South Georgia Island to Stromness, of how they heard the whistle at the whaling station and knew that they were so very close to being saved, and then deciding to take a treacherous route down the slope to save themselves a five-mile hike when they were near exhaustion. He would drop his voice then, and say to me 'Miss Emily'—he always called me Miss Emily, which was the name of his wife, as you know; it made me feel very grown-up, even though I was only eleven—'Miss Emily, I do not know how we did it. Yet afterwards we all said the same thing, those three of us who made that crossing: that there had been another with us, a secret one, who guided our steps and brought us to safety.' I used to think it a very comforting story, when I was a child, but now—I am not as sure."

"Why not?"

For a moment he thought that she had not heard. Her eyes, which until that moment had been sharp and blue as Antarctic ice, dimmed, reflecting each of her hundred-and-one years as she gazed at her father's photograph on the wall opposite. He had an idea that she was not even with him in her comfortable room, that she was instead back in the parlour of her parents' home in north London, ninety years earlier, listening to Ernest Shackleton talk of his miraculous escape after the sinking of the *Endurance*, or her father's no less amazing tales of his own Antarctic travels. He was about to get up and start putting away his recording equipment when she spoke.

"As I told you, my father would gladly speak about his time in Antarctica with the Mawson and Shackleton expeditions, but of the James Wentworth expedition aboard the *Fortitude* in 1910 he rarely talked. He used to become quite angry with me if I mentioned it, and I learned not to raise the subject. I will always remember one thing he *did* say of it: 'It was hard to know how many people were there. I sometimes felt that there were too many of us.' And it would be frightening to think, in that place where so few people are, that there was another with you who should not be."

The statement did not appear to require an answer, for which the thin man in jeans and rumpled sweater was glad. Instead he said, "If you remember anything else, or if, by chance, you should come across those journals from the 1910 expedition, please do contact me, Miss Edwards."

"Yes, I have your card." Emily nodded towards the small table beside her, where a crisp white card lay beside a small ceramic tabby cat, crouched as if eyeing a mouse in its hole. Her gaze rested on it for a moment before she picked it up.

"I had this when I was a child; I carried it with me everywhere. It's really a wonder that it has survived this long." She gazed at it for a moment, a half-smile on her lips. "Sir Ernest said that it put him in mind of Mrs. Chippy, the ship's cat." Her smile faded. "He was always very sorry, you know, about what he had to do, and sorry that it caused an estrangement between him and Mr. McNish; he felt that the carpenter never forgave him for having Mrs. Chippy and the pups shot before they embarked on their journey in the boats."

"It was rather cruel, though, wasn't it? A cat, after all; what harm could there have been in taking it with them?"

"Ah, well." Emily set it carefully back down on the table. "I thought that, too, when I was young; but now I see that Sir Ernest was quite right. There was no room for sentimentality, or personal feeling; his task was to ensure that his men survived. Sometimes, to achieve that, hard decisions must be made. One must put one's own feelings and inclinations aside, and act for the greater good."

He sensed a closing, as of something else she might have said but had decided against. No matter; it had been a most productive afternoon. At the door Emily smiled as she shook his hand.

"I look forward to reading your book when it comes out."

"Well"—he paused, somewhat embarrassed—"it won't be out for a couple of years yet. These things take time, and I'm still at an early stage in my researches."

Emily laughed; a lovely sound, like bells chiming. "Oh, I do not plan on going anywhere just yet. You must bring me a copy when it is published, and let me read again about those long ago days. The past, where everything has already happened and there can be no surprises, can be a very comforting place when one is old."

It was past six o'clock when the writer left, but Emily was not hungry. She made a pot of tea, then took her cup and saucer into the main room and placed it on the table by her chair, beside the ceramic cat. She looked at it for a moment, and ran a finger down its back as if stroking it; then she picked up the card and considered it for a few moments.

"I think that I was right not to show him," she said, as if speaking to someone else present in the room. "I doubt that he would have understood. It is for the best."

Thus reminded, however, she could not easily forget. She crossed the room to a small rosewood writing desk in one corner, unlocked it, and pulled down the front panel, revealing tidily arranged cubbyholes and drawers of various sizes. With another key she unlocked the largest of the drawers, and withdrew from it a notebook bound in leather, much battered and weathered, as with long use in difficult conditions. She returned with it to her armchair, but it was some minutes before she opened it, and when she did it was with an air almost of sadness. She ran her fingers over the faded ink of the words on the first page.

Robert James Edwards
Science Officer
H.M.S. *Fortitude*
1910–11

"No," she said aloud, as if continuing her last conversation, "there can be no surprises about the past; everything there has happened. One would like to think it happened for the best; but we can never be sure. And *that* is not comforting at all." Then she opened the journal and began to read from it, even though the story was an old one which she knew by heart.

* * * * *

20 November 1910: A relief to be here in Hobart, on the brink of starting the final leg of our sea voyage. The endless days of fundraising, organisation, and meetings in London are well behind us, and the Guvnor is in high spirits, and as usual has infected everyone with his enthusiasm. He called us all together this morning, and said that of the hundreds upon hundreds of men who had applied to take part in the expedition when it was announced in England, we had been hand-picked, and that everything he has seen on the journey thus far has reinforced the rightness of his choices; but that the true test is still to come—in the journey across the great Southern Ocean and along the uncharted coast of Antarctica. We will be seeing sights that no human has yet viewed and will, if all goes to plan, be in a position to furnish exact information which will be of inestimable value to those who come after us. Chief among this information will be noting locations where future parties can establish camps, so that they might use these as bases for exploring the great heart of this unknown land, and perhaps even establishing a preliminary base for Mawson's push, rumoured to be taking place in a year's time. We are not tasked with doing much in the way of exploring ourselves, save in the vicinity of any base we do establish, but we have the dogs and sledges to enable us at least to make brief sorties into that mysterious continent, and I think that all the men are as eager as I to set foot where no man has ever trodden.

Of course, we all realise the dangers inherent in this voyage; none more so than the Guvnor, who today enjoined anyone who had the least doubt to say so now, while there was still an opportunity to leave. Needless to say, no one spoke, until Richards gave a cry of "Three cheers for the *Fortitude*, and all who sail in her!"; a cheer which echoed to the very skies, and set the dogs barking on the deck, so furiously that the Guvnor singled out Castleton and called good-naturedly, "Castleton, quiet your dogs down, there's a good chap, or we shall have the neighbours complaining!", which elicited a hearty laugh from all.

22 November: Such a tumultuous forty-eight hours we have not seen on this voyage, and I earnestly hope that the worst is now behind us. Two days ago the Guvnor was praising his hand-picked crew, and I, too, was thinking how our party had pulled together on the trip from Plymouth, which boded well, I thought, for the trials which surely face us; and now we have said farewell to one of our number, and made room for another. Chadwick, whose excellent meals brightened the early part of our voyage, is to be left in Hobart following a freakish accident which none could have foreseen, he having been knocked down in the street by a runaway horse and cart. His injuries are not, thank Heaven, life threatening, but are sufficient to make it impossible for him to continue as part of the expedition.

It is undoubtedly a very serious blow to the fabric of our party; but help has arrived in the form of Charles De Vere, who was actually present when the accident occurred, and was apparently instrumental in removing the injured man to a place of safety following the incident. He came by the ship the next day, to enquire after Chadwick, and was invited aboard; upon meeting with the Guvnor he disclosed that he has, himself, worked as a ship's cook, having reached Hobart in that capacity. The long and the short of it is that after a long discussion, the Guvnor has offered him Chadwick's place on the expedition, and De Vere has accepted.

"Needs must when the devil drives," the Guvnor said to me, somewhat ruefully, when De Vere had left to collect his things. "We can't do without a cook. Ah well, we have a few days more here in Hobart, and shall see how this De Vere works out."

What the Guvnor did not add—but was, I know, uppermost in his mind—is that a few days on board a ship at dockside is a very different proposition to what we shall be facing once we depart. We must all hope for the best.

28 November: We are set to leave tomorrow; the last of the supplies have been loaded, the last visiting dignitary has toured the ship and departed—glad, no doubt, to be going home safe to down pillows and a comfortable bed—and the men have written their last letters home, to be posted when the *Fortitude* has left. They are the final words we shall be able to send our loved ones before our return, whenever that will be, and a thin thread of melancholy pervades the ship tonight. I have written to Mary, and enclosed a message for sweet little Emily; by the time I return home she will have changed greatly from the little girl—scarcely more than a babe in arms—whom I left. She will not remember her father; but she and Mary are never far from my mind, and their photographs gaze down at me from the tiny shelf in my cabin, keeping watch over me as I sleep.

I said that the men had written their last letters home; but there was one exception. De Vere had no letters to give me, and while I made no comment he obviously noted my surprise, for he gave a wintry smile. "I said my goodbyes long ago," was all he said, and I did not press him, for there is something about his manner that discourages chatter. Not that he is standoffish, or unfriendly; rather, there is an air about him, as of a person who has spent a good deal of time alone, and has thus become a solitude unto himself. The Guvnor is pleased with him, though, and I must say that the man's cooking is superb. He spends most of his time in the tiny galley; to acquaint himself with his new domain, he told me. The results coming from it indicate that he is putting his time to good use, although I hope he will not have many occasions to favour us with seal consommé or Penguin *à la* Emperor.

Castleton had the largest batch of letters to send. I found him on the deck as usual, near the kennels of his charges. He is as protective of his dogs as a mother is of her children, and with good cause, for on these half-wild creatures the sledge teams shall depend. His control over them is quite wonderful. Some of the men are inclined to distrust the animals, which seem as akin to the domesticated dogs we all know as tigers are to tabby cats; none more so than De Vere who, I notice, gives them a wide berth on the rare occasions when he is on the deck. This wariness appears to be mutual; Castleton says that it is because the dogs scent food on De Vere's clothing.

29 November: At last we are under way, and all crowded to the ship's rail as the *Fortitude* departed from Hobart, to take a last look at civilisation. Even De Vere emerged into the sunlight, sheltering his sage eyes with his hand as we watched the shore recede into the distance. I think it fair to say that despite the mingled wonder and excitement we all share about the expedition, the feelings of the men at thus seeing the known world slip away from us were mixed; all save De Vere, whose expression was one of relief before he retreated once more to his sanctum. I know that the Guvnor—whose judgement of character is second to none—is satisfied with the man, and with what he was able to find out about him at such short notice, but I cannot help but wonder if there is something which makes De Vere anxious to be away from Hobart.

20 December: The Southern Ocean has not been kind to us; the storms of the last three weeks have left us longing for the occasional glimpse of blue sky. We had some idea of what to expect, but as the Guvnor reminds us, we are charting new territory every day, and must be prepared for any eventuality. We have repaired most of the damage done to the bridge and superstructure by the heavy seas of a fortnight ago, taking advantage of a rare spell of relative calm yesterday to accomplish the task and working well into the night, so as to be ready should the wind and water resume their attack.

The strain is showing on all the men, and I am thankful that the cessation of the tumultuous seas has enabled De Vere to provide hot food once more; the days of cold rations, when the pitching of the ship made the galley unusable, told on all of us. The cook's complexion, which has always been pale, has assumed a truly startling pallor, and his face looks lined and haggard. He spent most of yesterday supplying hot food and a seemingly endless stream of strong coffee for all of us, and then came and helped with the work on deck, which continued well into the long Antarctic summer night. I had wondered if he was in a fit state to do such heavy labour, but he set to with a will, and proved he was the equal of any aboard.

22 December: Yet another accident has claimed one of our party; but this one with graver consequences than the one which injured Chadwick. The spell of calmer weather which enabled us to carry out the much-needed repairs to the ship was all too short, and it was not long after we had completed our work that the storm resumed with even more fury than before, and there was a very real possibility that the sea waves would breach our supply of fresh water, which would very seriously endanger the fate of the expedition. As it was, those of us who had managed to drop off into some kind of sleep awoke to find several inches of icy water around our feet; and the dogs were in a general state of uproar, having been deluged by waves. I stumbled on to the deck and began helping Castleton and one or two others who were removing the dogs to a more sheltered location—a difficult task given the rolling of the ship and the state of the frantic animals. I was busy concentrating on the task at hand, and thus did not see one of the kennels come loose from its moorings on the deck; but we all heard the terrible cry of agony which followed.

When we rushed to investigate we found young Walker crushed between the heavy wooden kennel and the rail. De Vere had reached the spot before us and, in a fit of energy which can only be described as superhuman, managed single-handedly to shift the kennel out of the way and free Walker, who was writhing and moaning in pain. Beddoes was instantly summoned, and a quick look at the doctor's face showed the gravity of the situation. Walker was taken below, and it was some time before Beddoes emerged, looking graver than before, an equally grim-faced Guvnor with him. The report is that Walker's leg is badly broken, and there is a possibility of internal injuries. The best that can be done is to make the injured man as comfortable as possible, and hope that the injuries are not as severe as they appear.

25 December: A sombre Christmas Day. De Vere, in an attempt to lighten the mood, produced a truly sumptuous Christmas dinner for us all, which did go some way towards brightening our spirits, and afterwards the Guvnor conducted a short but moving Christmas Day service for all the men save Walker, who cannot be moved, and De Vere, who volunteered to sit with the injured man. One thing for which we give thanks is that the storms which have dogged our journey thus far seem to have abated; we have had no further blasts such as the one which did so much damage, and the Guvnor is hopeful that it will not be very much longer before we may hope to see the coast of Antarctica.

28 December: De Vere has been spending a great deal of time with Walker, who is, alas, no better; Beddoes's worried face tells us all that we need know on that score. He has sunk into a restless, feverish sleep which does nothing to refresh him, and seems to have wasted away to a mere shell of his former self in a shockingly brief period of time. De Vere, conversely, appears to have shaken off the adverse effects which the rough weather had on him; I had occasion to visit the galley earlier in the day, and was pleased to see that our cook's visage has assumed a ruddy hue, and the haggard look has disappeared.

De Vere's attendance on the injured man has gone some way to mitigating his standing as the expedition's "odd man out." Several of the men have worked with others here on various voyages, and are old Antarctic hands, while the others were all selected by the Guvnor after careful consideration: not only of their own qualities, but with an eye to how they would work as part of the larger group. He did not, of course, have this luxury with De Vere, whose air of solitude has gone some way to making others keep their distance. Add to this the fact that he spends most of his time in the galley, and is thus excused from taking part in much of the daily routine of the ship, and it is perhaps not surprising that he remains something of a cipher.

31 December: A melancholy farewell to the old year. Walker is no better, and Beddoes merely shakes his head when asked about him. Our progress is slower than we anticipated, for we are plagued with a never-dissipating fog which wreathes the ship, reducing visibility to almost nothing. Brash ice chokes the sea: millions of pieces of it, which grind against the ship in a never-ceasing cacophony. We are making little more than three knots, for we dare not go any faster, and risk running the *Fortitude* against a larger piece which could pierce the hull; on the other hand, we must maintain speed, lest we become mired in a fast-freezing mass. It is delicate work, and Mr. Andrews is maintaining a near-constant watch, for as captain he bears ultimate responsibility for the ship and her crew, and is determined to keep us safe.

I hope that 1911 begins more happily than 1910 looks set to end.

3 January 1911: Sad news today. Walker succumbed to his injuries in the middle of last night. The Guvnor gathered us all together this morning to inform us. De Vere was with Walker at the end, so the man did not die alone, a fact for which we are all grateful. I think we all knew that there was little hope of recovery; I was with him briefly only yesterday, and was shocked by how pale and gaunt he looked.

There was a brief discussion as to whether or not we should bury Walker at sea, or wait until we made land and bury him ashore. However, we do not know when—or even if—we shall make landfall, and it was decided by us all to wait until the water around the ship is sufficiently clear of ice and bury him at sea.

5 January: A welcome break in the fog today, enabling us to obtain a clear view of our surroundings for the first time in many days. We all knew that we were sailing into these waters at the most treacherous time of the southern summer, when the ice breaking up in the Ross Sea would be swept across our path, but we could not wait until later when the way would be clearer, or we would risk being frozen in the ice before we completed our work. As it is, the prospect which greeted us was not heartening; the way south is choked, as far as the eye can see, with vast bergs of ice; one, which was directly in front of us, stretched more than a mile in length, and was pitted along its base by caves, in which the water boomed and echoed.

Though the icebergs separate us from our goal, it must be admitted that they are beautiful. When I tell people at home of them, they are always surprised to hear that the bergs and massive floes are not pure white, but rather contain a multitude of colours: shades of lilac and mauve and blue and green, while pieces which have turned over display the brilliant hues of the algae which live in these waters. Their majesty, however, is every bit as awesome as has been depicted, in words and in art; Coleridge's inspired vision in his "Ancient Mariner" being a case in point.

I was standing at the rail this evening, listening to the ice as it prowled restlessly about the hull, gazing out upon the larger floes and bergs surrounding us and thinking along these lines, when I became aware of someone standing at my elbow. It was De Vere, who had come up beside me as soundlessly as a cat. We stood in not uncompanionable silence for some moments; then, as if he were reading my thoughts, he said quietly, "Coleridge was correct, was he not? How does he put it:

'The ice was here, the ice was there
The ice was all around:

It cracked and growled, and roared and howled,
Like noises in a swound!'

"Quite extraordinary, for a man who was never here. And Doré's illustrations for the work are likewise inspired. Of course, he made a rather dreadful *faux pas* with his polar bears climbing up the floes, although it does make a fine illustration. He was not at all apologetic when his mistake was pointed out to him. 'If I wish to place polar bears on the southern ice I shall.' Well, we must allow as great an artist as Doré some licence."

I admitted that I had been thinking much the same thing, at least about Coleridge. De Vere smiled.

"Truly one of our greatest and most inspired poets. We must forever deplore that visitor from Porlock who disturbed him in the midst of 'Kubla Khan.' And 'Christabel'; what might that poem have become had Coleridge finished it? That is the common cry; yet Coleridge's fate was always to have a vision so vast that in writing of it he could never truly 'finish,' in the conventional sense. In that he must surely echo life. Nothing is ever 'finished,' not really, save in death, and it is this last point which plays such a central role in 'Christabel.' Is the Lady Geraldine truly alive, or is she undead? He would never confirm it, but I always suspected that Coleridge was inspired, in part, to write 'Christabel' because of his earlier creation, the Nightmare Life-in-Death, who 'thicks men's blood with cold.' When she wins the Mariner in her game of dice with Death, does he join her in a deathless state, to roam the world forever? It is a terrible fate to contemplate."

"Surely not," I replied; "only imagine all that one could see and do were one given eternal life. More than one man has sought it."

De Vere, whose eyes had focussed on the ice around us, turned and fixed me with a steady gaze. The summer night was upon us, and it was sufficiently dark that I could not see his face distinctly; yet his grey eyes were dark pools, which displayed a grief without a pang, one so old that the original sting had turned to dull, unvarying sorrow.

"Eternal life," he repeated, and I heard bitterness underlying his words. "I do not think that those who seek it have truly considered it in all its consequences."

I did not know how to respond to this statement. Instead I remarked on his apparent familiarity with the works of Doré and Coleridge. De Vere nodded.

"I have made something of a study of the literature of the undead, if literature it is. *Varney the Vampyre;* certainly not literature, yet possessed of a certain crude power, although not to be mentioned in the same breath as works such as Mr. Poe's 'Berenice' or the Irishman Le Fanu's sublime 'Carmilla.'"

I consider myself to be a well-read man, but not in this field, as I have never had an inclination for bogey stories. I made a reference to the only work with which I was familiar that seemed relevant, and my companion shook his head.

"Stoker's novel is certainly powerful; but he makes of the central character too romantic a figure. Lord Byron has much for which to answer. And such a jumble of legends and traditions and lore, picked up here and there and then adapted to suit the needs of the novelist! Stoker never seems to consider the logical results of the depredations of the Count; if he were as bloodthirsty as depicted, and leaving behind such a trail of victims who become, in time, like him, then our world would be overrun." He shook his head. "One thing that the author depicted well was the essential isolation of his creation. Stoker does not tell us how long it was before the Count realised how alone he was, even in the midst of bustling London. Not long, I suspect."

It was an odd conversation to be having at such a time, and in such a place. De Vere must have realised this, for he gave an apologetic smile.

"I am sorry for leading the conversation in such melancholy channels, especially in light of what has happened. Did you know Walker very well?"

"No," I replied; "I did not meet him until shortly before we sailed from England. This was his first Antarctic voyage. He hoped, if the Guvnor gave him a good report at the end of it, to sign on with Mawson's next expedition, or even with Shackleton or Scott. Good Antarctic hands are in short supply. I know that the Guvnor, who has never lost a man on any of his expeditions, appreciates the time that you spent with Walker, so that he did not die alone. We all do."

"Being alone is a terrible thing," said De Vere, in so soft a voice that I could scarce hear him. "I only wish that…" He stopped. "I wish that it could have been avoided, that I could have prevented it. I had hoped…" He stopped once more.

"But what could you have done?" I asked in some surprise, when he showed no sign, this time, of breaking the silence. "You did more than enough. As I said, we are all grateful."

He appeared not to hear my last words. "More than enough," he repeated, in a voice of such emptiness that I could make no reply; and before long the cook excused himself to tend his duties before retiring for the night. I stayed on deck for a little time after, smoking a pipe and reflecting on our strange conversation. That De Vere is a man of education and intelligence I had already guessed, from his voice and manner and speech; he is clearly not a common sailor or sea-cook. What had brought him to Australia, however, and in such a capacity, I do not know. Perhaps he is one of those men, ill-suited to the rank and expectations of his birth, who seeks to test himself in places and situations which he would not otherwise encounter; or one of the restless souls who finds himself constrained by the demands of society.

It was, by this time, quite late; the only souls stirring on deck were the men of the watch, whom it was easy to identify: Richards with his yellow scarf, about which he has taken some good-natured ribbing; Wellington, the shortest man in our crew but with the strength and tenacity of a bulldog; and McAllister, with his ferocious red beard. All eyes would, I knew, be on the ice, for an accident here would mean the end.

The dogs were agitated; I could hear whining and a few low growls from their kennels. I glanced in that direction, and was startled to see a man, or so I thought, standing in the shadows beside them. There was no one on the watch near that spot, I knew, and while it was not unthinkable that some insomniac had come up on deck, what startled me was the resemblance the figure bore to Walker: the thin, eager face, the manner in which he held himself, even the clothing called to mind our fallen comrade. I shook my head, to clear it, and when I looked again the figure was gone.

This is, I fear, what comes of talks such as the one which I had with De Vere earlier. I must banish such thoughts from my head, as having no place on this voyage.

7 January: There was a sufficient clearing of the ice around the ship today to enable us to commit Walker's body to the deep. The service was brief, but very moving, and the faces of the men were solemn; none more so than De Vere, who still seems somewhat distraught, and who lingered at the rail's edge for some time, watching the spot where Walker's remains slipped beneath the water.

The ice which is keeping us from the coastline is as thick as ever; yet we are noting that many of the massive chunks around us are embedded with rocky debris, which would seem to indicate the presence of land nearby. We all hope this is a sign that, before long, we will sight that elusive coastline which hovers just outside our view.

17 January: We have reached our El Dorado at last! Early this morning the watch wakened the Guvnor and Mr Andrews to announce that they had sighted a rocky beach which looked suitable for a base camp. This news, coming as it does on the heels of all that we have seen and charted in the last few days, has inspired a celebration amongst the expedition members that equals that which we displayed when leaving Plymouth to begin our voyage. The glad news spread quickly, and within minutes everyone was on deck—some of the men only half-dressed—to catch a glimpse of the spot, on a sheltered bay where the *Fortitude* will be able to anchor safely. There was an excited babble of voices, and even some impromptu dancing, as the prospect of setting foot in this unknown land took hold; I suspect that we will be broaching some of the twenty or so cases of champagne which we have brought with us.

And yet I found myself scanning the faces on deck, and counting, for ever since the evening of that conversation with De Vere I have half-convinced myself that there are more men on board the ship than there should be. Quite how and why this idea has taken hold I cannot say, and it is not something which I can discuss with anyone else aboard; but I cannot shake the conviction that this shadowy other is Walker. If I believed in ghosts I could think that our late crewmate has returned to haunt the scene of his hopes and dreams; but I do not believe, and even to mention the idea would lead to serious concerns regarding my sanity. De Vere's talk has obviously played on my mind. Bogeys indeed!

The man himself seems to have regretted his speech that night. He spends most of his time in the galley, only venturing out on deck in the late evening, but he has restricted his comments to commonplaces about the weather, or the day's discoveries. The dogs are as uncomfortable with him as ever, but De Vere appears to be trying to accustom them to his presence, for he is often near them, speaking with

Castleton. The dog master spends most of his time when not on watch, or asleep, with his charges, ensuring that they are kept healthy for when we need them for the sledging parties, a task which we are all well content to leave him to. "If he doesn't stop spending so much time alone with those brutes he'll soon forget how to talk, and start barking instead," said Richards one evening.

The dogs may be robust, but Castleton himself is not looking well; he appears pale, and more tired than usual. It cannot be attributed to anything lacking in our diet, for the Guvnor has ensured that our provisions are excellent, and should the need arise we can augment our supplies with seal meat, which has proven such an excellent staple for travellers in the north polar regions. It could be that some illness is doing the rounds, for De Vere was once again looking pale some days ago, but seems to have improved. I saw him only a few minutes ago on the deck, looking the picture of health. While the rest of us have focussed our gazes landward, the cook was looking back the way we had come, as if keeping watch for something he expected to see behind us.

20 January: It has been a Herculean task, landing all the supplies, but at last it is finished. The men who have remained on the beach, constructing the hut, have done yeomen's work and, when the *Fortitude* departs tomorrow to continue along the coast on its charting mission, we shall have a secure roof over our heads. That it shall also be warm is thanks to the work of De Vere. When we went to assemble the stove we found that a box of vital parts was missing. McAllister recalled seeing a box fall from the motor launch during one of its landings, and when we crowded to the water's edge we did indeed see the box lying approximately seven feet down, in a bed of the kelp which grows along the coast. As we debated how best to grapple it to the surface, De Vere quietly and calmly removed his outer clothing and boots and plunged into the icy water. He had to surface three times for great gulps of air before diving down once more to tear the kelp away from the box and then carry it to the surface. It was a heroic act, but he deflected all attempts at praise. "It needed to be done," he said simply.

I have erected a small shed for my scientific equipment, at a little distance from the main hut. The dogs are tethered at about the same distance in the other direction, and we are anticipating making some sledging runs soon, although Castleton advises that the animals will be difficult to handle at first, which means that only those with some previous skill in that area will go on the initial journeys. It is debatable whether Castleton himself will be in a fit state to be one of these men, for he is still suffering from some illness which is leaving him in a weakened state; it is all he can do to manage his tasks with the dogs, and De Vere has had to help him.

And still—I hesitate to confess it—I cannot shake myself of this feeling of someone with us who should not be here. With all the bustle of transferring the supplies and erecting the camp it has been impossible for me to keep track of everyone, but I am sure that I have seen movement beyond the science hut when there should be no one there. If these delusions—for such they must be—continue, then I shall have to consider treatment when we return to England, or risk being unable to take part in future expeditions. I am conscious it is hallucination, but it is a phantasm frozen in place, at once too fixed to dislodge and too damaging to confess to another. We have but seven weeks—eight at most—before the ship returns to take us back to Hobart, in advance of the Antarctic winter; I pray that all will be well until then.

24 January: Our first sledging mission has been a success; two parties of three men each ascended the pathway that we have carved from the beach to the plateau above and behind us, and from there we travelled about four miles inland, attaining an altitude of 1500 feet. The feelings of us all as we topped the final rise and saw inland across that vast featureless plateau are indescribable. We were all conscious that we were gazing upon land that no human eye has ever seen, as we gazed southwards to where the ice seemed to dissolve into a white, impenetrable haze. The enormity of the landscape, and our own insignificance within it, struck us all, for it was a subdued party that made its way back to the camp before the night began to draw in to make travel impossible; there are crevasses—some hidden, some not—all about, which will make travel in anything other than daylight impossible. We were prepared to spend the night on the plateau should the need arise, but we were all glad to be back in the icicled hut with our fellows.

The mood there was subdued also. Castleton assisted, this morning, in harnessing the dogs to the sledges, but a task of which he would have made short work only a month ago seemed almost beyond him; and the look in his eyes as he watched us leave, on a mission of which he was to have been a part, tore at the soul. De Vere's health contrasted starkly with the wan face of the man beside him, yet the cook had looked almost as stricken as the dog master as we left the camp.

1 February: I did not think that I would find myself writing these words, but the *Fortitude* cannot return too quickly. It is not only Castleton's health that is worrisome; it is the growing conviction that there is something wrong with *me*. The fancy that someone else abides here grows stronger by the day and, despite my best efforts, I cannot rid myself of it. I have tried, as delicately as possible, to raise the question with some of the others, but their laughter indicates that no one else is suffering. "Get better snow goggles, old man," was Richards's response. The only person who did not laugh was De Vere, whose look of concern told me that he, too, senses my anxiety.

6 February: The end has come, and while it is difficult to write this, I feel I must; as if setting it down on paper will go some way to exorcising it from my mind. I know, however, that the scenes of the last two days will be with me until the grave.

Two nights ago I saw Walker again, as plainly as could be. It was shortly before dark, and I was returning from the hut which shelters my scientific equipment. The wind, which howls down from the icy plateau above us, had ceased for a time, and I took advantage of the relative calm to light my pipe.

All was quiet, save for a subdued noise from the men in the hut, and the growling of one or two of the dogs. I stood for a moment, gazing about me, marvelling at the sheer immensity of where I was. Save for the *Fortitude* and her crew, and Scott's party—wherever they may be—there are no people within 1200 miles of us, and we are as isolated from the rest of the world and her bustle as if we were on the moon. Once again the notion of our own insignificance in this uninhabited land struck me, and I shivered, knocked the ashes out of my pipe, and prepared to go to the main hut.

A movement caught my eye, behind the shed containing my equipment; it appeared to be the figure of a man, thrown into relief against the backdrop of ice. I called out sharply "Who's there?" and, not receiving an answer, took a few steps in the direction of the movement; but moments later stopped short when the other figure in turn took a step towards me, and I saw that it was Walker.

And yet that does not convey the extra horror of what I saw. It was not Walker as I remembered him, either from the early part of the voyage or in the period just before his death; then he had looked ghastly enough, but it was nothing as to how he appeared before me now. He was painfully thin, the colour of the ice and snow behind him, and in his eyes was a terrible light; they seemed to glow like twin lucifers. His nose was eaten away, and his lips, purple and swollen, were drawn back from his gleaming teeth in a terrible parody of a smile; yet there was nothing of mirth in the look which was directed towards me. I felt that I was frozen where I stood, unable to move, and I wondered what I would do if the figure advanced any further towards me.

It was De Vere who saved me. A cry must have escaped my lips, and the cook heard it, for I was aware that he was standing beside me. He said something in a low voice, words that I was unable to distinguish, and then he was helping me—not towards the main hut, thank God, for I was in no state to present myself before the others, but to the science hut. He pulled open the door and we stumbled inside, and De Vere lit the lantern which was hanging from the ceiling. For a moment, as the match flared, his own eyes seemed to glow; then the lamp was sending its comforting light, and all was as it should be.

He was obviously concerned; I could see that in his drawn brow, in the anxious expression of his eyes. I found myself telling him what I had seen, but if I thought that he would immediately laugh and tell me that I was imagining things I was much mistaken. He again said some words in a low voice; guttural and harsh, in a language I did not understand. When he looked at me his grey eyes were filled with such pain that I recoiled slightly. He shook his head.

"I am sorry," he said in a quiet voice. "Sorry that you have seen what you did, and… for other things. I had hoped…"

His voice trailed off. When he spoke again it was more to himself than to me; he seemed almost to have forgotten my presence.

"I have lived a long time, Mr. Edwards, and travelled a great deal; all my years, in fact, from place to place, never staying long in one location. At length I arrived in Australia, travelling ever further south, away from civilisation, until I found myself in Hobart, and believed it was the end. Then the *Fortitude* arrived, bound on its mission even further south, to a land where for several months of the year it is always night. Paradise indeed, I thought." His smile was twisted. "I should have remembered the words of Blake: 'Some are born to sweet delight / Some are born to endless night.' It is not a Paradise at all."

I tried to speak, but he silenced me with a gesture of his hand and a look from those haunted eyes. "If I needed something from you, would you help me?" he asked abruptly. I nodded, and he thought for a moment. "There are no sledge trips tomorrow; am I correct?"

"Yes," I replied, somewhat bewildered by the sudden change in the direction of the conversation. "The Guvnor feels that the men need a day of rest, so no trips are planned. Why?"

"Can you arrange that a single trip should be made, and that it shall be only you and I who travel?"

"It would be highly irregular; usually there are three men to a sledge, because of the difficulty of…"

"Yes, yes, I understand that. But it is important that it should be just the two of us. Can it be managed?"

"If it is important enough, then yes, I should think so."

"It is more important than you know." He gave a small smile, and some of the pain seemed gone from his eyes. "Far more important. Tomorrow night this will be over. I promise you."

I had little sleep that night, and next day was up far earlier than necessary, preparing the sled and ensuring that all was in order. There had been some surprise when I announced that De Vere and I would be off, taking one of the sledges ourselves, but I explained it by saying that the cook merely wanted an opportunity to obtain a glimpse of that vast land for himself, and that we would not be travelling far. When De Vere came out to the sledge he was carrying a small bag. It was surprisingly heavy, but I found a place for it, and moments later the dogs strained into their harnesses, and we were away.

The journey up to the plateau passed uneventfully under the leaden sun, and we made good time on the trail, which was by now well established. When we topped the final rise I stopped the sledge, so that we could both look out across that vast wasteland of ice and snow, stretching away to the South Pole hundreds and hundreds of miles distant. De Vere meditated upon it for some minutes, then turned to me.

"Thank you for bringing me here," he said in his quiet voice. "We are about four miles from camp, I think you said?" When I concurred, he continued, "That is a distance which you can travel by yourself, is it not?"

"Yes, of course," I replied, somewhat puzzled.

"I thought as much, or I would not have brought you all this way. And I did want to see this"—he gestured at the silent heart of the continent behind us—"just once. Such a terrible beauty on the surface, and underneath, treachery. You say here there are crevasses?"

"Yes," I said. "We must be careful when breaking new trails, lest a snow bridge collapse under us. Three days ago a large crevasse opened up to our right"—I pointed—"and there was a very real fear that one of the sledges was going to be carried down into it. It was only some quick work on the part of McAllister that kept it from plunging through."

"Could you find the spot again?"

"Easily. We are not far."

"Good." He turned to the sledge, ignoring the movement and barking of the dogs; they had not been much trouble when there had been work to do, but now, stopped, they appeared restless, even nervous. De Vere rustled around among the items stowed on the sledge, and pulled out the bag he had given me. He hesitated for a moment; then he walked to where I stood waiting and passed it to me.

"I would like you to open that," he said, and when I did so I found a small, ornate box made of mahogany, secured with a stout brass hasp. "Open the box, and remove what is inside."

I had no idea what to expect; but any words I might have said failed me when I undid the hasp, opened the lid, and found inside the box a revolver. I looked up at De Vere, who wore a mirthless smile.

"It belonged to a man who thought to use it on me, some years ago," he said simply. "That man died. I think you will find, if you look, that it is loaded."

I opened the chamber, and saw that it was so. I am by no means an expert with firearms, but the bullets seemed to be almost tarnished, as with great age. I closed the chamber, and glanced at De Vere.

"Now we are going to go over to the edge of the crevasse, and you are going to shoot me." The words were said matter-of-factly, and what followed was in the same dispassionate tone, as if he were speaking of the weather, or what he planned to serve for dinner that evening. "Stand close, so as not to miss. When you return to camp you will tell them that we came too near to the edge of the crevasse, that a mass of snow collapsed under me, and that there was nothing you could do. I doubt that any blame or stigma will attach to you—not with your reputation—and while it may be difficult for you for a time, you will perhaps take solace in the fact that you will not see Walker again, and that Castleton's health will soon improve." He paused. "I am sorry about them both; more than I can say." Then he added some words in an undertone, which I did not quite catch; one word sounded like "hungry," and another like "tired," but in truth I was so overwhelmed that I was barely in a position to make sense of anything. One monstrous fact alone stood out hard and clear, and I struggled to accept it.

"Are you… are you ill, then?" I asked at last, trying to find some explanation at which my mind did not rebel. "Some disease that will claim you?"

"If you want to put it that way, yes; a disease. If that makes it easier for you." He reached out and put a hand on my arm. "You have been friendly, and I have not had many that I could call a friend. I thank you, and ask you to do this one thing for me; and, in the end, for all of you."

I looked into his eyes, dark as thunderclouds, and recalled our conversation on board the ship following Walker's death, and for a moment had a vision of something dark and terrible. I thought of the look on Walker's face—or the thing that I had thought was Walker—when I had seen it the night before. "Will you end up like him?" I asked suddenly, and De Vere seemed to know to what I referred, for he shook his head.

"No, but if you do not do this then others will," he said simply. I knew then how I must act. He obviously saw the look of resolution in my face, for he said again, quietly, "Thank you," then turned and began walking towards the crevasse in the ice.

I cannot write in detail of what followed in the next few minutes. I remained beside the crevasse, staring blankly down into the depths which now held him, and it was only with considerable effort that I finally roused myself enough to stumble back to the dogs, which had at last quietened. The trip back to camp was a blur of white, and I have no doubt that, when I stumbled down the final stretch of the path, I appeared sufficiently wild-eyed and distraught that my story was accepted without question.

The Guvnor had a long talk with me this morning when I woke, unrefreshed, from a troubled sleep. He appears satisfied with my answers, and while he did upbraid me slightly for failing to take a third person with us—as that might have helped avert the tragedy—he agreed that the presence of another would probably have done nothing to help save De Vere.

Pray God he never finds out the truth.

15 February: More than a week since De Vere's death, and I have not seen Walker in that time. Castleton, too, is much improved, and appears well on the way to regaining his full health.

Subsequent sledge parties have inspected the crevasse, and agree that it was a terrible accident, but one that could not have been avoided. I have not been up on the plateau since my trip with De Vere. My thoughts continually turn to the man whom I left there, and I recall what Cook wrote more than one hundred years ago. He was speaking of this place; but the words could, I think, equally be applied to De Vere: "Doomed by nature never once to feel the warmth of the sun's rays, but to be buried in everlasting snow and ice."

* * * * *

A soft flutter of leaves whispered like a sigh as Emily finished reading. The last traces of day had vanished, leaving behind shadows which pooled at the corners of the room. She sat in silence for some time, her eyes far away; then she closed the journal gently, almost with reverence, and placed it on the table beside her. The writer's card stared up at her, and she considered it.

"He would not understand," she said at last. "And they are all dead; they can neither explain nor defend themselves or their actions." She looked at her father's photograph, now blurred in the gathering darkness. "Yet you did not destroy this." She touched the journal with fingers delicate as a snowflake. "You left it for me to decide, keeping this a secret even from my mother. You must have thought that I would know what to do."

Pray God he never finds out the truth.

She remained in her chair for some moments longer. Then, with some effort, Emily rose from her chair and, picking up the journal, crossed once more to the rosewood desk and its shadows. She placed the journal in its drawer, where it rested beside a pipe which had lain unsmoked for decades. The ceramic cat watched with blank eyes as she turned out the light. In so doing she knocked the card to the floor, where it lay undisturbed.

INFESTATION

by Garth Nix

Garth Nix is the bestselling author of the Old Kingdom series, The Seventh Tower series, and The Keys to the Kingdom series. He is the winner of nine Aurealis Awards, given to best works of SF/fantasy by Australian writers. His short fiction has appeared in such venues as *Eidolon, The Magazine of Fantasy & Science Fiction, Jim Baen's Universe,* and in the anthology *Fast Ships, Black Sails.* Before becoming a full-time writer, he worked in a variety of careers in publishing, including publicist, editor, and literary agent.

Most authors imagine vampires skulking in the shadows, their existence suspected but never confirmed by the outside world. But there are notable exceptions. In Richard Matheson's classic *I Am Legend*, vampires have completely taken over the world, and a lone survivor uses science to try to puzzle out their nature. In Laurell K. Hamilton's Anita Blake series, various bureaucracies have grown up to deal with vampires, who live openly. This story is another in that mode. Here, vampires, law, and technology all intersect—in more ways than you might expect. You've probably never read a vampire story quite like this one.

They were the usual motley collection of freelance vampire hunters. Two men, wearing combinations of jungle camouflage and leather. Two women, one almost indistinguishable from the men though with a little more style in her leather armour accessories, and the other looking like she was about to assault the south face of a serious mountain. Only her mouth was visible, a small oval of flesh not covered by balaclava, mirror shades, climbing helmet and hood.

They had the usual weapons: four or five short wooden stakes in belt loops; snap-holstered handguns of various calibers, all doubtless chambered with Wood-N-Death® low-velocity timber-tipped rounds; big silver-edged bowie or other hunting knife, worn on the hip or strapped to a boot; and crystal vials of holy water hung like small grenades on pocket loops.

Protection, likewise, tick the usual boxes. Leather neck and wrist guards; leather and woven-wire reinforced chaps and shoulder pauldrons over the camo; leather gloves with metal knuckle plates; Army or climbing helmets.

And lots of crosses, oh yeah, particularly on the two men. Big silver crosses, little wooden crosses, medium-sized turned ivory crosses, hanging off of everything they could hang off.

In other words, all four of them were lumbering, bumbling mountains of stuff that meant that they would be easy meat for all but the newest and dumbest vampires.

They all looked at me as I walked up. I guess their first thought was to wonder what the hell I was doing there, in the advertised meeting place, outside a church at 4:30 pm on a winter's day while the last rays of the sun were supposedly making this consecrated ground a double no-go zone for vampires.

"You're in the wrong place, surfer boy," growled one of the men.

I was used to this reaction. I guess I don't look like a vampire hunter much anyway, and I particularly didn't look like one that afternoon. I'd been on the beach that morning, not knowing where I might head to later, so I was still wearing a yellow Quiksilver T-shirt and what might be loosely described as old and faded blue board shorts, but "ragged" might be more accurate. I hadn't had shoes on, but I'd picked up a pair of sandals on the way. Tan Birkenstocks, very comfortable. I always prefer sandals to shoes. Old habits, I guess.

I don't look my age, either. I always looked young, and nothing's changed, though "boy" was a bit rough coming from anyone under forty-five, and the guy who'd spoken was probably closer to thirty. People older than that usually leave the vampire hunting to the government, or paid professionals.

"I'm in the right place," I said, matter-of-fact, not getting into any aggression or anything. I lifted my 1968-vintage vinyl Pan-Am airline bag. "Got my stuff here. This is the meeting place for the vampire hunt?"

"Yes," said the mountain-climbing woman.

"Are you crazy?" asked the man who'd spoken to me first. "This isn't some kind of doper excursion. We're going up against a nest of vampires!"

I nodded and gave him a kind smile.

"I know. At least ten of them, I would say. I swung past and had a look around on the way here. At least, I did if you're talking about that condemned factory up on the river heights."

"What! But it's cordoned off—and the vamps'll be dug in till nightfall."

"I counted the patches of disturbed earth," I explained. "The cordon was off. I guess they don't bring it up to full power till the sun goes down. So, who are you guys?"

"Ten!" exclaimed the second man, not answering my question. "You're sure?"

"At least ten," I replied. "But only one Ancient. The others are all pretty new, judging from the spoil."

"You're making this up," said the first man. "There's maybe five, tops. They were seen together and tracked back. That's when the cordon was established this morning."

I shrugged and half-unzipped my bag.

"I'm Jenny," said the mountain-climber, belatedly answering my question. "The... the vampires got my sister, three years ago. When I heard about this infestation I claimed the Relative's Right."

"I've got a twelve-month permit," said the second man. "Plan to turn professional. Oh yeah, my name's Karl."

"I'm Susan," said the second woman. "This is our third vampire hunt. Mike's and mine, I mean."

"She's my wife," said the belligerent Mike. "We've both got twelve-month permits. You'd better be legal too, if you want to join us."

"I have a special licence," I replied. The sun had disappeared behind the church tower, and the street lights were flicking on. With the bag unzipped, I was ready for a surprise. Not that I thought one was about to happen. At least, not immediately. Unless I chose to spring one.

"You can call me J."

"Jay?" asked Susan.

"Close enough," I replied. "Does someone have a plan?"

"Yeah," said Mike. "We stick together. No hot-dogging off, or chasing down wounded vamps or anything like that. We go in as a team, and we come out as a team."

"Interesting," I said. "Is there… more to it?"

Mike paused to fix me with what he obviously thought was his steely gaze. I met it and after a few seconds he looked away. Maybe it's the combination of very pale blue eyes and dark skin, but not many people look at me directly for too long. It might just be the eyes. There've been quite a few cultures who think of very light blue eyes as the colour of death. Perhaps that lingers, resonating in the subconscious even of modern folk.

"We go through the front door," he said. "We throw flares ahead of us. The vamps should all be digging out on the old factory floor, it's the only place where the earth is accessible. So we go down the fire stairs, throw a few more flares out the door then go through and back up against the wall. We'll have a clear field of fire to take them down. They'll be groggy for a couple of hours yet, slow to move. But if one or two manage to close, we stake them."

"The young ones will be slow and dazed," I said. "But the Ancient will be active soon after sundown, even if it stays where it is—and it's not dug in on the factory floor. It's in a humungous clay pot outside an office on the fourth floor."

"We take it first, then," said Mike. "Not that I'm sure I believe you."

"It's up to you," I said. I had my own ideas about dealing with the Ancient, but they would wait. No point upsetting Mike too early. "There's one more thing."

"What?" asked Karl.

"There's a fresh-made vampire around, from last night. It will still be able to pass as human for a few more days. It won't be dug-in, and it may not even know it's infected."

"So?" asked Mike. "We kill everything in the infested area. That's all legal."

"How do you know this stuff?" asked Jenny.

"You're a professional, aren't you," said Karl. "How long you been pro?"

"I'm not exactly a professional," I said. "But I've been hunting vampires for quite a while."

"Can't have been that long," said Mike. "Or you'd know better than to go after them in just a T-shirt. What've you got in that bag? Sawn-off shotgun?"

"Just a stake and a knife," I replied. "I'm a traditionalist. Shouldn't we be going?"

The sun was fully down, and I knew the Ancient, at least, would already be reaching up through the soil, its mildewed, mottled hands gripping the rim of the earthenware pot that had once held a palm or something equally impressive outside the factory manager's office.

"Truck's over there," said Mike, pointing to a flashy new silver pick-up. "You can ride in the back, surfer boy."

"Fresh air's a wonderful thing."

As it turned out, Karl and Jenny wanted to sit in the back too. I sat on a tool box that still had shrink-wrap around it, Jenny sat on a spare tire and Karl stood looking over the cab, scanning the road, as if a vampire might suddenly jump out when we were stopped at the lights.

"Do you want a cross?" Jenny asked me after we'd gone a mile or so in silence. Unlike Mike and Karl she wasn't festooned with them, but she had a couple around her neck. She started to take a small wooden one off, lifting it by the chain.

I shook my head, and raised my T-shirt up under my arms, to show the scars. Jenny recoiled in horror and gasped, and Karl looked around, hand going for his .41 Glock. I couldn't tell whether that was jumpiness or good training. He didn't draw and shoot, which I guess meant good training.

I let the T-shirt fall, but it was up long enough for both of them to see the hackwork tracery of scars that made up a kind of "T" shape on my chest and stomach. But it wasn't a "T". It was a Tau Cross, one of the oldest Christian symbols and still the one that vampires feared the most, though none but the most ancient knew why they fled from it.

"Is that… a cross?" asked Karl.

I nodded.

"That's so hardcore," said Karl. "Why didn't you just have it tattooed?"

"It probably wouldn't work so well," I said. "And I didn't have it done. It was done to me."

I didn't mention that there was an equivalent tracery of scars on my back as well. These two Tau Crosses, front and back, never faded, though my other scars always disappeared only a few days after they healed.

"Who would—" Jenny started to ask, but she was interrupted by Mike banging on the rear window of the cab—with the butt of his pistol, reconfirming my original assessment that he was the biggest danger to all of us. Except for the Ancient Vampire. I wasn't worried about the young ones. But I didn't know which Ancient it was, and that was cause for concern. If it had been encysted since the drop it would be in the first flush of its full strength. I hoped it had been around for a long time, lying low and steadily degrading, only recently resuming its mission against humanity.

"We're there," said Karl, unnecessarily.

The cordon fence was fully established now. Sixteen feet high and lethally electrified, with old-fashioned limelights burning every ten feet along the fence, the sound of the hissing oxygen and hydrogen jets music to my ears. Vampires loathe limelight. Gaslight has a lesser effect, and electric light hardly bothers them at all. It's the intensity of the naked flame they fear.

The fire brigade was standing by because of the limelights, which though modernized were still occasionally prone to massive accidental combustion; and the local police department was there en masse to enforce the cordon. I saw the bright white bulk of the state Vampire Eradication Team's semi-trailer parked off to one side. If we volunteers failed, they would go in, though given the derelict state of the building and the reasonable space between it and the nearest residential area it was more likely they'd just get the Air Force to do a fuel-air explosion dump.

The VET personnel would be out and about already, making sure no vampires managed to get past the cordon. There would be crossbow snipers on the upper floors of the surrounding buildings, ready to shoot fire-hardened oak quarrels into vampire heads. It wasn't advertised by the ammo manufacturers, but a big old vampire could take forty or fifty Wood-N-Death® or equivalent rounds to the head and chest before going down. A good inch-diameter yard-long quarrel or stake worked so much better.

There would be a VET quick response team somewhere close as well, outfitted in the latest metal-mesh armour, carrying the automatic weapons the volunteers were not allowed to use—with good reason, given the frequency with which volunteer vampire hunters killed each other even when only armed with handguns, stakes and knives.

I waved at the window of the three-storey warehouse where I'd caught a glimpse of a crossbow sniper, earning a puzzled glance from Karl and Jenny, then jumped down. A police sergeant was already walking over to us, his long, harsh limelit shadow preceding him. Naturally, Mike intercepted him before he could choose who he wanted to talk to.

"We're the volunteer team."

"I can see that," said the sergeant. "Who's the kid?"

He pointed at me. I frowned. The kid stuff was getting monotonous. I don't look that young. Twenty at least, I would have thought.

"He says his name's Jay. He's got a 'special licence.' That's what he says."

"Let's see it then," said the sergeant, with a smile that suggested he was looking forward to arresting me and delivering a three-hour lecture. Or perhaps a beating with a piece of rubber pipe. It isn't always easy to decipher smiles.

"I'll take it from here, Sergeant," said an officer who came up from behind me, fast and smooth. He was in the new metal-mesh armour, like a wetsuit, with webbing belt and harness over it, to hold stakes, knife, WP grenades (which actually were effective against the vamps, unlike the holy water ones) and handgun. He had an H&K MP5-PDW slung over his shoulder. "You go and check the cordon."

"But Lieutenant, don't you want me to take—"

"I said check the cordon."

The sergeant retreated, smile replaced by a scowl of frustration. The VET lieutenant ignored him.

"Licences, please," he said. He didn't look at me, and unlike the others I didn't reach for the plasticated, hologrammed, data-chipped card that was the latest version of the volunteer vampire hunter licence.

They held their licences up and the reader that was somewhere in the lieutenant's helmet picked up the data and his earpiece whispered whether they were valid or not. Since he was nodding, we all knew they were valid before he spoke.

"OK, you're good to go whenever you want. Good luck."

"What about him?" asked Mike, gesturing at me with his thumb.

"Him too," said the lieutenant. He still didn't look at me. Some of the VET are funny like that. They seem to think I'm like an albatross or something. A sign of bad luck. I suppose it's because wherever the vampire infestations are really bad, then I have a tendency to show up as well. "He's already been checked in. We'll open the gate in five, if that suits you."

"Sure," said Mike. He lumbered over to face me. "There's something funny going on here, and I don't like it. So you just stick to the plan, OK?"

"Actually, your plan sucks," I said calmly. "So I've decided to change it. You four should go down to the factory floor and take out the vampires there. I'll go up against the Ancient."

"Alone?" asked Jenny. "Shouldn't we stick together like Mike says?"

"Nope," I replied. "It'll be out and unbending itself now. You'll all be too slow."

"Call this sl—" Mike started to say, as he tried to poke me forcefully in the chest with his forefinger. But I was already standing behind him. I tapped him on the shoulder, and as he swung around, ran behind him again. We kept this up for a few turns before Karl stopped him.

"See what I mean? And an Ancient Vampire is faster than me."

That was blarney. Or at least I hoped it was. I'd met Ancient Vampires who were as quick as I was, but not actually faster. Sometimes I did wonder what would happen if one day I was a fraction slower and one finally got me for good and all. Some days, I kind of hoped that it would happen.

But not this day. I hadn't had to go up against any vampires or anything else for over a month. I'd been surfing for the last two weeks, hanging out on the beach, eating well, drinking a little wine and even letting down my guard long enough to spend a couple of nights with a girl who surfed better than me and didn't mind having sex in total darkness with a guy who kept his T-shirt on and an old airline bag under the pillow.

I was still feeling good from this little holiday, though I knew it would only ever be that. A few weeks snatched out of…

"OK," panted Mike. He wasn't as stupid as I'd feared but he was a lot less fit than he looked. "You do your thing. We'll take the vampires on the factory floor."

"Good," I replied. "Presuming I survive, I'll come down and help you."

"What do… what do we do if we… if we're losing?" asked Jenny. She had her head well down, her chin almost tucked into her chest and her body-language screamed out that she was both scared and miserable. "I mean if there are more vampires, or if the Ancient one—"

"We fight or we die," said Karl. "No one is allowed back out through the cordon until after dawn."

"Oh, I didn't… I mean I read the brochure—"

"You don't have to go in," I said. "You can wait out here."

"I… I think I will," she said, without looking at the others. "I just can't… now I'm here, I just can't face it."

"Great!" muttered Mike. "One of us down already."

"She's too young," said Susan. I was surprised she'd speak up against Mike. I had her down as his personal doormat. "Don't give her a hard time, Mike."

"No time for anything," I said. "They're getting ready to power down the gate."

A cluster of regular police officers and VET agents were taking up positions around the gate in the cordon fence. We walked over, the others switching on helmet lights, drawing their handguns and probably silently uttering last-minute prayers.

The sergeant who'd wanted to give me a hard time looked at Mike, who gave him the thumbs up. A siren sounded a slow *whoop-whoop-whoop* as a segment of the cordon fence powered down, the indicators along the top rail fading from a warning red to a dull green.

"Go, go, go!" shouted Mike, and he jogged forward, with Susan and Karl at his heels. I followed a few metres behind, but not too far. That sergeant had the control box for the gate and I didn't trust him not to close it on my back and power it up at the same time. I really didn't want to know what 6,600 volts at 500 milliamps would do to my unusual physiology. Or show anyone else what didn't happen, more to the point.

On the other hand, I didn't want to get ahead of Mike and co, either, because I already know what being shot in the back by accident felt like, with lead and wooden bullets, not to mention ceramic-cased tungsten-tipped penetrator rounds, and I didn't want to repeat the experience.

They rushed the front door, Mike kicking it in and bulling through. The wood was rotten and the top panel had already fallen off, so this was less of an achievement than it might have been.

Karl was quick with the flares, confirming his thorough training. Mike, on the other hand, just kept going, so the light was behind him as he opened the fire door to the left of the lobby.

Bad move. There was a vampire behind the door, and while it was no ancient, it wasn't newly hatched either. It wrapped its arms around Mike, holding on with the filaments that lined its forelegs, though to an uneducated observer it just looked like a fairly slight, tattered rag-wearing human bear-hugging him with rather longer than usual arms.

Mike screamed as the vampire started chewing on his helmet, ripping through the Kevlar layers like a buzz-saw through softwood, pausing only to spit out bits of the material. Old steel helmets are better than the modern variety, but we live in an age that values only the new.

Vamps like to get a good grip around their prey, particularly ones who carry weapons. There was nothing Mike could do, and as the vamp was already backing into the stairwell, only a second or two for someone else to do something.

The vampire fell to the ground, its forearm filaments coming loose with a sticky popping sound, though they probably hadn't penetrated Mike's heavy clothes. I pulled the splinter out of its head and put the stake of almost two-thousand-year-old timber back in the bag before the others got a proper look at the odd silver sheen that came from deep within the wood.

Karl dragged Mike back into the flare-light as Susan covered him. Both of them were pretty calm, I thought. At least they were still doing stuff, rather than freaking out.

"Oh man," said Karl. He'd sat Mike up, and then had to catch him again as he fell backwards. Out in the light, I saw that I'd waited just that second too long, perhaps from some subconscious dislike of the man. The last few vampire bites had not been just of Mike's helmet.

"What… what do we do?" asked Susan. She turned to me, pointedly not looking at her dead husband.

"I'm sorry," I said. I really meant it, particularly since it was my slackness that had let the vamp finish him off. Mike was an idiot but he didn't deserve to die, and I could have saved him. "But he's got to be dealt with the same way as the vampires now. Then you and Karl have to go down and clean out the rest. Otherwise they'll kill you too."

It usually helps to state the situation clearly. Stave off the shock with the need to do something life-saving. Adrenalin focuses the mind wonderfully.

Susan looked away for a couple of seconds. I thought she might vomit, but I'd underestimated her again. She turned back, and still holding her pistol in her right hand, reached into a thigh pocket and pulled out a Quick-Flame™.

"I should be the one to do it," she said. Karl stepped back as she thumbed the Quick-Flame™ and dropped it on the corpse. The little cube deliquesced into a jelly film that spread over the torso of what had once been a man. Then, as it splashed on the floor, it woofed alight, burning blue.

Susan watched the fire. I couldn't see much of her face, but from what I could see, I thought she'd be OK for about an hour before the shock knocked her off her feet. Provided she got on with the job as soon as possible.

"You'd better get going," I said. "If this one was already up here, the others might be out and about. Don't get ahead of your flares."

"Right," muttered Karl. He took another flare from a belt pouch. "Ready, Susan?"

"Yes."

Karl tossed the flare down the stairs. They both waited to see the glow of its light come back up, then Karl edged in, working the angle, his pistol ready. He fired almost immediately, two double taps, followed by the sound of a vamp falling back down the stairs.

"Put two more in," I called out, but Karl was already firing again.

"And stake it before you go past!" I added as they both disappeared down the stair.

As soon as they were gone, I checked the smouldering remains of Mike. Quick-Flame™ cubes are all very well, but they don't always burn everything and if there's a critical mass of organic material left then the vamp nanos can build a new one. A little, slow one, but little slow ones can grow up. I doubted there'd been enough exchange of blood to get full infestation, but it's better to be sure, so I took out the splinter again and waved it over the fragments that were left.

The sound of rapid gunshots began to echo up from below as I took off my T-shirt and tucked it in the back of my board shorts. The Tau cross on my chest was already glowing softly with a silver light, the smart matter under the scars energizing as it detected vamp activity close by. I couldn't see the one on my back, but it would be doing the same thing. Together they were supposed to generate a field that repulsed the vampires and slowed them down if they got close, but it really only worked on the original versions. The latter-day generations of vampires were such bad copies that a lot of the original tech built to deter them simply missed the mark. Fortunately, being bad copies, the newer vampires were weaker, slower, less intelligent and untrained.

I took the main stairs up to the fourth floor. The Ancient Vampire would already know I was coming so there was no point skulking up the elevator shaft or the outside drain. Like its broodmates, it had been bred to be a perfect soldier at various levels of conflict, from the nanonic frontline where it tried to replicate itself in its enemies to the gross physical contest of actually duking it out. Back in the old days it might have had some distance weapons as well, but if there was one thing we'd managed right in the original mission it was taking out the vamp weapons caches and resupply nodes.

We did a lot of things right in the original mission. We succeeded rather too well, or at least so we thought at the time. If the victory hadn't been so much faster than anticipated, the boss would never have had those years to fall in love with humans and then work out his crazy scheme to become their living god.

Not so crazy perhaps, since it kind of worked, even after I tried to do my duty and stop him. In a half-hearted way, I suppose, because he was team leader and all that. But he was going totally against regulations. I reported it and I got the order, and the rest, as they say, is history…

Using the splinter always reminds me of him, and the old days. There's probably enough smart matter in the wood, encasing his DNA and his last download to bring him back complete, if and when I ever finish this assignment and can signal for pickup. Though a court would probably confirm HQ's original order and he'd be slowed into something close to a full stop anyway.

But my mission won't be over till the last vamp is burned to ash, and this infested Earth can be truly proclaimed clean.

Which is likely to be a long, long time, and I remind myself that daydreaming about the old days is not going to help take out the Ancient Vampire ahead of me, let alone the many more in the world beyond.

I took out the splinter and the silver knife and slung my Pan-Am bag so it was comfortable, and got serious.

I heard the Ancient moving around as I stepped into what was once the outer office. The big pot was surrounded by soil and there were dirty footprints up the wall, but I didn't need to see them to know to look up. The Vamps have a desire to dominate the high ground heavily programmed into them. They always go for the ceiling, up trees, up towers, up lamp-posts.

This one was spread-eagled on the ceiling, gripping with its foreleg and trailing leg filaments as well as the hooks on what humans thought were fingers and toes. It was pretty big as Vamps go, perhaps nine feet long and weighing in at around 200 pounds. The ultra-thin waist gave away its insectoid heritage, almost as much as a real close look at its mouth would. Not that you would want a real close look at a Vamp's mouth.

It squealed when I came in and it caught the Tau emissions. The squeal was basically an ultrasonic alarm oscillating through several wavelengths. The cops outside would hear it as an unearthly scream, when in fact it was more along the lines of a distress call and emergency rally beacon. If any of its brood survived down below, they'd drop whatever they might be doing—or chewing—and rush on up.

The squeal was standard operating procedure, straight out of the manual. It followed up with more orthodox stuff, dropping straight on to me. I flipped on my back and struck with the splinter, but the Vamp managed to flip itself in mid-air and bounce off the wall, coming to a stop in the far corner.

It was fast, faster than any Vamp I'd seen for a long time. I'd scratched it with the splinter, but no more than that. There was a line of silver across the dark red chitin of its chest, where the transferred smart matter was leeching the vampire's internal electrical potential to build a bomb, but it would take at least five seconds to do that, which was way too long.

I leapt and struck again and we conducted a kind of crazy ballet across the four walls, the ceiling and the floor of the room. Anyone watching would have got motion sickness or eyeball fatigue, trying to catch blurs of movement.

At 2.350 seconds in, it got a forearm around my left elbow and gave it a good hard pull, dislocating my arm at the shoulder. I knew then it really was ancient, and had retained the programming needed to fight me. My joints have always been a weak point.

It hurt. A lot, and it kept on hurting through several microseconds as the Vamp tried to actually pull my arm off and at the same time twist itself around to start chewing on my leg.

The Tau field was discouraging the Vamp, making it dump some of its internal nanoware, so that blood started geysering out of pinholes all over its body, but this was more of a nuisance for me than any major hindrance to it.

In mid-somersault, somewhere near the ceiling, with the thing trying to wrap itself around me, I dropped the silver knife. It wasn't a real weapon, not like the splinter. I kept it for sentimental reasons, as much as anything, though silver did have a deleterious effect on younger vamps. Since it was pure sentiment, I suppose I could have left it in coin form, but then I'd probably be forever dropping some in combat and having to waste time later picking them up. Besides, when silver was still the usual currency and they were still coins I'd got drunk a few times and spent them, and it was way too big a hassle getting them back.

The Vamp took the knife-dropping as more significant than it was, which was one of the reasons I'd let it go. In the old days I would have held something serious in my left hand, like a de-weaving wand, which the vampire probably thought the knife was—and it wanted to get it and use it on me. It partially let go of my arm as it tried to catch the weapon and at that precise moment, second 2.355, I feinted with the splinter, slid it along the thing's attempted forearm block, and reversing my elbow joint, stuck it right in the forehead.

With the smart matter already at work from its previous scratch, internal explosion occurred immediately. I had shut my eyes in preparation, so I was only blown against the wall and not temporarily blinded as well.

I assessed the damage as I wearily got back up. My left arm was fully dislocated with the tendons ripped away, so I couldn't put it back. It was going to have to hang for a day or two, hurting like crazy till it self-healed. Besides that, I had severe bruising to my lower back and ribs, which would also deliver some serious pain for a day or so.

I hadn't been hurt by a Vamp as seriously for a long, long time, so I spent a few minutes searching through the scraps of mostly disintegrated vampire to find a piece big enough to meaningfully scan. Once I got it back to the jumper I'd be able to pick it apart on the atomic level to find the serial number on some of its defunct nanoware.

I put the scrap of what was probably skeleton in my flight bag, with the splinter and the silver knife, and wandered downstairs. I left it unzipped, because I hadn't heard any firing for a while, which meant either Susan and Karl had cleaned up, or the vamps had cleaned up Susan and Karl. But I put my T-shirt back on. No need to scare the locals. It was surprisingly clean, considering. My skin and hair sheds vampire blood, so the rest of me looked quite respectable as well. Apart from the arm hanging down like an orangutang's that is.

I'd calculated the odds at about 5:2 that Susan and Karl would win, so I was pleased to see them in the entrance lobby. They both jumped when I came down the stairs, and I was ready to move if they shot at me, but they managed to control themselves.

"Did you get them all?" I asked. I didn't move any closer.

"Nine," said Karl. "Like you said. Nine holes in the ground, nine burned vampires."

"You didn't get bitten?"

"Does it look like we did?" asked Susan, with a shudder. She was clearly thinking about Mike.

"Vampires can infect with a small, tidy bite," I said. "Or even about half a cup of their saliva, via a kiss."

Susan did throw up then, which is what I wanted. She wouldn't have if she'd been bitten. I was also telling the truth. While they were designed to be soldiers, the vampires were also made to be guerilla fighters, working amongst the human population, infecting as many as possible in small, subtle ways. They only went for the big chow-down in full combat.

"What about you?" asked Karl. "You OK?"

"You mean this?" I asked, threshing my arm about like a tentacle, wincing as it made the pain ten times worse. "Dislocated. But I didn't get bitten."

Neither had Karl, I was now sure. Even newly infected humans have something about them that gives their condition away, and I can always pick it.

"Which means we can go and sit by the fence and wait till morning," I said cheerily. "You've done well."

Karl nodded wearily and got his hand under Susan's elbow, lifting her up. She wiped her mouth and the two of them walked slowly to the door.

I let them go first, which was kind of mean, because the VET have been known to harbour trigger-happy snipers. But there was no sudden death from above, so we walked over to the fence and then the two of them flopped down on the ground and Karl began to laugh hysterically.

I left them to it and wandered over to the gate.

"You can let me out now," I called to the sergeant. "My work here is almost done."

"No one comes out till after dawn," replied the guardian of the city.

"Except me," I agreed. "Check with Lieutenant Harman."

Which goes to show that I can read ID labels, even little ones on metal-mesh skinsuits.

The sergeant didn't need to check. Lieutenant Harman was already looming up behind him. They had a short but spirited conversation, the sergeant told Karl and Susan to stay where they were, which was still lying on the ground essentially in severe shock, and they powered down the gate for about thirty seconds and I came out.

Two medics came over to help me. Fortunately they were VET, not locals, so we didn't waste time arguing about me going to hospital, getting lots of drugs injected, having scans, etc. They fixed me up with a collar and cuff sling so my arm wasn't dragging about the place, I said thank you and they retired to their unmarked ambulance.

Then I wandered over to where Jenny was sitting on the far side of the silver truck, her back against the rear wheel. She'd taken off her helmet and balaclava, letting her bobbed brown hair spring back out into shape. She looked about eighteen, maybe even younger, maybe a little older. A pretty young woman, her face made no worse by evidence of tears, though she was very pale.

She jumped as I tapped a little rhythm on the side of the truck.

"Oh… I thought… aren't you meant to stay inside the… the cordon?"

I hunkered down next to her.

"Yeah, most of the time they enforce that, but it depends," I said. "How are you doing?"

"Me? I'm… I'm OK. So you got them?"

"We did," I confirmed. I didn't mention Mike. She didn't need to know that, not now.

"Good," she said. "I'm sorry… I thought I would be braver. Only when the time came…"

"I understand," I said.

"I don't see how you can," she said. "I mean, you went in, and you said you fight vampires all the time. You must be incredibly brave."

"No," I replied. "Bravery is about overcoming fear, not about not having it. There's plenty I'm afraid of. Just not vampires."

"We fear the unknown," she said. "You must know a lot about vampires."

I nodded and moved my flight bag around to get more comfortable. It was still unzipped, but the sides were pushed together at the top.

"How to fight them, I mean," she added. "Since no one really knows anything else. That's the worst thing. When my sister was in… infected and then later, when she was… was killed, I really wanted to know, and there was no one to tell me anything"

"What did you want to know?" I asked. I've always been prone to show-off to pretty girls. If it isn't surfing, it's secret knowledge. Though sharing the secret knowledge only occurred in special cases, when I knew it would go no further.

"Everything we don't know," sighed Jenny. "What are they, really? Why have they suddenly appeared all over the place in the last ten years, when we all thought they were just… just made-up."

"They're killing machines," I explained. "Bioengineered self-replicating guerilla soldiers, dropped here kind of by mistake a long time ago. They've been in hiding mostly, waiting for a signal or other stimuli to activate. Certain frequencies of radiowaves will do it, and the growth of cellphone use…"

"So what, vampires get irritated by cellphones?"

A smile started to curl up one side of her mouth. I smiled too, and kept talking.

"You see, way back when, there were these good aliens and these bad aliens, and there was a gigantic space battle—"

Jenny started laughing.

"Do you want me to do a personality test before I can hear the rest of the story?"

"I think you'd pass," I said. I had tried to make her laugh, even though it was kind of true about the aliens and the space battle. Only there were just bad aliens and even worse aliens, and the vampires had been dropped on Earth by mistake. They had been meant for a world where the nights were very long.

Jenny kept laughing and looked down, just for an instant. I moved at my highest speed—and she died laughing, the splinter working instantly on both human nervous system and the twenty-four-hours-old infestation of vampire nanoware.

We had lost the war, which was why I was there, cleaning up one of our mistakes. Why I would be on Earth for countless years to come.

I felt glad to have my straightforward purpose, my assigned task. It is too easy to become involved with humans, to want more for them, to interfere with their lives. I didn't want to make the boss's mistake. I'm not human and I don't want to become human or make them better people. I was just going to follow orders, keep cleaning out the infestation, and that was that.

The bite was low on Jenny's neck, almost at the shoulder. I showed it to the VET people and asked them to do the rest.

I didn't stay to watch. My arm hurt, and I could hear a girl laughing, somewhere deep within my head.

LIFE IS THE TEACHER

by Carrie Vaughn

Carrie Vaughn is the bestselling author of the Kitty Norville series, which started with *Kitty and the Midnight Hour*. The seventh Kitty novel, *Kitty's House of Horrors*, is due out in January 2010. Her short work has appeared many times in *Realms of Fantasy* and in a number of anthologies, such as *The Mammoth Book of Paranormal Romance* and *Fast Ships, Black Sails*, and is forthcoming in *Warriors*, edited by George R. R. Martin and Gardner Dozois.

Vaughn says that the modern seductive vampire is very different from the old-school folklore vampire. "It's an interesting evolution seeing how the one became the other in film and fiction," she said. "I think audiences are intrigued by the power—supernatural power, seductive power, political power—that vampires are made to wield. They become these avatars for the dangerous and alluring." This story, which first appeared in the anthology *Hotter Than Hell*, is about a new vampire learning to hunt, using her newfound powers of supernatural seduction.

Emma slid under the surface of the water and stayed there. She lay in the tub, on her back, and stared up at a world made soft, blurred with faint ripples. An unreal world viewed through a distorted filter. For minutes—four, six, ten—she stayed under water, and didn't drown, because she didn't breathe. Would never breathe again.

The world looked different through these undead eyes. Thicker, somehow. And also, strangely, clearer.

Survival seemed like such a curious thing once you'd already been killed.

This was her life now. She didn't have to stay here. She could end it any time she wanted just by opening the curtains at dawn. But she didn't.

Sitting up, she pushed back her soaking hair and rained water all around her with the noise of a rushing stream. Outside the blood-warm bath, her skin chilled in the air. She felt every little thing, every little current—from the vent, from a draft from the window, coolness eddying along the floor, striking the walls. She shivered. Put the fingers of one hand on the wrist of the other and felt no pulse.

After spreading a towel on the floor, she stepped from the bath.

She looked at herself: she didn't look any different. Same slim body, smooth skin, young breasts the right size to cup in her hands, nipples the color of a bruised peach. Her skin was paler than she remembered. So pale it was almost translucent. Bloodless.

Not for long.

She dried her brown hair so it hung straight to her shoulders and dressed with more care than she ever had before. Not that the clothes she put on were by any means fancy, or new, or anything other than what she'd already had in her closet: a tailored silk shirt over a black lace camisole, jeans, black leather pumps, and a few choice pieces of jewelry, a couple of thin silver chains and dangling silver earrings. Every piece, every seam, every fold of fabric, produced an effect, and she wanted to be sure she produced the right effect: young, confident, alluring. Without, of course, looking like she was *trying* to produce such an effect. It must seem casual, thrown together, effortless. She switched the earrings from one ear to the other because they didn't seem to lay right the other way.

This must be what a prostitute felt like.

Dissatisfied, she went upstairs to see Alette.

The older woman was in the parlor, waiting in a wingback chair. The room was decorated in tasteful antiques, Persian rugs, and velvet-upholstered furniture, with thick rich curtains hanging over the windows. Books crammed into shelves and a silver tea service ornamented the mantel. For all its opulent decoration, the room had a comfortable, natural feel to it. Its owner had come by the décor honestly. The Victorian atmosphere was genuine.

Alette spoke with a refined British accent. "You don't have to do this."

Alette was the most regal, elegant woman Emma knew. An apparent thirty years old, she was poised, dressed in a silk skirt and jacket, her brunette hair tied in a bun, her face like porcelain. She was over four hundred years old.

Emma was part of her clan, her Family, by many ties, from many directions. By blood, Alette was Emma's ancestor, a many-greats grandmother. Closer, Alette had made the one who in turn had made Emma.

That had been unplanned. Emma hadn't wanted it. The man in question had been punished. He was gone now, and Alette had taken care of her: mother, mentor, mistress.

"You can't bottle feed me forever," Emma replied. In this existence, that meant needles, IV tubes, and a willing donor. It was so clinical.

"I can try," Alette said, her smile wry.

If Emma let her, Alette would take care of her forever. Literally forever. But that felt wrong, somehow. If Emma was going to live like this, then she ought to live. Not cower like a child.

"Thank you for looking after me. I'm not trying to sound ungrateful, but—"

"But you want to be able to look after yourself."

Emma nodded, and again the wry smile touched Alette's lips. "Our family has always had the most awful streak of independence."

Emma's laugh startled her. She didn't know she still could.

"Remember what I've taught you," Alette said, rising from her chair and moving to stand with Emma. "How to choose. How to lure him. How to leave him. Remember how I've taught you to see, and to feel. And remember to only take a little. If you take it all, you'll kill him. Or risk condemning him to this life."

"I remember." The lessons had been difficult. She'd had to learn to see the world with new eyes.

Alette smoothed Emma's hair back from her face and arranged it over her shoulders—an uncharacteristic bit of fidgeting. "I know you do. And I know you'll be fine. But if you need anything, please—"

"I'll call," Emma finished. "You won't send anyone to follow me, will you?"

"No," she said. "I won't."

"Thank you."

Alette kissed her cheek and sent her to hunt alone for the first time.

Alette had given her advice: go somewhere new, in an unfamiliar neighborhood, where she wasn't likely to meet someone from her old life, therefore making her less likely to encounter complications of emotion or circumstance.

Emma didn't take this advice.

She'd been a student at George Washington University. Officially, she'd taken a leave of absence, but she wasn't sure she'd ever be able to continue her studies and finish her degree. There were always night classes, sure…but it was almost a joke, and like most anything worth doing, easier said than done.

There was a place, a bar where she and her friends used to go sometimes when classes got out. They'd arrive just in time for happy hour, when they could buy two-dollar hamburgers and cheap pitchers of beer. They'd eat supper, play a few rounds of pool, bitch about classes and papers they hadn't written yet. On weekends they'd come late and play pool until last call. A completely normal life.

That was what Emma found herself missing, a few months into this new life. Laughing with her friends. Maybe she should have gone someplace else for this, found new territory. But she wanted to see the familiar.

She came in through the front and paused, blinked a couple of times, took a deep breath through her nose to taste the air. And the world slowed down. Noise fell to a low hum, the lights seemed to brighten, and just by turning her head a little she could see it all. Thirty-four people packed into the first floor of this converted townhouse. Twelve sat at the bar, two worked behind the bar, splashing their way through the fumes of a dozen different kinds of alcohol. Their sweat mixed with those fumes, two kinds of heat blending with the third ashy odor of cigarette smoke. This place was hot with bodies. Five beating hearts played pool around two tables in the back, three more watched—these were female. Girlfriends. The smell of competing testosterone was ripe. All the rest crammed around tables or stood in empty spaces, putting alcohol into their bodies, their blood—Emma could smell it through their pores. She caught all this in a glance, in a second.

She could feel the clear paths by the way the air moved. Incredibly, she could feel the whole room, all of it pressing gently against her skin. As if she looked down on it from above. As if she commanded it. There—that couple at the table in the corner was fighting. The woman stared into her tumbler of gin and tonic while her foot tapped a nervous beat on the floor. Her boyfriend stared at her, frowning hard, his arms crossed, his scotch forgotten.

Emma could have him if she wanted. His blood was singing with need. He would be easy to persuade, to lure away from his difficulty. A chance meeting by the bathrooms, an unseen exit out the back—

No. Not like that.

A quartet of boisterous, drunken men burst into laughter in front of her. Raucous business school types, celebrating some exam or finished project. She knew how to get to them, too. Stumble perhaps. Lean an accidental arm on a shoulder, gasp an apology—and the one who met her gaze first would be the one to follow her.

Instead, she went to the bar, and despite the crowd, the press of bodies jostling for space, her path there was clear, and a space opened for her just as she arrived because she knew it would be there.

She wanted to miss the taste of alcohol. She could remember the taste of wine, the tang on the tongue, the warmth passing down her throat. She remembered great dinners, her favorite Mexican food, overstuffed burritos with sour cream and chile verde, with a big, salty margarita. She wanted to miss it with a deep and painful longing. But the memories turned her stomach. The thought of consuming anything made her feel sick. Anything except blood.

The glass of wine before her remained untouched. It was only for show.

She never would have done this in the old days. Sitting alone at the bar like this, staring into her drink—she looked like she was trying to get picked up.

Well, wasn't she?

When the door opened and a laughing crowd of friends entered, Emma turned and smiled in greeting. Even before the door had opened, she'd known somehow. She'd sensed the sound of a voice, the tone of a footstep, the scent of skin, a ripple in the air. She couldn't have remembered such fine details from her old life. But somehow, she'd known. She knew *them*.

"Emma!"

"Hey, Chris." Finally, her smile felt like her old smile. Her old friends gathered around, leaned in for hugs, and she obliged them. But the one who spoke to her, the one she focused on, was Chris.

He was six feet tall, with wavy blond hair and a clean-shaven, handsome face, still boyish but filling out nicely. He had a shy smile and laughing eyes.

"Where've you been? I haven't seen you in weeks. The registrar's office said you took a leave of absence."

She had her story all figured out. It wasn't even a lie, really.

"I've been sick," she said.

"You couldn't even call?"

"Really sick." She pressed her lips in a thin smile, hoping she sounded sad.

"Yeah, I guess." He took the cue not to press the question further. He brightened.

"But you look great now. Really great."

There it was, a spark in his eye, a flush in his cheek. She'd always wondered if he liked her. She'd never been sure. Now, she had tools. She had senses. And she looked great. It wasn't her, a bitter voice sounded inside her. It was this thing riding her, this creature inside her. It was a lure, a trap.

Looking great made men like Chris blush. Now, she could use it. She knew how to respond. She'd always been uncertain before.

She lowered her gaze, smiled, then looked at him warmly, searching. "Thanks."

"I—I guess you already have a drink."

The others had moved off to claim one of the pool tables. Chris remained, leaning on the bar beside her, nervously tapping his foot.

Compared to him, Emma had no trouble radiating calm. She was in control here.

"Let me get you something," she said.

For a moment—for a long, lingering, blissful moment—it felt like old times. They only talked, but the conversation was long and heartfelt. He really listened to her. So she kept talking—so much so that she almost got to the truth.

"I've had to reassess everything. What am I going to do with my life, what's the point of it all." She shrugged, letting the implications settle.

"You must have been really sick," he said, his gaze intent.

"I thought I was going to die," she said, and it wasn't a lie. She didn't remember much of it—the man, the monster's hand on her face, on her arms, pinning her to the bed. She wanted to scream, but the sound caught in her throat. And however frightened she was, her body responded to his touch, flushed, shuddered toward him, and this made her ashamed. She hoped that he would kill her rather than turn her. But she awoke again and the world was different.

"You make it sound like you're not coming back."

"Hm?" she murmured, startled out of her memory.

"To school. You aren't coming back, are you?"

"I don't know," she said, wanting to be honest, knowing she couldn't tell him everything. "It'd be hard, after what's happened. I just don't know." This felt so casual, so normal, that she almost forgot she had a purpose here. That she was supposed to be guiding this conversation. She surprised herself by knowing what to say next. "This is going to sound really cliché, but when you think you aren't going to make it like that, it really does change how you look at things. You really do try to live for the moment. You don't have time to screw around anymore."

Which was ironic, because really, she had all the time in the world.

Chris hung on her words. "No, it doesn't sound cliché at all. It sounds real."

"I just don't think I have time anymore for school. I'd rather, you know—live."

This sounded awful—so false and ironic. *Don't listen to me, I'm immortal*, part of her almost yelled. But she didn't, because another part of her was hungry.

When he spoke, he sounded uncertain. "Do—do you want to get out of here? Go to my place maybe?"

Her shy smile widened. She'd wanted him to say that. She wanted him to think this was his idea. She rounded her shoulders, aware of her posture, her body language, wanting to send a message that she was open, willing, and ready.

"Yeah," she said, touching his hand as she stood.

His skin felt like fire.

Chris took her back to his place. He lived within walking distance, in a garden-level unit in a block of apartments. A nice place, small but functional, and very student. It felt like a foreign country.

Emma watched Chris unlock the door and felt some trepidation. Nerves, that was all. Anticipation. Unknown territory—to be expected, going home with a new guy for the first time.

Chris fumbled with the key.

There was more to this than the unknown, or the thrill of anticipation. She stood on the threshold, literally, and felt something: a force outside of herself. Nothing solid, rather a feeling that made her want to turn away. Like a voice whispering, *Go, you are not welcome, this is not your place, your blood does not dwell here.*

She couldn't ignore it. The voice fogged her senses. If she turned away, even just a little—stepped back, tilted her head away—her mind cleared. She didn't notice when Chris finally unlocked the door and pushed his way inside.

She didn't know how long he'd been standing on the other side of the threshold, looking back at her expectantly. She simply couldn't move forward.

"Come on in," he said, giving a reassuring smile.

The feeling, fog, and voice disappeared. The unseen resistance fell away, the barrier was gone. She'd been invited.

Returning his smile, she went in.

Inside was what she'd expected from a male college student: the front room had a ripe, well-lived-in smell of dirty laundry and pizza boxes. Mostly, though, it smelled like him. In a moment, she took it all in, the walls and the carpet. Despite how many times the former had been repainted and the later replaced, the sense that generations of college students had passed through here lingered.

The years of life pressed against her skin, and she closed her eyes to take it all in, to feel it eddy around her. It tingled against her like static.

"Do you want something to drink?" Chris was sweating, just a little.

Yes. "No, I'm okay."

Seduction wasn't a quick thing. Though she supposed, if she wanted, she could just take him. She could feel in her bones and muscles that she could. He wouldn't know what hit him. It would be easy, use the currents of the room, slow down the world, move in the blink of an eye—

No. No speed, no fear, no mess. Better to do it cleanly. Nicer, for everyone. Now that they were alone, away from the crowd, her purpose became so very clear. Her need became crystalline. She planned it out: a brief touch on his arm, press her body close, and let him do the rest.

Fake. It was fake, manipulative... She liked him. She really did. She wished she'd done this months ago, she wished she'd had the nerve to say something, to touch his hand—before she'd been attacked and turned. Then, she hadn't had the courage, and now she wanted something else from him. It felt like deception.

This was why Alette had wanted her to find a stranger. She wouldn't be wishing that it had all turned out different. Maybe she wouldn't care. She wanted to like Chris—she didn't want to need him like this. Didn't want to hurt him. And she didn't know if she'd have been so happy to go home with anyone else. That was why she was here. That was why she'd gone to that particular bar and waited for him.

That doesn't matter, her instincts—new instincts, like static across her skin, like the heat of blood drawing her—told her. The emotion is a by-product of need. He is yours because you've won him. You've already won him, you have only to claim him.

She reached out—she could feel him without looking, by sensing the way the air folded around his body—and brushed her fingers across the back of his hand. He reacted instantly, curling his hand around hers, squeezing, pulling himself toward her, and kissing her—half on cheek, half on lip.

He pulled back, waiting for a reaction, his breath coming fast and brushing her cheek. She didn't breathe at all—would he notice? Should she gasp, to fool him into thinking she breathed, so he wouldn't notice that she didn't? Another deception.

Rather than debating the question, she lunged for him, her lips seeking his, kissing forcefully. Distract him. In a minute he wouldn't notice anything. She devoured him, and he was off balance, lagging behind as she sucked his lips and sought his tongue. She'd never been this hungry for someone before. The taste of his skin, his sweat, his mouth, burst inside her and fired her brain. He tasted so good on the outside, she couldn't wait to discover what the inside of him tasted like, that warm blood flushing just under the surface. Her nails dug into his arm, wanting to pull off the sleeves of his shirt, all his clothes, to be closer to his living skin. She wanted nothing more than to close her teeth, bite into him—

She pulled back, almost ripping herself away. Broke all contact and took a step back, so that she was surrounded by cool air and not flesh. She could hear the blood rushing in his neck.

This wasn't her. This wasn't her doing this. She couldn't do this.

Chris gave a nervous chuckle. "Wow. That was... Emma, what's wrong?"

She closed her eyes, took a moment to gather herself, drew breath to speak. It would look like a deep sigh to him.

"I'm sorry," she said. "I can't do this."

She couldn't look at him. If he saw her eyes, saw the way she looked at him, he'd know about the thing inside her, he'd know she only wanted to rip him open. How could she explain to him, without explaining?

"I had a really nice time... but I'm sorry."

Holding the collar of her jacket closed, she fled before he could say a word in argument.

Alette had had to force her to drink blood the first time. Emma hadn't wanted to become this thing. She'd threatened to leave the house at dawn and die in the sunlight. But Alette persuaded her to stay. A haunted need inside her listened to that, wanted to survive, and stayed inside, in the dark. Still, she gagged when the mistress showed her the glass tumbler full of viscous red. "It's only your first night in this life," she said. "You're too new to hunt. But you still need this." Alette had then stood behind her, embraced Emma and locked her arms tight with one hand while tipping the glass to her mouth with the other. Emma had struggled, fought to pull out of her grasp, but Alette was deceptively powerful, and Emma was still sick and weak.

Emma had recognized the scent of the blood even before it reached her lips: tangy, metallic, like a butcher's shop. Even as she rebelled, even as her mind quailed, part of her reached toward it. Her mouth salivated. This contradiction was what had caused her to break down, screaming that she didn't want this, that she couldn't do this, kicking and thrashing in Alette's grip. But Alette had been ready for it, and very calmly held her still, forced the glass between her lips, and made her drink. As much spilled out of her mouth and down her chin as slid down her throat. Then, she'd fallen still. Helpless, she'd surrendered, even as that single sip returned her strength to her.

Eventually, she could hold the glass herself and drain it. She even realized she should learn to find the blood herself. She thought she'd been ready.

Alette found her in the parlor, sitting curled up on one of the sofas. "What happened?"

Emma hugged her knees and stared into space. She'd spent hours here, almost until dawn, watching dust motes, watching time move. This was fascinating—the idea that she could see time move. Almost, if she concentrated, she could reach out and touch it. Twist it. Cross the room in a second. She would look like she was flying. She'd almost done it, earlier tonight. She'd have taken him so quickly he wouldn't have known...

Alette waited patiently for her to answer. Like she could also spend all night watching time move.

"I don't know." Even after all that had happened, her voice sounded like a little girl's. She still felt like a child. "I liked him. It was...it felt good. I thought..." She shook her head. The memory was a distant thing. She didn't want to revisit it. "I got scared. I had him in the palm of my hand. He was mine. I was strong. And this *thing* rose up in me, this amazing power—I could do anything. But it wasn't me. So I got scared and ran."

Poised and regal, Alette sat, hands crossed in her lap, the elegant noblewoman of an old painting. Nothing shook her, nothing shattered her.

"That's the creature. That's what you are now. How you control it will determine what your life will look like from now on."

It was a pronouncement, a judgment, a knell of doom.

Alette continued. "Some of our kind give free rein to it. They revel in it. It makes them strong, but often leaves them vulnerable. If you try to ignore it, it will consume you. You'll lose that part of yourself that is yours."

In her bones, in the tracks of her bloodless veins, Emma knew Alette was right, and this was what she feared: that she wasn't strong, that she wouldn't control it. That she would lose her self, her soul to the thing. Her eyes ached with tears that didn't fall.

How did Alette control it? How did she manage to sit so calm and dignified, with the creature writhing inside of her, desperate for power? Emma felt sure she wouldn't last long enough to develop that beautiful self-possession.

"Oh my dear, hush there." Alette moved to her side and gathered her in her arms. She'd seen Emma's anguish and now sought to wrap her in comfort. Emma clung to her, pressing her face against the cool silk of her jacket, holding tight to her arms. For just a moment, she let herself be a child, protected within the older woman's embrace. "I can't teach you everything. Some steps you must take alone. I can take care of you if you like—keep you here, watch you always, hold the creature at bay and bring you cups of blood. But I don't think you'd be happy."

"I don't know that I'll ever be happy. I don't think I can do this."

"The power is a tool you use to get what you need. It should not control you."

Not much of the night remained. Emma felt dawn tugging at her nerves—another new sensation to catalog with the rest. The promise of sunlight was a weariness that settled over her and drove her underground, to a bed in a sealed, windowless room. At least she didn't need a coffin. Small comfort.

"Come," Alette said, urging her to her feet. "Sleep for now. Vanquish this beast another night."

Her mind was still her own, and she still dreamed. The fluttering, disjointed scenes took place in daylight. Already, the sunlit world of her dreaming memories had begun to look odd to her, unreal and uncertain, as if these things could never really have happened.

At dusk, she woke and told herself all kinds of platitudes: she had to get back on the horse, if at first you don't succeed… But it came down to wanting to see Chris again. She wanted to apologize.

She found his phone number and called him, half hoping he wouldn't answer, so she could leave a message and not have to face him.

But he picked up. "Hi."

"Hi, Chris?"

"Emma?" He sounded surprised. And why wouldn't he be? "Hey. Are you okay?"

Her anxiety vanished, and she was glad that she'd called. "I'm okay. I just wanted to say I'm so sorry about last night. I got scared. I freaked. I know you'll probably laugh in my face, but I want to see you again."

I'd like to try again, an unspoken desire she couldn't quite give voice to.

"I wouldn't laugh. I was just worried about you. I thought maybe I'd done something wrong."

"No, no, of course you didn't. It's just…I guess since this was my first time out since I was sick, my first time being with anyone since then… I got scared, like I said."

"I don't know. It seemed like you were really into it." He chuckled nervously. "You were really hot."

"I was into it." She wasn't sure this was going to sound awkward-endearing or just awkward. She tried to put that lust, that power that she'd felt last night, into her voice. Like maybe she could touch him over the phone. She held that image in her mind. "I'd like to see you again."

The meaning behind the words said, *I need you.*

Somehow, he heard that. She could tell by the catch in his breath, an added huskiness in his voice. "Okay. Why don't you come over."

"I'll be right there." She shut the phone off, not giving him a chance to change his mind, not letting herself doubt.

Emma could screw this up again. There was a gnawing in her belly, an anxious thought that kept saying, *This isn't right.* I'm using him, and he doesn't deserve that. She was starting to think of that voice as the old Emma. The Emma who could walk in daylight and never would again.

The new Emma, the voice she had to listen to now, felt like she was about to win a race. She had the power here, and she was buzzed on it. Almost drunk. The new Emma didn't miss alcohol because she didn't need it.

It felt good. Everything she moved toward felt so physically, fundamentally good. All she had to do was let go of doubt and revel in it.

That near-ecstasy shone in her eyes when Chris opened the door. For a moment, they only looked at each other. He was tentative—expecting her to flee again. She caught his gaze, and he saw nothing but her. She could see him, see through him, everything about him. He wanted her—had watched her for a long time, dreaming of a moment like this, not thinking it would happen. Not brave enough to make it happen. Assuming she wasn't the kind of girl who would let him in.

Yet here she was. She saw all of this play behind his eyes.

She touched his cheek and gave him a shy smile. "Thanks for letting me come over."

Gazing at him through lowered lids, she pushed him over the edge.

He grabbed her hand and pulled her against him, bringing her lips to his, hungry, and she was ready for him, opening her mouth to him, letting him devour her with kisses and sending his passion back to him. He clutched at her, wrinkling the back of her shirt as if he were trying to rip through it to get to her skin, kneading, moving his hand low to pin her against him. These weren't the tender, careful, assured movements he might have used if he were attempting to seduce her—if he'd had to persuade her, if she had shown some hesitation. These were the clumsy, desperate gropings of a man who couldn't control himself. She made him lose control. If she could now pick up those reins that he had dropped—

She pulled back her head to look at him; kissed him lightly, then slowly—staying slow, forcing him to match her pace. She controlled his movements now. She unbuttoned his shirt, drawing out every motion, brushing the bare skin underneath with fleeting touches. Lingering. Teasing. Heightening his need, feeding his desire. Driving him mad. He was melting in her arms. She could feel his muscles tremble.

Taking hold of his hands—she practically had to peel them off her backside—she guided them to her breasts and pressed them there. His eyes widened, like he'd just won a prize, and she smiled, letting her head fall back, feeling the weight of her hair pull her back, rolling her shoulders and putting her chest even more firmly into his grasp. Quickly, he undid the buttons of her shirt, tugged aside her bra, and bent to kiss her, tracing her right breast with his tongue, taking her nipple between his teeth. For all that had happened, for all that she'd become, her nerves, her senses, still worked, still shuddered at a lover's touch. Her hands clenched on his shoulders, then tightened in his hair. She gasped with pleasure. She wanted this. She wanted this badly.

She pulled him toward the bedroom. Didn't stop looking at him; held his gaze, would not let him break it. Her own veins were fire—controlled fire, in a very strong furnace, directed to some great purpose, a driving machine. She needed him, the blood that flushed along his skin. His very capillaries opened for her. She did not have a heartbeat, but something in her breast cried out in triumph. He was hers, to do with as she pleased.

She ran her tongue along her top row of teeth, scraping it on needle sharp fangs.

He tugged at her shirt, searching for more bare skin. She shivered at his touch on the small of her back. His hands were hot, burning up, and for all her desire, her skin felt cold, bloodless.

She would revel in his heat instead.

She pushed his shirt off his shoulders and let it drop to the floor, then wrapped herself around him, pulling as much of that skin and heat to her as she could.

"You're so warm," she murmured, not meaning to speak at all. But she was amazed at the heat of him. She hadn't felt so much heat since before…before she became this thing.

He kept his mouth against her, lips working around her neck, pressing up to her ear, tasting every inch. Her nerves flared at the touch.

And suddenly, finally, she understood. It wasn't just the blood that drew her kind to living humans. It was the heat, the life itself. They were bright sunlight to creatures who lived in darkness. They held the energy that kept her kind alive and immortal—for there would always be people, an endless supply of people, to draw that energy from. She was a parasite and the host would never die.

Neither, then, would she.

With new reverence, she eased him to the bed, made him lay back, and finished

stripping him, tugging down his jeans and boxers, touching him at every opportunity, fingertips around his hips, along his thighs. She paused to regard him,
stretched out on his back, naked before her, member erect, whole body flush and
almost trembling with need. She had brought him to this moment, with desire
burning in his eyes. He would do anything she asked, now. She found herself
wanting to be kind—to reward him for the role he'd played in her education, in
bringing about the epiphany that so clarified her place in the world.

This exchange would be fair. She would not simply take from him. He would
have pleasure as well.

She rubbed her hands down his chest, down his belly. He moaned, shivered
under her touch but did not interfere. She traced every curve of his body: down
his ribs, his hips. Stretched out on the bed beside him, she took his penis in her
hand. Again, their mouths met. His kissing was urgent, fevered, and she kept pace
with him. He was growing slick with sweat and smelled of musk.

She laughed. The sound just bubbled out of her. Lips apart, eyes gleaming, she
found joy in this. She would live, she would not open the curtains on the dawn.
She had power in this existence and she would learn to use it.

"Oh my God," Chris murmured. He froze, his eyes wide, his blood suddenly
cooled. In only a second, she felt the sweat on his body start to chill as fear struck
him. He wouldn't even notice it yet.

He was staring at her, her open, laughing mouth, the pointed canine teeth she'd
been so careful to disguise until this moment, when euphoria overcame her.

In a moment of panic like this, it might all fall apart. An impulse to run struck
her, but she'd come too far, she was too close to success. If she fled now she might
never regain the nerve to try again.

"Shh, shh, it's all right," she whispered, stroking his hair, nuzzling his cheek,
breathing comfort against him. "It's fine, it'll be fine."

She brought all her nascent power to bear: seduction, persuasion. The creature's
allure. The ability to fog his mind, to erase all else from his thoughts but his desire
for her, to fill his sight only with her.

"It's all right, Chris. I'll take care of you. I'll take good care of you."

The fear in his eyes ebbed, replaced by puzzlement—some part of his mind
asking what was happening, who was she, what was she, and why was she doing
this to him. She willed him to forget those questions. All that mattered were her,
him, their joint passion that would feed them both: his desire, and her life.

He was still hard against her hand, and she used that. Gently, carefully, she urged
him back to his heat, brought him again to that point of need. She stroked him,
first with fingertips, then with her whole hand, and his groan of pleasure gratified
her. When he tipped back his head, his eyes rolling back a little, she knew he had
returned to her.

The next time she kissed him, his whole body surged against her.

She twined her leg around his; he moved against her, insistent. But she held him,
pinned him, and closed her mouth over his neck. There she kissed, sucked—felt
the hot river of his blood so close to his skin, just under her tongue. She almost

lost control, in her need to take that river into herself.

Oh so carefully, slowly, to make sure she did this right and made no mistakes, she bit. Let her needle teeth tear just a little of his skin.

The flow of blood hit her tongue with a shock and instantly translated to a delicious rush that shuddered through her body. Blood slipped down her throat like honey, burning with richness. Clenching all her muscles, groaning at the flood of it, she drank. Her hand closed tight around his erection, moved with him, and his body responded, his own wave of pleasure bringing him to climax a moment later.

She held him while he rocked against her, and she drank a dozen swallows of his blood. No more than that. Do not kill, Alette's first lesson. But a dozen mouthfuls would barely weaken him. He wouldn't even notice.

She licked the wound she'd made to hasten its healing. He might notice the marks and believe them to be insect bites. He would never know she'd been here.

His body radiated the heat of spent desire. She lay close to him, gathering as much of it as she could into herself. She now felt hot—vivid and alive. She could feel his blood traveling through her, keeping her alive.

Stroking his hair, admiring the lazy smile he wore, she whispered to him. "You won't remember me. You won't remember what happened tonight. You had a nice dream, that's all. A vivid dream."

"Emma," he murmured, flexing toward her for more. Almost, her resolve broke. Almost, she saw that pulsing artery in his neck and went to drink again.

But she continued, "If you see me again, you won't know me. Your life will go on as if you never knew me. Go to sleep. You'll sleep very well tonight."

She brushed his hair with her fingers, and a moment later he was snoring gently. She pulled a blanket over him. Kissed his forehead.

Straightening her bra, buttoning her blouse, she left the room. Made sure all the lights were off. Locked the door on her way out.

She walked home. It was the deepest, stillest hour of night, or early morning. Streetlights turned colors but no cars waited at intersections. No voices drifted from bars and all the storefronts were dark. A cold mist hung in the air, ghost-like. Emma felt that she swam through it.

The stillest part of night, and she had never felt more awake, more alive. Every pore felt the touch of air around her. Warm blood flowed in her veins, firing her heart. She walked without fear along dark streets, secure in the feeling that the world had paused to notice her passage through it.

She entered Alette's town home through the kitchen door in back rather than through the front door, because she'd always come in through the back in her student days when she studied in Alette's library and paid for school by being Alette's part-time housekeeper. That had all changed. Those days—nights—were finished. But she'd never stop using the back door.

"Emma?" Alette called from the parlor.

Self-conscious, Emma followed the voice and found Alette in her favorite chair in the corner, reading a book. Emma tried not to feel like a kid sneaking home after a night of mischief.

Alette replaced a bookmark and set the book aside. "Well?"

Her unnecessary coat wrapped around her, hands folded before her, Emma stood before the mistress of the house. Almost, she reverted to the teenager's response: "Fine, okay, whatever." Monosyllables and a fast exit.

But she felt herself smile broadly, happily. "It was good."

"And the gentleman?"

"He won't remember me."

"Good," Alette said, and smiled. "Welcome to the Family, my dear."

She went back to the bar once more, a week later. Sitting at the bar, she traced condensation on the outside of a glass of gin and tonic on the rocks. She hadn't sipped, only tasted, drawing a lone breath so she could take in the scent of it.

The door opened, bringing with it a cold draft and a crowd of college students. Chris was among them, laughing at someone's joke, blond hair tousled. He walked right by her on his way to the pool tables. Flashed her a hurried smile when he caught her watching him. Didn't spare her another glance, in the way of two strangers passing in a crowded bar.

Smiling wryly to herself, Emma left her drink at the bar and went out to walk in the night.

THE VECHI BARBAT

by Nancy Kilpatrick

Nancy Kilpatrick is the author of the Power of the Blood vampire series, which includes the novels *Child of the Night, Near Death, Reborn, Bloodlover*, and a fifth volume which is currently in progress. She is also the editor of several anthologies, including an all-new vampire anthology called *Evolve*, due out in 2010. She's a prolific author of short fiction as well, and her work is frequently nominated for awards. Nancy was a guest of honor at the 2007 World Horror Convention. She lives in Montréal, Québec.

This story is about the old world clashing with the modern world. "There are places in this world today, despite computers, cellphones, TV and other modern technologies, that still have a lot of cultural mythology and ancient lore embedded in the lives of the ordinary person who live, by our standards, very primitive lives," Kilpatrick said. "How much of a shock would it be for someone who comes from such a place and is thrust into the 'first' world, hauling with them every one of their beliefs learned at the knee of their mother into this more or less godless and myth-free zone of 2009?"

Nita sat hunched at the scarred table studying the black gouges in the wood made by knives, pens, fingernails hard as talons, thinking about the words and symbols. J.C. had been scratched in about the center, and a rough drawing of an eye with long lashes that looked mystical or psychotic, depending on how Nita let her mind wander. A cruder sketch of what might have been a penis but slightly deformed with two long eye teeth and "Bite Me" deeply carved into the birch had been positioned to the right. The letters *c-a-s-ă*, Romanian for "home," stretched above the rest.

"We are nearly ready," Dr. Sauers said, a bit gruffly to Nita's ear. Then, "*Sit liniște!*" telling her to sit quietly in her native tongue, as if that would have more impact. The doctor didn't really approve of having anyone else in the room and likely was worried that Nita would "misbehave" as she had warned her against so often. Not that she could. Even if there were no chains circling her wrists and ankles, the drugs they pumped into her kept her weighed down emotionally as if there were also heavy chains clamped to her heart. Sauers was a control freak, she preferred running the show by herself, Nita had quickly realized to her dismay.

Suddenly, Nita felt her heart grow even heavier. What had happened, it had escalated. She felt so alone. She didn't know if she could go over the events again. No one had believed her the first time. No one believed her now. Or cared. How she missed her home!

She glanced up at Dr. Sauers but the sharp-featured woman fiddling with the video camera did not return her look. Eventually, though, the older woman turned to the silver-haired man standing by the door; he couldn't have been more than forty; he had not yet been introduced to Nita. As if sensing her insecurities, he glanced at Nita and presented her with a quick benign smile, then faced Sauers to say in English, "Perhaps you should test the audio."

Sauers, scowling, twisted knobs on the tripod, aimed the small video camera's eye and adjusted the panel at the back of the camera, making sure the focus was on Nita. Was the camera lens the eye of God watching her, judging her? The doctor's long hard nail stabbed at a button on the camera twice. Maybe she was nudging God to pay attention too!

"Alright!" Dr. Sauers said abruptly, impatiently, jerking herself away from the equipment. She glanced at her watch with the large face. "We must begin." She sounded as if there had been a delay that Nita or maybe the grey-haired man was responsible for.

The doctor took a seat to the right of Nita, the man in the well-fitting grey suit took the chair directly in front of her, both of them out of the camera's view. Almost enough for a card game, Nita thought wryly. Her mind flew to the old beat-up decks of cards the men in her village played with as they drank the strong local brandy, and quickly jettisoned those images in favor of larger cards with faded pastel pictures that her grandmother—her *bunică*—kept hidden, wrapped in a soiled scrap of green satin, buried in the rich brown earth with a rock over top as if it were a grave hiding a body that refused to stay interred. In her memory Nita envisioned only one card, a black and white and grey picture with a few smudges the color of blood. *Bunică* patiently explained that this was artwork from five hundred or more years ago. "Danse Macabre," she had called it. A grisly skeleton with tufts of hair adhering to its skull and fragments of meat on its bones, holding the hand of a richly adorned King on one side of his boney body, and clutching about the waist what looked to be a peasant woman in rags on the other, the three drawn so that they appeared to be in motion. Nita thought the King and the woman were trying to get away from the skeleton, but *Bunică* interpreted it differently: "He leads the dance. We all must dance with him one day."

Nita smiled at the memory, so caught up in her mental picture of the stark yet mesmerizing image and of her *Bunică's* rough but soothing tone of voice that she missed the first part of what the man at the table was saying, which apparently had included his name.

"…and I understand you speak English. I'm a behavioral psychologist with the ICSCS, that's the International Centre for Studies of the Criminally—"

"But I'm not a criminal," Nita said flatly.

"You're a patient, convicted of a crime, in an institution for the criminally insane,"

Dr. Sauers reminded her, as if Nita might have forgotten about the trial, about being in jail, now the hospital, the humiliation, the alienation, about all of it.

She turned away from Sauers and stared at the man's cool ash-colored eyes which reminded her so much of the winter sky above the unforgiving mountains of her village. Mountains strong and permanent formed of orange and red molten rock that had burst forth from below the surface and forced its way upward towards the snowy clouds, piercing the steel-blue sky like stalagmites, until the heavens were dominated by soil and rock and trees that could withstand the fierce climate—survivor of every cataclysm. What had existed before she was born, before her grandmother, and her great great great grandmother—

A buzzer down the hall sounded and Nita jolted. Furtively she glanced around her at the sterile environment, its only richness in the dead gleam of stainless steel, its only life the color corpse-white. No, this was not the mountains. She had little power here; she looked down at her wrists chained together and her pale small hands clasped tightly in her lap as if all they could clutch, all they could hold onto to keep body and soul together was each other.

"We're not here about the legalities," the grey man whose name she had not learned said in a comforting tone accented by a slight smile. But Nita knew that both people in the room with her thought she was not just guilty but also insane. Hopelessly insane. Not much to do about that. *Bunică* believed you can't change people's minds with words, just with actions. "Trust only what you taste and touch and smell," she'd said. "What others believe, this cannot matter."

"I see your name is Luminita."

"Everyone calls me Nita."

"Yes, a diminutive. Very nice. What does Luminita mean? Something about light?"

"In Romanian it means 'little light.'"

"Meaning a bright personality?"

"Yes. But also someone who lights the way for others."

"A beacon."

Nita remembered her *Bunică* with so much longing. The woman after whom she had been named, who had meant the world to her, was gone now, and that thought stabbed Nita's heart like a rusty knife. *Bunică*, in Nita's youthful view, had always been old, snowy hair like goose down covered by a headscarf the color of the purple loostrife that grew in the wetlands, a face earth-brown and crinkly as Baltic fruit shriveled by a sudden frost. But her smile, that wasn't old at all. Her smile lit wise honey eyes and changed the wrinkles around her mouth until she appeared young to young Nita. As if they were sisters. And sometimes Nita believed that they were sisters, more than sisters, identical. As a child, she had wanted to grow up to be just like *Bunică*.

"And how do you feel about that?"

Nita's vision of the past cleared returning her to the present. The man had spoken and she had no idea what he was asking her.

"I'm sorry. Could you repeat that, please?" she said.

"*Wake sus!*" Sauers snapped.

The man said gently, "I asked if we could begin at the beginning. If you would be willing to tell me about how you came to be in Bucharest."

Nita knew this man had read her file and was aware of every bit of information about her that the courts and the doctors had been able to ascertain. Why he wanted it now, she did not know.

She was about to ask him this when Sauers ordered, "*Completat!*" and Nita decided that complying was in fact the easiest way to go. Once this was over she could return to the vomit-green cell they called her room in this small asylum and fall into the world inside her, where they could not penetrate.

"Let me ask you specific questions," the man said. "It might be easier that way. Why did you come to Bucharest?"

"To go to school."

She could see him struggle to recall the information from her files. "I seem to have read that you did very well in school. Exceptionally well."

"Yes. My grades were excellent."

He smiled. "It's unusual for a girl from a small mountain village to be accepted at university."

"I studied with my grandmother. She taught me to read three languages, and to learn numbers. She wanted me to be modern and well-educated."

"Your grandmother must have been very proud of you, earning a scholarship."

"Yes. The whole village took pride in me."

"I see. So you came here for university."

"No, I studied first at the secondary school level. I then matriculated to the university."

"I see."

She wondered if he saw much of anything. His dove eyes revealed nothing. Did he understand how life could be? How her life had been? Could he sense a clash of worlds? She doubted it.

"Did you enjoy school."

"Yes."

"Did you make friends?"

"Yes. A few." When she said no more he waited and she filled in the blank space hovering between them. "I had two girlfriends, Magda and Anya, and a guy, Toma. We all went to coffee houses together and clubs. We listened to music and danced and talked a lot. More than I was used to." She felt exhausted from talking now, as if all this depleted her. And to what end? She knew she was destined to be a name in some research study that a girl her age would read about in a text book one day.

"Did you have a boyfriend."

"No."

"What about the young man you just mentioned?"

"Toma and I were friends. Only friends."

"And the girls? Were you just friends as well?"

She did not know what he was implying and at first could not form an answer. Finally she took the easiest route. "We were friends only."

"Close?"

She hesitated. "I suppose."

"And did you confide in them?"

"Confide what?"

"Anything. Your thoughts. Feelings. Anything about your life. Your past."

He said "past" as if she might have accidentally conveyed to Anya or Magda a dark secret, or even Toma, but they had not talked of the past, only the present. And the future. A future that no longer existed. "We talked of school and movie stars and music." She hoped that would satisfy him, and it appeared to.

"Tell me, Nita, while you were in Bucharest, did you miss your village."

"Of course. Sometimes, not all the time. I had my studies."

The man had been making notes on a pad of paper and now turned the page. She wondered why he made notes when he would have the videotape.

In the pause, Nita snuck a glance at Dr. Sauers. The woman's manure eyes pierced her and threatened retribution but Nita did not know for what. Nita looked down again, but a small smile spread her lips apart as she thought to herself, "We all must dance with him one day."

"Nita, I'd like to hear what your village was like. Can you tell me something about it? I'm from North America, so this is all new to me."

She stared at him as he tried to look sincere. Yes, her village would not be known to him, and yet she wondered if he truly appreciated the differences. While she had not been to North America, or even to Western Europe, she had seen his land on television and in movies and knew how it looked, how people acted. He would have no such markers for her world. She could tell him anything and he would believe it. Of course, Sauers knew her village, or claimed to. The doctor was probably German or Austrian but clearly she spoke the language well and must have lived in Romania for some time. But even if she didn't know Nita's village, she would know the region; she would have passed through villages like Nita's. Although there was no village like Nita's, of that she was quite certain.

"A fi honest," Sauers said slowly.

Nita stared at the camera, the most humane element in the room to her thinking. At least the camera eye of God was not judgmental today. Or analytical. It recorded what was, without interpretation or hidden agendas. The way she had learned to think at the university.

"The village I grew up in was like many. Small, the people simple, kind and generous. They looked after one another. The people were old because the young ones moved away, like I did." She felt a short, sharp pain in her heart. An image floated to mind of the village, colorless, empty of living beings, the houses abandoned, the cold mountain breezes blowing through broken windows, forcing wooden shutters to bang against walls, the yards littered with the bones of dead chickens, paper and fabric rushing across the ground and into the nearby woods.

A village of ghosts. She felt tears forming in her right eye and looked down. She did not want either of these two to see her vulnerable.

"How many people lived there?" he asked.

"One hundred, no more."

"Your parents?"

"My mother…died when I was a child."

"And your father?"

She shook her head.

"Who looked after you?"

She felt annoyed. He must have read all this in the reports. Still, she tried to keep her voice from sounding impatient, which would only bring trouble. "My grandmother raised me. My mother's mother." Then she added before he could ask, "My father's family was from somewhere far away."

He nodded as if she had said or done something right. Nita did not dare look at Sauers.

The man continued but he could not disguise the energy in his voice, now that he thought he was onto something. "Was there anyone unusual in your village? Anyone different than the others?"

"Everyone was unique." She kept her smile hidden; she wanted to toy with him a little.

"Yes, of course. But what I meant was would you say there was anyone living in the village who maybe did not feel they belonged there? Who might have felt like a prisoner?"

She knew what he was getting at, and she knew what he wanted her to say. He wanted her to say it was her. Instead she told him, "Yes, one man. We called him *Vechi bărbat*. It means 'ancient man.'"

This was not what the grey-haired man was expecting. Out of the corner of her eye she saw him move back in his chair slightly, as if regrouping his thoughts. To her right, she heard Sauers make a small sound like a snake hissing.

They insisted she be here. They controlled her life. She had no options but this one: to play with them, as much as she could. And she would. They did not care about her, about her village, about *vechi bărbat*. And Nita did not care about them. Not at all. What could a prisoner feel but to desire the end of her captors?

The man at the table leaned forward and scribbled in his notebook. When he looked up at her she met his gaze, forcing her eyes to reflect innocence, guilelessness. In an instant his demeanor altered and he again looked hopeful, as if he had made a good decision and even before he spoke, she knew where he wanted to go.

"Tell me about this *vechi bărbat*," he said, badly mispronouncing the words. And she knew he had decided to humor her. She smiled, which from his reaction he interpreted as her being more at ease with him. But of course she did not trust him. Not at all.

"*Vechi bărbat* was old when my grandmother was young. She told me stories, what her grandmother had told her, and her grandmother before her."

"I see," the man said, jotting a note. He looked up at Nita with an encouraging smile. "Could you describe this *vechi bărbat* for me?"

"Grey hair like yours, but brittle," she said. "He was thin, very thin, because he did not eat much, and hunched, but I think he must have been shorter than me. His eyes could not focus well, and he had trouble with light, especially the sun."

"Where did he live? In the village, I mean. Did he have a house?"

"He lived with us. In a cage in the back room. My grandmother fed him from time to time, and let him out when she felt he was not a threat."

"What kind of threat?" The man's voice held anticipation, as if Nita were on the edge of divulging something important.

"He might hurt someone. If he were kept weak, he could not harm us. That's why my grandmother fed him little."

"And the rest of the villagers? Were they afraid of him?"

"No one was afraid of him."

"But if he was a danger—"

"When he was well fed. But he never was. And at night, but he was kept on chains and ropes. He was not dangerous in the day, and not when he was weak."

The man paused. "Did your grandmother ever keep you in the cage?"

"Of course not!" Nita snapped. She saw Sauers tense, ready for action. "I was not a threat. Only *vechi bărbat*."

"Alright. That makes sense," the man said, trying to mollify her, fearful that she would stop talking to him. "Tell me more about him. Did you ever speak with him?"

"No. Why should I? There was no reason to. And besides, he could not talk. He only knew the language of long ago. He had nothing to say."

"Did he ever try to speak to you?"

She thought for a moment. "Once. When I was very young. I had gone into the woods to hunt for mushrooms too late in the day and he appeared."

"You were not afraid?"

Nita looked at him with disdain. "Of course not. I told you I did not fear him."

"And what did he do?"

"He walked up to me and reached out his hand to touch my face, but I stepped back. And anyway, the chains and ropes were caught around a tree trunk, so he could not reach me. It was dark in those woods where the trees grew close together and little sunlight got through. He might have had more power."

"What did you do, when he tried to touch you?"

"I picked up my bucket and went home."

"Did he follow you?"

"Yes, for a while, when he unraveled himself."

"Did you tell anyone about this?"

"Yes, I told my grandmother."

"And what did she do?"

"She beat him."

They were all silent for a moment. Nita recalled watching the crimson welts form on *vechi bărbat*'s bare back as *Bunică* laid on the thick black leather strap. The blood was not red like Nita's and *Bunică*'s but pale, almost colorless, barely pink-tinged. *Vechi bărbat* took the beating with barely a sound coming from his lips, but his body hunched over even more until he was curled into a ball like a baby. Nita had felt sorry for him.

"How did you feel about that?"

"He had to be taught a lesson, my grandmother said. Otherwise he would cause harm to others."

The man took more notes. Dr. Sauers got up and checked the camera. Nita looked down at the shackles locking her wrists and ankles and thought that she was as much of a prisoner here as *vechi bărbat* had been in the village. She, too, was kept in a cage. Controlled not by near starvation but through drugs they injected into her daily. She knew how much *vechi bărbat* had longed to break free. She grew to understand him very well.

When Sauers returned to her seat and the man whose name she still did not know had finished his note taking, he turned to Nita and asked if she would like some water, or a juice.

"No. Thank you."

"All right then. Can we continue?"

She knew he did not expect an answer and she gave none. He would continue whether she wanted to or not. That was the nature of being held prisoner.

"I'd like to talk about the last time you visited your village. Back in the summer."

Her mind went to a picture. Like a postcard. An overview of the village, in shades of verdant green, with rich ochre mixed in, and the azure of the sky above. There were people: pretty, tan-skinned Oana and her four rosy-cheeked children and her belly swollen with the fifth. And Radu, her blond-haired, hard-working husband. Little Gheroghe, who played the flute so well, and Ilie who made such beautiful, well-constructed boots with his long, graceful fingers colored nearly black from the Russian cigarettes he liked to smoke. She saw them all as dabs of paint on a canvas, a human still-life, paralyzed in the thickness of time, depicted in her mind as they went about their day, as they had always done, as their children would, unless they left the village as Nita had.

"Tell me about that visit. Why did you go home?"

"My studies were complete for the year. I had gotten a position, serving food and drink in a *taverna* in Bucharest, but the owner did not need me for three weeks, until the tourists would come, so I went home to see my grandmother."

"Were you happy to be visiting her and your village?"

"Yes, of course."

"And how did everyone react to you?"

"They were all excited to see me. They wanted to know what it was like in Bucharest, and at the school."

"And what did you tell them?"

"That the city is full of people who dress in all the colors of the world and walk the narrow streets at every hour, and that lamp posts shine warm light at night like stars. I told them that the school gave me knowledge, and I learned about things I had not known existed."

"For example?"

"Mythologies. Legends. The stories of cultures."

The man checked a file report, obviously filled with information about her. "Ah, yes, you were studying cultural anthropology, is that correct?"

"Yes."

He closed the file folder, folded his arms on top of it and stared at her. She did not meet his gaze. "Were there legends, stories and myths in your village?"

"Yes." Suddenly she felt ashamed. Forlorn. How could she not have known what would happen?

"And one was about the *vechi bărbat*, was it not?"

"Yes," she said, struggling to release the dark memory and keep living in the present.

"Tell me the story of the *vechi bărbat*."

She sighed heavily, surprised at this new, even heavier weight she felt in her chest, as if her lungs had turned to pumice and the clear, pure air had trouble getting inside her.

Dr. Sauers tapped her fingernails on the table. She did not subscribe to "talk" therapy, as she called it. She believed in drugs. Sedate patients. Give them anti-psychotics. Gradually reduce their medication and see if they improved. If so, they were released. If not, up the meds. Since Nita would never be released, she had no hope in either direction.

"My grandmother told me the story of the *vechi bărbat*. He came to our village centuries ago. He had met a girl from the village, you see, by the river, and they fell in love. They married. Then the woman died of a fever that spread through the mountains killing humans and animals alike. It reduced the numbers in our small village to twenty only, plus the *vechi bărbat*, and the people did not know how to survive. The *vechi bărbat* was not the oldest in the village but he held the most power and was the one with a quick brain and he should have told the people what to do, but he was caught by grief and unable to lead. Another man who had survived became the leader and managed to save the remaining livestock, and the crops, so the people did not starve and could bear more children, and their numbers increased."

"And the *vechi bărbat*? You say he was grieving. For his lost wife?"

"Yes. He loved her very much. So much that he would do anything to be with her again. And did."

"What did he do?"

"He roamed the forest at night, calling on the bad spirits of the old gods, the ones from his life before the village when he lived with the Gypsies, before the Christian god became the one god. He begged the darkest elementals, the angriest spirits of nature to aid him. He promised them that he would do anything if they would allow him to again be with his wife."

Nita felt her heart race. She knew her eyes darted around the room, looking for what? Escape? Yes, she wanted to escape. This room, these people. The story that had gone so very wrong.

"Then what happened?"

"The storms came. The village is nestled in a valley, and the land flooded. Blinding lightning shot from the sky and struck the *vechi bărbat.* His skin blackened, and the pale brown color of his eyes turned white, as did his hair and beard. When he returned to the village he had become…different."

"Different how?"

She tried to avoid his questions. "The villagers, they were so busy trying to save themselves, the crops, the animals, to recapture their way of life. The flood forced mud down the side of the mountain that buried much of what had been rescued. Red-streaked mud, as if the mountain were bleeding. Their numbers dwindled further. They saw it as a sign, that there were demons in the village. The *vechi bărbat* had brought havoc to their lives when they were struggling to recover. Naturally they blamed him."

There was silence for a moment. The man said softly, "What did they do to the *vechi bărbat?"*

Nita swallowed hard. "They could not kill him. He had been with them many years and was now one of their own. But they had to protect themselves."

"From what?"

"From the curse."

"What curse is that?"

Nita felt her legs begin to tremble uncontrollably, rattling the chains under the table. The room seemed too hot, the color of scorching yellow. "I'd like some water now, if you please," she said, trying yet again to redirect the grey man.

He got up and went to a side table and poured a glass of clear water. He set it in front of her but she did not touch it.

Once he was seated again he said, "Tell me about the curse."

Maybe, she thought, maybe if I tell it now, here, maybe someone will understand. The others before, the police, the medical men, Dr. Sauers, they had all been impatient, believing what they wanted to believe, not the truth, and she knew the truth. This man with hair and eyes the color of a vole who said he was listening, maybe he was listening. Maybe he would believe her.

She heard Dr. Sauers' nails again, tapping on the table, talons painted violent purple eager to rend flesh.

"Dr. Sauers, would you mind terribly if I spoke with Nita alone for a few minutes?"

"Why?" Sauers snarled. "This is irregular."

"Yes, it is. But I wonder if I might try a technique I've found that has had great success. If you wouldn't mind…"

Reluctantly Sauers got up from the table and obviously she did not appreciate this shift in the plan.

Sauers checked the camera for film.

"Thank you," the grey-headed man said cheerfully.

The doctor went out the door, closing it loudly behind her, not acknowledging him.

When she was gone, the man turned his head and smiled at Nita. "There. Now you can take your time telling me what happened."

For some reason Nita found this both reassuring and intimidating. She picked up the water with shaking hands and took a small sip, then set the glass back down, spilling a little that she wiped up with her sleeve. She held onto the glass, as if letting go might leave her floating in a colorless universe.

"What did the villagers do to the *vechi bărbat?*"

"They put him in a cage and kept him there. He lived in the cage day and night. They fed him only a little blood, from time to time, to keep him alive, but this is how he existed."

"And when the original villagers died?"

"For the first season all the villagers cared for him, but soon, as winter approached, one woman offered to take the *vechi bărbat* into her home, and it was then that he lived in the cage all the time. She…looked after him, and then her daughter, and so on. It soon became the unspoken rule that only one took responsibility for him. One woman of each generation, the task handed down to the next in line, the eldest. Eventually my grandmother was responsible."

"And with your mother gone, you were next in line?"

Nita's hands trembled and felt white cold. "Yes."

The man paused. "And this responsibility, to take care of, to live with the *vechi bărbat*, is this something you wanted for yourself?"

"I…I don't know," she said. No one had asked her this. *Bunică* had not. It was assumed that Nita would go to school, then return home to the village and bear children, raising only one girl child, and that she would look after the ancient one who would live with her, in the cage, as it had been with all the women before her.

"Tell me, you said the *vechi bărbat* walked in the village, and he tried to touch you in the forest. So he was no longer in a cage."

"Somewhere back in time it was determined by a woman who cared for him that if he were not permitted to eat he would be weak and he could then be allowed to roam free at dusk, provided a chain was attached to his ankle with a long rope. This seemed to work out, and the villagers agreed. Anyway, he could not tolerate the sun and always returned to the cage during the day."

"Like a vampire," the grey-haired man said.

"Exactly like a vampire."

"And he was fed blood."

"Yes."

"What kind of blood?"

"The blood of the village."

The man looked a little shocked by this revelation. "Not animals?"

"No. His body could not tolerate their blood. Only human."

"Did he drink your blood?"

"Sometimes."

"How...how was this done? Did he bite you?"

"Of course not!" she said, feeling the tension building in her. "We would make cuts on our arms and legs, each person in the village taking a turn, and would provide a tin cup every day and he would drink that. It kept him alive."

"Why, over the centuries, did the villagers want to keep him alive?"

"Because it would be bad luck to kill him."

"But he'd brought disaster to the village, or so everyone thought?"

"But more disaster would come from killing him. He was a Gypsy. He had been in touch with the most evil spirits. They had come to him, heeded him, given him what he asked for. The villagers did not know what would happen if he were killed or released, but they knew they would be cursed and harm would come to them. They just did not know the nature of that harm."

"But you didn't believe that, did you? That his curse would bring disaster. That he was ancient. That he had brought back his dead wife."

A small sound slipped from Nita's lips. She felt a tear form in one eye and tried to brush it away but the sparkly multicolored drop slid down her cheek. Maybe...maybe he understood! "I...I... The university. They said it could not be so. That he was not old. That he was just a crazy man that everyone kept caged and starved, and that his dead wife had not returned but a woman in the village—my grandmother, and my mother—had slept with him to get pregnant."

"How did your mother die?"

That was too horrible. Nita could not bring herself to admit the suicide. Instead of answering his question, her mind raced on as if he hadn't interrupted. "The university professor said it was an example of a mythology that had gone terribly wrong, and the people wanted to blame someone for all their problems, and to torture him." She looked up at the grey man. "I went home to make it right."

The man nodded imperceptibly.

Now the words spilled from Nita, like the scorching lava that had formed the mountains. "I tried to tell the others. I told them that he could not be ancient. That he was not responsible for catastrophes. That the gods had not returned his wife to him. I explained that my grandmother who kept him, she was his wife. They would not believe me."

"What did you do?"

"After the sun set, I cut his chain and took him far from the village, up into the mountains, a night's journey by foot. I gave him food I had brought home with me, liquid food with nutrients, some blood because he was used to that, but other beverages, because he had not eaten solid food that I knew of. I tried to feed him grains but he could not digest them. And then I pointed to the much larger village just over the mountain peak and told him to go there, to begin a new life. That he was free. I told him that he would be caged no more."

Nita shook her head. Tears streamed down her face and though her voice wavered, she needed no encouragement to finish her story. "I returned to my village the following day. My grandmother was furious with me. She struck me and called me a fool, ranting that I had brought down the curse and put them all in danger. The villagers were angry and afraid. Some wanted to run away, others found weapons to defend themselves. One suggested I take the place of the *vechi bărbat* in the cage, as if that would make things right. I told them they had nothing to fear, that the old man, the *vechi bărbat*, was gone for good, and they were all free now. Just as I was free from the life that had awaited me. No more wrong legends to rule their lives, or mine. I could return to the university. I would not have to marry the *vechi bărbat*, or spend my life taking care of him.

"But the people were not pleased by this; they were so enraged. And terrified. My grandmother struggled to keep them from hurting me."

After a moment, the man said, "And then what happened?"

"He returned. Two nights later. He murdered people in their beds, outside their homes, as they fled into the forest. Women, children, men—even the strongest who tried to fight him off. My...my grandmother. He had been strengthened by the nourishment I'd provided, and he took blood until he became bloated, and then took more. He killed everyone, and it was my fault!"

Her body trembled uncontrollably. The room had become icy. The colors surrounding her, even the white, paled as if glaciers had formed over everything, and the opaqueness that reminded her of the *vechi bărbat*'s eyes as he stared into hers began to spin and swirl like a snowstorm.

"But he didn't kill *you*," the man said.

"No," she gasped. "He spared me."

"Why?"

She stared at him, watching his grey features shift and twist and the shape of his face change from human to animal then change again from animal to something dark and otherworldly until the images that formed petrified her.

"Nita, they found you covered with blood. *You*, not the *vechi bărbat*. You killed the villagers, because you felt trapped there, destined to a life you did not want."

Her head jerked from side to side.

"Nita, if there were a *vechi bărbat*, why wasn't he found? Where is he now?"

She screamed, "I—don't—know!"

"Take it easy. You're safe here."

But his words could not quell the horror that gripped her heart. "He disappeared. And I remained with the bodies, the blood-red bodies, stained by color that seeped into the hungry brown soil as if it were a mouth that had longed for this nourishment. The land of my foremothers, of the villagers, those who imprisoned the *vechi bărbat*. Don't you see? The blood went back into the earth. Where it should have gone centuries ago! Because they imprisoned him!"

Her raised voice brought Dr. Sauers storming into the room. "What's going on here? You're upsetting my patient!" She hit an intercom button on the wall and told a nurse to hurry with an injection.

"No! No more drugs! Let me be free!" Nita jumped to her feet. "Remove these chains! I did nothing to you, why are you holding me prisoner! Help! Someone help me! *Vechi bărbat* free me, as I freed you!"

But Nita's cries faded soon after the needle pierced her flesh. The world around her receded, the colors dimming and fading to nothing, until she could neither see nor hear those outside her with their demands and judgments and limitations. But she clearly heard the *vechi bărbat*, for now he could speak and he spoke to her, calling her his bride, assuring her that he would be with her always. That she would not be a prisoner forever. "One day," he promised, "you, too, must dance with me."

THE BEAUTIFUL, THE DAMNED

by Kristine Kathryn Rusch

Kristine Kathryn Rusch's most recent novel, *Diving into the Wreck*, will be published by Pyr Books in November. She is the author of more than fifty novels, including several in her popular Retrieval Artist series. Many of her novels belong to the mystery or romance genres and are published under the pen names Kristine Grayson, Kris Nelscott, and Kristine Dexter. Rusch is a prolific author of short fiction as well, much of which will be collected in the forthcoming book *Recovering Apollo 8 and Other Stories*. She has been nominated for the Hugo Award thirteen times, winning twice—once for writing and once for editing, making her the only person to ever win a Hugo Award in both categories. She has also won the World Fantasy Award, the Sidewise Award, and numerous Asimov's Readers Choice Awards.

Rusch describes this story as a kind of sequel to *The Great Gatsby*—with vampires. "For some reason, I reread *The Great Gatsby* every two or three years whether I need to or not," she said. "Like Nick Carraway, I am a child of the Middle West, a person who has moved away to a land that's not quite familiar and people who are a bit strange. I have always seen ties between vampirism and alcoholism (and I am the child of two alcoholics). I dealt with that tie in my novel *Sins of the Blood*, a vampire book, and I deal with it here too."

On one rereading of *Gatsby*, Rusch realized that the characters were metaphorical vampires, and that was all the inspiration she needed to come up with the tale that follows.

CHAPTER I

I come from the Middle West, an unforgiving land with little or no tolerance for imagination. The wind blows harsh across the prairies, and the snows fall thick. Even with the conveniences of the modern age, life is dangerous there. To lose sight of reality, even for one short romantic moment, is to risk death.

I didn't belong in that country, and my grandfather knew it. I was his namesake, and somehow, being the second Nick Carraway in a family where the name had a certain mystique had forced that mystique upon me. He had lived in the East during the twenties, and had had grand adventures, most of which he would not talk about. When he returned to St. Paul in 1928, he met a woman—my grandmother Nell—and with her solid, common sense had shed himself of the romance and imagination that had led to his adventures in the first place.

Although not entirely. For when I announced, fifty years later, that I intended to pursue my education in the East, he paid four years of Ivy League tuition. And, when I told him, in the early '80s, that, despite my literary background and romantic nature, I planned a career in the securities business, he regaled me with stories of being a bond man in New York City in the years before the crash.

He died while I was still learning the art of the cold call, stuck on the sixteenth floor of a windowless high rise, in a tiny cubicle that matched a hundred other tiny cubicles, distinguished only by my handprint on the phone set and the snapshots of my family thumbtacked to the indoor-outdoor carpeting covering the small barrier that separated my cubicle from all the others. He never saw the house in Connecticut which, although it was not grand, was respectable, and he never saw my rise from a cubicle employee to a man with an office. He never saw the heady Reagan years, although he would have warned me about the awful Black Monday well before it appeared. For despite the computers, jets, and televised communications, the years of my youth were not all that different from the years of his.

He never saw Fitz either, although I knew, later that year, when I read the book, that my grandfather would have understood my mysterious neighbor too.

My house sat at the bottom of a hill, surrounded by trees whose russet leaves are—in my mind—in a state of perpetual autumn. I think the autumn melancholy comes from the overlay of hindsight upon what was, I think, the strangest summer of my life, a summer which, like my grandfather's summer of 1925, I do not discuss, even when asked. In that tiny valley, the air always had a damp chill and the rich smell of loam. The scent grew stronger upon that winding dirt path that led to Fitz's house on the hill's crest—not a house really, but more of a mansion in the conservative New England style, white walls hidden by trees, with only the wide walk and the entry visible from the gate. Once behind, the walls and windows seemed to go on forever, and the manicured lawn with its neatly mowed grass and carefully arranged marble fountains seemed like a throwback from a simpler time.

The house had little life in the daytime, but at night the windows were thrown open and cars filled the driveway. The cars were all sleek and dark—blue Saabs and midnight BMWs, black Jaguars and ebony Carreras. Occasionally a white stretch limo or a silver DeLorean would mar the darkness, but those guests rarely returned for a second visit, as if someone had asked them to take their ostentation elsewhere. Music trickled down the hill with the light, usually music of a vanished era, waltzes and marches and Dixieland Jazz, music both romantic and danceable, played to such perfection that I envied Fitz his sound system until I saw several of the better known New York Philharmonic members round the corner near my house early on a particular Saturday evening.

Laughter, conversation and the tinkle of ice against fine crystal filled the gaps during the musicians' break, and in those early days, as I sat on my porch swing and stared up at the light, I imagined parties like those I had only seen on film—slender beautiful women in glittery gowns, and athletic men who wore tuxedos like a second skin, exchanging witty and wry conversation under a dying moon.

In those early days, I didn't trudge up the hill, although later I learned I could have, and drop into a perpetual party that never seemed to have a guest list. I still had enough of my Midwestern politeness to wait for an invitation and enough of my practical Midwestern heritage to know that such an invitation would never come.

Air conditioners have done little to change Manhattan in the summer. If anything, the heat from their exhausts adds to the oppression in the air, the stench of garbage rotting on the sidewalks, and the smell of sweaty human bodies pressed too close. Had my cousin Arielle not discovered me, I might have spent the summer in the cool loam of my Connecticut home, monitoring the markets through my personal computer, and watching Fitz's parties with a phone wedged between my shoulder and ear.

Arielle always had an ethereal, other-worldly quality. My sensible aunt, with her thick ankles and dishwater-blond hair, must have recognized that quality in the newborn she had given birth to in New Orleans, and committed the only romantic act of her life by deciding that Arielle was not a Mary or a Louise, family names that had suited Carraways until then.

I had never known Arielle well. At family reunions held on the shores of Lake Superior, she was always a beautiful, unattainable ghost, dressed in white gauze with silver-blond hair that fell to her waist, wide blue eyes, and skin so pale it seemed as fragile as my mother's bone china. We had exchanged perhaps five words over all those reunions, held each July, and always I had bowed my head and stammered in the presence of such royalty. Her voice was sultry and musical, lacking the long "a"s and soft "d"s that made my other relations sound like all their years of education had made no impression at all.

Why she called me when she and her husband Tom discovered that I had bought a house in a village only a mile from theirs I will never know. Perhaps she was lonely for a bit of family, or perhaps the other-worldliness had absorbed her, even then.

CHAPTER II

I drove to Arielle and Tom's house in my own car, a BMW, navy blue and spit-polished, bought used because all of my savings had gone into the house. They lived on a knoll in a mock-Tudor-style house surrounded by young saplings that had obviously been transplanted. The lack of tall trees gave the house a vulnerable air, as if the neighbors who lived on higher hills could look down upon it and find it flawed. The house itself was twice the size of mine, with a central living area flanked by a master bedroom wing and a guest wing, the wings more of an architect's affectation than anything else.

Tom met me at the door. He was a beefy man in his late twenties whose athletic build was beginning to show signs of softening into fat. He still had the thick neck, square jaw and massive shoulders of an offensive lineman which, of course, he had been. After one season with the Green Bay Packers—in a year unremarked for its lackluster performance—he was permanently sidelined by a knee injury. Not wanting to open a car dealership that would forever capitalize on his one season of glory, he took his wife and his inheritance and moved east. When he saw me, he clapped his hand on my back as if we were old friends when, in fact, we had only met once, at the last and least of the family reunions.

"Ari's been waiting ta see ya," he said, and the broad flat uneducated vowels of the Midwest brought with them the sense of the stifling summer afternoons of the reunions, children's laughter echoing over the waves of the lake as if their joy would last forever.

He led me through a dark foyer and into a room filled with light. Nothing in the front of the house had prepared me for this room, with its floor to ceiling windows, and their view of an English garden beyond the patio. Arielle sat on a loveseat beneath the large windows, the sunlight reflecting off her hair and white dress, giving her a radiance that was almost angelic. She held out her hand, and as I took it, she pulled me close and kissed me on the cheek.

"Nicky," she murmured. "I missed you."

The softness with which she spoke, the utter sincerity in her gaze made me believe her and, as on those summer days of old, I blushed.

"Not much ta do in Connecticut." Tom's booming voice made me draw back. "We been counting the nails on the walls."

"Now, Tom," Ari said without taking her hand from mine, "we belong here."

I placed my other hand over hers, capturing the fragile fingers for a moment, before releasing her. "I rather like the quiet," I said.

"You would," Tom said. He turned and strode across the hardwood floor, always in shadow despite the light pouring in from the windows.

His abruptness took me aback, and I glanced at Ari. She shrugged. "I think we'll eat on the terrace. The garden is cool this time of day."

"Will Tom join us?"

She frowned in a girlish way, furrowing her brow, and making her appear, for a moment, as if she were about to cry. "He will when he gets off the phone."

I hadn't heard a phone ring, but I had no chance to ask her any more for she placed her slippered feet on the floor and stood. I had forgotten how tiny she was, nearly half my height, but each feature perfectly proportioned. She took my arm and I caught the fresh scent of lemons rising from her warm skin.

"You must tell me everything that's happened to you," she said, and I did. Under her intense gaze my life felt important, my smallest accomplishments a pinnacle of achievement. We had reached the terrace before I had finished. A glass table, already set for three, stood in the shade of a maple tree. The garden spread before us, lush and green. Each plant had felt the touch of a pruning shears and were trimmed back so severely that nothing was left to chance.

I pulled out a chair for Ari and she sat daintily, her movements precise. I took the chair across from her, feeling cloddish, afraid that my very size would cause me to break something. I wondered how Tom, with his linebacker's build, felt as he moved through his wife's delicate house.

She shook out a linen napkin and placed it on her lap. A man appeared beside her dressed as a waiter—he had moved so silently that I hadn't noticed him—and poured water into our crystal glasses. He filled Tom's as well, and Ari stared at the empty place.

"I wish he wouldn't call her before lunch," she said. "It disturbs my digestion."

I didn't want to ask what Ari was referring to. I didn't want to get trapped in their private lives.

She sighed and brushed a strand of hair out of her face. "But I don't want to talk about Tom's awful woman. I understand you live next door to the man they call Fitz."

I nodded as the waiter appeared again, bringing fresh bread in a ceramic basket.

"I would love," she said, leaning forward just enough to let me know this was the real reason behind my invitation, "to see the inside of his home."

Tom never joined us. We finished our lunch, walked through the garden, and had mint juleps in the late afternoon, after which everything seemed a bit funnier than it had before. As I left in the approaching twilight, it felt as if Ari and I had been friends instead of acquaintances linked by a happenstance of birth.

By the time I got home, it was dark. The house retained the heat of the day, and so I went into the back yard and stared at the path that led up to Fitz's mansion. The lights blazed on the hillside, and the sound of laughter washed down to me like the blessing of a god. Perhaps Ari's casual suggestion put something in my mind, or perhaps I was still feeling the effects of the mint juleps, but whatever the cause, I walked up the path feeling drawn to the house like a moth to light.

My shoes crunched against the hardpacked earth, and my legs, unused to such strenuous exercise, began to ache. Midway up, the coolness of the valley had disappeared, and perspiration made my shirt cling to my chest. The laughter grew closer, and with it, snatches of conversation—women's voices rising with passion, men speaking in low tones, pretending that they couldn't be overheard.

I stopped at a small rock formation just before the final rise to Fitz's house. The rocks extended over the valley below like a platform, and from them, I could see the winding road I had driven that afternoon to Ari's house. A car passed below and I followed the trail of its headlights until they disappeared into the trees.

As I turned to leave the platform, my desire to reach the party gone, I caught a glimpse of a figure moving against the edge of the path. A man stood on the top of the rise, staring down at the road, as I had. He wore dark evening dress with a white shirt and a matching white scarf draped casually around his neck. The light against his back caused his features to be in shadow—only when he cupped his hands around a burning match to light a cigarette already in his mouth did I get a sense of his face.

He had an older beauty—clean-shaven, almost womanish, with a long nose, high cheekbones and wide, dark eyes. A kind of beauty that had been fashionable in men when my grandfather was young—the Rudolph Valentino, Leslie Howard look that seemed almost effete by the standards of today.

As he tossed the match away, a waltz started playing behind him, and it gave him context. He stared down at the only other visible point of light—Ari's knoll—and his posture suggested such longing that I half expected the music to swell, to add too much violin in the suggestion of a world half-forgotten.

I knew, without being told, that this was my neighbor. I almost called to him, but felt that to do so would ruin the perfection of the moment. He stared until he finished his cigarette, then dropped it, ground it with his shoe, and, slipping his hands in his pockets, wandered back to the party—alone.

CHAPTER III

The next afternoon I was lounging on my sofa with the air conditioning off, lingering over the book review section of the Sunday *Times*, when the crunch of gravel through the open window alerted me to a car in my driveway. I stood up in time to see a black Rolls Royce stop outside my garage. The driver's door opened, and a chauffeur got out, wearing, unbelievably, a uniform complete with driving cap. He walked up to the door, and I watched him as though he were a ghost. He clasped one hand behind his back and, with the other, rang the bell.

The chimes pulled me from my stupor. I opened the door, feeling ridiculously informal in my polo shirt and my stocking feet. The chauffeur didn't seem to notice. He handed me a white invitation embossed in gold and said, "Mr. Fitzgerald would like the pleasure of your company at his festivities this evening."

I stammered something to the effect that I would be honored. The chauffeur nodded and returned to the Rolls, backing it out of the driveway with an ease that suggested years of familiarity. I watched until he disappeared up the hill. Then I took the invitation inside and stared at it, thinking that for once, my Midwestern instincts had proven correct.

The parties began at sundown. In the late afternoon, I would watch automobiles with words painted on their sides climb the winding road to Fitz's mansion. *Apple Valley Caterers. Signal Wood Decorators.* Musicians of all stripes, and extra service personnel, preparing for an evening of work that would last long past dawn. By the time I walked up the hill, the sun had set and the lights strung on the trees and around the frame of the house sent a glow bright as daylight down the walk to greet me.

Cars still drove past—the sleek models this time—drivers often visible, but the occupants hidden by shaded windows. As I trudged, my face heated. I looked like a schoolboy, prowling the edges of an adult gathering at which he did not belong.

By the time I arrived, people flowed in and out of the house like moths chasing the biggest light. The women wore their hair short or up, showing off cleavage and dresses so thin that they appeared to be gauze. Most of the men wore evening clothes, some of other eras, long-waisted jackets complete with tails and spats. One man stood under the fake gaslight beside the door, his skin so pale it looked bloodless, his hair slicked back like a thirties gangster, his eyes hollow dark points in his empty face. He supervised the attendants parking the cars, giving directions with the flick of a bejeweled right hand. When he saw me, he nodded, as if I were expected and inclined his head toward the door.

I flitted through. A blond woman, her hair in a marcel, gripped my arm as if we had come together, her bow-shaped lips painted a dark wine red. The crowd parted for us, and she said nothing, just squeezed my arm, and then disappeared up a flight of stairs to the right.

It was impossible to judge the house's size or decor. People littered its hallways, sprawled along its stairs. Waiters, carrying trays of champagne aloft, slipped through the crowd. Tables heaped in ice and covered in food lined the walls. The orchestra played on the patio, and couples waltzed around the pool. Some of the people had a glossy aura, as if they were photographs come to life. I recognized a few faces from the jumble of Wall Street, others from the occasional evening at the Met, but saw no one I knew well enough to speak to, no one with whom to have even a casual conversation.

When I arrived, I made an attempt to find my host, but the two or three people of whom I asked his whereabouts stared at me in such an amazed way, and denied so vehemently any knowledge of his movements that I slunk off in the direction of the open bar—the only place on the patio where a single man could linger without looking purposeless and alone.

I ordered a vodka martini although I rarely drank hard liquor—it seemed appropriate to the mood—and watched the crowd's mood switch as the orchestra slid from the waltz to a jitterbug. Women dressed like flappers, wearing no-waisted fringed dresses and pearls down to their thighs, danced with an abandon I had only seen in movies. Men matched their movements, sweat marring the perfection of their tailored suits.

A hand gripped my shoulder, the feeling tight but friendly, unlike Tom's clap of the week before. As I looked up, I realized that the crowd of single men around the bar had eased, and I was standing alone, except for the bartender and the man behind me.

Up close, he was taller and more slender than he had looked in the moonlight. His cheekbones were high, his lips thin, his eyes hooded. "Your face looks familiar," he said. "Perhaps you're related to the Carraways of St. Paul, Minnesota."

"Yes," I said. The drink had left an unpleasant tang on my tongue. "I grew up there."

"And Nick Carraway, the bondsman, would be your—grandfather? Great-grandfather?"

That he knew my grandfather startled me. Fitz looked younger than that, more of an age with me. Perhaps there were family ties I did not know about. "Grandfather," I said.

"Odd," he murmured. "How odd, the way things grow beyond you."

He had kept his hand on my shoulder, making it impossible to see more than half of his face. "I wanted to thank you for inviting me," I said.

"It would be churlish not to," he said. "Perhaps, in the future, we'll actually be able to talk."

He let go of my shoulder. I could still feel the imprint of his hand as he walked away. He had an air of invisibleness to him, a way of moving unnoticed through a crowd. When he reached the edge of the dancers, he stopped and looked at me with a gaze piercing with its intensity.

"Next time, old sport," he said, the old-fashioned endearment tripping off his tongue like a new and original phrase, "bring your cousin. I think she might like the light."

At least, that was what I thought he said. Later, when I had time to reflect, I wondered if he hadn't said, "I think she might like the night."

CHAPTER IV

Men with little imagination often have a clarity of vision that startles the mind. For all their inability to imagine beauty, they seem able to see the ugliness that lies below any surface. They have a willingness to believe in the baser, cruder side of life.

On the following Wednesday afternoon, I found myself in a bar at the edge of the financial district, a place where men in suits rarely showed their faces, where the average clientele had muscles thick as cue balls and just as hard. Tom had corralled me as I left the office, claiming he wanted to play pool and that he knew a place, but as we walked in, it became clear that we were not there for a game, but for an alibi.

The woman he met was the antithesis of Ari. She was tall, big-chested with thick ankles, more a child of my aunt than Ari ever could be. The woman—Rita—wore her clothes like an ill-fitting bathrobe, slipping to one side to reveal a mound of flesh and a bit of nipple. Lipstick stained the side of her mouth and the edges of her teeth. She laughed loud and hard, like a man, and her eyes were bright with too much drink. She and Tom disappeared into the back, and I remained, forgotten, in the smoky haze.

I stuck my tie in my pocket, pulled off my suitjacket and draped it over a chair, rolling up my sleeves before I challenged one of the large men in a ripped t-shirt to a game of eight-ball. I lost fifty dollars to him before he decided there was no challenge in it; by then Tom and Rita had reappeared, her clothing straight and her lipstick neatly applied.

Tom clapped my back before I could step away, and the odors of sweat, musk and newly applied cologne swept over me. "Thanks, man," he said, as if my accompanying him on this trip had deepened our friendship.

I could not let the moment slide without exacting my price. "My neighbor asked that Ari come to one of his parties this week."

Rita slunk back as if Ari's name lessened Rita's power. Tom stepped away from me.

"Fitzgerald's a ghoul," he said. "They say people go ta his house and never come back."

"I was there on Sunday."

"You're lucky ta get out alive."

"Hundreds of people go each night." I unrolled my sleeves, buttoned them, and then slipped into my suitcoat. "I plan to take Ari."

Tom stared at me for a moment, the male camaraderie gone. Finally he nodded, the acknowledgment of a price paid.

"Next time you go," Rita said, addressing the only words she would ever say to me, "take a good look at his guests."

I drove Ari up in my car. Even though I spent the afternoon washing and polishing it, the car's age showed against the sleek new models, something in the lack of shine of the bumpers, the crude design of a model year now done. The attendant was polite as he took my place, but lacked the enthusiasm he had shown over a Rolls just moments before.

Ari stared at the house, her tiny mouth agape, her eyes wide. The lights reflected in her pupils like a hundred dancing stars. She left my side immediately and ran up the stairs as if I were not even there.

I tipped the attendant and strode in, remembering Rita's admonishment. The faces that looked familiar had a photographic edge to them—the patina of images I had seen a thousand times in books, in magazines, on film. But as I scanned, I could not see Ari. It was as if she had come into the mammoth house and vanished.

I grabbed a flute of champagne from a passing waiter and wandered onto the patio. The orchestra was playing "Alexander's Ragtime Band" and the woman with the marcel danced in the center, alone, as if she were the only one who understood the music.

Beside me, a burly man with dark hair and a mustache that absorbed his upper lip spoke of marlin fishing as if it were a combat sport. A lanky and lean man who spoke with a Mississippi accent told a familiar story about a barn-burning to a crowd of women who gazed adoringly at his face. Behind him, a tiny woman with an acid tongue talked in disparaging terms of the Algonquin, and another man with white hair, a face crinkled from too much drink, and a body so thin it appeared dapper, studied the edges of the conversation as if the words were written in front of him.

They all had skin as pale as Fitz's, and a life force that seemed to have more energy than substance.

There were others scattered among the crowd: a man with an unruly shock of white hair who spoke of his boyhood in Illinois, his cats, and the workings of riverboats powered by steam; the demure brown-haired woman wearing a long white dress, standing in a corner, refusing to meet anyone's gaze. "She's a poet," a young girl beside me whispered, and I nodded, recognizing the heart-shaped face, the quiet, steady eyes.

In that house, on that night, I never questioned their presence, as if being in the company of people long-dead were as natural as speaking to myself. I avoided them: they had nothing to do with me. I was drawn to none of them, except, perhaps, Fitz himself.

He was as invisible as Ari. I wandered through the manse three times, pushing past bodies flushed from dancing, bright with too much drink, letting the conversation flow over me like water over a stone. Most of my colleagues spoke of Fitz himself, how he had favored them in one way or another, with a commission or, in the case of the women, with time alone. They spoke with a sigh, their eyes a bit glazed, as if the memory were more of a dream, and as they spoke, they touched their throats, or played with pearl chokers around their necks. A shudder ran through me and I wondered what I had brought Arielle into.

I found her at 3 a.m., waltzing in the empty grand ballroom with Fitz. He wore an ice cream suit, perfectly tailored, his hair combed back, and she wore a white gown that rippled around her like her hair. She gazed at him like a lover, her lips parted and moist, her body pressed against his, and as they whirled to the imaginary music, I caught glimpses of his face, his brows brought together in concentration, his eyes sparkling and moist. He looked like a man caught in a dream from which he could not wake, a dream which had gone bad, a dream which, when he remembered it, he would term a nightmare.

Then she saw me, and her expression changed. "Nick," she said. "Nick Carraway." And she laughed. The voice was not hers. It had more music than before, but beneath it, a rasp older women gained from too many cigarettes, too much drink. "He will never leave us alone, Scott."

Fitz looked at me. If anything, he appeared paler than he had before. The sparkle in his eyes was not tears, but the hard glare of a man who could not cry. "Thanks for all your help, old man," he said, and with that I knew I had been dismissed.

CHAPTER V

About a week before, an ambitious young reporter appeared on Fitz's doorstep as one of the parties began. He managed to find Fitz at the edge of the pool and asked him if he had anything to say.

"About what?" Fitz asked.

"About anything."

It transpired after a few minutes that the young man had heard Fitz's name around the office in a connection he wouldn't or couldn't reveal and, it being his day off, had hurried out to Connecticut "to see."

It was a random shot and yet the reporter's instinct had been right. Fitz's reputation, as spread by the people who saw him, the people who came to his gatherings, had that summer fallen just short of news. Stories of his mysterious past persisted, and yet none came close to the truth.

You see, he did not die of a heart attack in 1940. Instead he fell in, as he later said, with the ghouls of the Hollywood crowd. Obsessed with immortality, glamour and youth, they convinced him to meet a friend, a person whose name remains forever elusive. He succumbed to the temptation, as he had so often before, and discovered, only after he had changed, that in giving up life he had given up living and that the needs which drove his fiction disappeared with his need for food and strong drink.

He watched his daughter from afar and occasionally brought others into the fold, as the loneliness ate at him. He began throwing large parties and in them found sustenance, and others like him who had managed to move from human fame into a sort of shadowed, mythical existence. But the loneliness did not abate, and over time he learned that he had only one more chance, another opportunity to make things right. And so he monitored the baby wards in the South, allowing his own brush with the supernatural to let him see when her soul returned. For his love affair with her was more haunting and tragic than those he wrote about, and he hoped, with his new understanding, that he could make amends.

Some of this I learned, and some of this he told me. I put it down here as a way of noting that the rumors about him weren't even close to the truth, that the truth is, in fact, as strange as fiction, and I would not believe it if I had not seen it with my own eyes. What he did tell me, he said at a time of great confusion, and I might not have believed him, even then, if later that year, I hadn't found the books, the novels, the biographies, that somehow even with my literary education, I had managed to overlook.

That night, I did not sleep. The phone rang three times, and all three times, the machine picked up. Tom's coarse accent echoed in the darkness of my bedroom, demanding to know why Ari had not returned home. Finally I slipped on a faded pair of jeans and loafers, and padded up the hill to see if I could convince her to leave before Tom created trouble.

Only the light in the ballroom remained on, casting a thin glow across the yard. The cars were gone as were their occupants. Discarded cigarette butts, broken champagne glasses, and one woman's shoe with the heel missing were the only evidence of the gaiety that had marked the evening. Inside, I heard Ari sobbing hysterically, and as I walked up the steps, a hand pushed against my chest.

I hadn't seen him in the dark. He had been sitting on the steps, staring at the detritus in the driveway, an unlit cigarette in his hands. "You can't help her," he said, and in his voice, I heard the weariness of a man whose dreams were lost.

Still, I pushed past him and went inside. Ari sat on the floor, her bare feet splayed in front of her, her dress still the white of pure snow. When she saw me, the crying stopped. "Nicky," she said in that raspy, not-her voice, and then the laughter started, as uncontrolled as the crying. I went to her, put my arm around her shoulder and tried to lift her up. She shook her head and pulled out of my grasp. For a moment, the horrible laughter stopped and she gazed up at me, her eyes as clear as the sky on a summer morning. "You don't understand, do you?" she asked. "When I'm here, this is where I belong."

Then the laughter began again, a harsh, almost childish sound too close to tears. Fitz glided past me, still wearing the white suit he had worn earlier. He picked her up and shushed her, and she buried her face against his shoulder as if he gave her strength.

Her thin, fragile neck was clear and unmarked. God help me, I checked. But he had not touched her, at least in that way.

He carried her to the plush sofa pushed back to the wall beneath the windows. Then he pushed the hair off her face, wiped the tears from her cheeks, and whispered to her, hauntingly: *sleep*. Her eyes closed and her breathing evened, and once again she was the Arielle I had always known, pink-cheeked and delicate.

He looked at me, and said, "This is why Daisy had to leave Gatsby, because he was wrong for her. The better part of me knew that being with me shattered her spirit. But we are not Daisy and Gatsby, and I could not let her go. You knew that, didn't you, old man? That I could not let her go?"

But I didn't know, and I didn't understand until much later. So I remained quiet. Wisely, as it turned out.

"Ah, Nick," he said, his fingers brushing her brow. "Your arrival surprised me. I never thought—I never realized—how the characters live on, even when the story's over. I could believe in my own transformation but not your existence. And I never understood the past, so here I am repeating it."

He smiled then, a self-deprecating smile that made all his words seem like the foolish ravings of a man who had had little sleep. And yet he continued, telling me some of the things of which I have already wrote, and others, which I shall never commit to the page.

"Go home, old sport," he finally said. "Everything will look different in the light of day."

I must have glanced at Arielle with concern, for he cupped her cheek possessively. "Don't worry," he said. "I'll take good care of her."

Something in the throb of his voice made me trust him, made me turn on my heel even though I knew it was wrong, and leave him there with her. Some warble, some imperative moved me, as if he were the creator and I the created. I wandered down the hill in the dark, and didn't return until the light of day.

CHAPTER VI

I had slept maybe twenty minutes when I woke to the sound of tires peeling on the road outside my house. An engine raced, powering a fast-moving car up the hill. As I sat up, brakes squealed and a voice raised in a shout that echoed down the valley. The shouts continued until they ended abruptly—mid-sentence—followed by a moment of silence and a woman's high-pitched scream.

It was still dark, although the darkness had that gray edge that meant dawn wasn't far away. I picked up the phone and called the police which, in my compulsion-fogged mind, felt like an act of defiance. Then I rose from my bed a second time, dressed, and ran out of the house.

I didn't think to take the car until I was halfway up the path. By then to run back and get it would have taken twice as long as continuing. The sun rose, casting orange and gold tendrils across the sky. The silence in Fitz's house unnerved me and I was shaking by the time I reached the driveway.

I had never seen the car before—a light gray sedan that lacked pretension—but the Wisconsin vanity plate made its ownership clear. It had parked on the shattered glasses. A woman's black glove lay beneath one of the tires. In the early morning glow, Fitz's manse seemed ancient and old: the lawn filled with bottles and cans from the night before; the shutters closed and unpainted; the steps cracked and littered with ashes and gum. The door stood open and I slipped inside, careful to touch nothing.

A great gout of blood rose in an arch along one wall and dripped to the tile below. Drops led me to the open French doors. Through them, I saw the pool.

Tiny waves still rippled the water. The laden air mattress moved irregularly along the surface, the man's dark suit already telling me this was not whom I had expected. His eyes were open and appeared to frown in confusion, his skin chalk-white, and his neck a gaping hole that had been licked clean of blood.

Of Ari and Fitz we never found a trace. A man who had lived on the fringes as long as he had known how to disappear. I had half hoped for an acknowledgment—a postcard, a fax, a phone message—something that recognized the dilemma he had put me in. But, as he said, an author never realizes that the characters live beyond the story, and I suspect he never gave me a second thought.

Although I thought of him as I read the articles, the biographies, the essays and dissertations based on his life—his true life. I saved his novels for last and his most famous for last of all. And in it, I heard my grandfather's voice, and understood why he never spoke of his life before he returned from the East all those years ago. For that life had not been his but a fiction created by a man my grandfather had never met. My grandfather's life began in 1925 and he lived it fully until the day he died.

I sold the house at the bottom of the hill, and moved back to the Middle West. I found that I prefer the land harsh and the winds of reality cold against my face. It reminds me that I am alive. And, although I bear my grandfather's name in a family where that name has a certain mystique, that mystique does not belong to me. Nor must I hold it hallowed against my breast. The current my grandfather saw drawing him into the past pushes me toward the future, and I shall follow it with an understanding of what has come before.

For, although we are all created by someone, that someone does not own us. We pick our own paths. To do anything else condemns us to a glittering world of all-night parties hosted by Fitz and his friends, the beautiful and the damned.

PINECONES

by David Wellington

David Wellington is the author of the zombie novels *Monster Island, Monster Nation,* and *Monster Planet,* and the vampire novels *13 Bullets, 99 Coffins, Vampire Zero,* and *23 Hours.* A werewolf novel, *Frostbite,* is due out in October.

Wellington says that for him, vampires have always been the ultimate predator. "We have no predators in our human world anymore—the only people who are ever attacked by bears or tigers are people who are doing stupid things to start with," he said. "But for a lot of human history we were prey animals. It's why we got so smart and so adaptable as a species, to survive in a hostile world. The vampire is the metaphor for what that must have been like, when there was something out there in the dark, stronger, faster, and far more deadly than you were. Something that only wanted to destroy you. So many modern vampire writers seem to miss this point, that vampire are supposed to be a threat, an enemy."

"Pinecones" is the story of the first American vampire—at the very beginning, at the Roanoke Colony, before Jamestown, before the Puritans, before the colonists even thought of themselves as Americans.

When I took my son Isaac away from the colony on Roanoke Island it was fear that drove me, & I freely admit it. I wished to save his life & my own. That is all.

In the year of our lord 1587 we came to this haunted place thinking God & Walter Raleigh would follow where good Christians first tread. We did not think to stop at Roanoke, but put in only to bring rescue & succor to the fifteen lonely men Richard Grenville had left there. We expected to find cheery faces, bright with the first white company they'd had in many a month. Instead we found the fortress of Roanoke abandoned. The men were gone, slaughtered by Americans surely, & only the bones of one man remaining, & those brining in a barrel as if to preserve them for a proper burial. This we provided & then returned to our ships. We would for the mainland of Virginia well to the south, where good land had been sighted, & there to become planters & farmers & wealthy gentlemen all.

Yet it was that the Navigator of our little fleet, one Simon Fernandez, refused to sail one league farther, for he must make for England at once or risk the storm season in the midst of the Ocean. Our entreaties & offers of shares in the Corporation were rebuffed & without ships we must make our colony on Roanoke, or swim for home.

All was well at first & our little community was blessed with a child, Virginia Dare, the first English child born in all the New World. It was only afterward the killing began, when September was shedding her radiant bounty of leaves upon the Earth, & the nights were already drawing long.

It was George Howe who died the first, while crabbing in Albemarle Sound. We found of him his nets & his kerchief & nothing else. When his body appeared at the shore of the island, returned to us by Leviathan, it was pale & bloodless but we thought nothing of it. Americans had butchered him, we believed, or else he had drowned.

When Patience Goode was found below an oak tree on Hatterask, her favor as pale & drawn as a good wax candle, there were murmurs. Governor White spoke with each man alone & when he came to me he asked if I'd grown jealous & wroth, for my wife was taken on the voyage by a Fever, & I was known to be lonesome. I spat at his feet & told him I was an Englishman, & no killer of women, & he said he believed me. The very next morning little Benjamin Holcombe was found in his bed, his neck torn & in some places broken, & his blood drained.

It was then we begged John White to return home, & fetch aid for our defense, a Company of soldiers to protect us from the Americans. His face grew sharp & he repeated the warnings of the blackguard Fernandez, that the storm season was upon us. Yet he went, for we were fearful, & in truth we knew it was too late already. Some claimed they saw signs of a wreck when the tide came in that very day, boards & sailcloth floating on the oily tide. For myself I saw nothing, & wished our Governor God's Speed.

The next day Robbie Caithness, the Scotch carpenter who had signed on with the Corporation only after we were well asea, knocked on my door as if he were pounding to get into Heaven on the Day of Judgment. His face was pale as death when I answered & in troth he lived but moments longer. His clothing was bloody but his skin was white as a new made shirt. "Ye bownes onlie we fownd," he said to me, before God took him.

The bones in the barrel, he meant, & I knew it. The next day I took Isaac, my son, & I told him we would leave the Colony & make a new establishment of our own elsewhere.

"Whut doth ye wright thir, son?" I asked when I found Isaac carving on a tree, one hour later only. I had been gathering up my nets & my gun, & as much food as we two could carry. I had set Issac to choosing our clothes & finding a tarpalling we might make into make-shift shelter during our journey. Instead I found him playing at wood-carving: CRO, he carved. He had made the letters tall & deep, so all could see them. I stopped him at once but it was his second effort, for on a post of the fort already he had written it out in full, our destination: CROATOAN. For such was the name of the Island where I thought to take my refuge. I clouted him on the ear but could not explain why. He begged of me why we should go alone, & why I wished none other of the Colony to follow, & I could tell him nothing.

We took a short boat out in the mists of day's first dawning, & paddled softly across the Sound, & walked inland, through the trees, all that day. There were Americans about, I was sure of it, yet I feared them less than the bones of a dead man set to brine in an oaken barrel.

Of the Colony at Roanoke, & what my friends & partners did after, I can not add more.

It was a fortnight afore we found good water & a place to make a home. We had been unassailed & for once I rested easy, thinking the Lord had provided. We made of our tarpalling a lean-to, a canvas roof under which to sleep, & Isaac built a good fire, for he was a fine boy & clever, if only ten years old. We ate a rabbit that I shot & prepared ourselves to sleep, & rise in the morning, & begin to construct a house fitting for two such gentlemen of Virginia as we.

I sent Isaac into the tent to say his prayers & lay himself down, while I poured out water on the fire & watched it steam. It hissed & spat & a half-burnt log cracked with a loud report, as of a gun firing, & I laughed so that Isaac would hear me & be not afraid.

It was then in the darkness between the trees, which were not well lit by the dying fire, that I was sure I spied some movement.

"Speeke up, that I shuld heere ye praye, lad," I called, thinking it was some simple animal, & would be frightened by man's speech.

"Our father whiche art in heuen, halowed be thy name," Isaac said, raising his voice to me & to the Father of us all. The motion in the woods stopped at once, & I was eased. It were some dumb animal surely, that was driven off by Christian prayers. "Let thy kingdome cum unto us. Thy wyll be fulfylled as well in erthe, as it is in heuen," Isaac said, & I thought to calm him, for he sounded afeared. Yet even as I turned to say somewhat, I saw red eyes, two of them, no more than one dozen yards from me, betwixt the trees. I turned to ice, & sat stock still, & did not move. The eyes blinked, lazily. Was it a wolf? Was it a bear, one of those titans of the forest that dwarf our English breed? The eyes were of a height above the ground that I thought it was no wolf.

"& lede vs nat in to temtacyon. But delyuer vs from euyll. So be it." As the words stopped & Isaac fell silent I felt a cold draught flood through the clearing, as if winter had come on at once.

The red eyes took one step closer to me.

I sought for something, some weapon, & for a missile I found pine cones only, which lay all about in good supply. I thurst forward my arm & cast the pine cone at the eyes. They disappeared at once. Yet in a moment I saw them again, this time a step to my right.

I grasped another pine cone, & threw it with all my strength, directly at the eyes. They blinked but this time they did not move. They took a step closer, in fact.

I slung one last missile & saw it fly through the dark air, & kept my eyes upon it. & thus I saw when a hand the color of bleached linen caught the cone in mid-flight. Caught it, & threw it back.

"Isaac," I shouted, "Isaac, sonne, saye ye praier againe," but already, I knew it was too late for us.

DO NOT HASTEN TO BID ME ADIEU

by Norman Partridge

Norman Partridge is a three-time Stoker Award-winner, and author of the novels *Saguaro Riptide, The Ten Ounce Siesta, Slippin' into Darkness, Wildest Dreams,* and *Dark Harvest,* which was named one of the 100 Best Books of 2006 by *Publishers Weekly.* Partridge's short fiction has been collected in three volumes: *Mr. Fox and Other Feral Tales, Bad Intentions,* and *The Man with the Barbed-Wire Fists.* A new collection is due out in October called *Lesser Demons,* which features an original vampire novella called "The Iron Dead."

This story, which first appeared in the landmark vampire anthology *Love in Vein,* riffs off Bram Stoker's *Dracula,* telling the story of Quincey Morris, the American cowboy who, along with Jonathan Harker, kills the count at the climax of the novel. "My version of the tale is different than Stoker's, and it involves Morris's Texas homecoming after the events of *Dracula,*" Partridge said. "It's about demons old and new, on both sides of the pond."

ONE

He was done up all mysterious-like—black bandana covering half his face, black duster, black boots and hat. Traveling incognito, just like that coachman who picked up Harker at the Borgo Pass.

Yeah. As a red man might figure it, that was many moons ago… at the beginning of the story. Stoker's story, anyway. But that tale of mannered woe and stiff-upper-lip bravado was as crazy as the lies Texans told about Crockett and his Alamo bunch. Harker didn't exist. Leastways, the man in black had never met him.

Nobody argued sweet-told lies, though. Nobody in England, anyhow. Especially with Stoker tying things up so neat and proper, and the count gone to dust and dirt and all.

A grin wrinkled the masked man's face as he remembered the vampire crumbling to nothing finger-snap quick, like the remnants of a cow-flop campfire worried by an unbridled prairie wind. Son of a bitch must have been *mucho* old. Count Dracula had departed this vale of tears, gone off to suckle the devil's own tit…though the man in black doubted that Dracula's scientific turn of mind would allow him to believe in Old Scratch.

You could slice it fine or thick—ultimately, the fate of Count Dracula didn't make no never mind. The man in black was one hell of a long way from Whitby, and his dealings with the count seemed about as unreal as Stoker's scribblings. Leastways, that business was behind him. This was to be *his* story. And he was just about to slap the ribbons to it.

Slap the ribbons he did, and the horses picked up the pace. The wagon bucked over ruts, creaking like an arthritic dinosaur. Big black box jostling in the back. Tired horses sweating steam up front. West Texas sky a quilt for the night, patched blood red and bruise purple and shot through with blue-pink streaks, same color as the meat that lines a woman's heart.

And black. Thick black squares in that quilt, too. More coming every second. Awful soon, there'd be nothing but those black squares and a round white moon.

Not yet, though. The man could still see the faint outline of a town on the horizon. There was Morrisville, up ahead, waiting in the red and purple and blue-pink shadows.

He wondered what she'd make of Morrisville. It was about as far from the stone manors of Whitby as one could possibly get. No vine-covered mysteries here. No cool salt breezes whispering from the green sea, blanketing emerald lawns, traveling lush garden paths. Not much of anything green at all. No crumbling Carfax estate, either. And no swirling fog to mask the night—everything right out in the open, just as plain as the nose on your face. A West Texas shitsplat. Cattle business, mostly. A match-stick kind of town. Wooden buildings—wind-dried, sun-bleached—that weren't much more than tinder dreading the match.

The people who lived there were the same way.

But it wasn't the town that made this place. He'd told her that. It was that big blanket of a sky, an eternal wave threatening to break over the dead dry husk of the prairie, fading darker with each turn of the wagon wheels—cresting, cresting—ready to smother the earth like a hungry thing.

Not a bigger, blacker night anywhere on the planet. When that nightwave broke, as it did all too rarely—wide and mean and full up with mad lightning and thunder—it was something to see.

He'd promised her that. He'd promised to show her the heart of a wild Texas night, the way she'd shown him the shadows of Whitby.

Not that he always kept his promises. But this one was a promise to himself as much as it was a promise to her.

He'd hidden from it for a while. Sure. In the wake of all that horror, he'd run. But finally he'd returned to Whitby, and to her. He'd returned to keep his promise.

And now he was coming home.

"Not another place like it anywhere, Miss Lucy. Damn sure not on this side of the pond, anyhow."

She didn't fake a blush or get all offended by his language, like so many of the

English missies did, and he liked that. She played right with him, like she knew the game. Not just knew it, but thrived on it. "No," she said. "Nothing here could possibly resemble your Texas, Quincey P. Morris. Because no one here resembles you."

She took him by the lapels and kissed him like she was so hungry for it, like she couldn't wait another moment, and then he had her in his arms and they were moving together, off the terrace, away from the house and the party and the dry rattle of polite conversation. He was pulling her and she was pushing him and together they were going back, back into the shadows of Whitby, deep into the garden where fog settled like velvet and the air carried what for him would always be the green scent of England.

And then they were alone. The party sounds were a world away. But those sounds were nothing worth hearing—they were dead sounds compared to the music secret lovers could make. Matched with the rustle of her skirts, and the whisper of his fingers on her tender thighs, and the sweet duet of hungry lips, the sounds locked up in the big stone house were as sad and empty as the cries of the damned souls in Dr. Seward's loony bin, and he drew her away from them, and she pushed him away from them, and together they entered another world where strange shadows met, cloaking them like fringed buckskin, like gathered satin.

Buckskin and satin. It wasn't what you'd call a likely match. They'd been dancing around it for months. But now the dancing was over.

"God, I want you," he said.

She didn't say anything. There was really nothing more to say. She gave. She took. And he did the same.

He reined in the horses just short of town. Everything was black but that one circle of white hanging high in the sky.

He stepped down from the driver's box and stretched. He drew the night air deep into his lungs. The air was dry and dusty, and there wasn't anything in it that was pleasant.

He was tired. He lay down on top of the big black box in the back of the wagon and thought of her. His fingers traveled wood warped in the leaky cargo hold of a British ship. Splinters fought his callused hands, lost the battle. But he lost the war, because the dissonant rasp of rough fingers on warped wood was nothing like the music the same rough fingers could make when exploring a young woman's thighs.

He didn't give up easy, though. He searched for the memory of the green scent of England, and the music he'd made there, and shadows of satin and buckskin. He searched for the perfume of her hair, and her skin. The ready, eager perfume of her sex.

His hands traveled the wood. Scurrying like scorpions. Damn things just wouldn't give up, and he couldn't help laughing

Raindrops beaded on the box. The nightwave was breaking.

No. Not raindrops at all. Only his tears.

The sky was empty. No clouds. No rain.

No lightning.

But there was lightning in his eyes.

TWO

The morning sunlight couldn't penetrate the filthy jailhouse window. That didn't bother the man in black. He had grown to appreciate the darkness.

Sheriff Josh Muller scratched his head. "This is the damnedest thing, Quincey. You got to admit that that Stoker fella made it pretty plain in his book."

Quincey smiled. "You believe the lies that Buntline wrote about Buffalo Bill, too?"

"Shit no, Quince. But, hell, that Stoker is a silver stickpin gentleman. I thought they was different and all—"

"I used to think that. Until I got to know a few of the bastards, that is."

"Well," the sheriff said, "that may be...but the way it was, was...we all thought that you had been killed by them Transylvanian gypsies, like you was in the book."

"I've been some places, before and since. But we never got to Transylvania. Not one of us. And I ain't even feelin' poorly."

"But in the book—"

"Just how stupid are you, Josh? You believe in vampires, too? Your bowels get loose thinkin' about Count Dracula?"

"Hell, no, of course not, but—"

"Shit, Josh, I didn't mean that like a question you were supposed to answer."

"Huh?"

Quincey sighed. "Let's toss this on the fire and watch it sizzle. It's real simple—I *ain't* dead. I'm *back*. Things are gonna be just like they used to be. We can start with this here window."

Quincey Morris shot a thumb over his shoulder. The sheriff looked up and saw how dirty the window was. He grabbed a rag from his desk. "I'll take care of it, Quince."

"You don't get it," the man in black said.

"Huh?"

Again, Quincey sighed. "I *ain't* dead. I'm *back*. Things are gonna be just like they used to be. And this *is* Morrisville, right?"

The sheriff squinted at the words painted on the window. He wasn't a particularly fast reader—he'd been four months reading the Stoker book, and that was with his son doing most of the reading out loud. On top of that, he had to read this backwards. He started in, reading right to left: O-W-E-N-S-V-I-L-L—

That was as far as he got. Quincey Morris picked up a chair and sent it flying through the glass, and then the word wasn't there anymore.

Morris stepped through the opening and started toward his wagon. He stopped in the street, which was like a river of sunlight, turned, and squinted at the sheriff. "Get that window fixed," he said. "Before I come back."

"Where are you headed?" The words were out of Josh Muller's mouth before he could stop himself, and he flinched at the grin Morris gave him in return.

"I'm goin' home," was all he said.

There in the shadows, none of it mattered, because it was only the two of them. Two creatures from different worlds, but with hearts that were the same.

He'd come one hell of a long way to find this. Searched the world over. He'd known that he'd find it, once he went looking, same as he'd known that it was something he had to go out and find if he wanted to keep on living. His gut told him, *Find it, or put a bullet in your brainpan.* But he hadn't known it would feel like this. It never had before. But this time, with this person...she filled him up like no one else. And he figured it was the same with her. "I want you."

"I think you just had me, Mr. Morris."

Her laughter tickled his neck, warm breath washing a cool patch traced by her tongue, drawn by her lips. Just a bruise, but as sure and real as a brand. He belonged to her. He knew that. But he didn't know—

The words slipped out before he could think them through. "I want you, forever."

That about said it, all right.

He felt her shiver, and then her lips found his.

"Forever is a long time," she said.

They laughed about that, embracing in the shadows.

They actually laughed.

She came running out of the big house as soon as he turned in from the road. Seeing her, he didn't feel a thing. That made him happy, because in England, in the midst of everything else, he'd thought about her a lot. He'd wondered just what kind of fuel made her belly burn, and why she wasn't more honest about it, in the way of the count. He wondered why she'd never gone ahead and torn open his jugular, the way a vampire would, because she sure as hell had torn open his heart.

Leonora ran through the blowing dust, her hair a blond tangle, and she was up on the driver's box sitting next to him before he could slow the horses—her arms around him, her lips on his cheek, her little flute of a voice all happy. "Quince! Oh, Quince! It *is* you! We thought you were dead!"

He shook his head. His eyes were on the big house. It hadn't changed. Not in the looks department, anyway. The occupants...now that was a different story.

"Miss me?" he asked, and his tone of voice was not a pleasant thing.

"I'm sorry." She said it like she'd done something silly, like maybe she'd spilled some salt at the supper table or something. "I'm glad you came back." She hugged him. "It'll be different now. We've both had a chance to grow up."

He chuckled at that one, and she got it crossed up. "Oh, Quince, we'll work it out...you'll see. We both made mistakes. But it's not too late to straighten them out." She leaned over and kissed his neck, her tongue working between her lips.

Quincey flushed with anger and embarrassment. The bitch. And with the box right there, behind them, in plain view. With him dressed head to toe in black. God, Leonora had the perceptive abilities of a blind armadillo.

He shoved her, hard. She tumbled off the driver's box. Her skirts caught on the seat, tearing as she fell. She landed in the dirt, petticoats bunched up around her waist.

She cussed him real good. But he didn't hear her at all, because suddenly he could see everything so clearly. The golden wedding band on her finger didn't mean much. Not to her it didn't, so it didn't mean anything to him. But the fist-sized bruises on her legs did.

He'd seen enough. He'd drawn a couple conclusions. Hal Owens hadn't changed. Looking at those bruises, that was for damn sure. And it was misery that filled up Leonora's belly—that had to be the answer which had eluded him for so long—and at present it seemed that she was having to make do with her own. Knowing Leonora as he did, he figured that she was probably about ready for a change of menu, and he wanted to make it real clear that he wasn't going to be the next course.

"You bastard!" she yelled. "You're finished around here! You can't just come walkin' back into town, big as you please! This ain't Morrisville, anymore, Quincey! It's Owensville! And Hal's gonna kill you! I'm his wife, dammit! And when I tell him what you did to me, he's gonna flat-out kill you!" She scooped up fistfuls of dirt, threw them at him. "You don't belong here anymore, you bastard!"

She was right about that. He didn't belong here anymore. This wasn't his world. His world was contained in a big black box. That was the only place for him anymore. Anywhere else there was only trouble.

Didn't matter where he went these days, folks were always threatening him.

Threats seemed to be his lot in life.

Take Arthur Holmwood, for instance. He was a big one for threats. The morning after the Westenra's party, he'd visited Quincey's lodgings, bringing with him Dr. Seward and a varnished box with brass hinges.

"I demand satisfaction," he'd said, opening the box and setting it on the table.

Quincey stared down at the pistols. Flintlocks. Real pioneer stuff. "Hell, Art," he said, snatching his Peacemaker from beneath his breakfast napkin (Texas habits died hard, after all), "let's you and me get real satisfied, then."

The doctor went ahead and pissed in the pot. "Look here, Morris. You're in England now. A man does things in a certain way here. A gentleman, I should say."

Quincey was sufficiently cowed to table his Peacemaker. "Maybe I am a fish out of water, like you say, Doc." He examined one of the dueling pistols. "But ain't these a little old-fashioned, even for England? I thought this kind of thing went out with powdered wigs and such."

"A concession to you." Holmwood sneered. "We understand that in your Texas, men duel in the streets quite regularly."

Quincey grinned. "That's kind of an exaggeration."

"The fact remains that you compromised Miss Lucy's honor."

"Who says?"

Seward straightened. "I myself observed the way you thrust yourself upon her last night, on the terrace. And I saw Miss Lucy leave the party in your charge."

"You get a real good look, Doc?" Quincey's eyes narrowed. "You get a right proper fly-on-a-dung-pile close-up view, or are you just telling tales out of school?"

Holmwood's hand darted out. Fisted, but he did his business with a pair of kid gloves knotted in his grip. The gloves slapped the Texan's left cheek and came back for his right, at which time Quincey Morris exploded from his chair and kneed Arthur Holmwood in the balls.

Holmwood was a tall man. He seemed to go down in sections. Doctor Seward trembled as Quincey retrieved his Peacemaker, and he didn't calm down at all when the Texan holstered the weapon.

Quincey didn't see any point to stretching things out, not when there was serious fence-mending to do at the Westenra's house. "I hope you boys will think on this real seriously," he said as he stepped over Holmwood and made for the door.

There was a Mexican kid pretending to do some work behind the big house. Quincey gave him a nickel and took him around front.

The kid wasn't happy to see the box. He crossed himself several times. Then he spit on his palms and took one end, delighted to find that the box wasn't as heavy as it looked.

They set it in the parlor. Quincey had to take a chair and catch his breath. After all that time on the ship, and then more time sitting on his butt slapping reins to a pair of sway-backs, he wasn't much good. Of course, this wasn't as tough as when he'd had to haul the box from the Westenra family tomb, all by his lonesome, but it was bad enough. By the time he remembered to thank the kid, the kid had already gone.

Nothing for it, then.

Nothing, but to do it.

The words came back to him, echoing in his head. And it wasn't the voice of some European doctor, like in Stoker's book. It was Seward's voice. *"One moment's courage, and it is done."*

He shook those words away. He was alone here. The parlor hadn't changed much since the day he'd left to tour the world. The curtains were heavy and dark, and the deep shadows seemed to brush his cheek, one moment buckskin-rough, next moment satin-smooth.

Like the shadows in the Westenra's garden. The shadows where he'd held Lucy to him. Held her so close.

No. He wouldn't think of that. Not now. He had work to do. He couldn't start thinking about how it had been, because then he'd certainly start thinking about how it might be, again...

One moment's courage, and it is done.

God, how he wanted to laugh, but he kept it inside.

His big bowie knife was in his hand. He didn't know quite how it had gotten there. He went to work on the lid of the box, first removing brass screws, then removing the hinges.

One moment's courage…

The lid crashed heavily to the floor, but he never heard it. His horror was too great for that. After all this time, the stink of garlic burned his nostrils, scorched his lungs. But that wasn't the hell of it.

The hell of it was that she had moved.

Oh, *she* hadn't moved. He knew that. He could see the stake spearing her poor breast, the breast that he had teased between his own lips. She couldn't move. Not with the stake there.

But the churning Atlantic had rocked a sailing ship, and that had moved her. And a bucking wagon had jostled over the rutted roads of Texas, and that had moved her. And now her poor head, her poor severed head with all that dark and beautiful hair, was trapped between her own sweet legs, nestled between her own tender thighs, just as his head had been.

Once. A long time ago.

Maybe, once again…

No. He wouldn't start thinking like that. He stared at her head, knowing he'd have to touch it. There was no sign of decay, no stink of corruption. But he could see the buds of garlic jammed into the open hole of her throat, the ragged gashes and severed muscles, the dangling ropes of flesh.

In his mind's eye, he saw Seward standing stiff and straight with a scalpel in his bloodstained grip.

And that bastard called himself a doctor.

There were shadows, of course, in their secret place in the Westenra garden. And he held her, as he had before. But now she never stopped shaking.

"You shouldn't have done it," she said. "Arthur is behaving like one of Seward's lunatics. You must be careful."

"You're the one has to be careful, Lucy," he said.

"No." She laughed. "Mother has disregarded the entire episode. Well, nearly so. She's convinced that I behaved quite recklessly—and this judging from one kiss on the terrace. I had to assure her that we did nothing more than tour the garden in search of a better view of the moon. I said that was the custom in Texas. I'm not certain that she accepted my story, but…" She kissed him, very quickly. "I've feigned illness for her benefit, and she believes that I am in the grip of a rare and exotic fever. Seward has convinced her of this, I think. Once I'm pronounced fit, I'm certain that she will forgive your imagined indiscretion."

"Now, Miss Lucy, I don't think that was my *imagination*," he joked.

She laughed, trembling laughter there in his arms. "Seward has consulted a specialist. A European fellow. He's said to be an expert in fevers of the blood. I'm to see him tomorrow. Hopefully that will put an end to the charade."

He wanted to say it. More than anything, he wanted to say, *Forget tomorrow. Let's leave here, tonight.* But he didn't say it, because she was trembling so.

"You English," he said. "You do love your charades."

Moonlight washed the shadows. He caught the wild look in her eye. A twin to the fearful look a colt gets just before it's broken.

He kept his silence. He *was* imagining things. He held her. It was the last time he would hold her, alive.

THREE

Quincey pushed through the double-doors of the saloon and was surprised to find it deserted except for a sleepy-eyed man who was polishing the piano.

"You the piano player?" Quincey asked.

"Sure," the fellow said.

Quincey brought out the Peacemaker. "Can you play 'Red River Valley'?"

"S-sure." The man sat down, rolled up his sleeves.

"Not here," Quincey said.

"H-huh?"

"I got a big house on the edge of town."

The man swallowed hard. "You mean Mr. Owens' place?"

"No. I mean my place."

"H-huh?"

"Anyway, you go on up there, and you wait for me." The man rose from the piano stool, both eyes on the Peacemaker, and started toward the double-doors.

"Wait a minute," Quincey said. "You're forgetting something."

"W-what?"

"Well, I don't have a piano up at the house."

"Y-you don't?"

"Nope."

"Well… Hell, mister, what do you want me to do?"

Quincey cocked the Peacemaker. "I guess you'd better start pushing."

"You mean…you want me to take the piano with me?"

Quincey nodded. "Now, I'll be home in a couple hours or so. You put the piano in the parlor, then you help yourself to a glass of whiskey. But don't linger in the parlor, hear?"

The man nodded. He seemed to catch on pretty quick. Had to be that he was a stranger in these parts.

Quincey moved on. He stopped off at Murphy's laundry, asked a few questions about garlic, received a few expansive answers detailing the amazing restorative power of Mrs. Murphy's soap, after which he set a gunnysack on the counter. He set it down real gentle-like, and the rough material settled over something kind of round, and, seeing this, Mr. Murphy excused himself and made a beeline for the saloon.

Next Quincey stopped off at the church with a bottle of whiskey for the preacher. They chatted a bit, and Quincey had a snort before moving on, just to be sociable.

He had just stepped into the home of Mrs. Danvers, the best seamstress in town, when he glanced through the window and spotted Hal Owens coming his way, two men in tow, one of them being the sheriff.

Things were never quite so plain in England. Oh, they were just as dangerous, that was for sure. But, with the exception of lunatics like Arthur Holmwood, the upper-crust of Whitby cloaked their confrontational behavior in a veil of politeness.

Three nights running, Quincey stood alone in the garden, just waiting. Finally, he went to Lucy's mother in the light of day, hat literally in hand. He inquired as to Lucy's health. Mrs. Westenra said that Lucy was convalescing. Three similar visits, and his testiness began to show through.

So did Mrs. Westenra's. She blamed Quincey for her daughter's poor health. He wanted to tell her that the whole thing was melodrama, and for her benefit, too, but he held off.

And that was when the old woman slipped up. Or maybe she didn't, because her voice was as sharp as his bowie, and it was plain that she intended to do damage with it. "Lucy's condition is quite serious," she said. "Her behavior of late, which Dr. Seward has described in no small detail… Well, I mean to tell you that Lucy has shown little consideration for her family or her station, and there is no doubt that she is quite ill. We have placed her in hospital, under the care of Dr. Seward and his associates."

Mrs. Westenra had torn away the veil. He would not keep silent now. He made it as plain as plain could be. "You want to break her. You want to pocket her, heart and soul."

She seemed to consider her answer very carefully. Finally, she said, "We only do what we must."

"Nobody wants you here," Owens said.

Quincey grinned. Funny that Owens should say that. Those were the same words that had spilled from Seward's lips when Quincey confronted him at the asylum.

Of course, that had happened an ocean away, and Dr. Seward hadn't had a gun. But he'd had a needle, and that had done the job for him right proper.

Quincey stared down at Mrs. Danvers' sewing table. There were needles here, too. Sharp ones, little slivers of metal. But these needles weren't attached to syringes. They weren't like Dr. Seward's needles at all.

Something pressed against Quincey's stomach. He blinked several times, but he couldn't decide who was standing in front of him. Owens, or Seward, or…

Someone said, "Get out of town, or I'll make you wish you *was* dead." There was a sharp click. The pressure on Quincey's belly increased, and a heavy hand dropped onto his shoulder.

The hand of Count Dracula. A European nobleman and scientist. Stoker had split him into two characters—a kindly doctor and a hellborn monster. But Quincey knew that the truth was somewhere in between.

"Start movin', Quince. Otherwise, I'll spill your innards all over the floor."

The count had only held him. He didn't make idle threats. He didn't use his teeth. He didn't spill a single drop of Quincey's blood. He let Seward do all the work, jabbing Quincey's arm with the needle, day after day, week after week.

That wasn't how the count handled Lucy, though. He had a special way with Dr. Seward's most combative patient, a method that brought real results. He emptied her bit by bit, draining her blood, and with it the strength that so disturbed Lucy's mother and the independent spirit that so troubled unsuccessful suitors such as Seward and Holmwood. The blind fools had been so happy at first, until they realized that they'd been suckered by another outsider, a Transylvanian bastard with good manners who was much worse than anything that had ever come out of Texas.

They'd come to him, of course. The stranger with the wild gleam in his eyes. Told him the whole awful tale. Cut him out of the straitjacket with his own bowie, placed the Peacemaker in one hand. A silver crucifix and an iron stake jammed in a cricketing bag filled the other.

"You make your play, Quince," Owens said. "I'm not goin' to give you forever."

"Forever is a long time."

"You ain't listenin' to me, Quince."

"A moment's courage, and it is done."

Count Dracula, waiting for him in the ruins of the chapel at Carfax. His fangs gleaming in the dark…fangs that could take everything…

The pistol bucked against Quincey's belly. The slug ripped straight through him, shattered the window behind. Blood spilled out of him, running down his leg. Lucy's blood on the count's lips, spilling from her neck as he took and took and took some more. Quincey could see it from the depths of Seward's hell, he could see the garden and the shadows and their love flowing in Lucy's blood. Her strength, her dreams, her spirit…

"This is my town," Owens said, his hand still heavy on Quincey's shoulder. "I took it, and I mean to keep it."

Quincey opened his mouth. A gout of blood bubbled over his lips. He couldn't find words. Only blood, rushing away, running down his leg, spilling over his lips. It seemed his blood was everywhere, rushing wild, like once-still waters escaping the rubble of a collapsed dam.

He sagged against Owens. The big man laughed.

And then the big man screamed.

Quincey's teeth were at Owens' neck. He ripped through flesh, tore muscle and artery. Blood filled his mouth, and the Peacemaker thundered again and again in his hand, and then Owens was nothing but a leaking mess there in his arms, a husk of a man puddling red, washing away to nothing so fast, spurting red rich blood one second, then stagnant-pool dead the next.

Quincey's gun was empty. He fumbled for his bowie, arming himself against Owens' compadres.

There was no need.

Mrs. Danvers stood over them, a smoking shotgun in her hands.

Quincey released Owens' corpse. Watched it drop to the floor.

"Let me get a look at you," Mrs. Danvers said.

"There ain't no time for that," he said.

Dracula chuckled. "I can't believe it is you they sent. The American cowboy. The romantic."

Quincey studied the count's amused grin. Unnatural canines gleamed in the moonlight. In the ruined wasteland of Carfax, Dracula seemed strangely alive.

"Make your play," Quincey offered.

Icy laughter rode the shadows. "There is no need for such melodrama, Mr. Morris. I only wanted the blood. Nothing else. And I have taken that."

"That ain't what Seward says." Quincey squinted, his eyes adjusting to the darkness. "He claims you're after Miss Lucy's soul."

Again, the laughter. "I am a man of science, Mr. Morris. I accept my condition, and my biological need. Disease, and the transmission of disease, make for interesting study. I am more skeptical concerning the mythology of my kind. Fairy stories bore me. Certainly, powers exist which I cannot explain. But I cannot explain the moon and the stars, yet I know that these things exist because I see them in the night sky. It is the same with my special abilities—they exist, I use them, hence I believe in them. As for the human soul, I cannot see any evidence of such a thing. What I cannot see, I refuse to believe."

But Quincey could see. He could see Dracula, clearer every second. The narrow outline of his jaw. The eyes burning beneath his heavy brow. The long, thin line of his lips hiding jaws that could gape so wide.

"You don't want her," Quincey said. "That's what you're saying."

"I only want a full belly, Mr. Morris. That is the way of it." He stepped forward, his eyes like coals. "I only take the blood. Your kind is different. You want everything. The flesh, the heart, the...soul, which of course has a certain tangibility fueled by *your* belief. You take it all. In comparison, I demand very little—"

"We take. But we give, too."

"That is what your kind would have me believe. I have seen little evidence that this is the truth." Red eyes swam in the darkness. "Think about it, Mr. Morris. They have sent you here to kill me. They have told you how evil I am. But who are they—these men who brought me to your Miss Lucy? What do they want?" He did not blink; he only advanced. "Think on it, Mr. Morris. Examine the needs of these men, Seward and Holmwood. Look into your own heart. Examine your needs."

And now Quincey smiled. "Maybe I ain't as smart as you, Count." He stepped forward. "Maybe you could take a look for me...let me know just what you see."

Their eyes met.

The vampire stumbled backward. He had looked into Quincey Morris' eyes. Seen a pair of empty green wells. Bottomless green pits. Something was alive there, undying, something that had known pain and hurt, and, very briefly, ecstasy.

Very suddenly, the vampire realized that he had never known real hunger at all.

The vampire tried to steady himself, but his voice trembled. "What I can see...I believe."

Quincey Morris did not blink.

He took the stake from Seward's bag.

"I want you to know that this ain't something I take lightly," he said.

FOUR

He'd drawn a sash around his belly, but it hadn't done much good. His jeans were stiff with blood, and his left boot seemed to be swimming with the stuff. That was his guess, anyway—there wasn't much more than a tingle of feeling in his left foot, and he wasn't going to stoop low and investigate.

Seeing himself in the mirror was bad enough. His face was so white. Almost like the count's.

Almost like her face, in death.

Mrs. Danvers stepped away from the coffin, tucking a pair of scissors into a carpet bag. "I did the best I could," she said.

"I'm much obliged, ma'am." Quincey leaned against the lip of the box, numb fingers brushing the yellow ribbon that circled Lucy's neck.

"You can't see them stitches at all," the whiskey-breathed preacher said, and the seamstress cut him off with a glance.

"You did a fine job, Mrs. Danvers." Quincey tried to smile. "You can go on home now."

"If you don't mind, I think I'd like to stay."

"That'll be fine," Quincey said.

He turned to the preacher, but he didn't look at him. Instead, he stared through the parlor window. Outside, the sky was going to blood red and bruise purple.

He reached into the box. His fingers were cold, clumsy. Lucy's delicate hand almost seemed warm by comparison.

Quincey nodded at the preacher. "Let's get on with it."

The preacher started in. Quincey had heard the words many times. He'd seen people stand up to them, and he'd seen people totter under their weight, and he'd seen plenty who didn't care a damn for them at all.

But this time it was him hearing those words. Him answering them. And when the preacher got to the part about taking...*do you take this woman*...Quincey said, "Right now I just want to give."

That's what the count couldn't understand, him with all the emotion of a tick. Seward and Holmwood, even Lucy's mother, they weren't much better. But Quincey understood. Now more than ever. He held tight to Lucy's hand.

"If you've a mind to, you can go ahead and kiss her now," the preacher said.

Quincey bent low. His lips brushed hers, ever so gently. He caught a faint whiff of Mrs. Murphy's soap, no trace of garlic at all.

With some effort, he straightened. It seemed some time had passed, because the preacher was gone, and the evening sky was veined with blue-pink streaks.

The piano player just sat there, his eyes closed tight, his hands fisted in his lap.

"You can play it now," Quincey said, and the man got right to it, fingers light and shaky on the keys, voice no more than a whisper:

"Come and sit by my side if you love me,
Do not hasten to bid me adieu,
But remember the Red River Valley,
And the cowboy who loved you so true."

Quincey listened to the words, holding Lucy's hand, watching the night. The sky was going black now, blacker every second. There was no blood left in it at all.

Just like you, you damn fool, he thought.

He pulled his bowie from its sheath. Seward's words rang in his ears: *"One moment's courage, and it is done."*

But Seward hadn't been talking to Quincey when he'd said those words. Those words were for Holmwood. And Quincey had heard them, but he'd been about ten steps short of doing something about them. If he hadn't taken the time to discuss philosophy with Count Dracula, that might have been different. As it was, Holmwood had had plenty of time to use the stake, while Seward had done his business with a scalpel.

For too many moments, Quincey had watched them, too stunned to move. But when he did move, there was no stopping him.

He used the bowie, and he left Whitby that night.

He ran out. He wasn't proud of that. And all the time he was running, he'd thought, *So much blood, all spilled for no good reason. Dracula, with the needs of a tick. Holmwood and Seward, who wanted to be masters or nothing at all.*

He ran out. Sure. But he came back. Because he knew that there was more to the blood, more than just the taking.

One moment's courage...

Quincey stared down at the stake jammed through his beloved's heart, the cold shaft spearing the blue-pink muscle that had thundered at the touch of his fingers. The bowie shook in his hand. The piano man sang:

"There never could be such a longing,
In the heart of a poor cowboy's breast,
As dwells in this heart you are breaking,
While I wait in my home in the West."

Outside, the sky was black. Every square in the quilt. No moon tonight.

Thunder rumbled, rattling the windows.

Quincey put the bowie to his neck. Lightning flashed, and white spiderwebs of brightness danced on Lucy's flesh. The shadows receded for the briefest moment, then flooded the parlor once more, and Quincey was lost in them. Lost in shadows he'd brought home from Whitby.

One moment's courage...

He sliced his neck, praying that there was some red left in him. A thin line of blood welled from the wound, overflowing the spot where Lucy had branded him with eager kisses.

He sagged against the box. Pressed his neck to her lips.

He dropped the bowie. His hand closed around the stake.

One moment's courage…

He tore the wooden shaft from her heart, and waited.

Minutes passed. He closed his eyes. Buried his face in her dark hair. His hands were scorpions, scurrying everywhere, dancing to the music of her tender thighs.

Her breast did not rise, did not fall. She did not breathe.

She would never breathe again.

But her lips parted. Her fangs gleamed. And she drank.

Together, they welcomed the night.

FOXTROT AT HIGH NOON

by Sergei Lukyanenko

Translated from Russian by Michael M. Naydan and Slava I. Yastremski

Russian writer Sergei Lukyanenko is the author of the international bestselling vampire novels *Night Watch* and *Day Watch*, which were adapted to film by Russian filmmaker Timur Bekmambetov. The third book in the series, *Twilight Watch*, is currently in production. The fourth and final book in the series, *Last Watch*, was published in January. He is among the most popular Russian science fiction/fantasy writers, and is the author of several other novels as well, but to date only the Watch books have been translated into English.

Lukyanenko's short work has appeared in English only once so far, in James and Kathryn Morrow's *SFWA European Hall of Fame* anthology. That story, like this one, was translated by Michael M. Naydan and Slava I. Yastremski.

This story appears here for the first time. It tells the story of a lone stranger, in a post-apocalyptic future, coming to a town overrun by lawlessness.

The town was lost between the mountains and the sea, like a man between the earth and heaven.

The train moved along the shore all night, and the rattle of the wheels merged with the sound of the surf in a single unending melody. In the freight car, Denis was barely able to sleep. He lay on boards that smelled of hay and horse dung, watching the infrequent flashes of stars through the holes in the slotted roof of the car. There were no horses here—the livestock pens were empty—but a little bit of hay remained, and he raked it under his head. Before going to sleep, Denis had undressed, and now wore only his undershorts. Boots stood beside his feet; jeans, a plaid shirt, and a velvet jacket hung off the side rail of the livestock pen. His left hand rested atop a heavy revolver in a frayed holster.

The wheels of the train knocked out their song. Denis began to stir, and whispered:

"The train is rushing—what a beaut,
The wheels are knocking—tra ta toot toot!"

—then dozed off for a short time.

Denis awoke as the car was gripped by the morning chill. He stood, grabbed his weapon, and walked from the end of the car to the caboose platform. In one of the pens, a vagrant lay still and unmoving in the shadows. Denis averted his eyes.

Daybreak. The door to the train car was open; he had entered the train through it last night. Outside, on the platform, he unhurriedly relieved himself, then sat down, hanging his legs off the side of the car, an endless ladder spreading out beneath him, the rails like twin steel bow strings and the rungs of the cross-ties dark from creosote. If you lay your head back it seemed as if the train were gliding down from the sky itself.

"The wheels are knocking tra-ta-toot," Denis repeated.

A quarter of an hour later, when the train had stopped in a small town, Denis stood in the open doors of the freight car finishing a cigarette. The train pulled onto track number one; on track two, a long freight train with tanks and storage containers began to sing and toot and started off in the opposite direction. Denis jumped down without waiting for the train to come to a full stop and teetered, but kept his balance.

"It's a one-minute stop," said the stationmaster, who was standing by the tracks with a red flag in his hand. He looked suspiciously at the empty car. He was alone on the platform, his uniform—like his face—old and crumpled, his eyes dull and dead.

"I've already arrived," Denis said.

A gleam of curiosity appeared in the eyes of the stationmaster. He looked over Denis from head to toe, then asked: "Got a pistol?"

"Revolver."

"Licensed?"

"No."

The locomotive whistled and started to move. The stationmaster rolled up the signal flag and slid it into a tube. He glanced at the departing train.

"What about your traveling companion?" the stationmaster said, pointing. Denis saw that the vagrant's foot was visible through the open door of the train car.

He'd asked as if by inertia, in exactly the same way that he had stepped out to meet the train, in exactly the way he had rolled up the flag. The man had observed this kind of behavior before. Too many times.

"He's going farther," Denis answered. "Is your town a big one?"

"Two hundred thirty people," the stationmaster said. "And there's an infant, too, the daughter of a schoolteacher. But she was born sickly." He shrugged his shoulders. "I don't know whether she counts."

The knocking of the wheels grew silent in the distance and only the whisper of the sea remained. "My name is Denis."

"Pyotr," the stationmaster said. He extended his hand—mechanically, lifeless. Denis pressed his palm—firmly, steadily. "Oh, you're completely frozen," Pyotr said, some emotion, at least, appearing in his voice. "Let's go inside. I'll make you some tea."

Denis nodded and followed him into the station—a small, one-story building made of red brick, the roof covered in tile.

They drank tea in the cold, dilapidated office. In the corner, old red banners with golden letters gathered dust—awards for victories in some kind of Socialist labor competitions from the previous century. On the desk was a black plastic telephone, out-of-place, incongruent—a relic of a time before everything turned to shit.

"Does that thing work?" Denis asked, and gulped down the hot tea.

"You've got to be joking." Pyotr didn't even smile. "But we're supposed to have one. Nobody rescinded the rule."

"Is there electricity in the town?"

"There's a generator in the hospital. They've been bringing in a little bit of oil," the stationmaster said cautiously. "The fishermen have a wind turbine. An old one."

"How do you get by?"

"Like everybody else," Pyotr said, with no trace of resentment. "We do whatever we need to. We poke around in the soil, but there's very little good soil around here. We catch fish. During the day the freight train will come by; we will send ten barrels of fish to the city."

"Salted?"

"Fresh. We interlay them with wet grass—seaweed. They'll last a day."

"What else?"

The stationmaster hemmed and hawed. "Well, in general, nothing. There's no work. There was no point for you to get off the train here."

"I always find work," Denis said. He poured himself more tea from a fat nickel teapot. It was the only clean and well-conditioned object in the office. And the tea brew was the real thing, as though from a past life.

"Unfortunately, there's no sugar left," Pyotr said. "There's never enough sugar."

"I don't drink it sweet."

The stationmaster raised his tired and pleading eyes: "You should go. The freight train will set off in the afternoon—I'll put you on it. I can talk to the engineer, he'll let you in the cabin, you can go as—"

He failed to explain the word "as"—as right then there was a knock at the door, and someone entered the office.

"Well, now," Pyotr whispered as he stood.

Denis finished drinking his tea, then turned around.

A young man was standing at the door—thin, black-haired, with brash, lively eyes, and bright-red lips, as though they had been painted with lipstick. He was wearing a black leather coat with shining silver braid-studs and black leather pants that fit tightly over wiry legs. In his left hand, he held an automatic pistol by his side—carelessly, with boyish defiance.

"Who's he?" the young man asked.

"He's just passing through," the stationmaster said. "He got off the morning train. He was riding in the freight car; he was completely frozen. He's leaving in mid-afternoon."

The young man remained silent and bit his lip.

"Who's this?" Denis asked the stationmaster. "Some kind of pretty boy?"

Pyotr choked on his tea and shook his head.

The young man's eyes became big and round from the insult. He didn't say a thing—for which Denis mentally complimented him—but he immediately began to raise his weapon. The stationmaster dove under the desk.

The revolver in Denis's hand shot just once. A hole appeared in the young man's black leather jacket, and the air smelled tartly of gunpowder. The youth glanced at Denis—hurt, like a child forbidden to play a game—and fell heavily to the floor.

"You go," Denis said to Pyotr. "I'll clean up here."

"What have you done?" the stationmaster began, as he crawled out from under the desk. "What have you done? You should have just peacefully left in the afternoon…"

"You're not sick of living this way?"

"Everybody's living this way, it's bad for everyone now."

"No, not everyone's living *this way*," Denis said resolutely. "Go."

The stationmaster set off for the door in an arc, but the young man's boots—heavy, laced-up army boots—were lying right on the doorstep, and he was forced to step over the body.

"Is this one a newcomer, or one of yours?" Denis asked.

The stationmaster stopped, awkwardly leaning over the body. He licked his lips, took off his service cap with raspberry-colored piping and crumpled it in his hand.

"One of ours. The doctor's son."

"Where can I find him?"

"The doctor? Take this street," the stationmaster said, and flicked his hand so that it was clear right away there was only one street in the town and it goes from the station to the sea. "There's a little hospital, halfway down the street. A clinic, of course, not a hospital. We just call it that."

"You go home," Denis suggested. "Go, go. I'll clean up everything."

The hospital was very small, but even so, it was a little bigger than the train station. It was two stories tall, but on the second story, parts of broken window panes were awkwardly patched with clear plastic. Denis walked back and forth on the porch, finishing his cigarette. Finally he made up his mind, gave a short knock on the door and, without waiting for an answer, entered.

The doctor must have lived in the hospital—otherwise why would he be in his office so early? Fairly old and heavy, he was sitting at his desk. A stethoscope, the symbol of his profession, was in the corner. He was eating a watermelon.

"Have a seat," the doctor said, pushing a plate at Denis. "Eat. We have sandy soil, the watermelons are really good. They help your kidneys."

"I'm not worried about my kidneys," Denis said. "Your son—"

"I know," the doctor didn't raise his eyes to look at him. "Pyotr stopped by earlier."

Denis remained silent.

"What do you expect?" The doctor asked. "I can't say 'thank you' to you. But I'm not going to begin to accuse you of anything. Yes, certainly, it's good that this torment has ended. To watch your son being turned into a monster—it… burns up the soul."

"I can imagine," Denis said.

The doctor set aside the green rind and started on the next piece of melon. "Just what have you achieved?" he mumbled. "Now they'll kill you. And punish us for the fact that we didn't kill you ourselves."

"How many of them are there?" Denis asked.

"Twenty or so."

"Can you be more precise?"

"Eighteen," he said, red juice trickling from his lips. "Not counting my son."

"We don't have to count him," Denis confirmed. "There are about a hundred men in the city, couldn't you handle this yourself?"

"It's not a hundred," the doctor shook his head. "If we count just the adults, it's about seventy."

"Well? There are only eighteen of them."

"That's easy for you to say," the doctor shrugged his shoulders. "Eighteen. Fifteen of them are our children."

"Initially there was just three?"

"Yes. They settled in. Everything began little by little. They promised to protect us and for a while they really did protect us. Then one our boys went over to them, then another, then a third…"

"You should've done something about it before the first went over to them," Denis said firmly. "How many men, how many women?"

"They have about two women," the doctor winced. "But that's not a problem for them. If they get bored, they come take our women."

"What is the name of this gang?" Denis asked.

"They call themselves the 'High Noon Vampires.' They come to harass us every day at noon, like clockwork."

"And the leader?"

"His name is Anton Pavlovich."

Denis stood and went to the door. "I could never understand this. A handful of bloodsuckers puts the entire town on its knees…and everyone sits in the corner like sheep," he said. He was quiet for a moment, then said: "Where can I get something to eat?"

"There's a café across the street." He already had finished another slice of watermelon and was now gnawing on the rind unconsciously. "We have just one café."

The owner of the café was the first person with living eyes Denis had met in the town. When he entered, there were three people sitting in the dining room, but they immediately got up and left, as though a nasty odor were hovering around Denis.

A woman, not yet old, but with hair streaked with gray, came up to him, peered into his eyes for a second, and then nodded her head: "Kill as many as you can," she said. "I'm begging you."

"I'll kill them all," Denis answered simply. "What can I have to drink?"

"Just something to drink or 'have a drink'?"

"Just drink. I can't stand alcohol."

"Coffee?"

Denis just smiled, as if she were making a joke.

But the woman went behind the bar, jingled some keys and opened a drawer. She took out a small bag, generously poured coffee beans into a hand grinder and started solemnly rotating the lever as if she were performing a sacred ritual. To a certain degree, it was just that.

Denis waited, looking as if he were enchanted.

The coffee that the woman brought to him in a big red mug was boiling hot. But the most important thing was the fact that it smelled like coffee.

"Where did this luxury come from?" Denis asked, after taking a sip.

"From past life. There is always something left from the past life."

Denis nodded silently.

"Do you want to have a bite to eat?" The woman asked. "I'm not offering you a banquet—you can't fight on a full stomach. But they'll come to the city at noon; you'll have time for a snack."

"Okay," Denis said, although he was full. "What can you recommend?"

"I hate fish," the woman said. "But I have good steaks. Honestly."

"Give me one—well-done and not too big." A young girl peeked into the dining hall from the kitchen. She had a pale face and tightly pursed lips. "Is she afraid of me?"

"She's afraid of everyone," the woman answered without turning. "Ever since she was dragged away last year. They kept her for three days."

The girl was about fourteen or fifteen. "Don't you worry," Denis said, although he knew that the woman would not believe him, "I *will* kill all of them."

"There are eighteen of them," the woman answered. He liked her precision.

"I know. That's not too many."

Her look changed ever so slightly, as if she had begun to believe him.

"Take this." The woman's hand dove into the neck of her dress and pulled out a chain. "This is an icon of the Mother of God. I believe it was what saved my daughter."

"No," Denis said, and gently but firmly stopped her hand. "I can't take it. But you'll help me immensely if in a half-hour you bring me another cup of coffee."

"If you kill them all, I'll make you a cappuccino," the café owner said. "With foam."

They drove into town from the sea side, the side of the pier where, in a leisurely manner, they set a couple of old barns on fire. The fishermen had long ago gone off to sea in their little boats, taking their wives, children, and more or less all of their valuable household possessions.

Five of the gang rode horses, the rest huddled on two horse-drawn carts. In one of the carts a machine gun was set on a turret, and behind the machine gun, sitting on an old office chair, a young woman was stooped over—all decked out in black leather with silver buttons glistening in the sun. Denis watched her with amusement. Vampires, of course, aren't afraid of either the sun or silver. They can be killed just like people—it's just…more difficult.

The town had become deserted. The residents did not dare look at what was happening even out of the corners of their eyes. However—in one of the windows of the café the drape was moving slightly. Denis smiled in that direction then returned his attention to the two carts and five riders.

When they saw Denis standing in the middle of the street, they slowed down slightly and began to move more cautiously, looking from side to side, cocking their rifles, and switching off the safeties on their revolvers and automatic weapons. Denis waited patiently until they completely surrounded him. The girl with the machine gun was chewing gum and gave him a look of scorn, but without animosity.

"What is this, some kind of fucking cowboy…" the leader—Anton Pavlovich, Denis remembered—said. He was middle-aged but not old—strong, with keen, intelligent eyes. He wore a gun in an open holster and rode the best horse. Since it wasn't a question, Denis preferred to remain silent. "It was you who killed Andrei," Pavlovich said.

"Me," Denis said.

Pavlovich nodded, thinking. "Well," he said, "if that was your way of asking to join our gang, I'll take you. I was tired of that *soplyak* anyway."

"Are you the Master?" Denis asked.

"What?"

"Are—you—the Master? That's what the leader of a vampire pack is called. Or don't you even know that much?"

A fat man riding beside Pavlovich laughed. The girl with the machine gun smiled.

Pavlovich sighed: "Kill him!"

The first bullet struck the girl with the machine gun right between the eyes.

Denis side-stepped right, pulling Pavlovich's second-in-command down from his horse and throwing him onto the cart, knocking down the other gang members as if they were bowling pins. At the end of the cart, he lay still, his neck broken.

The second bullet tore through the heart of a man holding an automatic rifle.

The third targeted the face of a girl holding a shotgun. At the very last moment she jerked and the bullet tore off part of her ear, and so Denis had to shoot a fourth time.

The fifth and sixth bullets felled two guys with revolvers who were the spitting image of each other (brothers? twins?).

The last one, the seventh, entered the stomach of a man who'd tried to jump Denis—an Asian with shortly cropped hair and cold, merciless eyes.

Someone shot and missed.

Someone screamed.

The horses neighed and reared.

Denis danced between and among his remaining adversaries, breaking the necks of two of them and, with a single strike of his hand, tearing out the heart of a third. A teenager on the cart saw this, put his lips around the muzzle of his revolver, and shot himself.

The girl with the shotgun was hanging limply off the side of the cart, the weapon falling out of her dead fingers. Denis grabbed it and discharged one barrel into the head of a man on a horse; his head exploded into red mist.

"Tra-ta-ta-ta, tra-ta-ta-ta, tra-ta-ta-ta," Denis hummed like the rhythm of a foxtrot, counting the dead enemies. He decided not to count the young one who shot himself. The leader did not fit into the rhythm either; another end awaited him.

The remaining High Noon Vampires ran in all directions.

But the dance wasn't over yet.

The second shotgun shell hit the guy with the hunting rifle in the back. He fell, writhing in the road's dust. Denis then drove the butt of the gun into the forehead of a scrawny man with crazed eyes who'd been running backwards, deftly shuffling his feet and giggling madly as if he had seen something amazingly funny.

"Tra-ta…" Denis said.

Three horses rushed along the road toward the sea. Denis switched the revolver to his other hand, emptied out the shells, and snapped three bullets in.

"Tra-ta…" Denis finished humming and shot. Two of the horses started galloping faster, dislodging their deceased riders. One of the riders' feet got caught in the stirrup, and he was dragged for a few meters, then lost his boot and remained on the road, motionless.

Only the leader remained. With a little regret in his heart, Denis planted a bullet into the leg of the man's horse. With surprising deftness, Pavlovich leapt down, but did not even try to get up—he just turned on his back and glared at Denis as he approached.

Denis slowly walked toward him.

Pavlovich pulled out a gun and fired off a single shot, but Denis kicked the weapon out of his hand, and grabbed Pavlovich's jacket and pulled it tightly around him. "You missed," he said.

Denis shackled Pavlovich's hands with his own belt, gagged his mouth with a handkerchief, and started dragging him toward the rail station.

The woman came out of the café when they were passing by, holding a coffee cup somewhat shakily in her hands.

Denis looked into it. A cappuccino.

"You are quick," he said.

"You are even quicker," the woman said. Her daughter stood behind her, smiling.

"We must finish the horse off," Denis said. "Will you be able to do it? There are a lot of weapons back there."

"No more deaths," the woman said. "Even a lame horse is a living horse."

Denis drank his cappuccino. Pavlovich wheezed something unintelligible into his gag.

"Please, go away. Go away for God's sake!" The woman shouted; her nerves couldn't stand it any more.

"It will be better for you not to tell anyone exactly what you saw here," Denis said. He returned the unfinished cup to her and walked away, dragging the leader to the train station.

Barrels of fish stood on the platform, but there was no one around. Denis signaled to the approaching train himself and loaded the barrels onto a cargo car at the end of the train. He then threw the leader into the car and climbed aboard.

The train whistled and started off.

Denis stood for a while by the open door, looking at the town receding into the distance. Without looking, he caught Pavlovich as he made an attempt to jump off the train, and tossed him back into the car. Denis closed the door, approached the man, and pulled the gag out of his mouth.

"You god damned *pridurok!*" Pavlovich shouted. He was so terrified that he no longer was afraid of anything. "You *pridurok!* We're not vampires! We just called ourselves 'High Noon Vampires'! We're an ordinary gang, understand? An ordinary gang!"

"I understand," Denis nodded.

"And this is our town!"

"*Was* your town," Denis said.

Pavlovich fell silent. He looked at Denis's face for a moment, then stared at his chest. "I didn't miss," he muttered. "I couldn't have missed!"

Denis took off his jacket, revealing a hole from which slowly oozed a dark, dark liquid…that quite recently, just that morning, had been flowing in the veins of the doctor's son. The cold, gray flesh surrounding the wound was already starting to heal.

"You didn't miss," Denis said. "But it's really difficult to kill us. Those who have died already don't like to die again."

He was silent for a moment, looking at Pavlovich's neck, then continued: "My Master doesn't like it when a gang of con men call themselves vampires. We don't like to kill very much. But we have to, sometimes; that's what we are. But if we have a choice, we always choose to kill those who are even worse than we are."

The train's wheels tapped out—tra-ta-ta-ta, tra-ta-ta-ta—and the rhythmical crash of the surf could be heard off in the distance.

The fish, layered with moist seaweed, stirred listlessly in the barrels.

Unlike Pavlovich, they lived all the way to the city.

THIS IS NOW

by Michael Marshall Smith

Michael Marshall Smith is the author of several novels, including *Only Forward*, which won the Philip K. Dick Award and the British Fantasy Award, and *The Servants*, which was a finalist for the World Fantasy Award. He also publishes under the name Michael Marshall; his most recent novels under that pen name are *Bad Things* and *The Intruders*, the latter of which is being adapted into a miniseries to air on the BBC. His short fiction has been collected in three volumes, most recently in *More Tomorrow & Other Stories*.

This story, which first appeared in the BBC's *Vampire Cult Magazine*, tells the story of a small group of friends, as they recall a formative event in their lives. It explores how big a gap there is between then and now, and all the things that can fall through that gap.

"Okay," Henry said. "So now we're here."

He was using his "So entertain me" voice, and he was cold but trying not to show it. Pete and I were cold too. We were trying not to show it either. Being cold is not manly. You look at your condensing breath as if it's a surprise to you, what with it being so balmy and all. Even when you've known each other for over thirty years, you do these things. Why? I don't know.

"Yep," I agreed. It wasn't my job to entertain Henry.

Pete walked up to the thick wire fence. He tilted his head back until he was looking at the top, four feet above his head. A ten-foot wall of tautly criss-crossed wire.

"Who's going to test it?"

"Well, hey, you're closest." Like the others, I was speaking quietly, though we were half a mile from the nearest road or house or person.

This side of the fence, anyhow.

"I did it last time."

"Long while ago."

"Still," he said, stepping back. "Your turn, Dave."

I held up my hands. "These are my tools, man."

Henry sniggered. "*You're* a tool, that's for sure."

Pete laughed too, I had to smile, and for a moment it was like it *was* the last time. Hey presto: time travel. You don't need a machine, it turns out, you just need a

189

friend to laugh like a teenager. Chronology shivers.

And so—quickly, before I could think about it—I flipped my hand out and touched the fence. My whole arm jolted, as if every bone in it had been tapped with a hammer. Tapped hard, and in different directions.

"Christ," I hissed, spinning away, shaking my hand like I was trying to rid myself of it. "Goddamn *Christ* that hurts."

Henry nodded sagely. "This stretch got current, then. Also, didn't we use a stick last time?"

"Always been the brains of the operation, right, Hank?"

Pete snickered again. I was annoyed, but the shock had pushed me over a line. It had brought it all back much more strongly.

I nodded up the line of the fence as it marched off into the trees. "Further," I said, and pointed at Henry. "And you're testing the next section, bro."

It was one of those things you do, one of those stupid, drunken things, that afterwards seem hard to understand. You ask yourself why, confused and sad, like the ghost of a man killed though a careless step in front of a car.

We could have not gone to The Junction, for a start, though it was a Thursday and the Thursday session is a winter tradition with us, a way of making January and February seem less like a living death. The two young guys could have given up the pool table, though, instead of bogarting it all night (by being better than us, and efficiently dismissing each of our challenges in turn): in which case we would have played a dozen slow frames and gone home around eleven, like usual—ready to get up the next morning feeling no more than a little fusty. This time of year it hardly matters if Henry yawns over the gas pump, or Pete zones out behind the counter in the Massaqua Mart, and I can sling a morning's home fries and sausage in my sleep. We've been doing these things so long that we barely have to be present. Maybe that's the point. Maybe that's the real problem right there.

By quarter after eight, proven pool-fools, we were sitting at the corner table. We always have, since back when it was Bill's place and beer tasted strange and metallic in our mouths. We were talking back and forth, laughing once in a while, none of us bothered about the pool but yes, a little bit bothered all the same. It wasn't some macho thing. I don't care about being beat by some guys who are passing through. I don't much care about being beat by anyone. Henry and Pete and I tend to win games about equally. If it weren't that way then probably we wouldn't play together. It's never been about winning. It was more that I just wished I was better. Had *assumed* I'd be better, one day, like I expected to wind up being something other than a short order cook. Don't get me wrong: you eat one of my breakfasts, you're set up for the day and tomorrow you'll come back and order the same thing. It just wasn't what I had in mind when I was young. Not sure what I *did* have in mind—I used to think maybe I'd go over the mountains to Seattle, be in a band or something, but the thought got vague after that—but it certainly wasn't being first in command at a hot griddle. None of ours are bad jobs, but they're the kind held by people in the background. People who are getting by. People who don't play pool that well.

It struck me, as I watched Pete banter with Nicole when she brought round number four or five, that I was still smoking. I had been assuming I would have given it up by now. Tried, once or twice. Didn't take. Would it happen? Probably not. Would it give me cancer sooner or later? Most likely. Better try again, then. At some point.

Henry watched Nicole's ass as it accompanied her back to the counter. "Cute as hell," he said, approvingly, not for the first time.

Pete and I grunted, in the way we would if he'd observed that the moon was smaller than the Earth. Henry's observation was both true and something that had little bearing on our lives. Nicole was twenty-three. We could give her fifteen years each. That's not the kind of gift that cute girls covet.

So we sat and talked, and smoked, and didn't listen to the sound of balls being efficiently slotted into pockets by people who weren't us.

You walk for long enough in the woods at night, you start getting a little jittery. Forests have a way of making civilisation seem less inevitable. In sunlight they may make you want to build yourself a cabin and get back to nature, get that whole Davy Crockett vibe going on. In the dark they remind you what a good thing chairs and hot meals and electric light really are, and you thank God you live now instead of then.

Every once in a while we'd test the fence—using a stick now. The current was on each time we tried. So we kept walking. We followed the line of the wire as it cut up the rise, then down into a shallow streambed, then up again steeply on the other side.

If you were seeing the fence for the first time, you'd likely wonder at the straightness of it, the way in which the concrete posts had been planted at ten-yard intervals, deep into the rock. You might ask yourself if national forests normally went to these lengths, and you'd soon remember they didn't, that for the most part a cheerful little wooden sign by the side of the road was all that was judged to be required. If you kept on walking deeper, intrigued, sooner or later you'd see a notice attached to one of the posts. The notices are small, designed to convey authority rather than draw attention.

"No Trespassing," they say. "Military Land."

That could strike you as a little strange, perhaps, because you might have believed that most of the marked-off areas were down over in the moonscapes of Nevada, rather than up here at the quiet northeast corner of Washington State. But who knows what the military's up to, right? Apart from protecting us from foreign aggressors, of course, and The Terrorist Threat, and if that means they need a few acres to themselves then that's actually kind of comforting. The army moves in mysterious ways, our freedoms to defend. Good for them, you'd think, and you'd likely turn and head back for town, having had enough of tramping through snow for the day. In the evening you'd come into Ruby's and eat hearty, some of my wings or a burger or the brisket—which, though I say so myself, isn't half bad. Next morning you'd drive back south.

I remember when the fences went up. Thirty years ago. 1985. Our parents knew what they were for. Hell, we were only eight and *we* knew.

There was a danger, and it was getting worse: the last decade had proved that. Four people had disappeared in the last year alone. One came back and was sick for a week, in an odd and dangerous kind of way, and then died. The others were never seen again. My aunt Jean was one of those.

But there's a danger to going in abandoned mine shafts, too, or talking to strangers, or juggling knives when you're drunk. So… you don't do it. You walk the town in pairs at night, and you observe the unspoken curfew. You kept an eye out for men who didn't blink, for slim women whose strides were too short—or so people said. There was never that much passing trade in town. Massaqua isn't on the way to anywhere. Massaqua is a single guy who keeps his yard tidy and doesn't bother anyone. The tourist season up here is short and not exactly intense. There is no ski lodge or health spa and the motel frankly isn't up to much. The fence seemed to keep the danger contained and out of town, and within a few years its existence was part of life. It wasn't like it was right there on the doorstep. No big-city reporter heard of it and came up looking to make a sensation—or, if they did, they didn't make it all the way here.

Life went on. Years passed. Sometimes small signs work better than great big ones.

As we climbed deeper into the forest, Pete was in front, I was more-or-less beside him, and Henry lagged a few steps behind. It had been that way the last time, too, but then we hadn't had hip flasks to keep us fuelled in our intentions. We hadn't needed to stop to catch our breath so often either.

"We just going to keep on walking?"

It was Henry asked the question, of course. Pete and I didn't even answer.

At quarter after ten we were still in the bar. The two guys remained at the pool table. When one leaned down, the other stood silently, judiciously sipping from a bottled beer. They weren't talking to each other, just slotting the balls away. Looked like they're having a whale of a time.

We were drinking steadily, and the conversation was often two-way while one or other of us trekked back and forth to empty our bladder. By then we were resigned to sitting around. We were a little too drunk to start playing pool, even when the table became free. There was no news to catch up on. We felt aimless. We already knew that Pete was ten years married, that they had no children and it was likely going to stay that way. His wife is fine, and still pleasant to be with, though her collection of dolls is getting exponentially bigger. We knew that Henry was married once too, had a little boy, and that though the kid and his mother now lived forty miles away, relations between them remained cordial. Neither Pete nor I are much surprised that he has achieved this. Henry can be a royal pain in the ass at times, but he wouldn't still be our friend if that's all he was.

"Same again, boys? You're thirsty tonight."

It was Pete's turn in the gents so it was Henry and I who looked up to see Nicole smiling down at us, thumb hovering over the REPEAT button on her pad. Deprived of Pete's easy manner (partly genetic, also honed over years of chatting while totting and bagging groceries), our response was cluttered and vague.

Quick nods and smiles, I said thanks and Henry got in a "Hell, yes!" that came out a little loud.

Nicole winked at me and went away again, as she has done many times over the last three years. As she got to the bar I saw one of the pool-players looking at her, and felt a strange twist of something in my stomach. It wasn't because they were strangers, or because I suspected they might be something else, something that shouldn't be here.

They were just younger guys, that's all.

Of course they're going to look at her. She's probably going to want them to.

I lit another cigarette and wondered why I still didn't really know how to deal with women. They've always seemed so different to me. So confident, so powerful, so in themselves. Kind of scary, even. Most teenage boys feel that way, I guess, but I had assumed age would help. That being older might make a difference. Apparently not. The opposite, if anything. "Cute just don't really cover it," Henry said, again not for the first time. "Going to have to come up with a whole new word. Supercute, how's that. Hyperhot. Ultra—"

How about just beautiful?

For a horrible moment I thought I'd said this out loud. I guess in a way I did, because what pronouncements are louder than the ones you make in your own head?

Pete returned at the same time as the new beers arrived, and with him around it was easier to come across like grown-ups. He came back looking thoughtful, too.

He waited until the three of us were alone again, and then he reached across and took one of my Marlboro: like he used to, back in the day, when he couldn't afford his own. He didn't seem to be aware he'd done it. He looked pretty drunk, in fact, and I realised that I was too. Henry is generally at least a little drunk.

Pete lit the cigarette, took a long mouthful of beer, and then he said:

"You remember that time we went over the fence?"

The stick touched, and nothing happened.

I did it again. Same result. We stopped walking. My legs ached and I was glad for the break. Pete hesitated a beat, then reached out and brushed the thick black wire with his hand. When we were kids he might have pretended it was charged, and jiggered back and forth, eyes rolling and tongue sticking out.

He didn't now. He just curled his fingers around it, gave it a light tug.

"Power's down," he said, quietly.

Henry and I stepped up close. Even with Pete standing there grasping it, you still had to gird yourself to do the same.

Then all three of us were holding the fence, holding it with both hands, looking in.

That close up, the wire fuzzed out of focus and it was almost as if it wasn't there. You just saw the forest beyond it: moonlit trunks, snow; you heard the quietness. If you stood on the other side and looked out, the view would be exactly the same.

With a fence that long, it could be difficult to tell which side was in, which was out.

This, too, was what had happened the previous time, when we were fifteen. We'd heard that sometimes a section went down, and so we went looking. With animals, snow, the random impacts of falling branches and a wind that could blow hard and cold at most times of year, once in a while a cable stopped supplying the juice to one ten-yard stretch. The power was never down for more than a day. There was a computer that kept track, and—somewhere, nobody knew where—a small station from which a couple of military engineers could come to repair the outage. It had happened back then. It had happened now.

We stood, this silent row of older men, and remembered what had happened then.

Pete had gone up first. He shuffled along to one of the concrete posts, so the wire wouldn't bag out, and started pulling himself up. As soon as his feet left the ground I didn't want to be left behind, so I went to the other post and went up just as quickly.

We reached the top at around the same time. Soon as we started down the other side—lowering ourselves at first, then just dropping, Henry started his own climb.

We all landed silently in the snow, with bent knees.

We were on the other side, and we stood very still. Far as we knew, no one had ever done this before.

To some people, this might have been enough.

Not to three boys.

Moving very quietly, hearts beating hard—just from the exertion, none of us were scared, not exactly, not enough to admit it anyway—we moved away from the fence. After about twenty yards I stopped and looked back.

"You chickening out?"

"No, Henry," I said. His voice had been quiet and shaky. I took pains that mine sound firm. "Memorising. We want to be able to find that dead section again."

He'd nodded. "Good thinking, smart boy."

Pete looked back with us. Stand of three trees close together there. Unusually big tree over on the right. Kind of a semi-clearing, on a crest. Shouldn't be hard to find.

We glanced at each other, judged it logged, then turned and headed away, into a place no one had been for nearly ten years.

The forest floor led away gently. There was just enough moonlight to show the ground panning down towards a kind of high valley lined with thick trees.

As we walked, bent over a little with unconscious caution, part of me was already relishing how we'd remember this in the future, leaping over the event into retrospection. Not that we'd talk about it, outside the three of us. It was the kind of thing which might attract attention to the town, including maybe attention from this side of the fence.

There was one person I thought I might mention it to, though. Her name was

Lauren and she was very cute, the kind of beautiful that doesn't have to open its mouth to call your name from across the street. I had talked to her a couple times, finding bravery I didn't know I possessed. It was she who had talked about Seattle, said she'd like to go hang out there someday. That sounded good to me, good and exciting and strange. What I didn't know, that night in the forest, was that she would do this, and I would not, and that she would leave without us ever having kissed.

I just assumed… I assumed a lot back then.

After a couple of hundred yards we stopped, huddled together, shared one of my cigarettes. Our hearts were beating heavily, even though we'd been coming down-hill. The forest is hard work whatever direction it slopes. But it wasn't just that. It felt a little colder here. There was also something about the light. It seemed to hold more shadows. You found your eyes flicking from side to side, checking things out, wanting to be reassured, but not being sure that you had been after all.

I bent down to put the cigarette out in the snow. It was extinguished in a hiss that seemed very loud.

We continued in the direction we'd been heading. We walked maybe another five, six hundred yards.

It was Henry who stopped.

Keyed up as we were, Pete and I stopped immediately too. Henry was leaning forward a little, squinting ahead.

"What?"

He pointed. Down at the bottom of the rocky valley was a shape. A big shape.

After a moment I could make out it was a building. Two wooden storeys high, and slanting. You saw that kind of thing, sometimes. The sagging remnant of some pioneer's attempt to claim an area of this wilderness and pretend it could be a home.

Pete nudged me and pointed in a slightly different direction. There was the rem-nants of another house further down. A little fancier, with a fallen-down porch.

And thirty yards further, another: smaller, with a false front.

"Cool," Henry said, and briefly I admired him.

We sidled now, a lot more slowly and heading along the rise instead of down it. Ruined houses look real interesting during the day. At night they feel different, especially when lost high up in the forest. Trees grow too close to them, pressing in. The lack of a road, long overgrown, can make the houses look like they were never built but instead made their own way to this forgotten place, in which you have now disturbed them; they sit at angles which do not seem quite right.

I was beginning to wonder if maybe we'd done enough, come far enough, and I doubt I was the only one.

Then we saw the light.

After Pete asked his question in the bar, there was silence for a moment. Of course we remembered that night. It wasn't something you'd forget. It was a dumb question unless you were really asking something else, and we both knew

Pete wasn't dumb.

Behind us, on the other side of the room, came the quiet, reproachful sound of pool balls hitting each other, and then one of them going down a pocket.

We could hear each other thinking. Thinking it was a cold evening, and there was thick snow on the ground, as there had been on that other night. That the rest of the town had pretty much gone to bed. That we could get in Henry's truck and be at the head of a hiking trail in twenty minutes, even driving drunkard slow.

I didn't hear anyone thinking a reason, though. I didn't hear anyone think *why* we might do such a thing, or what might happen.

By the time Pete had finished his cigarette our glasses were empty. We put on our coats and left and crunched across the lot to the truck.

Back then, on that long-ago night, suddenly my heart hadn't seemed to be beating at all. When we saw the light in the second house, a faint and curdled glow in one of the downstairs windows, my whole body suddenly felt light and insubstantial.

One of us tried to speak. It came out like a dry click. I realised there was a light in the other house too, faint and golden. Had I missed it before, or had it just come on?

I took a step backwards. The forest was silent but for the sound of my friends breathing. "Oh, no," Pete said. He started moving backwards, stumbling. Then I saw it too.

A figure, standing in front of the first house.

It was tall and slim, like a rake's shadow. It was a hundred yards away but still it seemed as though you could make out an oval shape on its shoulders, the colour of milk diluted with water. It was looking in our direction.

Then another was standing near the other house.

No, two.

Henry moaned softly, we three boys turned as one, and I have never run like that before or since.

The first ten yards were fast but then the slope cut in and our feet slipped, and we were down on hands half the time, scrabbling and pulling—every muscle working together in a headlong attempt to be somewhere else.

I heard a crash behind and flicked my head to see Pete had gone down hard, banging his knee, falling on his side.

Henry kept on going but I made myself turn around and grab Pete's hand, not really helping but just pulling, trying to yank him back to his feet or at least away.

Over his shoulder I glimpsed the valley below and I saw the figures were down at the bottom of the rise, speeding our way in jerky blurred-black movements, like half-seen spiders darting across an icy window pane.

Pete's face jerked up and I saw there what I felt in myself, and it was not a cold fear but a hot one, a red-hot meltdown as if you were going to rattle and break apart.

Then he was on his feet again, moving past me, and I followed on after him towards the disappearing shape of Henry's back. It seemed so much further than we'd walked. It was uphill and the trees no longer formed a path and even the wind seemed to be pushing us back. We caught up with Henry and passed him, streaking up the last hundred yards towards the fence. None of us turned around. You didn't have to. You could feel them coming, like rocks thrown at your head, rocks glimpsed at the last minute when there is time to flinch but not to turn.

I was sprinting straight at the fence when Henry called out. I was going too fast and didn't want to know what his problem was. I leapt up at the wire.

It was like a truck hit me from the side.

I crashed the ground fizzing, arms sparking and with no idea which way was up. Then two pairs of hands were on me, pulling at my coat, cold hands and strong.

I thought the fingers would be long and pale and milky but then I realised it was my friends and they were pulling me along from the wrong section of the fence, dragging me to the side, when they could have just left me where I fell and made their own escape.

The three of us jumped up at the wire at once, scrabbling like monkeys, stretching out for the top. I rolled over wildly, grunting as I scored deep scratches across my back that would earn me a long, hard look from my mother when she happened to glimpse them a week later. We landed heavily on the other side, still moving forward, having realised that we'd just given away the location of a portion of dead fence. But now we had to look back, and what I saw—though my head was still vibrating from the shock I'd received, so I cannot swear to it—was at least three, maybe five, figures on the other side of the fence. Not right up against it, but a few yards back.

Black hair was whipped up around their faces, and they looked like absences ill-lit by moonlight.

Then they were gone.

We moved fast. We didn't know why they'd stopped, but we didn't hang around. We didn't stick too close to the fence either, in case they changed their minds.

We half-walked, half-ran, and at first we were quiet but as we got further away, and nothing came, we began to laugh and then to shout, punching the air, boys who had come triumphantly out the other side.

The forest felt like some huge football field, applauding its heroes with whispering leaves. We got back to town a little after two in the morning. We walked down the middle of the deserted main street, slowly, untouchable, knowing the world had changed: that we were not the boys who had started the evening, but men, and that the stars were there to be touched. That was then.

As older men we stood together at the fence for a long time, recalling that night.

Parts of it are fuzzy now, of course, and it comes down to snapshots: Pete's terrified face when he slipped, the first glimpse of light at the houses, Henry's shout as he tried to warn me, narrow faces the colour of moonlight. They most likely remembered other things, defined that night in different ways and were the centre of their recollections. As I looked now through the fence at the other forest I was thinking how long a decade had seemed back then, and how you could learn that it was no time at all.

Henry stepped away first. I wasn't far behind. Pete stayed a moment longer, then took a couple of steps back. Nobody said anything. We just looked at the fence a little longer, and then we turned and walked away.

Took us forty minutes to get back to the truck.

The next Thursday Henry couldn't make it, so it was just me and Pete at the pool table. Late in the evening, with many beers drunk, I mentioned the fence.

Not looking at me, chalking his cue, Pete said that if Henry hadn't stepped back when he did, he'd have climbed it.

"And gone over?"

"Yeah," he said.

This was bullshit, and I knew it. "Really?"

There was a pause. "No," he said, eventually, and I wished I hadn't asked the second time. I could have left him with something, left us with it. Calling an ass cute isn't much, but it's better than just coming right out and admitting you'll never cup it in your hand.

The next week it was the three of us again, and our walk in the woods wasn't even mentioned. We've never brought it up since, and we can't talk about the first time any more either. I think about it sometimes, though.

I know I could go out walking there myself some night, and there have been slow afternoons and dry, sleepless small hours when I think I might do it: when I tell myself such a thing isn't impossible now, that I am still who I once was. But I have learned a little since I was fifteen, and I know now that you don't need to look for things that will suck the life out of you. Time will do that all by itself.

BLOOD GOTHIC

by Nancy Holder

Nancy Holder is the author of more than eighty novels, including *Pretty Little Devils, Daughter of the Flames,* and *Dead in the Water,* which won the Bram Stoker Award for best novel. She's also written a number of media tie-in novels, for properties such as *Buffy the Vampire Slayer, Highlander,* and *Smallville.* Writing as Chris P. Flesh, Holder is the author of the Pretty Freekin Scary series of books for children. A new paranormal romance novel, *Son of the Shadows,* was released last August. The latest in her young adult series, Wicked (co-authored with Debbie Viguié), *Wicked: Witch & Curse,* is currently a *New York Times* bestseller. Holder's short fiction—which has appeared in anthologies such as *Borderlands, Confederacy of the Dead, Love in Vein,* and *The Mammoth Book of Dracula*—has won her the Stoker Award three times.

Many of the stories in this anthology show vampires to be apex predators, with humanity as their prey. This story, however, demonstrates that perhaps the most dangerous predator of all is unfulfilled and unrelenting desire.

She wanted to have a vampire lover. She wanted it so badly that she kept waiting for it to happen. One night, soon, she would awaken to wings flapping against the window and then take to wearing velvet ribbons and cameo lockets around her delicate, pale neck. She knew it.

She immersed herself in the world of her vampire lover: She devoured Gothic romances, consumed late-night horror movies. Visions of satin capes and eyes of fire shielded her from the harshness of the daylight, from mortality and the vain and meaningless struggles of the world of the sun. Days as a kindergarten teacher and evenings with some overly eager, casual acquaintance could not pull her from her secret existence: always a ticking portion of her brain planned, proceeded, waited.

She spent her meager earnings on dark antiques and intricate clothes. Her wardrobe was crammed with white negligees and ruffled underthings. No crosses and no mirrors, particularly not in her bedroom. White tapered candles stood in pewter sconces, and she would read late into the night by their smoky flickerings, she scented and ruffled, hair combed loosely about her shoulders. She glanced at the window often.

She resented lovers—though she took them, thrilling to the fullness of life in them, the blood and the life—who insisted upon staying all night, burning their breakfast toast and making bitter coffee. Her kitchen, of course, held nothing but fresh ingredients and copper and ironware; to her chagrin, she could not do without ovens or stoves or refrigerators. Alone, she carried candles and bathed in cool water.

She waited, prepared. And at long last, her vampire lover began to come to her in dreams. They floated across the moors, glided through the fields of heather. He carried her to his crumbling castle, undressing her, pulling off her diaphanous gown, caressing her lovely body until, in the height of passion, he bit into her arched neck, drawing the life out of her and replacing it with eternal damnation and eternal love.

She awoke from these dreams drenched in sweat and feeling exhausted. The kindergarten children would find her unusually quiet and self-absorbed, and it frightened them when she rubbed her spotless neck and smiled wistfully. *Soon and soon and soon,* her veins chanted, in prayer and anticipation. *Soon.*

The children were her only regret. She would not miss her inquisitive relatives and friends, the ones who frowned and studied her as if she were a portrait of someone they knew they were supposed to recognize. Those, who urged her to drop by for an hour, to come with them to films, to accompany them to the seashore. Those, who were connected to her—or thought they were—by the mere gesturing of the long and milky hands of Fate. Who sought to distract her from her one true passion; who sought to discover the secret of that passion. For, true to the sacredness of her vigil for her vampire lover, she had never spoken of him to a single earthly, earthbound soul. It would be beyond them, she knew. They would not comprehend a bond of such intentioned sacrifice.

But she would regret the children. Never would a child of their love coo and murmur in the darkness; never would his proud and noble features soften at the sight of the mother and her child of his loins. It was her single sorrow.

Her vacation was coming. June hovered like the mist and the children squirmed in anticipation. Their own true lives would begin in June. She empathized with the shining eyes and smiling faces, knowing their wait was as agonizing as her own. Silently, as the days closed in, she bade each of them a tender farewell, holding them as they threw their little arms around her neck and pressed fervent summertime kisses on her cheeks.

She booked her passage to London on a ship. Then to Romania, Bulgaria, Transylvania. The hereditary seat of her beloved; the fierce, violent backdrop of her dreams. Her suitcases opened themselves to her long, full skirts and her brooches and lockets. She peered into her hand mirror as she packed it. "I am getting pale," she thought, and the idea both terrified and delighted her.

She became paler, thinner, more exhausted as her trip wore on. After recovering from the disappointment of the raucous, modern cruise ship, she raced across the Continent to find refuge in the creaky trains and taverns she had so yearned for. Her heart thrilled as she meandered past the black silhouettes of ruined fortresses and ancient manor houses. She sat for hours in the mists, praying for the howling wolf to find her, for the bat to come and join her.

She took to drinking wine in bed, deep, rich, blood-red burgundy that glowed in the candlelight. She melted into the landscape within days, and cringed as if from the crucifix itself when flickers of her past life, her American, false existence, invaded her serenity. She did not keep a diary; she did not count the days as her summer slipped away from her. She only rejoiced that she grew weaker.

It was when she was counting out the coins for a Gypsy shawl that she realized she had no time left. Tomorrow she must make for Frankfurt and from there fly back to New York. The shopkeeper nudged her, inquiring if she were ill, and she left with her treasure, trembling.

She flung herself on her own rented bed. "This will not do. This will not do." She pleaded with the darkness. "You must come for me tonight. I have done everything for you, my beloved, loved you above all else. You must save me." She sobbed until she ached.

She skipped her last meal of veal and paprika and sat quietly in her room. The innkeeper brought her yet another bottle of burgundy and after she assured him that she was quite all right, just a little tired, he wished his guest a pleasant trip home.

The night wore on; though her book was open before her, her eyes were riveted to the windows, her hands clenched around the wineglass as she sipped steadily, like a creature feeding. Oh, to feel him against her veins, emptying her and filling her!

Soon and soon and soon...

Then, all at once, it happened. The windows rattled, flapped inward. A great shadow, a curtain of ebony, fell across the bed, and the room began to whirl, faster, faster still; and she was consumed with a bitter, deathly chill. She heard, rather than saw, the wineglass crash to the floor, and struggled to keep her eyes open as she was overwhelmed, engulfed, taken.

"Is it you?" she managed to whisper through teeth that rattled with delight and cold and terror. "Is it finally to be?"

Freezing hands touched her everywhere: her face, her breasts, the desperate offering of her arched neck. Frozen and strong and never-dying. Sinking, she smiled in a rictus of mortal dread and exultation. Eternal damnation, eternal love. Her vampire lover had come for her at last.

When her eyes opened again, she let out a howl and shrank against the searing brilliance of the sun. Hastily, they closed the curtains and quickly told her where she was: home again, where everything was warm and pleasant and she was safe from the disease that had nearly killed her.

She had been ill before she had left the States. By the time she had reached Transylvania, her anemia had been acute. Had she never noticed her own pallor, her lassitude?

Anemia. Her smile was a secret on her white lips. So they thought, but he *had* come for her, again and again. In her dreams. And on that night, he had meant to take her finally to his castle forever, to crown her the best-beloved one, his love of the moors and the mists.

She had but to wait, and he would finish the deed.

Soon and soon and soon.

She let them fret over her, wrapping her in blankets in the last days of summer. She endured the forced cheer of her relatives, allowed them to feed her rich food and drink in hopes of restoring her.

But her stomach could no longer hold the nourishment of their kind; they wrung their hands and talked of stronger measures when it became clear that she was wasting away.

At the urging of the doctor, she took walks. Small ones at first, on painfully thin feet. Swathed in wool, cowering behind sunglasses, she took tiny steps like an old woman. As she moved through the summer hours, her neck burned with an ungovernable pain that would not cease until she rested in the shadows. Her stomach lurched at the sight of grocery-store windows. But at the butcher's, she paused, and licked her lips at the sight of the raw, bloody meat.

But she did not go to him. She grew neither worse nor better.

"I am trapped," she whispered to the night as she stared into the flames of a candle by her bed. "I am disappearing between your world and mine, my beloved. Help me. Come for me." She rubbed her neck, which ached and throbbed but showed no outward signs of his devotion. Her throat was parched, bone-dry, but water did not quench her thirst.

At long last, she dreamed again. Her vampire lover came for her as before, joyous in their reunion. They soared above the crooked trees at the foothills, streamed like black banners above the mountain crags to his castle. He could not touch her enough, worship her enough, and they were wild in their abandon as he carried her in her diaphanous gown to the gates of his fortress.

But at the entrance, he shook his head with sorrow and could not let her pass into the black realm with him. His fiery tears seared her neck, and she thrilled to the touch of the mark even as she cried out for him as he left her, fading into the vapors with a look of entreaty in his dark, flashing eyes.

Something was missing; he required a boon of her before he could bind her against his heart. A thing that she must give to him...

She walked in the sunlight, enfeebled, cowering. She thirsted, hungered, yearned. Still she dreamed of him, and still he could not take the last of her unto himself.

Days and nights and days. Her steps took her finally to the schoolyard, where once, only months before, she had embraced and kissed the children, thinking never to see them again. They were all there, who had kissed her cheeks so eagerly. Their silvery laughter was like the tinkling of bells as dust motes from their games and antics whirled around their feet. How free they seemed to her who was so troubled, how content and at peace.

The children.

She shambled forward, eyes widening behind the shields of smoky glass.

He required something of her first.

Her one regret. Her only sorrow.

She thirsted. The burns on her neck pulsated with pain.

Tears of gratitude welled in her eyes for the revelation that had not come too late. Weeping, she pushed open the gate of the schoolyard and reached out a skeleton-limb to a child standing apart from the rest, engrossed in a solitary game of cat's cradle. Tawny-headed, ruddy-cheeked, filled with the blood and the life.

For him, as a token of their love.

"My little one, do you remember me?" she said softly.

The boy turned. And smiled back uncertainly in innocence and trust.

Then, as she came for him, swooped down on him like a great, winged thing, with eyes that burned through the glasses, teeth that flashed, once, twice...

soon, soon, soon.

MAMA GONE

by Jane Yolen

Jane Yolen is the bestselling author of nearly 300 books, including fiction for all ages, from picture books to middle-grade readers to adult novels. She has also edited several anthologies and written several books of non-fiction, as well as numerous volumes of poetry. Her books and stories have won the prestigious Caldecott Medal and have been nominated for the National Book Award. She is also a winner of the Nebula, Locus, and World Fantasy awards. Her latest novel is *Dragon's Heart*, the fourth volume in her Pit Dragon chronicles.

We know that certain types of brain injuries can turn nice people into sociopaths. At the flick of a switch these people, through no fault of their own, lose their basic sense of restraint, of remorse, of empathy. Vampirism seems to work the same way. So if a bump on the head or a bite on the neck turns you bad, are you still you? And if a bump on the head or a bite on the neck *can* turn you bad, are you ever really you? Such questions are especially perplexing for the affected person's family—particularly when the individual in question is feasting on the local children.

Mama died four nights ago, giving birth to my baby sister Ann. Bubba cried and cried, "Mama gone," in his little-boy voice, but I never let out a single tear.

There was blood red as any sunset all over the bed from that birthing, and when Papa saw it he rubbed his head against the cabin wall over and over and over and made little animal sounds. Sukey washed Mama down and placed the baby on her breast for a moment. "Remember," she whispered.

"Mama gone," Bubba wailed again.

But I never cried.

By all rights we should have buried her with garlic in her mouth and her hands and feet cut off, what with her being vampire kin and all. But Papa absolutely refused.

"Your Mama couldn't stand garlic," he said when the sounds stopped rushing out of his mouth and his eyes had cleared. "It made her come all over with rashes. She had the sweetest mouth and hands."

And that was that. Not a one of us could make him change his mind, not even Granddad Stokes or Pop Wilber or any other of the men who come to pay their last respects. And as Papa is a preacher, and a brimstone man, they let it be. The onliest thing he would allow was for us to tie red ribbons round her ankles and wrists, a kind of sign like a line of blood. Everybody hoped that would do.

But on the next day, she rose from out her grave and commenced to prey upon the good folk of Taunton.

Of course she came to our house first, that being the dearest place she knew. I saw her outside my window, gray as a gravestone, her dark eyes like the holes in a shroud. When she stared in, she didn't know me, though I had always been her favorite.

"Mama, be gone," I said and waved my little cross at her, the one she had given me the very day I'd been born. "Avaunt." The old Bible word sat heavy in my mouth.

She put her hand up on the window frame, and as I watched, the gray fingers turned splotchy pink from all the garlic I had rubbed into the wood.

Black tears dropped from her black eyes, then. But I never cried.

She tried each window in turn and not a person awake in the house but me. But I had done my work well and the garlic held her out. She even tried the door, but it was no use. By the time she left, I was so sleepy, I dropped down right by the door. Papa found me there at cockcrow. He never did ask what I was doing, and if he guessed, he never said.

Little Joshua Greenough was found dead in his crib. The doctor took two days to come over the mountains to pronounce it. By then the garlic around his little bed to keep him from walking, too, had mixed with the death smells. Everybody knew. Even the doctor, and him a city man. It hurt his mama and papa sore to do the cutting. But it had to be done.

The men came to our house that very noon to talk about what had to be. Papa kept shaking his head all through their talking. But even his being preacher didn't stop them. Once a vampire walks these mountain hollers, there's nary a house or barn that's safe. Nighttime is lost time. And no one can afford to lose much stock.

So they made their sharp sticks out of green wood, the curling shavings littering our cabin floor. Bubba played in them, not understanding. Sukey was busy with the baby, nursing it with a bottle and a sugar teat. It was my job to sweep up the wood curls. They felt slick on one side, bumpy on the other. Like my heart.

Papa said, "I was the one let her turn into a night walker. It's my business to stake her out."

No one argued. Specially not the Greenoughs, their eyes still red from weeping.

"Just take my children," Papa said. "And if anything goes wrong, cut off my hands and feet and bury me at Mill's Cross, under the stone. There's garlic hanging in the pantry. Mandy Jane will string me some."

So Sukey took the baby and Bubba off to the Greenoughs' house, that seeming the right thing to do, and I stayed the rest of the afternoon with Papa, stringing garlic and pressing more into the windows. But the strand over the door he took down.

"I have to let her in somewhere," he said. "And this is where I'll make my stand." He touched me on the cheek, the first time ever. Papa never has been much for show.

"Now you run along to the Greenoughs', Mandy Jane," he said. "And remember how much your mama loved you. This isn't her, child. Mama's gone. Something else has come to take her place. I should have remembered that the Good Book says, The living know that they shall die; but the dead know not anything.'"

I wanted to ask him how the vampire knew to come first to our house, then, but I was silent, for Papa had been asleep and hadn't seen her.

I left without giving him a daughter's kiss, for his mind was well set on the night's doing. But I didn't go down the lane to the Greenoughs' at all. Wearing my triple strand of garlic, with my cross about my neck, I went to the burying ground, to Mama's grave.

It looked so raw against the greening hillside. The dirt was red clay, but all it looked like to me was blood. There was no cross on it yet, no stone. That would come in a year. Just a humping, a heaping of red dirt over her coffin, the plain pinewood box hastily made.

I lay facedown in that dirt, my arms opened wide. "Oh, Mama," I said, "the Good Book says you are not dead but sleepeth. Sleep quietly, Mama, sleep well." And I sang to her the lullaby she had always sung to me and then to Bubba and would have sung to Baby Ann had she lived to hold her.

"*Blacks and bays,*
Dapples and grays,
All the pretty little horses."

And as I sang I remembered Papa thundering at prayer meeting once, "Behold, a pale horse: and his name that sat on him was Death." The rest of the song just stuck in my throat then, so I turned over on the grave and stared up at the setting sun.

It had been a long and wearying day, and I fell asleep right there in the burying ground. Any other time fear might have overcome sleep. But I just closed my eyes and slept.

When I woke, it was dead night. The moon was full and sitting between the horns of two hills. There was a sprinkling of stars overhead. And Mama began to move the ground beneath me, trying to rise.

The garlic strands must have worried her, for she did not come out of the earth all at once. It was the scrabbling of her long nails at my back that woke me. I leaped off that grave and was wide awake.

Standing aside the grave, I watched as first her long gray arms reached out of the earth. Then her head, with its hair that was once so gold, now gray and streaked with black and its shroud eyes, emerged. And then her body in its winding sheet, stained with dirt and torn from walking to and fro upon the land. Then her bare feet with blackened nails, though alive Mama used to paint those nails, her one vanity and Papa allowed it seeing she was so pretty and otherwise not vain.

She turned toward me as a hummingbird toward a flower, and she raised her face up and it was gray and bony. Her mouth peeled back from her teeth and I saw that they were pointed and her tongue was barbed.

"Mama gone," I whispered in Bubba's voice, but so low I could hardly hear it myself.

She stepped toward me off that grave, lurching down the hump of dirt. But when she got close, the garlic strands and the cross stayed her.

"Mama."

She turned her head back and forth. It was clear she could not see with those black shroud eyes. She only sensed me there, something warm, something alive, something with the blood running like satisfying streams through the blue veins.

"Mama," I said again. "Try and remember."

That searching awful face turned toward me again, and the pointy teeth were bared once more. Her hands reached out to grab me, then pulled back.

"Remember how Bubba always sucks his thumb with that funny little noise you always said was like a little chuck in its hole. And how Sukey hums through her nose when she's baking bread. And how I listened to your belly to hear the baby. And how Papa always starts each meal with the blessing on things that grow fresh in the field."

The gray face turned for a moment toward the hills, and I wasn't even sure she could hear me. But I had to keep trying.

"And remember when we picked the blueberries and Bubba fell down the hill, tumbling head-end over. And we laughed until we heard him, and he was saying the same six things over and over till long past bed."

The gray face turned back toward me and I thought I saw a bit of light in the eyes. But it was just reflected moonlight.

"And the day Papa came home with the new ewe lamb and we fed her on a sugar teat. You stayed up all the night and I slept in the straw by your side."

It was as if stars were twinkling in those dead eyes. I couldn't stop staring, but I didn't dare stop talking either.

"And remember the day the bluebird stunned itself on the kitchen window and you held it in your hands. You warmed it to life, you said. To life, Mama."

Those stars began to run down the gray cheeks.

"There's living, Mama, and there's dead. You've given so much life. Don't be bringing death to these hills now." I could see that the stars were gone from the sky over her head; the moon was setting.

"Papa loved you too much to cut your hands and feet. You gotta return that love, Mama. You gotta."

Veins of red ran along the hills, outlining the rocks. As the sun began to rise, I took off one strand of garlic. Then the second. Then the last. I opened my arms. "Have you come back, Mama, or are you gone?"

The gray woman leaned over and clasped me tight in her arms. Her head bent down toward mine, her mouth on my forehead, my neck, the outline of my little gold cross burning across her lips.

She whispered, "Here and gone, child, here and gone," in a voice like wind in the coppice, like the shaking of willow leaves. I felt her kiss on my cheek, a brand.

Then the sun came between the hills and hit her full in the face, burning her as red as earth. She smiled at me and then there was only dust motes in the air, dancing. When I looked down at my feet, the grave dirt was hardly disturbed but Mama's gold wedding band gleamed atop it.

I knelt down and picked it up, and unhooked the chain holding my cross. I slid the ring onto the chain, and the two nestled together right in the hollow of my throat. I sang:

"Blacks and bays,
Dapples and gray…"

and from the earth itself, the final words sang out,

"All the pretty little horses."

That was when I cried, long and loud, a sound I hope never to make again as long as I live.

Then I went back down the hill and home, where Papa still waited by the open door.

ABRAHAM'S BOYS

by Joe Hill

Joe Hill is the bestselling author of the novel *Heart-Shaped Box* and the short story collection *20th Century Ghosts*, both of which won the Bram Stoker Award. He is currently at work on a comic book called *Locke & Key* with artist Gabriel Rodriguez.

The vampire hunter Abraham Van Helsing first appeared in the most famous vampire novel of them all, Bram Stoker's classic *Dracula*, and served as the inspiration for editor Jeanne Cavelos's 2004 anthology *The Many Faces of Van Helsing*, which features new stories about this intriguing and enigmatic figure.

Joe Hill's "Abraham's Boys," from that anthology, provides a new literary interpretation of this classic character by way of nods to such contemporary issues as domestic abuse and post-traumatic stress disorder. The story also calls to mind Nietzsche's famous dictum, "Whoever fights monsters should see to it that in the process he does not become a monster."

We also note that, like his protagonist, the author is the son of a famous man (author Stephen King) and also has a younger brother (author Owen King). This is most assuredly just a coincidence.

Maximilian searched for them in the carriage house and the cattle shed, even had a look in the springhouse, although he knew almost at first glance he wouldn't find them there. Rudy wouldn't hide in a place like that, dank and chill, no windows and so no light, a place that smelled of bats. It was too much like a basement. Rudy never went in their basement back home if he could help it, was afraid the door would shut behind him, and he'd find himself trapped in the suffocating dark.

Max checked the barn last, but they weren't hiding there either, and when he came into the dooryard, he saw with a shock dusk had come. He had never imagined it could be so late.

"No more this game," he shouted. "Rudolf! We have to go." Only when he said *have* it came out *hoff*, a noise like a horse sneezing. He hated the sound of his own voice, envied his younger brother's confident American pronunciations. Rudolf had been born here, had never seen Amsterdam. Max had lived the first five years of his life there, in a dimly lit apartment that smelled of mildewed velvet curtains, and the latrine stink of the canal below.

Max hollered until his throat was raw, but in the end, all his shouting brought only Mrs. Kutchner, who shuffled slowly across the porch, hugging herself for warmth, although it was not cold. When she reached the railing she took it in both hands and sagged forward, using it to hold herself up.

This time last fall, Mrs. Kutchner had been agreeably plump, dimples in her fleshy cheeks, her face always flushed from the heat of the kitchen. Now her face was starved, the skin pulled tight across the skull beneath, her eyes feverish and bird-bright in their bony hollows. Her daughter, Arlene—who at this very moment was hiding with Rudy somewhere—had whispered that her mother kept a tin bucket next to the bed, and when her father carried it to the outhouse in the morning to empty it, it sloshed with a quarter inch of bad-smelling blood.

"You'n go on if you want, dear," she said. "I'll tell your brother to run on home when he crawls out from whatever hole he's in."

"Did I wake you, Mrs. Kutchner?" he asked. She shook her head, but his guilt was not eased. "I'm sorry to get you out of bed. My loud mouth." Then, his tone uncertain: "Do you think you should be up?"

"Are you doctorin me, Max Van Helsing? You don't think I get enough of that from your daddy?" she asked, one corner of her mouth rising in a weak smile.

"No ma'am. I mean, yes ma'am."

Rudy would've said something clever to make her whoop with laughter and clap her hands. Rudy belonged on the radio, a child star on someone's variety program. Max never knew what to say, and anyway, wasn't suited to comedy. It wasn't just his accent, although that was a source of constant discomfort for him, one more reason to speak as little as possible. But it was also a matter of temperament; he often found himself unable to fight his way through his own smothering reserve.

"He's pretty strict about havin you two boys in before dark, isn't he?"

"Yes ma'am," he said.

"There's plenty like him," she said. "They brung the old country over with them. Although I would have thought a doctor wouldn't be so superstitious. Educated and all."

Max suppressed a shudder of revulsion. Saying that his father was superstitious was an understatement of grotesquely funny proportions.

"You wouldn't think he'd worry so much about one like you," she went on. "I can't imagine you've ever been any trouble in your life."

"Thank you, ma'am," said Max, when what he really wanted to say was he wished more than anything she'd go back inside, lie down and rest. Sometimes it seemed to him he was allergic to expressing himself. Often, when he desperately wanted to say a thing, he could actually feel his windpipe closing up on him, cutting off his air. He wanted to offer to help her in, imagined taking her elbow, leaning close enough to smell her hair. He wanted to tell her he prayed for her at night, not that his prayers could be assumed to have value; Max had prayed for his own mother, too, but it hadn't made any difference. He said none of these things. *Thank you, ma'am* was the most he could manage.

"You go on," she said. "Tell your father I asked Rudy to stay behind, help me clean up a mess in the kitchen. I'll send him along."

"Yes, ma'am. Thank you, ma'am. Tell him hurry please."

When he was in the road he looked back. Mrs. Kutchner clutched a handkerchief to her lips, but she immediately removed it, and flapped it in a gay little wave, a gesture so endearing it made Max sick to his bones. He raised his own hand to her and then turned away. The sound of her harsh, barking coughs followed him up the road for a while—an angry dog, slipped free of its tether and chasing him away.

When he came into the yard, the sky was the shade of blue closest to black, except for a faint bonfire glow in the west where the sun had just disappeared, and his father was sitting on the porch waiting with the quirt. Max paused at the bottom of the steps, looking up at him. His father's eyes were hooded, impossible to see beneath the bushy steel-wool tangles of his eyebrows.

Max waited for him to say something. He didn't. Finally, Max gave up and spoke himself. "It's still light."

"The sun is down."

"We are just at Arlene's. It isn't even ten minutes away."

"Yes, Mrs. Kutchner's is very safe. A veritable fortress. Protected by a doddering farmer who can barely bend over, his rheumatism pains him so, and an illiterate peasant whose bowels are being eaten by cancer."

"She is not illiterate," Max said. He heard how defensive he sounded, and when he spoke again, it was in a tone of carefully modulated reason. "They can't bear the light. You say so yourself. If it isn't dark there is nothing to fear. Look how bright the sky."

His father nodded, allowing the point, then said, "And where is Rudolf?"

"He is right behind me."

The old man craned his head on his neck, making an exaggerated show of searching the empty road behind Max.

"I mean, he is coming," Max said. "He stops to help clean something for Mrs. Kutchner."

"Clean what?"

"A bag of flour I think. It breaks open, scatters on everything. She's going to clean herself, but Rudy say no he wants to do it. I tell them I will run ahead so you will not wonder where we are. He'll be here any minute."

His father sat perfectly still, his back rigid, his face immobile. Then, just when Max thought the conversation was over, he said, very slowly, "And so you left him?"

Max instantly saw, with a sinking feeling of despair, the corner he had painted himself into, but it was too late now, no talking his way back out of it. "Yes sir."

"To walk home alone? In the dark?"

"Yes sir."

"I see. Go in. To your studies."

Max made his way up the steps, towards the front door, which was partly open. He felt himself clenching up as he went past the rocking chair, expecting the quirt. Instead, when his father lunged, it was to clamp his hand on Max's wrist, squeezing so hard Max grimaced, felt the bones separating in the joint.

His father sucked at the air, a sissing indraw of breath, a sound Max had learned was often prelude to a right cross. "You know our enemies? And still you dally with your friends until the night come?"

Max tried to answer, but couldn't, felt his windpipe closing, felt himself choking again on the things he wanted, but didn't have the nerve, to say.

"Rudolf I expect not to learn. He is American, here they believe the child should teach the parent. I see how he look at me when I talk. How he try not to laugh. This is bad. But you. At least when Rudolf disobey, it is deliberate, I feel him *engaging* me. You disobey in a stupor, without considering, and then you wonder why sometime I can hardly stand to look at you. Mr. Barnum has a horse that can add small numbers. It is considered one of the great amazements of his circus. If you were once to show the slightest comprehension of what things I tell you, it would be wonder on the same order." He let go of Max's wrist, and Max took a drunken step backwards, his arm throbbing. "Go inside and out of my sight. You will want to rest. That uncomfortable buzzing in your head is the hum of thought. I know the sensation must be quite unfamiliar." Tapping his own temple to show where the thoughts were.

"Yes sir," Max said, in a tone—he had to admit—which sounded stupid and churlish. Why did his father's accent sound cultured and worldly, while the same accent made himself sound like a dull-witted Scandinavian farmhand, someone good at milking the cows maybe, but who would goggle in fear and confusion at an open book. Max turned into the house, without looking where he was going, and batted his head against the bulbs of garlic hanging from the top of the door frame. His father snorted at him.

Max sat in the kitchen, a lamp burning at the far end of the table, not enough to dispel the darkness gathering in the room. He waited, listening, his head cocked so he could see through the window and into the yard. He had his English Grammar open in front of him, but he didn't look at it, couldn't find the will to do anything but sit and watch for Rudy. In a while it was too dark to see the road, though, or anyone coming along it. The tops of the pines were black cutouts etched across a sky that was a color like the last faint glow of dying coals. Soon even that was gone, and into the darkness was cast a handful of stars, a scatter of bright flecks. Max heard his father in the rocker, the soft whine-and-thump of the curved wooden runners going back and forth over the boards of the porch. Max shoved his hands through his hair, pulling at it, chanting to himself, *Rudy, come on*, wanting more than anything for the waiting to be over. It might've been an hour. It might've been fifteen minutes.

Then he heard him, the soft chuff of his brother's feet in the chalky dirt at the side of the road; he slowed as he came into the yard, but Max suspected he had just been running, a hypothesis that was confirmed as soon as Rudy spoke. Although he tried for his usual tone of good humor, he was winded, could only speak in bursts.

"Sorry, sorry. Mrs. Kutchner. An accident. Asked me to help. I know. Late."

The rocker stopped moving. The boards creaked, as their father came to his feet.

"So Max said. And did you get the mess clean up?"

"Yuh. Uh-huh. Arlene and I. Arlene ran through the kitchen. Wasn't looking. Mrs. Kutchner—Mrs. Kutchner dropped a stack of plates—"

Max shut his eyes, bent his head forward, yanking at the roots of his hair in anguish.

"Mrs. Kutchner shouldn't tire herself. She's unwell. Indeed, I think she can hardly rise from bed."

"That's what—that's what I thought. Too." Rudy's voice at the bottom of the porch. He was beginning to recover his air. "It's not really all the way dark yet."

"It isn't? Ah. When one get to my age, the vision fail some, and dusk is often mistake for night. Here I was thinking sunset has come and gone twenty minutes ago. What time—?" Max heard the steely snap of his father opening his pocket watch. He sighed. "But it's too dark for me to read the hands. Well. Your concern for Mrs. Kutchner, I admire."

"Oh it—it was nothing—" Rudy said, putting his foot on the first step of the porch.

"But really, you should worry more about your own well-being, Rudolf," said their father, his voice calm, benevolent, speaking in the tone Max often imagined him employing when addressing patients he knew were in the final stages of a fatal illness. It was after dark and the doctor was in.

Rudy said, "I'm sorry, I'm—"

"You're sorry now. But your regret will be more palpable momentarily."

The quirt came down with a meaty smack, and Rudy, who would be ten in two weeks, screamed. Max ground his teeth, his hands still digging in his hair; pressed his wrists against his ears, trying vainly to block out the sounds of shrieking, and of the quirt striking at flesh, fat and bone.

With his ears covered he didn't hear their father come in. He looked up when a shadow fell across him. Abraham stood in the doorway to the hall, hair disheveled, collar askew, the quirt pointed at the floor. Max waited to be hit with it, but no blow came.

"Help your brother in."

Max rose unsteadily to his feet. He couldn't hold the old man's gaze so he lowered his eyes, found himself staring at the quirt instead. The back of his father's hand was freckled with blood. Max drew a thin, dismayed breath.

"You see what you make me do."

Max didn't reply. Maybe no answer was necessary or expected.

His father stood there for a moment longer, then turned, and strode away into the back of the house, toward the private study he always kept locked, a room in which they were forbidden to enter without his permission. Many nights he nodded off there, and could be heard shouting in his sleep, cursing in Dutch.

"Stop running," Max shouted. "I catch you eventually."

Rudolf capered across the corral, grabbed the rail and heaved himself over it, sprinted for the side of the house, his laughter trailing behind him.

"Give it back," Max said, and he leaped the rail without slowing down, hit the ground without losing a step. He was angry, really angry, and in his fury possessed an unlikely grace; unlikely because he was built along the same lines as his father, with the rough dimensions of a water buffalo taught to walk on its back legs.

Rudy, by contrast, had their mother's delicate build, to go with her porcelain complexion. He was quick, but Max was closing in anyway. Rudy was looking back over his shoulder too much, not concentrating on where he was going. He was almost to the side of the house. When he got there, Max would have him trapped against the wall, could easily cut off any attempt to break left or right.

But Rudy didn't break to the left or right. The window to their father's study was pushed open about a foot, revealing a cool library darkness. Rudy grabbed the windowsill over his head—he still held Max's letter in one hand—and with a giddy glance back, heaved himself into the shadows.

However their father felt about them arriving home after dark, it was nothing compared to how he would feel to discover either one of them had gained entry to his most private sanctum. But their father was gone, had taken the Ford somewhere, and Max didn't slow down to think what would happen if he suddenly returned. He jumped and grabbed his brother's ankle, thinking he would drag the little worm back out into the light, but Rudy screamed, twisted his foot out of Max's grasp. He fell into darkness, crashed to the floorboards with an echoing thud that caused glass to rattle softly against glass somewhere in the office. Then Max had the windowsill and he yanked himself into the air—

"Go slow, Max, it's a… " his brother cried.

—and he thrust himself through the window.

"Big drop," Rudy finished.

Max had been in his father's study before, of course (sometimes Abraham invited them in for "a talk," by which he meant he would talk and they would listen), but he had never entered the room by way of the window. He spilled forward, had a startling glance of the floor almost three feet below him, and realized he was about to dive into it face first. At the edge of his vision he saw a round end table, next to one of his father's armchairs, and he reached for it to stop his fall. His momentum continued to carry him forward, and he crashed to the floor. At the last moment, he turned his face aside and most of his weight came down on his right shoulder. The furniture leaped. The end table turned over, dumping everything on it. Max heard a bang, and a glassy crack that was more painful to him then the soreness he felt in either head or shoulder.

Rudy sprawled a yard away from him, sitting on the floor, still grinning a little foolishly. He held the letter half-crumpled in one hand, forgotten.

The end table was on its side, fortunately not broken. But an empty inkpot had smashed, lay in gleaming chunks close to Max's knee. A stack of books had been flung across the Persian carpet. A few papers swirled overhead, drifting slowly to the floor with a swish and a scrape.

"You see what you make me do," Max said, gesturing at the inkpot. Then he flinched, realizing that this was exactly what his father had said to him a few nights before; he didn't like the old man peeping out from inside him, talking through him like a puppet, a hollowed-out, empty-headed boy of wood.

"We'll just throw it away," Rudy said.

"He knows where everything in his office is. He will notice it missing."

"My balls. He comes in here to drink brandy, fart in his couch and fall asleep. I've been in here lots of times. I took his lighter for smokes last month and he still hasn't noticed."

"You what?" Max asked, staring at his younger brother in genuine surprise, and not without a certain envy. It was the older brother's place to take foolish risks, and be casually detached about it later.

"Who's this letter to, that you had to go and hide somewhere to write it? I was watching you work on it over your shoulder. 'I still remember how I held your hand in mine.'" Rudy's voice swooping and fluttering in mock-romantic passion.

Max lunged at his brother, but was too slow, Rudy had flipped the letter over and was reading the beginning. The smile began to fade, thought lines wrinkling the pale expanse of his forehead; then Max had ripped the sheet of paper away.

"Mother?" Rudy asked, thoroughly nonplussed.

"It was assignment for school. We were ask if you wrote a letter to anyone, who would it be? Mrs. Louden tell us it could be someone imaginary or—or historic figure. Someone dead."

"You'd turn that in? And let Mrs. Louden read it?"

"I don't know. I am not finish yet." But as Max spoke, he was already beginning to realize he had made a mistake, allowed himself to get carried away by the fascinating possibilities of the assignment, the irresistible *what if* of it, and had written things too personal for him to show anyone. He had written *you were the only one I knew how to talk to* and *I am sometimes so lonely*. He had really been imagining her reading it, somehow, somewhere—perhaps as he wrote it, some astral form of her staring over his shoulder, smiling sentimentally as his pen scratched across the page. It was a mawkish, absurd fantasy and he felt a withering embarrassment to think he had given in to it so completely.

His mother had already been weak and ill when the scandal drove their family from Amsterdam. They lived for a while in England, but word of the terrible thing their father had done (whatever it was—Max doubted he would ever know) followed them. On they had gone to America. His father believed he had acquired a position as a lecturer at Vassar College, was so sure of this he had ladled much of his savings into the purchase of a handsome nearby farm. But in New York City they were met by the dean, who told Abraham Van Helsing that he could not, in good conscience, allow the doctor to work unsupervised with young ladies who were not yet at the age of consent. Max knew now his father had killed his mother as surely as if he had held a pillow over her face in her sickbed. It wasn't the travel that had done her in, although that was bad enough, too much for a woman who was both pregnant and weak with a chronic infection of the blood which caused her to bruise at the slightest touch. It was humiliation. Mina had not been able to survive the shame of what he had done, what they were all forced to run from.

"Come on," Max said. "Let's clean up and get out of here."

He righted the table and began gathering the books, but turned his head when Rudy said, "Do you believe in vampires, Max?"

Rudy was on his knees in front of an ottoman across the room. He had hunched over to collect a few papers which had settled there, then stayed to look at the battered doctor's bag tucked underneath it. Rudy tugged at the rosary knotted around the handles.

"Leave that alone," Max said. "We need to clean, not make bigger mess."

"Do you?"

Max was briefly silent. "Mother was attacked. Her blood was never the same after. Her illness."

"Did *she* ever say she was attacked, or did he?"

"She died when I was six. She would not confide in a child about such a thing."

"But... do you think we're in danger?" Rudy had the bag open now. He reached in to remove a bundle, carefully wrapped in royal purple fabric. Wood clicked against wood inside the velvet. "That vampires are out there, waiting for a chance at us. For our guard to drop?"

"I would not discount possibility. However unlikely."

"However unlikely," his brother said, laughing softly. He opened the velvet wrap and looked in at the nine-inch stakes, skewers of blazing white wood, handles wrapped in oiled leather. "Well I think it's all bullshit. *Bullll*-shit." Singing a little.

The course of the discussion unnerved Max. He felt, for an instant, light-headed with vertigo, as if he suddenly found himself peering over a steep drop. And perhaps that wasn't too far off. He had always known the two of them would have this conversation someday and he feared where it might take them. Rudy was never happier than when he was making an argument, but he didn't follow his doubts to their logical conclusion. He could say it was all bullshit, but didn't pause to consider what that meant about their father, a man who feared the night as a person who can't swim fears the ocean. Max almost *needed* it to be true, for vampires to be real, because the other possibility—that their father was, and always had been, in the grip of a psychotic fantasy—was too awful, too overwhelming.

He was still considering how to reply when his attention was caught by a picture frame, slid halfway in under his father's armchair. It was face down, but he knew what he'd see when he turned it over. It was a sepia-toned calotype print of his mother, posed in the library of their townhouse in Amsterdam. She wore a white straw hat, her ebon hair fluffed in airy curls beneath it. One gloved hand was raised in an enigmatic gesture, so that she almost appeared to be waving an invisible cigarette in the air. Her lips were parted. She was saying something, Max often wondered what. He for some reason imagined himself to be standing just out of the frame, a child of four, staring solemnly up at her. He felt that she was raising her hand to wave him back, keep him from wandering into the shot. If this was so, it seemed reasonable to believe she had been caught forever in the act of saying his name.

He heard a scrape and a tinkle of falling glass as he picked the picture frame up and turned it over. The plate of glass had shattered in the exact center. He began wiggling small gleaming fangs of glass out of the frame and setting them aside, concerned that none should scratch the glossy calotype beneath. He pulled a large wedge of glass out of the upper corner of the frame, and the corner of the print came loose with it. He reached up to poke the print back into place... and then hesitated, frowning, feeling for a moment that his eyes had crossed and he was seeing double. There appeared to be a second print behind the first. He tugged the photograph of his mother out of the frame, then stared without understanding at the picture that had been secreted behind it. An icy numbness spread through his chest, crawling into his throat. He glanced around and was relieved to see Rudy still kneeling at the ottoman, humming to himself, rolling the stakes back up into their shroud of velvet.

He looked back at the secret photograph. The woman in it was dead. She was also naked from the waist up, her gown torn open and yanked to the curve of her waist. She was sprawled in a four-poster bed—pinned there by ropes wound around her throat, and pulling her arms over her head. She was young and maybe had been beautiful, it was hard to tell; one eye was shut, the other open in a slit that showed the unnatural glaze on the eyeball beneath. Her mouth was forced open, stuffed with an obscene misshapen white ball. She was actually biting down on it, her upper lip drawn back to show the small, even row of her upper palate. The side of her face was discolored with bruise. Between the milky, heavy curves of her breasts was a spoke of white wood. Her left rib-cage was painted with blood.

Even when he heard the car in the drive, he couldn't move, couldn't pry his gaze from the photograph. Then Rudy was up, pulling at Max's shoulder, telling him they had to go. Max clapped the photo to his chest to keep his brother from seeing. He said go, I'll be right behind you, and Rudy took his hand off his arm and went on.

Max fumbled with the picture frame, struggling to fit the calotype of the murdered woman back into place... then saw something else, went still again. He had not until this instant taken notice of the figure to the far left in the photograph, a man on the near side of the bed. His back was to the photographer, and he was so close in the foreground that his shape was a blurred, vaguely rabbinical figure, in a flat-brimmed black hat and black overcoat. There was no way to be sure who this man was, but Max *was* sure, knew him from the way he held his head, the careful, almost stiff way it was balanced on the thick barrel of his neck. In one hand he held a hatchet. In the other a doctor's bag.

The car died with an emphysemic wheeze and tinny clatter. He squeezed the photograph of the dead woman into the frame, slid the portrait of Mina back on top of it. He set the picture, with no glass in it, on the end table, stared at it for a beat, then saw with horror that he had stuck Mina in upside down. He started to reach for it.

"*Come on!*" Rudy cried. "*Please, Max.*" He was outside, standing on his tiptoes to look back into the study.

Max kicked the broken glass under the armchair, stepped to the window, and screamed. Or tried to—he didn't have the air in his lungs, couldn't force it up his throat.

Their father stood behind Rudy, staring in at Max over Rudy's head. Rudy didn't see, didn't know he was there, until their father put his hands on his shoulders. Rudolf had no trouble screaming at all, and leaped as if he meant to jump back into the study.

The old man regarded his eldest son in silence. Max stared back, head half out the window, hands on the sill.

"If you like," his father said. "I could open the door and you could effect your exit by the hallway. What it lacks in drama, it makes up in convenience."

"No," Max said. "No thank you. Thank you. I'm—we're—this is—mistake. I'm sorry."

"Mistake is not knowing capital of Portugal on a geography test. This is something else." He paused, lowering his head, his face stony. Then he released Rudy, and turned away, opening a hand and pointing it at the yard in a gesture that seemed to mean, *step this way.* "We will discuss what at later date. Now if it is no trouble, I will ask you to leave my office."

Max stared. His father had never before delayed punishment—breaking and entering his study at the least deserved a vigorous lashing—and he tried to think why he would now. His father waited. Max climbed out, dropped into the flower bed. Rudy looked at him, eyes helpless, pleading, asking him what they ought to do. Max tipped his head towards the stables—their own private study—and started walking slowly and deliberately away. His little brother fell into step beside him, trembling continuously.

Before they could get away, though, his father's hand fell on Max's shoulder.

"My rules are to protect you always, Maximilian," he said. "Maybe you are tell me now you don't want to be protect any longer? When you were little I cover your eyes at the theater, when come the murderers to slaughter Clarence in *Richard.* But then, later, when we went to *Macbeth*, you shove my hand away, you *want* to see. Now I feel history repeats, nuh?"

Max didn't reply. At last his father released him.

They had not gone ten paces when he spoke again. "Oh I almost forget. I did not tell you where or why I was gone and I have piece of news I know will make sad the both of you. Mr. Kutchner run up the road while you were in school, shouting doctor, doctor, come quick, my wife. As soon as I see her, burning with fever, I know she must travel to Dr. Rosen's infirmary in town, but alas, the farmer come for me too late. Walking her to my car, her intestines fall out of her with a *slop*." He made a soft clucking sound with his tongue, as of disapproval. "I will have our suits cleaned. The funeral is on Friday."

Arlene Kutchner wasn't in school the next day. They walked past her house on the way home, but the black shutters were across the windows, and the place had a too-silent, abandoned feel to it. The funeral would be in town the next morning, and perhaps Arlene and her father had already gone there to wait. They had family in the village. When the two boys tramped into their own yard, the Ford was parked alongside the house, and the slanted double doors to the basement were open.

Rudy pointed himself towards the barn—they owned a single horse, a used-up nag named Rice, and it was Rudy's day to muck out her stable—and Max went into the house alone. He was at the kitchen table when he heard the doors to the cellar crash shut outside. Shortly afterwards his father climbed the stairs, appeared in the basement doorway.

"Are you work on something down there?" Max asked.

His father's gaze swept across him, but his eyes were deliberately blank.

"Later I shall unfold to you," he said, and Max watched him while he removed a silver key from the pocket of his waistcoat, and turned it in the lock to the basement door. It had never been used before and until that moment, Max had not even known a key existed.

Max was on edge the rest of the afternoon, kept looking at the basement door, unsettled by his father's promise: *Later I shall unfold to you.* There was of course no opportunity to talk to Rudy about it over dinner, to speculate on just *what* might be unfolded, but they were also unable to talk afterward, when they remained at the kitchen table with their schoolbooks. Usually, their father retired early to his study to be alone, and they wouldn't see him again until morning. But tonight he seemed restless, always coming in and out of the room, to wash a glass, to find his reading glasses, and finally, to light a lantern. He adjusted the wick, so a low red flame wavered at the bottom of the glass chimney, and then set it on the table before Max.

"Boys," he said, turning to the basement, unlocking the bolt. "Go downstairs. Wait for me. Touch nothing."

Rudy threw a horrified, whey-faced look at Max. Rudy couldn't bear the basement, its low ceiling and its smell, the lacy veils of cobwebs in the corners. If Rudy was ever given a chore there, he always begged Max to go with him. Max opened his mouth to question their father, but he was already slipping away, out of the room, disappearing down the hall to his study.

Max looked at Rudy. Rudy was shaking his head in wordless denial.

"It will be all right," Max promised. "I will take care of you."

Rudy carried the lantern, and let Max go ahead of him down the stairs. The reddish-bronze light of the lamp threw shadows that leaned and jumped, a surging darkness that lapped at the walls of the stairwell. Max descended to the basement floor and took a slow, uncertain look around. To the left of the stairs was a worktable. On top of it was a pile of something, covered in a piece of grimy white tarp—stacks of bricks maybe, or heaps of folded laundry, it was hard to tell in the gloom without going closer. Max crept in slow, shuffling steps until he had crossed most of the way to the table, and then he stopped, suddenly knowing what the sheet covered.

"We need to go, Max," Rudy peeped, right behind him. Max hadn't known he was there, had thought he was still standing on the steps. "We need to go right now." And Max knew he didn't mean just get out of the basement, but get out of the house, run from the place where they had lived ten years and not come back.

But it was too late to pretend they were Huck and Jim and light out for the territories. Their father's feet fell heavily on the dusty wood planks behind them. Max glanced up the stairs at him. He was carrying his doctor's bag.

"I can only deduce," their father began, "from your ransack of my private study, you have finally develop interest in the secret work to which I sacrifice so much. I have in my time kill six of the Undead by my own hand, the last the diseased bitch in the picture I keep hid in my office—I believe you have both see it." Rudy cast a panicked look at Max, who only shook his head, *be silent*. Their father went on: "I have train others in the art of destroying the vampire, including your mother's unfortunate first husband, Jonathan Harker, Gott bless him, and so I can be held indirectly responsible for the slaughter of perhaps fifty of their filthy, infected kind. And it is now, I see, time my own boys learn how it is done. How to be sure. So you may know how to strike at those who would strike at you."

"I don't want to know," Rudy said.

"He didn't see picture," Max said at the same time.

Their father appeared not to hear either of them. He moved past them to the worktable, and the canvas covered shape upon it. He lifted one corner of the tarp and looked beneath it, made a humming sound of approval, and pulled the covering away.

Mrs. Kutchner was naked, and hideously withered, her cheeks sunken, her mouth gaping open. Her stomach was caved impossibly in beneath her ribs, as if everything in it had been sucked out by the pressure of a vacuum. Her back was bruised a deep bluish violet by the blood that had settled there. Rudy moaned and hid his face against Max's side.

Their father set his doctor's bag beside her body, and opened it.

"She isn't, of course, Undead. Merely dead. True vampires are uncommon, and it would not be practicable, or advisable, for me to find one for you to rehearse on. But she will suit for purposes of demonstration." From within his bag he removed the bundle of stakes wrapped in velvet.

"What is she doing here?" Max asked. "They bury her tomorrow."

"But today I am to make autopsy, for purposes of my private research. Mr. Kutchner understand, is happy to cooperate, if it mean one day no other woman die in such a way." He had a stake in one hand, a mallet in the other.

Rudy began to cry.

Max felt he was coming unmoored from himself. His body stepped forward, without him in it; another part of him remained beside Rudy, an arm around his brother's heaving shoulders. Rudy was saying, *Please I want to go upstairs.* Max watched himself walk, flat-footed, to his father, who was staring at him with an expression that mingled curiosity with a certain quiet appreciation.

He handed Max the mallet and that brought him back. He was in his own body again, conscious of the weight of the hammer, tugging his wrist downward. His father gripped Max's other hand and lifted it, drawing it towards Mrs. Kutchner's meager breasts. He pressed Max's fingertips to a spot between two ribs and Max looked into the dead woman's face. Her mouth open as to speak. *Are you doctorin' me, Max Van Helsing?*

"Here," his father said, folding one of the stakes into his hand. "You drive it in here. To the hilt. In an actual case, the first blow will be follow by wailing, profanity, a frantic struggle to escape. The accursed never go easily. Bear down. Do not desist from your work until you have impale her and she has give up her struggle against you. It will be over soon enough."

Max raised the mallet. He stared into her face and wished he could say he was sorry, that he didn't want to do it. When he slammed the mallet down, with an echoing bang, he heard a high, piercing scream and almost screamed himself, believing for an instant it was her, still somehow alive; then realized it was Rudy. Max was powerfully built, with his deep water buffalo chest and Scandinavian farmer's shoulders. With the first blow he had driven the stake over two-thirds of the way in. He only needed to bring the mallet down once more. The blood that squelched up around the wood was cold and had a sticky, viscous consistency.

Max swayed, his head light. His father took his arm.

"*Goot,*" Abraham whispered into his ear, his arms around him, squeezing him so tightly his ribs creaked. Max felt a little thrill of pleasure—an automatic reaction to the intense, unmistakable affection of his father's embrace—and was sickened by it. "To do offense to the house of the human spirit, even after its tenant depart, is no easy thing, I know."

His father went on holding him. Max stared at Mrs. Kutchner's gaping mouth, the delicate row of her upper teeth, and found himself remembering the girl in the calotype print, the ball of garlic jammed in her mouth.

"Where were her fangs?" Max said.

"*Hm?* Whose? What?" his father said.

"In the photograph of the one you kill," Max said, turning his head and looking into his father's face. "She didn't have fangs."

His father stared at him, his eyes blank, uncomprehending. Then he said, "They disappear after the vampire die. *Poof.*"

He released him and Max could breathe normally again. Their father straightened.

"Now, there remain one thing," he said. "The head must be remove, and the mouth stuff with garlic. Rudolf!"

Max turned his head slowly. His father had moved back a step. In one hand he held a hatchet, Max didn't know where it had come from. Rudy was on the stairs, three steps from the bottom. He stood pressed against the wall, his left wrist shoved in his mouth to quell his screaming. He shook his head, back and forth, frantically.

Max reached for the hatchet, grabbed it by the handle. "I do it." He would too, was confident of himself. He saw now he had always had it in him: his father's brusque willingness to puncture flesh and toil in blood. He saw it clear, and with a kind of dismay.

"No," his father said, wrenching the hatchet away, pushing Max back. Max bumped the worktable, and a few stakes rolled off, clattering to the dust. "Pick those up."

Rudy bolted, but slipped on the steps, falling to all fours and banging his knees. Their father grabbed him by the hair and hauled him backwards, throwing him to the floor. Rudy thudded into the dirt, sprawling on his belly. He rolled over. When he spoke his voice was unrecognizable.

"*Please!*" he screamed. "*Please don't! I'm scared. Please father don't make me.*"

The mallet in one hand, half a dozen stakes in the other, Max stepped forward, thought he would intervene, but his father swiveled, caught his elbow, shoved him at the stairs.

"Up. Now." Giving him another push as he spoke.

Max fell on the stairs, barking one of his own shins.

Their father bent to grab Rudy by the arm, but he squirmed away, crabwalking over the dirt for a far corner of the room.

"Come. I help you," their father said. "Her neck is brittle. It won't take long."

Rudy shook his head, backed further into the corner by the coal bin.

His father flung the axe in the dirt. "Then you will remain here until you are in a more complaisant state of mind."

He turned, took Max's arm and thrust him towards the top of the steps.

"*No!*" Rudy screamed, getting up, lunging for the stairs.

The handle of the hatchet got caught between his feet, though, and he tripped on it, crashed to his knees. He got back up, but by then their father was pushing Max through the door at the top of the staircase, following him through. He slammed it behind them. Rudy hit the other side a moment later, as their father was turning that silver key in the lock.

"Please!" Rudy cried. "I'm scared! I'm scared I want to come out!"

Max stood in the kitchen. His ears were ringing. He wanted to say stop it, open the door, but couldn't get the words out, felt his throat closing. His arms hung at his sides, his hands heavy, as if cast from lead. No—not lead. They were heavy from the things in them. The mallet. The stakes.

His father panted for breath, his broad forehead resting against the shut door. When he finally stepped back, his hair was scrambled, and his collar had popped loose.

"You see what he make me do?" he said. "Your mother was also so, just as unbending and hysterical, just as in need of firm instruction. I tried, I—"

The old man turned to look at him, and in the instant before Max hit him with the mallet, his father had time to register shock, even wonder. Max caught him across the jaw, a blow that connected with a bony clunk, and enough force to drive a shivering feeling of impact up into his elbow. His father sagged to one knee, but Max had to hit him again to sprawl him on his back.

Abraham's eyelids sank as he began to slide into unconsciousness, but they came up again when Max sat down on top of him. His father opened his mouth to say something, but Max had heard enough, was through talking, had never been much when it came to talk anyway. What mattered now was the work of his hands; work he had a natural instinct for, had maybe been born to.

He put the tip of the stake where his father had showed him and struck the hilt with the mallet. It turned out it was all true, what the old man had told him in the basement. There was wailing and profanity and a frantic struggle to get away, but it was over soon enough.

NUNC DIMITTIS

by Tanith Lee

Tanith Lee, a two-time winner of the World Fantasy Award, is the author of more than 100 books. These include the Piratica Series and the Wolf Tower/Claidi Journals series, among many others. She's written several vampiric novels, including *Vivia, Sabella,* and her Blood Opera series, which began with *Dark Dance.* Her Flat Earth series is now being brought back into print, and the publisher, Norilana Books, will be bringing out two new volumes in the series as well. Lee also has several new short stories forthcoming in various magazines and anthologies. Her most recent book is a new story collection, *Tempting the Gods.*

The Biblical phrase "nunc dimittis servum tuum"—"now dismiss your servant"—evokes images of selfless sacrifice. But so often when we tear away the mask of "You need me," we find underneath the face of "I need you."

We sometimes describe a certain type of person as an "emotional vampire." For all their romance and dangerous magnetism, vampires are at heart blood-suckers—that is to say, parasites. A parasite cannot live without attaching itself to a host organism.

After reading this story, ask yourself how many vampires are in it. Are you sure? Maybe you should count again.

The Vampire was old, and no longer beautiful. In common with all living things, she had aged, though very slowly, like the tall trees in the park. Slender and gaunt and leafless, they stood out there, beyond the long windows, rain-dashed in the grey morning. While she sat in her high-backed chair in that corner of the room where the curtains of thick yellow lace and the wine-coloured blinds kept every drop of daylight out. In the glimmer of the ornate oil lamp, she had been reading. The lamp came from a Russian palace. The book had once graced the library of a corrupt pope named, in his temporal existence, Roderigo Borgia. Now the Vampire's dry hands had fallen upon the page. She sat in her black lace dress that was one hundred and eighty years of age, far younger than she herself, and looked at the old man, streaked by the shine of distant windows.

"You say you are tired, Vassu. I know how it is. To be so tired, and unable to rest. It is a terrible thing."

"But, Princess," said the old man quietly, "it is more than this. I am dying."

The Vampire stirred a little. The pale leaves of her hands rustled on the page. She stared, with an almost childlike wonder.

"Dying? Can this be? You are sure?"

The old man, very clean and neat in his dark clothing, nodded humbly.

"Yes, Princess."

"Oh, Vassu," she said, "are you glad?"

He seemed a little embarrassed. Finally he said:

"Forgive me, Princess, but I am very glad. Yes, very glad."

"I understand."

"Only," he said, "I am troubled for your sake."

"No, no," said the Vampire, with the fragile perfect courtesy of her class and kind. "No, it must not concern you. You have been a good servant. Far better than I might ever have hoped for. I am thankful, Vassu, for all your care of me. I shall miss you. But you have earned…" she hesitated. She said, "You have more than earned your peace."

"But you," he said.

"I shall do very well. My requirements are small, now. The days when I was a huntress are gone, and the nights. Do you remember, Vassu?"

"I remember, Princess."

"When I was so hungry, and so relentless. And so lovely. My white face in a thousand ballroom mirrors. My silk slippers stained with dew. And my lovers waking in the cold morning, where I had left them. But now, I do not sleep, I am seldom hungry. I never lust. I never love. These are the comforts of old age. There is only one comfort that is denied to me. And who knows. One day, I too…" She smiled at him. Her teeth were beautiful, but almost even now, the exquisite points of the canines quite worn away. "Leave me when you must," she said. "I shall mourn you. I shall envy you. But I ask nothing more, my good and noble friend."

The old man bowed his head.

"I have," he said, "a few days, a handful of nights. There is something I wish to try to do in this time. I will try to find one who may take my place."

The Vampire stared at him again, now astonished. "But Vassu, my irreplaceable help—it is no longer possible."

"Yes. If I am swift."

"The world is not as it was," she said, with a grave and dreadful wisdom.

He lifted his head. More gravely, he answered:

"The world is as it has always been, Princess. Only our perceptions of it have grown more acute. Our knowledge less bearable."

She nodded.

"Yes, this must be so. How could the world have changed so terribly? It must be we who have changed."

He trimmed the lamp before he left her.

Outside, the rain dripped steadily from the trees.

The city, in the rain, was not unlike a forest. But the old man, who had been in many forests and many cities, had no special feeling for it. His feelings, his senses, were primed to other things.

Nevertheless, he was conscious of his bizarre and anachronistic effect, like that of a figure in some surrealist painting, walking the streets in clothes of a bygone era, aware he did not blend with his surroundings, nor render them homage of any kind. Yet even when, as sometimes happened, a gang of children or youths jeered and called after him the foul names he was familiar with in twenty languages, he neither cringed nor cared. He had no concern for such things. He had been so many places, seen so many sights; cities which burned or fell in ruin, the young who grew old, as he had, and who died, as now, at last, he too would die. This thought of death soothed him, comforted him, and brought with it a great sadness, a strange jealousy. He did not want to leave her. Of course he did not. The idea of her vulnerability in this harsh world, not new in its cruelty but ancient, though freshly recognised—it horrified him. This was the sadness. And the jealousy… that, because he must try to find another to take his place. And that other would come to be for her, as he had been.

The memories rose and sank in his brain like waking dreams all the time he moved about the streets. As he climbed the steps of museums and underpasses, he remembered other steps in other lands, of marble and fine stone. And looking out from high balconies, the city reduced to a map, he recollected the towers of cathedrals, the star-swept points of mountains. And then at last, as if turning over the pages of a book backwards, he reached the beginning.

There she stood, between two tall white graves, the chateau grounds behind her, everything silvered in the dusk before the dawn. She wore a ball dress, and a long white cloak. And even then, her hair was dressed in the fashion of a century ago; dark hair, like black flowers.

He had known for a year before that he would serve her. The moment he had heard them talk of her in the town. They were not afraid of her, but in awe. She did not prey upon her own people, as some of her line had done.

When he could get up, he went to her. He had kneeled, and stammered something; he was only sixteen, and she not much older. But she had simply looked at him quietly and said: "I know. You are welcome." The words had been in a language they seldom spoke together now. Yet always, when he recalled that meeting, she said them in that tongue, and with the same gentle inflexion.

All about, in the small café where he had paused to sit and drink coffee, vague shapes came and went. Of no interest to him, no use to her. Throughout the morning, there had been nothing to alert him. He would know. He would know, as he had known it of himself.

He rose, and left the café, and the waking dream walked with him. A lean black car slid by, and he recaptured a carriage carving through white snow—

A step brushed the pavement, perhaps twenty feet behind him. The old man did not hesitate. He stepped on, and into an alleyway that ran between the high buildings. The steps followed him; he could not hear them all, only one in seven, or eight. A little wire of tension began to draw taut within him, but he gave no sign. Water trickled along the brickwork beside him, and the noise of the city was lost.

Abruptly, a hand was on the back of his neck, a capable hand, warm and sure, not harming him yet, almost the touch of a lover.

"That's right, old man. Keep still. I'm not going to hurt you, not if you do what I say."

He stood, the warm and vital hand on his neck, and waited.

"All right," said the voice, which was masculine and young and with some other elusive quality to it. "Now let me have your wallet."

The old man spoke in a faltering tone, very foreign, very fearful. "I have—no wallet."

The hand changed its nature, gripped him, bit.

"Don't lie. I can hurt you. I don't want to, but I can. Give me whatever money you have."

"Yes," he faltered, "yes—yes—"

And slipped from the sure and merciless grip like water, spinning, gripping in turn, flinging away—there was a whirl of movement.

The old man's attacker slammed against the wet grey wall and rolled down it. He lay on the rainy debris of the alley floor, and stared up, too surprised to look surprised.

This had happened many times before. Several had supposed the old man an easy mark, but he had all the steely power of what he was. Even now, even dying, he was terrible in his strength. And yet, though it had happened often, now it was different. The tension had not gone away.

Swiftly, deliberately, the old man studied the young one.

Something struck home instantly. Even sprawled, the adversary was peculiarly graceful, the grace of enormous physical coordination. The touch of the hand, also, impervious and certain—there was strength here, too. And now the eyes. Yes, the eyes were steady, intelligent, and with a curious lambency, an innocence—

"Get up," the old man said. He had waited upon an aristocrat. He had become one himself, and sounded it. "Up. I will not hit you again."

The young man grinned, aware of the irony. The humour flitted through his eyes. In the dull light of the alley, they were the colour of leopards—not the eyes of leopards, but their *pelts*.

"Yes, and you could, couldn't you, granddad."

"My name," said the old man, "is Vasyelu Gorin. I am the father to none, and my nonexistent sons and daughters have no children. And you?"

"My name," said the young man, "is Snake."

The old man nodded. He did not really care about names, either.

"Get up, Snake. You attempted to rob me, because you are poor, having no work and no wish for work. I will buy you food, now."

The young man continued to lie, as if at ease, on the ground.

"Why?"

"Because I want something from you."

"What? You're right. I'll do almost anything, if you pay me enough. So you can tell me."

The old man looked at the young man called Snake, and knew that all he said was a fact. Knew that here was one who had stolen and whored, and stolen again when the slack bodies slept, both male and female, exhausted by the sexual vampirism he had practised on them, drawing their misguided souls out through their pores as later he would draw the notes from purse and pocket. Yes, a vampire. Maybe a murderer, too. Very probably a murderer.

"If you will do anything," said the old man, "I need not tell you beforehand. You will do it anyway."

"Almost anything, is what I said."

"Advise me then," said Vasyelu Gorin, the servant of the Vampire, "what you will not do. I shall then refrain from asking it of you."

The young man laughed. In one fluid movement he came to his feet. When the old man walked on, he followed.

Testing him, the old man took Snake to an expensive restaurant, far up on the white hills of the city, where the glass geography nearly scratched the sky. Ignoring the mud on his dilapidated leather jacket, Snake became a flawless image of decorum, became what is always ultimately respected, one who does not care. The old man, who also did not care, appreciated this act, but knew it was nothing more. Snake had learned how to be a prince. But he was a gigolo with a closet full of skins to put on. Now and then the speckled leopard eyes, searching, wary, would give him away.

After the good food and the excellent wine, the cognac, the cigarettes taken from the silver box—Snake had stolen three, but, stylishly overt, had left them sticking like porcupine quills from his breast pocket—they went out again into the rain.

The dark was gathering, and Snake solicitously took the old man's arm. Vasyelu Gorin dislodged him, offended by the cheapness of the gesture after the acceptable one with the cigarettes.

"Don't you like me any more?" said Snake. "I can go now, if you want. But you might pay for my wasted time."

"Stop that," said Vasyelu Gorin. "Come along."

Smiling, Snake came with him. They walked, between the glowing pyramids of stores, through shadowy tunnels, over the wet paving. When the thoroughfares folded away and the meadows of the great gardens began, Snake grew tense. The landscape was less familiar to him, obviously. This part of the forest was unknown.

Trees hung down from the air to the sides of the road.

"I could kill you here," said Snake. "Take your money, and run."

"You could try," said the old man, but he was becoming weary. He was no longer certain, and yet, he was sufficiently certain that his jealousy had assumed a tinge of hatred. If the young man were stupid enough to set on him, how simple it would be to break the columnar neck, like pale amber, between his fleshless hands. But then, she would know. She would know he had found for her, and destroyed the finding. And she would be generous, and he would leave her, aware he had failed her, too.

When the huge gates appeared, Snake made no comment. He seemed, by then, to anticipate them. The old man went into the park, moving quickly now, in order to outdistance his own feelings. Snake loped at his side.

Three windows were alight, high in the house. Her windows. And as they came to the stair that led up, under its skeins of ivy, into the porch, her pencil-thin shadow passed over the lights above, like smoke, or a ghost.

"I thought you lived alone," said Snake. "I thought you were lonely."

The old man did not answer any more. He went up the stair and opened the door. Snake came in behind him, and stood quite still, until Vasyelu Gorin had found the lamp in the niche by the door, and lit it. Unnatural stained glass flared in the door panels, and the window-niches either side, owls and lotuses and far-off temples, scrolled and luminous, oddly aloof.

Vasyelu began to walk toward the inner stair.

"Just a minute," said Snake. Vasyelu halted, saying nothing. "I'd just like to know," said Snake, "how many of your friends are here, and just what your friends are figuring to do, and how I fit into their plans."

The old man sighed.

"There is one woman in the room above. I am taking you to see her. She is a Princess. Her name is Darejan Draculas." He began to ascend the stair.

Left in the dark, the visitor said softly:

"What?"

"You think you have heard the name. You are correct. But it is another branch."

He heard only the first step as it touched the carpeted stair. With a bound, the creature was upon him, the lamp was lifted from his hand. Snake danced behind it, glittering and unreal.

"Dracula," he said.

"Draculas. Another branch."

"A vampire."

"Do you believe in such things?" said the old man. "You should, living as you do, preying as you do."

"I never," said Snake, "pray."

"Prey," said the old man. "Prey upon. You cannot even speak your own language. Give me the lamp, or shall I take it? The stair is steep. You may be damaged, this time. Which will not be good for any of your trades."

Snake made a little bow, and returned the lamp.

They continued up the carpeted hill of stair, and reached a landing and so a passage, and so her door.

The appurtenances of the house, even glimpsed in the erratic fleeting of the lamp, were very gracious. The old man was used to them, but Snake, perhaps, took note. Then again, like the size and importance of the park gates, the young thief might well have anticipated such elegance.

And there was no neglect, no dust, no air of decay, or, more tritely, of the grave. Women arrived regularly from the city to clean, under Vasyelu Gorin's stern command; flowers were even arranged in the salon for those occasions when the Princess came downstairs. Which was rarely, now. How tired she had grown. Not aged, but bored by life. The old man sighed again, and knocked upon her door.

Her response was given softly. Vasyelu Gorin saw, from the tail of his eye, the young man's reaction, his ears almost pricked, like a cat's.

"Wait here," Vasyelu said, and went into the room, shutting the door, leaving the other outside it in the dark.

The windows which had shone bright outside were black within. The candles burned, red and white as carnations.

The Vampire was seated before her little harpsichord. She had probably been playing it, its song so quiet it was seldom audible beyond her door. Long ago, nonetheless, he would have heard it. Long ago—

"Princess," he said, "I have brought someone with me."

He had not been sure what she would do, or say, confronted by the actuality. She might even remonstrate, grow angry, though he had not often seen her angry. But he saw now she had guessed, in some tangible way, that he would not return alone, and she had been preparing herself. As she rose to her feet, he beheld the red satin dress, the jewelled silver crucifix at her throat, the trickle of silver from her ears. On the thin hands, the great rings throbbed their sable colours. Her hair, which had never lost its blackness, abbreviated at her shoulders and waved in a fashion of only twenty years before, framed the starved bones of her face with a savage luxuriance. She was magnificent. Gaunt, elderly, her beauty lost, her heart dulled, yet—magnificent, wondrous.

He stared at her humbly, ready to weep because, for the half of one half-moment, he had doubted.

"Yes," she said. She gave him the briefest smile, like a swift caress. "Then I will see him, Vassu."

Snake was seated cross-legged a short distance along the passage. He had discovered, in the dark, a slender Chinese vase of the *yang ts'ai* palette, and held it between his hands, his chin resting on the brim.

"Shall I break this?" he asked.

Vasyelu ignored the remark. He indicated the opened door.

"You may go in now."

"May I? How excited you're making me."

Snake flowed upright. Still holding the vase, he went through into the Vampire's apartment. The old man came into the room after him, placing his black-garbed body, like a shadow, by the door, which he left now standing wide. The old man watched Snake.

Circling slightly, perhaps unconsciously, he had approached a third of the chamber's length towards the woman. Seeing him from the back, Vasyelu Gorin was able to observe all the play of tautening muscles along the spine, like those of something readying itself to spring, or to escape. Yet, not seeing the face, the eyes, was unsatisfactory. The old man shifted his position, edged shadow-like along the room's perimeter, until he had gained a better vantage.

"Good evening," the Vampire said to Snake. "Would you care to put down the vase? Or, if you prefer, smash it. Indecision can be distressing."

"Perhaps I'd prefer to keep the vase."

"Oh, then do so, by all means. But I suggest you allow Vasyelu to wrap it up for you, before you go. Or someone may rob you on the street."

Snake pivotted, lightly, like a dancer, and put the vase on a side-table. Turning again, he smiled at her.

"There are so many valuable things here. What shall I take? What about the silver cross you're wearing?"

The Vampire also smiled.

"An heirloom. I am rather fond of it. I do not recommend you should try to take that."

Snake's eyes enlarged. He was naive, amazed.

"But I thought, if I did what you wanted, if I made you happy—I could have whatever I liked. Wasn't that the bargain?"

"And how would you propose to make me happy?"

Snake went close to her; he prowled about her, very slowly. Disgusted, fascinated, the old man watched him. Snake stood behind her, leaning against her, his breath stirring the filaments of her hair. He slipped his left hand along her shoulder, sliding from the red satin to the dry uncoloured skin of her throat. Vasyelu remembered the touch of the hand, electric, and so sensitive, the fingers of an artist or a surgeon.

The Vampire never changed. She said:

"No. You will not make me happy, my child."

"Oh," Snake said into her ear. "You can't be certain. If you like, if you really like, I'll let you drink my blood."

The Vampire laughed. It was frightening. Something dormant yet intensely powerful seemed to come alive in her as she did so, like flame from a finished coal. The sound, the appalling life, shook the young man away from her. And for an instant, the old man saw fear in the leopard-yellow eyes, a fear as intrinsic to the being of Snake as to cause fear was intrinsic to the being of the Vampire.

And, still blazing with her power, she turned on him.

"What do you think I am?" she said, "some senile hag greedy to rub her scaly flesh against your smoothness; some hag you can, being yourself without sanity or fastidiousness, corrupt with the phantoms, the left-overs of pleasure, and then murder, tearing the gems from her fingers with your teeth? Or I am a perverted hag, wanting to lick up your youth with your juices. Am I that? Come now," she said, her fire lowering itself, crackling with its amusement, with everything she held in check, her voice a long, long pin, skewering what she spoke to against the farther wall. "Come now. How can I be such a fiend, and wear the crucifix on my breast? My ancient, withered, fallen, empty breast. Come now. What's in a name?"

As the pin of her voice came out of him, the young man pushed himself away from the wall. For an instant there was an air of panic about him. He was accustomed to the characteristics of the world. Old men creeping through rainy alleys could not strike mighty blows with their iron hands. Women were moths that burnt, but did not burn, tones of tinsel and pleading, not razor blades.

Snake shuddered all over. And then his panic went away. Instinctively, he told something from the aura of the room itself. Living as he did, generally he had come to trust his instincts.

He slunk back to the woman, not close, this time, no nearer than two yards.

"Your man over there," he said, "he took me to a fancy restaurant. He got me drunk. I say things when I'm drunk I shouldn't say. You see? I'm a lout. I shouldn't be here in your nice house. I don't know how to talk to people like you. To a lady. You see? But I haven't any money. None. Ask him. I explained it all. I'll do anything for money. And the way I talk. Some of them like it. You see? It makes me sound dangerous. They like that. But it's just an act." Fawning on her, bending on her the groundless glory of his eyes, he had also retreated, was almost at the door.

The Vampire made no move. Like a marvelous waxwork she dominated the room, red and white and black, and the old man was only a shadow in a corner.

Snake darted about and bolted. In the blind lightlessness, he skimmed the passage, leapt out in space upon the stairs, touched, leapt, touched, reached the open area beyond. Some glint of star-shine revealed the stained glass panes in the door. As it crashed open, he knew quite well that he had been let go. Then it slammed behind him and he pelted through ivy and down the outer steps, and across the hollow plain of tall wet trees.

So much, infallibly, his instincts had told him. Strangely, even as he came out of the gates upon the vacant road, and raced towards the heart of the city, they did not tell him he was free.

"Do you recollect," said the Vampire, "you asked me, at the very beginning, about the crucifix."

"I do recollect, Princess. It seemed odd to me, then. I did not understand, of course."

"And you," she said. "How would you have it, after—" She waited. She said, "After you leave me."

He rejoiced that his death would cause her a momentary pain. He could not help that, now. He had seen the fire wake in her, flash and scald in her, as it had not done for half a century, ignited by the presence of the thief, the gigolo, the parasite.

"He," said the old man, "is young and strong, and can dig some pit for me."

"And no ceremony?" She had overlooked his petulance, of course, and her tact made him ashamed.

"Just to lie quiet will be enough," he said, "but thank you, Princess, for your care. I do not suppose it will matter. Either there is nothing, or there is something so different I shall be astonished by it."

"Ah, my friend. Then you do not imagine yourself damned?"

"No," he said. "No, no." And all at once there was passion in his voice, one last fire of his own to offer her. "In the life you gave me, I was blessed."

She closed her eyes, and Vasyelu Gorin perceived he had wounded her with his love. And, no longer peevishly, but in the way of a lover, he was glad.

Next day, a little before three in the afternoon, Snake returned.

A wind was blowing, and seemed to have blown him to the door in a scurry of old brown leaves. His hair was also blown, and bright, his face wind-slapped to a ridiculous freshness. His eyes, however, were heavy, encircled, dulled. The eyes showed, as did nothing else about him, that he had spent the night, the forenoon, engaged in his second line of commerce. They might have drawn thick curtains and blown out the lights, but that would not have helped him. The senses of Snake were doubly acute in the dark, and he could see in the dark, like a lynx.

"Yes?" said the old man, looking at him blankly, as if at a tradesman.

"Yes," said Snake, and came by him into the house.

Vasyelu did not stop him. Of course not. He allowed the young man, and all his blown gleamingness and his wretched roué eyes, to stroll across to the doors of the salon, and walk through. Vasyelu followed.

The blinds, a sombre ivory colour, were down, and the lamps had been lit; on a polished table hothouse flowers foamed from a jade bowl. A second door stood open on the small library, the soft glow of the lamps trembling over gold-worked spines, up and up, a torrent of static, priceless books.

Snake went into and around the library, and came out.

"I didn't take anything."

"Can you even read?" snapped Vasyelu Gorin, remembering when he could not, a wood-cutter's fifth son, an oaf and a sot, drinking his way or sleeping his way through a life without windows or vistas, a mere blackness of error and unrecognised boredom. Long ago. In that little town cobbled together under the forest. And the chateau with its starry lights, the carriages on the road, shining, the dark trees either side. And bowing in answer to a question, lifting a silver comfit box from a pocket as easily as he had lifted a coin the day before…

Snake sat down, leaning back relaxedly in the chair. He was not relaxed, the old man knew. What was he telling himself? That there was money here, eccentricity to be battened upon. That he could take her, the old woman, one way or another. There were always excuses that one could make to oneself.

When the Vampire entered the room, Snake, practised, a gigolo, came to his feet. And the Vampire was amused by him, gently now. She wore a bone-white frock that had been sent from Paris last year. She had never worn it before. Pinned at the neck was a black velvet rose with a single drop of dew shivering on a single petal: a pearl that had come from the crown jewels of a czar. Her tact, her peerless tact.

Naturally, the pearl was saying, *this is why you have come back. Naturally. There is nothing to fear.*

Vasyelu Gorin left them. He returned later with the decanters and glasses. The cold supper had been laid out by people from the city who handled such things, pâté and lobster and chicken, lemon slices cut like flowers, orange slices like suns, tomatoes that were anemones, and oceans of green lettuce, and cold, glittering ice. He decanted the wines. He arranged the silver coffee service, the boxes of different cigarettes. The winter night had settled by then against the house, and, roused by the brilliantly lighted rooms, a moth was dashing itself between the candles and the coloured fruits. The old man caught it in a crystal goblet, took it away, let it go into the darkness. For a hundred years and more, he had never killed anything.

Sometimes, he heard them laugh. The young man's laughter was at first too eloquent, too beautiful, too unreal. But then, it became ragged, boisterous; it became genuine.

The wind blew stonily. Vasyelu Gorin imagined the frail moth beating its wings against the huge wings of the wind, falling spent to the ground. It would be good to rest.

In the last half hour before dawn, she came quietly from the salon, and up the stair. The old man knew she had seen him as he waited in the shadows. That she did not look at him or call to him was her attempt to spare him this sudden sheen that was upon her, its direct and pitiless glare. So he glimpsed it obliquely, no more. Her straight pale figure ascending, slim and limpid as a girl's. Her eyes were young, full of a primal refinding, full of utter newness.

In the salon, Snake slept under his jacket on the long white couch, its brocaded cushions beneath his cheek. Would he, on waking, carefully examine his throat in a mirror?

The old man watched the young man sleeping. She had taught Vasyelu Gorin how to speak five languages, and how to read three others. She had allowed him to discover music, and art, history and the stars; profundity, mercy. He had found the closed tomb of life opened out on every side into unbelievable, inexpressible landscapes. And yet, and yet. The journey must have its end. Worn out with ecstasy and experience, too tired any more to laugh with joy. To rest was everything. To be still. Only she could continue, for only she could be eternally reborn. For Vasyelu, once had been enough.

He left the young man sleeping. Five hours later, Snake was noiselessly gone. He had taken all the cigarettes, but nothing else.

Snake sold the cigarettes quickly. At one of the cafés he sometimes frequented, he met with those who, sensing some change in his fortunes, urged him to boast. Snake did not, remaining irritatingly reticent, vague. It was another patron. An old man who liked to give him things. Where did the old man live? Oh, a fine apartment, the north side of the city.

Some of the day, he walked.

A hunter, he distrusted the open veldt of daylight. There was too little cover, and equally too great cover for the things he stalked. In the afternoon, he sat in the gardens of a museum. Students came and went, seriously alone, or in groups riotously. Snake observed them. They were scarcely younger than he himself, yet to him, another species. Now and then a girl, catching his eye, might smile, or make an attempt to linger, to interest him. Snake did not respond. With the economic contempt of what he had become, he dismissed all such sexual encounters. Their allure, their youth, these were commodities valueless in others. They would not pay him.

The old woman, however, he did not dismiss. How old was she? Sixty, perhaps—no, much older. Ninety was more likely. And yet, her face, her neck, her hands were curiously smooth, unlined. At times, she might only have been fifty. And the dyed hair, which should have made her seem raddled, somehow enhanced the illusion of a young woman.

Yes, she fascinated him. Probably she had been an actress. Foreign, theatrical—rich. If she was prepared to keep him, thinking him mistakenly her pet cat, then he was willing, for a while. He could steal from her when she began to cloy and he decided to leave.

Yet, something in the uncomplexity of these thoughts disturbed him. The first time he had run away, he was unsure now from what. Not the vampire name, certainly, a stage name—*Draculas*—what else? But from something—some awareness of fate for which idea his vocabulary had no word, and no explanation. Driven once away, driven thereafter to return, since it was foolish not to. And she had known how to treat him. Gracefully, graciously. She would be honourable, for her kind always were. Used to spending money for what they wanted, they did not baulk at buying people, too. They had never forgotten flesh, also, had a price, since their roots were firmly locked in an era when there had been slaves.

But. But he would not, he told himself, go there tonight. No. It would be good she should not be able to rely on him. He might go tomorrow, or the next day, but not tonight.

The turning world lifted away from the sun, through a winter sunset, into darkness. Snake was glad to see the ending of the light, and false light instead spring up from the apartment blocks, the cafés.

He moved out on to the wide pavement of a street, and a man came and took his arm on the right side, another starting to walk by him on the left.

"Yes, this is the one, the one calls himself Snake."

"Are you?" the man who walked beside him asked.

"Of course it is," said the first man, squeezing his arm. "Didn't we have an exact description? Isn't he just the way he was described?"

"And the right place, too," agreed the other man, who did not hold him. "The right area."

The men wore neat nondescript clothing. Their faces were sallow and smiling, and fixed. This was a routine with which both were familiar. Snake did not know them, but he knew the touch, the accent, the smiling fixture of their masks. He had tensed. Now he let the tension melt away, so they should see and feel it had gone.

"What do you want?"

The man who held his arm only smiled.

The other man said, "Just to earn our living."

"Doing what?"

On either side the lighted street went by. Ahead, at the street's corner, a vacant lot opened where a broken wall lunged away into the shadows.

"It seems you upset someone," said the man who only walked. "Upset them badly."

"I upset a lot of people," Snake said.

"I'm sure you do. But some of them won't stand for it."

"Who was this? Perhaps I should see them."

"No. They don't want that. They don't want you to see anybody." The black turn was a few feet away.

"Perhaps I can put it right."

"No. That's what we've been paid to do."

"But if I don't know—" said Snake, and lurched against the man who held his arm, ramming his fist into the soft belly. The man let go of him and fell. Snake ran. He ran past the lot, into the brilliant glare of another street beyond, and was almost laughing when the thrown knife caught him in the back.

The lights turned over. Something hard and cold struck his chest, his face. Snake realized it was the pavement. There was a dim blurred noise, coming and going, perhaps a crowd gathering. Someone stood on his ribs and pulled the knife out of him and the pain began.

"Is that it?" a choked voice asked some way above him: the man he had punched in the stomach.

"It'll do nicely."

A new voice shouted. A car swam to the kerb and pulled up raucously. The car door slammed, and footsteps went over the cement. Behind him, Snake heard the two men walking briskly away.

Snake began to get up, and was surprised to find he was unable to.

"What happened?" someone asked, high, high above.

"I don't know."

A woman said softly, "Look, there's blood—"

Snake took no notice. After a moment he tried again to get up, and succeeded in getting to his knees. He had been hurt, that was all. He could feel the pain, no longer sharp, blurred, like the noise he could hear, coming and going. He opened his eyes. The light had faded, then came back in a long wave, then faded again. There seemed to be only five or six people standing around him. As he rose, the nearer shapes backed away.

"He shouldn't move," someone said urgently.

A hand touched his shoulder, fluttered off, like an insect.

The light faded into black, and the noise swept in like a tide, filling his ears, dazing him. Something supported him, and he shook it from him—a wall—

"Come back, son," a man called. The lights burned up again, reminiscent of a cinema. He would be all right in a moment. He walked away from the small crowd, not looking at them. Respectfully, in awe, they let him go, and noted his blood trailing behind him along the pavement.

The French clock chimed sweetly in the salon; it was seven. Beyond the window, the park was black. It had begun to rain again.

The old man had been watching from the downstairs window for rather more than an hour. Sometimes, he would step restlessly away, circle the room, straighten a picture, pick up a petal discarded by the dying flowers. Then go back to the window, looking out at the trees, the rain and the night.

Less than a minute after the chiming of the clock, a piece of the static darkness came away and began to move, very slowly, towards the house.

Vasyelu Gorin went out into the hall. As he did so, he glanced towards the stairway. The lamp at the stairhead was alight, and she stood there in its rays, her hands lying loosely at her sides, elegant as if weightless, her head raised.

"Princess?"

"Yes, I know. Please hurry, Vassu. I think there is scarcely any margin left."

The old man opened the door quickly. He sprang down the steps as lightly as a boy of eighteen. The black rain swept against his face, redolent of a thousand memories, and he ran through an orchard in Burgundy, across a hillside in Tuscany, along the path of a wild garden near St. Petersburg that was St. Petersburg no more, until he reached the body of a young man lying over the roots of a tree.

The old man bent down, and an eye opened palely in the dark and looked at him.

"Knifed me," said Snake. "Crawled all this way."

Vasyelu Gorin leaned in the rain to the grass of France, Italy and Russia, and lifted Snake in his arms. The body lolled, heavy, not helping him. But it did not matter. How strong he was, he might marvel at it, as he stood, holding the young man across his breast, and turning, ran back towards the house.

"I don't know," Snake muttered, "don't know who sent them. Plenty would like to—How bad is it? I didn't think it was so bad."

The ivy drifted across Snake's face and he closed his eyes.

As Vasyelu entered the hall, the Vampire was already on the lowest stair. Vasyelu carried the dying man across to her, and laid him at her feet. Then Vasyelu turned to leave.

"Wait," she said.

"No, Princess. This is a private thing. Between the two of you, as once it was between us. I do not want to see it, Princess. I do not want to see it with another."

She looked at him, for a moment like a child, sorry to have distressed him, unwilling to give in. Then she nodded. "Go then, my dear."

He went away at once. So he did not witness it as she left the stair, and knelt beside Snake on the Turkish carpet newly coloured with blood. Yet, it seemed to him he heard the rustle her dress made, like thin crisp paper, and the whisper of the tiny dagger parting her flesh, and then the long still sigh.

He walked down through the house, into the clean and frigid modern kitchen full of electricity. There he sat, and remembered the forest above the town, the torches as the yelling aristocrats hunted him for his theft of the comfit box, the blows when they caught up with him. He remembered, with a painless unoppressed refinding, what it was like to begin to die in such a way, the confused anger, the coming and going of tangible things, long pulses of being alternating with deep valleys of non-being. And then the agonised impossible crawl, fingers in the earth itself, pulling him forward, legs sometimes able to assist, sometimes failing, passengers which must be dragged with the rest. In the graveyard at the edge of the estate, he ceased to move. He could go no farther. The soil was cold, and the white tombs, curious petrified vegetation over his head, seemed to suck the black sky into themselves, so they darkened, and the sky grew pale.

But as the sky was drained of its blood, the foretaste of day began to possess it. In less than an hour, the sun would rise.

He had heard her name, and known he would eventually come to serve her. The way in which he had known, both for himself and for the young man called Snake, had been in a presage of violent death.

All the while, searching through the city, there had been no one with that stigma upon them, that mark. Until, in the alley, the warm hand gripped his neck, until he looked into the leopard-coloured eyes. Then Vasyelu saw the mark, smelled the scent of it like singed bone.

How Snake, crippled by a mortal wound, bleeding and semi-aware, had brought himself such a distance, through the long streets hard as nails, through the mossy garden-land of the rich, through the colossal gates, over the watery, night-tuned plain, so far, dying, the old man did not require to ask, or to be puzzled by. He, too, had done such a thing, more than two centuries ago. And there she had found him, between the tall white graves. When he could focus his vision again, he had looked and seen her, the most beautiful thing he ever set eyes upon. She had given him her blood. He had drunk the blood of Darejan Draculas, a princess, a vampire. Unique elixir, it had saved him. All wounds had healed. Death had dropped from him like a torn skin, and everything he had been—scavenger, thief, brawler, drunkard, and, for a certain number of coins, *whore*—each of these things had crumbled away. Standing up, he had trodden on them, left them behind. He had gone to her, and kneeled down as, a short while before, she had kneeled by him, cradling him, giving him the life of her silver veins.

And this, all this, was now for the other. Even her blood, it seemed, did not bestow immortality, only longevity, at last coming to a stop for Vasyelu Gorin. And so, many many decades from this night the other, too, would come to the same hiatus. Snake, too, would remember the waking moment, conscious another now endured the stupefied thrill of it, and all that would begin thereafter.

Finally, with a sort of guiltiness, the old man left the hygienic kitchen and went back towards the glow of the upper floor, stealing out into the shadow at the light's edge.

He understood that she would sense him there, untroubled by his presence—had she not been prepared to let him remain?

It was done.

Her dress was spread like an open rose, the young man lying against her, his eyes wide, gazing up at her. And she would be the most beautiful thing that he had ever seen. All about, invisible, the shed skins of his life, husks he would presently scuff uncaringly underfoot. And she?

The Vampire's head inclined toward Snake. The dark hair fell softly. Her face, powdered by the lampshine, was young, was full of vitality, serene vivacity, loveliness. Everything had come back to her. She was reborn.

Perhaps it was only an illusion.

The old man bowed his head, there in the shadows. The jealousy, the regret were gone. In the end, his life with her had become only another skin that he must cast. He would have the peace that she might never have, and be glad of it. The young man would serve her, and she would be huntress once more, and dancer, a bright phantom gliding over the ballroom of the city, this city and others, and all the worlds of land and soul between.

Vasyelu Gorin stirred on the platform of his existence. He would depart now, or very soon; already he heard the murmur of the approaching train. It would be simple, this time, not like the other time at all. To go willingly, everything achieved, in order. Knowing she was safe.

There was even a faint colour in her cheeks, a blooming. Or maybe, that was just a trick of the lamp.

The old man waited until they had risen to their feet, and walked together quietly into the salon, before he came from the shadows and began to climb the stairs, hearing the silence, their silence, like that of new lovers.

At the head of the stair, beyond the lamp, the dark was gentle, soft as the Vampire's hair. Vasyelu walked forward into the dark without misgiving, tenderly.

How he had loved her.

HUNGER

by Gabriela Lee

Gabriela Lee is a graduate of the University of the Philippines with a B.A. in Creative Writing, and received her Master's degree in Literary Studies from the National University of Singapore. She is based in Singapore and works for an online gaming company, developing content. Lee's fiction has appeared in the anthology *A Time for Dragons*, edited by Vincent Simbulan, in the *Dark Blue Southern Seas 2009* literary anthology from Silliman University, and in an anthology of Filipino fiction called *A Different Voice*, in which this story first appeared.

"Hunger" deals with the vampiric *mananaggal* myth, which, in Philippine mythology, is a blend of old-school Western vampiric myths and native superstition. "In myths, she's a beautiful woman who can separate the upper half of her body from her lower half," Lee said. "The lower half stays rooted in one place while the upper half goes on a feeding frenzy—usually sucking the unborn fetus from a pregnant woman. If you look at the duality of such a creature, it serves as the perfect metaphor for adolescent hunger."

You feel like a small star orbiting around a center of gravity as you step out of the car and instinctively move towards Kian. He smiles at you: that kind of smile reserved for best friends and childhood confidants, and for once you wish that you hadn't known him since first grade, when you squished a sugary ice cream cone into Joseph Bulaong's nose because he was beating Kian up in the middle of the school playground.

"Good gig," he says, giving you a thumbs-up sign. "Your rendition of that Buckley song was amazing." You blush and grin, batting away the compliment with one blue-manicured hand. He is the bassist for Hands Down; you are the lead singer. You see him three gigs a week, the last of which is usually at Hole-In-The-Wall, a small smoky bar with faux 1960s American diner-style interiors and a bathroom that flooded every fourth toilet flush. You resist the urge to step closer to him; instead, you wait until Lia and Paolo step out of the car and make their way towards Ababu. It is past two in the morning, and you're sure your parents will have a hissy fit when they smell your clothes (they reek of cigarette smoke, courtesy of the patrons at the Hole) but that it's all right: more time spent with Kian is definitely time spent well.

The small neighborhood Persian-esque eatery is filled with students and other night owls—your group has to stand at the curb for ten minutes before a free seat emerges, floating like an empty glass bottle in the middle of the sea of people. You move towards it, quickly manipulating an extra chair to fit the four of you around the monobloc table. You already know what you want, and wave the waitress away. Shawarma at this time of the night is always a treat.

Paolo and Kian immediately fall into conversation regarding the set: Paolo you've known since your freshman year at the Ateneo, where he mistakenly thought you were a high school student looking for the Office of Admissions and kindly directed you to Kostka Hall. Both of you were in Comm; Lia, whom you met through friends of friends, was a part-time model and no-time student. Kian, you've known since forever. (A Sarah Geronimo song suddenly plays in your head, and you want to smash your internal radio for even considering such a cheesy song to describe…oh never mind. Forever really isn't enough, anyway.)

The food arrives, courtesy of a sleepy-eyed waitress in shorts and a pink cotton shirt. Another rerun of a bad Filipino action movie plays on the TV mounted at the corner of Ababu, where nobody pays any attention (well, except the *manongs* who would usually sit at the proper angle, just to watch the rapid-fire exchange between Fernando Poe Jr. and Max Alvarado). Paolo scarfs down his food, occasionally squirting the fiery-hot red chili sauce liberally across the mound of white rice on his plate. Lia eats delicately, drinking her Diet Coke with a pinky slightly raised in the air; if you didn't know where the place was, you're sure you'd have thought that Lia was eating at one of those five-star restaurant chains that her father owns.

Surreptitiously, you watch Kian scoop up the rice and meat into his spoon and put it in his mouth. You watch his lips surround the neck of the spoon, the silver giving way to warm pink flesh. You watch his tongue swirl slightly around the depression of the spoon, cleaning the surface and making sure that the savory white sauce was gone from the utensil. You feel a shiver run down your spine. (*God, am I being turned on by watching him eat?*)

"Rachel, are you all right? You're not eating your food." Paolo peers into your face, his eyes wide behind his glasses. Despite his pudgy, well-dressed exterior, he was the best damn drummer you had ever met; drum sticks were lightning bolts in his hand, hurled at the next beat with deadly accuracy. Kian glances at you sideways but doesn't say anything. His eyes are dark behind the long, stylish bangs.

"Oh, I'm fine," you say, flustered. You cover up the fact that you've been checking out your best friend for the last five minutes by grabbing the chili sauce and pouring it into the shawarma. "I was just thinking—"

"We all know what you're thinking," cut in Lia suddenly.

"We do?" Paolo asks, raising an eyebrow.

You feel panic rise inside your throat, acid green bubbling just up your windpipe. (*Fuck.*)

"What are we thinking of?" Kian seconds. You feel like you're suddenly part of a hive mind.

"That Rachel fudged up the second verse to that Jack Johnson song. She went too fast. She was half a beat early."

(*Breathe. Breathe. Everything's fine.*)

You mentally count to ten, and then turn to look at Kian. His eyebrows were slightly raised, the corners of his lips curved slightly in a smile of suppressed mirth. You are briefly reminded of one of those battery-operated dolls that grinned (evilly, you think) whenever you pressed a button. He doesn't suspect a thing. Grinning, you bite into your shawarma, savoring the bite of onions and tomatoes and lettuce/cabbage (you're never sure which is which) and the sweet, sweet essence of the meat. You wonder briefly if that is how Kian will taste in your mouth: a riot of flavors, clamoring for attention, slipping/sliding across your tongue.

You don't have a gig tonight.

You open the windows of your bedroom and let the night breeze play with the tassels of your curtains, the tips of your hair. You parents are out late; another charity event, this time for the pediatrics ward. You managed to excuse yourself from tonight's festivities, claiming a headache. Your mother tells you that maybe it's the pain from not doing anything (except that "damn band"), but you barely hear her. Tonight, the winds are calling. The stars are now within your reach.

You lift up your shirt and run your fingers across the smooth line that neatly bisects your stomach, just below your navel. The cut is clean and there is almost no bleeding now. You close your eyes and allow everything that is dark and bright to resurface. You can't see it now, but the slice of pain across your mind tells you that your wings have emerged from beneath your skin: warm and leathery, smelling of old streets and older shadows. You give them an experimental flap, feeling the gust of wind lift you slightly off the ground, your toes scraping the floor. Your shoulder blades complain of the exertion, and you return to the surface, your heels conforming with the flat wooden surfaces.

Carefully, you inch your way towards the window. Your wings beat faster, and you hear a swift crack as your bones sever themselves. You feel lighter suddenly, half flesh and skin, the human side stripped away as you abandon yourself to another creature, feral and wild. A scream rips from your mouth, and you hear others answer. The wind whips around you, invisible fingers running through your hair. Pale and wide-eyed, you prepare to fly.

You take a deep breath. Hunger returns: stomach pangs stronger than any need for human food. (*Well, there is such a thing as "human" food.*) Your mouth tastes imagined blood, sweet/thick, and you know that tonight will be a feast.

Candy-coated words dribble out of your mouth as you lean into the microphone, your hands running around the slender neck of the stand as you would encircle your fingers around a lover's arm. Around you, the stage lights sweep across the tiny stage, creating a chiaroscuro effect. The beat consumes you: everything moves from one melody to the next. The riffs leave you sweaty, your heart pounding to song. You know that everything you do is dictated by the cycle of words and music—every thrust of your hip, every movement of your head, the flow of your arms and legs. This is the closest you can get to heaven, to a high, to falling in love.

You know Kian finds you beautiful when you sing—some residual psychic abilities remain at least twenty-four hours after you feed. You give him your patent come-hither look that you use whenever you sing "Hanggang Saan." That was the latest song you guys had penned, and your most popular to date—NU 107 has been playing it constantly, rumor has it that labels have been wanting to snap up your band. The ripple of excitement from hardcore fans (they were with you ever since college—orgmates and classmates, high school friends and indie audiences) was palpable. You and your bandmates try to downplay it, but even (the ice-queen) Lia can't help but break into a silly grin once in a while.

But tonight, you are focused on Kian. You run the tip of your tongue across the edges of your teeth, and pretend you aren't looking at him while he's looking at you. He's dressed up for tonight's gig: pressed midnight blue jeans and a button-down polo (you were with him when you bought this at People Are People) with a Tasmanian Devil tie. His sneakers are newly washed, and he smells like soap and deodorant, clean and smooth, like clear river water constantly washing over the shiny pebble shores.

You are feeding more often now, at least once every two days. The siren call is harder and harder to ignore. Your mother finally notices the dark circles under your eyes, fingerprints of a night spent without sleep, and your chalk-white cheeks. You wander around your house barefoot, dragging your legs, tired. Your father presses the back of his hand on your forehead, an act of concern. You try and stop yourself from tilting your head back and forcing his fingers into your mouth, a small snack in the middle of the day.

Your back is constantly sore, and drops of blood pepper your sheets. Your mother asks you if it's anything she could help you with, and you smile sweetly and tell her no, perhaps it's just dysmenorrhea. (You know you're a good liar.)

You tell the band that you're having a case of the stomach flu, and if Lia could sub first while you deal with the pain. They acquiesce, understanding that pain is a part of your life. Kian visits you often, bringing rolls of *ensaymada* from Red Ribbon, and complimenting your mother on her new hairdo. She simpers and smiles and asks him if he has a girlfriend, and you know where the conversation is going and start wishing a hole in the ground would open up and swallow you alive. Or your mother. Your stomach starts hurting again, like there is an invisible dwarf with a silver knife that is slowly peeling away layers of flesh, and dammit, you know that tonight, you have to fly again.

> Until when are we going to walk
> Arm in arm, hand in hand, friends?
> Are we only fooling each other
> Because neither wants to speak?
> —"Until When," Hands Down

When Kian first introduces you to Katherine, it is all you can do to stop from breaking her delicate little fingers in your grip. She gives you a Barbie Doll smile and tells you that she's happy to meet you and that Christopher (*Christopher?* He had never used that name since high school.) has told her so much about his best friend Rachel. You want to roll your eyes so far into your head that you might be drowned in the dark, but Kian quickly steers her away from you and towards the small round table near the amps. Lia passes by and takes you by the elbow, then frog-marches you towards the girls' toilets.

Inside the ceramic-tiled room, she proceeds to tell you how much she *hates* Kian's new girl and that if she had it her way, she would allow her latent Chinese side (the side that loves pain and torture, which then makes you wonder just how is hers and Paolo's sex life, and if the rope burn rumors are true) to take over and just slice off Katherine's flesh, one sliver at a time, until she's flayed a million times over and blood is dripping on the floor in heart-shaped droplets.

You kindly thank Lia for her thoughtful words as you lean towards the counter and position your hands underneath the sink. Water automatically gushes out from the tap and you turn your wrists, letting the cool, clear liquid wash away the memory of Katherine's touch. A part of you feels that this is a dream, a hallucinatory experience. Your stomach feels like a thousand tiny balloons straining against a net, and you're afraid that you're ready to explode.

There is a knock on the door, and you can hear Raffy, your manager, asking in his disconcertingly nasal voice (even though he says he's not gay) that it's five minutes before the set starts. Lia hollers that you're ready, that you two are just freshening up. You grip the edge of the sink with both hands, and watch in detached fascination as the color of your fingernails slowly seep away, almost matching the pale egg white surface of the sink.

You feel Lia's strong hands on your back, and you dry heave into the sink. You tell her it's just nerves, that you can't remember performing in front of an audience this large, and in a venue this popular—the Hole was like home, but a newer, larger venue, with possible scouts is something else—but Lia just rubs your back harder, until you feel the balloons carefully pop.

You now feed with a vengeance, your wings ripping through the air like sharp claws across a stretch of fine dark silk. Your tongue continually snakes out from between your lips, tasting invisible molecules, your body constantly angled, a stubborn compass needle pointing towards the next prey.

Before, when you were just starting out and you were unaccustomed to the taste of meat, you decided to just have a meal a night. You were careful to choose only the mothers who never wanted their child, or those who prayed fervently each night that they would be a good girl, that they would never allow *that man* into their beds and inside their hearts, those who were too frightened of the *hilot* or the Quiapo vendors who sold herbal concoctions beside the church. You would listen carefully to the susurrus of voices in your head, carefully separating strand from strand, allowing the most fearful to surface inside your head, like a drop of oil in a bowl of water.

But now you are ravenous. Anger fuels your hunt, and it is only after the fifth feeding that you feel slightly satisfied. You lick the blood coating your lips, run your fingers lightly across your incisors in order to check for any stray bits of meat. Carefully, you poise yourself from the edge of the corrugated tin rooftop, ready to take flight. Beneath you, the girl sleeps soundly in a small pool of dark blood, the color of the evening tide. You stretch out your wings and leap on the back of the wind. The thrill of flight still excites you, even after all these years, and you abandon yourself to the moment, the patterns of the wind at midnight, the way the city lights seem to mirror the constellation of stars scattered across the sky.

It has been six months since Kian (or Christopher, as he has decided to be called again) and Katherine hooked up. Each time that you see them, it's like a needle is being driven deeper and deeper into your chest, just above where your heart is located. You are waiting for the day when, in the middle of singing "Hanggang Saan," you suddenly keel over the microphone stand, tangling up in the skeins of wires swirling around your feet. When your bandmates turn you over, they will find a small hole just above your left breast, trickling blood down your chest and soaking your blouse. It's an appealing thought, you decide, while watching Kian steal a kiss from Katherine's lips.

You decide to turn your back on them and help Paolo out with the equipment. Since Katherine started following Kian around like a faithful (puppy?) girlfriend, their nights out as a group has been severely limited. You feel like the odd one out: Paolo and Lia have been a couple since the beginning of time, and Katherine would rather have Kian tied to a pole than leave her line of sight for more than five minutes. Sure, there are boys, and you've gone out on a few dates, only to realize that you have an annoying tendency to compare each and every reasonably interested, hot-blooded male with Kian. It's a depressing thought, and you decided to stop being masochistic by just pretending to be lesbian. Lia gleefully joins into the fray of pretense, to the point of almost kissing you on the lips after a gig, which forever made Paolo disconcerted about his girlfriend's sexual orientation and Kian laughing so hard that he had to gulp down several glasses of water just to calm down.

Tonight's different, though. Kian offers you a ride home, even though Katherine lives in Parañaque and he lives in Makati now, while you are still at your old neighborhood in La Vista. He shrugs off your protestations and instead gallantly escorts you and Katherine to his car. Paolo and Lia wave goodbye, and you find yourself sitting at the back seat of his souped-up Toyota Corolla, sharing the space with the long, hard length of Tobey, his guitar, because the front seat has been taken over by The Girlfriend.

The drive is silent along EDSA, with only Death Cab for Cutie playing on the CD player. Katherine is half-asleep, and the digital read-out on the dashboard tells you it's past two in the morning, and your parents have gotten used to you going home even later (or earlier, whichever strikes your fancy) and have resigned themselves to that fact. Kian hums along, his thumbs occasionally following the beat on the rim of the steering wheel. You are lulled by the lamp lights sweeping past the window at regular intervals, and Kian pushing the car to almost ninety, and the way the car flows along the avenue, almost as if it were flying.

Katherine lives on a sleepy street inside an exclusive subdivision. The guard already knows Kian, and waves him inside without an ID (just like at your place). The gate is white and tall, and the greenery outside is trim and neat. Beyond the fence, you can see an expanse of brick and glass. Kian carefully wakes Katherine up and kisses her tenderly. You stare out the window, focus on the stray dog wandering down the opposite sidewalk, occasionally raising up one hind leg and pissing on the side of the wall. The street lamp makes the dog's coat shine like amber. You bite your bottom lip, playing with the tender bit of flesh. They said that in the olden days, when food was scarce, your kind would feed on dogs to survive. You are glad that you have never had to deal with such a problem.

You move into the front seat when Katherine vacates it; you give her a friendly peck on the cheek and resist drawing blood. The door closes with a definitive click as you slide into the front. Kian keeps the engine on as the both of you wait until the gate opens for Katherine. Then Kian puts the car into gear, and you feel it growl to life.

The drive is smooth until you hit EDSA again, just past the Magallanes Station. For some reason, the stretch is filled with heavy-loading trucks and busloads of people on their way north, and half of the avenue is blocked by workmen and piles of rubble. Kian swears and swerves to another lane, only to be hit by another tangle in the mounting traffic jam.

"I don't think we'll get you back home so quickly, Chel," he says sleepily. You can recognize the warning signs from when you were younger—Kian would become more talkative in an effort to stave off the drowsiness. "I'm sorry."

"You can just drop me off at the next station," you say nervously. "At least you can go home and sleep, right? Not a problem."

"What kind of a best friend would I be if I don't bring you home properly?"

You laugh. "The kind that would kill us in a traffic jam because he could barely keep his eyes open."

"Well, either way, your parents would kill me," he says, rubbing his eyes with the back of his hands and leaning to the front (Sign Number Two). "I can't leave you here, but I sure as hell don't think that it will clear up soon."

"Who knows?" you tell him, falsely optimistic. "Maybe it will clear up after this stretch."

But thirty minutes later, the car barely moved ten meters. The world seems to have stopped. Kian is staring straight ahead. You adjust your skirt modestly around your thighs, clasping your hands in the middle like a proper Catholic schoolgirl. The air conditioning sputters and spits out small clouds of cool air. The CD has stopped; the interior is quieter than what you imagined a tomb to be like.

Kian peers outside. "My turn's coming up soon. I don't think this traffic will clear up."

You shrug. "If you have a couch and a spare toothbrush, I don't mind crashing over at your place."

He looks exceptionally relieved that the suggestion came from you. "If you're sure…" he says, his voice trailing off hopefully.

You nod, your fingers surreptitiously trailing across the fabric of your shirt, right above the scar. He knows about the operation, but he has never seen the scar. You hope the night won't come to that.

You were fifteen and stupid, and already three months into the pregnancy when you discovered the situation. The boy was also fifteen and stupid, and promptly stopped returning your increasingly panicky phone calls and text messages. Twice, you went to his house, but the maid answered both times and denied emphatically the presence of the Drs. Hernandezes' *único hijo*.

Desperate, you remember the story of one of your friends about the illegal clinics that litter the side streets of the city, and resolve to visit one of them. You bring three thousand pesos and the girl who told you the story, and take a jeep to Sta. Mesa. It started raining lightly then, making the streets look like pea soup, the street canals carrying with it the vestiges of the city: candy wrappers, plastic wrappers of all colors of the rainbow, dead rats and bloody cats gutted by careless drivers.

You didn't know what pain was until you fainted from it. Later on, you remember your friend telling you that there was blood, too much blood, and they had to give you a transfusion. But it was a black market clinic, and the blood was tainted, and it was only three weeks after the operation that you realized that it wasn't just any kind of disease known to man, but something other than of this world.

At first, the bleeding refused to stop. You had to buy rolls of gauze and change your bandages every hour just to avoid staining your clothes. Suspicious, your parents assigned a chaperone, Ate Babing, who spent more time chatting up the tricycle drivers at the corner store than watch you go off with your friends. There was no pain, which surprised you, just a damp feeling around your midsection, like a patch of grass after a summer shower.

And then you learned about others of your kind. They came to you just as the clock struck midnight: all women, with hair flowing like forest vines around their faces and leathery, batlike wings. All of them were also able to separate their upper halves from their lower halves, the edges of their stomachs distended and glittering from a night's frenzied feeding. You wanted to weep when you saw them, floating outside your window, looking at you with dead eyes, calling you forward. You knew what they were, you knew the stories, half-whispered to children in order to fear the dark, the beat of shadow wings. You thought that being in the city would make you safe.

But you had to accept it. A part of you knew that this was all your fault, and you had to learn how to accept consequences. And if this was punishment for that one night of bliss, then so be it.

Kian's apartment was no bigger than a large walk-in closet. Two steps forward and you were in the kitchen, two steps back and you were almost stumbling into the bed. There was no couch. You look at him expectantly. "Bathroom's over there," he says, waving carelessly at a wooden door that was held shut by a length of chain. He rummages inside a synthetic textile closet, the one with a zipper for a door, and hands you a rumpled t-shirt and a pair of cotton shorts. You thank him quietly and close the bathroom door behind you. In the dim light of a single orange electric bulb, you pour the freezing cold water over your head from a pail. There are warning bells going off inside your head, but you force them to be quiet, to still. Kian won't touch you, and you certainly will (try) not to have any physical contact with him.

(*He has a girlfriend!*)

You stumble out of the bathroom and into utter darkness. "Sorry," came his disembodied voice from somewhere to your left. "I'm too tired. I'll take a shower in the morning."

"Did you even change?" you tease, keeping your voice light.

"Of course," he says. "Come to bed, Chel."

You carefully maneuver around the plastic furniture and the plastic bags of clothes and groceries scattered on the floor. Your fingers encounter a soft material, which means you've probably reached the bed already. You slip into the space Kian has provided, painfully aware of the dip in the center of the mattress, which means that he's already on the other side. Positioning yourself on the edge, you cross your hands over your chest and turn your back towards him. You're not sure whether your eyes are open or closed; it doesn't make much of a difference.

Behind you, Kian moves forward and wraps his around your waist, pulling you to him. You whisper worriedly, wondering what's wrong, but he simply buries his face at the back of your neck. You feel something warm and wet trickle down your nape, and you turn around to face him. "Are you crying?" you ask quietly, wrapping your arms around his shuddering shoulders. His face is in your shirt, burrowed between the valley of your breasts, and you have never held him like this, not even when Anita, the love of his life and his first girlfriend, left him for her classmate Jasmine Toledo. He had also cried then, and refused to eat anything but Meat Lovers' Pizza from Pizza Hut (because that was the last meal that he and Anita had shared) for two weeks.

You hold him to you (*it's not so bad after all*), until you feel him shift slightly and his lips press against your skin, through the fabric. You look down, and he looks up, and then you are reminded of the way the *Titanic* slammed against the icebergs—the impact was enough to bring the mighty ship shuddering to its knees. Kian's kiss feels that way: breaking all the barriers, refusing to acknowledge their existence, cracking the walls that you have surrounded yourself with. (*Twelve years' worth…*) You bite down on the flesh of his lower lip; your tongue swipes the drop of blood that wells across the surface. He tastes of metal and cinnamon, bitter and pungent, the salt of the seas. You store the memory inside your mind, where later on, when you are alone, you will roll it over and over in your mind, like a particularly beautiful and intricate plaything.

You gasp as his hands slip underneath your shirt, stroking the flat of your stomach, tracing the line of your wound. "Is this it?" he whispers, his voice grating the still night air. You nod desperately, squirming underneath his touch, everything be damned.

He lowers his head and you feel the tip of his tongue, like a flower petal dipped in morning dew, slipping/sliding across the cut, tasting your blood. You tangle your fingers into his hair, allow him to uncover your skin beneath the clothes, his hands memorizing the language of your movements. You know you are sinking, that you have abandoned all hope of resurfacing, You, who have known flight, known the names of all the winds that encircle the city—now, you know how it feels to drown. The waters are slowly, slowly closing over your head.

In your mind, there will be no chance for redemption, so you will decide to run away. You will change your city, your name, your face. But to the women, the others of your kind, the foulest of blood that flows hotly through your veins will still sound a clarion call, and everywhere you go, they will gather outside your window, waiting for you like ghosts at a funeral.

You will taste the blood on your mouth, feed because you need to live, but there is no more pleasure in the succulent liquid taste of meat. Even flight has lost its pleasure: every time you take to the air, you remember the fall into his arms, and everything is made bittersweet by the memory.

When you feed for the last time, you will find yourself crouched on the rooftop of a beautiful white house in the outskirts of the village where you are currently hiding in. You will hear the fervent prayers of the woman in your mind. She does not want this child. Carefully, you will unfurl your tongue and search for a gap in the roof. You can smell her already: strong and warm, full of flesh and life. Your tongue enters her belly, laps up the scarlet-and-sunset child that will never know light; only the warm beat of the darkness. You will swirl the liquid inside your mouth, and realize that it tastes of metal and cinnamon, bitter and pungent, the salt of the seas—

(*I know this taste.*)

ODE TO EDVARD MUNCH

by Caitlín R. Kiernan

Caitlín R. Kiernan is the author of seven novels, including *Silk*, *Murder of Angels*, *Daughter of Hounds*, *The Red Tree*, and the vampire novel *The Five of Cups*. Her short fiction has been collected in *A is for Alien*, and in several other volumes. She has also published two collections of erotica, and a third, *Confessions of a Five-Chambered Heart*, will be released in 2010. She lives in Providence, Rhode Island.

This tale was inspired, in part, by Edvard Munch's painting, *The Vampire*. "But I was much more interested in writing a story about immortality and time, about our smallness in the face of the passage and the gulf of time, than I was in writing a traditional vampire story," Kiernan said.

Kiernan says that she usually accounts for the prevalence of the vampire in modern literature to the marriage of sex and death. "In the vampire tale, and especially in the more romantic sort, we have a sort of socially sanctioned necrophilia," she said. "A vampire is essentially a cannibalistic corpse, through which a 'kiss' combines the act of feeding and copulation. To be preyed upon by a vampire is to become Death's lover, and it's hard to imagine a more powerful frisson."

I find her, always, sitting on the same park bench. She's there, no matter whether I'm coming through the park late on a Thursday evening or early on a Monday evening or in the first grey moments of a Friday morning. I play piano in a martini bar at Columbus and 89th, or I play *at* the piano, mostly for tips and free drinks. And when I feel like the long walk or can't bear the thought of the subway or can't afford cab fare, whenever I should happen to pass that way alone in the darkness and the interruptions in the darkness made by the lampposts, she's there. Always on that same bench, not far from the Ramble and the Bow Bridge, just across the lake. They call that part of the park Cherry Hill. The truth is that I haven't lived in Manhattan long enough to know these things, and, anyway, I'm not the sort of man who memorizes the cartography of Central Park, but she *told* me it's called Cherry Hill, because of all the cherry trees growing there. And when I looked at a map in a guidebook, it said the same thing.

You might mistake her for a runaway, sixteen or maybe seventeen; she dresses all in rags, or clothes so threadbare and dirty that they may as well be rags, and I've never seen her wearing shoes, no matter the season or the weather. I've seen her barefoot in snow. I asked her about that once, if she would wear shoes if I brought her a pair, and she said no, thank you, but no, because shoes make her claustrophobic.

I find her sitting there alone on the park bench near the old fountain, and I always ask before I sit down next to her. And always she smiles and says of course, of course you can sit with me. You can always sit with me. Her shoulder-length hair has been dyed the color of pomegranates, and her skin is dark. I've never asked, but I think she may be Indian. India Indian, I mean. Not Native American. I once waited tables with a girl from Calcutta, and her skin was the same color, and she had the same dusky brown-black eyes. But if she is Indian, the girl on Cherry Hill, she has no trace of an accent when she talks to me about the fountain or her favorite paintings in the Met or the exhibits she likes best at the Museum of Natural History.

The first time she smiled…

"You're a vampire?" I asked, as though it were the sort of thing you might ask any girl sitting on a park bench in the middle of the night.

"That's an ugly word," she said and scowled at me. "That's a silly, ugly word." And then she was silent a long moment, and I tried to think of anything but those long incisors, like the teeth of a rat filed down to points. It was a freezing night near the end of January, but I was sweating, nonetheless. And I had an erection. And I realized, then, that her breath didn't fog in the cold air.

"I'm a daughter of Lilith," she said.

Which is as close as she's ever come to telling me her name, or where she's from, or anything else of the sort. *I'm a daughter of Lilith*, and the *way* she said it, with not even a trace of affectation or humor or deceit, I knew that it was true. Even if I had no idea what she meant, I knew that she was telling me the truth.

That was also the first night that I let her kiss me. I sat with her on the bench, and she licked eagerly at the back of my neck. Her tongue was rough, like a cat's tongue.

She smelled of fallen leaves, that dry and oddly spicy odor which I have always associated with late October and jack-o'-lanterns. Yes, she smelled of fallen leaves, and her own sweat and, more faintly, something which I took to be woodsmoke. Her breath was like frost against my skin, colder even than the long winter night. She licked at the nape of my neck until it was raw and bleeding, and she whispered soothing words in a language I could neither understand nor recognize.

"It was designed in 1860," she said, some other night, meaning the fountain with its bluestone basin and eight frosted globes. "They built this place as a turnaround for the carriages. It was originally meant to be a drinking fountain for horses. A place for thirsty things."

"Like an oasis," I suggested, and she smiled and nodded her head and wiped my blood from her lips and chin.

"Sometimes it seems all the wide world is a desert," she said. "There are too few places left where one may freely drink. Even the horses are no longer allowed to drink here, though it was built for them."

"Times change," I told her and gently touched the abraded place on my neck, trying not to wince, not wanting to show any sign of pain in her presence. "Horses and carriages don't much matter anymore."

"But horses still get thirsty. They still need a place to drink."

"Do you like horses?" I asked, and she blinked back at me and didn't answer my question. It reminds me of an owl, sometimes, that slow, considering way she blinks her eyes.

"It will feel better in the morning," she said and pointed at my throat. "Wash it when you get home." And then I sat with her a while longer, but neither of us said anything more.

She takes my blood, but never more than a mouthful at a time, and she's left me these strange dreams in return. I have begun to think of them as a sort of gift, though I know that others might think them more a curse. Because they are not entirely pleasant dreams. Some people would even call them nightmares, but things never seem so cut and dried to me. Yes, there is terror and horror in them, but there is beauty and wonder, too, in equal measure—a perfect balance that seems never to tip one way or the other. I believe the dreams have flowed into me on her rough cat's tongue, that they've infected my blood and my mind like a bacillus carried on her saliva. I don't know if the gift was intentional, and I admit that I'm afraid to ask. I'm too afraid that I might pass through the park late one night or early one morning and she wouldn't be waiting for me there on her bench on Cherry Hill, that asking would break some brittle spell which I can only just begin to comprehend. She has made me superstitious and given to what psychiatrists call "magical thinking," misapprehending cause and effect, when I was never that way before we met. I play piano in a martini bar, and, until now, there's never been anything in my life which I might mistake for magic. But there are many things in her wide sienna eyes which I might mistake for many *other* things, and now that uncertainty seems to cloud my every waking thought. Yet I believe that it's a small price to pay for her company, smaller even than the blood she takes.

I thought that I should write down one of the dreams, that I should try to make mere words of it. From this window beside my bed, I can see Roosevelt Island beyond the rooftops, and the East River and Brooklyn and the hazy blue-white sky that can mean either summer or winter in this city. It makes me think of her, that sky, though I'm at a loss to explain why. At first, I thought that I would write it down and then read it to her the next time I see her. But then I started to worry that she might not take it the way I'd intended, simply as reciprocation, my gift to repay hers. She might be offended, instead, and I don't think I could bear the world without her. Not after all these nights and mornings, and all these dreams.

I'm stalling. Yes, I am.

There's the silhouette of a city, far off, past the sand and smoke that seem to stretch away in all directions except that one which would lead to the city. I know I'll never go that far, that going as far as that, I'd never again find my way home. The city is for other beings. I know that she's seen the city, that she's walked its streets and spoken all its dialects and visited its brothels and opium dens. She knows the stink of its sewers and the delicious aromas of its markets. She knows all the high places and all the low places. And I follow her across the sand, up one dune and down another, these great waves of wind-sculpted sand which tower above me, which I climb and then descend. In this place, the jackals and the vultures and the spiny black scorpions are her court, and there is no place here for thirsty horses.

Sometimes I can see her, through stinging veils of sand. And other times it seems I am entirely alone with the wailing Sirocco gale, and the voice of that wind is a thousand women crying for their men cut down on some Arabian battlefield a thousand years before my birth. And it is also the slow creep of the dunes across the face of the wasteland, and it is my heart pounding loudly in my ears. I'm lost in the wild, and I think I'll never see her again, but then I catch a glimpse of her through the storm, crouched in the lee of ruins etched and defaced by countless millennia of sand and wind and time. She might almost be any animal, anything out looking for its supper or some way to quench its thirst.

She waits there for me in the entrance to that crumbling temple, and I can smell her impatience, like dashes of turmeric. I can smell her thirst and her appetite, and the wind drives me forward.

She leads me down into the earth, her lips pressed to my ear, whispering so I can hear her over the storm. She tells me the name of the architect who built the fountain on Cherry Hill, that his name was Jacob Wrey Mould, and he came to New York in 1853, or 1854, or 1855, to design and build All Soul's Church. He was a pious man, she tells me, and he illustrated Thomas Grey's "Elegy in a Country Church-Yard" and "Book of Common Prayer." She says he died in 1886, and that he too was in love with a daughter of Lilith, that he died with no other thought but her. I want to ask where she learned all these things, if, perhaps, she spends her days in libraries, and I also want to ask if she means that she believes that I'm in love with her. But then the narrow corridor we've been following turns left and opens abruptly on a vast torch-lit chamber.

"Listen," she whispers. "This is one of my secrets. I've guarded this place for all my life."

The walls are built from great blocks of reddish limestone carved and set firmly in place without the aid of mortar, locking somehow perfectly together by a forgotten masonic art. The air reeks of frankincense, and there is thick cinnamon-colored dust covering everything; I follow her down a short flight of steps to the floor. It occurs to me that we've gone so deep underground that the roar of the wind should not still be so loud, but it is, and I wonder if maybe the wind has found its way *inside* me, if it's entered through one of the wounds she leaves on my throat.

"This was the hall of my mother," she says.

And now I see the corpses, heaped high between the smoky braziers. They are nude, or they are half-dressed, or they've been torn apart so completely, or are now so badly decomposed, that it's difficult to tell whether they're clothed or not. Some are men, and others are women, and not a few are children. I can smell them even through the incense, and I might cover my nose and mouth. I might begin to gag. I might take a step back towards the stairs leading up to the long corridor and the bloodless desert night beyond. And she blinks at me like a hungry, watchful owl.

"I cannot expect you to understand," she says.

And there are other rooms, other chambers, endless atrocities that I can now only half recall. There are other secrets which she keeps for her mother in the deep places beneath shifting sands. There are the ghosts of innumerable butcheries. There are demons held in prisons of crystal and iron, chained until some eventual apocalypse; their voices are almost indistinguishable from the voice of the wind.

And then we have descended into some still greater abyss, a cavern of sparkling stalactite and stalagmite formations, travertine and calcite glinting in the soft glow of phosphorescent vegetation which has never seen and will never have need of sunlight. We're standing together at the muddy edge of a subterranean pool, water so still and perfectly smooth, an ebony mirror, and she's already undressed and is waiting impatiently for me to do the same.

"I can't swim," I tell her and earn another owl blink.

If I *could* swim, I cannot imagine setting foot in that water, that lake at the bottom of the world.

"No one has asked you to swim," she replies and smiles, showing me those long incisors. "At this well, men only have to drown. You can do that well enough, I suspect." And then I'm falling, as the depths of that terrible lake rise up around me like the hood of some black desert cobra and rush over me, bearing me down and down and down into the chasm, driving the air from my lungs. Stones placed one by one upon my chest until my lungs collapse, constricting coils drawing tighter and tighter about me, and I try to scream. I open my mouth, and her sandpaper tongue slips past my lips and teeth. She tastes of silt and dying and loss. She tastes of cherry blossoms and summer nights in Central Park. She wraps herself about me, and the grey-white wings sprouting from her shoulders open wider than the wings of any earthly bird. Those wings have become the sky, and her feathers brush aside the fire of a hundred trillion stars.

Her teeth tear at my lower lip, and I taste my own blood.

This wind howling in my ears is the serpent flood risen from out that black pool, and is also icy solar winds, and the futile cries of bottled demons.

"Don't be afraid," she whispers in my ear, and her hand closes around my penis. "One must only take very small drinks. One must not be greedy in these dry times."

I gasp and open my eyes, unable to remember having shut them, and now we're lying together on the floor of the abattoir at the end of the long corridor below the temple ruins. This is the only one of her secrets she's shown me, and anything else must have been my imagination, my shock at the sight of so much death. There is rain, rain as red and sticky as blood, but still something to cool my fever, and I wrap my legs around her brown thighs and slide inside her. She's not made like other women, my raggedy girl from Cherry Hill, and she begins to devour me so slowly that I will still be dying in a thousand years.

She tells me she loves me.

There are no revelations here.

My eyes look for the night sky somewhere beyond the gore and limestone and sand, but there are only her wings, like Heaven and Hell and whatever might lie in between, and I listen to the raw and bitter laughter of the wind...

Some nights, I tell myself that I will walk around the park, and never mind the distance and inconvenience. Some nights, I pretend I hope that she *won't* be there, waiting by the fountain. But I'm not even as good a liar as I am a pianist, and it hardly matters, because she's always there.

Last night, for instance.

I brought her an old sweater I never wear, a birthday present from an ex-girl-friend, and she thanked me for it. I told her that I can bring her other things, whatever she might need, that she only has to ask, and she smiled and told me I'm very kind. My needs are few, she said, and pulled the old sweater on over whatever tatters she was already wearing.

"I worry about you," I said. "I worry about you all the time these days."

"That's sweet of you," she replied. "But I'm strong, stronger than I might seem." And I wondered if she knows about my dreams, and if our conversations were merely a private joke. I wonder if she only accepted the sweater because she feels sorry for me.

We talked, and she told me a very funny story about her first night in the park, almost a decade before I was born. And then, when there were no more words, when there was no longer the *need* for words, I leaned forward and offered her my throat. Thank you, she said, and I shut my eyes and waited for the scratch of her tongue against my skin, for the prick of those sharp teeth. She was gentle, because she is always gentle, lapping at the hole she's made and pausing from time to time to murmur reassurances I can understand without grasping the coarser, literal meaning of what she's said. I get the gist of it, and I know that's all that matters. When she was done, when she'd wiped her mouth clean and thanked me again for the sweater, when we'd said our usual good-byes for the evening, I sat alone on the bench and watched as she slipped away into the maze of cherry trees and azaleas and forsythia bushes.

I don't know what will become of these pages.

I may never print them. Or I may print them out and hide them from myself.

I could slip them between the pages of a book in the stacks at NYU and leave them there for anyone to find. I could do that. I could place them in an empty wine bottle and drop them from the Queensboro Bridge, so that the river would carry them down to the sea. The sea must be filled with bottles...

FINDERS KEEPERS
by L. A. Banks

L. A. Banks is the bestselling author of the Vampire Huntress Legend series, which consists of twelve volumes. She is currently working on a graphic novel and manga scripts based on the series, and a young adult trilogy set in the same milieu is due out in 2010. Earlier this year, the latest in her Crimson Moon werewolf series, *Undead on Arrival*, was released. In 2008, Banks was named the *Essence Magazine* Storyteller of the Year.

Having thoroughly explored the hip-hop, urban vampires in the Vampire Huntress Legends, with this story Banks wanted to try her hand at a historical vampire tale, in the vein of the classic vampire sagas. "'Finders Keepers' is about a centuries-old vampire who finds herself alone in the modern world," Banks said. "It was fun going back in time and dealing with the prejudices against women, minorities, as well as a lot of the social power paradigms that existed then (and now). There's always a thread of social justice that runs through my work, wanting to see those who probably will never (in real life) be brought to justice get their due."

ATLANTIC CITY, NEW JERSEY

She kissed his forehead, tasting the thin sheen of salty moisture that still lingered on his skin, considering him before she gently closed his eyes. He had a handsome face, that of a Roman; dark lashes that rested against his now porcelain-pale skin; a strong, aristocratic nose; rugged square jaw. But he wasn't a keeper.

Slightly forlorn, she peeled herself away from his nude, lifeless body with a sigh, studying the tall, athletic form in repose on the bed as she took her time to dress. A thread-width finger of crimson seeped from his wound, the scarlet beacon drawing her back to his side to taste the last of him. His body twitched from the invasion; she kissed his lips as a goodbye and a thank you, leaving a red print of his essence against his mouth. But he wasn't a keeper.

Death was like delicious prose when delivered with elegance and style. It had a prologue, a body, and then an epilogue, no less than fine dining replete with an appetizer, entrée, followed by dessert. The composition of it all was quiet, pleasurable, and perfect. She felt no guilt as she turned toward the terrace doors and faced the moon. She would shower later, back at her lair. This man's death was an elegant kill, as always. Society was the better for it, she was the better for it, and if there was an Ultimate Maker, then the drained man on the bed could hash out the particulars with the judge of creation regarding whether or not his life had been lived in vain.

It was always a philosophical question that niggled her—would a so-called victim dare ask the Divine for recompense, after having killed so many men himself for blood money? One less mob enforcer lost at a casino would not imperil the world. Perhaps she provided a true service to mankind. The man her feed would have killed tonight had been given a night of reprieve... an honest man would therefore get one more night to live—she just hoped he'd made the most of the time.

A slight smile graced her lips, exposing a hint of fang as she retracted them. Her logic was sound in her own mind as she leaped up on the terrace railing, balancing on it for a moment before allowing the night to pull her into its dark folds of freedom.

Wind rushed through her hair and buffeted her face. Plummeting helped her remember being alive, the joy, the fear, the pain.

But after a few moments, she finally allowed the fierceness of the wind to abate so she could hover on the gentleness of the evening breeze. Floating high above the Atlantic City boardwalk, her thoughts drifted to her human days. Back then, it was the humans who were beasts. Things were not so different now, she reasoned, spying the antlike creatures that dotted the boardwalk and streets below. Humans killed more of their own than her kind did, and for much more senseless reasons. Men who'd wanted her called her a witch—when she denied their advances; women who'd envied her beauty joined in their persecution. Murderous group thinking prevailed over logic, as was the human way.

The verdict was simple and heartless. It was in everyone's best interest that she be exterminated, everyone's best interest but hers. Mysterious deaths had been blamed on her sorcery, when all she'd had was the gift, or curse, of second sight. No one had given a single thought to the nobleman stranger that had recently come ashore with his ship and largess. He was above the law and above their suspicion or contempt. They had been elegantly glamoured.

People. She hated that she even needed them for blood.

The midnight blue horizon drew her attention. Moonlight sent shards of opalescence to ripple against the blue-black water. It was so beautiful. If she could stay airborne all night, she would.

Memories rolled across her mind in unrelenting waves. Haiti was a small lush place then... too small to hide in. Who would risk their life to give sanctuary to a motherless child? No one was that brave when a mob came calling. They'd easily found her, had mercilessly beaten and violated her, and then dragged her to a pyre to cover their shame. Already half-dead from the abuse and hemorrhaging badly, they'd lit tinder around her. Flames quickly caught the hem of her ragged dress. Heat raced up her legs, but she was too weak to move and could barely scream. Her protest came out as a deep, resounding moan of agony. She would have been their bonfire that night, had a man with honor not shown up. Maybe that's why she loved the weightlessness of vapor so.

That was how Alfonse had come to her, as vapor.

Searing heat had given way to cool relief. The jeers and curses all around her had turned into screams of terror. Something that no human mind could fathom had rescued her from the flames, and now the townspeople knew beyond a shadow of a doubt that there was more on the island to fear than her. The least likely person, the nobleman of means, wielded the wrath and destructive power of an entity that they were horrified to name.

Humans fled. The beach had returned to a place of peace beneath the moon. A gentle hand had cradled her skull, lifting her throat to his mouth. A gentle whisper offered her a choice with a promise, "I will not hurt you; do you want to live?"

Something human within her recoiled as she swallowed her own blood, but that feral, primal animus within knew she was dying, and it fought with all its might to survive. Blood choked her words; all she could do was nod. But her mind screamed a thousand questions as his beautiful lips parted and the moonlight glinted off his fangs.

Yet, his murmur was so serene. "Relax. I must do this now before your heart stops beating or it will be too late, *chérie*."

She remembered her *making* as though it were only moments ago. More than two hundred years still could not eclipse the horror of what people had done to her, nor could she ever forget what Alfonse had given her.

Through his sanguine kiss, her broken bones and violated flesh had begun to knit as her muscles relaxed. Raw nail beds from fighting rapists and aggressors began to heal. Pain literally ceased with his kiss, and then there was only sweet pressure at her neck. Life was draining out of her with each suckle; the world slowed down, her hearing dulled, her eyes closed against the moon. The burns that had engulfed her legs cooled, the puffiness of her swollen face eased. For a moment, there was a velvet cloak of dark peace that enveloped her, a totality of nothingness so peaceful that if she could have, she would have wept. Initially, she could feel him, then see him within her mind's eye as he threw his head back with his eyes closed, ecstasy staining his expression, chest heaving from the exertion, moonlight casting crimson prisms in saliva and blood against porcelain canines. He was horrifying and gorgeous, this nobleman that had claimed her.

"Breathe," he'd commanded.

A gasp shuddered through her and relief made him hug her.

Tears stung her eyes as she searched for a place to discreetly land amongst the modern day humans that strolled the Atlantic City boardwalk so carefree at night. It was time to return her thoughts to the present. Without Alfonse, the past was a place of pain.

But the memories had a stranglehold on her. Her first question upon her awakening in Alfonse's arms had been so naïve.

"I will live?"

His dark eyes had flashed with both triumph and remorse. "*Non*. You will exist." He'd then touched her disheveled hair with reverence. "I'm sorry, it was the only way."

Even then she hadn't fully understood. All she was sure of was that a strange nobleman had found her and had saved her at her darkest hour. His handsome face still haunted her… deeply intense, dark eyes… thick brows furrowed in a frown of concern. Square jaw owning a slight cleft. Strong, Romanesque nose. A shock of glistening brunette hair spilling across his shoulders when the wind tired of it. His mouth lush and ruby-stained, punished by the suckle.

"Why didn't you just let me die?" It had seemed fair enough a question then.

"Because you'd fought so hard to live, and what they'd accused you of was a lie. I am a man of principle. Without principles, we are all just animals."

His admission became a sensual murmur that bonded them forever. "I have watched you since I came to this island… you are an exquisite beauty that I could never allow to endure the sentence for my sins. Even being what I am, there is a code of ethics. Never take more than you need, never take from those who are innocent, *ma chérie*. Break no hearts; cull the herd of its own beasts. Feed from the damned and don't allow them to wake up. They'd blamed you for my feeds, a convenient scapegoat to give them license to act out their lusts and anger. Fools, the lot of them. How could they think a woman who walks in the sunlight amongst them could be capable of such crimes?"

Still, she wasn't sure of what he'd admitted, but she did understand how a woman of no pedigree, no social standing, born at the wrong time to the wrong majority could be blamed. Her response had pained him as she'd taken up his hand within hers.

"Look at my hand, look at yours. What do you see? Look at your clothes, look at mine. That is enough of a reason for them to excuse you and to lynch me."

She'd expected him to snatch his hand away in offense, but her simple truth had gentled his expression from outrage at the mob that had violated her humanity to something else that she, even now, couldn't describe. His words had become tender like his touch, his fingers dappling the pleasure of a caress against her cheek as he'd spoken in a gentle timbre.

"I see beautiful, cinnamon-hued skin perfumed by oils and flavors of the earth. I see deep, amber-brown, expressive eyes, so gorgeous and with depth so vast that they rival the jewel-blue sea. I see thick, lush tendrils of mahogany hair that appears to be as velvet under the night sky. I see a face of an angel, a mouth so inviting I tremble."

He looked away out toward the surf, his voice becoming distant as he spoke a truth that was hard to bear. "I've also sadly witnessed a soul that was pure have to flee its earthly housing well before its time, heard a heart that was loving stop beating while you were in my arms… then, as now, I see a body created in majesty that is still yearning for affection beyond lust. I see a brilliant mind trapped in an era of ignorance, straining for recognition and release. I see a woman held captive by circumstance and accident of birth, a hostage of men who have no right to own another living soul. The small attention I gave you upon arriving here at night caused them to hate you more… jealousy is a tireless monster that no one can understand."

It was her turn to look away then. Tears mixed with rage as she remembered the respectful attention the new nobleman had given her, and the way men with lesser wealth had resented her reciprocated charm. Women on the island, black and white, hated her because of the attention she'd garnered from the wealthy stranger. Men on the island seethed with outrage, those of all hues taking offense that she would be so enamored with a stranger that she'd deny their advances.

She hadn't thought she was better, or that they were lesser; Alfonse duBenet had given her a jewel that no man had offered. Respect set in kindness. He didn't presume to own her, hadn't presumed that due to her station versus his that he could simply take her. He'd actually tried to begin the slow process of courting her. That is what had been viewed as scandalous. That was where the true crime had been committed, according to the locals. And she'd blossomed under Alfonse's gifts of emotional tenderness. She'd seen that as his difference, the respect and tenderness he'd offered. Not until the night he'd rescued her had she realized that he was something beyond human. But, then again, so were they.

It was humans that had ultimately abused her, had tried to murder her. A vampire had killed her, but in so doing had saved her. The simplicity of it was both profound and perverse.

Alfonse had released a sigh of frustration when he saw her thinking too hard and had then given her his hand. "Be my bride and let us seek our revenge by outliving them all. We will have to go to the mainland. They now know what I am, as well as will correctly assume you are that, too. If we stay on this small island, they will find us by daylight… we must leave tonight, *chérie.*"

His human crew was already waiting. The ship had been loaded, the hull of it prepared. Protection sealed it. That was the first time she'd crossed the sea. New Orleans eventually became her home, but not before he'd shown her the world. She missed Alfonse so terribly that her heart still contracted with phantom pains when she thought about him.

Shaking the memory, she alighted on a deserted section of boardwalk. The night was still young as she considered the moon. Only a little after midnight. Normally she didn't hunt so early and preferred being out in the ocean breeze as long as possible. But the man she'd fed on so reminded her of Alfonse. Yet his physical attributes were where the similarity had begun and ended. The man's mind was repugnant. His thoughts pedestrian… common. She had done a good deed—freeing a beautiful body of a stagnant soul. At least the physical work of art could decompose in peace and not be mocked by adulterous misuse from the banal mind that had controlled it. He wasn't even a good lover, thus not worthy of being a vampire.

The shadow of a building provided her reentry into solid form near humans. A quick autumn breeze took up the edges of her little black dress as she stepped into the light, giving passerby men a glimpse of her long, sleek legs and a flash of red thong. Brief curiosity and lust filled their eyes. She dismissed them mentally while she listened to their life stories in her head as she walked toward the boardwalk rails to stare out at the ocean. All average Joes; none worth pursuing, and she'd just eaten. Never take more than you need. The casinos here were just not like those in Monaco. The beaches here so unlike the Caribbean or the Mediterranean. Losing Alfonse was a tragedy.

Tears rose in her eyes and then burned away. Time had bled out the tears, but not the pain or the memory. Nightly survival was a game of chance; the casinos were that as well. The baccarat tables and high rollers' dens were filled with men who thrived on risk and survived. That was the energy that drew her and ignited her. That was the energy that disappointed her.

Bored insane she wondered if she might try a new milieu this century… politicians, perhaps. Most were duplicitous, foul creatures that were predatory in nature, so why not? It would be no different than hand-picking criminals to feed from.

However, hiding their deaths would be more problematic. Siphoning a hit-man dry would not create a full-scale investigation. It would go into a cold-case homicide file; police wouldn't expend too much manpower on it. The organization her feed hailed from would retaliate, if necessary, against their assumed enemies, which would allow her to feed off the opposing side for a while until they retaliated—and the authorities would be none the wiser. A beautiful cycle until she moved on. It would all remain in the province of organized crime. Simple, elegant. Going after white-collar political criminals with high-profile posts would be messy, even if more satisfying. Maybe one day.

For now she was stuck in North America until she could develop a foolproof plan to cross the forbidding sea. Daylight was the barrier. One could travel as vapor only so far before depleting one's energy. The specter of being lost at sea at sunrise, decomposing and burning in the water, was compelling enough of a reason to stay on shore. Alfonse had taught her that, too, had taught her how to glamour human helpers to keep their coffins closed in the cargo hull until night. But with new technology and Homeland Security, new maritime laws, as well as the ineptness of this era's baggage handlers were she to dare a plane flight, would mean she'd surely fry in their care. She allowed her shoulders to slump. For now she was not just stuck, but trapped on this continent since Alfonse's demise.

Pushing away from the rail with renewed annoyance, she headed toward the bright lights, not caring which casino she entered. They were all the same; just like the feeds had been. Vegas was a notch up from where she was now, but it lacked a beach, and being a spawn of the Caribbean, the night air for her required surf. Down in the delta the feeds that came into the casinos were so po'boy-southern fried that they threatened to make her kill sloppily in outrage. She'd had to move from there, and her beloved New Orleans just wasn't the same since the flood.

Miami had potential, but there was so much competition to feed on the drug lords that often territorial plunder wars broke out amongst her kind, and she didn't need the hassle. Each coven was so protective of its land rights. Same with LA; California was another world. The northeastern seaboard held the greatest potential at the moment, as did the Connecticut tract, or going up into Michigan and over into Canada. Still, one had to be careful of regional vampire politics.

She was older than most, but was also made by Alfonse—whom many had ill feelings about because he'd been merciless in enforcing his code of ethics: *Never the innocent, never take more than you need.* Gorging orgies had been put to a stop in his region. Making children was considered heresy in Alfonse's book.

He had garnered formidable enemies because of his extreme views… because of his extreme mercy toward humans. For that mercy, they had colluded to mercilessly expose him to sunlight in a devastating coup. The only thing that had saved her was another male wanted her for himself. Her face became tight as thoughts of vengeance tainted her mood. Yes, she'd played along until she could return the favor of sunlight exposure, but that had left her alone, an outcast from polite vampire society. That was the main reason she couldn't trust a cargo ship or flight abroad.

However, Montreal was beautiful and Quebec was her refuge when she needed a taste of Europe, albeit neither was a seaside town. But up there, any death of a local human was a big deal in that pristine environment and created too much attention. So, until circumstances changed, or her code of feeding off those who'd been predators changed, she was stuck.

How did one stop missing a man that she'd loved for more than two hundred years?

She kept walking until the click of her high heels against the marble pierced her senses. Sometimes she lived so deeply inside her own head that she had to remember where she was and had to remember to keep up the tedious façade of being engaged in the moment, caring about the mundane goings on of human existence. Had to fit in, be unobtrusive in their world. Had to stay away from the mirrors and reflective surfaces that were all the rage in the chic hotels. Wanted a vodka martini and hated that she had to find a feed who was drinking one and then had to entice him somewhere for just a sip from his veins. All this waiting, when she was a woman of action. Tonight, she wanted to be anywhere but here, but Atlantic City would just have to do.

Frustrated, she found a black jack table and sat with a flop.

"Bad night?" the dealer asked with a smile.

She stared at his warm hazel eyes and dark brown skin, enjoying the way his mouth moved for a moment before she materialized a stack of chips in her clutch bag and then withdrew them to slide them onto the table. "Just a slow start, but the night is young."

He nodded, appraising her physique for a second and then dealt her cards. She studied him before looking down at her cards; he couldn't have been more than twenty-five, with his sexy chocolate self.

"Black jack," she said quietly, and then pushed the five thousand dollars worth of chip winnings back in his direction as a tip. He was cute. Too young with too much of a future to dine on. She stood as he gaped.

"You sure, Miss?" He looked from the stack to her and then over to his pit boss.

"As ever," she murmured, blowing him a sexy kiss. "Do something positive with it. A mind is a terrible thing to waste." She made eye contact with the older pit boss to be sure the young dealer wouldn't get in trouble—he hadn't stolen the chips, it was her tip, her choice. The pit boss nodded. Now she could leave. This is what acute boredom did, made one find little stupid things to engage in to give one's life meaning.

She turned to leave but the young dealer's energy reached out to try to hold her. She could feel him summoning the nerve to ask a simple question, curiosity about to cost him dearly. Curiosity always killed the cat, and sometimes satisfaction brought it back. He was a handsome cat, even if curiosity had the potential to kill him. But he wasn't a keeper, not likely to get brought back.

"What's your name?"

She half turned and offered him a half-smile. "Not important. And... no... I don't want to meet you later when you get off your shift. Just enjoy the cash and stay healthy, baby."

"Okay, I can do that," he said, seeming disappointed as she strode away.

She shook her head and chuckled softly to herself. Men. They always wanted more than the bargain. Five grand wasn't enough; he wanted sex, too? Maybe she would just head toward the poker tables... or just go out to sit under the stars to allow the night to pass without incident.

He stared at the security monitors, running back the images that didn't make sense. A chair had moved away from the table by itself. Chips had appeared on the table and the dealer looked as though he was talking to himself. He'd dealt, and cards flipped where no one was seated. Then what looked like five thousand in winnings had gotten pushed back to the dealer. The kid had even checked with the pit boss, who nodded. Chips slid toward him as he spoke to the nothingness.

It was time to take a break.

Obviously his head was all screwed up. Either someone had slipped him a mickey or he was finally having that nervous breakdown that he should have had five years ago. But he was so fuckin' close! No one else had seemed to notice; it had gone by in a flash.

"Yo, Tony, you okay?" A burly member of the security team stared at him seeming worried. "All of a sudden you don't look so good. Like you seen a ghost, or somethin'."

He dabbed at the sweat beading his brow. "I'm cool, man, just need a few. Cover for me? I need to go take a walk."

Several pairs of eyes regarded him, eyes he knew he could never fully trust. He wasn't one of them, but had worked his way inside their organization through years of deception. And still, he was only in the outer layers of their hierarchy.

"Sure thing, man. Take ten."

He nodded, studying their predatory eyes before slipping out of the casino floor monitoring room. Maybe he was losing it, if they could see it so clearly. Sharks could always sense blood in the water from miles away, and from what Fat Joe had said and the expression on his face, it was obvious he was bleeding to death. But the big question was, had his cover been blown somehow? And ultimately, did that matter? If he was a traitor, he was dead; if he was perceived as a liability, he was dead. Sharks would eat their own if one of them was weak or injured.

Right now he seemed weak, seemed injured. He knew his eyes had given him away. His sweat in a cool, air-conditioned room had telegraphed to them that something out of the blue had made him freak. He could have replayed the images, but what if what he saw was all in his head? Then there'd be questions, deeper digging into his background. He couldn't fully trust his own, either. There had been a leak back at the Federal Task Force on Organized Crime, Jersey Division.

After what they'd done to his Meghan, his partner, and his partner's wife, there was no time for so-called healing. He kept walking. If they snuffed him in the men's room, then he'd take several of them with him.

Checking the stalls briefly, he walked past the urinals and went to the sinks splashing water on his face quickly so that his senses remained alert. He grabbed a paper towel and stared in the mirror as he wiped away the water, not seeing himself, but the fire before he turned away.

His partner, Nate, was the inside man, he'd worked the logistics in the office. Their wives were dear friends. That day, Meghan had gone over to personally tell Carol the good news… she was pregnant. Tony briefly closed his eyes. The kids, thank God, were in the yard when Carol turned on the burner under a tea kettle. Both women were at ground zero when the blast rocked the kitchen. Nate heard it on the police band. Evidence of the charred radio told them that. He'd never made it home to collect his devastated children or to bury his wife. They'd duct-taped explosives to Nate's chair, and then allowed the warehouse to go up like a Fourth of July display.

He needed a drink, even though that was thoroughly against casino policy. Fuck it. No wonder he was seeing things. Following the rules had never been his forte, at least not after what went down had gone down.

Heading toward the elevators, he kept his gaze scanning.

He'd known all along that there had to be a leak, no matter what the internal investigation revealed. His own personal investigation told him otherwise. Some people even suggested that he rest, stop asking questions, take a vacation, take time off to grieve Meghan. There were a lot of people who didn't want the Gambiotti family to have any legal problems. Political incorrectness was entrenched in the system, as was payola. He took their advice for three months, took time off to do what he had to do. So when bodies within the department started dropping, they never suspected it was one of their own making a surgical strike. It wasn't murder, in his mind; it was a matter of principle.

Chaos bred panic. Those within the department left in the chain of command wanted the loose ends tied up quickly before death came to their door. They wanted him back on the job, back in play; suddenly, they didn't care about his healing or his loss. Survival instinct was a motherfucker. They knew that a man with nothing to lose was a dangerous thing, so they set him on the other side like a rabid dog—never the wiser about who was hitting dirty feds—and they sicced him on the side that had given the hit order. He could go after the Gambiottis with impunity, as long as he yielded results… but if he was caught doing anything outside the scope of the law, he was on his own, a rogue that they would necessarily disavow.

The bell sounding the elevator arrival gave him a start. He stepped inside, glad it was empty, and went down to the casino floor. He *had* to talk to that black jack dealer and pit boss before he left to go out for a smoke. A small dive bar around the corner was calling his name, but so was the need to know.

He approached the table carefully, watching the patrons and the dealer until the young man noticed him. After the hand, he shut the table down.

"Yo, man, I knew y'all was coming—ask Stan, the chick said it was my tip. Y'all ain't breaking my legs for no bullshit. I don't steal from the house, never have."

"The kid is clean, Tony," Stan said, his voice low as he entered the quiet but intense conversation.

"I haven't said a word and you all have jumped to a defense," Tony said coolly, regarding both men.

"C'mon, Tony. What are we supposed to think? One of you guys comes down here from the monitoring booth, shuts down the table, and whatever, right after the kid gets a big tip." The old man lifted his chin. "It ain't right."

"What did the woman look like?" Tony waited, knowing the cameras were now on him. If there was something shaky going on, then he had to solidify the family's trust in him by going to handle it directly. Maybe he would run back those digital images. He could show the boys in the room the thing that had triggered his reaction, and they would see him now down on the floor.

But both men looked puzzled for a moment.

"You saw the broad from the monitors," old Stan challenged, running his thick fingers through his snow-white hair.

"She was fine," the dealer said, keeping his voice low and his eyes darting around like a trapped rabbit's. "You know, man, the money type. Five ten, skin flawless. Designer black dress on. Diamond earrings, the real shit, not no CZs. Single gold bangle with some real weight. Legs that go on for miles, stilettos making her ass even hotter when she walks. Beautiful set of tits, V-neck serving it all up, but not in a hoochie type of way. But she didn't remind me of a pro, at least not the ones around here I've seen. She had a real classy vibe, man, like she wasn't from around here—belonged in fucking Vegas or Monaco, or off some runway in Paris, but not down at the damned Jersey shore… like she had money to play with. Seemed like she was bored as hell, too, if you feel me. Hey, if she stole it, y'all can have it back—but *I* didn't steal it."

"The kid is only twenty-six, Tony. He didn't steal from the drawer; that I witnessed with my own eyes. He's not lying, the broad was old money."

The desperation in the young man's voice and fear in his eyes told him what he needed to know. One—there hadn't been a theft. Two—there was a woman at that table. But then why hadn't she shown up on the monitors? That was the part that made him question his sanity. Unnerved, he let the two men waiting on his judgment off the hook.

"All right. Keep the chips, but point out which way she went. I have some questions for her."

"Shit, you shut my table down and I'll walk you to her over by the poker tables." The young dealer seemed unconvinced that his life was no longer in jeopardy. Stan nodded and he quickly came around the edge of his table. "I don't want no problems, man, no bullshit whatsoever. Aw'ight. So, I'ma take you to her, you can ask her yourself whether or not she gave me the tip. Cool? Then you guys will have that on tape and I don't have to worry about getting into my car in the parking lot, right?"

"That'll work," Tony said calmly as the young dealer came to his side, looked around, and then shook his hand.

"There she go," he said, beginning to walk. "Can't miss her… ain't nothing like her in this joint."

Tony stared behind the kid for a moment before he began walking. Again, he hadn't lied. Sensuality personified oozed from her very being. The way her graceful hand took up a card and added it to her fan, the way her mesmerizing eyes studied them and the dealer, sent the temperature of the entire casino up a notch. Her face was gorgeous, and that added to the unbelievable curves she owned made her a knockout, drop-dead, to-die-for beauty. Not since Meghan had he been so drawn to a woman. A roll in the hay with a pro was one thing, simply a matter of releasing the primal—something he'd indulged in when he had more drinks than advisable. But this woman…

Then, as though sensing his approach, she looked up and stared at him. There was no question she was staring at him—it was more than a visual recognition, *he felt it*. He watched her fold her hand, rake in the winnings, and stand, leaving the game.

She'd sensed someone staring at her, but until the crowd parted a bit, she wasn't sure of where the energy pull was coming from. She spotted the young dealer, whose entire aura radiated stress and flight-or-fight hormone that was palpable. Yes, he'd been the one staring at her, but there was a darker presence, a more sensual, mysterious creature behind the kid. The moment she saw the source, she froze.

His dark brown hair was pulled back in a ponytail; she wondered if it was held by a dark leather thong or a simple rubber band. She briefly closed her eyes, no longer than a slow blink, perceiving as much as she could about him in seconds. Leather held his hair. Broad shoulders filled out his black leather jacket and concealed a gun. She could taste the metallic change in the air and smell the gunpowder in the clip. He wore a black t-shirt beneath the butter soft leather, black slacks, black slip-on Cole Haans. No jewelry, just a fine gold watch made by Rolex. A pair of intense, dark eyes pierced her, asking questions in a thunder of human thoughts. A strong jaw was set hard, but his mouth was still beautiful, not a tight line of anger. His athletic body moved through the crowd with the stealth of a cat… he was hunting her… interesting. Yet there was no guile aimed at her to be found in his presence, but this was a man of mysteries.

As he neared her, it all became so clear—he was the honest man she'd saved earlier by feeding on the assassin. The irony made her smile.

"Excuse me, Miss, may I have a word with you?"

She turned and regarded the near breathless dealer and then the man that stood behind him.

She nodded, already knowing what the problem was. "I had hoped it wouldn't come to this," she said, looking past the dealer into the eyes of pure intrigue. "I was bored, gave him a large tip of my own volition. He didn't steal anything from your casino." She flashed a purse full of chips worth close to fifty thousand dollars. "Look, I have more." She pulled out another five grand and handed it to the dealer. "Just so you gentlemen who watch transactions can be clear that I did tip the man."

"See, see what I mean, Tony!" The dealer held the chips out to Tony to take, still nervous.

"You're straight, you can go back to your table and open up," Tony said quietly, not looking at the dealer, his eyes transfixed on her. "Buy you a drink?"

She gave him a half-smile. "Mind if we get out of here and go somewhere less frenetic? This place is giving me a headache."

"Great minds think alike. I'm Tony."

"Pleased to meet you, Antonio. I am Odette."

"How did you know my full name was Antonio and not just plain Anthony?"

"Because you are a complicated man and Anthony is way too simplistic for you."

"How about that drink… somewhere out of here?"

"I would adore a Vodka martini."

He nodded. "My favorite."

"Good," she murmured. "*Très bon.*"

Fat Joe took the phone away from his ear slowly, every man in the booth watching Tony leave the casino alone after money had again changed hands. "They just found Donny all fucked up in his room over at the Trump. Can't figure out what the fuck happened to him. Wasn't an ounce of blood in 'im."

"That shit is crazy," Lou said, standing. "Tony had to know Donny was gonna do 'im tonight… 'cuz look at the segment of floor activity he was checking out before he got all weird on us."

Fat Joe came around the desks, moving his heft swiftly to lean in and see where Lou pointed. Other henchmen in the room joined in.

"Look at that shit. I don't understand it, but somehow he must have either erased the person's image or somethin'. The dealer looks nervous, five large goes across the table. The dealer asks old Stan something, and then our boy shuts down his monitors, goes downstairs, right. He has a little talk, the dealer walks with him away from the black jack area over toward poker, they put more cash in the dealer's hand and he leaves."

"So, the black kid is working undercover with him and they got old Stan to turn a blind eye, you think?" Fat Joe stood up straight, outrage making his face turn red.

"Yeah, and helping himself to a little pocket lining just like the other feds... but how he got to Donny, that's what I wanna know."

Fat Joe looked at Lou. "Does that matter how they did it? They tried to infiltrate us, are stealing money from us—even if it is a punk ass amount, and they killed a good man. The boss said to be sure that crazy bastard Tony got put down hard tonight. We can't have undercover cops thinking they can violate us like that. So, it's good he's off the premises. Saves us the trouble of having to ask him to go for a little ride."

"I'll round up the fellas," Lou said with a slight smile.

The place where he'd taken her was a dive, but it was quiet. The short walk away from the casino district had allowed her thoughts to gather along with her impressions of him. Pain so deep and so profound cloaked him and she'd almost reached out to touch him to try to dispel it.

"You're an honest man," she said, once the bartender had taken their drink orders. "Noble."

"No man is without sin," he replied, staring into her eyes. "Sin stains nobility."

"I didn't say you were without sin, I said you were an honest man. To kill those who have brutalized those you love is an honest emotion."

Her words made him draw back and a frown replaced his once serene expression. "You need to talk to me—quickly."

She smiled. "I am not your nemesis, nor your enemy." She released a sigh as their drinks came, knowing she'd never be able to sip hers without a bit of blood mixer. "There was a man in the hotel, over at the Trump Taj Mahal... Donny, I think his name was."

"Was?" Tony leaned in to her and grabbed her arm.

"Was," she said flatly. "He knew who you were; they all do, I suppose, if they sent him to kill you."

"He's dead?" Tony slowly let go of her arm and then cautiously downed half his martini. "How do you know all of this?"

"Because I eliminated him."

Incredulous, he simply stared at her for a moment. "You work for them and you've now set me up?"

She shook her head no. "Have the rest of your martini. I don't work for anyone, haven't in *years*. He was an asshole, a very bad man, the type I despise, so..."

"Then how do you know all of this—like how you knew my name?" Tony's voice was a low, threatening rumble.

"If I told you, you'd never believe me."

"Try me. You just told me you killed a man and know way too much about me for comfort."

She searched his face, seeing kind eyes behind their angry veneer, seeing where the pain began and what had chased him into the arms of fate.

"They took your wife's life," she murmured. "Your partner's and his wife. The baby." Odette shook her head and then shivered. "Beasts. Humans can be animals—I've died at their hands, had that which was precious taken from me. You and I are not so different."

"Lady, stop talking in riddles," he said, now grabbing her arm again as he roughly set down his glass.

"You aren't ready for the truth… ask yourself, didn't you find it strange that you couldn't see me on the monitors? The moment I saw you pushing the young dealer in my direction, with you dressed in security staff black, I figured that the technology had betrayed me."

"What *the fuck* is going on, lady?"

She inclined her head toward the mirror behind the bar, motioning toward it with her chin. "I don't show up in reflections, mirrored surfaces, or even in photographs. I don't exist, but I do exist. I don't appear dangerous, but I'm deadly. And I'm so much older than you think. But I'm not evil, although everything you've been taught says that I am… even though some like me definitely are. You and I are the same, rogues, an enigma, cloaked in pain and invisible to most others. We cull the herds, you and I, in our own way; we keep the beasts away from the innocent. Be careful tonight—it's getting late, I need to go."

His hand had fallen away from her arm as his jaw went slack. He didn't offer protest as he stared in the mirror and she stood and walked away, too stunned to immediately gather himself. By the time his body and mind caught up to each other, allowing him to toss a twenty on the bar and dash out the door to find her, she was gone.

But a black Escalade careened over the curb, its door opened before he could draw his weapon, and beefy hands had him. Duct tape went over his mouth; nylon cuffed his wrists as the vehicle sped to a deserted section of beach. Hardened eyes told him Odette hadn't lied. How could he have been so stupid!

His shoulder collided with the ground, the searing pain racing through his skeleton. A pair of dead, young eyes stared at him, open, glassy… the kid was only twenty-six. Hell, he was only thirty-seven. Struggling just made the men around him laugh. Trying to speak made them draw their weapons.

"Take the tape off and lemme hear what this sonofabitch has to say," Lou growled, leveling a nine millimeter toward Tony's face. "We've known you were a cop for months."

Another henchman ripped off the tape. Tony took a huge inhale, and then began shouting, spittle flying.

"Fuck you!" he yelled out, trying to sit up. "You kill my pregnant wife and think I'm not coming for you? You kill my partner and think there'd be no retribution?" Chest heaving, death eminent, he refused to beg them, wanted them to know that he'd take this grudge with him to hell and back. "I'll haunt you motherfuckers! This ain't over!"

The men around him laughed and shook their heads.

"Sorry, I ain't superstitious," one said.

"Yeah, me neither," Lou said, shrugging his shoulders and poking out his barrel chest. "But sorry about the wife, little bitch wasn't supposed to be at the house when it blew. Our bad."

"I'll kill you!" Tony shouted.

"Yeah, we're so scared," Lou said, and then squeezed the trigger twice.

The back of his head exploded in pain and colors for a second and then everything went dark. There was no light, no sound; he could no longer feel the sand or the wind. The chill of the night air was gone. He'd failed. It was so quick, a blink of time. He was floating and weeping inside his shattered mind. Pressure at his throat made his muscles twitch. Something tightened around him and then became light, making him feel like he was flying away. Time stood still and yet he could feel its passage. Water now pelted his body, his forehead rested against something soft. He opened his eyes slowly to a dark angel, the shower spray blurring his vision.

Butter-cream-soft hands traced his back; cinnamon-hued breasts cushioned his chest as his knees buckled. A warm mouth sought his in a tender kiss. He had to be in heaven, because he'd just left hell on the beach. Everything was now surreal. His stomach churned and then pain soon gripped him, making him stagger backward to claw the wall, his wail an agonized echo that bounced off the tiles.

"I tried but got there too late to save the boy, that young dealer. They are animals," a familiar voice murmured. "You must eat to regain your strength, and then heal today... tonight we will work together."

Frantic, he looked around at the exquisite marble and gold fixtures, and then his gaze settled on Odette. "Where am I?"

"At my home, far away from them."

"You saved me?" he panted. "The last thing I remember is Lou unloaded two slugs into the back of my head." Tony's hand gingerly touched his skull and then when he felt no wound, panicked.

"I perceived that you wanted to live more than anything else, in order to avenge this travesty of justice."

"I did, but... but how?" He stepped out of the walk-in shower, bumping into the glass and staggering to the far side of the spacious bathroom. "I heard the shots, felt the impact, passed out. How in the fuck don't I have a huge hole in my head!" He looked around, noticing something was missing. "Where's the mirror? Where's the goddamned mirror, Odette!"

"I don't have any in the mansion," she said calmly, turning off the water and covering her nudity with a large, white Turkish towel. "They upset me."

"Why! What's going on?"

She tossed him a towel and watched him grab it swiftly. "I'm sorry, it was the only way to save you. But once you eat, you'll understand all."

"Eat? Eat! Are you insane?" He wound the towel around his waist and struggled to stand without the aid of the double sink. "I'm not hungry, I'm about to lose my mind. My brains just got blown out, but I'm not dead, this ain't a hospital, and I don't know why I'm even alive." Pain doubled him over again.

"You're not. Eat," she whispered, offering him her wrist.

He seemed confused, and then became horrified as her French manicured finger broke the skin and fangs filled his mouth at the first sight of her blood.

Tears stung his eyes but the scent of blood saturated the bathroom, drawing him to her beyond his control. He closed his eyes as he took her arm and brought it to his lips, her fingers threading through his hair, petting him as he greedily suckled, colors staining the inside of his lids, pleasure careening through his system until he could stand it no more. He threw his head back and released a moan. Her embrace opened the floodgate on years of hurt along with a torrent of tears.

Sobs of remorse choked him, a tender mouth swallowed them away. Velvet tresses were in his fist, his fingers wending their way through dripping curls. Hands so graceful, so soft removed pain from his aura with each gentle caress until towels fell away and skin burned against skin. This woman had saved him, had pulled his essence of existence away from the blackness. He had another chance to complete the mission he'd begun. Her story exploded inside his mind and he wept for her as his story entered her and she wept for him, their honesty becoming raw passion that slammed against the walls and melted down to body-slicked heat on the towel-strewn floor.

The storm of emotions and pleasure was so swift that it left them both breathless. He stared down at her, tracing the edge of her beautiful brows and then cradled her cheek.

"Why did you come back for me?" he murmured, still out of breath.

"Because you were a keeper. I found you after a very long search. A nobleman... and it has been centuries since I'd found someone worth saving." A gentle smile eased out of hiding on her face. "Plus, I so badly wanted a Vodka martini."

He paused to catch his breath, his mind laboring under the new knowledge it had just received. "What they did to you was unforgivable."

"I became what I am, much like you did tonight," she murmured, touching his cheek, her smile fading. "Someone cared enough about me to give me another chance and I loved him for that... and for whom he was."

He understood what Odette was telling him, he loved Meghan that way. But it was becoming so difficult to hold onto the memory or to nurse it to life.

"Imagine after more than two hundred years... the memories fade and all you have left is the pain." Her stare was so hypnotic, so open, and for all that she was and all that she had done, she possessed serenity.

"I have to finish this, tomorrow night, then I can move on."

"I know you have to redress what happened to you," she said quietly, briefly closing her eyes. "Just as one day I'll route out the rest of those in the coven that participated in the coup against Alfonse."

"I know," he murmured, moving against her slowly and now appreciating the unhurried pleasure of their union. She was a beautiful woman, but there was something beyond that, something still so genuine inside her very being. It had been so long since he'd witnessed that or had allowed himself to experience the possibility it existed beyond Meghan. The fact that he felt the way he did almost seemed like a betrayal.

"It's not a betrayal," Odette murmured, brushing his mouth with hers. "They would have wanted us to go on, to thrive, and not merely survive. If we exist tortured, then the others have also won."

A gasp escaped him as Odette's slick sheath tightened around him. He studied her face as he loved her slowly, kissing her throat, then her breasts, paying delicate homage to her erect Hershey nipples with tiny suckles until she moaned. Satiny legs encircled his waist as she arched and offered him her throat. The strike into her jugular was swift but tender, her gasp sending a shudder through him that made him cry out.

The night wore on, their lovemaking an anthem, to survival, to renewal, that took them from the floor of the vast bathroom to the sprawl of her king-sized bed. He watched semi-dazed as the steel door to the basement sanctuary closed and pure darkness surrounded them, but yet he could still see.

"Rest," she whispered. "Later tonight will be ours. We have the benefit now of time, power, and stealth."

He pulled her against his chest in the darkness, finding it new that no heartbeats meshed and only cool skin now touched. The heat was gone, but not his loyalty to the one who'd saved him. The seeds of a long-time love had been planted. One that wouldn't grow old, one that understood him more than the former love of his life ever had, one that shared his altruism and even his dark side.

"I'm glad you found me," he said quietly. "I didn't want to die."

She nodded and kissed his chest. "I am glad, too. This is rare… it is magic."

"Finders keepers." For the first time in years, he closed his eyes with a smile.

They entered the casino just as they had left, but no monitors could perceive them. Old Stan looked at Tony and then glanced away.

"Wait here," he said to Odette. "I have to clear this up."

She nodded and perused the floor watching as her lover tried to make an old man understand. But that was pointless, people believed what they wanted to. Finally, she saw Tony hail her with a slight lift of his jaw.

"Ask Odette," he said calmly, placing a hand on Stan's shoulder.

She already knew the direction of the conversation. "He didn't kill the young dealer, they did. Tony used to work for the feds."

Stan straightened. "Then get the fuck away from me, would ya!" He spoke through his teeth. "I don't wanna wind up like that kid, and I don't wanna know what's going on—but I don't want them to see me ever talking to you."

Tony nodded. "No problem, you live well."

Odette took his arm. "There is much I have to teach you about the use of your power."

"Just get me up into the security area without them seeing me."

"Vapor?" she said with a wide grin. "Follow me to the shadows. You just don't do that on an open casino floor in polite company."

She took his hand and then pulled him into an alcove, kissing him passionately as passersby glanced at them once, and then they were gone.

Drifting replaced body weight, and then vents became passageways. Silence echoed all around him until Odette's voice entered his head.

Bullets will hurt but not kill you. However, the rage is controlling you right now, you must control the rage. Decide before you go in there whether or not you want to rip them to shreds with your bare hands and start an entirely crazy investigation, or if you want to just shoot them all so that it looks like a human-on-human crime.

Before he could answer her, he was standing inside the room and could feel her presence invisibly monitoring his first foray as a vampire.

They were eating take-out from the restaurants below. Laughter filled the room, total entitlement to joy surrounded them like his life and death and that of an innocent kid's never matter, never happened. They didn't even see him.

"I told you I would haunt you," Tony said in a low growl.

"Oh, shit!" Lou jumped up and grabbed his gun.

Four henchmen cursed and scrambled for weapons.

"I thought you whacked this bastard!" Fat Joe shouted.

In that moment, Tony decided. He didn't want to shoot them. Hand-to-hand combat just felt too good. Ripping Lou's arm out of its socket and then shooting him in the head, just felt like the right thing to do. But wisdom and vampire speed prevailed, as he unloaded his clip.

"Feed before you leave," Odette said, materializing behind him. "Or else, it's a waste."

They sat hand in hand under the stars on a bench watching the surf. A thousand questions pummeled his mind but he was grateful he didn't have to verbalize any of them for her to understand.

"It is a sexy, glorious emotion, revenge, but just like sex with a lover you don't love, once you climax, it all feels so hollow."

He nodded. Leave it to a woman to so eloquently define what was raging within him. "Now what?" he whispered. "There are so many more of them, so many I could go after, and will… but it all seems so pointless."

She laid her head on his shoulder. "This is why I haven't destabilized the coven. After I repaid Gustav for what he'd done to Alfonse, I sadly realized, it would never bring him back." Her soft palm stroked his chest as she looked out to the moon. "Alfonse and I decimated the town back in Haiti before we left that fateful night of my *making*. We settled all old debts, but in the end, none of that made us feel better beyond the moment of the blood-letting."

"Sorta like a crack high… for the moment it's an adrenaline rush like you cannot believe, and then…"

"And then you crash."

He stared at her. "So how do you go on living now?"

"As time passes you'll realize that the greatest thing you have is someone to share that passage of time with… for what felt like eons I focused on the ugliness so much that I could never see the beauty of life. Once I died I forgot how to do that."

"I had forgotten that while I was still living," he said in a sad murmur.

"I have seen the dawn of so much, though… cars, telephones, airplanes; I could go on and on. But also wars."

He smiled, and then chuckled sadly. "So, what do we do, become philanthropists?"

She smiled and shrugged. "Why not. We can be whatever we want to be, can right wrongs, can help or hurt. What do you want to be?"

"I don't want to hurt people," he said quietly, his voice so sad that it drew her.

She stared into his eyes and nodded, touching his lips with one finger. "Enough lessons for one night. Enough vengeance for one era. Let us focus on beauty."

He took her mouth in a slow dissolve of pleasure. He was her greatest find, something precious that she would vow to keep, and she knew that she was that for him. The irony of that truth not lost on either of them.

AFTER THE STONE AGE

by Brian Stableford

Brian Stableford's latest novels, all new this year, include *Sherlock Holmes and the Vampires of Eternity, The Dragon Man,* and *The Moment of Truth.* He is well-known in vampire circles for his novels *The Hunger and Ecstasy of Vampires, The Empire of Fear,* and *Young Blood,* and for his translations of French author Paul Féval, père's nineteenth-century works of vampire fiction (which pre-date Bram Stoker's *Dracula*). He has also authored many other novels and French translations, as well as numerous works of non-fiction about science fiction.

About vampire fiction, Stableford says: "It's probably popular because it imagines a kind of charisma, a subspecies of angst and an insidious variety of violence of which humans are incapable, thus providing a temporary distraction from the charismatic void, ineffably tedious angst and mere brutality that constitute the quotidian human condition. I became interested in it when the history of the subgenre took an interesting turn in the 1970s, when assumptions of monstrosity formerly taken more-or-less for granted were challenged and interrogated in various quirky ways, presumably reflecting—albeit in a distorting mirror—contemporary sociological shifts in attitudes to sexuality."

This tale, which first appeared in the BBC's *Cult Vampire Magazine,* is about the potential utility of vampirism as a "natural" substitute for liposuction.

Mina had tried them all: WeightWatchers, Conley, grapefruit, Atkins, hypnotherapy and pumping iron. On the day she decided, after three grueling months, that the Stone Age diet was doing her more harm than good—just like all the rest—she felt that she had hit rock bottom in the abyss of despair. She clocked in at sixteen stone five pounds, just six pounds lighter than the day she had embarked on the Stone Age with such steely determination. By the end of March she would doubtless crack the seventeen stone barrier, going in the wrong direction.

Younger people, she supposed, calculated in kilograms but she had never contrived to adjust. Mercifully, she was in public finance rather than the commercial sector, so she rarely had to audit accounts that were connected, even in the remotest degree, with the EU. She never traveled abroad, because she couldn't bear the thought of an airplane seat, let alone stripping down to a bikini on a beach in

Marbella. She had never lost the habits of embarrassment gained in childhood, and now she had the prospect of middle-age spread looming before her.

Mina hadn't an atom of proof that she had been passed over for promotion because of the way she looked. The fact that her newly imported line manager, Lucy Stanwere, had a figure like Paula Radcliffe as well as being ten years younger might have been coincidence. The fact that Lucy was able to wear four-inch heels, thus allowing her to tower over those condemned by gravity to flat soles, might also be irrelevant to her rapid ascent of the status ladder. The fact that Mina was due to see Lucy for her annual appraisal the morning after she fell off the Stone Age wagon and gorged herself on Welsh rarebit and chocolate milk was, however, definitely not a coincidence. Anxiety had always been a key factor in Mina's comfort eating.

Lucy's office was, of course, incredibly neat. It wasn't just that the cleaners made more effort there than in the open-plan, but that Lucy's own personal neatness radiated out from her size-ten suit to bathe her entire environment with a kind of bloodless perfection. Simply being there made Mina feel even more like a rubbish-heap than usual; from the moment she stepped through the door her one ambition was to escape as soon as possible, no matter how much criticism she had to absorb and acknowledge in order to do it.

She didn't, of course, dare to entertain the ambition that she might accomplish that escape without some slighting reference being made to her appearance—in fact, the first thing Lucy said, after "Please sit down, Miss Mint," was "Are you unwell?" That, in health-fascist-ese, meant: "How can you even breathe when you're carrying so much excess baggage, you disgusting calorie-addict?"

"I've had a little tummy trouble recently," Mina admitted, "but it's sure to clear up now."

"Coming off the Stone Age?" Lucy asked, in a tone that sounded almost sympathetic.

Mina had never talked to Lucy in a non-work context, so she couldn't claim to know her well, but she certainly hadn't expected sympathy. She decided that it must be an illusion.

"Yes, actually," Mina admitted.

"I thought so," Lucy said. "The trouble with all these theories about what evolution shaped our digestive systems to do is that humans are so exceedingly adaptable. We grow up on grains and dairy products, and our bodies learn to love them. If there's one thing that separates humans from all the other animals, it's the ability to learn to love. Don't you agree?"

The chance would be a fine thing, Mina thought. What she said aloud was: "Yes, Miss Stanwere."

"It's Lucy. Look, Mina, I don't want to seem presumptuous, and I'll understand if you want to confine our discussion to the nerves and sinews of auditing practice and Gordon Brown's latest wrinkles, but there's a better way to lose weight, if you really want to. It's about time that you were let in on the secret."

Mina had long suspected that there must be a vast conspiracy of the fit and thin whose precious secrets were sternly withheld from people like her, but she had never expected to be let into it. She said nothing.

"I know what you're thinking," Lucy Stanwere said, when the pause had passed from pregnant to eggbound. "How would I know? Well, I do." She took up her handbag. Any normal person would have had to root about for at least thirty seconds to find what she wanted, but Lucy only required a mere moment to pluck the desired item from its innermost depths. She handed Mina a photograph.

Mina stared at the snapshot in frank disbelief. It wasn't so much the sixteen stone version of Lucy Stanwere that startled and appalled her so much as the expression the teenager was wearing: an expression of profound shame and terror of exposure that Mina had only ever seen at WeightWatchers—or in a mirror.

When she looked up again, Mina saw her superior with entirely new eyes. She could find but one word: "How?"

Lucy's perfectly manicured fingers dipped into the mysterious bag for a second time, and produced another slim item. At first, Mina judged from its size that it was a business-card, but it was glossy and black, and bore an image of two magnificently athletic individuals dancing what appeared to be the tango, above the red-lettered inscription: THE AFTER DARK CLUB. The postcode attached to the address was suggestive of Mayfair.

"Meet me there at ten-thirty," Lucy said. "I'll tell the desk to expect you, and I'll take you in."

"A night club?" Mina said, aghast. "I can't go to a night club."

"Ten-thirty," Lucy Stanwere repeated, insistently. "Be on time."

Mina had nothing suitable to wear, but the situation was so surreal that it didn't seem to matter. She was usually curled up in bed with a Mills and Boon not long after ten-thirty, once she'd watched the news on the BBC, so she went to catch the Central Line tube at Ealing Broadway with the kind of disturbed feeling that changes in a familiar routine always bring on.

She had never realized that the urban wilderness between Piccadilly and Oxford Street had so many hidden trails and discreet coverts but her pocket A-to-Z eventually guided her to an unmarked door with a discreet intercom and bell-push. Mina almost turned round and went home right then, but eventually plucked up courage to press the button. When a fuzzy voice said "Yes?" she blurted out "Is-that-the-After-Dark-Club-Lucy-Stanwere-asked-me-to-meet-her-here?" without the slightest pause for breath.

There was an eerie buzzing sound—more like a swarm of angry wasps than placid bees, but no less welcome for that—punctuated by a click. Mina pushed the door open, and entered a gloomy corridor which led to a flight of stairs. At the top of the stairs was a desk, manned by a teenage male in an absurdly old-fashioned suit. "Miss Mint?" he said, before she could gather her breath. "We've been expecting you. It's a pleasure to meet you."

Mina had not had time to frame a reply when the burgundy-colored door to the left of the desk opened and Lucy Stanwere came out, accompanied by two other men, each as callow as the receptionist, both complexioned like Turks or Italians. They too were wearing black suits cut to standards of formality that had surely gone out with the last King George, or maybe Queen Victoria.

Lucy, by contrast, was dressed in a very now manner that was far more relaxed—louche, even—than her everyday office-wear. "Mina, darling!" she said, with a brazen bonhomie that contrasted just as sharply with the flinty face of public finance. "I want you to meet Marcian and Szandor. You'll have to forgive Szandor—I'm afraid his English is a trifle rusty—but Marcian will translate for him. Come through, won't you?"

Mina was unable to respond to this invitation immediately, because Marcian and Szandor were busy kissing her hands, so enthusiastically that they hadn't waited to take turns, seizing one apiece. Nor did they let go when they had finished, arranging themselves to either side of her with an affectionate politeness that she had never encountered before.

She had, of course, avoided making eye-contact, her embarrassment being so intense that she had all but closed her eyes, but as she stole sidelong glances to her left and right she observed that both of them were looking at her with expressions that betrayed not the slightest hint of disgust, contempt, scorn or disapproval.

If she had only dared, she might have felt a surge of joy, but she had lived in the world too long to be free of the suspicion that she was about to suffer some humiliating reversal of fortune.

Marcian and Szandor escorted her through the doorway, although it didn't seem humanly possible that there was room enough for either to pass through it beside her, let alone both. She was swept along another purple-carpeted corridor to another darkly varnished door, while Lucy followed.

The image on the card had left Mina with the impression that there might be a ballroom swirling with exotic couples, all engaged in a furiously erotic tango, but the whole building seemed silent, insulated from the unceasing noise of the capital; the room in which Mina now found herself was actually a bedroom.

My God! Mina thought, as she contemplated the king-sized four-poster with the red velvet curtains. It's not a night club at all. It's a knocking-shop for chubby-chasers!

So far as she was concerned, chubby-chasers were creatures of legend, one of whom she had always longed to meet. Like unicorns, which refused to have anything to do with anyone but virgins, men who were sexually attracted to fat women were exceedingly thin on the ground in Ealing. Then Mina remembered Lucy, who was only half the woman now that she had been as a teenager, and realized that there must be more to the situation than had yet met her eye. She turned, opening her fearful eyes sufficiently to demand an explanation.

"It's all right, Mina," Lucy said. "There's nothing to be afraid of. No one's gong to do anything to you that you don't want them to do. But the time has come for you to ask yourself the question: *Do I sincerely want to be thin?*"

Mina swallowed a hysterical laugh. The consequent frog in her throat made it impossible to do anything but croak: "Yes."

It seemed a pitifully feeble expression of her desire, but Lucy seemed satisfied. "Good," she said. "I'll cut to the chase, then—no point in beating about the bush. Marcian and Szandor are vampires. Given a few months of weekly sessions, they can literally drink your superfluous flesh away. You'll need to take iron tablets to facilitate the manufacture of new blood, but their enzymes will do the rest—re-orientate your metabolism to convert your adipose deposits, that kind of thing. It won't make you feel bad—quite the reverse. You'll feel better than you've ever felt before: full of energy, in more ways than one. Natural selection is a wonderful thing, and we talked only this morning about the marvelous ability of human beings to adapt themselves.

"Marcian and Szandor are human too, of course—you'll have to forget all that superstitious nonsense about the undead rising from their graves and canine teeth becoming fangs. Vampires are just another natural species, near relatives of ours in the genus *Homo*, who accompanied us to the brink of extinction more than once, but are now on the increase again. They're not quite ready to come out of hiding yet—like us, they're not entirely free of their old instincts—but they're making discreet diplomatic moves at every level, taking one step at a time in the tedious business of winning hearts and minds."

Mina hadn't noticed Lucy Stanwere's cliché-addiction before, but she tried to concentrate her attention on the more important aspects of the speech. Apparently, she wasn't going to be required to dance the tango in any literal sense. Instead, she was going to lie down on the bed while Marcian and Szandor drank her blood, presumably relieving her of forty fluid ounces or so, while pumping some kind of enzymes into her that would retune her metabolism to mobilize her fat reserves and set her on the road to paradise, or at least size twelve.

All in all, it was difficult to see a downside.

Eyes wide open now, Mina found herself staring at Lucy's neck, looking for tell-tale holes.

Lucy smiled. "That stuff about fangs is just Hammer horror," Lucy said. "It's more sucking than biting, actually. It doesn't even leave a love-bite, because there are no leftovers. You'll feel a slight numbness for a day or two, and your complexion might be a trifle pale, but you'll feel a lot better in yourself."

Mina belatedly thought of a potential downside. "Will I turn into a vampire too?" she asked, surprised at the lack of faintness in her own voice.

"No, silly," Lucy replied. "I told you, they're just another human species. You can't turn into one of them any more than they can turn into wolves or bats. It's symbiosis. They obtain sustenance from us; we get fitness and an amazing sense of well-being in return. Mutual profit—the ultimate expression of free-market economics at its finest. There's no rush; you can have all the time you need to think about it. All we ask is a little discretion."

"Discretion?" Mina echoed, with a confidence she had never felt before. "To hell with discretion. Let's get on with it!"

In the next two hours Mina discovered why the After Dark Club's card depicted two dancing figures. The movement was internal and emotional, and there were three people involved rather than two, but it was rhythmic as well as hectic, measured as well as erotic.

Marcian and Szandor never touched her below the waist, but that didn't matter. Mina understood well enough, by the time she went to catch the night bus back to Ealing, why sophisticated people said that the most important sexual organ was the brain.

She didn't see Lucy Stanwere before she left. Presumably, that wonderful woman and perfect friend was still engaged in a languorous horizontal tarantella of her own, probably with a single partner given that she no longer had the stored-up wealth to satisfy two. Marcian saw her to the door, bid her a fond goodnight, and made another date with her for the following Tuesday.

The old Mina would have asked, anxiously, whether she'd be ready for another session quite so soon, but the new Mina took it for granted that she could raise her blood to the required pressure with time to spare.

Marcian's conversation had been mostly devoted to technical matters and mild warnings, so Mina felt that he hadn't really warmed to her as yet, but Szandor—who had been silent apart from a few incomprehensible mumblings—had been free to indulge himself in fond stares and tactile explorations, and Mina felt that they had already built a delicate rapport. Although she was besotted with them both, she couldn't help feeling a little fonder of Szandor.

They seemed such nice young men, so expert in their arcane art, that she would have been more than happy to see them again even if the pounds hadn't started to melt away with such awesome rapidity.

It wasn't until the Tuesday, when Mina plucked up enough nerve to make a feeble joke about Dracula, that she discovered how old the seemingly young men actually were.

"Old Vlad!" Marcian said, with a delighted chuckle that was a fine compliment to her joke. "I remember him. Not one of us, of course—just a…how do you say?…a groupie. Thought he might become immortal if we would only teach him the trick. Poor sap!"

Her experience was so ecstatic that it took Mina ten minutes to realize that she too was a groupie: someone who hung around vampires, avidly offering blood. Twenty more were required to disclose that "poor sap" wasn't an Americanism. "Sap" was a vampire colloquialism for *Homo sapiens*; Marcian referred to his own kind as "ultras"—that being a contraction of *Homo ultrasapiens*, which, loosely translated, meant "man the extremely wise." It wasn't until it was nearly time to go home that it occurred to Mina to wonder how old Marcian actually was, given that he had obviously been around for centuries, but it didn't seem polite to ask forthrightly. After all, he'd been polite enough not to ask her age. She resolved to make discreet and indirect inquiries on the following Sunday, for which they made a third date.

By the time Friday night arrived, eight days after Mina's introduction to the joys of vampire victimhood, she felt that her life had undergone a fabulous transformation.

As she said good night to Lucy Stanwere she gloried in the conspiratorial glance that they exchanged—a pleasure in which she had never indulged with any other colleague, of either sex, during her entire career in public finance. At work, of course, they behaved with strict formality, never making the slightest mention of their secret, but as they stepped over the threshold each evening they made their silent acknowledgements.

Mina went straight from work to the gym, where she went to work, first on the rowing machine and then on the cycling machine. She sometimes caught other people staring at her, but that didn't make her feel self-conscious any more. Once, they would merely have been appalled by her bulk; now she was content to assume that they were amazed at her capacity for exercise. Regenerating the blood she required to feed Marcian and Szandor was no mere matter of stuffing herself with calories and iron tablets; she had to crank up her retuned metabolism, rebalancing the energy-economy of her physical and spiritual being. Even fake rowing and fake cycling were beginning to give her a sense of furious speed and steadfast endurance that was remarkably satisfying—though not, of course, anywhere near as satisfying as lying on the curtained four-poster while Marcian and Szandor sucked their sustenance from her flesh with such obvious avidity and appreciation.

On Sunday, she observed that it must have been hard for vampires living through times of plague, famine and religious persecution.

"The Black Death was bad," Marcian admitted, "but the Church wasn't too inconvenient. Bishops grow as fat as members of any other priviligentsia. Civilization is a fine thing; life was harder before there were cities."

"You must have very good memories to recall a time when there wasn't," Mina suggested, delicately.

"Ach, it's more tradition than memory," Marcian admitted. "We make up stories to remind ourselves of all the things we're bound to forget. We all feel nostalgic about the good old days before you saps wiped out the Neanderthals, but it's legend-based. Nobody really remembers anything much before the fall of Troy, and it's all momentary flashes until the last two hundred years or so."

"The price of living forever, I suppose," Mina said, pensively.

Marcian actually raised his head then, to look her in the eye—as fondly as Szandor, but also a trifle darkly.

"Nobody lives forever, Mina," he said. "Ultras don't age or suffer from disease, but we all die in the end: drowned or decapitated, burned or blown up. Every living thing dies."

In the early hours of that Monday morning Mina stepped on the scales to find that she had broken fifteen-seven for the first time in three years, going in the right direction. She couldn't expect to continue to shed weight at more than a pound a day for very long, of course, but even as the rate of loss tailed off she could reasonably expect to be below fourteen stone by the end of April and below twelve by the end of June. Come Hallowe'en, she might be the woman of her dreams, not an ounce over nine stone and fit as a flea.

Mina had rarely contemplated the future in any frame of mind but abject horror, but she found herself wondering now about very serious questions. When, for instance, would she no longer be able to feed two hungry vampires? Would she have to choose between Marcian and Szandor, or would they settle her fate between themselves? And what, then, would be her long-term prospects? How long could a sap continue to feed a single vampire, if she made every possible effort to maximize her blood-production? Years? Decades? A whole sap lifetime?

Marcian would have known all the answers, but Mina felt that she needed a different perspective. One Friday when she wasn't due at the After Dark, she asked Lucy Stanwere if they could meet up for a drink. Lucy looked her up and down, as if trying to decide whether Mina had lost sufficient weight to be fit company in a sap-filled wine-bar, but eventually nodded. "Let's have dinner," she said. "Do you know the Arlequino Andante in Marylebone High Street? It's late to make a booking, but they'll let me in if I ring."

Mina didn't know the restaurant, but she promised to find it and meet Lucy there at eight.

"I've been meaning to have an in-depth chat to find out how you were getting along," Lucy said, when they'd ordered, "but you know how it is. It's obviously working. Happy?"

"Never been happier," Mina agreed. "It's just that I've been wondering about a few things, and I don't like to trouble Marcian with too much chat while he's…drinking."

"Oh, Marcy wouldn't mind. He's a real chatterbox by comparison with my Otto. What is it? The not-going-out-in-daylight business?"

"That too," Mina agreed, although it had not been among the items praying on her mind.

"They don't catch fire and shrivel up or anything Hammery like that," Lucy told her. It's just a matter of ingrained habit. Evolution shaped them as nocturnal hunters, like most other vampiric species—bats, bedbugs and the like. They could give it up if they wanted to, but they don't."

That prompted Mina to think of another question. "If natural selection gave them such long lives," she said, "why did we poor saps get stuck with seventy years?"

"Why did the chimps get stuck with all that hair and no brains? Small differences in DNA can easily be amplified into big differences of lifestyle. We've outstripped chimps because human babies are born at a relatively early stage of development, so our brains gain from experience as they grow. The older we grow the more benefit we get from that experience, so natural selection favors living longer—but we poor saps never got the benefit of the mutation that freed the ultras from the burden of ageing. The corollary is that they reproduce very slowly—ultra males and females don't mix much and only have sex once or twice a millennium—and there's the nutritional limitation too. It has to be human blood, you see—no other species will do. It's almost as if they were our extra selves, formed entirely from our spare flesh—but maybe that's a bit too philosophical. The Parma ham's good, isn't it? Nice texture."

Mina found the ham a trifle chewy, and it had a tendency to stick to her teeth, so it wasn't until she was tucking into her veal Marsala that she raised the question of where her new relationship might be headed, medium-term-wise.

"Didn't Marcy tell you?" Lucy asked. "You only had to ask. Szandor will take you on eventually—I hope that's not a disappointing prospect. His English is improving, I hope? He's supposed to be doing night-classes at the City Lit. Marcy runs the Club—he's the fixer for the entire London community. He'll put you on home visits soon if that's okay—just Szandor, I suppose, although Marcy might drop in occasionally. He kept tabs on me for a while, once he'd set me up with Otto. I love Otto. Good job we no longer live in an era when lifelong spinsters were automatically assumed to be consorting with the devil, isn't it?"

"Yes it is," Mina agreed. "When you say lifelong…?"

"Don't worry about that," Lucy said. "It's not really a matter of living fast, dying young and leaving a beautiful corpse. What if we do get used up by fifty or fifty-five? We'll look as good as we possibly can until then, and all you'll ever have to do to reconcile yourself to it is consider the alternative."

Even the new Mina didn't quite have courage enough to ask exactly how old Lucy really was, although she had concluded that appearances were probably deceptive and that Lucy's CV might not be honest about such details as date of birth. It didn't seem to matter much; the crucial datum, so far as Mina was concerned, was her own age, which was thirty-three. If feeding a vampire meant that she was likely to die at fifty-something rather than the contemporary female average of seventy-nine, that didn't seem too high a price to pay for twenty years of better-than-normal slenderness. Anyway, who could tell how many years of life-expectancy her obesity might have cost her if she'd stayed on the boom-and-bust diet carousel?

Mina did, however, summon enough courage to ask whether Lucy had sap boyfriends as well as Otto.

"I had a few, when I still wanted to catch up on all the sex I thought I'd missed out on," Lucy admitted, frankly. "It didn't take long to realize that I hadn't missed anything at all, compared to the real thing. You'll find that out for yourself, I dare say."

Mina did find out for herself. Indeed, everything transpired as Lucy had prophesied. Szandor's English improved enough for him to ask her himself whether he might visit her at home, once a week to begin with, and Mina readily agreed. Marcian dropped in on her too, once a month or so, more for a chat than a feed. On one such occasion, in August, he mentioned to her that the club had moved, but he didn't give her a card with the new address. Soon after that, Lucy announced that she was moving on again too, having been promoted to a senior position in Newcastle.

Mina breezed through the interview panel for Lucy's job, so the farewell party was a double celebration. It got so wild by midnight that some jumped-up office-boy from Procurement blurted out the office rumor which held that Mina and Lucy were lesbian lovers. Far from feeling appalled or insulted, Mina was delighted that she should be thought so versatile, so desirable and so interesting. She told Szandor about it when he visited her on the following Sunday—Sundays having now become their regular date—but he didn't laugh. It wasn't that vampires didn't have a sense of humor, just that they found different things amusing.

"Anyway," Mina said, "the promotion will mean a hike in salary, so I'll be able to buy a house. You could move in if you wanted to—it might be more convenient."

He laughed at that. "Sank you very much," he said, "but it vouldn't be right."

"Where do you live now?" she asked, for the first time. "Do you have a job of your own—night security or something."

Szandor's gaze, though still fond, became troubled. "I cannot tell you vere I liff," he said. "As for jops, ve liff as ve liffed in the old country, as communists—real communists, not those Soffiet bastards. Effer since…." He broke off.

"Ever since what?" Mina prompted, assuming he was thinking about something that had happened after the collapse of communism, in Bosnia or Chechnya or wherever he had recently come from.

"Effer since the Stone Age," he said. "Ven you began to vork in bronze…ve vere neffer a part of that. The vorld of vork, of jops…is not ours."

Mina realized then how little she actually knew about the vampire way of life, and how they occupied themselves when they were not feeding. She realized, too, how wide the gulf between the two human species must be, if all of history since the end of the Stone Age had been sap history, never recognizing, let alone involving the ultras, except as myth and shadow, mystery and threat. And yet, the ultras lived in a world that saps had remade, an ecosphere that saps had spoiled, on the edges of a global civilization organized and driven by sap machines and money.

Mina nearly asked Szandor what the communist vampires did for money, but realized that she didn't have to. They obtained their money as they obtained their blood, from their sapient groupies—not, evidently, in weekly handouts, but at intervals nevertheless adequate to their peculiar needs. In all probability, they were content to wait until their victims were used up; who else, after all, but her one and only dependent was a groupie likely to appoint as her heir?

Vampires could afford to be patient, and had certainly had abundant opportunity to acquire the habit.

How many victims, Mina wondered, had Szandor had before her? Far more, she guessed, than she had had hot dinners of her own…that being, at the end of the day, exactly what she was. It wouldn't be right for him to move in with her, she realized, for exactly the same reasons that it wouldn't be right for her to move into a battery cage or a veal crate. She was no longer the fat cow she had been in spring, but she would be a cow for as long as she might live.

After that reverie there was only one question that she needed to ask.

"Szandor," she said, "do you love me? Do you really love me?"

The ultra paused in his appreciation of the wonderfully appetizing blood that he was sucking from her breast to say: "Yes, my darlink. I loff you ferry much."

Mina knew that it was true. He loved her, not as a boy-child is obliged to love the mother at whose teat he sucks, nor as a farmer is obliged to love his prize cattle, nor as saps were obliged by their carefully selected hormones to love one another, but freely. He loved her in his own unique way, as only a vampire could love a member of his sister species, who provided the substance of his life in a single miraculous red stream.

When her lover had gone, after kissing her hand as any over-polite European might have done in saying *au revoir*, Mina went to the full-length mirror that she had bought only the previous day, and stood naked before it to make a critical study of the skin that sagged loosely about her ten stone two pound frame.

There was still a way to go, but she was getting there.

The skin would tighten up in time; even at thirty-three she still had enough adaptability to continue tightening its grip on her compacted flesh.

She would never reach perfection, but every day, in every way, she was getting better and better—and how many hard-working saps could honestly say that…except for all the others who were secretly in bed with the real reds?

All in all, she told herself, more in self-congratulation than in a spirit of self-discipline, *it's quite impossible to see a downside.*

MUCH AT STAKE

by Kevin J. Anderson

Bestselling author Kevin J. Anderson has written nearly 100 novels, many of them co-written with Doug Beason, with his wife Rebecca Moesta, or with Brian Herbert, with whom he continues Frank Herbert's Dune saga. His most recent original projects are the Saga of Seven Suns series, which concluded with last year's *The Ashes of Worlds*, and his nautical fantasy epic Terra Incognita, the first of which, *The Edge of the World*, came out in June. A Batman/Superman tie-in novel was also released earlier this year, and a new Dune novel, *The Winds of Dune*, is due in August.

Anderson says that one of the appeals of vampire fiction is that the mythos has grown so rich and varied over the past century or so, it gives writers plenty of room to operate with their imaginations. "My story takes place on the periphery of actual vampire fiction…more a story about vampires than a story with vampires," he said.

"Much at Stake" is a different sort of Dracula story; its protagonist is famed actor Bela Lugosi, the star of the original 1931 *Dracula* film, and explores some of his personal background as well as the history behind vampire legends.

Bela Lugosi stepped off the movie set, listening to his shoes thump on the papier-mâché flagstones of Castle Dracula. He swept his cape behind him, practicing the liquid, spectral movement that always evoked shrieks from his live audiences.

The film's director, Tod Browning, had called an end to shooting for the day after yet another bitter argument with Karl Freund, the cinematographer. The egos of both director and cameraman made for frequent clashes during the intense seven weeks that Universal had allotted for the filming of *Dracula*. They seemed to forget that Lugosi was the star, and he could bring fear to the screen no matter what camera angles Karl Freund used.

With all the klieg lights shut down, the enormous set for Castle Dracula loomed dark and imposing. Universal Studios had never been known for its lavish productions, but they had outdone themselves here. Propmen had found exotic old furniture around Hollywood, and masons built a spooky fireplace big enough for a man to stand in. One of the most creative technicians had spun an eighteen-foot rubber-cement spiderweb from a rotary gun. It now dangled like a net in the dim light of the closed-down set.

On aching legs, Lugosi walked toward his private dressing room. He never spoke much to the others, not his costars, not the director, not the technicians. He had too much difficulty with his English to enjoy chitchat, and he had too many troubling thoughts on his mind to seek out company.

Even during his years of portraying Dracula in the stage play, he had never socialized with the others. Perhaps they were afraid of him, seeing what a frightening monster he could become in his role. After 261 sell-out performances on Broadway, then years on the road with the show, he had sequestered himself each time, maintaining the intensity he had built up as Dracula, the Prince of Evil, drawing on the pain in his own life, the fear he had seen with his own eyes. He projected that fear to the audiences. The men would shiver; the women would cry out and faint, and then write him thrilling and suggestive letters. Lugosi embodied fear and danger for them, and he reveled in it. Now he would do the same on the big screen.

He closed the door of the dressing room. All of the others would be going home, or to the studio cafeteria, or to a bar. Only Dwight Frye remained late some nights, practicing his Renfield insanity. Lugosi thought about going home himself, where his third wife would be waiting for him, but the pain in his legs felt like rusty nails, twisting beneath his kneecaps, reminding him of the old injury. The one that had taught him fear.

He sat down on the folding wooden chair—Universal provided nothing better for the actors, not even for the film's star—but Lugosi turned from the mirror and the lights. Somehow, he couldn't bear to look at himself every time he did this.

He reached to the back of his personal makeup drawer, fumbling with clumsy fingers until he found the secret hypodermic needle and his vial of morphine taped out of sight.

The filming of *Dracula* had been long and hard, and he had needed the drug nearly every night. He would have to acquire more soon.

Outside on the set, echoing through the thin walls of his dressing room, Lugosi could hear Dwight Frye practicing his Renfield cackle. Frye thought his portrayal of the madman would make him a star in front of the American audiences.

But though they screamed and shivered, none of them understood anything about fear. Lugosi had found that he could mumble his lines, wiggle his fingers, and leer once or twice, and the audiences still trembled. They enjoyed it. It was so easy to frighten them.

Before Universal decided to film *Dracula*, the script readers had been very negative, crying that the censors would never pass the movie, that it was too frightening, too horrifying. "This story certainly passes beyond the point of what the average person can stand or cares to stand," one had written.

As if they knew anything about fear! He stared at the needle, sharp and silver, with a flare of yellow reflected from the makeup lights—and Van Helsing thought a wooden stake would be Lugosi's bane! He filled the syringe with morphine. His legs tingled, trembled, aching for the relief the drug would give him. It always did, like Count Dracula consuming fresh blood.

Lugosi pushed the needle into his skin, finding the artery, homing in on the silver point of pain… and release. He closed his eyes.…

In the darkness behind his thoughts, he saw himself as a young lieutenant in the 43rd Royal Hungarian Infantry, fighting in the trenches in the Carpathian Mountains during the Great War. Lugosi had been a young man, frightened, hiding from the bullets but risking his life for his homeland—he had called himself Bela Blasko then, from the Hungarian town of Lugos.

The bullets sang around him in the air, mixed with the explosions, the screams. The air smelled thick with blood and sweat and terror. The mountain peaks, backlit at night by orange explosions, looked like the castle spires of some ancient Hungarian fortress, more frightening by far than the crumbling stones and cobwebs the set builders had erected on the studio lot.

Then the enemy bullets had crashed into his thigh, his knee, shattering bone, sending blood spraying into the darkness. He had screamed and fallen, thinking himself dead. The enemy soldiers approached, ready to kill him… but one of his comrades had dragged him away during the retreat.

Young Lugosi had awakened from his long, warm slumber in the army hospital. The nurses there gave him morphine, day after day, long after the doctors required it—one of the nurses had recognized him from the Hungarian stage, his portrayal of Jesus Christ in the "Passion Play." She had given Lugosi all the morphine he wanted. And outside, in a haze of sparkling painlessness, the Great War had continued.…

Now he winced in the dressing room, snapping his eyes open and waiting for the effects of the drug to slide into his mind. Through the thin walls of the dressing room, he could hear Dwight Frye doing Renfield again, "Heh hee hee hee HEEEEE!" Lugosi's mind grew muddy; flares of color appeared at the edges.

When the rush from the morphine kicked in, the pleasure detached his mind from the chains of his body. A liquid chill ran down his spine, and he felt suddenly cold.

The makeup lights in his dressing room winked out, plunging him into claustrophobic darkness. He drew a sharp breath that echoed in his head.

Outside, Dwight Frye's laugh changed into the sound of distant, agonized screams.

Blinking and disoriented, he tried to comprehend exactly what had altered around him. As if walking through gelatin, Lugosi shuffled toward the dressing room door and opened it. The morphine made fright and uneasiness drift away from him. He experienced only a melting curiosity to know what had happened, and in his mind he questioned nothing. His Dracula costume felt alive on him, as if it had become more than just an outfit.

The set for Castle Dracula appeared even more elaborate now, more solid, dirtier. And he saw no end to it, no border where the illusion stopped and the cameras set up, where Karl Freund and Tod Browning would argue over the best way to photograph the action. No booms, no klieg lights, no catwalks.

The fire in the enormous hearth had burned low, showing only orange embers; sharp smoke drifted into the greatroom. He smelled old feasts, dampness and mildew in the corners, the leavings of animals in the scattered straw on the floor. Torches burned in iron holders on the wall. The cold air raised goosebumps on his morphine-numbed flesh.

The moans and screams continued from outside.

Moving with a careful, driven gait, Lugosi climbed the wide stone staircase, much like the one on which he met Renfield in the film. His shoes made clicking sounds on the flagstones, solid stones now, not mere papier-mâché. He listened to the screams. He followed them.

He knew he was no longer in Hollywood.

Reaching the upper level, Lugosi trailed a cold draft to an open balcony that looked down onto a night-shrouded hillside. Stars shone through wisps of high clouds in an otherwise clear sky. Four bonfires raged near clusters of soldiers and drab tents erected at the base of the knoll. Though the stench of rotting flesh reached him at once, it took Lugosi's eyes a moment to adjust from the brightness of the fires to see the figures spread out on the slope.

At first, he thought it was a vineyard, with hundreds of stakes arranged in rows, radiating from concentric circles of other stakes. But one of the "vines" moved, a flailing arm, and the chorus of the moans increased. Suddenly, like a camera coming into focus, Lugosi recognized that the stakes contained human forms impaled on the sharp points. Some of the points were smeared with blood that looked oily black in the darkness; other stakes still shone wicked and white, as if they had been trimmed once again after the victims had been thrust down upon them.

Lugosi gasped, and even the morphine could not numb him to this. Many of the human shapes stirred, waving their arms, clutching the wounds where the stakes protruded through their bodies. They had not been allowed to die quickly.

Dim winged shapes fluttered about the bodies—vultures feasting even at night, so gorged they could barely fly, ignoring the soldiers by the tents and bonfires, ignoring the fact that many of the victims were not even dead. Ravens, nearly invisible in the blackness, walked along the bloodstained ground, pecking at dangling limbs. A group of the soldiers broke out in laughter from some game they played.

Lugosi squeezed his eyes shut and shivered. Revulsion, confusion, and fear warred within his mind. This must all be some illusion, a twisted nightmare. The morphine had never affected him like this before!

Some of the victims had been skewered head down, others sideways, others feet down. The stakes rose to various heights, high and low, as if in a morbid caste system of death. A rushing wail of pain swept along the garden of bloody stakes, sounding like a choir.

From the corridor behind Lugosi, a quiet voice murmured. "Listen to them—like children of the night. Do you enjoy the music they make?" Lugosi whirled and stumbled, slumping against the stone wall; the numbness seemed to put his legs at a greater distance from his body.

Behind him stood a man with huge black eyes that reflected tears in the torchlight.

His face appeared beautiful, yet seemed to hide a deep agony, like a doe staring into a broken mirror. Rich brown locks hung curling to his shoulders. He wore a purple embroidered robe lined with spotted fur; some of the spots were long smears of brown, like dried spots of blood wiped from wet blades. His full lips trembled below a long, dark mustache.

"What is this place?" Lugosi croaked, then realized that he had answered automatically in the stranger's own tongue, a language as familiar to Lugosi as his childhood, as most of his life. "You are speaking Hungarian!"

The stranger widened his eyes in indignation. Outside, the chorus of moans grew louder, then quiet, like the swell of the wind. "I speak Hungarian now that I am no longer a prisoner of the Turks. We will obliterate their scourge. I will strike such fear in their hearts that the sultan himself will run cowering back to Constantinople!"

One of the vultures swooped close to the open balcony, and then flew back toward its feeding ground. Startled, Lugosi turned around, then back to face the stranger who had frightened him. "Who are you?" he asked.

The Hungarian words fit so naturally in his mouth again. Lugosi had forced his native language aside to learn English, phonetically at first, delivering his lines with power and menace to American audiences, though he could not understand a word of what he was saying. Understanding came much later.

The haunted stranger took a hesitant step toward Lugosi. "I am… Vlad Dracula. I bid you welcome. I have waited for you a long time."

Lugosi lurched back and held his hand up in a warding gesture, as if reenacting the scene when Van Helsing shows him a box containing wolfsbane. From childhood Lugosi had heard horrible stories of Vlad the Impaler, the real Dracula, rumored to be a vampire himself, known to be a bloodthirsty butcher who had slaughtered hundreds of thousands of Turks—and as many of his own people.

In the torchlit shadows, Vlad Dracula paid no attention to Lugosi's reaction. He walked up beside him and stood on the balcony, curling his hands on the stone half-wall. Gaudy rings adorned each of his fingers.

"I knew you would come," Dracula said. "I have been smoking the opium pipe, a trick I learned during my decade of Turkish captivity. The drug makes my soul rest easier. It makes me open for peace and eases the pain. I thought at such a time you might be more likely to appear."

Vlad Dracula turned and locked eyes with Bela Lugosi. The dark, piercing stare seemed more powerful, more menacing than anything Lugosi had mimed in hundreds of performances as the vampire. He could not shirk away. He knew now how the Mina character must feel when he said "Look into my eyes…"

"What do you want from me?" Lugosi whispered.

Vlad Dracula did not try to touch him, but turned away, speaking toward the countless victims writhing below. "Absolution," he said.

"Absolution!" Lugosi cried. "For this? Who do you think I am?"

"How are you called?" Dracula asked.

Lugosi, disoriented yet accustomed to having his name impress guests, answered,

"Bela Lugos—no, I am Bela Blasko of the town of Lugos." He drew himself up, trying to feel imposing in his own Dracula costume, but the enormity of Vlad the Impaler's presence seemed to dwarf any imaginary impressiveness Lugosi could command.

Vlad Dracula appeared troubled. "Bela Blasko—that is an odd name for an angel. Are you perhaps one of my fallen countrymen?"

"An angel?" Lugosi blinked. "I am no angel. I cannot grant you forgiveness. I do not even believe in God." He wished the morphine would wear off. This was growing too strange for him, but as he held his hand on the cold stone of the balcony it felt real to him. Too real. The sharp stakes below would be just as solid, and just as sharp.

He looked down at the ranks of tortured people covering the hillside, and he knew from the legends about the Impaler that this was but a tiny fraction of all the atrocities Vlad Dracula had already done. "Even if I could, I would not grant you absolution for all of this."

Vlad Dracula's eyes became wide, but he shrank away from Lugosi. "But I have built monasteries and churches, restored shrines and made offerings. I have surrounded myself with priests and abbots and bishops and confessors. I have done everything I know how." He gazed at the bloodied stakes, but seemed not to see them.

"You killed all these people, and many many more! What do you expect?" Lugosi felt the fear grow in him again, real fear, as he had experienced that war-torn night in the Carpathian Mountains. What would Vlad Dracula do to him?

Some of those victims below were Lugosi's own countrymen—the simple peasants and farmers, the bakers and bankers, craftsmen—just like those Lugosi had fought with in the Great War, just like those who had rescued him after he had been shot in the legs, who had dragged him off to safety, where the nurses tended him, gave him morphine. Vlad Dracula had killed them all.

"There are far worse things awaiting man… than death," the Impaler said. "I did all this for God, and for my country."

Lugosi felt the words catch in his throat. For his country! His own mind felt like a puzzle, with large pieces of memory breaking loose and fitting together in new ways. Lugosi himself had done things for his country, for Hungary, that others had called atrocities.

Back in 1918 he had embraced Communism and the revolution. Proudly, he had bragged about his short apprenticeship as a locksmith, then had formed a union of theater workers, fighting and propagandizing for the revolution that thrust Bela Kun into power. But Kun's dictatorship lasted only a few months, during which Romania attacked the weakened country, and Kun was ousted by the counterrevolution. All supporters of Bela Kun were hunted down and thrown into prison or executed. Lugosi had fled for his life to Vienna with his first wife, and from there, penniless, he had traveled to Berlin seeking acting jobs.

Lugosi had scorned his faint-hearted American audiences because they proved too weak to withstand anything but safe, insignificant frights—yet now he didn't believe he could stomach what he saw of the Impaler. But Vlad Dracula thought he was doing this for his people, to free Wallachia and the towns that would become great Hungarian cities.

"I fight the Turks and use their own atrocities against them. They have taught me all this!" Vlad Dracula wrung his hands, then snatched a torch free from its holder on the wall. He pushed it toward Lugosi, letting the fire crackle. Lugosi flinched, but he felt none of the heat. It seemed important for Dracula to speak to Lugosi, to justify everything.

"Can you not *hear* me? I care not if you are not the angel I expected. You have come to me for a reason. The Turks held me hostage from the time I was a boy. To save his own life, my father Dracul the Dragon willingly delivered me to the sultan, along with my youngest brother Radu. Radu turned traitor, became a Turk in his heart. He grew fat from harem women, and rich banquets, and too much opium. My father then went about attacking the sultan's forces, knowing that his own sons were bound to be executed for it!"

Vlad Dracula held his hands over the torch flame; the heat licked his fingers, but he seemed not to notice. "Day after day, the sultan promised to cut me into small pieces. He promised to have horses pull my legs apart while he inserted a dull stake through my body the long way! Several times he even went so far as to tie me to the horses, just to frighten me. Day after day, Bela of Lugos!" He lowered his voice. "Yes, the Turks taught me much about the extremes one can do to an enemy!"

Vlad Dracula hurled the torch out the window. Lugosi watched it whirl and blaze as it dropped through the air to the ground, rolled, then came to rest against a rock. Without the torch, the balcony alcove seemed smothered with shadows, lit only by the starlight and distant fires from the slaughter on the hillside.

"After I escaped, I learned that my father and my brother, Mircea, had been ambushed and murdered by John Hunyadi, a Hungarian who should have shared their loyalty! Hunyadi captured my father and brother so he could gain lordship over the principalities my father controlled. He struck my father with seventy-three sword strokes before he dealt the mortal blow. He claimed that he had tortured my brother Mircea to death and buried him in the public burial grounds." Dracula shook his head, and Lugosi saw real tears hovering there.

"Mircea had fought beside John Hunyadi for three years, and had saved his life a dozen times. When I was but a boy, Mircea taught me how to fish and ride a horse. He showed me the constellations in the stars that the Greeks had taught him." Dracula scraped one of his rings down the stone wall, leaving a white mark.

"When I became Prince again, I ordered his coffin to be opened so that I could give him a proper burial, with priests and candles and hymns. We found his head twisted around, his hands had scraped long gouges on the top of his coffin. John Hunyadi had buried him alive!"

Vlad Dracula glanced behind him, as if to make certain no one else wandered the castle halls so late at night, and then he allowed himself to sob. He mumbled his brother's name.

"Just a few months ago, in my castle on the Arges River in Transylvania, the Turks laid siege to me and fired upon the battlements with their cherrywood cannons. One Turkish slave forewarned me, and I was able to escape by picking my way along the ice and snow of a terrible pass. My own son fell off his horse during the flight, and I have never seen him again. My wife could not come with us, and so rather than being captured by the Turks, she climbed the stairs of our tallest tower overlooking the sheer gorge, and she cast herself out of the window. She was my wife, Bela of Lugos. Do you know what it is like to lose a wife like that?"

Lugosi felt cold from the breeze licking over the edge of the balcony. "Not… like that. But I can understand the loss."

In exile from Hungary back in 1920, Lugosi had left his wife Ilona in Vienna, while he tried to find work in Berlin in German cinema or on the stage. He had written to her every other day, but she had never replied. He learned later that her father, the executive secretary of a Budapest bank, had convinced her to divorce him, to flee back to Hungary and to avoid her husband at all costs because of the awful things he had done against his own country. Dracula's wife had chosen a different way out.

Outside, Lugosi heard distant shouts and the jingling of horses approaching at a gallop. He saw the soldiers break away from their tents, scattering the bonfires and snatching up their weapons. The Impaler seemed not to notice.

"I do not know who you are, or why you have come," Vlad Dracula said. "I prayed for an angel, a voice who could remove these demons of guilt from within me." He snatched out at Lugosi's vampire costume, but his hand passed directly through the actor's chest.

Lugosi shrank back, feeling the icy claw of a spectral hand sweep through his heart. Vlad Dracula widened his enormous dark eyes with superstitious terror. "You truly must be a spirit come to torment me, since you refuse to grant me absolution."

Lugosi did not know how to answer. He delivered his answer with a stuttering, uncertain cadence. "I… I am neither of those things. I am only a traveler, a dream to you perhaps, from a time and place far from here. I have not lived my life yet. I will be born many centuries from now."

"You come not to judge me, then? Or punish me?" Vlad Dracula looked truly terrified. He looked down at the hand that had passed through Lugosi's body.

"No, I am just an actor—an entertainer. I perform for other people. I try to make them afraid." He shook his head. "But I was wrong. What I do has no bearing on real fear. The acting I do, the frights I give to my audience, are a sham. That fear has no consequences." He leaned out over the balcony, then squeezed his eyes shut at the scores of maimed corpses, and those victims not fortunate enough to have died yet. "Seeing this convinces me I know nothing about real fear."

In the courtyard directly below, shouting erupted. Marching men hurried out into the night. Someone blasted a horn. Lugosi heard the sounds of a fight, swords clashing. Vlad Dracula glanced at it, dismissed the commotion for a moment, then locked his hypnotic gaze with Lugosi's again. The anguish behind the Impaler's eyes made Lugosi want to squirm.

"That is all? I have prayed repeatedly for an apparition, and you claim to have learned something from *me?* About fear? All is lost. I have been abandoned. God is making a joke with me." His shoulders hunched into the fur-lined robe, and he reddened with anger.

Lugosi had the crawling feeling that if he had been corporeal to the Impaler, Vlad Dracula would have thrust him upon a vacant stake on the hillside. "I do not know what to tell you, Vlad Dracula. I am not your conscience. I have destroyed enough things in my own life by trying to do what I thought was right and best. But I can tell you what I think."

Vlad Dracula cocked an eyebrow. Below, a clattering sound signaled a portcullis opening. Booted feet charged across the flagstone floor as someone hurried into the receiving hall. "My Lord Prince!"

Lugosi spoke rapidly. "The Turks have taught you well, as your atrocities show. But you have perhaps gone too far. You cannot undo the things you have already done, the thousands already slain. But you can change how you act from now on. Your brutal, bloodthirsty reputation is already well-earned. Mothers will frighten their children with stories of Vlad the Impaler for five hundred years! Now perhaps you have built enough terror that you no longer need the slaughter. The mere mention of your name and the terror it evokes may be enough to accomplish your aims, to save Hungary from the Turks. If this is how you must be, try to govern with *fear*, not with death. Then your God may give your conscience some rest."

Vlad Dracula made a puzzled frown. "Perhaps we are together because I needed to learn something about fear as well." The Impaler laughed with a sound like breaking glass. "For one who has not lived even a single lifetime, you are a wise man, Bela of Lugos."

They both turned at the sound of a running man hurrying up the stone steps to the upper level where Lugosi and Vlad Dracula stood side by side. The messenger scraped his sword against the stone wall, clattering. He swept his cloak back, looking from side to side until he spotted Dracula in the shadowy alcove. Sweat and blood smeared his face.

"My Lord Prince! You did not respond!" the man cried. A crimson badge on his shoulder identified him as a retainer from one of the boyars serving Vlad Dracula.

"I have been in conversation with an important representative," Dracula said, nodding to Lugosi. Surprised, but falling back on his training, Lugosi sketched a formal bow to the messenger. But the retainer looked toward where Lugosi stood, blinked, and frowned.

"I see nothing, my Lord Prince."

In a rage, Vlad Dracula snatched out a dagger from his fur-lined robe. The messenger blanched and stumbled backward, warding off the death from the knife, but also showing a kind of sick relief that his end would be quick, not moaning and bleeding for days on a stake as the vultures circled about.

"Dracula!" Lugosi snapped, bringing to bear all the power and command he had used during his very best performances as the vampire. Vlad Dracula stopped, holding the knife poised for its strike. The retainer trembled, staring with wide blank eyes, but afraid to flee.

"Look at how terrified you have made this man. The fear you create is a powerful thing. You need not kill him to accomplish your purpose."

Vlad Dracula heard Lugosi, but kept staring at the retainer, making his eyes blaze brighter, his leer more vicious. The retainer began to sob.

"I need not explain my actions to you," he said to the man. "Your soul is mine to crush whenever I wish. Now tell me your news!"

"The sultan's army has arrived. It appears to be but a small vanguard attacking under cover of darkness, but the remaining Turks will be here by tomorrow. We can stand strong against this vanguard—many of them have already fled upon seeing their comrades impaled on this hillside, my Lord Prince. They will report back. It will enrage the sultan's army."

Vlad Dracula pinched his full lips between his fingers. He looked at Lugosi, who stood watching and waiting. The messenger seemed confused at what the Impaler thought he saw.

"Or it will strike *fear* into the sultan's army. We can use this. Go out to the victims on the stakes. Cut off the heads of those dead or mortally wounded—and be quick about it!—and catapult the heads into the Turkish vanguard. They will see the faces of their comrades and know that this will happen to them if they fight me. Find those whose injuries may still allow them to live and set them free of the stakes. Send them back to the sultan to tell how monstrous I am. Then he will think twice about his aggression against me and against my land."

The retainer blinked in astonishment, still trembling from having his life returned to him, curious about these new tactics Vlad Dracula was attempting. "Yes, my Lord Prince!" He scrambled backward and ran to the stone steps.

Lugosi felt the walls around him growing softer, shimmering. His knees felt watery. His body felt empty. The morphine was wearing off.

Dracula tugged at his dark mustache. "This is interesting. The sultan will think it just as horrible, but God will know how merciful I have been. Perhaps next time I smoke the opium pipe, He will send me a true angel."

Lugosi stumbled, feeling sick and dizzy. Warm flecks of light roared through his head. Dracula seemed to loom larger and stronger.

"I cannot see you as clearly, my friend. You grow dim, and I can barely feel the effects of the opium pipe. Our time together is at an end. Now that we have learned what we have learned, it would be best for you to return to your own country.

"But I must dress for battle! If we are to fight the sultan's vanguard, I want them to see exactly who has brought them such fear! Farewell, Bela of Lugos. I will try to do as you suggest."

Lugosi tried to shake the thickening cobwebs from his eyes. "Farewell, Vlad Dracula," he said, raising his hand. It passed through the solid stone of the balcony wall....

The lights flickered around his makeup mirror, dazzling his eyes. Lugosi drew in a deep breath and stared around his tiny dressing room. A shiver ran through him, and he pulled the black cape close around him, seeking some warmth.

Outside, Dwight Frye attempted his long Renfield laugh one more time, but sneezed at the end. Frye's dressing room door opened, and Lugosi heard him walking away across the set.

On the small table in front of him, Lugosi saw the empty hypodermic needle and the remaining vial of morphine. Fear. The silver point looked like a tiny stake to impale himself on. Morphine had always given him solace, a warm and comfortable feeling that made him forget pain, forget trouble, forget his fears.

But he had used it too much. Now it transported him to a place where he could see only the thousands of bloodied stakes and moaning victims, vultures circling, ravens pecking at living flesh. And the mad, tormented eyes of Vlad the Impaler.

He did not want to think where the morphine might take him next—the night in the Carpathians during the Great War? Or his secret flight across the Hungarian border after the overthrow of Bela Kun, knowing that his life was forfeit if he stopped? Or just the pain of learning that Ilona had abandoned him while he worked in Berlin? The possibilities filled him with fear—not the fear without consequences that sent shivers through his audiences, but a real fear that would put his sanity at risk. He had brought the fear upon himself, cultivated it by his own actions.

Bela Lugosi dropped the syringe and the small vial of morphine onto the hard floor of his dressing room. Slowly, with great care, he ground them both to shards under the heel of his Count Dracula shoes.

His legs ached again from the old injury, but it made him feel solid and alive. The pain wasn't so bad that he needed to hide from it. What he found in his drug-induced hiding place might be worse than the pain itself.

Lugosi opened his dressing room and saw Dwight Frye just leaving through the large doors. He called out for the other actor to wait, remembering to use English again, though the foreign tongue seemed cumbersome to him.

"Mr. Frye, would you care to join me for a bit of dinner? I know it is late, but I would enjoy your company."

Frye stopped, and his eyes widened to show how startled he was. For a moment he looked like the madman Renfield again, but when he chuckled the laugh carried delight, not feigned insanity.

"Yes, I would sure like that, Mr. Lugosi. It's good to see you're not going to keep to yourself again. The rest of us don't bite, you know. Nothing to be afraid of."

Lugosi smiled sardonically and stepped toward him. The pain in his legs faded into the background. "You're right, Mr. Frye. There is nothing to fear."

HOUSE OF THE RISING SUN

by Elizabeth Bear

Elizabeth Bear's recent books include *All the Windwracked Stars* and *Seven for a Secret*. A new novel, *By the Mountain Bound*, is due out this fall. Other novels include *Carnival*, which was a finalist for the Philip K. Dick Award, *Undertow*, and the Jenny Casey trilogy—*Hammered*, *Scardown*, and *Worldwired*—which won the Locus Award for best first novel. She is a prolific short story writer as well, much of which has been collected in *The Chains That You Refuse*. Additionally, she is one of the creative minds behind *Shadow Unit* (www.shadowunit.org), an ongoing, hyperfiction serial. Bear is a winner of the Hugo Award and the John W. Campbell Award for Best New Writer.

This story first appeared in the UK magazine *The Third Alternative* (which is now known as *Black Static*). It follows a man who used to be the most famous person in the world, living a life of anonymity that still has strange echoes of his fame. To say more than that might give too much away, but let's just say that as a result of writing this story, Bear knows a lot more about the history of blues, gospel, and rock and roll than she used to.

Sycorax smiled at me through the mantilla shadowing her eyes: eyes untouched by that smile. She lolled against a wrought-iron railing, one narrow hip thrust out, dyed red hair tumbling out of the black spiderweb of her shawl, looking like a Mac Rebennack song come to life.

The dead quickly grow thin.

She licked her lips with a long pale tongue and even the semblance of amusement fell away. "You're pale, Tribute. No coup tonight?"

"Nothing appealed." Tribute wasn't my real name any more than Sycorax was hers.

She leaned into me, pressed a hand to my throat. Her flesh lay like ice against the chill of my skin. "I told you to hunt."

"I hunted." Backing away, red nails trailing down my chest. I hunted. Hunted and returned empty-handed. It's as much how you hear the orders as how they're given.

She followed close on my steps, driving me before her. Ragged black chiffon clung and drifted around her calves; she reached up to lace china fingers in the fine hairs at the nape of my neck. Her face against my throat was waxen: too long unfed. "You weaken me on purpose, Tribute. Give me what you have."

She needed me, needed me to feed. Old as she was, she had to have the blood more often and she couldn't take it straight from a human anymore. She needed someone like me to purge the little taints and poisons from it first—and even then, I had to be careful what I brought home. So sensitive, the old.

She caught at my collar, pulled it open with fumbling hands. I leaned down to her—chattel, blood of her blood, no more able to resist her will than her own right hand, commanded to protect and feed her. At least this time, I knew what sort of predator I served, although I had less choice about it.

I figured things out too late, again.

Sycorax curled cold lips back from fangs like a row of perfect icicles, sank her teeth into my flaccid vein and tried to drink. All that pain and desire spiked through me—every time like the first time—and on its heels a hollowness. Sycorax hissed, drew back. She turned her head and spat transparent fluid on the cobbles. I smiled as she turned on me, spreading my hands like Jesus on a hilltop, still backing slowly away. I had made very sure that I had nothing to feed her on.

Petty, I know. And she'd make me pay for it before dawn.

Down the narrow lane, a club's red door swung open and I turned with a predator's eye, attracted to the movement. Spill of light cut like a slice of cake, booted feet crunching on glittering glass. Girls. Laughing, young, drunk. I remembered what that felt like.

I raked a hand through my forelock and looked away, making the mistake of catching Sycorax's china-blue eye.

"Those," she said, jerking her chin.

I shook my head. "Too easy, baby. Let me get you something more challenging." I used to have an accent—down-home Mississippi. Faded by the years, just like everything else. I suspected I sounded pan-European now, like Sycorax; I've put some effort into changing my speech patterns. Her lips, painted pale to match china-white skin, curled into a sulk.

"Tribute. After a quarter of a century, you ought to know I mean what I say."

I tugged my collar, glancing down.

"Them." Sycorax twisted a stiletto-heeled boot, crushing the litter of cracked glass against the bricks.

She enjoyed the hunt a little too much. But who but a madwoman would have drained *my* living body and made me hers? Just fetching my corpse from the grave would have taken insane effort.

"I'm hungry," she complained while I sharpened my teeth on my lip to stop a malicious smile.

If I could buy a little time, the girls might make it to the street and I could lose them in the crowds and tangled shadows of the gaslamp district. Footsteps receded down the alley; I spread my hands in protest, cocking my head to one side and giving her the little half-smile that used to work so well on my wife. "Something with a little more fight in it, sweetie."

My wife was a hell of a lot younger than Sycorax. "Those two girls. Bring me their blood, Tribute. That's an order."

And that was the end of the argument. I turned to obey.

"Tribute."

Coming back around slowly, her gaze—catching mine—flat and pale. "Sycorax."

"I could just spike your pretty eyes out on my pinkie finger and eat them, lovely boy," she purred. "Hazel, aren't they?"

"Blue."

She shrugged and made an irritated, dismissive gesture, hands white as wax. "It's so hard to tell in the dark."

The girls made it to the street before Sycorax ended the discussion, but I had to follow them anyway. I paced my ordained prey, staying to the shadows, the collar of the black leather trenchcoat that Sycorax had picked out for me tugged up to half-hide the outline of my jaw. I never would have bought that coat for myself. You'd think anybody who'd been dead for any time at all would have had enough of blackness and shadows, thank you very much. Sycorax reveled in it. If she were three hundred years younger, she'd have been a gothchick.

It was a good night: nobody turned for a second look.

People are always dying, and human memory is short. In a hundred years, I shall probably be able to walk down any street in the world without raising an eyebrow.

As long as the sun is down.

Sycorax didn't bother to follow. I had no choice but to do as I was bid. It's more than a rule; it's a fact. I expected there were still a few women I knew who would get a kick out of that.

My girls staggered somewhat, weaving. One was a blonde, brittle dyed hair and a red beret. The other one had glossy chestnut brown waves and the profile of a little girl. I tracked them through the district toward the ocean, neon glow and littered sidewalks. A door would open and music would issue forth, and it wasn't long before I found myself mouthing the words to one particular song.

There's something gloriously ironic in a man charting a number-one hit twenty-five years after he's dead. *Otis Redding, eat your heart out.*

My quarry paused at an open-air patio where a live band played the blues. Girl singer, open coat and a spill of curls like wicked midnight: performing old standards, the kind I've always loved. *Mama, tell my baby sister, not to do what I have done. I'll spend my life in sin and misery, in the House of the Rising Sun.* A song that was already venerable when Eric Burdon made it famous.

There's all kinds of whoredom, aren't there? And all kinds of bloodsuckers, too.

The singer nailed "Amazing Grace" a capella like heartbreak, voice sharp and gritty as little Mary Johnson doing "Cold, Cold Heart." I caught myself singing along and slashed my tongue with needle teeth before someone could overhear. Still no blood. I hadn't fed in a long time and it hurt more than it should have.

The girls sat down at a table and ordered food. I smelled beer, hot wings, eye-watering garlic. I suddenly very badly wanted a peanut butter sandwich and a milkshake.

Leaning against the high black iron fence, I watched the girls watching the band until a passerby in her fifties turned to get a startled better look at me. I stood up straight and met her gaze directly, giving her the crooked little-kid smile. It almost always works, except on Sycorax.

Trying to hide your face only convinces them they've seen something.

"Sorry," she said, waving me away with a smile. A moment later, she turned back. "You know you look like…."

"People say," I answered, pitching my voice high.

"Amazing." She nodded cheerfully, gave me a wide wondering grin, and continued on her way. I watched her go, chattering with her friends, shaking their heads.

The girls didn't stay for "King of the Road," although I would have liked to hear the version.

Kids.

I almost turned away when they walked past. They stank of garlic-stuffed mushrooms and beer. The reek of the herb knotted my stomach and seared my eyes. I actually tried to take a half-step away before the compulsion Sycorax had laid on me locked my knees and forced me back into pursuit.

They walked arm in arm, skinny twenty-year-olds with fake IDs and black vinyl miniskirts. Cheap boots, too much eyeliner. The one with the brown hair broke my heart every time she tossed her head, just that way. I let myself drift ahead of them, taking a gamble on where they would cut across the residential neighborhood near the ocean: a dangerous place for girls to be.

I ducked down a side street to cut them off and waited in the dark of an unlit doorway. Sycorax's control permitted that much. I leaned against the wall, scrubbing my face against my hands. It felt like a waxen mask, cold and stiff. My hands weren't much better.

They weren't long. I was unlucky. They picked the better of the two routes through the brownstones, the one I had been able to justify choosing, and just that innocently chose their fate.

The scent of bougainvillea and jacaranda filled the spaces of the night. I watched them skipping from streetlight to streetlight, shadows stretched out behind them, catching up, and then reaching before. The brown-haired one walked a few steps ahead of the bleach-blonde, humming to herself.

I couldn't help it. It wasn't one of my standards, but every blues singer born knows the words to that one. Hell, I used to have a horse by that name.

I picked up the tune.

I had to.

"....they call the Rising Sun. It's been the ruin of many a poor boy. And me, O God, I'm one!"

Their heads snapped up. Twenty, maybe. I was dead before they were born. Gratifying that they recognized my voice.

"Fellas, don't believe what a bad woman tells you—though her eyes be blue, or brown...." I strolled out of the shadows, ducking my head and smiling, letting the words trail away.

The dark-haired girl did a double take. She had a lovely nose, pert and turned up. The blonde blinked a couple of times, but I don't think she made the connection. I'd changed my appearance some, and I'd lost a lot of weight.

The stench of garlic on their breath would have thickened my blood in my veins if I had any left. I swallowed hard, remembering all those songs about wandering ghosts and unquiet graves. Ghosts that all seem to want the same thing: revenge, and to lay down and rest.

I smiled wider. *What the lady wants, the lady gets.*

"Oh, wow," the darker girl said. "Do you have any idea how much you look like...."

The street was empty, dark and deserted. I came up under the streetlight, close enough to reach out and touch the tip of that nose if I wanted. I dropped them a look that used to melt hearts, sidelong glance under lowered lashes. "People say," I answered.

And, sick to my stomach, I broke their necks before I fed.

It was the least I could do.

Poison roiled in my belly when I laid them out gently in the light of that streetlamp, in the rich dark covering the waterfront, close enough to smell the sea. I straightened their spines so they wouldn't look so terrible for whoever found them, but at least *they* wouldn't be coming back.

It was happening already: my limbs jerked and shook. My flesh crawled with ripples like fire, my tongue numb as a drunk's. *I'm going back to New Orleans, to wear that ball and chain....*

Not this time. Struggling to smooth each step, to hide the venom flooding my veins, I hurried back to my poor, *hungry* mistress. I stole the brunette's wallet. I stopped and bought breath mints at the all-night grocery.

I beat Sycorax home.

A STANDUP DAME

by Lilith Saintcrow

Lilith Saintcrow's most recent books are *Hunter's Prayer*, the latest in her Jill Kismet series, and *Strange Angels* (as by Lili St. Crow), the first in a new series for young adults. The third Jill Kismet book is due out around the same time as this anthology. Her other work includes the Dante Valentine series, as well as several other novels.

Saintcrow says each generation invents and reinvents different variations on the vampire theme. "Blood, sex, love, death, repression, liberation from the confines of civilization or meditation upon the link between Eros and Thanatos—vampires are tremendously versatile," she said. "They endure because we can (and do) remake them with every generation. To Bram Stoker's readers, vampires were about disturbing untrammeled female sexuality, discomfort with modernity, and the excesses of colonization. Since then they've gone through several incarnations, as filthy corpses, investment bankers, androgynous sexy avatars, you name it. The strength of the vampire is her ability to shapeshift for each new set of popular neuroses."

This story is an homage to the noir gumshoe greats—Hammett and Chandler. "I was working on a very dark, ugly book and needed something shorter and a little more hopeful," Saintcrow said. "Not too hopeful, though. Noir isn't very hopeful."

When a man wakes up in his own grave, he sometimes reconsiders his choice of jobs.

If he's smart, that is. Me, I'm dumb as a box of rocks and my skull felt like a cannonade was going off inside. The agony in my head was rivaled only by the thirst. Aching thirst in every nerve and vein, my throat scorched and my eyes hot marbles. It was raining, but the water from the sky falling into my open mouth did nothing for the dry nails twisting in my larynx. I struggled up out of clods of rain-churned clay mud, slick and dirty as a newborn pig. My clothes were ruined and the monster in my head roared.

I fell backward, still trapped to my knees in wet earth, padded hammers of rain smashing along the length of my body, and screamed. The spasm passed, leaving only the parched desert plains inside every inch of me.

A few moments of effort got me kicking free, the last of the wet clay collapsing in a body-shaped hole now that the body was above ground. I opened my mouth, rain beating my dirty face, and got only a mouthful of muck.

Coughing, gagging, I made it to hands and knees. My head was a swollen pumpkin balanced on a thin aching stick, and the headache receded between waves of scorching, unbearable, agonizing *thirst*.

There were pines all around me, singing and sighing as the sodden wind slapped them around. It took me two tries to stand up, and another two tries before I remembered my name.

Jack. Jack Becker. That's me. That's who I am.

And I've got to find the dame in the green dress.

Outside the city limits and I'm a duck out of water. The mud wouldn't dry, not in this downpour, it just kept smearing over the ruin of my shirt and suit pants. Even Chin Yun's laundry wouldn't be able to get it out of the worsted. Slogging and slipping, I made it down a hill the size of the Chrysler building and found the dirt road turned off the highway, and there was a mile marker right there.

Twelve miles to the city. Cramps screamed from my empty belly. Maybe getting shot in the head works up a man's appetite. Every time I reached up to touch my noggin it was tender, a puckered hole above my right eye full of even more mud.

I wasn't going to get far. The idea of stumbling off the side of the road and drowning in a ditch was appealing—except for the dame in the green dress.

Think about that, Jack. One thing at a time.

Thunder rumbled somewhere far away. Miss Dale would be at home, probably talking to her cat or making a nice hot cup of tea. The thought made my insides clench like they were going to turn into a meat grinder, and my breath made a funny whistling sound through my open mouth. My nose was plugged, and in any case, I was gasping for air. Sometimes it rains hard enough to drown you out here.

That was when I saw the light.

It was beautiful, it was golden, it was a diner. Not just any diner, but the Denton's Dandy Diner, eleven miles from the city limits. I couldn't go in there looking like this. It took me a while to fumble for my wallet and I nearly ended up in the ditch anyway, my feet tangling together.

The wallet—last year's Christmas present from Miss Dale—was still in my pocket and held all the usuals, plus nineteen dollars and twenty cents. They hadn't taken any money. Interesting.

Think about that later, Jack.

My shirt was wet enough to shed the mud, my suit jacket nowhere in evidence. Stinging pellets warned me the rain was turning to ice.

But the crazy thing was, I wasn't cold. Just thirsty as hell. Maybe the idea of the dame in green was warming me up.

Neon blinked in the diner's windows. It was closed, goddammit, and just when I could have used a phone. I could even *see* the phone box, smearing my muddy mitts on the window and blinking every time the *Cold Drinks* sign blinked as well. The phone was at the end of the hall, right near the crapper.

My legs nearly gave out.

This is turning out to be a bad night, Jackie boy.

I found a rock I could lift without busting myself and heaved it. The glass on the door went to pieces, and I carefully unlocked it. The long slugtrail of mud I left toward the phone might have been funny if I'd been in a grinning mood.

A man like me knows his secretary's home number. Any dame dumb enough to work for a case like me probably wouldn't be out dancing at a nightclub. Dale didn't have any suitors—not that she talked, of course. She was a tall thin number with interesting eyes, but that was as far as it went.

Not like the dame in green, no sir.

I hung onto the phone box with fingers that looked swollen and bruised. Dirt still slimed my palms. Under it I was fishbelly white, almost glowing in the dim lighting. The Dentons were going to find their diner not quite so dandy in the cold light of dawn, and I was sorry about that.

"Hello?" She repeated herself, because I was trying to make my mouth work. "Hello?"

"Dale," I managed through the obstruction in my mouth. Sounded like they'd broken my jaw, or like I was sucking on candy.

"Mr. Becker?" A note of alarm, now. "*Jack?*"

"You got to come pick me up, dollface." I sounded drunk.

"Where have you—oh, never mind. Where are you?" I could almost see her perched on her settee, that cup of tea steaming gently on an endtable, and her ever-present steno pad appearing. "Jack? Where are you right *now?*"

"Denton," I managed. "Dandy Diner, about eleven miles out of the city. You got the keys to my Studebaker?"

"Your car is impounded, Mr. Becker." Now she sounded like the Miss Dale I knew. Cool, calm, efficient. Over the phone she sounded smoky and sinful, just like Bacall. I might've hired her just for that phone voice alone, but she turned out to be damned efficient and not likely to yammer her yap off all the time, which meant I paid her even when I couldn't eat.

You don't find secretaries like that every day, after all.

"Never mind, I'll bring my car. Denton's Dandy, hm? That's west out of town, right?"

"Sure it is." My legs buckled again, I hung onto the box for all I was worth. "I'll be waiting out front."

"I'm on my way." And she hung up, just like that.

What a gal.

The pain in my gut crested as Miss Dale peered over the seat. I'd barely managed to get the door open, and as soon as I was in the car she took off; I wrestled the door shut and the windshield wipers made their idiot sound for about half a mile as I lay gasping in the back seat.

The car smelled like Chanel No. 5 and Chesterfields. And it smelled of Miss Dale, of hairspray and powder and a thousand other feminine things you usually have to get real close to a dame to get a whiff of. It also smelled like something else.

Something warm, and coppery, and salty, and so good. The windshield wipers went ka-thump ka-thump, and her Ford must've had something going on with the engine, because there was another regular thumping, high and hard and fast. My mouth wouldn't close all the way. I kept making that wheezing sound, and she finally risked another look over the seat at me.

"I'm taking you to Samaritan General," she said, and I stared at the sheen of her dark hair. "You sound terrible."

"No." Thank God, it was one word I could say without whatever was wrong with my mouth interfering. "No hospital." The slurring was back, like my jaw was broken but I wasn't feeling any pain. As a matter of fact, now that the headache was gone, the only thing bothering me was how *thirsty* I was.

Another mile squished under the tires. She turned the defroster up, and that regular thumping sounded like her car was about to explode, it was going so fast. "Mr. Becker, you are beginning to worry me." She lit a Chesterfield, keeping her eyes on the road, and when she opened the window to blow the smoke out the smell of the rain came through and I realized what that thumping was.

It was Miss Dale's pulse. I was hearing her heartbeat. And the tires touching the road. And each raindrop smacking the hardtop. The hiss of flame as she lit the cigarette showed the fine sheen of sweat on her forehead, and I realized Miss Dale was nervous.

"Don't worry, dollface. Everything's fine. Take me..."

Where can you go, Jack? The lady in green knows your office, and if she thinks you're dead—

"Take me to your house." Only it was more like *hauwsch*, like I was a goddamn German deli-owner, and when I ran my tongue along the inside of my teeth everything got interesting. My tongue rasped, and I lost whatever it was Miss Dale would have said because the taste of copper filled my mouth and I suddenly knew what I was thirsty for.

The knowledge might have made me scream if I hadn't gone limp against the seat as if someone had sapped me, because it was warm and the twisting in my gut receded a little bit, and because goddammit, after a man claws his way up out of his own grave and breaks into a diner, he deserves a little rest.

The green dress hugged her curves like the Samaritan freeway hugs the coast, and under the little veil on her hat those eyes were green too. She even had green gloves, and she accepted a light from me with a small nod and raised eyebrows, settling her emerald velvet clutch purse in her lap.

"You come highly recommended, Mr. Becker." A regular Bryn Mawr purr, over the sound of Miss Dale typing in the front. The lady kept her back straight as a ruler and

the lamp on my desk made her out to be pale, not one of those sun-bunnies.

Miss Dale stopped typing.

"Glad to hear that." I made it noncommittal, as casual as my shoes on the desk. It was five o'clock and already dark, the middle of winter, and I was behind on the rent.

"Mr. Becker?" Miss Dale stood tall and angular in the doorway. "Will you be needing anything else?" Her cat-tilted dark eyes met mine, and she had a sheaf of files in her capable, narrow hands. If she got a little more meat on her, she'd be a knockout. If, that is, you could chip through the ice.

Right now she was giving me the chance to say we were closing and the dame in green could come back another time. I waved a languid hand. "No thanks, Miss Dale. I'll see you in the morning."

"Very good, sir." Frosty as a Frigidaire. Miss Dale spent a few moments moving around the office, locking the files in the front cabinet, and the dame in green said nothing until my secretary left, locking the door behind her and her heels click-tapping down the hall, as efficiently as the rest of her.

The sign outside my office window blinked. We were up over an all-night lunch counter and newsstand, and the big neon arrow drenched the room with waves of yellow and red after dark once Miss Dale turned the lights off. The couch opposite my desk looked inviting, and it would have looked even more inviting if I hadn't been looking eviction in the face, I suppose.

"So what do you want me to do, Mrs....?" I made it into a question.

"Kendall. Mrs. Arthur Kendall. Mr. Becker, I want you to follow my husband."

It smelled like Chanel and dirt. And even though I was under a pile of blankets, I was lying on something soft and I shot up straight, swallowing a scream. It was the sound a bullet makes when it hits a skull, the explosion that was death.

My fingers were around something soft, but with a harder core. My other hand flashed up, catching Miss Dale's other wrist as she tried to slap me. Silk fluttered—she was dressed in a wrapper, a red kimono with a sun-yellow dragon breathing orange fire.

She yelped, and I realized I was half-naked, only in a pair of mud-crusted skivvies. Someone had undressed me and put me in a bed made of pink fluff, pillows spilling over the edges. The Chanel was her, and the dirt? That was me, stinking up a nice dame's bed.

"Mr. Becker," she said, and it was my imperturbable secretary again, the belt of her kimono loosened enough to show a strap of her—well, I'm only human, of course I looked. "Mr. Becker, let go of me at once."

The nightmare receded. I let go of her wrists. She retreated two steps, bumping her hip against a bedside table loaded with a jar of cold cream and a stack of big leatherbound books that looked straight out of Dr. Caligari's library, as well as a lamp with a frilly pink shade and an economy-sized box of Kleenex. We stared at each other, and the fine damp texture of her skin looked better than it ever had.

She rubbed at her right wrist, the one I'd grabbed first. "You were screaming," she whispered.

For once, I had no smart-aleck thing to say. Of course I'd been screaming.

Miss Dale drew herself up, tightening her kimono with swift movements. She was barefoot, and her dark hair wasn't pinned back. It tumbled down to her shoulders in a mass of curls, and it looked nice that way. She folded her arms and tried her best glare on me, and if I hadn't been lounging half-naked in what I suspected was her bed, it might have worked.

"I'm sorry." It was all I could say.

"You'd better be. You're wanted for murder."

I closed my mouth with a snap and started thinking furiously.

"You disappeared three days ago, Mr. Becker. The police tore apart your office. I am sad to report they also took your last three bottles of Scotch. They questioned me rather extensively, too."

My throat was dry. The thirst was worse than ever, and that distracting sound was back, the high hard thumping. It was her pulse, and it sounded like water in the desert. It sounded like the chow bell in basic training.

Her heart going that fast meant she was terrified. But there she stood, high color on her cheeks, arms folded and shoulders back, ready to take me to task once again.

Three days? "Murder?" I husked.

"The murder of Arthur Kendall, Mr. Becker. His widow identified you as the killer." Hung on the bedroom wall behind her was a Photoplay page of Humphrey Bogart in a fedora, leering at the camera like the bum he was. I was beginning to suspect my practical Miss Dale had a soft spot for leering bums.

"The Kendall job." It was difficult to think through the haze in my head and the sound of her pulse, calming down a little now, thank God.

There was something very wrong with me.

"The Kendall job," she echoed. "Naturally I have an extra copy of the file you prepared. And *naturally* I didn't mention it to the police, especially to Lieutenant Grady. I think you are many things, Mr. Becker—a disgraceful drunk and an immoral and unethical investigator, just to mention a few. But a murderer? Not the man who does widow cases for free." She rubbed at her right wrist.

So I'm a sucker for dames with hard stories. So what? "I didn't kill anyone." It was a relief to say it. "You've got the file?"

"*Naturally.*" She dropped her arms. "I would appreciate an explanation, but I'm only your secretary."

"You're a stand-up doll," I managed. "The Kendall job went bad, Miss Dale. I didn't kill him."

Being that practical type, she got right down to brass tacks. "Then who did, Mr. Becker?"

Even though the thirst was getting worse by the second and the sound of her pulse wasn't helping, I knew the answer to that one. "Get me that file, Dale. And while you're at it, can I have some clothes or am I just going to swing around like Tarzan?"

If she'd muttered something unladylike under her breath as she swept from the room I wouldn't have blamed her.

I cleaned the rest of the mud off in her pink-and-yellow bathroom. She had an apartment on the seedier side of Parth Street, but everything was neat and clean and prim as you'd expect from the woman I'd once caught alphabetizing my incoming mail. She even had a suit hanging on the back of the door for me, one of mine. The door didn't shut quite tight, and I could hear her moving around the kitchen, and hear that maddening, delicious, irresistible thumping.

I looked like I'd been dug up that morning. Which, if you think about it, I had. There was an ugly flushed-red mark over my right eye, a divot I could rest my fingertip in. It was tender, and pressing on it made my whole head feel like a pumpkin again. The back of my skull was sore too, seamed and scarred under my short wet hair. There were bruised bags of flesh under my eyes, and my cheeks had sunken in, and I looked yellow as a jaundiced Chinaman.

I peeled away my shirt collar and looked. A fresh, bruised mark above the collarbone, two holes that looked like a tiny pair of spikes had gone into my throat. The bruise was fever-hot, and when I touched it, the rolling thunder of a heartbeat roared in my ears so loud I grabbed at Miss Dale's scrubbed-white sink and had to fight to retain consciousness.

What the hell happened to me?

The last thing I remembered was Letitia Kendall wiping her mouth and the skinny, nervous redhead putting the barrel of the gun to my forehead. Right where that livid mark was, the one with speckles of dark grit in an orbit around its sunken redness. Then that sound, like an artillery shell inside my skull…

…and waking up in a cold, cold grave. Wanting a drink, but not my usual drink. Not the kind that went down the gullet like liquid fire and detonated in the belly, wrapping a warm haze between me and the rest of the world.

You're insane, Jack. You got shot in the head.

The trouble with that was, I shouldn't be insane. I should be *dead.*

But I had a pulse too. Just like Miss Dale. Who was starting to smell less like Chanel and more like…

Food.

A sizzling sound drifted down the hall. I tied the shoes she'd thoughtfully left right outside the bathroom door and saw her front door, and the warm light of the kitchen, a square of yellow sanity. She had her back turned and was fiddling with the stove, and a steak waited on a plate on the drainboard. She poked at the pan with a fork, and I was moving up quietly, just as if I was going to sap her.

Three steps. Two.

She never even turned around.

I reached out, saw my hand, yellow in the yellow light, shaking as it brushed past Miss Dale's hip…and fastened on the plate with the steak.

She jumped, the fork went clattering, and I retreated to the table. If I hadn't been so cold I would have been sweating buckets. I dropped down in one of Miss Dale's two straight-backed, frill-cushioned chairs next to her cheap gold-speckled kitchen table, and I found out why my mouth hadn't been working properly.

It was because the fangs had grown, and I licked the plate clean of bloody juice before burying my teeth in the raw meat and sucking as if it was mother's milk.

Dale's hand clapped over her mouth. She pinched so hard her cheeks blanched white from the pressure of her fingers, and her cat-tilted dark eyes turned big as the landlord's on rent day. The pan sizzled, I sucked and sucked, and the two sounds almost managed to drown out the thunder of her pulse again.

Her free hand shot out and jerked the pan from the stove. The gas flame kept burning, a hissing circle of blue, and Miss Dale stared at me, holding the pan like she intended to storm the barricades with it.

I kept sucking. It wasn't nearly enough, but the thirst retreated. *This* was what I wanted. When it was as tasteless as dry paper, I finished licking the plate clean, and I dropped the wad of drained meat down.

I looked at Miss Dale. She looked at me. I searched for something to say. Dames on her salary don't buy steak every day. She must've thought I'd be hungry.

"I still need a secretary, dollface."

Her throat worked as she swallowed. Then she put the pan down on an unlit burner. She peeled her fingers away from her mouth, the bruise still a dark bracelet on her right wrist. It took her two tries before she could get the words out.

"There's another steak in the fridge, Jack. It's…raw."

Winter nights last forever, and the rain was still coming down. Dale's wrist was swelling, but she wrapped it in an Ace and told me in no uncertain terms she was fine. She drove the Ford cautiously, the wipers ticking, just like her pulse. I spread the file out in my lap and checked for tails—we were clean.

Down on Cross Street, she parked where we had a good view of The Blue Room, and I paged through the file. Pictures of Arthur Kendall, millionaire, who had come back from Europe with a young wife who had begun to suspect him of fooling around.

If I hadn't been so interested in the greenbacks she fanned out on my desktop, I wouldn't have taken the job. Divorce jobs aren't my favorites. They end up too sticky.

This one had just gotten stickier. Kendall wasn't just a millionaire, he was as dirty as they come. I'd been careful, sure, but I'd gotten priceless little shots of him canoodling with the heavies in town—Lefty Schultz who ran the prostitution racket, Big Buck Beaudry who provided muscle, Papa Ginette whose family used to run gin and now ran dope. Big fan of tradition, Papa Ginette.

I'd thought I was just getting into a dicey situation until I snapped a few shots of Kendall and his wife at a pricey downtown joint where the jazz was hot and the action was hotter. The Blue Room had a waiting list ten years long, but money talks—and it was Willie Goldstein's place. If Goldstein hadn't owned more than half the cops in town, he'd have been in Big Sing years ago.

Another late-night appointment, and the dame in green waltzed in my door just as Miss Dale was waltzing out. I spread the shots out and told her Kendall wasn't cheating. She'd married a dirty son of an unmentionable, but he wasn't hanging out with the ladies.

Those green eyes narrowed, and she picked up the glossy of the crowd outside Goldstein's. There they were, Kendall and the missus and the redheaded, ratfaced gent who followed Kendall like glue. He wasn't heavy muscle—his name was Shifty Malloy, and he had a dope habit the size of Wrigley Field—but he was dapper in a suit and lit Kendall's cigarettes.

Mrs. Kendall set the photo down again, and smiled at me. She crushed her cigarette out in the ashtray and I glanced down at the pictures again. Something very strange occurred to me.

I remember thinking that for a dame who wore green so much, she had awfully red lips. I remember snapping the shot, and I remember the flash of white calf as she turned to follow her husband past the velvet ropes and into the restaurant.

But there in black and white was Kendall, and Malloy, and a crowd of other schmucks thinking it was hot stuff to pay five bucks for a steak and ogle the other rich schmucks, and there was a space where the dame in green should have been.

But Letitia Kendall wasn't in the picture. She was sitting across the desk from me, the last ghost of her cigarette rising in the air, and her face suddenly shifted under its little green veil. She came over the desk at me like a feral tiger, and everything went black…

"There he is," Dale whispered. "The redhead."

And sure enough, there was Shifty Malloy, dapper as ever in tails, getting out of a shiny new Packard. The Blue Room had a long awning to keep the rich dry, but the ratfaced bum actually unfolded an umbrella and held his hand out to help a lady out of the backseat. Miles of white, white leg through a slit in her dress, and she rose up out of the back of the car like a dream. Only she wasn't in green. The dame was in mourning like midnight, her red lips a slash on the white powder of her face, and I wondered how long it would take people to catch on that she liked to sleep in all day. I wondered if anyone would know her hands were cold as ice cubes under the satin gloves, and I wondered if anyone would guess how Arthur Kendall gurgled when she had her teeth in his throat.

Because if I hadn't killed him, that only left one suspect, didn't it.

It was cold. I lay on the floor and looked at the shapes in front of me—a wall full of splinters and long handles ending in metal shapes. It was the type of shack you have when you've got a pool and a garden and you need somewhere to store all the unattractive bits needed to keep it clipped and pretty—a lawnmower, shovels, all sorts of things.

"You'll do as I say," Letitia Kendall said.

"Aw Jesus." Shifty Malloy whined. "Jesus Christ."

Then a dainty foot in a green satin pump stepped into view. I blinked. Felt like I'd been hit by a train, throat was burning, couldn't take a deep breath, and I couldn't even squirm. My hands were tied back and my feet felt like lead blocks. She bent down, the dame in green, and she wasn't wearing her pretty face anymore. The smear of crimson on her lips was fresh, and she wiped at it with one white, white hand as her other hand came down, snagged a handful of my suit coat and shirt, and hauled me up like I weighed nothing.

"You have to cut off the head," she said. "It's very important. If you don't, you won't get any more."

Malloy was sweating. "Got it. Cut off the head."

"Use a shovel. They do well." Her head tilted a little to the side, like a cat's considering its prey. "It is very important, Edward, to cut off the head."

If I could have opened my mouth, I might have said that asking Shifty Malloy to decapitate someone was like asking a politician to be honest. I knew the bum. Malloy might shoot a man in the back, but he was squeamish about cockroaches, for Christ's sake.

"All right, already." Malloy stepped into view, and his ridiculous little pasted-on moustache was limp as a dead caterpillar with sweat. He raised the gun, a serviceable little derringer, and put it to my forehead. "You might wanna put him down. This is going to make a mess."

"Just do it." Letitia gave me an impatient little shake. My feet dangled like a puppet's. "I have a party to attend tonight."

When I came back from the war some bum asked me what the worst thing about it was. I told him it was the goddamn food in the service. But the worst thing in the war was the not knowing, in the smoke and the chaos, where the next bullet was coming from.

The only thing worse than that is knowing where it's coming from, and when that gun is to your head and nothing comes out of your crushed and dry throat but a little sound like nuh-nuh-muh.

Then the world exploded.

"Wait until I get around the corner," I said, handing her the file. "Then go home. You're a standup dame, Dale."

"For Christ's sake." She slid down in the seat, as if afraid someone would see us parked here. "Call me Sophie, Jack. How long have I worked for you?"

"Three years." *Kept me on time and kept that office from going under, too.*

"I deserve a raise." Her pulse was thumping again. Like a rabbit's. The thirst was back. It scorched the back of my throat like bile from the worst hangover ever, and it smelled her. Chanel and softness and the steak she'd cooked, and my fingers twitched like they wanted to cross the air between us and catch at her dress. It was a pretty blue dress, high in the collar and tight in the waist, and she looked good.

Never noticed before how easy on the eyes Miss Dale was. Yeah, I'm an unobservant bum.

"Go home, Sophie." It was getting hard to talk again, the teeth were coming out. *Shophie*, I mangled her name the first time I ever said it. "You're a doll. A real doll."

"What are you going to do?" She had never asked me that before. Plenty of questions, like, *where did you put that file* and *do you want coffee* and *what should I tell Boyleston when he calls about the rent?* But that particular one she'd never asked.

"I'm going to finish the Kendall job." I slid out of the car and closed the door softly, headed down the street. She waited, just like I'd told her, for me to reach the corner. Then the Ford's engine woke and she pulled away. I could hear the car, but the biggest relief came when I couldn't hear her pulse anymore.

Instead, I heard everyone else's. The drumbeats were a jungle, and here I was, the thirst burning a hole in me and the rain smacking at the top of my unprotected head. I flipped up the collar of my coat, wished like hell a bottle of Scotch could take the edge off the burning, and headed for Chinatown.

You can find anything in Chinatown. They eat anything down there, and I have a few friends. Still, it's amazing how a man who won't balk when you ask him to hide a dead body or a stack of bloodstained clothes might get funny ideas when you ask him to help you find…blood.

That's what butchers are for. And after a while I found what I was looking for. I had my nineteen dollars and the thirty in pin money from Miss Dale's—Sophie's—kitchen jar. She said I was good for it, and she would take it on her next paycheck.

I would worry about getting her another paycheck as soon as I finished this out. It might take a little doing.

After two bouts of heaving as my body rebelled, the thirst took over and I drank nearly a bucket of steaming copper, and then I fell down and moaned like a doper on the floor of a filthy Chinatown slaughterhouse. It felt good, slamming into the thirst in my gut and spreading in waves of warmth until I almost cried.

I paid for another bucket. Then I got the hell out of there, because even yellow men will stop looking the other way for *some* things.

It's amazing what you can do once a dame in a green dress kills you and pins you for murder.

The next thing I needed was a car. On the edge of Chinatown sits Benny's Garage, and I rousted Benny by the simple expedient of jimmying his lock and dragging him out of bed. He didn't know why I wanted the busted-down pickup and twelve jerrycans of kerosene. "I don't want to know," he whined at me. "Why'd'ja have to bust the door down? Jeez, Becker, you—"

"Shut up." I peeled a ten-spot off my diminishing bankroll and held it in front of him, made it disappear when he snatched at it. "You never saw me, Benny."

He grabbed the ten once I made it reappear. "I *never* goddamn see you, Jack. I never wanta see you again, neither." He rubbed at his stubble, the rasp of every hair audible to me, and the sound of his pulse was a whack-whack instead of the sweet music of Sophie's. How long would his heart work through all the blubber he had piled on?

I didn't care. I drove away and hoped like hell Benny wouldn't call the cops. With a yard full of stolen cars and up to his ass in hock to Papa Ginette, it would be a bad move for him.

But still, I worried. I worried all the way up into Garden Heights and the quiet manicured mansions of the rich, where I found the house I wanted and had to figure out how to get twelve jerrycans over a nine-foot stone wall.

The house was beautiful. I almost felt bad, splishing and splashing over parquet floors, priceless antiques, and a bed that smelled faintly of copper and talcum powder. There was a whole closetful of green dresses. I soaked every goddamn one of them. Rain pounded the roof, gurgled through the gutters, hissed against the walls.

I carried two jerrycans downstairs to the foyer—a massive expanse of checkered black and white soon swimming in the nose-cleaning sting of kerosene—and settled myself to wait by the door to a study that probably had been Arthur Kendall's favorite place. I could smell him in there, cigars and fatheaded, expensive cologne. I ran my hands down the shaft of the shovel while I waited, swung it a few experimental times, and tapped it on the floor. It was a flathead shovel, handily available in any garden shed—and every immaculate lawn needs a garden shed, even if you get brown or yellow people out to clean it up for you.

I'm good at waiting, and I waited a long time. The fumes got into my nose and made me lightheaded, but when the Packard came purring up the drive I was pouring the last half of a jerrycan, lit a match and a thin trail of flame raced away up the stairs like it was trying to outrun time. Even if her nose was as acute as mine she might not smell the smoke through the rain, and I bolted through the study, which had a floor-length window I'd been thoughtful enough to unlock. Around the corner, moving so fast it was like being back in the war again, hardly noticing where either foot landed as long as I kept moving, and the shovel whistled as I crunched across the gravel drive and smacked Shifty Malloy right in the face with it, a good hit with all my muscle behind it. He had gotten out of the car, the stupid bum, and he went down like a ton of bricks while Letitia Kendall fumbled at the doorhandle inside, scratching like a mad hen.

The house began to whoosh and crackle. Twelve jerries is a lot of fuel, and there was a lot to burn in there. Even if it was raining like God had opened every damn tap in the sky.

She fell out of the Packard, the black dress immediately soaked and flashes of fishbelly flesh showing as she scrabbled on gravel. Her crimson mouth worked like a landed fish's, and if I was a nice guy I suppose I might have given her a chance to explain. Maybe I might have even let her get away by being a stupid dick like you see in the movies, who lets the bad guy make his speech.

But I'm not a good guy. The shovel sang again, and the sound she made when the flat blade chopped three-quarters of the way through her neck was between a gurgle and a scream. The rain masked it, and she was off the gravel and on the lawn now, on mud as I followed, jabbing with the shovel while her head flopped like a defective Kewpie doll's. I chopped the way we used to chop rattlers back on the farm, and when her body stopped flopping and the gouts and gouts of fresh steaming blood had soaked a wide swatch of rain-flattened grass I dropped the shovel and dragged her strangely heavy carcass back toward the house. I tossed it in the foyer, where the flames were rising merrily in defiance of the downpour, and I tossed the shovel in too. Then I had to stumble back, eyes blurring and skin peeling, and I figured out right then and there that fire was a bad thing for me, whatever I was now.

She was wet and white where the black dress was torn, and the flames wanted to cringe away. I didn't stick around to see if she went up, because the house began to burn in earnest, the heat scratching at my skin with thousands of scraping gold pins, and there was a rosy glow in the east that had nothing to do with kerosene.

It was dawn, and I didn't know exactly what had happened to me, but I knew I didn't want to be outside much longer.

Of course she hadn't gone to sleep. As soon as I got near her door, trying to tread softly on the worn carpet and smelling the burned food and dust smell of working folks in her apartment building, it opened a crack and Sophie peered through. She was chalk-white, trembling, and she retreated down the hall as I shambled in. It was still raining and I was tired. The thirst was back, and my entire body was shot through with lead. The pinpricks on my throat throbbed like they were infected, but the divot above my right eye wasn't inflamed anymore. But my skin cracked and crackled with the burning, still, and the thirst was back, burrowing in my veins.

I shut her door and locked it. I stood dripping on her welcome mat and looked at her.

She hadn't changed out of the blue dress. She had nice legs, by God, and those cat-tilted eyes weren't really dark. They were hazel. And her wrist was still bruised where I'd grabbed her, she had peeled the Ace off and it was a nice dark purple. It probably hurt like hell.

Her hands hung limp at her sides.

I searched for something to say. The rain hissed and gurgled. Puddles in the street outside were reflecting old neon and newer light edging through gray mist. "It's dawn."

She just stood there.

"You're a real doll, Sophie. If I didn't have—"

"How did it happen?" She swallowed, the muscles in her throat working. Under that high collar her pulse was still like music. "Your...you..." She fluttered one hand helplessly. For the first time since she walked into my office three years ago and announced the place was a dump, my Miss Dale seemed nonplussed.

"I got bit, sugar." I peeled my sodden shirt collar away. "I don't want to make any trouble for you. I'll figure something out tomorrow night."

Thirty of the longest seconds of my life passed in her front hallway. I dripped, and I felt the sun coming the way I used to feel storms moving in on the farm, back when I was a jugeared kid and the big bad city was a place I only heard about in church.

"Jack, you ass," Sophie said. "So it's a bite?"

"And a little more."

Miss Dale lifted her chin and eyed me. "I don't have any more steak." Her pulse was back. It was thundering. It was hot and heavy in my ears and I already knew I wasn't a nice guy. Wasn't that why I'd come here?

"I'll go." I reached behind me and fumbled for the knob.

"Oh, no you will *not*." It was Miss Dale again, with all her crisp efficiency. She reached up with trembling fingers, and unbuttoned the very top button of her collar.

"Sophie—"

"How long have I been working for you, Jack?" She undid another button, slender fingers working, and I took a single step forward. Burned skin crackled, and my clothes were so heavy they could have stood up by themselves. "Three years. And it wasn't for the pay, and certainly not because you've a personality that recommends itself."

Coming from her, that was a compliment. "You've got a real sweet mouth there, Miss Dale."

She undid her third button, and that pulse of hers was a beacon. Now I knew what the thirst wanted, now I knew what it felt like, now I knew what it could do—

"Mr. Becker, shut up. If you don't, I'll lose my nerve."

Sophie is on her pink frilly bed. The shades are drawn, and the apartment's quiet. It's so quiet. Time to think about everything.

When a man wakes up in his own grave, he can reconsider his choice of jobs. He can do a whole lot of things.

It's so goddamn quiet. I'm here with my back to the bedroom door and my knees drawn up. Sophie is so still, so pale. I've had time to look over every inch of her face and I wonder how a stupid bum like me could have overlooked such a doll right under his nose.

It took three days for me. Two days ago the dame in the black dress choked her last and her lovely mansion burned. It was in all the papers as a tragedy, and Shifty Malloy choked on his own blood out in the rain too. I think it's time to find another city to gumshoe in. There's Los Angeles, after all, and that place does three-quarters of its business after dark.

Soon the sun's going to go down. Sophie's got her hands crossed on her chest and she's all tucked in nice and warm, the coverlet up to her chin and the lamp on so she won't wake up like I did, in the dark and the mud.

The rain has stopped beating the roof. I can hear heartbeats moving around in the building.

Jesus, I hope she wakes up.

TWILIGHT

by Kelley Armstrong

Kelley Armstrong is the bestselling author of the Otherworld urban fantasy series, which began with *Bitten*, and the latest of which, *Frostbitten*, comes out in October. She is also the author of the Darkest Powers trilogy, a young-adult series that began last year with *The Summoning*. Armstrong is currently in the midst of writing a five-issue arc for Joss Whedon's *Angel* comic book series.

Armstrong says that the most obvious appeal of vampire fiction is the mingling of sex and death. "But for me, the appeal has always been the concept of immortality," she said. "Particularly the problems with it, and the sacrifices we would—or wouldn't—make to retain it."

This story, which features Cassandra DuCharme from Armstrong's Otherworld series, was written for *Many Bloody Returns*, an anthology with a vampires-and-birthdays theme. "When I think birthdays in regards to my vampires, I think rebirth day, which is the anniversary of the day they became vampires and, each year at that time, they must take a life to continue their semi-immortality," Armstrong said. "Cassandra has never had a problem fulfilling her annual bargain, but this year, she does."

Another life taken. Another year to live.

That is the bargain that rules our existence. We feed off blood, but for three hundred and sixty-four days a year, it is merely that: feeding. Yet on that last day—or sometime before the anniversary of our rebirth as vampires—we must drain the lifeblood of one person. Fail and we begin the rapid descent into death.

As I sipped white wine on the outdoor patio, I watched the steady stream of passersby. Although there was a chill in the air—late autumn coming fast and sharp—the patio was crowded, no one willing to surrender the dream of summer quite yet. Leaves fluttering onto the tables were lauded as decorations. The scent of a distant wood-fire was willfully mistaken for candles. The sun, almost gone despite the still early hour, only added romance to the meal. All embellishments to the night, not signs of impending winter.

I sipped my wine and watched night fall. At the next table, a lone businessman eyed me. He was the sort of man I often had the misfortune to attract—

middle-aged and prosperous, laboring under the delusion that success and wealth were such irresistible lures that he could allow his waistband and jowls to thicken unchecked.

Under other circumstances, I might have returned the attention, let him lead me to some tawdry motel, then take *my* dinner. He would survive, of course, waking weakened, blaming it on too much wine. A meal without guilt. Any man who took such a chance with a stranger—particularly when he bore a wedding band—deserved an occasional bout of morning-after discomfort.

He did not, however, deserve to serve as my annual kill. I can justify many things, but not that. Yet I found myself toying with the idea more than I should have, prodded by a niggling voice that told me I was already late.

I stared at the glow over the horizon. The sun had set on the anniversary of my rebirth, and I hadn't taken a life. Yet there was no need for panic. I would hardly explode into dust at midnight. I would weaken as I began the descent into death, but I could avoid that simply by fulfilling my bargain tonight.

I measured the darkness, deemed it enough for hunting, then laid a twenty on the table and left.

A bell tolled ten. Two hours left. I chastised myself for being so dramatic. I loathe vampires given to theatrics—those who have read too many horror novels and labor under the delusion that's how they're supposed to behave. I despise any sign of it in myself and yet, under the circumstances, perhaps it could be forgiven.

In all the years that came before this, I had never reached this date without fulfilling my obligation. I had chosen this vampiric life and would not risk losing it through carelessness.

Only once had I ever neared my rebirth day, and then only due to circumstances beyond my control. It had been 1867… or perhaps 1869. I'd been hunting for my annual victim when I'd found myself tossed into a Hungarian prison. I hadn't been caught at my kill—I'd never made so amateurish a mistake even when I'd been an amateur.

The prison sojourn had been Aaron's fault, as such things usually were. We'd been hunting my victim when he'd come across a nobleman whipping a servant in the street. Naturally, Aaron couldn't leave well enough alone. In the ensuing confusion of the brawl, I'd been rousted with him and thrown into a pest-infested cell that wouldn't pass any modern health code.

Aaron had worked himself into a full-frothing frenzy, seeing my rebirth anniversary only days away while I languished in prison, waiting for justice that seemed unlikely to come swiftly. I hadn't been concerned. When one partakes of Aaron's company, one learns to expect such inconveniences. While he plotted, schemed and swore he'd get us out on time, I simply waited. There was time yet and no need to panic until panic was warranted.

The day before my rebirth anniversary, as I'd begun to suspect that a more strenuous course of action might be required, we'd been released. I'd compensated for the trouble and delay by taking the life of a prison guard who'd enjoyed his work far more than was necessary.

This year, my only excuse for not taking a victim yet was that I hadn't gotten around to it. As for why, I was somewhat... baffled. I am nothing if not conscientious about my obligations. Yet, this year, delays had arisen, and somehow I'd been content to watch the days slip past and tell myself I would get around to it, as if it was no more momentous than a missed salon appointment.

The week had passed and I'd been unable to work up any sense of urgency until today, and even now, it was only an oddly cerebral concern. No matter. I would take care of it tonight.

As I walked, an old drunkard drew my gaze. I watched him totter into the shadows of an alley and thought: "There's a possibility..." Perhaps I could get this chore over with sooner than expected. I could be quite finicky—refusing to feed off sleeping vagrants—yet as my annual kill, this one was a choice I could make.

Every vampire deals with our "bargain" in the way that best suits his temperament and capacity for guilt and remorse. I cull from the edges—the sick, the elderly, those already nearing their end. I do not fool myself into thinking this is a just choice. There's no way to know whether that cancer-wracked woman might have been on the brink of remission or if that elderly man had been enjoying his last days to the fullest. I make the choice because it is one I can live with.

This old drunkard would do. As I watched him, I felt the gnawing in the pit of my stomach, telling me I'd already waited too long. I should follow him into that alley, and get this over with. I *wanted* to get it over with—that there was no question of that, no possibility I was conflicted on this point. Other vampires may struggle with our bargain. I do not.

Yet even as I visualized myself following the drunk into the alley, my legs didn't follow through. I stood there, watching him disappear into the darkness. Then I moved on.

A block farther, a crowd poured from a movie theater. As it passed, its life force enveloped me. I wasn't hungry, yet I could still feel that tingle of anticipation, of hunger. I could smell their blood, hear the rush of it through their veins. The scent and sound of life.

Twenty steps later, and they were still passing, an endless stream of humanity disgorged by a packed theater. How many seats were inside? Three hundred, three fifty? As many years as had passed since my rebirth?

One life per year. It seems so moderate a price... until you looked back and realized you could fill a movie theater with your victims. A sobering thought, even for one not inclined to dwell on such things. No matter. There wouldn't be hundreds more. Not from this vampire.

Contrary to legend, our gift of longevity comes with an expiry date. Mine was drawing near. I'd felt the signs, the disconnect from the world, a growing disinterest in all around me. For me, that was nothing new. I'd long since learned to keep my distance from a world that changed while I didn't.

After some struggle with denial, I'd accepted that I had begun the decline toward death. But it would be slow, and I still had years left, decades even. Or, I would, if I could get past this silly bout of ennui and make my rebirth kill.

As the crowd dwindled, I looked over my shoulder to watch them go and considered taking a life from them. A random kill. I'd done it once before, more than a century ago, during a particularly bleak time when I hadn't been able to rouse enough feeling to care. Yet later I'd regretted it, having let myself indulge my darkest inclinations simply because I'd been in a dark place myself. Unacceptable. I wouldn't do it again.

I wrenched my gaze from the dispersing crowd. This was ridiculous. I was no angst-ridden cinema vampire, bemoaning the choice she'd made in life. I was no flighty youngster, easily distracted from duty, abhorring responsibility. I was Cassandra DuCharme, senior vampire delegate to the interracial council. If any vampire had come to me with this problem—"I'm having trouble making my annual kill"—I'd have shown her the sharp side of my tongue, hauled her into the alley with that drunk and told her, as Aaron might say, to "piss or get off the pot."

I turned around and headed back to the alley.

I'd gone only a few steps when I picked up a sense of the drunkard. Excitement swept through me. I closed my eyes and smiled. That was more like it.

The quickening accelerated as I slid into the shadows. My stride smoothed out, each step taken with care, rolling heel to toe, making no sound.

That sense of my prey grew stronger with each step, telling me he was near. I could see a recessed emergency exit a dozen feet ahead. A shoe protruded from the darkness. I crept forward until I spotted a dark form crumpled inside.

The rush of his blood vibrated through the air. My canines lengthened and I allowed myself one shudder of anticipation, then shook it off and focused on the sound of his breathing.

A gust whipped along the alley, scattering candy wrappers and leaflets, and the stink of alcohol washed over me. I caught the extra notes in his breathing—the deep, almost determined rhythm. Passed out drunk. He'd probably stumbled into the first semi-sheltered place he'd seen and collapsed.

That would make it easier.

Still, I hesitated, telling myself I needed to be sure. But the rhythm of his breathing stayed steady. He was clearly asleep and unlikely to awake even if I bounded over there and shouted in his ear.

So what was I waiting for? I should be in that doorway already, reveling in the luck of finding so easy a victim.

I shook the lead from my bones and crossed the alley.

The drunkard wore an army jacket, a real one if I was any judge. I resisted the fanciful urge to speculate, to imagine him as some shell-shocked soldier turned to drink by the horrors of war. More likely, he'd bought the jacket at a thrift shop. Or stolen it.

His hair was matted, so filthy it was impossible to tell the original color. Above the scraggly beard, though, his face was unlined. Younger than I'd first imagined. Significantly younger.

That gave me pause, but while he was not the old drunkard I'd first imagined, he was certainly no healthy young man. I could sense disease and wasting, most likely cirrhosis. Not my ideal target, but he would do.

And yet...

Almost before I realized it, I was striding toward the road.

He wasn't right. I was succumbing to that panic, and that was unnecessary, even dangerous. If I made the wrong choice, I'd regret it. Better to let the pressure of this ominous date pass and find a better choice tomorrow.

I slid into the park and stepped off the path. The ground was hard, so I could walk swiftly and silently.

As I stepped from the wooded patch, my exit startled two young men huddled together. Their gazes tripped over me, eyes glittering under the shadows of their hoods, like jackals spotting easy prey. I met the stronger one's gaze. He broke first, grumbling deep in his throat. Then he shuffled back and waved his friend away as he muttered some excuse for moving on.

I watched them go, considering... then dismissing.

It was easy to separate one victim from a group. Not nearly so simple when the "group" consisted of only two people. As the young men disappeared, I resumed my silent trek across the park.

My goal lay twenty paces away. Had I not sensed him, I likely would have passed by. He'd ignored a park bench under the light and instead had stretched out upon the top of a raised garden, hidden under the bushes and amidst the dying flowers.

He lay on his back with his eyes closed. His face was peaceful, relaxed. A handsome face, broad and tanned. He had thick blond hair and the healthy vitality of a young man in his prime. A big man, too, tall and solid, his muscular arms crossed behind his head, his slim hips and long denim-clad legs ending in work boots crossed at the ankles.

I circled north to sneak up behind his head. He lay completely motionless, even his chest was still, not rising and falling with the slow rhythm of breathing. I crossed the last few feet between us and stopped just behind his head. Then I leaned over.

His eyes opened. Deep brown eyes, the color of rich earth. He snarled a yawn.

"'Bout time, Cass," he said. "Couple of punks been circling to see if I'm still conscious. Another few minutes, and I'd have had to teach them to let sleeping vamps lie."

"Shall I go away then? Let you have your fun?"

Aaron grinned. "Nah. They come back? We can both have fun." He heaved his legs over the side of the garden wall, and sat up, shaking off sleep. Then, catching a glimpse of my face, his grin dropped into a frown. "You didn't do it, did you?"

"I couldn't find anyone."

"Couldn't find—?" He pushed to his feet, towering over me. "Goddamn it, what are you playing at? First you let it go until the last minute, then you 'can't find anyone'?"

I checked my watch. "It's not the last minute. I still have ten left. I trust that if I explode at midnight, you'll be kind enough to sweep up the bits. I would like to be scattered over the Atlantic but, if you're pressed for time, the Charleston River will do."

He glowered at me. "A hundred and twenty years together, and you never got within a week of your rebirth day without making your kill."

"Hungary. 1867."

"Sixty-eight. And I don't see any bars this time. So what was your excuse?"

"Among others, I was busy researching that council matter Paige brought to my attention. I admit I let things creep up on me this year, and a century ago that would never have happened, but while we were apart, I changed—"

"Bullshit. You never change. Except to get more imperious, more pigheaded and more cranky."

"The word is 'crankier.'"

He muttered a few more descriptors under his breath. I started down the path.

"You'd better be going off to find someone," he called after me.

"No, I'm heading home to bed. I'm tired."

"Tired?" He strode up beside me. "You don't get tired. You're—"

He stopped, mouth closing so fast his teeth clicked.

"The word is 'dying,'" I said. "And, while that is true, and it is equally true that my recent inability to sleep is a symptom of that, tonight I am, indeed, tired."

"Because you're late for your kill. You can't pull this shit, Cassandra, not in your condition."

I gave an unladylike snort and kept walking.

His fingers closed around my arm. "Let's go find those punks. Have some fun." A broad, boyish grin. "I think one has a gun. Been a long time since I got shot."

"Another day."

"A hunt then."

"I'm not hungry."

"Well, I am. Maybe you couldn't find someone suitable, but I can. I know what you look for. We'll hunt together. I'll get a snack; you'll get another year. Fair enough?"

He tried to grin, but I could see a hint of panic behind his eyes. I felt an answering prickle of worry, but told myself I was being ridiculous. I'd simply had too much on my mind lately. I was tired and easily distracted. I needed to snap out of this embarrassing lethargy and make this kill, and I would do so tomorrow, once Aaron had gone back to Atlanta.

"It's not the end of the world—or *my* world—if I don't take a life tonight, Aaron. You've been late yourself, when you couldn't find someone suitable. I haven't—and perhaps I'd simply like to know what that's like." I touched his arm. "At my age, new experiences are few and far between. I take them where I can."

He hesitated, then nodded, mollified, and accompanied me from the park.

Aaron followed me home. That wasn't as nearly as exciting a prospect as it sounds. These days we were simply friends. His choice. If I had my way, tired or not, I would have found the energy to accommodate him.

When I first met Aaron, less than a year after his rebirth, he'd accused me of helping him in his new life because he looked like something to "decorate my bed with." True enough.

Even as a human, I had never been able to rouse more than a passing interest in men of my own class. Too well-mannered, too gently spoken, too *soft*. My tastes had run to stable boys and, later, to discreet working men.

Finding Aaron as a newly reborn vampire, a big strapping farm boy with hands as rough as his manners, I will admit that my first thought was indeed carnal. He was younger than I liked, but I'd decided I could live with that.

So I'd trained him in the life of a vampire. In return, I'd received friendship, protection… and endless nights alone, frustrated beyond reason. It was preposterous, of course. I'd never had any trouble leading men to my bed and there I'd been, reduced to chasing a virile young man who strung me along as if he were some coy maiden. I told myself it wasn't his fault—he was English. Thankfully, when he finally capitulated, I discovered he wasn't nearly as repressed as I'd feared.

Over a hundred years together. It was no grand romance. The word "love" never passed between us. We were partners in every sense—best friends, hunting allies and faithful lovers. Then came the morning I woke, looked over at him, and imagined *not* seeing him there, tried to picture life without him. I'd gone cold at the thought.

I had told myself I'd never allow that again. When you've lost everyone, you learn the danger of attachments. As a vampire, you must accept that every person you ever know will die, and you are the only constant in your life, the only person you can—and should—rely on. So I made a decision.

I betrayed Aaron. Not with another man. Had I done that, he'd simply have flown into a rage and, once past it, demanded to know what was really bothering me. What I did instead was a deeper betrayal, one that said, more coldly than I could ever speak the words "I don't want you anymore."

After over half a century apart, happenstance had brought us together again. We'd resisted the pull of that past bond, reminded ourselves of what had happened the last time and yet, gradually, we'd drifted back into friendship. Only friendship. Sex was not allowed—Aaron's way of keeping his distance. Given the choice between having him as a friend and not having him in my life at all, I'd gladly choose the former… though that didn't keep me from hoping to change his mind.

That night I slept. It was the first time I'd done more than catnapped in over a year. While I longed to seize on this as some sign that I wasn't dying, I knew Aaron's assessment was far more likely—I was tired because I'd missed my annual kill.

Was this what happened, then, when we didn't hold up our end of the bargain? An increasing lethargy that would lead to death? I shook it off. I had no intention of exploring the phenomenon further. Come sunset, I would end this foolishness and take a life.

As I entered my living room that morning, I heard a dull slapping from the open patio doors. Aaron was in the yard, building a new retaining wall for my garden.

When he'd been here in the spring, he'd commented on the crumbling wall, and said, "I could fix that for you." I'd nodded and said, "Yes, I suppose you could." Three more intervening visits. Three more hints about the wall. Yet I refused to ask for his help. I had lost that right when I betrayed him. So yesterday, he'd shown up on my doorstep, masonry tools in one hand, suitcase in the other, and announced he was building a new wall for my rebirth day.

That meant he had a reason to stay until he'd finished it. Had he simply decided my rebirth day made a good excuse? Or was there more than that? When I'd spoken to him this week, had something in my voice told him I had yet to take my annual victim?

I watched Aaron through the patio doors. The breeze was chilly, but the sun beat down and he had his shirt off as he worked, oblivious to all around him. This was what he did for a living—masonry, the latest in a string of "careers." I chided him that, after two hundred years, one should have a healthy retirement savings plan. He only pointed the finger back at me, declaring that I too worked when I didn't need to. But I was self-employed, and selling art and antiques was certainly not in the same category as the physically demanding jobs he undertook. Yet another matter on which we disagreed—with vigor and enthusiasm.

I watched him for another minute, then headed for the kitchen to make him an iced tea.

I went out later to check a new shipment at an antique shop. When I got home, Aaron was sitting on the couch, a pile of newspapers on the table and one spread in his hands.

"I hope you didn't take those from my trash."

"I wouldn't have had to, if you'd recycle." He peered around the side of the paper. "That blue box in the garage? That's what it's for, not holding garden tools."

I waved him off. "Three hundred and fifty years and I have never been deprived of a newspaper or book by want of paper. I'm not going to start recycling now. I'm too old."

"Too stubborn." He gave a sly grin. "Or too lazy."

He earned a glare for that one. I walked over and snatched up a stray paper from the carpet before it stained.

"If you're that desperate for reading material, just tell me and I'll walk to the store and buy you a magazine."

He folded the paper and laid it on the coffee table, then patted the spot next to him. I hesitated, sensing trouble, and took a place at the opposite end, perched on the edge. He reached over, his hand going around my waist, and dragged me until I was sitting against him.

"Remember when we met, Cass?"

"Vaguely."

He laughed. "Your memory isn't *that* bad. Remember what you did for me? My first rebirth day was coming, and I'd decided I wasn't doing it. You found me a victim, a choice I could live with." With his free hand, he picked up a paper separated from the rest and dropped it onto my lap. "Found you a victim."

I sighed. "Aaron, I don't need you to—"

"Too late." He poked a calloused finger at the top article. "Right there."

The week-old story told of a terminally ill patient fighting for the right to die. When I looked over at Aaron, he was grinning, pleased with himself.

"Perfect, isn't it?" he said. "Exactly what you look for. She wants to die. She's in pain."

"She's in a palliative care ward. How would I even get in there, let alone kill her?"

"Is that a challenge?" His arm tightened around my waist. "Because if it is, I'm up for it. You know I am."

He was still smiling, but behind it lurked a shadow of desperation. Again, his worry ignited mine. Perhaps this added incentive was exactly what I needed. It wouldn't be easy, but it could be interesting, particularly with Aaron's help.

Any other time, I'd have pounced on the idea, but now, even as I envisioned it, I felt only a spark of interest, buried under an inexplicable layer of lethargy, even antipathy, and all I could think was "Oh, but it would just be so much *work*."

My hackles rose at such indolence, but I squelched my indignation. I *was* determined to take a life tonight. I would allow nothing to stand in the way of that. Therefore, I could not enter into a plan that might prove too difficult. Better to keep this simple, so I would have no excuse for failure.

I lay the paper aside. "Are you hungry?"

A faint frown.

"Last night, you said you were hungry," I continued. "If you were telling the truth, then I presume you still need to feed, unless you slipped out last night."

"I thought we'd be hunting together later. So I waited."

"Then we'll hunt tonight. But not—" A wave at the paper. "—in a hospital."

We strolled along the sidewalk. It was almost dark now, the sun just a red-tinged memory along the horizon. As I watched a flower-seller clear her outdoor stock for the night, Aaron snapped his fingers.

"Flowers. That's what's missing in your house. You always have flowers."

"The last arrangement wilted early. I was going to pick up more when I was out today, but I didn't get the chance."

He seemed to cheer at that, as if reading some hidden message in my words.

"Here then," he said. "I'll get some for you now."

I arched my brows. "And carry bouquets on a hunt?"

"Think I can't? Sounds like a challenge."

I laughed and laid my fingers on his forearm. "We'll get some tomorrow."

He took my hand and looped it through his arm as we resumed walking.

"We're going to Paris this spring," he said after a moment.

"Are we? Dare I ask what prompted that?"

"Flowers. Spring. Paris."

"Ah. A thoughtful gesture, but Paris in the spring is highly overrated. And overpriced."

"Too bad. I'm taking you. I'll book the time off when I get home, and call you with the dates."

When I didn't argue, he glanced over at me, then grinned and quickened his pace, launching into a "remember when" story of our last spring in Paris.

We bickered over the choice of victim. Aaron wanted to find one to suit my preference, but I insisted we select his type. Finally, he capitulated.

The fight dampened the evening's mood, but only temporarily. Once Aaron found a target, he forgot everything else.

In the early years, Aaron had struggled with vampiric life. He'd died rescuing a stranger from a petty thug. And his reward? After a life spent thinking of others, he'd been reborn as one who fed off them. Ironic and cruel.

Yet we'd found a way for him to justify—even relish—the harder facts of our survival. He fed from the dregs of society, punks and criminals like those youths in the park. For his annual kill, he condemned those whose crimes he deemed worthy of the harshest punishment. And so he could feel he did some good in this parasitic life.

As he said, I'd found his first victim. Now, two hundred years later, he no longer scoured newspapers or tracked down rumors, but seemed able to locate victims by intuition alone, as I could find the dying. The predatory instinct will adapt to anything that ensures the survival of the host.

Tonight's choice was a drug dealer with feral eyes and a quick switchblade. We watched from the shadows as the man threatened a young runner. Aaron rocked on the balls at his feet, his gaze fixed on that waving knife, but I laid my hand on his arm. As the runner loped toward the street, Aaron's lips curved, happy to see him go, but even happier with what the boy's safe departure portended—not a quick intervention but a true hunt.

We tracked the man for over an hour before Aaron's hunger won out. With no small amount of regret, he stopped toying with his dinner and I lured the drug dealer into an alleyway. An easy maneuver, as such things usually were with men like this, too greedy and cocksure to feel threatened by a middle-aged woman.

As Aaron's fangs sank into the drug dealer's throat, the man's eyes bugged in horror, unable to believe what was happening. This was the most dangerous point of feeding, that split second where they felt our fangs and felt a nightmare come to life. It is but a moment, then the sedative in our saliva takes hold and they pass out, those last few seconds wiped from memory when they wake.

The man lashed out once, then slumped in Aaron's grasp. Still gripping the man's shirtfront, Aaron began to drink, gulping the blood. His eyes were closed, face rapturous, and I watched him, enjoying the sight of his pleasure, his appetite.

He'd been hungrier than he'd let on. Typical for Aaron, waiting that extra day or two, not to practice control or avoid feeding, but to drink heartily. Delayed gratification for heightened pleasure. I shivered.

"Cass?"

He licked a fallen drop from the corner of his mouth as he held the man out for me.

This was how we hunted—how Aaron liked it, not taking separate victims but sharing. He always made the disabling bite, drank some, then let me feed to satiation. If I took too much for him to continue feeding safely, he'd find a second victim. There was no sense arguing that I could find my own food—he knew that, but continued, compelled by a need to protect and provide.

"You go on," I said softly. "You're still hungry."

He thrust the man to me. "Yours."

His jaw set and I knew his insistence had nothing to do with providing sustenance.

As Aaron held the man up for me, I moved forward. My canines lengthened, throat tightening, and I allowed myself a shudder of anticipation.

I lowered my mouth to the man's throat, scraped my canines over the skin, tasting, preparing. Then, with one swift bite, my mouth filled with—

I jerked back, almost choking. I resisted the urge to spit, and forced—with effort—the mouthful down, my stomach revolting in disgust.

It tasted like… blood.

When I became a vampire, I thought this would be the most unbearable part: drinking blood. But the moment that first drop of blood touched my tongue, I'd realized my worries had been for naught. There was no word for the taste; no human memory that came close. I can only say that it was so perfect a food that I could never tire of it nor wish for something else.

But this tasted like *blood*, like my human memory of it. Once, before I'd completed the transition to vampire, I'd filled a goblet with cow's blood and forced it down, preparing for my new life. I could still taste the thick, metallic fluid that had coated my mouth and tongue, then sat in my stomach for no more than a minute before returning the way it had gone down.

Now, after only a mouthful of this man's blood, I had to clamp my mouth shut to keep from gagging. Aaron dropped the man and grabbed for me. I waved him aside.

"I swallowed wrong."

I rubbed my throat, lips curving in a moue of annoyance, then looked around, and found the man at my feet. I steeled myself and bent. Aaron crouched to lift the man for me, but I motioned him back, and shielded my face, so he wouldn't see my reaction. Then I forced my mouth to the man's throat.

The bleeding had already stopped. I bit his neck again, my nails digging into my palms, eyes closed, letting the disgusting taste fill my mouth, then swallowing. Drink, swallow. Drink, swallow. My nails broke my skin, but I felt no pain. I wished I could, if only to give me something else to think about.

It wasn't only the taste. That I could struggle past. But my whole body rebelled at the very sensation of the blood filling my stomach, screaming at me to stop, as if what I was doing was unnatural, even dangerous.

I managed one last swallow. And then… I couldn't. I simply couldn't. I hung there, fangs still in the man's neck, willing myself to suck, to fill my mouth, to finish this, mentally screaming, raging against the preposterousness of it. I was a vampire; I drank blood. And even if I didn't want to, by God, I would force every drop down my throat—

My stomach heaved. I swallowed hard.

I could sense Aaron behind me. Hovering. Watching. Worrying.

Another heave. If I took one more sip, I'd vomit and give Aaron reason to worry, to panic, and give *myself* reason to panic.

It was the victim. God only knew what poisons this drug dealer had swimming through his veins and, while such things don't affect vampires, I am a delicate feeder, too sensitive to anomalies in the blood. I've gone hungry rather than drink anything that tastes "off." There was no sense asking Aaron to confirm it—he could swill week-old blood and not notice.

That was it, then. The victim. Just the victim.

I sealed the wound with my tongue and stepped back.

"Cass…" Aaron's voice was low with warning. "You need to finish him."

"I—" The word "can't" rose to my lips, but I swallowed it back. I couldn't say that. Wouldn't. This was just another temporary hurdle. I'd rest tonight and find a victim of my own choosing tomorrow.

"He isn't right," I said, then turned and headed down the alley.

After a moment, I heard Aaron pitch the unconscious man into a heap of trash bags and storm off in the opposite direction.

Any other man would have thrown up his hands and left me there. I arrived at my car to find Aaron waiting by the driver's door. I handed him the keys and got in the passenger's side.

At home, as I headed toward my room, Aaron called after me. "I hope you're not going to tell me you're tired again."

"No, I'm taking a bath to scrub off the filth of that alley. Then, if you aren't ready to retire, we could have a glass of wine, perhaps light the fire. It's getting cool."

He paused, still ready for a fight, but finding no excuse in my words.

"I'll start the fire," he said.

"Thank you."

No more than ten minutes after I got into the tub, the door banged open with such a crash that I started, sloshing bubbles over the side. Aaron barreled in and shoved a small book at me. My appointment book.

"I found this in your desk."

"Keen detective work. Practicing for your next council investigation?"

"*Our* next council investigation."

I reached for my loofah brush. "My mistake. That's what I meant."

"Is it?"

I looked up, trying to understand his meaning, but seeing only rage in his eyes. He was determined to find out what had happened in that alley, and somehow this was his route there. My stomach clenched, as if the blood was still pooled in it, curdling. I wouldn't have this conversation. I wouldn't.

Ostensibly reaching for the loofah brush, I rose, letting the bubbles slide from me. Aaron's gaze dropped from my face. I tucked my legs under, took hold of the side of the tub and started to rise. He let me get halfway up, then put his hand on my head and firmly pushed me down.

I reclined into the tub again, then leaned my head back, floating, breasts and belly peeking from the water. Aaron watched for a moment, before tearing his gaze away with a growl.

"Stop that, Cass. I'm not going to run off and I'm not going to be distracted. I want to talk to you."

I sighed. "About my appointment book, I presume."

He lifted it. "Last week. On the day marked 'birthday.' The date you must have planned to make your kill. There's nothing else scheduled."

"Of course not. I keep that day open—"

"But you said you were busy. That's why you didn't do it."

"I don't believe I said that. I said things came up."

"Such as...?"

I raised a leg onto the rim and ran the loofah brush down it. Aaron's eyes followed, but after a second, he forced his gaze back to mine and repeated the question.

I sighed. "Very well. Let's see. On that particular day, it was a midnight end-of-season designer clothing sale. As I was driving out of the city to make my kill, I saw the sign and stopped. By the time I left, it was too late to hunt."

He glowered at me. "That's not funny."

"I didn't say it was."

The glower deepened to a scowl. "You postponed your annual kill to *shop?* Bullshit. Yeah, you like your fancy clothes, and you're cheap as hell. But getting distracted by a clothing sale?" He snorted. "That's like a cop stopping a high speed chase to grab donuts."

I went quiet for a moment, then said, as evenly as I could. "Perhaps. But I did."

He searched my eyes, finding the truth there. "Then something's wrong. Very wrong. And you know it."

I shuttered my gaze. "All I know is that you're making too big a deal of this, as always. You take the smallest—"

"Cassandra DuCharme skips her annual kill to go *shopping?* That's not small. That's apocalyptic."

"Oh, please, spare me the—"

He shoved the open book in my face. "Forget the sale. Explain the rest of it. You had nothing scheduled all week. You had no excuse. You didn't forget. You didn't get distracted." His voice dropped as he lowered himself to the edge of the tub. "You have no intention of taking a life."

"You… you think I'm trying to kill myself?" I laughed, the sound almost bitter. "Do you forget how I became what I am, Aaron? I *chose* it. I risked everything to get this life, and if you think I'd throw that away one minute before my time is up—"

"How you came into this life is exactly why you're hell-bent on leaving it like this." He snagged my gaze and held it. "You cheated death. No, you *beat* it—by sheer goddamned force of will. You said 'I won't die.' And now, when it's coming around again, you're damned well not going to sit back and let it happen. You chose once. You'll choose again."

I paused, looked away, then back at him. "Why are you here, Aaron?"

"I came to fix your wall—"

"At no prompting from me. No hints from me. You came of your own accord, correct?"

"Yeah, but—"

"Then, if I'd planned to let myself die, presumably, you wouldn't have seen me again." I met his gaze. "Do you think I would do that? Of everyone I know in this world, would I leave you without saying goodbye?"

His jaw worked, but he said nothing. After a moment, he pushed to his feet, and walked out.

I lay in bed, propped on my pillows, staring at the wall. Aaron was right. When the time came, I would leave this vampiric life as I'd come into it: by choice. But this was not that time. There was no doubt of that, no possibility that I was subconsciously trying to end my life. That was preposterous. I had no qualms about suicide. Fears… perhaps. Yet no different than my fear of death itself.

When the time came, yes. But I would never be so irresponsible as to end my life before my affairs were in order. My estate would need to be disposed of in advance, given to those I wished to see benefit. Of equal concern was the discovery and disposal of my body. To leave that to chance would be unforgivably irresponsible.

I would make my peace with Aaron and make amends for my betrayal or, at the very least, ensure he understood that whatever I had done to him, the reason for it, the *failing* behind it, had been mine.

Then there was the council. Aaron was already my co-delegate, but I had to ready him to take my senior position and ready the vampire community to accept that change. Moreover, as the senior overall council member, it was my duty to pass on all I knew to Paige, as the keeper of records, something I'd been postponing, unwilling to accept that my time was ending.

Ending.

My stomach clenched at the thought. I closed my eyes and shuddered.

I had never lacked for backbone and never stood for the lack of it in others. Now I needed to face and accept this reality. I was dying. Not beginning a lengthy descent, but at the end of the slope.

I now knew how a vampire died. A rebirth date came and we discovered, without warning, that we couldn't fulfill our end of the bargain. Not *would* not, but *could* not.

If I could not overcome this, I would die. Not in decades, but days.

Panic surged, coupled with an overwhelming wave of raw rage. Of all the ways to die, could any be more humiliating in its sublime ridiculousness? Not to die suddenly, existence snuffed out as my time ended. Not to die, beheaded, at the hands of an enemy. Not to grow ill and fade away. Not even to pass in my sleep. Such deaths couldn't be helped, and while I would have raged against that, the injustice of it, such a fate was nothing compared to this—to die because I inexplicably lacked the will to do something I'd done hundreds of times before.

No, that wasn't possible. I wouldn't *let* it be possible.

I would get out of this bed, find a victim and force myself to drain his blood if I vomited up every mouthful.

I envisioned myself standing, yanking on clothing, striding from the room…

Yet I didn't move.

My limbs felt leaden. Inside, I was spitting mad, snarling and cursing, but my body lay as still and calm as if I'd already passed.

I pushed down the burbling panic.

Consider the matter with care and logic. I should have taken Aaron's victim, while I still had the strength, but now that I'd missed my opportunity, I couldn't chance waiting another day. I'd rest for an hour or so, until Aaron had retired.

Better for him not to know. I wouldn't let him pity and coddle me simply because it was in his nature to help the sick, the weak, the needy. I would not be needy.

I'd stay awake and wait until the house grew quiet. Then I'd do this—alone.

I fixed my gaze on the light, staring at it to keep myself awake. Minutes ticked past, each feeling like an hour. My eyes burned. My body begged for sleep. I refused. It threatened to pull me under even with my eyes wide. I compromised. I'd close them for a moment's rest and then I'd leave.

I shut my eyes and all went dark.

I awoke to the smell of flowers. I usually had some in the house, so the smell came as no surprise, and I drowsily stretched, rested and refreshed.

Then I remembered I hadn't replaced my last flowers and I was seized by the sudden vision of my corpse lying on my bed, surrounded by funeral wreaths. I bolted upright and found myself staring in horror at a room of flowers… before realizing that the fact I was sitting upright would suggest I was not dead.

With a deep sigh, I looked around. Flowers did indeed fill my room. There were at least a dozen bouquets, each a riot of blooms, with no unifying theme of color, shape or type. I smiled. Aaron.

My feet lit on the cool hardwood as I crossed to a piece of paper propped against the nearest bouquet. An advertisement for flights to France. Beside another was a list of hotels. A picture of the Eiffel Tower adorned a third. Random images of Parisian travel littered the room, again with no obvious theme, simply pages hurriedly printed from websites. Typically Aaron. Making his point with all the finesse of a sledgehammer wielded with equal parts enthusiasm and determination.

Should I still fail to be swayed, he'd scrawled a note with letters two inches high, the paper thrust into a bouquet of roses. Paige had called. She was still working on that case and needed my help. In smaller letters below, he informed me that today's paper carried another article on the palliative care patient who wanted to die.

I dressed, then tucked two of the pages into my pocket, and slipped out the side door.

I didn't go to the hospital Aaron had suggested. It was too late for that. If I was having difficulty making this kill, I could not compound that by choosing one that would itself be difficult.

So I returned to the alley where I'd found—and dismissed—my first choice two nights ago. The drunkard wasn't there, of course. No one was. But I traversed the maze of alleys and back roads in search of another victim. I couldn't wait for nightfall. I couldn't risk falling asleep again or I might not wake up.

When an exit door swung open, I darted into an alley to avoid detection and spotted my victim. A woman, sitting in an alcove, surrounded by grocery bags stuffed with what looked like trash but, I presumed, encompassed the sum of her worldly belongings. Behind me, whoever opened that door tossed trash into the alley, and slammed it shut again. The woman didn't move. She stared straight ahead, gaze vacant. Resting before someone told her to move on.

Even as I watched her, evaluated her and decided she would do, something deep in me threw up excuses. Not old enough. Not sick enough. Too dangerous a location. Too dangerous a time of day. Keep looking. Find someone better, someplace safer. But if I left here, left *her*, I would grow more tired, more distracted and more disinterested with every passing hour.

She would do. She had to. For once, not a choice I could live with, but the choice that would let me live.

There was no way to approach without the woman seeing me. Unlike Aaron, I didn't like to let my victims see the specter of death approach, but today I had no choice. So I straightened and started toward her, as if it was perfectly natural for a well-dressed middle-aged woman to cut through alleyways.

Out of the corner of my eye, I saw her look up as I passed. She tensed, then relaxed, seeing no threat. I turned, as if just noticing her. Then with a brisk nod, I took a twenty from my wallet.

A cruel ruse? Or making her last memory a pleasant one? Perhaps both. As expected, she smiled, her guard lowering even more. I reached down, but let go of the bill too soon. As it fluttered to the ground, I murmured an apology and bent, as if to retrieve it, but she was already snatching it up. I kept bending, still apologizing... and sank my fangs into the back of her neck.

She gave one gasp before the sedative took effect and she fell forward. I tugged her into the alcove, propped her against the wall and crouched beside her still form.

As my fangs pierced her jugular, I braced myself. The blood filled my mouth, as thick, hot and horrible as the drug dealer's the night before. My throat tried to seize up, rejecting it, but I swallowed hard. Another mouthful. Another swallow. Drink. Swallow. Drink. Swallow.

My stomach heaved. I pulled back from the woman, closed my eyes, lifted my chin and swallowed the blood. Another heave, and my mouth filled, the taste too horrible to describe. I gritted my teeth and swallowed.

With every mouthful now, some came back up. I swallowed it again. Soon my whole body was shaking, my brain screaming that this wasn't right, that I was killing myself, drowning.

My stomach gave one violent heave, my throat refilling. I clamped my hand to my mouth, eyes squeezed shut as I forced myself to swallow the regurgitated blood.

Body shaking, I crouched over her again. I opened my eyes and saw the woman lying there. I couldn't do this. I couldn't—

One hand still pressed to my mouth, I tugged the pages from my pocket. I unfolded them and forced myself to look. Paris. Aaron. Paige. The council. I wasn't done yet. Soon... but not yet.

I squeezed my eyes shut, then slammed my fangs into the woman's throat and drank.

Her pulse started to fade. My stomach was convulsing now, body trembling so hard I could barely keep my mouth locked on her neck. Even as I pushed on, seeing the end in sight, I knew this wasn't success. I'd won only the first round of a match I was doomed to lose.

The last drops of blood filled my mouth. Her heart beat slower, and slower, then... stopped.

Another life taken. Another year to live.

IN DARKNESS, ANGELS

by Eric Van Lustbader

Eric Van Lustbader is the bestselling author of *The Ninja* and the others in the Nicholas Linnear cycle, as well as The Pearl Saga and The Sunset Warrior cycle, and a number of other novels. His latest books are the presidential thriller *First Daughter* and *The Bourne Deception*, the latest in Robert Ludlum's Bourne series, which Lustbader took over after Ludlum's death. The next Bourne novel, *The Bourne Objective*, is due to be published in June 2010.

Vampires are scary. And you know what else is scary? In-laws. So it stands to reason that this is going to be one scary story. We fall in love with individuals, but we don't always appreciate that in the bargain we'll be getting their family too—a whole web of relationships and past events that are unknown to us. And when those past events stretch back *centuries*? Let's just say that you may have been in relationships where you felt like your lover's family members were out for blood. But probably never quite like this.

If I had known then what I know now.

How those words echo on and on inside my mind, like a rubber ball bouncing down an endless staircase. As if they had a life of their own. Which, I suppose, they do now.

I cannot sleep but is it any wonder ? Outside, blue-white lightning forks like a giant's jagged claw and the thunder is so loud at times that I feel I must be trapped inside an immense bell, reverberations like memory unspooling in a reckless helix, making a mess at my feet.

If I had known then what I know now. And yet….

And yet I return again and again to that windswept evening when the ferry deposited me at the east end of the island. It had once been, so I had been told by the rather garrulous captain, a swansneck peninsula. But over time, the water had gradually eaten away at the rocky soil until at last the land had succumbed to the ocean's cool tidal embrace, severing itself from the mainland a mile away.

Of course the captain had an entirely different version of what had transpired. "It's them folks up there," he had said, jerking his sharp unshaven chin toward the castle high atop the island's central mount. "Didn't want no more interference from the other folks hereabouts." He gave a short barking laugh and spat over the boat's side. "Just as well, I say," he observed as he squinted heavily into the last of the dying sun's watery light. "Them rocks were awfully sharp." He shook his head as if weighed down by the memory. "Kids were always darin one another t'do their balancin act goin across, down that long spit o land." He turned the wheel hard over and spuming water rushed up the bow of the ferry. "Many's the night we'd come out with the searchlights, tryin to rescue some fool boy'd gone over."

For just a moment he swung us away from the island looming up on our starboard side, getting the most out of the crosswinds. "Never found em, though. Not a one." He spat again. "You go over the side around here, you're never seen again."

"The undertow," I offered.

He whipped his ruddy windburned face around, impaling me with one pale-gray eye. "Undertow, you say?" His laugh was harsh now and unpleasant. "You gotta lot t'learn up there at Fuego del Aire, boyo. Oh, yes indeed!"

He left me on the quayside with no one around to mark my arrival. As the wide-beamed ferry tacked away, pushed by the strong sunset wind, I thought I saw the captain raise an arm in my direction.

I turned away from the sea. Great stands of pine, bristly and dark in the failing light, marched upward in majestic array toward the castle high above me. Their tops whipsawed, sending off an odd melancholy drone.

I felt utterly, irretrievably alone and for the first time since I had sent the letter I began to feel the queasy fluttering of reservations. An odd kind of inner darkness had settled about my shoulders like a vulture descending upon the flesh of the dead.

I took a deep breath and shook my head to clear it. The captain's stories were only words strung one after the other—all the legends just words and nothing more. Now I would see for myself. After all, that was what I wanted.

The last of the sunset torched the upper spires so that for a moment they looked like bloody spears. Imagination, that's all it was. A writer's imagination. I clutched at my battered weekender and continued onward, puffing, for the way was steep. But I had arrived at just the right time of the day when the scorching sun was gone from the sky and night's deep chill had not yet settled over the land.

The air was rich with the scents of the sea, an agglomeration so fecund it took my breath away. Far off over the water, great gulls twisted and turned in lazy circles, skimming over the shining face of the ocean only to whirl high aloft, disappearing for long moments into the fleecy pink and yellow clouds.

From the outside, the castle seemed stupendous. It was immense, thrusting upward into the sky as if it were about to take off in flight. It was constructed—obviously many years ago—from massive blocks of granite laced with iridescent chips of mica that shone like diamonds, rubies and sapphires in the evening's light.

A fairy tale castle it surely looked with its shooting turrets and sharply angled spires, horned and horrific. However, on closer inspection, I saw that it had been put together with nothing more fantastic than mortar.

Below me, a mist was beginning to form, swiftly climbing the route I had taken moments before as if following me. Already the sight of the quay had been snuffed out and the cries of the gulls, filtered through the stuff, were eerie and vaguely disquieting.

I climbed the basalt steps to the front door of the castle. The span was fully large enough to drive a semi through. It was composed of a black substance that seemed to be neither stone nor metal. Cautiously, I ran my hand over its textured surface. It was petrified wood. In its center was a circular scrollwork knocker of black iron and this I used.

There was surprisingly little noise but almost immediately the door swung inward. At first I could see nothing. The creeping mist had curled itself around the twilight, plunging me into a dank and uncomfortable night.

"Yes?" It was a melodious voice, light and airy. A woman's voice.

I told her my name.

"I am so sorry," she said. "We tend to lose track of time at Fuego del Aire. I am Marissa. Of course you were expected. My brother will be extremely angry that you were not met at the quay."

"It's all right," I said. "I thoroughly enjoyed the walk."

"Won't you come in."

I picked up my suitcase and crossed the threshold, felt her slim hand slip into mine. The hallway was as dark as the night outside. I did not hear the door swing shut but when I looked back the sky and the rolling mist were gone.

I heard the rustling of her just in front of me and I could smell a scent like a hillside of flowers at dusk. Her skin was as soft as velvet but the flesh beneath was firm and supple and I found myself suddenly curious to find out what she looked like. Did she resemble the image in my thoughts? A thin, pale waif-like creature, faint blue traceries of veins visible beneath her thin delicate skin, her long hair as black as a raven's wings.

After what seemed an interminable time, we emerged into a dimly lighted chamber from which all other rooms on this floor seemed to branch. Directly ahead of us, an enormous staircase wound upward. It was certainly wide enough for twenty people to ascend abreast.

Torches flickered and the smoky, perfumed air was thick with the scent of burning tallow and whale oil. Uncomfortable looking furniture lined the walls: bare, wooden stiff-backed benches and chairs one might find in a Methodist church. Huge, heavy banners hung limply but they were so high above my head and the light so poor I could not make out their designs.

Marissa turned to face me and I saw that she was not at all as I had imagined her.

True, she was beautiful enough. But her cheeks were ruddy, her eyes cornflower blue and her hair was the color of sun-dazzled honey, falling in thick, gentle waves from a thin tortoise-shell band that held it from her face, back over her head, across her shoulders, cascading all the way down to the small of her back.

Her coral lips pursed as if she could not help the smile that now brightened her face. "Yes," she said softly, musically, "you are truly surprised."

"I'm sorry," I said. "Am I staring?" I gave an unnatural laugh. Of course I was staring. I could not stop.

"Perhaps you are weary from your climb. Would you like some food now? A cool drink to refresh you?"

"I would like to meet Morodor," I said, breaking my eyes away from her gaze with a concerted effort. She seemed to possess an ability to draw emotion out of me, as if she held the key to channels in myself I did not know existed.

"In time," she said. "You must be patient. There are many pressing matters that need attending to. Only he can see to them. I am certain you understand."

Indeed I did not. To have come this far, to have waited so long... all I felt was frustration. Like a hurt little boy, I had wanted Morodor to greet me at the front door by way of apology for the discourtesy of the utter stillness at the quay when I arrived. But no. There were more important matters for him.

"When I wrote to your brother—"

Marissa had lifted her long pale palm. "Please," she said, smiling. "Be assured that my brother wishes to aid you. I suspect that is because he is a writer himself. There is much time here at Fuego del Aire and lately his contemplation has found this somewhat more physical outlet."

I thought of the grisly stories the ferryboat captain had heaped on me—and others, over time, that had come my way from other loquacious mouths—and felt a chill creeping through my bones at the idea of Morodor's physical outlets.

"It must be fascinating to be able to write novels," Marissa said. "I must confess that I was quite selfishly happy when I learned of your coming. Your writing has given me much pleasure." She touched the back of my hand as if I might be a sculpture of great artistry. "This extraordinary talent must make you very desirable in... your world."

"You mean literary circles... entertainment...."

"Circles, yes. You are quite special. My brother doubtless divined this from your letter." She took her fingertips from me. "But now it is late and I am certain you are tired. May I show you to your room? Food and drink are waiting for you there."

That night there was no moon. Or rather no moon could be seen. Nor the stars nor even the sky itself. Peering out the window of my turret room, I could see nothing but the whiteness of the mist. It was as if the rest of the world had vanished.

Gripping the edge of the windowsill with my fingers, I leaned out as far as I dared, peering into the night in an attempt to pick up any outline, any shape. But not even the tops of the enormous pines could poke their way through the pall.

I strained to hear the comforting hiss and suck of the ocean spending itself on the rocky shore so far below me. There was nothing of that, only the odd intermittent whistling of the wind through the stiff-fingered turrets of the castle.

At length I went back to bed, but for the longest time I could not fall asleep. I had waited so long for Morodor's reply to my letter, had traveled for so many days just to be here now, it seemed impossible to relax enough for sleep to overtake me.

I was itchy with anticipation. Oh more. I was burning.... In the days after I had received his affirmative answer, the thought of coming here, of talking to him, of learning his secrets had, more and more, come to stand for my own salvation.

It is perhaps difficult enough for any author to be blocked in his work. But for me… I lived to write. Without it, there seemed no reason at all to live, for I had found during this blocked time that the days and nights passed like months, years, centuries, as ponderous as old elephants. They had become my burden.

I had been like a machine, feverishly turning out one book after another—one a year—for… how many years now? Fifteen? Twenty? You see, the enfant terrible has lost count already. Mercifully.

Until this year when there was nothing, a desert of paper, and I grew increasingly desperate, sitting home like a hermit, traveling incessantly, bringing smiling girls home, abstaining, swinging from one extreme to the other like a human pendulum in an attempt to get the insides in working order again.

Nothing.

And then one drunken night I had heard the first of the stories about Fuego del Aire and, even through the vapors of my stupor, *something* had penetrated. An idea, perhaps or, more accurately at that point, the ghost of an idea. Of lost love, betrayal and the ultimate horror. As simple as that. And as complex. But I knew that imagination was no longer enough, that I would have to seek out this place myself. I had to find Morodor and somehow persuade him to see me….

Sleep. I swear to you it finally came, although, oddly, it was like no slumber I had ever had, for I dreamed that I was awake and trying desperately to fall asleep. I knew that I was to see Morodor in the morning, that I had to be sharp and that, sleepless, I would fall far short of that.

In the dream I lay awake, clutching the bedspread up around my chest, staring at the ceiling with such intensity that I suspected at any minute I would be able to see right through it.

I opened my eyes. Or closed them and opened them again to find the dawnlight streaming through the tall narrow window. I had forgotten to close the curtains before going to bed.

For just an instant I had the strangest sensation in my body. It was as if my legs had gone dead, all the strength flowing out of my muscles and into the wooden floor of my room. But the paralysis had somehow freed my upper torso so that I felt an enormous outpouring of energy.

A brief stab of fear rustled through my chest and my heart fluttered. But as soon as I sat up, the sensation went away. I rose, washed, dressed and went down to breakfast.

Food was waiting in steaming array along the length of an immense wooden table. In fact, now that I had my first good look at Fuego del Aire in the light of day, I saw that everything was of wood: the paneled walls, the floor where you could see it between the series of dark-patterned carpets, the cathedral ceilings; door handles, windowsills, even the lighting fixtures. If I had not seen the outside of the castle myself, I would have sworn the place had been built entirely of wood.

Two formal settings were laid out, one at the head of the table and the other by its left side. Assuming the first was for Morodor, I settled into the side chair and began to help myself.

But it was not Morodor who came down the wide staircase; it was Marissa. She was, that morning, a sight to make the heart pound. It was as if the sun had detached itself from its prescribed route across the heavens and had descended to earth. She wore a sky-blue tunic, wrapped criss-cross between her breasts and around her narrow waist with a deep green satin sash. On her feet she wore rope sandals. I saw that one of her toes was girdled by a tiny gold ring.

Her smile as she approached had the warmth of summer itself. And her hair! How can I adequately describe the way her hair shone in the daylight, sparkling and glittering as if each strand were itself some mysterious source of light. Those waves of golden honey acted as if they had a life of their own.

"Good morning," she said easily. "Did you sleep well?"

"Yes," I lied. "Perfectly." I lifted a bowl of green figs. "Fruit?"

"Yes, please. Just a bit." But even with that she left more on her plate than she ate.

"I was hoping to find your brother already awake," I said, finishing up my meal.

She smiled sweetly. "Unfortunately, he is not an early riser. Be patient. All will be well." She rose. "If you are finished, I imagine you are quite curious about Fuego del Aire. There is much here to see."

We went out of the main hall, through corridors and chambers one after another, so filled, so disparate that I soon became dizzied with wonder. The place seemed to go on forever.

At length we emerged into a room that, judging by its accouterments, must once have been a scullery. We crossed it quickly and went through a small door I did not see until Marissa pulled it open.

The mist of last night had gone completely and above was only an enormous cerulean sky clear of cloud or bird. I could hear the distant sea hurling itself with ceaseless abandon at the jagged base of the mount. But lowering my gaze I saw only foliage.

"The garden," Marissa breathed, slipping her hand into mine. "Come on." She took me past a field of tiger lilies, rows of flowering woodbine; through a rose garden of such humbling perfection, it took my breath away.

Beyond, we came upon a long sculptured hedge half again as tall as I stand. There was a long narrow opening through which she led me and immediately we were surrounded by high walls of hedges. They were lushly verdant and immaculately groomed so that it was impossible to say where one left off and another began, seamless on and on and—

"What is this place?" I said.

But Marissa did not answer until, after many twistings and turnings, we were deep within. Then she faced me and said, "This is the labyrinth. My brother had it constructed for me when I was just a child. Perhaps he thought it would keep me out of trouble."

"There *is* a way out," I said uneasily, looking around me at the dark-green screens looming up on every side.

"Oh yes." She laughed, a bell-like silvery tone. "It is up here." And tapped the side of her head with a slender forefinger. "This is where I come to think, when I am sad or distraught. It is so peaceful and still and no one can find me here if I choose to remain hidden, not even Morodor. This is my domain."

She began to lead me onward, through switchbacks, past cul-de-sacs, moving as unerringly as if she were a magnet being drawn toward the North Pole. And I followed her silently; I was already lost.

"My brother used to say to me, 'Marissa, this labyrinth is unique in all the world for I have made it from the blueprint of your mind. All these intricate convolutions... the pattern corresponds to the eddies and whorls of your own brain.'"

She stared at me with those huge mocking eyes, so blue it seemed as if the noonday sky were reflected there. The hint of a smile played at the corners of her lips. "But of course I was only a child then and always trying to do what he did... to be like him." She shrugged. "He was most likely trying to make me feel special... don't you think?"

"He wouldn't need this place to do that," I said. "How on earth do you find your way out of here?" Nothing she had said had lessened my uneasiness.

"The years," she said seriously, "have taken care of that."

She pulled at me and we sat, our torsos in the deep shade of the hedges, our stretched-out legs in the buttery warmth of the sunlight. Somewhere, close at hand, a bumblebee buzzed fatly, contentedly.

I put my head back and watched the play of light and shadow on the hedge opposite us. Ten thousand tiny leaves moved minutely in the soft breeze as if I were watching a distant crowd fluttering lifted handkerchiefs at the arrival of some visiting emperor. A kind of dreamy warmth stole over me and at once my uneasiness was gone.

"Yes," I told her. "It *is* peaceful here."

"I am glad," she said. "You feel it too. Perhaps that is because you are a writer. A writer feels things more deeply, is that not so?"

I smiled. "Maybe some, yes. We're always creating characters for our stories so we have to be adept at pulling apart the people we meet. We have to be able to get beyond the world and, like a surgeon, expose their workings."

"And you're never frightened of such things?"

"Frightened? Why?"

"Of what you'll find there."

"I've discovered many things there over the years. How could all of them be pleasant? Why should I want them to be? I sometimes think that many of my colleagues live off the *un*pleasant traits they find beneath the surface." I shrugged. "In any event, nothing seems to work well without the darkness of conflict. In life as well as in writing."

Her eyes opened and she looked at me sideways. "Am I wrong to think that knowledge is very important to you?"

"What could be more important to a writer? I sometimes think there is a finite amount of knowledge—not to be assimilated—but that can be used."

"And that is why you have come here."

"Yes."

She looked away. "You have never married. Why is that?"

I shrugged while I thought about that for a moment. "I imagine it's because I've never fallen in love."

She smiled at that. "Never ever. Not in all the time—"

I laughed. "Now wait a minute! I'm not that old. Thirty-seven is hardly ancient."

"Thirty-seven," she mouthed softly, as if she were repeating words alien to her. "Thirty-seven. Really?"

"Yes." I was puzzled. "How old are you?"

"As old as I look." She tossed her hair. "I told you last night. Time means very little here."

"Oh yes, day to day. But I mean you must—"

"No more talk now," she said, rising and pulling at my hand. "There is too much to see."

We left the labyrinth by a simple enough path, though, left to myself, I undoubtedly would have wandered around in there until someone had the decency to come and get me.

Presently we found ourselves at a stone parapet beyond which the peak dropped off so precipitously that it seemed as if we were standing on the verge of a rift in the world.

This was the western face of the island, one that I had not seen on my journey here. Far below us—certainly more than a thousand feet—the sea creamed and sucked at the jagged rocks, iced at their base by shining pale-gray barnacles. Three or four large lavender and white gulls dipped and wheeled through the foaming spray as they searched for food.

"Beautiful, isn't it?" Marissa said.

But I had already turned from the dark face of the sea to watch the planes and hollows of her own shining face, lit by the soft summer light, all rose and golden, radiating a warmth....

It took me some time to understand the true nature of that heat. It stemmed from the same spot deep inside me from which had leaped that sharp momentary anger.

"Marissa," I breathed, saying her name as if it were a prayer.

And she turned to me, her cornflower blue eyes wide, her full lips slightly parted, shining. I leaned over her, coming closer inch by inch until I had to shut my eyes or cross them. Then I felt the brush of her lips against mine, so incredibly soft, at first cool and fragrant, then quickly warming to blood-heat.

"No," she said, her voice muffled by our flesh. "Oh, don't." But her lips opened under mine and I felt her hot tongue probing into my mouth.

My arms went around her, pulling her to me as gently as I would handle a stalk of wheat. I could feel the hard press of her breasts, the round softness of her stomach, and the heat. The heat rising....

And with the lightning comes the rain. That's from an old poem my mother used to sing to me late at night when the storms woke me up. I cannot remember any more of it. Now it's just a fragment of truth, an artifact unearthed from the silty riverbed of my mind. And I the archeologist of this region as puzzled as everyone else at what I sometimes find. But that, after all, is what has kept me writing, year after year. An engine of creation.

The night is impenetrable with cloud and the hissing downpour. But still I stand at my open window, high up above the city, at the very edge of heaven.

I cannot see the streets below me—the one or two hurrying people beneath their trembling umbrellas or the lights of the cars, if indeed there are any out at this ungodly hour—just the spectral geometric patterns, charcoal-gray on black, of the buildings' tops closest to mine. But not as high. None of them is as high.

Nothing exists now but this tempest and its fury. The night is alive with it, juddering and crackling. Or am I wrong? Is the night alive with something else? I know. *I know.*

I hear the sound of them now....

The days passed like the most intense of dreams. The kind where you can recall every single detail any time you wish, producing its emotions again and again with a conjurer's facility.

Being with Marissa, I forgot about my obsessive desire to seek out Morodor. I no longer asked her where he was or when I would get to see him. In fact, I hoped I never would, for, if there were any truth to the legends of Fuego del Aire, they most assuredly must stem from his dark soul and not from this creature of air and light who never left my side.

In the afternoons we strolled through the endless gardens—for she was ill at ease indoors—and holding her hand seemed infinitely more joyous than looking upon the castle's illimitable marvels. I fully believe that if we had chanced upon a griffin during one of those walks I would have taken no more notice of it than I would an alley cat.

However, no such fabled creature made its appearance, and as the time passed I became more and more convinced that there was no basis at all to the stories that had been told and re-told over the years. The only magical power Marissa possessed was the one that enabled her to cut to the very core of me with but one word or the merest touch of her flesh against mine.

"I lied to you," I told her one day. It was late afternoon. Thick dark sunlight slanted down on our shoulders and backs, as slow-running as honey. The cicadas wailed like beaten brass and butterflies danced like living jewels in and out of the low bushes and the blossoms as if they were a flock of children playing tag.

"About what?"

"When I said that I had never been in love." I turned over on my back, staring up at a fleecy cloud piled high, a castle in the sky. "I was. Once."

I took her hand, rubbed my thumb over the delicate bones ribbing the back. "It was when I was in college. We met in a child psychology class and fell in love without even knowing it."

For a moment there was a silence between us and I thought perhaps I had made a mistake in bringing it up.

"But you did not marry her."

"No."

"Why not?"

"We were from different... backgrounds." I turned to see her face peering at me, seeming as large as the sun in the sky. "I think it would be difficult to explain to you, Marissa. It had something to do with religion."

"Religion." Again she rolled a word off her tongue as if trying to *get* the taste of a new and exotic food. "I am not certain that I understand."

"We believed in different things—or, more accurately, she believed and I didn't."

"And there was no room for... compromise?"

"In this, no. But the ironic part of all of it is that now I have begun to believe, if just a little bit; and she, I think, has begun to disbelieve some of what she had always held sacred."

"How sad," Marissa said. "Will you go back to her?"

"Our time has long passed."

Something curious had come into her eyes. "Then you believe that love has a beginning and an end, always."

I could no longer bear to have those fantastic eyes riveting me. "I had thought so."

"Why do you look away?"

"I—" I watched the sky. The cloud-castle had metamorphosed into a great humpbacked bird. "I don't know."

Her eyes were very clear, piercing though the natural light was dusky. "We are explorers," she said, "at the very precipice of time." Something in her voice drew me. "Can there really be a love without end?"

Now she began to search my face in detail as if she were committing it to memory, as if she might never see me again. And that wild thought brought me fully out of my peaceful dozing.

"Do you love me?"

"Yes," I whispered with someone else's voice. Like a dry wind through sere reeds. And pulled her down to me.

At night we seemed even closer. It was as if I had taken a bit of the sun to bed with me: she was as radiant at night as she was during the day, light and supple and so eager to be held, to be caressed. To be loved.

"Feel how I feel," she whispered, trembling, "when I am close to you." She stretched herself over me. "The mouth can lie with words but the body cannot.

This heat is real. All love flows out through the body, do you know that?"

I was beyond being able to respond verbally.

She moved her fingertips on me, then the petal softness of her palms. "I feel your body. How you respond to me. Its depth. As if I were the moon and you the sea." Her lips were at my ear, her esses sibilant. "It is important. More important than you know."

"Why?" I sighed.

"Because only love can mend my heart."

I wondered at the scar there. I moved against her, opening her legs.

"Darling!"

I met Morodor on the first day of my second week at Fuego del Aire. And then it seemed quite by chance.

It was just after breakfast and Marissa had gone back to her room to change. I was strolling along the second-floor balustrade when I came across a niche in the wall that I had missed before.

I went through it and found myself on a parapet along the jutting north side of the castle. It was like hanging in mid-air and I would have been utterly stunned by the vista had I not almost immediately run into a dark towering shape.

Hastily I backed up against the stone wall of the castle, thinking I had inadvertently run into another outcropping of this odd structure.

Then, quite literally, it seemed as if a shadow had come to life. It detached itself from the edge of the parapet and now I could see that it was the figure of a man.

He must have been nearly seven feet tall and held about him a great ebon cape, thick and swirling, that rushed down his slender form so that it hissed against the stone floor when he moved.

He turned toward me and I gasped. His face was long and narrow, as bony as a corpse's, his skin fully as pale. His eyes, beneath darkly furred brows, were bits of bituminous matter as if put there to plug a pair of holes into his interior. His nose was long and thin to the point of severity but his lips were full and rubicund, providing the only bit of color to his otherwise deathly pallid face.

His lips opened infinitesimally and he spoke my name. Involuntarily, I shuddered and immediately saw something pass across his eyes: not anger or sorrow but rather a weary kind of resignation.

"How do you do."

The greeting was so formal that it startled me and I was tongue-tied. After all this time, he had faded from my mind and now I longed only to be with Marissa. I found myself annoyed with him for intruding upon us.

"Morodor," I said. I had the oddest impulse to tell him that what he needed most was a good dose of sunshine. That almost made me giggle. Almost.

"Pardon me for saying this but I thought... that is, to see you up and around, outside in the daylight—" I stopped, my cheeks burning, unable to go on. I had done it anyway. I cursed myself for the fool that I was.

But Morodor took no offense. He merely smiled—a perfectly ghastly sight—and inclined his head a fraction. "A rather common misconception," he said in his disturbing, rumbling voice. "It is in fact *direct* sunlight that is injurious to my health. I am like a fine old print." His dark hair brushed against his high forehead. "I quite enjoy the daytime, otherwise."

"But surely you must sleep sometime."

He shook his great head. "Sleep is unknown to me. If I slept, I would dream and this is not allowed me." He took a long hissing stride along the parapet. "Come," he said. "Let us walk." I looked back the way I had come and he said, "Marissa knows we are together. Do not fear. She will be waiting for you when we are finished."

Together we walked along the narrow parapet. Apparently, it girdled the entire castle, for I saw no beginning to it and no end.

"You may wonder," Morodor said in his booming, vibratory voice, "why I granted you this interview." His great cape swept around him like the coils of a midnight sea so that it seemed as if he kept the night around him wherever he went. "I sensed in your writing a certain desperation." He turned to me. "And desperation is an emotion with which I can empathize."

"It was kind of you to see me."

"Kind, yes."

"But I must confess that things have… changed since I wrote that letter."

"Indeed." Was that a vibratory warning?

"Yes," I plunged onward. "In fact, since I came here, I—" I paused, not knowing how to continue. "The change has come since I arrived at Fuego del Aire."

Morodor said nothing and we continued our perambulation around the perimeter of the castle. Now I could accurately judge just how high up we were. Perhaps that mist I had seen the first night had been a cloud passing us as if across the face of the moon. And why not? All things seemed possible here. It struck me as ridiculous that just fifty miles from here there were supertankers and express trains, Learjets and paved streets lined with shops dispensing sleekly packaged products manufactured by multinational corporations. Surely all those modern artifacts were part of a fading dream I once had.

The sea was clear of sails for as far as the horizon. It was a flat and glittering pool there solely for the pleasure of this man.

"I'm in love with your sister." I had blurted it out and now I stood stunned, waiting, I suppose, for the full brunt of his wrath.

But instead, he stopped and stared at me. Then he threw his head back and laughed, a deep booming sound like thunder. Far off, a gull screeched, perhaps in alarm.

"My dear sir," he said. "You really are the limit!"

"And she's in love with me."

"Oh oh oh. I have no doubt that she is."

"I don't—"

His brows gathered darkly like stormclouds. "You believe your race to be run."

He moved away. "But fear, not love, ends it." Through another niche, he slid back inside the castle. It was as if he had passed through the wall.

"If I had known that today was the day," Marissa said, "I would have prepared you."

"For what?"

We were sitting in a bower on a swing-chaise. Above our heads arched brilliant hyacinth and bougainvillea, wrapped around and around a white wooden trellis. It was near dusk and the garden was filled with a deep sapphire light that was almost luminescent. A westerly wind brought us the rich scent of the sea.

"For him. We are not… very much alike. At least, superficially."

"Marissa," I said, taking her hand, "are you certain that you *are* Morodor's sister?"

"Of course I am. What do you mean?"

"Well, it's obvious, isn't it?" But when she looked at me blankly, I was forced to go on. "What I mean is, he's precisely… what he's supposed to be. At least the way the legends describe… what he is."

Her eyes grew dark and she jerked her hand away. She gave me a basilisk stare. "I should have known." Her voice was filled with bitter contempt. "You're just like the rest. And why shouldn't you be?" She stood. "You think he's a monster. Yes, admit it. A monster!"

Her eyes welled up with tears. "And that makes me a monster too, doesn't it. Well, to hell with you!" And she whirled away.

"Marissa!" I cried in anguish. "That's not what I meant at all."

And I ran after her knowing that it was a lie, that it was what I had meant after all. Morodor was all the legends had said he should be. And more. My God but he was hideous. Pallid and cold as the dead. An engine of negative energy, incapable of any real feeling; of crying or true humor. Or love.

Only love can mend my heart.

I *had* meant it. How could this golden girl of air and sunlight bear any family ties to that great looming figure of darkness? Where was the sense in it? The rationality? She had feelings. She laughed and cried, felt pleasure and pain. And she loved. She loved.

"Marissa!" I called again, running. "Marissa, come back!" But she had vanished into the labyrinth and I stood there on the threshold, the scent of roses strong in my nostrils, and peered within. I called out her name over and over again but she did not appear and, unguided, I could not bring myself to venture farther.

Instead, I stormed back to the castle, searching for Morodor. It was already dark and the lights had been lit. As if by magic. In just the same way that the food was prepared, the wine bottles uncorked, my bed turned down in the evening and made in the morning, my soiled clothes washed, pressed and laid out with the professional's precision. And all done without my seeing a soul.

I found Morodor in the library. It was a room as large as a gallery: at least three floors of books, rising upward until the neat rows were lost in the haze of distance.

Narrow wooden walkways circled the library at various levels, connected by a complex network of wide wooden ladders.

He was crouched on one of these, three or four steps off the floor. It seemed an odd position for a man of his size.

He was studying a book as I came in but he quietly closed it when he heard me approach.

"What," I said, rather nastily, "no leather bindings?"

His hard ebon eyes regarded me without obvious emotion. "Leather," he said softly, "would mean the needless killing of animals."

"Oh, I see." My tone had turned acid. "It's only humans who need fear you."

He stood up and I backed away, abruptly fearful as he unfolded upward and upward until he stood over me in all his monstrous height.

"Humans," he said, "fear me only because they choose to fear me."

"You mean you haven't given them any cause to fear you?"

"Don't be absurd." He was as close to being annoyed as I had seen him. "I cannot help being what I am. Just as you cannot. We are both carnivores."

I closed my eyes and shuddered. "But with what a difference!"

"To some I have been a god."

"Such a dark god." My eyes flew open.

"There is a need for that, too." He put the book way. "Yet I am a man for all that."

"A man who can't sleep, who doesn't dream."

"Who cannot die."

"Not even if I drive a stake through your heart?" I did not know whether or not I was serious.

He went across the room to where a strip of the wooden paneling intervened between two bookshelves. His hand merged from the folds of his voluminous cape and for the first time I saw the long talon-like nails exposed. I shivered as I saw them dig into the wood with ferocious strength. But not in any hot animal way. The movement was as precise as a surgeon peeling back a patient's peritoneum.

Morodor returned with a shard of wood perhaps eighteen inches in length. It was slightly tapered at one end, not needle sharp but pointed enough to do its work. He thrust it into my hands. "Here," he said harshly. "Do it now."

For an instant, I intended to do just that. But then something inside me cooled. I threw the stake from me. "I'll do no such thing."

He actually seemed disappointed. "No matter. That part of the legend, as others, is incorrect." He went back to his perch on the ladder, his long legs drawn up tightly beneath the cape, the outline of his bony knees like a violent set of punctuation marks on a blank page.

"Legends," he said, "are like funerals. They both serve the same purpose. They give comfort without which the encroachment of terrifying entropy would snuff out man's desire—his absolute hunger—for life."

He looked from his long nails up into my face. "Legends are created to set up their own kind of terror. But it is a terror very carefully bounded by certain limitations: the werewolf can be killed by a silver bullet, the medusa by seeing her own reflection in a mirror.

"You see? Always there is a way out for the intrepid. It is a necessary safety valve venting the terror that lurks within all mankind—atavistic darkness, the unconscious. And death."

He rested his long arms in his lap. "How secure do you imagine mankind would feel if all of them out there knew the reality of it? That there is no escape for me. No stake through the heart."

"But you said direct sunlight—"

"Was injurious to me. Like the flu, nothing more." He smiled wanly. "A week or two in bed and I am fit again." He laughed sardonically.

"Assuming I believe you, why are you telling me this? By your own admission, mankind could not accept the knowledge."

"Then you won't tell them, will you?"

"But *I* know."

He took a deep breath and for the first time his eyes seemed to come to life, sparking and dancing within their deep fleshless sockets. "Why did you wish to come here, my friend?"

"Why, I told you in the letter. I was blocked, out of ideas."

"And now?"

I stared at him quizzically while it slowly began to wash over me. "I can tell them, can't I?"

He smiled sphinx-like. "You are a writer. You can tell them anything you wish."

"When I told you before that I was a man, I meant it."

I was sitting with Morodor high up in one of the castle's peaks, in what he called the cloud room. Like all the other chambers I had been in here, it was paneled in wood.

"I have a hunger to live just like all the rest of the masses." He leaned back in his chair, shifting about as if he were uncomfortable. To his left and right, enormous windows stood open to the starry field of the night. There were no shutters, no curtains; they could not be closed. A sharp, chill wind blew in, ruffling his dark hair but he seemed oblivious to the caress. "But do not mistake my words. I speak not as some plutocrat bloated on wealth. It is only that I am... special."

"What happened?"

His eyes flashed and he shifted again. "In each case, it is different. In mine... well, let us say that my hunger for life outweighed my caution." He smiled bleakly. "But then I have never believed that caution was a desirable trait."

"Won't you tell me more."

He looked at me in the most avuncular fashion. "I entered into a wager with... someone."

"And you won."

"No. I lost. But it was meant that I should lose. Otherwise, I would not be here now." His eyes had turned inward and in so doing had become almost wistful. "I threw the dice one time, up against a wall of green baize."

"You crapped out."

"No. I entered into life."

"And became *El Amor Brujo*. That's what you're sometimes called: the love sorcerer."

"Because of my… hypnotic effect on women." He moved minutely and his cape rustled all about him like a copse of trees stirred by a midnight wind. "A survival trait. Like seeing in the dark or having built-in radar."

"Then there's nothing magical—"

"There is," he said, "magic involved. One learns… many arts over the years. I have time for everything."

I shivered, pulled my leather jacket closer about me. He might not mind the chill, but I did. I pointed to the walls. "Tell me something. The outside of Fuego del Aire is pure stone. But here, inside, there is only wood. Why is that?"

"I prefer wood, my friend. I am not a creature of the earth and so stone insults me; its density inhibits me. I feel more secure with the wood." His hand lifted, fluttered, dropped back into his lap. "Trees." He said it almost as if it were a sacred word.

In the ensuing silence, I began to sweat despite the coldness. I knew what I at least was leading up to. I rubbed my palms down the fabric of my trousers. I cleared my throat.

"Morodor…."

"Yes." His eyes were half-shut as if he were close to sleep.

"I really do love Marissa."

"I know that." But there seemed no kindness in his voice.

I took a deep breath. "We had a row. She thinks I see you as a monster."

He did not move, his eyes did not open any wider, for which I was profoundly grateful. "In a world where so many possibilities exist, this is true. Yet I am also a man. And I am Marissa's brother. I am friend… foe; master… servant. It is all in the perception." Still he did not move. "What do *you* see, my friend?"

I wished he'd stop calling me that. I said nothing.

"If you are not truthful with me, I shall know it." His ruby lips seemed to curve upward at their corners. "Something else you may add to the new legend… if you choose to write about it."

"I've no wish to deceive you, Morodor. I'm merely trying to sort through my own feelings." I thought he nodded slightly.

"I confess… to finding your appearance… startling."

"I appreciate your candor."

"Oh, hell, I thought you were hideous."

"I see."

"You hate me now."

"Why should I hate you? Because you take the world view?"

"But that was at first. Already you've changed before my eyes. God knows I've tried but now I don't even find your appearance odd."

As if divining my thoughts, he said, "And this disturbs you."

"It does."

He nodded his head again. "Quite understandable. It will pass." He looked at me. "But you are afraid of that too."

"Yes," I said softly.

"Soon you shall meet my sister again."

I shook my head. "I don't understand."

"Of course you don't." Now his voice sounded softer. "Have patience, my friend. You are young enough still to rush headlong over the precipice merely to discover what is beyond it."

"That's why I came here."

"I know. But that time has passed. Now life has you by the throat and it will be a struggle to the end." His eyes flew open, seeming as hot as burning coals. "And who shall be the victor, my friend? When you have the answer to that, you shall understand it all."

I ate dinner alone that night. I had spent hours searching the castle for Marissa but it was as if she had vanished. Weary at last, I returned to the dining hall and availed myself of vast quantities of the hot food.

I was terrified and I thought that this would act as an inhibitor on my appetite. But, strangely, just the opposite was happening. I ate and ate as if this alone could assuage my fear.

It was Morodor I was terrified of, I knew that. But was it because I feared him or liked him?

Afterward, it was all I could do to drag myself up the staircase. I stumbled down the hallway and into bed without even removing my clothes.

I slept a deep dreamless sleep but when I opened my eyes it was still dark out. I turned over, about to return to sleep, when I heard a sound. I sat bolt upright, the short hairs at the back of my neck stiff and quivering.

Silence.

And out of the silence a weird, thin cry. I got off the bed about to open the door to the hallway when it came again and I turned. It was coming from outside in the blackness of the night.

I threw open the shutters wide and leaned out just as I had on my first night here. This time there was no mist. Stars shone intermittently through the gauzy cloud cover with a fierce cold light, blinking on and off as if they were silently appealing for help.

At first I saw nothing, hearing only the high soughing of the wind through the pines. Then, off to my left, so high up that I mistook it for another cloud, something moved.

I turned my head in that direction and saw a shape a good deal darker than a cloud. It blossomed with sickening speed, blacker even than the night. Wraith or dream, which was it? The noise of the flapping wings, leathery, horned and—what?—scabbed, conjured up in my mind the image of a giant bat.

Precariously, I leaned farther out, saw that it was heading for the open apertures of the cloud room. I hurled myself across the room and out the door, heading up the stairs in giant bounds.

Consequently, I was somewhat out of breath by the time I launched myself through the open doorway to the aerie and there found only Morodor.

He turned quickly from his apparent contemplation of the sky. "You should be asleep," he said. But something in his tone told me that I had been expected.

"Something woke me."

"Not a nightmare, I trust."

"A sound from the night. It was nothing to do with me."

"It is usually quite still here. What kind of sound?"

"It sounded like a scream… a terrible cry."

Morodor only stared at me, unblinking, until I was forced to go on.

"I went to the window and looked out. I… saw a shape I could not clearly identify; I heard the awful sound of bat wings."

"Oh," Morodor said, "that's quite impossible. We have none here, I've seen to that. Bats are boring, really. As with octopi, I'm afraid their ferocious reputation has been unjustly thrust upon them."

"Just what the hell did I see then?"

Morodor's hand lifted, fell, the arch of a great avian wing. "Whatever it was, it brought you up here."

"Then there *was* something there!" I said in triumph. "You admit it."

"I admit," said Morodor carefully, "that I wanted to see you. The fact is you are here."

"You and I," I said. "But what of Marissa? I have been looking for her all evening. I must see her."

"Do you think it wise to see her now, to… continue what has begun, knowing what you do about me?"

"But she is nothing like you. You two are the shadow and the light."

Morodor's gaze was unwavering. "Two sides of the coin, my friend. The same coin."

I was fed up with his oblique answers. "Perhaps," I said sharply, "it's just that you don't want me to see her. After all, I'm an outsider. I don't belong at Fuego del Aire. But if that's the case, let me warn you, I won't be balked!"

"That's the spirit!' His hand clenched into a fist. "Forget all about that which you saw from your bedroom window. It has nothing to do with you." His tone was mocking.

"A bird," I said uncertainly. "That's all it was."

"My friend," he said calmly, "there is no bird as large as the one you saw tonight."

And he reached out for the first time. I felt his chill touch as his long fingers gripped my shoulder with a power that made me wither inside. "Come," he commanded. "Over here at the windowledge."

I stood there, dazed with shock as he let go of me and leaped out into the night.

I screamed, reaching out to save him, thinking that, after all, his apparent melancholy signaled a wish to die. Then I saw his great ebon cape ballooning out like a sail, drawn upward by the crosscurrents and, for the first time, I saw what had been hidden beneath its voluminous folds.

I had thought he wore the thing as an affectation, because it was part of the legend. But now I understood. What care had he for legends? He wore the cape for practical reasons.

For now from under it spread a pair of the most extraordinary wings I had ever seen. They were glossy and pitch black, as far away from bat's wings as you could get. For one thing, they were feathered or at least covered in long silky strips that had the appearance of feathers. For another, they were as supple as a hummingbird's and quite as beautiful. And made even more so by the thick, muscular tendons by which they were attached to his back. It was like seeing the most beautifully developed torso: hard muscle tone combined with sleek line. And yet. And yet there was more, in the most literal sense, because more musculature was required in order for those massive wings to support the weight of the rest of the body.

Those wings! Sharply angled and hard, delicate as brushstrokes, they beat at the air like heroic engines. They were a magnificent creation, nothing less than a crowning achievement, an evolutionary pinnacle of the Creator.

But out of the wonder came terror and I thought: Marissa! My God! My God! He means to turn her into this. *El Amor Brujo.*

Without a word, I turned and bolted from the room. Taking the steps three at a time, I returned to the second floor and there found Marissa asleep in her own bed.

My heart beating like a triphammer, I brought a light close to her face. But no. An exhalation hissed from my mouth. There was no change. But still I feared Morodor and what he could do to her.

"Marissa!" I whispered urgently. "Marissa! Wake up!" I shook her but she would not waken. Hurling the light aside, I bent and scooped her up in my arms. Turning, I kicked the door wide and hurried down the stairs. Where I thought to go at that moment remains a mystery to me still. All I know was that I had to get Marissa away from that place.

The way to the disused scullery I knew and this was the route I took. Outside, the wind ruffled my hair but Marissa remained asleep.

I carried her through the field of tiger lilies and the woodbine, down the center aisle of the vast rose garden, to the verge of the labyrinth. Without thinking, I took her inside.

It was dark there. Darker than the night with the high ebon walls, textured like stucco, looming up on every side. I stumbled down the narrow pathways, turning now left or right at random until I knew that I was truly lost. But at least Morodor could not find us and I had with me this place's only key.

Panting, my muscles aching, I knelt on the grass and set Marissa down beside me. I looked around. All I could hear was the far-off whistle of the wind as if diminished by time. Even the booming surf was beyond hearing now.

I sat back and wiped my brow, staring down at that golden face, so innocent in repose, so shockingly beautiful. I could not allow—

Marissa's eyes opened and I helped her to sit up.

"What has happened?"

"I was awakened by a strange sound," I told her. "I saw your brother outside the castle. I thought at first it was a bird but when I went to find out, I saw him."

She looked at me but said nothing.

I gripped her shoulders. I had begun sweating again. "Marissa," I said hoarsely. "He was flying."

Her eyes brightened and she leaned toward me, kissed me hard on the lips. "Then it's happened! The time is here."

"Time," I echoed her stupidly. "Time for what?"

"For the change," she said as if talking to a slow-witted child.

"Yes," I said. "I suspected as much. That's why I've brought you into the labyrinth. We're safe here."

Her brows furrowed. "Safe? Safe from what?"

"From Morodor," I said desperately. "He can't touch you here. Now he cannot change you. You'll stay like this forever. You'll never have to look like him."

For the first time, I saw fright in her eyes. "I don't understand." She shivered. "Didn't he tell you?"

"Tell me what?" I hung on to her. "I ran out of there as soon as I saw him—"

"Oh no!" she cried. "It's all destroyed now. All destroyed!" She put her face in her hands, weeping bitterly.

"Marissa," I said softly, holding her close. "Please don't cry. I can't bear it. I've saved you. Why are you crying?"

She shook me off and stared wide-eyed at me. Even tear-streaked she was exquisitely beautiful. It did not matter that she was filled with pain. No emotion could alter those features. Not even, it seemed, time itself. Only Morodor, her haunted brother.

"He was supposed to tell you. To prepare you," she said between sobs. "Now it has all gone wrong."

"Marissa," I said, stroking her, "don't you know I love you? I've said it and I meant it. Nothing can change that. As soon as we get out of here, we'll—"

"Tell me, how deep is your love for me?" She was abruptly icily calm.

"How deep can any emotion be? I don't think it can be measured."

"Do not be so certain of that," she whispered, "until you've heard me out." She put her hands up before her body, steepling them as if they were a church's spire. "It is not Morodor who will work the change. It is you."

"Me?"

"And it has already begun."

My head was whirling and I put the flat of my hand against the ground as if to balance myself. "What are you saying?"

"The change comes only when we are in love and that love is returned. When we find a mate. The emotion and its reflection releases some chemical catalyst hidden deep inside our DNA helices which has remained dormant until triggered."

Her fingers twined and untwined anxiously. "This is not a... state that can be borne alone; it is far too lonely. So this is how it is handled. An imperative of nature."

"No!" I cried. "No no no! What you're telling me is impossible. It's madness!"

"It is life, and life only."

"Your life! Not mine!"

I stood up, stumbled, but I could not escape the gaze of her lambent eyes. I stared at her in mounting horror. "Liar!" I cried. "Where is Morodor's mate if this is true?"

"Away," she said calmly. "Feeding."

"My God!" I whirled away. "My God!" And slammed into the prickly wall of a hedge.

"Can love hold so much terror for you?" she asked. "You have a responsibility. To yourself as well as to me. Isn't that what love is?"

But I could no longer think clearly. I only knew that I must get away from them both. *The change has already begun,* she had said. I did not think that I wanted to see the fruits of that terrible metamorphosis. Not after having known her and loved her like this, all air and sunlight.

Two sides of the coin. Wasn't that what I had said to Morodor? How he must have laughed at that. Yes. Two sides. But of the same coin.

"Don't you see?" I heard her voice but could no longer see her. "You have nothing to fear. It is your destiny—*our* destiny, together."

Howling, I clawed my way from her, staggering, tripping as I ran through the labyrinth. My only coherent thought was to somehow get to the sea and then to hurl myself into its rocking embrace.

To swim. To swim. And if I were lucky I would at last be thrown up onto the soft sand of some beach far, far away.

But the night had come alive with shadows drenched in my own terror. And, like a mirror, they threw up to me the ugly writhing apparitions from the very bottom of my soul, thrusting them rudely into the light for me to view.

And above me the sound of.... .

Wings.

Even through the horrendous tattoo of the storm I can make out that sound. It's the same sound that reached down into my heavy slumber that night in Fuego del Aire and wrenched me awake. I did not know it then but I know it now.

But I know many things now that I did not then. I have had time to think. To think and to write. Sometimes they are one and the same. Like tonight.

Coming to terms. I have never been able to do that. I have never *wanted* to do that. My writing kept me fluid, moving in and out as the spirit took me. New York today, Capri the next. The world was my oyster.

But what of *me?*

The sound is louder now: that high keening whistle like the wind through the pines. It buzzes through my brain like a downed bottle of vintage champagne. I feel lightheaded but more than that. Light-bodied. Because I know. *I know.*

There is nothing but excitement inside me now. All the fear and the horror I felt in the labyrinth leached away from me. I have had six months to contemplate my destiny. Morodor was right: For each one, it is different. The doorway metamorphoses to suit the nature of the individual.

For me it is love. I denied that when Marissa confronted me with the process of her transmogrification. Such beauty! How could I lose that? I thought. It took me all of this time to understand that it was not her I feared losing but myself. Marissa will always be Marissa.

But what of me? Change is what we fear above all else and I am no different.

Was no different. I have already forgotten the golden creature of Fuego del Aire: she haunts my dreams still but I remember only her inner self. It is somehow like death, this acceptance of life. Perhaps this is where the legends began.

All around me the city sleeps on, safe and secure, wrapped in the arms of the myths of its own creation. Shhh! Don't bother to disturb it. No one would listen anyway.

The beating of the wings is very loud now, drowning out even the heavy pulsing of the rain. It reverberates in my mind like a heartbeat, dimming sight, taste, touch, smell. It dominates me in a way I thought only my writing could.

My shutters are open wide. I am drenched by the rain, buffeted by the chill wind. I am buoyed up by them both. I tremble at the thought. I love. *I love.* Those words a river of silver turning my bones hollow.

And now I lift my head to the place where last night the full moon rode calm and clear, a ghostly ideogram written upon the air, telling me that it is time for me to let go of all I know, to plunge inward toward the center of my heart. Six months have passed and it is time. *I know.* For now the enormous thrumming emanates from that spot. Beat-beat. Beat-beat. Beat-beat.

The heart-sound.

At last. There in the night, I see her face as she comes for me.

SUNRISE ON RUNNING WATER

by Barbara Hambly

Barbara Hambly is the bestselling author of dozens of books, including the vampire novels *Those Who Hunt the Night, Traveling with the Dead,* and *Renfield.* She has written many other novels as well, such as the popular *Dragonsbane* and its sequels, as well as media tie-in projects for *Star Trek* and *Star Wars,* and original non-genre novels of historical fiction, mystery, and romance. She is also the editor of the vampire anthology *Sisters of the Night.*

This story is about a vampire who is unfortunate enough to be on the *Titanic* on that ship's maiden and only voyage. "The genesis of the story was simple logistics: the *Titanic* loaded in dusk at Cherbourg, sank in darkness, and the rescue-boats made their appearance only minutes after full dawn," Hambly said. "If a vampire had been in one of the boats, he'd have been totally without powers—being upon running water (having shipped himself as Dracula did in a box of earth)—and would have been faced with the horrible choice of spontaneously auto-combusting at the first touch of sunlight, or dropping overboard in the deepest portion of the Atlantic ocean, to lie paralyzed upon the ocean floor—conscious and unable to either move or die—possibly forever."

The damn ship was supposed to be unsinkable.

Do you think I'd have set foot on the wretched tub if it weren't?

I embarked at Cherbourg for a number of reasons, chief among them being that the *Titanic* entered port from Southampton at sunset, and loaded in the dusk. I've never liked the thought of shipping myself in my coffin like a parcel, with the attendant risks of inquisitive customs-inspectors, moronic baggage-handlers, and all the tedious beforehand wrangling with a living accomplice who might or might not take the trouble to make sure one's coffin (or trunk—most of us prefer extra-large double trunks for travel) hasn't been installed in the hold lid-down under several thousand pounds of some imbecilic American dowager's frocks. Half the time one has to kill the accomplice anyway. Usually it's a pleasure.

"Are you sure you wish to do this, Napier?" inquired Simon, who had come down to the docks in a closed car to see me off. Being a century and a half older among the UnDead than I—one of the oldest in Europe, in fact—he is able to tolerate even more twilight, waking slightly earlier and, if need presses, can prolong his wakefulness for a short time into the morning hours, though of course only with adequate protection from the sun's destructive light. "You won't be able to hunt once you're on board, you know. The White Star Line keeps very accurate manifests of its passengers, even in third class. It isn't like the old days."

"Simon," I joked, and laid my hand on his gloved wrist, "you've been vampire too long. You're turning into a cautious old spook—what do they call them these days? A *fuddy-duddy*." I knew all about the passenger manifests. I'd studied them closely.

We'd hunted the night before, close to sunrise. I'd killed twice. I knew it was going to be a long voyage. Seven or eight days, from Cherbourg to New York. A span of time that bordered on dangerous, for such as we.

I hoped I wasn't one of those vampires who turn crazy after four or five days without a kill—who are so addicted to the pleasure of the death, as well as to its simple nourishment—that they hunt under conditions which are sure to bring them to the attention of authorities: for instance, among a limited and closely watched group of people. But quite frankly, I didn't know. Without a kill every few days, we start to lose our ability to deceive and ensorcel the minds of the living, a situation I had never permitted to occur.

This was the first time in a hundred and forty years that I'd traveled very far from London. The first time since I had become vampire in 1772 that I had crossed the ocean.

When the UnDead travel, they are horribly vulnerable. Money has always provided some protection in the form of bribes, patent locks, servants, and social pressure (Why do you think it's always Evil Lord So-and-So in the penny dreadfuls? It's astonishing how much interest bonds accumulate if allowed to mature for two centuries). But, as I was shortly to learn, accidents do happen. And the longer the journey, the more the chances accumulate that something will go fearfully wrong.

"There's a new world across the ocean, Simon," I said, making my voice grave. "Face it, Europe cannot go on as it is. War is going to break out. The Kaiser is practically jostling statesmen in doorways in the hopes of being challenged. You've seen the new weapons they have. Airships, incendiary bombs, cannon that can demolish a city from miles away. It's a wise man who knows when to make his break for safety."

Ninety-five hours later I was kicking myself for those words, but who knew?

Simon smiled, something he rarely does. "Perhaps you are correct, my friend. Be that so, I trust you will act in the nature of a scout, and send me word of the promised land. Now go, if not with God, at least with the blessing of an indifferent Fate, my Evil Lord…" He checked my papers for the name: "…Lord Sandridge." He put on his black-tinted spectacles and accompanied me to the barrier, where he added the subtle influence of his mind to mine in the task of getting my luggage through unchecked. I ascended the gangway, and from the rail saw him wave, a slim small form in dark gray, perhaps my only friend among the UnDead.

We are not, you understand, particularly pleasant company, even for one another.

Then I went down to the first-class luggage hold to make sure my coffin-trunk was both accessible and inconspicuous. Simon, I presume, returned home and slaughtered some unsuspecting immigrant en route for breakfast.

We put in at Queenstown on the Irish coast in the morning, before our final embarkation over the deep. It's always a damnable struggle to remain awake in one's coffin for even a short time after the sun is in the sky, but I was determined to make the effort, and it's a good thing I did. Shortly after I'd locked myself in for the day—we were still several hours from Queenstown at that point—I heard stealthy steps on the deck, and smelled the stink of a man's nervous sweat.

Of course someone had noticed the obsessive care I'd taken in bestowing my trunk, and had drawn the usual stupid conclusion that the living are prone to. Greedy sods. Skeleton keys rattled close to my head. I forced down both grogginess and the quick flash of panic in my breast—the hold was absolutely sheltered from any chance of penetration by sunlight—and fought to accumulate enough energy to act.

Get away from here, you stupid bastard! The living have no idea how commanding are the rhythms of vampire flesh; I felt as I had when in mortal life I'd gotten myself sodden-drunk on opium at the Hellfire Club. *This ship stinks with American millionaires and you're trying to rob the trunk of a mere Evil Lord?*

The outer lid opened, then the inner. I gazed up into a round unshaven face and brown eyes stretched huge with shock and fright.

I heaved myself up with what I hoped was a terrifying roar, wrenched the skeleton keys out of the young man's hand, and dropped back into the coffin, hauling the lid down after me and slamming shut its inner bolt. I heard outside a stifled gasping whimper, then heavy shoes hammering away across the deck and up the metal stairs.

I understand he abandoned ship at Queenstown and thus missed all subsequent events. A pity. Drowning was too good for the little swine.

It wasn't fear of robbery, however, that made me struggle to remain awake through the boarding-process at Queenstown, listening with a vampire's preternatural senses to every sound, every voice, every footfall in the ship around me. I had to know who was getting on the ship.

Because of course I had not been completely truthful with Simon as to my reasons for leaving England, or for embarking at Cherbourg for that matter. One never likes to admit when one has made a very foolish mistake.

Which brings me to the subject of Miss Alexandra Paxton.

I don't know under what name she boarded the *Titanic*. She knew, you see, that I'd be keeping an eye on the passenger lists, and would have changed my own travel plans had I suspected she was on board.

It is another truism of the more puerile examples of horror fiction that the victims of Evil Lord So-and-So or the wicked Countess Blankovsky are generally of the upper, or at worst the professional, classes. This is sheer foolishness, for these people keep track of one another, particularly in a small country like England. (Another motive for choosing America.)

Vampires for the most part live on the poor. We kill people whom no one will miss. Regrettably, these people tend to be dirty, smelly, undernourished, frequently gin-soaked, and conversationally uninteresting. And we *do* enjoy the chase, the cat-and-mouse game: the long slow luring, for days and weeks at a time.

Which is how I'd happened to meet, and court, and flirt with, and take to the opera, and eventually kill Miss Cynthia Engle, only a few days before she was to have wed Lionel Paxton.

Lionel and his sister had sounded like a remarkably boring pair when Miss Engle had told me about them at our clandestine meetings, edged with danger and champagne. I hadn't allowed for my lovely victim's craving for the melodramatic, which discounted her suitor's native shrewdness. In any case, after a train of events too complicated and messy to go into, I had been obliged to kill Lionel as well.

Alexandra had been dogging me ever since.

She came aboard at Queenstown, at the last possible moment. This was an unnecessary inconvenience on her part, since, as I've said, the sun was high in the sky and I couldn't have come up out of the hold even if I'd been awake. But I was aware of her, as I lay in the strange, clear awareness of the vampire sleep: smelled the distinctive vanilla and sandalwood of her dusting-powder, heard the sharp click of her stride on the decks.

And my heart sank.

There was no way I could kill her on board the *Titanic* without causing a tremendous fuss and possibly being locked in a cabin which might contain a window, which really *would* give the good Captain Smith something to write about in his log.

But *her* goal, on the other hand, was not survival. I knew from a previous encounter that she wore about her neck and wrists silver chains that would effectively sear my flesh should I come in contact with them, and carried a revolver loaded with silver bullets which she would not have the slightest hesitation about firing.

I also knew she was an extremely accurate shot.

I can't tell you exactly how the UnDead know when it's safe to emerge from their hiding-places. There are those of us who can step forth in lingering Nordic twilights with no more than frantic itching of the skin and a sense of intolerable panic, others whose flesh will auto-combust while the last morning stars are still visible in the sky. Our instinct in this matter is very strong, however—and those of us who lack it generally don't remain vampires very long.

I quit my coffin-trunk the minute I felt I could do so safely, around seven-thirty Thursday night, and ascended the several flights of steps past the squash court and through the seamen's and third-class quarters, down the long crew corridor known as "Scotland Road," and through a maze of passages and emergency ladders eventually reached my own B Deck stateroom in First-Class. The advertising for the *Titanic* had strongly implied that no first-class passenger need be even aware that such things as lesser mortals existed on the ship—another reason I'd chosen the vessel for my escape. Sharp-eyed stewards abounded to make sure those who paid for elevation above the Great Unwashed achieved it, but they, like most of the living (thank God) were prey to appearances. I was deep in conversation with the young and extremely pretty wife of an elderly American millionaire when the door of the stair from below opened and Miss Paxton slipped through.

She was clothed in a gown that must have cost her at least half of what her unfortunate brother had to leave: blue velvet with a bodice of cream-colored lace. A little aigret of blue gems and cream-colored feathers adorned the springy thickness of her mouse-brown hair. She was a tall girl, of the sort referred to by Americans as a "fine, strapping lass"; her jaw was long, her nose narrow, and her blue-gray eyes cool and daunting. She carried a blue velvet handbag and a trailing mass of lace shawl draped in such a fashion as to conceal her right hand and whatever might have been in it, and I fled like a rabbit before she even got a glimpse of me.

"That young person," I said to the head steward as I pressed a hundred dollars American into his hand, "is an impostor, a confidence trickster who has been harassing me for a number of months. I do not know under what pretext she will attempt to get near me nor do I wish to know. Only keep her away from me, or from any room that I am in, for the duration of this voyage. Understand?"

"Yes, sir. Certainly, Lord Sandridge."

As I slipped through into the dining saloon an American matron's Pekingese lunged at me in a fury of yapping. They really should keep those nasty little vermin locked up.

Of course that wasn't the end of Miss Paxton. Having guessed I'd be traveling first-class, she had invested God knows how much in a first-class wardrobe, so I was never sure I could avoid her merely by sticking to the A Deck promenades. Nor could I afford to keep to my stateroom during the night hours when I was up and about. She would, I guessed, be looking for me. By whispers overheard from the cabin stewards and maids—and believe me, a vampire can hear whispers through both locked doors and the conversation of American socialites—I guessed she had garnered allies among them by some tale of disinheritance, persecution, and attempted rape.

She stalked me most of that first night, for she had a constitution of iron; I was eventually reduced to donning an inconspicuous pair of trousers and a tweed jacket and hiding out on the third-class deck among the Irish.

At sunrise I retired to my coffin-trunk again, but I did not sleep with anything resembling peace.

All through that day and the next I heard her footfalls, smelled her blood and dusting-powder, in the dark of my dreams as she moved through the holds.

I dreamed about her.

And I dreamed about the sea.

As Mr. Stoker so obligingly pointed out in his book *Dracula*, we—the Un-Dead—cannot cross running water, except at the hour of astronomical midnight, and at the moment when the tide turns. He is quite right. It was more than dread that seized me, when I and my vampire master stood on the threshold of London Bridge and he ordered me across. It was a sickness, a weakness that paralyzed me, as if death itself were rising from the moving river below us like poisoned mist. My master laughed at me, the bastard, and we took a hackney cab across the river to hunt. In later years we'd take the Underground. He'd keep me talking, to school me to focus my mind against the panicky disorientation that flowing water produces, but like all vampires I hate the temporary loss of my powers over the minds of the living.

That was the thing that most worried me during that April voyage. That while I could cajole, or manipulate, or charm, or bribe those luscious-smelling, warm-blooded, rosily glowing morsels with whom I was surrounded every night, I couldn't alter their perceptions of me, or of what was going on around them.

I couldn't make them fall in love with me, so they'd be eager to do my bidding.

I couldn't lure them in a trance into nooks and corners of the hold, nor could I stand outside their cabin doors and tamper with their dreams.

Except for the fact that I retained some, though not all, of the superhuman strength of a vampire, I was to all intents and purposes human again, and indeed a trifle less so. The touch of silver would sear and blister my flesh; the touch of sunlight set me ablaze like a screaming torch.

And if this wretched young woman—who was as tall as I, and strong for a mortal—managed somehow to tip me overside, once in the water I would be paralyzed. I would sink like a stone, Simon had warned me, for the vampire state changes the UnDead flesh and we become physically perfect: all muscle, no fat.

Fat is what floats a body. (Simon knows things like that. He's made a scientific study of our state, and is fond of parading his knowledge, solicited or not.) Even in the sunless black of the deep ocean, I would not die, though crushed by the pressure of the water and frozen by its cold. Nor would I be able to move, save for the few minutes after midnight, or when the moon passed directly overhead and turned the tidal flow. Then the magnetism of the moving water would conquer again, and the sluggish currents push me where they would.

I would be conscious, Simon had assured me. (How the hell would *he* know?) I could think of no state closer to those described by Dante in his book of Hell.

And if Miss Paxton shot me with a silver bullet, even if it did not strike my heart, the logical place for her to dump my then-unresisting body would be into the drink.

All these things wove in and out of my dreams, with the clack of her shoe-heels on the storage-hold deck.

It was altogether not a pleasant voyage, even *before* 11:39 pm on the night of April 14.

I'd put in a brief appearance in the dining-room that Sunday night, enough so that no over-solicitous fellow-passenger or cabin steward would come inquiring for my health during the daytime. My story was that I was too sea-sick to eat. Most older vampires come to despise the stench of human food. I enjoyed it, and enjoyed too the spectacle of my table-mates shoveling away quantities of poached salmon with mousseline sauce, roast duckling, squabs and cress, asparagus vinaigrette, foie gras and éclairs—to say nothing of gallons of cognac and wines. The flavors linger for many hours in the blood, another reason, incidentally, that we prefer to sup when we can on the rich rather than the poor.

My custom on the *Titanic* was to spend most of my night moving from place to place in the first-class accommodation. I hadn't seen Miss Paxton anywhere on the A or B Decks since Thursday night, but twice, once in the Palm Court outside the First-Class Smoking Room and once in the corridor near my suite, I'd caught the lingering whiff of her dusting-powder. She was still finding her way up onto the First-Class Decks.

She could be waiting for me, gun in hand, around any corner

For that reason I was on the bow deck of the ship—as far forward on B Deck as I could get and a goodly distance from what might have been supposed to be a gentlemanly lurking-place in the First-Class Smoking Room—when I saw a dark mass of almost-clear ice lying straight in the path of the ship.

Being on open water hadn't affected my ability to see in the dark, any more than it affected my ability to detect Miss Paxton's cologne. The iceberg, though several miles away, would be almost invisible to human eyes, for there was no moon that night and the ocean lay flat calm, eliminating even the telltale froth of waves breaking around the dark ice's base. The previous night, in my ramblings around the ship, I'd heard the men discussing a warning of heavy pack ice received from an American steamer coming east, and around dinner-time the temperature of the air had dropped.

I worried no more than did anybody else on-board about the *Titanic* actually sinking, of course. Her hull was divided into water-tight compartments that could be closed at the touch of a button. But I did worry about there being a period of confusion in which one passenger—that is to say myself—might easily be incapacitated (say, with a silver bullet in the back) and dropped overboard without anyone seeing it happen. An investigation might later focus on Miss Paxton's purported vengefulness, but that wouldn't do *me* any good.

I descended to the C Deck well and down the stairs to the cargo-holds, where the "Scotland Road" corridor would lead me, eventually, to the Grand Staircase, and so up again eventually to the Boat Deck, at the rear of which lay the bridge.

And there she was, stepping out of the door of a servants' stair, blocking my path.

She said softly, "I have you, villain."

I said, just as softly, "Bugger."

She brought up her hand and I saw the gun in it. Down here surrounded by the crew quarters the sound of a shot would have brought everyone running, but at thirty feet it wasn't likely she'd miss. If she didn't get me through the heart the silver would cause such extraordinary damage as to both incapacitate me wherever it hit, and to cause great curiosity in the ship's doctor. On land I could have rushed her before she fired.

But I didn't trust my reflexes. I wheeled and plunged for the transverse passageway that would take me—I hoped—down the smaller crew corridor, and so to another stairway up. Her heels clattered in pursuit as I darted around the corner, fled down the brightly lighted white tunnel. I debated for a moment simply stepping into the shadow beside the nearest stairway and taking her as she came past—this late at night it would be easy to drop *her*, unconscious (or dead—I hadn't fed in four days and I was ravenous), over the side.

But she had the gun. And I knew from the past that she was a lusty screamer. I darted to the nearest downward stairway, and found myself lost in the mazes around the squash court and the quarters of lesser crew on F Deck. I could hear her behind me still, though farther off, it seemed. It was astonishing how those metal corridors re-echoed and tangled sound, and down here the thumping of the engines confused even the uncanny hearing of the UnDead. The main stairway led up through the third-class dining-hall but that, I knew, would be the logical place for her to cut me off. There was another, smaller stair by the Turkish Bath, and that's where I was, halfway up, when a shuddering impact made the whole ship tremble and knocked me, reeling, off my feet and nearly to the bottom of the steps again.

I don't think I doubted for an instant that we'd hit that wretched iceberg.

Only a human could have missed it that long. It towered above the ship, for Heaven's sake, glistening but dark: it was almost clear ice, as I'd seen, not the powdery white of ice that's been exposed to the air. I understand (again, from Simon, who wasted not a moment after I finally reached London again in telling me, *I told you so*) that when the upper sides of icebergs melt sufficiently to alter their balance they sometimes flip over, exposing faces that are far less reflective, especially on a moonless night. Even so...

I clung for a moment to the stair-rail, listening. The lights still blazed brightly, and after the first long, grinding jar there was no further shaking. But as I stretched my senses out—out and down, to the decks below me—I could hear the dim confusion of men's voices, the clatter of frenzied activity.

And the pounding roar of water shooting into the ship as if forced from a fire-hose.

I thought, *Damn it, if it floods the First-Class luggage hold I'm sunk.* I blush to say that was the very expression that formed itself in my mind, though at the time I thought only in terms of my light-proof double trunk and the two handsome windows in my stateroom. I had no idea what the White Star Line procedure was for keeping track of passengers and luggage on a disabled ship until another vessel could come alongside to take everyone off, but there was no guarantee that any of that would happen until after daylight.

On the other hand, I thought, depending on how much confusion there was, it would now be very easy to dispose of Miss Paxton without anyone being the wiser.

Trunk first.

First-Class luggage was on G Deck, at the bow. The gangways were sufficiently wide to get the trunk up at least as far as the C Deck cargo well. I was striding forward along a corridor still largely deserted—crewmembers sleep whenever they can, the lazy bastards—when the heavy beat of the engines ceased.

Silence and utter stillness, for the first time since we'd lain at Queenstown, filled the ship, seeming louder than any thunder.

I wasn't the only one to find the silence more disturbing than impact with thousands of tons of ice. Doors began opening along the corridor, men and women—most of them young and all of them tousled from sleep—emerged. "What is it?" "Why're we stopped?"

"Hit an iceberg," I said. I pulled a roll of banknotes from the pocket of my tuxedo jacket, and added, "I'll need assistance getting my trunk from the First-Class hold. It contains papers that I cannot risk having soaked." I could have carried the trunk by myself, of course, but if seen doing so I could kiss good-by any chance of remaining unnoticed, unquestioned, or uninvestigated for the rest of the trip.

"I'm sorry, Lord Sandridge." Fourth Officer Boxhall appeared behind me, uniformed and worried-looking. "We may need the crew to stand by and help with the mailroom, if the water comes up onto the Orlop Deck. If you'll return to your stateroom, I'll have a man come there the moment we know one can be spared. At the moment there doesn't seem to be much damage, but we should know more within half-an-hour."

I could have told him there was water pouring into what sounded like several of the water-tight compartments down below, but reasoned he'd have the truth very shortly. One of the stewardesses was looking closely at me, a thick-chinned, fair-haired Yorkshire girl whom I'd seen more than once in conversation with Miss Paxton. She moved off swiftly down the corridor, slipping between the growing gaggles of crewmen. So much for any hope of waiting in my stateroom.

Still, I thought, midnight was only ten minutes off. If there were crewmen hauling sacks of mail out of the way of floodwaters in the First-Class cargo hold, I'd be able to divert their attention from me while I rescued the trunk myself.

Or killed Miss Paxton.

And by long before sunrise, I reflected as I strode toward the stair, I'd know whether I was going on another vessel, or staying hidden in some sun-proof, locked nook on the *Titanic* while repairs were effected. With any luck I'd be able to get an immigrant or two in the confusion as well.

Miss Paxton would be up on B Deck, headed for my stateroom. On C Deck some of the Swedes and Armenians from steerage were still laughing and playing with chunks of the ice that had been scraped off the iceberg. On the B Deck promenade a few people were prowling about, dressed in their coats and their thickest sweaters; a young man in evening-clothes showed me a piece of ice, then dropped it in his highball: "Saw the thing go past. Bloody amazing!"

"You don't think there's been any damage to the ship?" asked an elderly lady, doddering by on the arm of her superannuated spouse.

"Good Lord, no. God himself couldn't sink this ship."

Simon would have crossed himself, vampire or no.

If I ever find myself in a similar situation again—God forbid!—I will do so, too.

By this time I realized—and the UnDead are more sensitive to such matters than the living—that the deck under my feet was just slightly out of true. With all that water in the compartments below that didn't surprise or upset me. I climbed to the Marconi shack on the Boat Deck—the room where the telegraphers sat pecking frantically at their electric keys. "We've sent word to the *Californian*, but she hasn't replied," said one of the young men, when I asked. "Probably turned off his set and went to bed. Bastard nearly blew my ears off earlier tonight, when I was trying to deal with the passenger messages. The *Carpathian's* about sixty miles south of us. She'll be here in four or five hours, to take the passengers off."

Four hours would put its arrival in darkness, I reflected as I made my way toward my own stateroom and what I hoped would be a rendezvous with my pursuer. Five hours, at dawn.

Which meant that the moment Miss Paxton was safely out of the way I would have to get that trunk, one way or another. And be where I could get into it come first light. Never, I vowed, would I travel again if I could help it: it was just one damn complication after another.

I could scent Miss Paxton's dusting-powder as I entered the corridor leading to my stateroom. The scent was strong, but she was nowhere in sight. In the other cabins I heard the murmur of voices—a woman complained about having to go out on deck in the cold, which was prodigious—but there was certainly neither panic nor concern. I took a few steps along the corridor, listening, sniffing.

She was in my stateroom.

Of course. She'd got the maid to let her in.

This would be easier than I'd thought.

I closed my eyes as midnight moved into the icy heavens overhead. Reached out my mind to hers, where she waited in the comfortable darkness of my room. Laid on her mind, one by one, the fragile veils of sleep.

Gently, gently… I'd done this to her before, back in London, and had to be all the more subtle because she knew what it felt like, and would resist if she recognized the sensations again. But she was tired from prowling the ship by night in quest of a clear shot at me, by day in search of my trunk. I could feel her slipping into dream. I murmured to her in the voice of the River Cher, beside which she and her idiot brother Lionel had played as children; whispered to her as the breeze had whispered among the willow-leaves on its bank.

Sleep… sleep… you're home and safe. Your parents are watching over you, no harm can come to you….

One has only about ten minutes, at the very outside, at those turning-hours of noon and midnight, when the positions of earth and stars (as Simon has explained it to me) are strong enough to counterbalance the terrible influence of the tides. It was excruciating, keeping still, concentrating my thoughts on those of the young woman in my stateroom. Feeling those seconds of power tick away, calculating how many I'd need to stride down the hall, open the door, and bury my fangs in her neck…

An image I had to keep stringently from my thoughts while my mind whispered to hers. *Sleep—rest—you'll sleep much easier if you take off those itchy heavy silver chains around your neck. It's safe to do so—you're safe… They're so heavy and annoying….*

I felt her fumble sleepily with her collar-buttons (Why do women persist in wearing garments that button up the back?). Saw her in the eyes of my heart, head pillowed on velvety hair half-unbound on the leather of the armchair. Fingers groping clumsily at her throat… *Sleep—*

The catch was large, solid, and complicated. Bugger. She must have chosen it so, knowing it wasn't easy to undo in half-sleep or trance. Damn, how many minutes—how many seconds—left…?

Gentle, gentle, Lionel is asking for the necklaces. *You have to take them off to give them to him—*

I heard her whisper in her heart, *Lionel,* and tears trickled down her face. In her dreams she saw her brother, plump and fatuous as he'd been in life, holding out his hand to her. *Got to have silver to wear to my wedding, old girl. Not legal if the groom's not wearing silver. New rules.*

She let the revolver slide from her fingers, brought up both hands. The catch gave, silver links sliding down her breasts. Seconds left, but enough—

I strode forward down the corridor and that God-cursed, miserable, miniaturized hair-farm of an American matron's Pekingese threw itself out of the door of a nearby stateroom and fastened his teeth in my ankle. The teeth of such a creature would hardly imperil a soggy toast-point, much less a vampire in full pursuit of undefended prey, but the UnDead are as likely as any other subject of Lord Gravity to trip if their feet come in contact with a ten-pound hairball mid-stride. I went sprawling, and although I caught myself as a cat does, with preternatural speed, the damage was done. The Peke braced his tiny feet and let out a salvo of barks, his mistress appeared in the stateroom door just as I was readying a kick that would have caved in the little abortion's skull, and shrieked at me, "How *dare* you, sir! Come to mummy, Sun!"

And the next second Miss Paxton, collar unbuttoned, hair tumbling over her shoulders, and gun in hand, was in the door of my stateroom, taking aim at a distance of six feet…

And midnight was over.

I fled. Mrs. Harper (I think that was her name), straightening up with her struggling hell-hound in her arms, effectively blocked the corridor for the instant that it took me to get out of the line of fire, and I pelted down the staircase, into the nearest corridor, with Miss Paxton like a silent fury at my heels.

There were people in the corridors now, my fellow-passengers in every imaginable variation of pyjamas, sweaters, coats, bath-robes, and life-jackets, all of them carping about having to go out on the boat-decks and all of them impeding Miss Paxton from taking aim at me—and me from getting far enough ahead to lose her. I strode, dodged, slithered bow-wards along the B Deck corridor, making for the cargo-well that would give me swift access to the bowels of the ship. The lights were still on, but if they went out—as I thought they must, with the holds flooding—she would surely be mine.

The deck was definitely sloped underfoot when I reached "Scotland Road" on D Deck again, now milling with crewmen. At the head of the spiral stair going down to E and F, I stopped short with a jolt of sickened shock. Beneath me a pit of green water churned, eerily illuminated by the lights that still burned on the levels below.

That water looked awfully *high*.

The gun cracked behind me and I spun; there were still crewmen in the corridor but none were between me and the emergency-ladder from which Miss Paxton had just emerged and not a single one attempted to stop her. I don't think the mad bitch would have cared if they had. Maybe her tales of my perfidy had spread widely among the crew: maybe they had a better idea of what was going on below our feet than the passengers or I did. The fact remained that she had a gun and a clear shot and I knew that even a glancing wound from it could prove fatal. I hadn't drunk the blood of thousands of grimy peasants, factory-workers, prostitutes and street-urchins over the course of fourteen decades to let myself be put out of the way by an enraged middle-class virago.

I did the only thing possible.

As she fired I fell against the rail, tipped over it, and dropped straight down into that seething jade-green seawater hell.

It was every bit as cold as I'd been led to expect.

My mind seemed to fracture, to go numb. I screamed, and my mouth and lungs flooded with water—it's a damn good thing I'd quit breathing many years previously. I remember staring up through the green water and seeing Alexandra Paxton looking down at me, gun still in her hand.

I was conscious, but I felt my ability to act at all—to summon my limbs to obey my disoriented mind—bleeding out of me like gore from a severed femoral artery. I couldn't move until she left, until she was convinced that I was dead, and she seemed to stand there—gloating, I expect, the miserable cow!—forever.

Then she spit at me, and turned away.

It took what felt like minutes of slow, clumsy thrashing before I could thrust myself to the door into what I think was F Deck. My fingers were like cricket bats and I don't know how long I spent simply trying to get the door open. My brain was like a cricket bat, too, trying to fish a single wet noodle of orientation—where the hell was the stairway up to E Deck?—from the swirling maelstrom of horror, shock, terrifying weakness and nightmare panic.

And I knew with blinding certainty that, watertight compartments be damned, the ship was going down.

Voices, impossibly distant, came to me from all parts of the ship.

Voices that said, "She's sinking by the head."

Voices that said, "You must get in the boat, Mary. I shall follow later."

Voices that said, "Get back there, you. Women and children first."

Nearer, feet thudded amid a frightened yammering of Swedish, Gaelic, Arabic, Japanese: third-class passengers trying to find their way up the maze of stairways to the decks above. Crewmen shouted at them to go back, to stay in their cabins, they'd be called when it was time for them to get in the lifeboats. But I'd gone to sea, God help me, as a living man all those years ago, and I knew jolly well how many people could fit into a boat the size of the mere sixteen that were in *Titanic*'s davits.

I had to get up to the decks before they started letting those foreign swine take up boat-space that I'd paid for with my first-class ticket. And I had to get there before the foreign swine realized that there wasn't going to be enough room for them in the boats, and took matters out of the crew's hands and into their own dirty paws.

The struggle was literally Hellish: I refer specifically to the Fifth Circle of Dante's Hell, where the Sullen bubble in eternal stasis in the mud beneath the waters of the River Styx. I can only assume that the Styx is warmer than the Atlantic Ocean in mid-April. Water at a temperature of thirty degrees has exactly the same effect on the UnDead as it would on the living, only, of course, more prolonged, since the living wouldn't survive more than a few minutes even were breathing not an issue. Beyond the paralyzing cold, there was the sheer hammering disorientation of ocean water—living water—itself. For long periods I became simply immobilized, my brain shrieking, fighting to make a hand move, a foot thrust against the metal walls that hemmed me in; it was like trying to remain awake in the final extremities of exhaustion. I'd come out of it, twist and thrash and wrench myself to push along a foot or so, then sink back into an inactivity I couldn't break no matter how frantically I tried.

Those periods got longer, the moments of clumsy, horrified lucidity shorter and shorter. And around me I could feel the walls, the hull, the decking tilting, tilting, as the weight of the water in the bow doubled and quadrupled and quintupled, and I hung there helpless, aware of the sheer, horrifying *depth* of the ocean below.

I wonder I didn't go mad. Not with fear that I would die when that final hideous tipping-point was at last reached and the ship began her lightless plunge to the bottom: with the appalling certainty that *I would not and could not.*

Ever.

Whether because the water conducted sound, or for some other cause, as I spastically, intermittently, agonizingly crept and pushed my way toward the stairways and survival, I was completely aware of everything that was passing on the decks above. Even above the cheerful ragtime being pumped out by the ship's band, I could hear with nightmarish clarity every conversation, every footfall, every creak of the tackle as the crew loaded up the lifeboats and lowered them to the surface of the sea far below. The ship's officers kept saying *Women and children first* and the women and children—brainless cretins!—kept finding reasons to remain on the main vessel where it was warm. A number of men got into those early boats unchallenged, since there were so many women who weren't interested: I learned later one of them was sent off with only twelve people in it. The miserable Mrs. Harper got off accompanied not only by her husband but by her wretched Pekingese.

But around me the walls changed their angle, with what to me seemed to be fearful speed, until even those first-class idiots on deck (I use the term advisedly) realized there was something greatly wrong. By the time I dragged myself at last, shaking and dripping, up a maintenance ladder onto D Deck, and stumbled toward an unguarded crew ladder to go above, the bow of the ship was underwater and all but four of the boats were gone.

I won't go into a detailed description of the behavior of the some two thousand men and women in competition for the approximately one hundred and sixty available passes out of the jaws of death. Anyone who has lived for close to two centuries in a major city like London has had ample occasion to view the behavior of mobs, and the passengers of the *Titanic* actually acquitted themselves fairly mildly, all things considered. Yes, the crew members had to form a cordon around one boat and threaten to shoot any non-lady who tried to board; yes, the men did rush another of the boats (I was too far back in the mob to get on, damn those other selfish bastards to hell).

Astonishingly, the lights remained on and the band continued to play, giving an eerie disjointedness to the scene but somehow, I think, keeping everyone just on the human side of total panic. God knows what it would have been like in darkness, with no sound but the groaning of the ship's overstrained armature readying itself to snap. I had long since given up any thought of getting my trunk to safety, or of Alexandra Paxton. I learned much later she'd gone straight from shooting me (as she thought) to the Boat Deck, and had gotten off fairly early in the proceedings. She returned to England and lived, I regret to say, happily ever after.

The bitch.

For my part, my only thought was getting into a boat and trusting to luck that the rescue ship would arrive while night still lay upon the ocean. The richest people in the world were aboard the *Titanic*, for God's sake! Other vessels must be racing one another to pick them up.

Mustn't they?

In addition to the regular lifeboats the *Titanic* carried four canvas collapsible boats, and two of these were assembled and put in the lifeboat davits as the last of the wooden boats was lowered away. The other two, lashed uselessly to the top of the officers' quarters, were too tangled up in rope to be dragged to the side, but men swarmed over them, trying to get them into shape to be floated off if and when, God help us all, the ship went under.

And under she would go. I knew it, could hear with the hyper-acute senses of the UnDead the snapping creak of her skeleton cracking under the weight of water pulling her down, and the whole stern end of her—God knows how many tons!—that was by this time lifted completely clear of the glass-smooth, obsidian ocean. The lights were beginning to glow red as the generators began to fail. As I fought my way through the mob to one of the collapsibles, a dapper little gentleman who'd been helping with the ropes turned to the officer in charge and said, "I'm going aboard." When the officer—who'd been fighting off would-be male boarders for some minutes—opened his mouth to protest, the dapper gentleman said, "I'm Bruce Ismay; President of the White Star Line." He stepped into the boat.

As it swung clear of the deck I reached the rail: *You may be President of the White Star Line but if there's room for you, there's room for me...*

And I froze. I could have batted aside any of the officers who tried to prevent me, and the leap would have been nothing. For one moment, just before the men began to lower, less than two feet separated the boat's gunwale from the rail; with a vampire's altered muscle and inhuman strength, I've cleared gaps four and five times that with ease.

Two feet of space, with running water not all that far below.

Had I been assured of the return of my immortal soul by so doing, I could not have made that jump.

And by the time I fought my way to the place where the other serviceable collapsible was being lowered, it was away. A number of passengers jumped at this point, when the boats were close enough to have picked them up. If you walked forward, it wasn't all that far to the surface of the sea. I made my way to the roof of the officers' quarters and joined the struggle to get the remaining two collapsibles unraveled from the snarl of ropes, get their canvas sides put up (the designer of the damned things is another on the long list of persons I hope will rot in hell), and get them to the rails: if one fell upside-down (which it did) it was too heavy and too clumsy to be righted. I could feel the angle of the deck steepening, could tell by the dark water's advance that the ship was being pulled forward and down.

At 2:15 the bridge went under. A rolling wave of black water swept over the roof of the officers' quarters and floated the right-side-up collapsible free. I scrambled aboard, fighting and clawing the army of other men trying to do the same thing; glancing back I could see the *Titanic*'s stern, swarming with humanity like ants on a floating branch, lift high out of the ocean. It was a fearful sight. Voices were screaming all around me and if I'd ever had a doubt that a vampire could pray, and pray sincerely, it was put to rest in that moment. I shrieked God's name with the best of them as I threw myself into that miserable canvas tub and we oared away, gasping, from the great ship as she snapped in half—dear God, with what a sound!—and her stern crashed back, the wave propelling our boat on its way.

I saw her lights beneath the water as the bow pulled down, dragging the stern after it. The stern rose straight up for a moment, venting steam at every orifice and wreathed in the despairing wails of those wretches still trapped aboard; pointed briefly like a stumpy accusing finger at the beacon-cold blazons of the icy stars...

...then sank.

With my trunk aboard.

And no rescue-boat in sight.

It was twenty minutes after two in the morning. Dawn in the North Atlantic comes, in mid-April, at roughly five a.m.; first light about a half-hour before that.

Dear God, was all I could think. *Dear God.*

The men—mostly crewmen—around me in the boat were praying, but I was at something of a loss for words. What I really wanted was for a light-proof, unsinkable coffin to drop down out of the heavens so I could go on killing people and drinking their blood for another few centuries. Even in my extremity, I didn't think God would answer that one.

So I waited.

The collapsible's sides never had been properly put up. We started shipping water almost immediately and barely dared stir at the oars, for fear of altering the boat's precarious balance and sending us all down into those black miles of abyss. This consideration at least kept the men in the boat from rowing back to pick up swimmers, whose voices hung over the water like the humming of insects on a summer night. Some sixteen hundred people went into the sub-freezing water that night—I'm told most of the other boats, even those lightly laden, held off for fear of being swamped. One American woman tried to organize the other ladies in her boat to stage a rescue at this point and was roundly snubbed: so much for the tender-heartedness of the fair sex.

The cries subsided after twenty minutes or so. The living don't last long, in water that cold.

Then we could only wait, in fear perhaps more excruciating than we'd left behind us on the *Titanic*, for the canvas boat to slowly fill with water, and sink away beneath our feet.

Or in my case, for the earth to turn, and the sun to rise, and my flesh to spontaneously ignite in unquenchable fire.

It was small consolation to reflect that such an event would briefly keep my fellow passengers warm and, one hoped, would take their minds off their own upcoming immersion.

Should the boat sink before I burst into flames, I found myself thinking, my best chance would be to guide myself, as best I could, toward the *Titanic* wreck. The short periods of volition permitted by even a long succession of noons and midnights would never be enough to counteract the movement of the slow, deep-flowing ocean currents. Staying in the wreck itself would be my best and only chance.

I could hear Simon's voice in my mind, speculating about how divers were already learning to search for ships foundered in shallow waters, for the sunken treasures of the Spanish Main and the ancient Mediterranean. *In time I fancy they shall discover even Atlantis, or at the very least whatever galleons went down chock-full of treasure in mid-ocean. You can be sure that whatever science can invent, treasure-hunters will not be long in adapting to their greed.*

The richest men and women in the world had been my fellow passengers. Very few of them stuffed their jewels in their pockets before getting into the lifeboats. Of course the treasure-hunters would come, as soon as science made it possible for them to do so.

And even as I thought this, I sent up the feeblest of human prayers: *Please, God, no....*

As if He'd listen.

At 3:30, far off to the southeast, a flicker of white light pierced the blackness, followed by a cannon's distant boom.

A slight breeze had come up, making the ocean choppy and the air yet more bitterly cold. Tiny as a nail-clipping, a new moon hung over the eastern horizon. Men had begun to fall off the collapsible, which was now almost up to its gunwales in seawater that hovered right around the temperature of ice: fall silently, numb, dead within sight of salvation. I could see all around us the ocean filled with the pale-gleaming blobs of what the sailors called "trash" and "growlers," miniature icebergs the size of motorcars or single-story houses, ghostly in the starlight. Among them, or west and south in the clearer water, I could make out the dark shapes of the other lifeboats. Could hear the voices of the passengers in them, tiny occasional drops of sound, like single crickets in the night.

It wanted but an hour till first light. I think I would have wept, had it been possible for vampires to shed tears.

The sky was staining gray when one of the lifeboats was sighted, slowly inching toward us. How far we'd drifted I don't know; I'd sunk into a lethargy of horror, watching the slow growing of the light. It might have been the effect of the water in the boat, which was up to our knees by this time; there were only a dozen men left, and a woman from third class. I could barely move my head to follow the lifeboat's agonizingly lentitudinous approach.

Everything seemed to have slowed to the gluey pace of a helpless dream. It was as if time itself were slowly jelling to immobility with the cold. Far across the water—perhaps a mile or two, in the midst of the floating ice—loomed the dark bulk of a small freighter. All around it the lifeboats were creeping inward, some from miles away, like nearly frozen insects painfully dragging themselves toward the jam-pot that is the Heaven of their tiny lives.

And I could see that, even if the lifeboat reached us—and each second it seemed that we'd go down under their very noses—there was no way under God's pitiless sky that it would reach the freighter before full light.

Don't make me do this, God. Don't make me…

Like the laughter of God, light flushed up into the gray sky, turning all the icebergs to silver, the water to sapphire of incredible hardness and depth. At the same time my frozen flesh was suffused with unbearable heat, my skin itching, writhing… my flesh readying to burst into flame.

Hiding in a boiler on the wreck, curled in some corner of the grand staircase or the Palm Court Lounge, I would have only to wait for the treasure-hunters to come.

The cold and darkness would only *seem* eternal.

Would hope in those circumstances be more cruel than the comfort of despair?

I closed my eyes, tipped myself backward over the side.

I was about to find out.

HIT

by Bruce McAllister

Bruce McAllister is the author of the novels *Dream Baby* and *Humanity Prime* and more than fifty short stories. His short work has been collected in *The Girl Who Loved Animals and Other Stories*, and has appeared in numerous anthologies, including the prestigious *Best American Short Stories* series. His stories have also been nominated for both the Hugo and Nebula awards. He's currently working on two "quiet fantasy" novels, both of which incorporate vampire elements.

McAllister says that he suspects vampire stories are Christianity flipped to its dark alter-self. "In communion we do drink blood, and we're promised immortality, so in one sense vampirism is communion and immortality but without God's grace," he said. "So that plays a role in the attraction, as does the neo-Romantic gothic feel of it."

This story, which first appeared in the online magazine *Aeon*, is inspired by classic and contemporary hard-boiled fiction. But while the characters of Dashiell Hammett and Robert Parker may have found themselves in similar situations, none of them ever had a client or a mark quite like this…

I'm given the assignment by an angel—I mean that, an angel—one wearing a high-end Armani suit with an Ermenegildo Zegna tie. A loud red one. Why red? To project confidence? Hell, I don't know. I'm having lunch at Parlami's, a mediocre bistro on Melrose where I met my first ex, when in he walks with what looks like a musical instrument case—French horn or tiny tuba, I'm thinking—and sits down. We do the usual disbelief dialogue from the movies: He announces he's an angel. I say, "You're kidding." He says, "No. Really." I ask for proof. He says, "Look at my eyes," and I do. His pupils are missing. "So?" I say. "That's easy with contacts." So he makes the butter melt on the plate just by looking at it, and I say, "Any demon could do that." He says, "Sure, but let's cut the bullshit, Anthony. God's got something He wants you to do, and if you'll take the job, He'll forgive everything." I shrug and tell him, "Okay, okay. I believe. Now what?" Everyone wants to be forgiven, and it's already sounding like any other contract.

  He reaches for the case, opens it right there (no one's watching—not even the two undercover narcs—the angel makes sure of that) and hands it to me. It's got a brand-new crossbow in it. Then he tells me what I need to do to be forgiven.

"God wants you to kill the oldest vampire."

"Why?" I ask and can see him fight to keep those pupilless eyes from rolling. Even angels feel boredom, contempt, things like that, I'm thinking, and that makes it all that more convincing.

"Because *He* can't do it."

"And why is that?" I'm getting braver. Maybe they *do* need me. I'm good—one of the three best repairmen west of Vegas, just like my sainted dad was—and maybe guys who say *yes* to things like this aren't all that common.

"Because the fellow—the oldest bloodsucker—is the son of...well, you know..."

"No, I don't."

"Does 'The Prince of Lies' ring a bell?"

"Oh." I'm quiet for a second. Then I get it. It's like the mob and the police back in my uncle's day in Jersey. You don't take out the don because then maybe they take out your chief.

I ask him if this is the reasoning.

The contempt drops a notch, but holds. "No, but close enough."

"And where do I do it?"

"The Vatican."

"The Holy City?"

"Yes."

"Big place, but doesn't have to be tricky." I'd killed men with a wide range of appliance—the angel knew that—and suddenly this wasn't sounding any trickier. Crossbow. Composite frame, wooden arrows—darts—whatever they're called. One to the heart. I'd seen enough movies and TV.

"Well," he says, "maybe. But most of the Jesuits there are vampires too."

"Oh."

"That's the bad news. The good news is they're pissed at him—the oldest vampire, I mean. They think he wants to turn mortal. He's taken up with some twenty-eight-year-old *bambina* who knows almost as many languages as he does—a Vatican interpreter—and they've got this place in Siena—Tuscany, no less—and he hasn't bitten her, and it's been making the Brothers, his great-great-great-grandchildren, nervous for about a month now. Handle it right and she just might help you even if they don't."

"You serious?"

"Yes."

"Why?"

"Because she wants to be one, too—she's very Euro-goth—you know the type—and he just won't bite her."

No, I don't know the type, but I say, "She's that vindictive?"

"What woman isn't?"

This sounds awfully sexist for an angel, but I don't argue. Maybe angels get dumped too.

"Does he really?" I ask.

"Does he really what?"

"Want to be mortal again."

"He never was mortal."

"He was born that way?"

The eyes—which suddenly have pupils now, majorly dark blue ones—are starting to roll again. "What do *you* think? Son of You Know Who—who's not exactly happy with the traditional wine and wafer thing, but likes the idea of blood and immortality."

"Makes sense," I say, eyeing the narcs, who are eyeing two Fairfax High girls, "but why does God need someone to kill him if he wants to flip?"

He takes a breath. *What an idiot*, the pupils say. "Remember when China tried to give Taiwan a pair of pandas?"

I'm impressed. This guy's up on earthly news. "No."

"Taiwan couldn't take them."

"Why not?"

He takes another breath and I hear him counting to ten.

"Okay, okay," I say. "I get it. If they took the pandas, they were in bed with China. They'd have to make nice with them. You accept cute cuddly creatures from someone and it looks like love, right?"

"Basically."

"If You Know Who's son flips—goes mortal—God has to accept him."

"Right."

"And that throws everything off. No balance. No order. Chaos and eventually, well, Hell?"

The angel nods, grateful, I can tell, that I'm no stupider than I am.

I think for a moment.

"How many arrows do I get?"

I think he'll laugh, but he doesn't.

"Three"

"*Three?*" I don't like the feeling suddenly. It's like some Bible story where the guy gets screwed so that God can make some point about fatherly love or other form of sacrifice. Nice for God's message. Bad for the guy.

"It's a holy number," he adds.

"I get that," I say, "but I don't think so. Not three."

"That's all you get."

"What makes you think three will do it—even if they're all heart shots?"

"You only need one."

The bad feeling jumps a notch.

"Why?"

He looks at me and blinks. Then nods. "Well, each has a point made from a piece of the Cross, Mr. Pagano. We were lucky to get even that much. It's hidden under three floors and four tons of tile in Jerusalem, you know."

"What is?"

"The Cross. You know which one."

I blink. "Right. That's the last thing he needs in the heart."

"Right."

"So all I've got to do is hit the right spot."

"Yes."

"Which means I need practice. How much time do I have?"

"A week."

I take a breath. "I'm assuming you—and He—know a few good crossbow schools, ones with weekly rates."

"We've got special tutors for that."

I'm afraid to ask. "And what do these tutors usually do?"

"Kill vampires."

"And you need *me* when you've got a team of them?"

"He'd spot them a mile away. They're his kids, you might say. He's been around 2000 years and he's had kids and his kids have had kids—in the way that they have them—you know, the biting and sucking thing—and they can sense each other a mile away. These kids—the ones working for us—are ones who've come over. Know what I mean?"

"And they weren't enough to throw off the—the 'balance.'"

Now he laughs. "No, they're little fish. Know what I mean?"

I don't really, but I nod. He's beginning to sound like my other uncle—Gian Felice—the one from Teaneck, the one with adenoids. *Know what I mean?*

I go home to my overpriced stucco shack in Sherman Oaks and to my girlfriend, who's got cheekbones like a runway model and lips that make men beg, but wears enough lipstick to stop a truck, and in any case is sick and tired of what I do for a living and probably has a right to be. I should know something besides killing people, even if they're people the police don't mind having dead and I'm as good at it as my father wanted me to be. It's too easy making excuses. Like a pool hustler who never leaves the back room. You start to think it's the whole world.

She can tell from my face that I've had one of those meetings. She shakes her head and says, "How much?"

"I'm doing it for free."

'No, Anthony, you're not.'

"I am."

"Are you trying to get me to go to bed with your brother? He'd like that. Or Aaron, that guy at the gym? Or do you just want me to go live with my sister?"

She can be a real harpy.

"No," I tell her, and mean it.

"You must really hate me."

"I don't hate you, Mandy. I wouldn't put up with your temper tantrums if I hated you." The words are starting to hurt—the ones she's using and the ones I'm using. I *do* love her, I'm telling myself. I wouldn't live with her if I didn't love her, would I?

"And I live on what while you're away, Anthony?"

"I'll sell the XKE?"

"To who?"

"My cousin. He wants it. He's wanted it for years."

She looks at me for a moment and I see a flicker of—kindness. "You in trouble?"

"No."

"Then you're lying or you're crazy but anyway it comes down to the same thing: You don't love me. If you did, you'd take care of me. I'm moving out tomorrow, Anthony Pagano, and I'm taking the Jag."

"Please…."

"If you'll charge for the work."

"I can't."

"You *are* in trouble."

"No."

How do you tell her you've got to kill a man who isn't really a man but wants to be one, and that if you do God will forgive you all the other killings?

She heads to the bedroom to start packing.

I get the case out, open it, touch the marbleized surface of the thing, and hope to hell that God wants a horny assassin because I'm certainly not seeing any action this night or any other before I leave for Rome, and action does help steady my finger. Which Mandy knows. Which every woman I've ever been with knows.

When I get up the next morning, she's gone. The note on the bathroom mirror, in slashes of that lipstick of hers, says, "I hope you miss my body so bad you can't walk or shoot straight, Anthony."

We do the instruction at a dead-grass firing range in Topanga Canyon. My tutor is a no-nonsense kid—maybe twenty—with Chinese characters tattooed around his neck like a dog collar, naked eyebrows, pierced tongue, nose, lower lip. He's serious and strict, but seems happy enough for a vampire killer. He picks me up in his Tundra and on the way to the canyon, three manikins (that holy number) bouncing in the truck bed, he says, "Yeah, I like it—even if it's not what you'd think from a *Buffy* re-run or a John Carpenter flick—you know, like that one shot in Mexico. More like CSI—not the Bruckheimer, but the Discovery Channel. Same way that being an investigative journalist isn't as much fun as you think it'll be—at least that's what I hear. All those hours Googling the public record. In my line of work, it's the tracking and casing and light-weapons prep. But you know more about that than I do, Mr. Pagano. Wasn't your dad—"

"Sounds like you've been to college, Kurt," I say.

"A year at a community college—that's it. But I'm a reader. Always have been."

How do you answer that? I've read maybe a dozen books in my life, all of them short and necessary, and I'm sitting with this kid who reads probably three fat ones a week. Not only is he more literate than I am, he's going to teach *me* how to kill—something I really thought I knew how to do.

"Don't worry," he says. "You'll pick it up. Your—shall we say 'previous training and experience'—should make up for your age, slower reflexes, *you* know."

What can I say? I've got fifteen years on him and we both know it. My reflexes *are* slower than his.

As we hit the Ventura Freeway, he tells me what I'm packing. "In the case beside you, Mr. Pagano, you've got a Horton Legend HD with a Talon Ultra-Light trigger, DP2 CamoTuff limbs, SpeedMax riser, alloy cams, Microflight arrow groove, and Dial-a-Range trajectory compensator—with LS MX aluminum arrows and Hunter Elite 3-arrow quivers. How does that make you feel?"

"Just wonderful," I tell him.

The firing range is upscale and very hip. There are dozens of trophy wives and starlets wearing $300 Scala baseball caps, newsboy caps and sun visors. There are almost as many very metro guys wearing $600 aviator shades and designer jungle cammies. And all of them are learning Personal Protection under the tutelage of guys who are about as savvy about what they're doing as the ordinary gym trainer. They're all trying their best to hit fancy bull's-eye, GAG, PMT, and other tactical targets made for pros, but I'm looking like an even bigger idiot trying to hit, with my handfuls of little crossbow darts, the manikins the kid has lined up for me at fifty yards. The other shooters keep rubbernecking to get a look at us. The kid stares them down and they look away. If they only knew.

"Do the arrows made from the other material—" I begin. "Do they—uh—act…?" I ask.

"Arrows with wood made from the Cross act the same," the kid says, very professional. "We balance them the way we'd balance any arrow."

"When it hits—"

"When it hits a vampire, I'm sure it doesn't feel like ordinary wood. I've never taken one myself."

"Glad to hear it."

"Actually, someone did try an arrow once. Deer bow. Two inches off the mark. I've got a scar. Want to see it?"

"Not really. How would it feel to *us?*"

"You mean mortals?"

"Right."

"It would probably hurt like hell, and if you happened to die I doubt it would get you a free pass to Heaven."

"That's too bad."

"Isn't it."

When I've filled the manikins with ten quivers' worth of arrows and my heart-shot rate is a sad 10%, we quit for the day. It's getting close to sunset, one of those gorgeous smoggy ones. The other shooters have hit the road in their Escalades, H3s, and Land Sharks and the kid is acting distracted.

"Date?"

"What?"

"You know. Two people. Dinner and a movie. Clubbing. Whatever."

"You could say that. But it's a threesome. Can't stand the guy—he's a Red-State crewcut ex-Delta-Forcer—but the girl, she's so hot she'll melt your belt buckle."

He can tell I'm not following.

"A job. It'll take the three of us about three hours. You know, holy number."

"Yeah, I know."

"Two Hollywood producers. Both vampires. They've got two very sexy, very coollow-budget vampire flicks—ones where the vampires win because, hey, if you're cool and sexy you should win, right?—-in post-production, two more in production and three in development. These flicks will seduce too many teens to the Dark Side, He says, so He wants us to take out their makers. They'll be having late poolside dinner at Blue-on-Blue tonight. We'll be interrupting it."

"I see," I say. I'm staring at him and he beats me to it.

"You want to know what we eat if we can't drink blood."

"Yes, I do."

"We eat what you eat. We don't need blood since we came over."

"Which means you don't—how to put it?—you don't perpetuate the species."

"Right."

"Which can't make the elders very happy."

"No, it can't."

By the end of the sixth day my heart-shot rate is 80% and the kid's nodding, doing a dance move or two in his tight black jeans, and saying, "You're the man, Anthony. You're the man." I shouldn't admit it, but what he thinks does matter.

When I get there, courtesy of Alitalia (the angel won't pay for Lufthansa), the city of Siena, in lovely Tuscany, country of my forefathers, is a mess. It's just after the horserace, the one where a dozen riders—each of them repping a neighborhood known for an animal (snail, dolphin, goose—you get the picture)—beat each other silly with little riding crops to impress their local Madonna. There's trash everywhere. I've got the crossbow in its case, and a kid on a Vespa tries to grab it as he sails by, but I'm ready. I know kids—I was one once—and I nail him with a kick to his knee. The Vespa skids and he flies into a fountain not far away. The fountain is a big sea shell—a scallop—which I know from reading my *Fodor's* must be this neighborhood's emblem for the race. He gets up crying, gives me the *va-funcu* with his arm and fist, and screams something in native Sienese—which isn't at all the Italian I grew up with but which I'm sure means, "I'm going to tell my dad and brothers, you asshole!"

The apartment is not in the Neighborhood of the Scallop, but in the Neighborhood of the Salmon, and the girl who answers the door is stunning. Tall. The kind of blonde who tans better than a commercial. Eyes like shattered glass, long legs, cute little dimple in her chin. I don't see how he can keep his teeth off her.

This is Euro-goth? I don't think so.

"So you're the one," she says. Her English is perfect, just enough accent to make it sexy.

"Yeah. Anthony Pagano." I stick out my hand. She doesn't take it.

"Giovanna," she says. "Giovanna Musetti. And that's what you're going to do it with?" She gestures with her head at my case. She can't take her eyes off it.

"Yeah."

"*Please don't do it*," she says suddenly.

I don't know what to say.

"You're supposed to want him dead."

She looks at me like I'm crazy.

"Why would I want him dead?"

"Because you want him to bite you—because you want to be one too—and he—he won't oblige."

"Who told you that?"

"The—the angel who hired me."

"I know that angel. He was here. He interviewed me."

"You don't want him dead?"

"Of course not. I love him."

I sit down on the sofa. They've got a nice place. Maybe they enjoy the horseraces. Even if they don't, the tourists aren't so bad off-season according to *Fodor's*. And maybe when you're the oldest vampire, you don't have to obey the no-daylight rule. Maybe you get to walk around in the day—in a nice, clean, modern medieval city—maybe one you knew when you were only a thousand years old and it was being built and a lot trashier—and feel pretty mortal and normal. Who knows?

"Why did my employer get it wrong?"

She's got the same look the angel did. "The angel didn't get it wrong, Mr. Pagano. He *lied*."

"Why?" I'm thinking: *Angels are allowed to do that? Lie? Sure, if God wants them to.*

"Why?" I ask again.

"I don't know. That's one of the things I love about Frank—"

"Your man's name is Frank?"

"It is now. That's what he's gone by for the last hundred years, he says, and I believe him. That's one of the things I love."

"What?"

"That he doesn't lie. That he doesn't need to. He's seen it all. He's had all the power you could want and he doesn't want it anymore. He's bitten so many people he lost count after a century, and he doesn't want to do it anymore. He's tired of living the lie any vampire has to live. He's very human in his heart, Mr. Pagano—in his soul—so human you wouldn't believe it—and he's tired of doing his father's bidding, the darkness, the blasphemy, all of that. I don't think he was ever really into it, but he had to do it. He was his father's son, so he had to do it. Carry on the tradition—the business. Do you know what that's like?"

"Yes. I do."

I'm starting to like her, of course—really like her. She's great eye candy, but it isn't just that. The more she talks, the more I like what's inside. She understands—she understands the mortal human heart.

"But I'm supposed to kill him," I say.

"Why?"

"Because of—because of 'balance.'"

"What?"

"That's what my employer said. Even though Frank wants to flip, and you'd think that would be a plus, it wouldn't be. It would throw things off."

"You really believe that, Anthony?"

Now we're on first-name basis, and I don't mind.

I don't say a thing for a second.

"I don't know."

"It sounds wrong, doesn't it."

"Yeah, it does."

We sit silent for a while. I'm looking at her hard, too interested, so I make myself look away.

"Do I make you self-conscious?" she asks gently.

That turns me red. "It's not you. It's me. You look awfully good. It's just me."

"That's sweet." Now she's doing the looking away, cheeks a little red, and when she looks backs, she says, "Any idea why God would *really* want him killed?"

"None whatsoever."

"But you've still got to do it."

"There was this promise."

"I know."

"You do?"

"Sure. If you do it, He'll forgive everything. They offered me that too if I helped you."

"And you said no?"

"Yes."

She loves this guy—this vampire—this son of You Know Who—so much she'll turn down an offer like that? Now I'm *really* looking at her. She's not just beautiful, she's got *coglioni*. She'll stand up to God for love.

I'm thinking these things and also wondering whether the angel lied about her because maybe she stiffed him. Because *he's* the vindictive one.

"There's nothing I can say to stop you?" she's asking. She doesn't say "nothing I can *do*." She says "nothing I can *say*," and that's all the difference in the world.

"Wish there were, but there isn't. Where is he?"

"You know."

"Yeah, I guess I do. He's in the Vatican somewhere trying to convince those Jesuit vampires that it's okay if he turns."

"That's where he said he was going when he left a week ago, so I'm sure it's true. Like I said, he—"

"Never lies. I know."

I get up.

"I'm sorry."
"Me too."

I'm depressed when I get to Rome and not because the city is big and noisy and feels like LA. (My dad's people were from Calabria and they never had a good thing to say about *Romani*, so I'm biased.) It's because—well, just because. But when I reach the Vatican, I feel a lot better. Now this—this is beautiful. St. Peter's. The church, the square, marble everywhere, sunlight blinding you like the flashlight of God. Even the silly little Fiats going round and round the circle like they're trapped and can't get off are nice.

He's not going to be in the basilica, I know. That's where the Pope is—that new strict guy, Benedict—and it's visiting day, dispensations, blessings, the rest. I don't even try to go through the main Vatican doorway on the opposite side. Too many tourists there too. Instead I go to a side entrance, Via Gerini, where there's no one. Construction cones, sidewalk repair, a big door with carvings on it. Why this entrance, I don't know. Just a hunch.

I know God can open any door for me that He wants to, so if my hunch is right why isn't the door opening? Maybe there'll be a mark on the right door—you know, a shadow that looks like the face of Our Lady, or the number 333, something—but before I can check the door for a sign, something starts flapping above my head and scares the shit out of me. I think it's a bat at first—that would make sense—but it's just a pigeon. No, a dove. Doves are smaller and pigeons aren't this white.

I know my employer thinks I'm slow, but a *white dove?*

The idiot bird keeps flapping two feet from my head and now I see it—a twig of something in its beak. I don't want to know.

The bird flies off, stops, hovers, and waits. I'm supposed to follow, so I do.

The door it's stopped at is the third one down from mine, of course. No face of Our Lady on it, but when I step up to it, it of course clicks and swings open.

We go through the next doorway, and the next, and the next, seven doorways in all—from a library to a little museum, then another library, then an office, then an archive with messy files, then a bigger museum. Some of the rooms are empty—of people, I mean—and some aren't, and when they're not, the people, some in suits and dresses and some in clerical outfits—give me a look like, "Well, he certainly seems to know where he's going with his musical instrument. Perhaps they're having chamber music with *espresso* for *gli ufficiali*. And of course that can't really be a pure white dove with an olive twig in its beak flapping in front of him, so everything's just fine. *Buon giorno, Signore.*"

When the bird stops for good, hovering madly, it's a really big door and it doesn't open right off. But I know this is it—that my guy is on the other side. Whatever he's doing, he's there and I'd better get ready. He's a vampire. Maybe he's confused—maybe he doesn't want to be one any longer—but he's still got, according to the angel, superhuman strength and super-senses and the rest.

When the door opens—without the slightest sound, I note—I'm looking down this spiral staircase into a gorgeous little chapel. Sunlight is coming through the stained-glass windows, so there's got to be a courtyard or something just outside, and the frescoes on the ceiling look like real Michelangelos. Big muscles. Those steroid bodies.

The bird has flown to the ceiling and is perched on a balustrade, waiting for the big event, but that's not how I know the guy I'm looking down at is Frank. It isn't even that he's got that distinguished-gentleman look that old vampires have in the movies. It's what he's doing that tells me.

He's kneeling in front of the altar, in front of this big golden crucifix with an especially bloody Jesus, and he's very uncomfortable doing it. Even at this distance I can tell he's shaking. He's got his hands out in prayer and can barely keep them together. He's jerking like he's being electrocuted. He's got his eyes on the crucifix, and when he speaks, it's loud and his voice jerks too. It sounds confessional—the tone is right—but it's not English and it's not Italian. It may not even be Latin, and why should it be? He's been around a long time and probably knows the original.

I'm thinking the stained-glass light is playing tricks on me, but it's not. There really *is* a blue light moving around his hands, his face, his pants legs—blue fire—and this, I see now, it's what's making him jerk.

He's got to be in pain. I mean, here in a chapel—in front of an altar—sunlight coming through the windows—making about the biggest confession any guy has ever made. Painful as hell, but he's doing it, and suddenly I know why she loves him. Hell, *anyone* would.

Without knowing it I've unpacked my crossbow and have it up and ready. This is what God wants, so I probably get some help doing it. I'm shaking too, but go ahead and aim the thing. *I need forgiveness, too, you know*, I want to tell him. You can't bank your immortal soul, no, but you do get to spend it a lot longer.

I put my finger on the trigger, but don't pull it yet. I want to keep thinking.

No, I don't. I don't want to keep thinking at all.

I lower the crossbow and the moment I do I hear a sound from the back of the chapel where the main door's got to be, and I crane my neck to see.

It's the main door all right. Heads are peeking in. They're wearing black and I think to myself: *Curious priests. That's all.* But the door opens up more and three of them—that holy number—step in real quiet. They're wearing funny Jesuit collars—the ones the angel mentioned—and they don't look curious. They look like they know exactly what they're doing, and they look very unhappy.

Vampires have this sixth sense, I know. One of them looks up at me suddenly, smiles this funny smile, and I see sharp little teeth.

He says something to the other two and heads toward me. When he's halfway up the staircase I shoot him. I must have my heart in it because the arrow nearly goes through him, but that's not what really bothers him. It's the *wood*. There's an explosion of sparks, the same blue fire, and a hole opens up in his chest, grows, and in no time at all he's just not there anymore.

Frank has turned around to look, but he's dazed, all that confessing, hands in prayer position and shaking wildly, and he obviously doesn't get what's happening.

The other two Jesuits are heading up the stairs now, and I nail them with my last two arrows.

The dove has dropped like a stone from its perch and is flapping hysterically in front of me, like *Wrong vampires! Wrong vampires!* I'm tired of its flapping, so I brush it away, turn and leave, and if it takes me (which it will) a whole day to get out of the Vatican without that dove to lead me and make doors open magically, okay. When you're really depressed, it's hard to give a shit about anything.

Two days later I'm back at Parlami's. I haven't showered. I look like hell. I've still got the case with me. God knows why.

I've had two martinis and when I look up, there he is. I'm not surprised, but I sigh anyway. I'm not looking forward to this.

"So you didn't do it," he says.

"You know I didn't, asshole."

"Yes, I do. Word does get out when the spiritual configuration of the universe doesn't shift the way He'd like it to."

I want to hit his baby-smooth face, his perfect nose and collagen lips, but I don't have the energy.

"So what happens now?" I ask.

"You really don't know?"

"No."

He shakes his head. Same look of contempt.

"I guess you wouldn't."

He takes a deep breath.

"Well, the Jesuits did it for you. They killed him last night."

"What?"

"They've got crossbows too. Where do you think we got the idea?"

"Same wood?"

"Of course. They handle it with special gloves."

"*Why?*"

"Why kill him? Same line of thought. If he flips, things get thrown off balance. Order is important for them, too, you know. Mortals are the same way, you may have noticed. You all need order. Throw things off and you go crazy. That's why you'll put up with despots—even choose them over more benign and loving leaders—just so you don't have to worry. Disorder makes for a lot of worry, Anthony."

"You already knew it?"

"Knew what?"

"That I wouldn't do it and the Jesuits would instead."

"Yes."

"Then why send me?"

Again the look, the sigh. "Ah. Think hard."

I do, and, miracle of miracles, I see it.

"Giovanna is free now," I say.

"Yes. Frank, bless his immortal soul—which God has indeed agreed to do—is gone in flesh."

"So He wants me to hook up with her?"

The angel nods. "Of course."

"Why?"

"Because she'll love you—*really* love you, innocent that you are—just the way she loved him."

"That's it?"

"Not exactly… Because she'll love you, you'll have to stop. You'll have to stop killing people, Anthony. It's just not right."

"No, I won't."

"Yes, you will."

"I don't think so."

"But you will—because, whether you know it yet or not, you love her, too."

What do you say to that?

The angel's gotten up, straightened his red Zegna, picked up the case, and is ready to leave.

"By the way," he adds, "He says He forgives you anyway."

I nod, tired as hell. "I figured that."

"You're catching on."

"About time," I say.

"He said that too."

"And the whole 'balance' thing—"

"What do *you* think?"

Pure bullshit is what I'm thinking.

"You got it," he says, reading my mind because, well, angels can do that.

Twenty-four hours later I'm back in Siena, shaved and showered, and she doesn't seem surprised to see me. She's been grieving—that's obvious. Red eyes. Perfect hair tussled, a mess. She's been debriefed by the angel—that I can tell—and I don't know whether she's got a problem with The Plan or not, or even whether there is a Plan. The angel may have been lying about that too. But when she says quietly, "Hello, Anthony," and gives me a shy smile, I *know*—and my heart starts flapping like that idiot bird.

UNDEAD AGAIN

by Ken MacLeod

Ken MacLeod's most recent novels are *The Execution Channel* and *The Night Sessions*, and a new book, *The Restoration Game*, is due out later this year. He is also the author of several other novels and short stories, including *The Sky Road*, which won the British Science Fiction Award. He is also the winner of the Prometheus Award, the Sidewise Award, and the Seiun Award, and has been a finalist for the Hugo, Nebula, and John W. Campbell Memorial awards. He is currently serving as Writer in Residence for the ESRC Genomics Policy and Research Forum at Edinburgh University.

This story, about a vampire who chooses cryonic preservation in the hope of a cure, first appeared in the science journal *Nature*, as part of their Futures series of short-short stories. MacLeod says that it was originally inspired by thinking about viruses that spread through changes they make in the host's behavior.

It's 2045 and I'm still a vampire. Damn.

The chap from Alcor UK is droning through his orientation lecture. New age of enlightenment, new industrial revolution, many changes, take some time to adjust, blah blah blah. I'm only half-listening, being too busy shifting my foot to keep it out of the beam of direct sunlight millimetering across the floor, and trying not to look at his neck.

I feel like saying: *I've only been dead forty years, for Chr—*

For crying out loud. I saw the *first* age of enlightenment. I worked nights right through the original Industrial Revolution. I remember being naive enough to get excited about mesmerism, galvanism, spiritualism, socialism, Roentgen rays, rationalism, radium, Mendelism, Marconi, relativity, feminism, the Russian Revolution, the Bomb, nightclubs, feminism (again), Apollo 11, socialism (again), the fall of Saigon and the fall of the Wall.

The last dodgy nostrum I fell for was cryonics.

So don't give me this future shock shit, sunshine. The most disconcerting thing I've come across so far in 2045 is the latest ladies' fashion: the old sleeveless mini-dress. The ozone hole has been fixed, and folk are frolicking in the sun. I hug myself with bare arms, and slide the castored chair back another inch.

Under the heel of my left wrist, I feel the thud of my regenerated heart. It beats time to the artery visible under the tanned skin of the resurrection man's neck. The rest of my nature is unregenerate. I feel somewhat thwarted. This is not, this is definitely not, what I died for. And it seemed such a good idea at the time.

It always does.

By 1995 we thought we had a handle on the thing. It's a virus. In all respects but one, it's benign: it prevents aging, and stimulates regeneration of any tissue damage short of, well, a stake through the heart. But it has a very low infectivity, so it takes a lot of mingling of fluids to spread. Natural selection has worked that one hard. Hence the unfortunate impulses. And by 1995, I can tell you, I was getting pretty sick of them. I cashed in my six Scottish Widows life insurance policies (let's draw a veil over how I acquired them), signed up for cryonic preservation in the event of my death, and after a discreet ten years, met an unfortunate and bloody end at the hand of the coven senior, Kelvin.

"You'll thank me later," he said, just before he pushed home the point.

"See you in the future," I croaked.

The last thing I saw was his grin. That, and the pavement below the spiked railings beside the steps of my flat. A tragic accident. The coroner, I just learned, blamed it on the long skirt. Vampires, always the fashion victims.

I leave the orientation room, hang around until dusk under the pretext of catching up with the news, and go out and find a vintage clothes shop. I walk out in Victorian widow's weeds. They fit so well I suspect they were once mine.

"It didn't work," I tell Kelvin.

He sips his bloody mary and looks defensive.

"It did in a way," he says. "There are no viruses in your blood."

That word again. I look away. We're in some kind of goth club, which covers for the mode but doesn't improve my mood.

"So why do I still feel… hungry?"

"Have a *tapas*," he says. "But seriously… the way we figure it, the virus has to have transcribed itself into our DNA. So the nanotech cell-repair just replicates it without a second thought."

"So we're stuck with it," I say. "Living in the dark and every so often—"

"Not quite," he says. "Now it's been established that cryonics really does work, there's been a whole new interest in a very old idea…"

The coffin lid opens. Kelvin's looking down, as I expect. The real shock is the light, full-spectrum and warm. It feels like something my skin has missed for centuries. I sit up, naked, and bask for a moment.

The overhead lights reproduce the spectrum of Alpha Centauri, which is where we're going. The whole coven is here, all thirteen of them, happier and better fed than I've ever seen them. It's taken us a lot of planning, a lot of money, and a lot of lying to get here, but we're on our way.

"Welcome back," says Kevin. He grins around at the coven.

"Let's thaw one out for her," he says. "She must be hungry."

As far as I can see stretch rows and rows of cryonic coffins containing interstellar colonists in what they euphemistically call cold sleep. Thousands of them. Enough to keep us going until we reach that kinder sun.

PEKING MAN

by Robert J. Sawyer

Robert J. Sawyer is the author of twenty novels, including *Hominids*, which won the Hugo Award, *The Terminal Experiment*, which won the Nebula Award, and *Mindscan*, which won the John W. Campbell Memorial Award. He has also won ten Aurora Awards, three Seiun Awards, and is the only three-time winner of Spain's prestigious UPC Award, which bestows the largest cash prize in all of science fiction.

Sawyer's novel *Flashforward* is currently being adapted for television and is scheduled to air on ABC this fall. His latest novel project is the WWW trilogy, consisting of *Wake*, *Watch*, and *Wonder*. The first volume, *Wake*, was recently serialized in the pages of *Analog* and was released in hardcover in April.

Although Sawyer is best known for his science fiction, he's written a number of works that deal with fantastic themes, such as this story, which won the Aurora Award and first appeared in the anthology *Dark Destiny III*. But, as you might guess from the title, this one doesn't see Sawyer straying too far from his science fiction roots…

The lid was attached to the wooden crate with eighteen nails. The return address, in blue ink on the blond wood, said, "Sender: Dept. of Anatomy, P.U.M.C., Peking, China." The destination address, in larger letters, was:

Dr. Roy Chapman Andrews
The American Museum of Natural History
Central Park West at 79th Street
New York, N.Y. U.S.A.

The case was marked "Fragile!" and "REGISTERED" and "*Par Avion.*" A brand had burned the words "Via Hongkong and by U.S. Air Service" into the wood.

Andrews had waited anxiously for this arrival. Between 1922 and 1930, he himself had led the now-famous Gobi Desert expeditions, searching for the Asian cradle of humanity. Although he'd brought back untold scientific riches—including the first-ever dinosaur eggs—Andrews had failed to discover a single ancient human remain.

But now a German scientist, Franz Weidenreich, had shipped to him a treasure trove from the Orient: the complete fossil remains of *Sinanthropus pekinensis*. In this very crate were the bones of Peking Man.

Andrews was actually salivating as he used a crowbar to pry off the lid. He'd waited so long for these, terrified that they wouldn't survive the journey, desperate to see what humanity's forefathers had looked like, anxious—

The lid came off. The contents were carefully packed in smaller cardboard boxes. He picked one up and moved over to his cluttered desk. He swept the books and papers to the floor, laid down the box, and opened it. Inside was a ball of rice paper, wrapped around a large object. Andrews carefully unwrapped the sheets, and—

White.

White?

No—no, it couldn't be.

But it was. It was a skull, certainly—but *not* a fossil skull. The material was bright white.

And it didn't weigh nearly enough.

A plaster cast. Not the original at all.

Andrews opened every box inside the wooden crate, his heart sinking as each new one yielded its contents. In total, there were fourteen skulls and eleven jawbones. The skulls were subhuman, with low foreheads, prominent brow ridges, flat faces, and the most unlikely looking perfect square teeth. Amazingly, each of the skull casts also showed clear artificial damage to the foramen magnum.

Oh, some work could indeed be done on these casts, no doubt. But where were the original fossils? With the Japanese having invaded China, surely they were too precious to be left in the Far East. What was Weidenreich up to?

Fire.

It was like a piece of the sun, brought down to earth. It kept the tribe warm at night, kept the saber-toothed cats away—and it did something wonderful to meat, making it softer and easier to chew, while at the same time restoring the warmth the flesh had had when still part of the prey.

Fire was the most precious thing the tribe owned. They'd had it for eleven summers now, ever since Bok the brave had brought out a burning stick from the burning forest. The glowing coals were always fanned, always kept alive.

And then, one night, the Stranger came—tall, thin, pale, with red-rimmed eyes that somehow seemed to glow from beneath his brow ridge.

The Stranger did the unthinkable, the unforgivable.

He doused the flames, throwing a gourd full of water on to the fire. The logs hissed, and steam rose up into the blackness. The children of the tribe began to cry; the adults quaked with fury. The Stranger turned and walked into the darkness. Two of the strongest hunters ran after him, but his long legs had apparently carried him quickly away.

The sounds of the forest grew closer—the chirps of insects, the rustling of small

animals in the vegetation, and—
  A flapping sound.
  The Stranger was gone.
  And the silhouette of a bat fluttered briefly in front of the waning moon.

Franz Weidenreich had been born in Germany in 1873. A completely bald, thickset man, he had made a name for himself as an expert in hematology and osteology. He was currently Visiting Professor at the University of Chicago, but that was coming to an end, and now he was faced with the uncomfortable prospect of having to return to Nazi Germany—something, as a Jew, he desperately wanted to avoid.

And then word came of the sudden death of the Canadian paleontologist Davidson Black. Black had been at the Peking Union Medical College, studying the fragmentary remains of early man being recovered from the limestone quarry at Chou Kou Tien. Weidenreich, who once made a study of Neanderthal bones found in Germany, had read Black's papers in *Nature* and *Science* describing *Sinanthropus*.

But now, at fifty, Black was as dead as his fossil charges—an unexpected heart attack. And, to Weidenreich's delight, the China Medical Board of the Rockefeller Foundation wanted him to fill Black's post. China was a strange, foreboding place—and tensions between the Chinese and the Japanese were high—but it beat all hell out of returning to Hitler's Germany...

At night, most of the tribe huddled under the rocky overhang or crawled into the damp, smelly recesses of the limestone cave. Without the fire to keep animals away, someone had to stand watch each night, armed with a large branch and a pile of rocks for throwing. Last night, it had been Kart's turn. Everyone had slept well, for Kart was the strongest member of the tribe. They knew they were safe from whatever lurked in the darkness.

When daybreak came, the members of the tribe were astounded. Kart had fallen asleep. They found him lying in the dirt, next to the cold, black pit where their fire had once been. And on Kart's neck there were two small red-rimmed holes, staring up at them like the eyes of the Stranger...

During his work on hematology, Weidenreich had met a remarkable man named Brancusi—gaunt, pale, with disconcertingly sharp canine teeth. Brancusi suffered from a peculiar anemia, which Weidenreich had been unable to cure, and an almost pathological photophobia. Still, the gentleman was cultured and widely read, and Weidenreich had ever since maintained a correspondence with him.

When Weidenreich arrived in Peking, work was still continuing at the quarry. So far, only teeth and fragments of skull had been found. Davidson Black had done a good job of cataloging and describing some of the material, but as Weidenreich went through the specimens he was surprised to discover a small collection of sharp, pointed fossil teeth.

Black had evidently assumed they weren't part of the *Sinanthropus* material, as he hadn't included them in his descriptions. And, at first glance, Black's assessment seemed correct—they were far longer than normal human canines, and much more sharply pointed. But, to Weidenreich's eye, the root pattern was possibly hominid. He dropped a letter to his friend Brancusi, half-joking that he'd found Brancusi's great-to-the-*n*th grandfather in China.

To Weidenreich's infinite surprise, within weeks Brancusi had arrived in Peking.

Each night, another member of the tribe stood watch—and each morning, that member was found unconscious, with a pair of tiny wounds to his neck.

The tribe members were terrified. Soon multiple guards were posted each night, and, for a time, the happenings ceased.

But then something even more unusual happened…

They were hunting deer. It would not be the same, not without fire to cook the meat, but, still, the tribe needed to eat. Four men, Kart included, led the assault. They moved stealthily amongst the tall grasses, tracking a large buck with a giant rack of antlers. The hunters communicated by sign language, carefully coordinating their movements, closing in on the animal from both sides.

Kart raised his right arm, preparing to signal the final attack, when—

—a streak of light brown, slicing through the grass—

—fangs flashing, the roar of the giant cat, the stag bolting away, and then—

—Kart's own scream as the saber-tooth grabbed hold of his thigh and shook him viciously.

The other three hunters ran as fast as they could, desperate to get away. They didn't stop to look back, even when the cat let out the strangest yelp…

That night, the tribe huddled together and sang songs urging Kart's soul a safe trip to heaven.

One of the Chinese laborers found the first skull. Weidenreich was summoned at once. Brancusi still suffered from his photophobia, and apparently had never adjusted to the shift in time zones—he slept during the day. Weidenreich thought about waking him to see this great discovery, but decided against it.

The skull was still partially encased in the limestone muck at the bottom of the cave. It had a thick cranial wall and a beetle brow—definitely a more primitive creature than Neanderthal, probably akin to Solo Man or Java Man…

It took careful work to remove the skull from the ground, but, when it did come free, two astonishing things became apparent.

The loose teeth Davidson Black had set aside had indeed come from the hominids here: this skull still had all its upper teeth intact, and the canines were long and pointed.

Second, and even more astonishing, was the foramen magnum—the large opening in the base of the skull through which the spinal cord passes. It was clear from its chipped, frayed margin that this individual's foramen magnum had been artificially widened—

—meaning he'd been decapitated, and then had something shoved up into his brain through the bottom of his skull.

Five hunters stood guard that night. The moon had set, and the great sky river arched high over head. The Stranger returned—but this time, he was not alone. The tribesmen couldn't believe their eyes. In the darkness, it looked like—

It was. Kart.

But—but Kart was dead. They'd seen the saber-tooth take him.

The Stranger came closer. One of the men lifted a rock, as if to throw it at him, but soon he let the rock drop from his hand. It fell to the ground with a dull thud.

The Stranger continued to approach, and so did Kart.

And then Kart opened his mouth, and in the faint light they saw his teeth—long and pointed, like the Stranger's.

The men were unable to run, unable to move. They seemed transfixed, either by the Stranger's gaze, or by Kart's, both of whom continued to approach.

And soon, in the dark, chill night, the Stranger's fangs fell upon one of the guard's necks, and Kart's fell upon another…

Eventually, thirteen more skulls were found, all of which had the strange elongated canine teeth, and all of which had their foramen magnums artificially widened. Also found were some mandibles and skull fragments from other individuals—but there was almost no post-cranial material. Someone in dim prehistory had discarded here the decapitated heads of a group of protohumans.

Brancusi sat in Weidenreich's lab late at night, looking at the skulls. He ran his tongue over his own sharp teeth, contemplating. These subhumans doubtless had no concept of mathematics beyond perhaps adding and subtracting on their fingers. How would they possibly know of the problem that plagued the Family, the problem that every one of the Kindred knew to avoid?

If all those who feel the bite of the vampire themselves become vampires when they die, and all of those new vampires also turn those they feed from into vampires, soon, unless care is exercised, the whole population will be undead. A simple geometric progression.

Brancusi had long wondered how far back the Family went. It wasn't like tracing a normal family tree—oh, yes, the lines were bloodlines, but not as passed on from father to son. He knew his own lineage—a servant at Castle Dracula before the Count had taken to living all alone, a servant whose loyalty to his master extended even to letting him drink from his neck.

Brancusi himself had succumbed to pneumonia, not an uncommon ailment in the dank Carpathians. He had no family, and no one mourned his passing.

But soon he rose again—and now he did have Family.

An Englishman and an American had killed the Count, removing his head with a kukri knife and driving a bowie knife through his heart. When news of this reached Brancusi from the gypsies, he traveled back to Transylvania. Dracula's attackers had simply abandoned the coffin, with its native soil and the dust that the Count's body had crumbled into. Brancusi dug a grave on the desolate, wind-swept grounds of the Castle, and placed the Count's coffin within.

Eventually, over a long period, the entire tribe had felt the Stranger's bite directly or indirectly.

A few of the tribefolk lost their lives to ravenous bloodthirst, drained dry. Others succumbed to disease or giant cats or falls from cliffs. One even died of old age. But all of them rose again.

And so it came to pass, just as it had for the Stranger all those years before, that the tribe had to look elsewhere to slake its thirst.

But they had not counted on the Others.

Weidenreich and Brancusi sat in Weidenreich's lab late at night. Things had been getting very tense—the Japanese occupation was becoming intolerable. "I'm going to return to the States," said Weidenreich. "Andrews at the American Museum is offering me space to continue work on the fossils."

"No," said Brancusi. "No, you can't take the fossils."

Weidenreich's bushy eyebrows climbed up toward his bald pate. "But we can't let them fall into Japanese hands."

"That is true," said Brancusi.

"They belong somewhere safe. Somewhere where they can be studied."

"No," said Brancusi. His red-rimmed gaze fell on Weidenreich in a way it never had before. "No—no one may see these fossils."

"But Andrews is expecting them. He's dying to see them. I've been deliberately vague in my letters to him—I want to be there to see his face when he sees the dentition."

"No one can know about the teeth," said Brancusi.

"But he's expecting the fossils. And I have to publish descriptions of them."

"The teeth must be filed flat."

Weidenreich's eyes went wide. "I can't do that."

"You can, and you will."

"But—"

"You can and you will."

"I—I can, but—"

"No buts."

"No, no, there *is* a but. Andrews will never be fooled by filed teeth; the structure of teeth varies as you go into them. Andrews will realize at once that the teeth have been reduced from their original size." Weidenreich looked at Brancusi. "I'm sorry, but there's no way to hide the truth."

The Others lived in the next valley. They proved tough and resourceful—and they could make fire whenever they needed it. When the tribefolk arrived it became apparent that there was never a time of darkness for the Others. Large fires were constantly burning.

The tribe had to feed, but the Others defended themselves, trying to kill them with rock knives.

But that didn't work. The tribefolk were undeterred.

They tried to kill them with spears.

But that did not work, either. The tribefolk came back.

They tried strangling the attackers with pieces of animal hide.

But that failed, too. The tribefolk returned again.

And finally the Others decided to try everything they could think of simultaneously.

They drove wooden spears into the hearts of the tribefolk.

They used stone knives to carve off the heads of the tribefolk.

And then they jammed spears up into the severed heads, forcing the shafts up through the holes at the bases of the skulls.

The hunters marched far away from their camp, each carrying a spear thrust vertically toward the summer sun, each one crowned by a severed, pointed-toothed head. When, at last, they found a suitable hole in the ground, they dumped the heads in, far, far away from their bodies.

The Others waited for the tribefolk to return.

But they never did.

"Do not send the originals," said Brancusi.

"But—"

"The originals are mine, do you understand? I will ensure their safe passage out of China."

It looked for a moment like Weidenreich's will was going to reassert itself, but then his expression grew blank again. "All right."

"I've seen you make casts of bones before."

"With plaster of Paris, yes."

"Make casts of these skulls—and then file the teeth on the casts."

"But—"

"You said Andrews and others would be able to tell if the original fossils were altered. But there's no way they could tell that the casts had been modified, correct?"

"Not if it's done skillfully, I suppose, but—"

"Do it."

"What about the foramen magnums?"

"What would you conclude if you saw fossils with such widened openings?"

"I don't know—possibly that ritual cannibalism had been practiced."

"Ritual?"

"Well, if the only purpose was to get at the brain, so you could eat it, it's easier just to smash the cranium, and—"

"Good. Good. Leave the damage to the skull bases intact. Let your Andrews have that puzzle to keep him occupied."

The casts were crated up and sent to the States first. Then Weidenreich himself headed for New York, leaving, he said, instructions for the actual fossils to be shipped aboard the S.S. *President Harrison*. But the fossils never arrived in America, and Weidenreich, the one man who might have clues to their whereabouts, died shortly thereafter.

Despite the raging war, Brancusi returned to Europe, returned to Transylvania, returned to Castle Dracula.

It took him a while in the darkness of night to find the right spot—the scar left by his earlier digging was just one of many on the desolate landscape. But at last he located it. He prepared a series of smaller holes in the ground, and into each of them he laid one of the grinning skulls. He then covered the holes over with dark soil.

Brancusi hoped never to fall himself, but, if he did, he hoped one of his own converts would do the same thing for him, bringing his remains home to the Family plot.

NECROS

by Brian Lumley

Brian Lumley is the bestselling author of dozens of novels, including the Necro-scope and Vampire World series, and his Titus Crow and Dreamlands series, both of which take place in H. P. Lovecraft's Cthulhu mythos. He's also written more than 100 short stories, which have been collected in numerous volumes, such as the vampire-centric *A Coven of Vampires*, and recent releases *The Taint and Other Novellas* and *Haggopian and Other Stories*. Lumley is a winner of the British Fantasy Award, and in 1998, he was named a Grand Master by the World Horror Society.

It raised eyebrows when twenty-six-year-old *Playboy* model Anna Nicole Smith married eighty-nine-year-old oil tycoon J. Howard Marshall. It seemed such a shameless example of a relationship built on mutual exploitation rather than mutual affection. But is that really so different from most relationships? Is it the case, as one character in this story ponders, that "all relationships are bargains of sorts"? Maybe so, maybe not. But in the case of this story, most definitely so.

1.

An old woman in a faded blue frock and black head-square paused in the shade of Mario's awning and nodded good-day. She smiled a gap-toothed smile. A bulky, slouch-shouldered youth in jeans and a stained yellow T-shirt—a slope-headed idiot, probably her grandson—held her hand, drooling vacantly and fidgeting beside her.

Mario nodded good-naturedly, smiled, wrapped a piece of stale focaccia in greaseproof paper and came from behind the bar to give it to her. She clasped his hand, thanked him, turned to go.

Her attention was suddenly arrested by something she saw across the road. She started, cursed vividly, harshly, and despite my meager knowledge of Italian, I picked up something of the hatred in her tone. "Devil's spawn!" She said it again. "Dog! Swine!" She pointed a shaking hand and finger, said yet again: "Devil's spawn!" before making the two-fingered, double-handed stabbing sign with which the Italians ward off evil. To do this it was first necessary that she drop her salted bread, which the idiot youth at once snatched up.

Then, still mouthing low, guttural imprecations, dragging the shuffling, focaccia-

396

munching cretin behind her, she hurried off along the street and disappeared into an alley. One word that she had repeated over and over again stayed in my mind: "Necros! Necros!" Though the word was new to me, I took it for a curse-word. The accent she put on it had been poisonous.

I sipped at my Negroni, remained seated at the small circular table beneath Mario's awning and stared at the object of the crone's distaste. It was a motor car, a white convertible Rover and this year's model, inching slowly forward in a stream of holiday traffic. And it was worth looking at if only for the girl behind the wheel. The little man in the floppy white hat beside her—well, he was something else too. But she was—just something else.

I caught just a glimpse, sufficient to feel stunned. That was good. I had thought it was something I could never know again: that feeling a man gets looking at a beautiful girl. Not after Linda. And yet—

She was young, say twenty-four or -five, some three or four years my junior. She sat tall at the wheel, slim, raven-haired under a white, wide-brimmed summer hat which just missed matching that of her companion, with a complexion cool and creamy enough to pour over peaches. I stood up—yes, to get a better look—and right then the traffic came to a momentary standstill. At that moment, too, she turned her head and looked at me. And if the profile had stunned me...well, the full-frontal knocked me dead. The girl was simply, classically beautiful.

Her eyes were of a dark green but very bright, slightly tilted and perfectly oval under straight, thin brows. Her cheekbones were high, her lips a red Cupid's bow, her neck long and white against the glowing yellow of her blouse. And her smile—

—Oh, yes, she smiled.

Her glance, at first cool, became curious in a moment, then a little angry, until finally, seeing my confusion—that smile. And as she turned her attention back to the road and followed the stream of traffic out of sight, I saw a blush of color spreading on the creamy surface of her cheek. Then she was gone.

Then, too, I remembered the little man who sat beside her. Actually, I hadn't seen a great deal of him, but what I had seen had given me the creeps. He too had turned his head to stare at me, leaving in my mind's eye an impression of beady bird eyes, sharp and intelligent in the shade of his hat. He had stared at me for only a moment, and then his head had slowly turned away; but even when he no longer looked at me, when he stared straight ahead, it seemed to me I could feel those raven's eyes upon me, and that a query had been written in them.

I believed I could understand it, that look. He must have seen a good many young men staring at him like that—or rather, at the girl. His look had been a threat in answer to my threat—and because he was practiced in it, I had certainly felt the more threatened!

I turned to Mario, whose English was excellent. "She has something against expensive cars and rich people?"

"Who?" he busied himself behind his bar.

"The old lady, the woman with the idiot boy."

"Ah!" he nodded. "Mainly against the little man, I suspect."

"Oh?"

"You want another Negroni?"

"OK—and one for yourself—but tell me about this other thing, won't you?"

"If you like—but you're only interested in the girl, yes?" He grinned.

I shrugged. "She's a good-looker...."

"Yes, I saw her." Now he shrugged. "That other thing—just old myths and legends, that's all. Like your English Dracula, eh?"

"Transylvanian Dracula," I corrected him.

"Whatever you like. And Necros: that's the name of the spook, see?"

"Necros is the name of a vampire?"

"A spook, yes."

"And this is a real legend? I mean, historical?"

He made a fifty-fifty face, his hands palms up. "Local, I guess. Ligurian. I remember it from when I was a kid. If I was bad, old Necros sure to come and get me. Today," again the shrug, "it's forgotten."

"Like the bogeyman." I nodded.

"Eh?"

"Nothing. But why did the old girl go on like that?"

Again he shrugged. "Maybe she think that old man Necros, eh? She crazy, you know? Very backward. The whole family."

I was still interested. "How does the legend go?"

"The spook takes the life out of you. You grow old, spook grows young. It's a bargain you make: he gives you something you want, gets what he wants. What he wants is your youth. Except he uses it up quick and needs more. All the time, more youth."

"What kind of bargain is that?" I asked. "What does the victim get out of it?"

"Gets what he wants," said Mario, his brown face cracking into another grin. "In your case the girl, eh? If the little man was Necros...."

He got on with his work and I sat there sipping my Negroni. End of conversation. I thought no more about it—until later.

2.

Of course, I should have been in Italy with Linda, but...I had kept her "Dear John" for a fortnight before shredding it, getting mindlessly drunk and starting in on the process of forgetting. That had been a month ago. The holiday had already been booked and I wasn't about to miss out on my trip to the sun. And so I had come out on my own. It was hot, the swimming was good, life was easy and the food superb. With just two days left to enjoy it, I told myself it hadn't been bad. But it would have been better with Linda.

Linda... She was still on my mind—at the back of it, anyway—later that night as I sat in the bar of my hotel beside an open bougainvillea-decked balcony that looked down on the bay and the seafront lights of the town. And maybe she wasn't all that far back in my mind—maybe she was right there in front—or else I was just plain daydreaming. Whichever, I missed the entry of the lovely lady and her shriveled companion, failing to spot and recognize them until they were taking their seats at a little table just the other side of the balcony's sweep.

This was the closest I'd been to her, and—

Well, first impressions hadn't lied. This girl was beautiful. She didn't look quite as young as she'd first seemed—my own age, maybe—but beautiful she certainly was. And the old boy? He must be, could only be, her father. Maybe it sounds like I was a little naive, but with her looks this lady really didn't need an old man. And if she did need one it didn't have to be this one.

By now she'd seen me and my fascination with her must have been obvious. Seeing it, she smiled and blushed at one and the same time, and for a moment turned her eyes away—but only for a moment. Fortunately her companion had his back to me or he must have known my feelings at once; for as she looked at me again—fully upon me this time—I could have sworn I read an invitation in her eyes, and in that same moment any bitter vows I may have made melted away completely and were forgotten. God, please let him be her father!

For an hour I sat there, drinking a few too many cocktails, eating olives and potato crisps from little bowls on the bar, keeping my eyes off the girl as best I could, if only for common decency's sake. But...all the time I worried frantically at the problem of how to introduce myself, and as the minutes ticked by it seemed to me that the most obvious way must also be the best.

But how obvious would it be to the old boy?

And the damnable thing was that the girl hadn't given me another glance since her original—invitation? Had I mistaken that look of hers—or was she simply waiting for me to make the first move? God, let him be her father!

She was sipping martinis, slowly; he drank a rich red wine, in some quantity. I asked a waiter to replenish their glasses and charge it to me. I had already spoken to the bar steward, a swarthy, friendly little chap from the South called Francesco, but he hadn't been able to enlighten me. The pair were not resident, he assured me; but being resident myself I was already pretty sure of that.

Anyway, my drinks were delivered to their table; they looked surprised; the girl put on a perfectly innocent expression, questioned the waiter, nodded in my direction and gave me a cautious smile, and the old boy turned his head to stare at me. I found myself smiling in return but avoiding his eyes, which were like coals now, sunken deep in his brown, wrinkled face. Time seemed suspended—if only for a second—then the girl spoke again to the waiter and he came across to me.

"Mr. Collins, sir, the gentleman and the young lady thank you and request that you join them." Which was everything I had dared hope for—for the moment.

Standing up, I suddenly realized how much I'd had to drink. I willed sobriety on myself and walked across to their table. They didn't stand up but the little chap said, "Please sit." His voice was a rustle of dried grass. The waiter was behind me with a chair. I sat.

"Peter Collins," I said. "How do you do, Mr.—er?—"

"Karpethes," he answered. "Nichos Karpethes. And this is my wife, Adrienne." Neither one of them had made the effort to extend their hands, but that didn't dismay me. Only the fact that they were married dismayed me. He must be very, very rich, this Nichos Karpethes.

"I'm delighted you invited me over," I said, forcing a smile, "but I see that I was mistaken. You see, I thought I heard you speaking English, and I—"

"Thought we were English?" she finished it for me. "A natural error. Originally I am Armenian, Nichos is Greek, of course. We do not speak each other's tongue, but we do both speak English. Are you staying here, Mr. Collins?"

"Er, yes—for one more day and night. Then—" I shrugged and put on a sad look, "—back to England, I'm afraid."

"Afraid?" the old boy whispered. "There is something to fear in a return to your homeland?"

"Just an expression," I answered. "I meant, I'm afraid that my holiday is coming to an end."

He smiled. It was a strange, wistful sort of smile, wrinkling his face up like a little walnut. "But your friends will be glad to see you again. Your loved ones—?"

I shook my head. "Only a handful of friends—none of them really close—and no loved ones. I'm a loner, Mr. Karpethes."

"A loner?" His eyes glowed deep in their sockets and his hands began to tremble where they gripped the table's rim. "Mr. Collins, you don't—"

"We understand," she cut him off. "For although we are together, we too, in our way, are loners. Money has made Nichos lonely, you see? Also, he is not a well man, and time is short. He will not waste what time he has on frivolous friendships. As for myself—people do not understand our being together, Nichos and I. They pry, and I withdraw. And so, I too, am a loner."

There was no accusation in her voice, but still I felt obliged to say: "I certainly didn't intend to pry, Mrs.—"

"Adrienne," she smiled. "Please. No, of course you didn't. I would not want you to think we thought that of you. Anyway I will tell you why we are together, and then it will be put aside."

Her husband coughed, seemed to choke, struggled to his feet. I stood up and took his arm. He at once shook me off—with some distaste, I thought—but Adrienne had already signaled to a waiter. "Assist Mr. Karpethes to the gentleman's room," she quickly instructed in very good Italian. "And please help him back to the table when he has recovered."

As he went, Karpethes gesticulated, probably tried to say something to me by way of an apology, choked again and reeled as he allowed the waiter to help him from the room.

"I'm...sorry," I said, not knowing what else to say.

"He has attacks." She was cool. "Do not concern yourself. I am used to it."

We sat in silence for a moment. Finally I began: "You were going to tell me—"

"Ah, yes! I had forgotten. It is a symbiosis."

"Oh?"

"Yes. I need the good life he can give me, and he needs…my youth. We supply each other's needs." And so, in a way, the old woman with the idiot boy hadn't been wrong after all. A sort of bargain had indeed been struck. Between Karpethes and his wife. As that thought crossed my mind I felt the short hairs at the back of my neck stiffen for a moment. Goose-flesh crawled on my arms. After all, "Nichos" was pretty close to "Necros", and now this youth thing again. Coincidence, of course. And after all, aren't all relationships bargains of sorts? Bargains struck for better or for worse.

"But for how long?" I asked. "I mean, how long will it work for you?"

She shrugged. "I have been provided for. And he will have me all the days of his life."

I coughed, cleared my throat, gave a strained, self-conscious laugh. "And here's me, the non-pryer!"

"No, not at all, I wanted you to know."

"Well," I shrugged, "—but it's been a pretty deep first conversation."

"First? Did you believe that buying me a drink would entitle you to more than one conversation?"

I almost winced. "Actually, I—"

But then she smiled and my world lit up. "You did not need to buy the drinks," she said. "There would have been some other way."

I looked at her inquiringly. "Some other way to—?"

"To find out if we were English or not."

"Oh!"

"Here comes Nichos now," she smiled across the room. "And we must be leaving. He's not well. Tell me, will you be on the beach tomorrow?"

"Oh—yes!" I answered after a moment's hesitation. "I like to swim."

"So do I. Perhaps we can swim out to the raft…?"

"I'd like that very much."

Her husband arrived back at the table under his own steam. He looked a little stronger now, not quite so shriveled somehow. He did not sit but gripped the back of his chair with parchment fingers, knuckles white where the skin stretched over old bones. "Mr. Collins," he rustled, "—Adrienne, I'm sorry…."

"There's really no need," I said, rising.

"We really must be going." She also stood. "No, you stay here, er, Peter? It's kind of you, but we can manage. Perhaps we'll see you on the beach." And she helped him to the door of the bar and through it without once looking back.

3.

They weren't staying at my hotel, had simply dropped in for a drink. That was understandable (though I would have preferred to think that she had been looking for me) for *my* hotel was middling tourist-class while theirs was something else. They were up on the hill, high on the crest of a Ligurian spur where a smaller, much more exclusive place nestled in Mediterranean pines. A place whose lights spelled money when they shone up there at night, whose music came floating down from a tiny open-air disco like the laughter of high-living elementals of the air. If I was poetic it was because of her. I mean, that beautiful girl and that weary, wrinkled dried-up walnut of an old man. If anything, I was sorry for him. And yet in another way I wasn't.

And let's make no pretence about it—if I haven't said it already, let me say it right now—I wanted her. Moreover, there had been that about our conversation, her beach invitation, which told me that she was available.

The thought of it kept me awake half the night....

I was on the beach at 9.00 a.m.—they didn't show until 11.00. When they did, and when she came out of her tiny changing cubicle—

There wasn't a male head on the beach that didn't turn at least twice. Who could blame them? That girl, in that costume, would have turned the head of a sphinx. But—there was something, some little nagging thing, different about her. A maturity beyond her years? She held herself like a model, a princess. But who was it for? Karpethes or me?

As for the old man: he was in a crumpled lightweight summer suit and sunshade hat as usual, but he seemed a bit more perky this morning. Unlike myself he'd doubtless had a good night's sleep. While his wife had been changing he had made his way unsteadily across the pebbly beach to my table and sun umbrella, taking the seat directly opposite me; and before his wife could appear he had opened with: "Good morning, Mr. Collins."

"Good morning," I answered. "Please call me Peter."

"Peter, then," he nodded. He seemed out of breath, either from his stumbling walk over the beach or a certain urgency which I could detect in his movements, his hurried, almost rude "let's get down to it" manner.

"Peter, you said you would be here for one more day?"

"That's right," I answered, for the first time studying him closely where he sat like some strange garden gnome half in the shade of the beach umbrella. "This is my last day."

He was a bundle of dry wood, a desiccated prune, a small, umber scarecrow. And his voice, too, was of straw, or autumn leaves blown across a shady path. Only his eyes were alive. "And you said you have no family, few friends, no one to miss you back in England?"

Warning bells rang in my head. Maybe it wasn't so much urgency in him—which usually implies a goal or ambition still to be realized—but eagerness in that the goal was in sight. "That's correct. I am, was, a student doctor. When I get home I shall seek a position. Other than that there's nothing, no one, no ties."

He leaned forward, bird eyes very bright, claw hand reaching across the table, trembling, and—

Her shadow suddenly fell across us as she stood there in that costume. Karpethes jerked back in his chair. His face was working, strange emotions twisting the folds and wrinkles of his flesh into stranger contours. I could feel my heart thumping against my ribs…why, I couldn't say. I calmed myself, looked up at her and smiled.

She stood with her back to the sun, which made a dark silhouette of her head and face. But in that blot of darkness her oval eyes were green jewels. "Shall we swim, Peter?"

She turned and ran down the beach, and of course I ran after her. She had a head start and beat me to the water, beat me to the raft, too. It wasn't until I hauled myself up beside her that I thought of Karpethes: how I hadn't even excused myself before plunging after her. But at least the water had cleared my head, bringing me completely awake and aware.

Aware of her incredible body where it stretched, almost touching mine, on the fibre deck of the gently bobbing raft.

I mentioned her husband's line of inquiry, gasping a little for breath as I recovered from the frantic exercise of our race. She, on the other hand, already seemed completely recovered. She carefully arranged her hair about her shoulders like a fan, to dry in the sunlight, before answering.

"Nichos is not really my husband," she finally said, not looking at me. "I am his companion, that's all. I could have told you last night, but…there was the chance that you really were curious only about our nationality. As for any 'veiled threats' he might have issued: that is not unusual. He might not have the vitality of younger men, but jealousy is ageless."

"No," I answered, "he didn't threaten—not that I noticed. But jealousy? Knowing I have only one more day to spend here, what has he to fear from me?"

Her shoulders twitched a little, a shrug. She turned her face to me, her lips inches away. Her eyelashes were like silken shutters over green pools, hiding whatever swam in the deeps. "I am young, Peter, and so are you. And you are very attractive, very…eager? Holiday romances are not uncommon."

My blood was on fire. "I have very little money," I said. "We are staying at different hotels. He already suspects me. It is impossible."

"What is?" she innocently asked, leaving me at a complete loss.

But then she laughed, tossed back her hair, already dry, dangled her hands and arms in the water. "Where there's a will…." she said.

"You know that I want you—" The words spilled out before I could control or change them.

"Oh, yes. And I want you." She said it so simply, and yet suddenly I felt seared. A moth brushing the magnet candle's flame.

I lifted my head, looked towards the beach. Across seventy-five yards of sparkling water the beach umbrellas looked very large and close. Karpethes sat in the shade just as I had last seen him, his face hidden in shadow. But I knew that he watched.

"You can do nothing here," she said, her voice languid—but I noticed now that she, too, seemed short of breath.

"This," I told her with a groan, "is going to kill me!"

She laughed, laughter that sparkled more than the sun on the sea. "I'm sorry," she said more soberly. "It's unfair of me to laugh. But—your case is not hopeless."

"Oh?"

"Tomorrow morning, early, Nichos has an appointment with a specialist in Geneva. I am to drive him into the city tonight. We'll stay at a hotel overnight."

I groaned my misery. "Then my case is quite hopeless. I fly tomorrow."

"But if I sprained my wrist," she said, "and so could not drive…and if he went into Geneva by taxi while I stayed behind with a headache—because of the pain from my wrist—" Like a flash she was on her feet, the raft tilting, her body diving, striking the water into a spray of diamonds.

Seconds for it all to sink in—and then I was following her, laboring through the water in her churning wake. And as she splashed from the sea, seeing her stumble, go to her hands and knees in Ligurian shingle—and the pained look on her face, the way she held her wrist as she came to her feet. As easy as that!

Karpethes, struggling to rise from his seat, stared at her with his mouth agape. Her face screwed up now as I followed her up the beach. And Adrienne holding her "sprained" wrist and shaking it, her mouth forming an elongated "O". The sinuous motion of her body and limbs, mobile marble with dew of ocean clinging saltily….

If the tiny man had said to me: "I am Necros. I want ten years of your life for one night with her," at that moment I might have sealed the bargain. Gladly. But legends are legends and he wasn't Necros, and he didn't, and I didn't. After all, there was no need….

4.

I suppose my greatest fear was that she might be "having me on," amusing herself at my expense. She was, of course, "safe" with me—in so far as I would be gone tomorrow and the "romance" forgotten, for her, anyway—and I could also see how she was starved for young companionship, a fact she had brought right out in the open from the word go.

But why me? Why should I be so lucky?

Attractive? Was I? I had never thought so. Perhaps it was because I was so safe: here today and gone tomorrow, with little or no chance of complications. Yes, that must be it. If she wasn't simply making a fool of me. She might be just a tease—

But she wasn't.

At 8.30 that evening I was in the bar of my hotel—had been there for an hour, careful not to drink too much, unable to eat—when the waiter came to me and said there was a call for me on the reception telephone. I hurried out to reception where the clerk discreetly excused himself and left me alone.

"Peter?" Her voice was a deep well of promise. "He's gone. I've booked us a table, to dine at 9.00. Is that all right for you?"

"A table? Where?" my own voice, breathless.

"Why, up here, of course! Oh, don't worry, it's perfectly safe. And anyway, Nichos knows."

"Knows?" I was taken aback, a little panicked. "What does he know?"

"That we're dining together. In fact he suggested it. He didn't want me to eat alone—and since this is your last night…."

"I'll get a taxi right away," I told her.

"Good. I look forward to…seeing you. I shall be in the bar."

I replaced the telephone in its cradle, wondering if she always took an aperitif before the main course….

I had smartened myself up. That is to say, I was immaculate. Black bow-tie, white evening jacket (courtesy of C & A), black trousers and a lightly frilled white shirt, the only one I had ever owned. But I might have known that my appearance would never match up to hers. It seemed that everything she did was just perfectly right. I could only hope that that meant literally everything.

But in her black lace evening gown with its plunging neckline, short wide sleeves and delicate silver embroidery, she was stunning. Sitting with her in the bar, sipping our drinks—for me a large whisky and for her a tall Cinzano—I couldn't take my eyes off her. Twice I reached out for her hand and twice she drew back from me.

"Discreet they may well be," she said, letting her oval green eyes flicker towards the bar, where guests stood and chatted, and back to me, "but there's really no need to give them occasion to gossip."

"I'm sorry. Adrienne," I told her, my voice husky and close to trembling, "but—"

"How is it," she demurely cut me off, "that a good-looking man like you is—how do you say it?—'going short'?"

I sat back, chuckled. "That's a rather unladylike expression," I told her.

"Oh? And what I've planned for tonight is ladylike?"

My voice went huskier still. "Just what is your plan?"

"While we eat," she answered, her voice low, "I shall tell you." At which point a waiter loomed, napkin over his arm, inviting us to accompany him to the dining room.

Adrienne's portions were tiny, mine huge. She sipped a slender, light white wine, I gulped blocky rich red from a glass the waiter couldn't seem to leave alone. Mercifully I was hungry—I hadn't eaten all day—else that meal must surely have bloated me out. And all of it ordered in advance, the very best in quality cuisine.

"This," she eventually said, handing me her key, "fits the door of our suite." We were sitting back, enjoying liqueurs and cigarettes. "The rooms are on the ground floor. Tonight you enter through the door, tomorrow morning you leave via the window. A slow walk down to the seafront will refresh you. How is that for a plan?"

"Unbelievable!"

"You don't believe it?"

"Not my good fortune, no."

"Shall we say that we both have our needs?"

"I think," I said, "that I may be falling in love with you. What if I don't wish to leave in the morning?"

She shrugged, smiled, said: "Who knows what tomorrow may bring?"

How could I ever have thought of her simply as another girl? Or even an ordinary young woman? Girl she certainly was, woman, too, but so…knowing! Beautiful as a princess and knowing as a whore.

If Mario's old myths and legends were reality, and if Nichos Karpethes were really Necros, then he'd surely picked the right companion. No man born could ever have resisted Adrienne, of that I was quite certain. These thoughts were in my mind—but dimly, at the back of my mind—as I left her smoking in the dining-room and followed her directions to the suite of rooms at the rear of the hotel. In the front of my mind were other thoughts, much more vivid and completely erotic.

I found the suite, entered, left the door slightly ajar behind me.

The thing about an Italian room is its size. An entire suite of rooms is vast. As it happened, I was only interested in one room, and Adrienne had obligingly left the door to that one open.

I was sweating. And yet…I shivered.

Adrienne had said fifteen minutes, time enough for her to smoke another cigarette and finish her drink. Then she would come to me. By now the entire staff of the hotel probably knew I was in here, but this was Italy.

5.

I shivered again. Excitement? Probably.

I threw off my clothes, found my way to the bathroom, took the quickest shower of my life. Drying myself off, I padded back to the bedroom.

Between the main bedroom and the bathroom a smaller door stood ajar. I froze as I reached it, my senses suddenly alert, my ears seeming to stretch themselves into vast receivers to pick up any slightest sound. For there had been a sound. I was sure of it, from that room….

A scratching? A rustle? A whisper? I couldn't say. But a sound, anyway.

Adrienne would be coming soon. Standing outside that door I slowly recommenced toweling myself dry. My naked feet were still firmly rooted, but my hands automatically worked with the towel. It was nerves, only nerves. There had been no sound, or at most only the night breeze off the sea, whispering in through an open window.

I stopped toweling, took another step towards the main bedroom, heard the sound again. A small, choking rasp. A tiny gasping for air.

Karpethes? What the hell was going on?

I shivered violently, my suddenly chill flesh shuddering in an uncontrollable spasm. But…I forced myself to action, returned to the main bedroom, quickly dressed (with the exception of my tie and jacket) and crept back to the small room.

Adrienne must be on her way to me even now. She mustn't find me poking my nose into things, like a suspicious kid. I must kill off this silly feeling that had my skin crawling. Not that an attack of nerves was unnatural in the circumstances, on the contrary, but I wasn't about to let it spoil the night. I pushed open the door of the room, entered into darkness, found the light switch. Then—

I held my breath, flipped the switch.

The room was only half as big as the others. It contained a small single bed, a bedside table, a wardrobe. Nothing more, or at least nothing immediately apparent to my wildly darting eyes. My heart, which was racing, slowed and began to settle towards a steadier beat. The window was open, external shutters closed—but small night sounds were finding their way in through the louvers. The distant sounds of traffic, the toot of horns—holiday sounds from below.

I breathed deeply and gratefully, and saw something projecting from beneath the pillow on the bed. A corner of card or of dark leather, like a wallet or—

Or a passport!

A Greek passport, Karpethes', when I opened it. But how could it be? The man in the photograph was young, no older than me. His birth date proved it. But there was his name: Nichos Karpethes. Printed in Greek, of course, but still plain enough. His son?

Puzzling over the passport had served to distract me. My nerves had steadied up. I tossed the passport down, frowned at it where it lay upon the bed, breathed deeply once more...then froze solid!

A scratching, a hissing, a dry grunting—from the wardrobe.

Mice? Or did I in fact smell a rat?

Even as the short hairs bristled on the back of my neck I knew anger. There were too many unexplained things here. Too much I didn't understand. And what was it I feared? Old Mario's myths and legends? No, for in my experience the Italians are notorious for getting things wrong. Oh, yes, notorious....

I reached out, turned the wardrobe's doorknob, yanked the doors open.

At first I saw nothing of any importance or significance. My eyes didn't know what they sought. Shoes, patent leather, two pairs, stood side by side below. Tiny suits, no bigger than boys' sizes, hung above on steel hangers. And—my God, my God—a waistcoat!

I backed out of that little room on rubber legs, with the silence of the suite shrieking all about me, my eyes bulging, my jaw hanging slack—

"Peter?"

She came in through the suite's main door, came floating towards me, eager, smiling, her green eyes blazing. Then blazing their suspicion, their anger, as they saw my condition. "Peter!"

I lurched away as her hands reached for me, those hands I had never yet touched, which had never touched me. Then I was into the main bedroom, snatching my tie and jacket from the bed, (don't ask me why) and out of the window, yelling some inarticulate, choking thing at her and lashing out frenziedly with my foot as she reached after me. Her eyes were bubbling green hells. "Peter?"

Her fingers closed on my forearm, bands of steel containing a fierce, hungry heat. And strong as two men, she began to lift me back into her lair!

I put my feet against the wall, kicked, came free and crashed backwards into shrubbery. Then up on my feet, gasping for air, running, tumbling, crashing into the night. Down madly tilting slopes, through black chasms of mountain pine with the Mediterranean stars winking overhead, and the beckoning, friendly lights of the village seen occasionally below....

In the morning, looking up at the way I had descended and remembering the nightmare of my panic-flight, I counted myself lucky to have survived it. The place was precipitous. In the end I had fallen, but only for a short distance. All in utter darkness, and my head striking something hard. But....

I did survive. Survived both Adrienne and my flight from her.

Waking with the dawn, stiff and bruised and with a massive bump on my forehead, I staggered back to my hotel, locked the door behind me—then sat there trembling and moaning until it was time for the coach.

Weak? Maybe I was, maybe I am.

But on my way into Geneva, with people round me and the sun hot through the coach's windows, I could think again. I could roll up my sleeve and examine that claw mark of four slim fingers and a thumb, branded white into my suntanned flesh, where hair would never grow again on skin sere and wrinkled.

And seeing those marks I could also remember the wardrobe and the waistcoat—and what the waistcoat contained.

That tiny puppet of a man, alive still but barely, his stick-arms dangling through the waistcoat's arm holes, his baby's head projecting, its chin supported by the tightly buttoned waistcoat's breast. And the large bulldog clip over the hanger's bar, its teeth fastened in the loose, wrinkled skin of his walnut head, holding it up. And his skinny little legs dangling, twig-things twitching there; and his pleading, pleading eyes!

But eyes are something I mustn't dwell upon.

And green is a color I can no longer bear....

EXSANGUINATIONS:

A HANDBOOK FOR THE EDUCATED VAMPIRE

by Anna S. Oppenhagen-Petrescu

translated from the Romanian by Catherynne M. Valente

Catherynne M. Valente is the critically acclaimed author of *The Orphan's Tales*, the first volume of which, *In the Night Garden*, won the Tiptree Award and was a finalist for the World Fantasy Award. She is also the author of the novels *The Labyrinth*, *Yume No Hon: The Book of Dreams*, and *The Grass-Cutting Sword*. Her latest novel, *Palimpsest*—which she describes as "a baroque meeting of science fiction and fantasy"—was published in February. In May, her first science fiction story, "Golubash, or Wine-Blood-War-Elegy" appeared in my anthology, *Federations*.

This next piece, translated by Valente, is an excerpt from *Exsanguinations: A Handbook for the Educated Vampire*, the indispensable tome of vampire legends and lore by noted vampire scholar Anna-Silvia Oppenhagen-Petrescu of the University of Budapest.

Valente originally published this prefatory and press material on her website, annapetrescu.catherynnemvalente.com. It appears here in print for the first time. Look for *Exsanguinations* at fine purveyors of Demonic Texts throughout Europe and America in October 2009.

AN IDEAL VAMPIRE: PREFATORY NOTES

Death is such a Victorian conceit.

Death is solemn, it is colorless. The unfortunate maiden is laid in a long bed with a silk scarf at the neck, scented with oils so that her stink does not offend delicate nostrils, her hair brushed to a lustre never achieved in life, skin powdered pale and smooth, lips drawn in obscene red: all to give the appearance of life just snuffed out, so recently that the body has not yet realized it has not merely dozed off in the midst of a pleasant afternoon. Why, her eyelashes never laid so coyly dark upon her cheek! Her color was never so high and fever-flushed! Her teeth

409

never sat so white upon her scarlet lips, her curls never clustered so black around her seraphic face!

In short, all effort has been made to make the poor corpse appear immortal, to dress it as a vampire. After all, it is not a proper funeral if she does not look so fresh that she could leap at any moment from the coffin and affix her teeth to a relative's jugular. It is a fetish, really, the just-dead virgin. As if death were a door from which she must emerge a whore, demoniac, and hungry.

The vampire, on the contrary, is essentially Byronic. It walks in beauty like the night, and through the night, and in it, it is always windswept and brooding, dandified by the accessories of death—the cross, the coffin, the shroud. But these things are merely fashion, no more intrinsic to the vampire self than a widow's peak or a Lugosian laugh. What is necessary is the predatory instinct, and the eternal study of death, since the vampire is its most skilled practitioner. The vampire is not half in love with easeful death, it *is* easeful death, and it has some small duty to make of death an art, an ecstasy, a philosophy. Else why be a demon? Certainly mortals cannot get away with such pretension. One might casually wonder whether the vampire was a product of the Gothic imagination, or the Gothic imagination was a product of the vampire—if one were predisposed to ponder such questions. The vampire, by its nature, does so. Unable to see itself in a looking-glass, it is the vainest of all creatures, and considers its own nature incessantly. These days, there are night-conferences in Bulgaria and Romania, with endless papers and sample chapters of promised masterpieces.

Of course, being Byronic, the ideal vampire is male, heroic in his way, a frontiersman braving the wilds of humanity, piling high his carcasses on the plains.

I am not an ideal vampire.

But surely my curls were never so black and shining as the day they lay me in the dirt. I listened to them mumble the old 23rd and counted like sheep the thud-falls of shoveled earth on the lid of what I must assume was a very expensive coffin. Death, as I have said, is Victorian—thus, no family would allow themselves to be seen in public with sub-par funerary rites.

I will not here indulge in that most vulgar of recent fashions, autobiography. Suffice it to say that I, along with every other vampire since the classical age of our Slavic forefathers, clawed my way out of that very well-appointed coffin and into the inevitably moonlit night. I availed myself, as so many of us do, of the graveyard caretaker as my first victim—how many of us recall the awkwardness of that first exsanguination! It is so much like making love for the first time; one has no clear idea what goes where, but clutches stiffly to whatever seems more or less correct, spraying fluids all over one's best evening clothes and mumbling apologies to the hapless partner, who no doubt experienced none of the crude pleasure one hoards to oneself. Of course, the experience of feeding is hardly the psycho-sexual revelation recent extra-cultural authors have claimed—do you, dear reader, find yourself in involuntary climax when ingesting a plate of pasta and a modest red wine? Certainly not. Yet certain in vogue lady novelists would have their deluded readership believe our own furtive suppers are orgiastic communions of the highest order.

Ah, but I have forgotten the tiresome necessity of all vampiric literature—I have not given my credentials. I ought to simply attach a notice of my parentage to my lapel or my Curriculum Vitae, perhaps even have it notarized like the breeding papers of a half-feeble spaniel. But certainly, without credentials, I can have nothing of importance to say. Very well.

I was sponsored by a very beguiling old debauch by the name of Ambrose Mosshammer who asked me to stay after his Herodotus seminar for special instruction. I fully expected to be accosted in his windowless eighth floor office—though when I imagined his skeletal hand groping my breasts and tearing my new wool skirt, I did not quite realize that he would simultaneously be whispering the tale of Gyges in my ear and divining the path of my jugular with his tongue before slashing into my throat with his gnarled, ancient teeth. It was certainly not what I had been led to expect young ladies experienced behind the closed doors of the offices of elderly colleagues. (I beg the forgiveness of any vampiric readers, for whom this recitation must be as tedious and gauche as a human reading about the expulsion of the placenta from his mother's womb. But the forms must be followed.)

Ambrose's blood tasted faintly of dust and the glue of book-bindings, as well as a peculiar undertaste of sandalwood and tobacco. It was not unpleasant, but I was rather in a rush to finish the process, once I realized what was afoot. There is no need to dwell in ritual—that sort of decadence can be safely left to Catholicism. He proffered his wrist in a most gentlemanly manner, and I availed myself of the necessary blood. I cannot overstate his professionalism and patience, truly, the old ones have a gravitas the younger generation of fiends cannot match.

I left his office with a rumpled skirt and a torn blouse, carried by his graduate students out to the parking lot, where I could safely be assumed to have been a victim of an over-zealous mugger. A few days later, I had risen from my grave and thusly embarked on my postdoctoral career.

—Anna S. Oppenhagen-Petrescu
University of Budapest
Night Campus

ABOUT THE AUTHOR

Anna-Silvia Oppenhagen-Petrescu was born in 1948 to Danish-Romanian parents, Adrian Petrescu and Marie Oppenhagen. Adrian and Marie had immigrated from the Continent whilst Marie was pregnant to the quiet London suburb of Kensington, where they raised their only daughter in relative tranquility[1].

The life of a young scholar is often tediously predictable, and young Anna was educated in the usual single-sex boarding schools before entering the equally homogenous St. Hilda's College, Oxford University. She studied Classics there under the watchful eye of Dr. Ambrose K. Mosshammer, who in her final year of study graciously Converted her in recognition of her great talent[2].

Once Anna had graduated, her interest shifted from the roots of human civilization in Ancient Greece to the roots of Vampiric civilization in the Slavic states and Central Europe. Her unromantic and strictly researched work in the field of Proto-History is widely recognized as having been one of the foundations of the field. In 1983, she helped to establish the Order of the Ivory Tooth, an association of literary historians who set out to archive the entirety of the Vampiric Corpus—that is, the sum total of all literature involving Vampires in the West. While this goal is far from complete, the Order is now one of the most highly respected institutions among the Vampiric elite, and its work, and ritual conferences, are watched with great interest.

In the early eighties, while a humble lecturer at the University of the Danube[3], Anna was also involved in the Eden Project, a think-tank which aimed to definitively prove or debunk the ever-popular claims of pre-Slavic heritage through Lilith. In recent years, the Edenites have shifted their focus to documenting the Dark Ages of the Classical World and Early Semitic Culture, in which the records of Vampiric activity are so scarce as to be by and large discounted by the academic majority. The "Lilith Question," a now-ubiquitous term coined by Dr. Moira Russell, Anna's partner in Edenism, was never qualitatively answered, and the two disagree on the subject to this day.

In 1986, Anna was hired as a tenure-track professor at the University of Constantinople, where she produced her enormous and definitive critical work, *She Drained Me of My Very Marrow: The Female Vampire in History and Literature*[4]. The success and influence of this work cannot be overestimated, and continues to be the bedrock of Black Feminism[5], a movement which has become something of a juggernaut in recent years. In fact, it was largely due to the popularity of this "lay" history that the loose confederation of Night Campuses organized the first of its annual Conferences in Madrid, in 1993. Of course there are many other conferences around the world, and meetings of various Societies, but the general Conference of Shadow-Academia is by far the largest, most prestigious, and well-attended. It is, nowadays, simply referred to as "The Conference[6]."

Disagreements arose between Anna and the Faculty of Sanguinary History at Constantinople, largely revolving around Anna's involvement with the Edenites and her insistence on encouraging her graduate students to generate texts of their own to counter the horde of human literature on the subject of Vampires[7]. In 1991, she left Constantinople and took the prestigious Geisslerin Chair at the University of Budapest, where she teaches to this day.

Anna remains unmarried[8].

---

[1] It is considered somewhat gauche to reference one's mortal parentage when in polite society. Most modern vampires trace their heritage purely through the line of Conversion, often in the Spanish style, in which case Anna's rather baroque moniker would be Anna-Silvia Oppenhagen-Petrescu y Mosshammer y Chamberlain, etc. Nevertheless, for the sake of the

laity, she has chosen to briefly recount the flotsam and jetsam of her pre-Conversion existence here. Those of standing in the Community may feel secure in passing by this piece of historical curiosity.

[2] Dr. Mosshammer has kindly agreed to write an introduction to Dr. Petrescu's forthcoming work, *Exsanguinations: A Handbook for the Educated Vampire*. (University of Csejthe Press, 2005). The apprentice-master relationship between many vampires and the quasi-parental figures who Converted them is well-documented, but Dr. Mosshammer has been particularly supportive, and the editors of this site wish to take this opportunity to publicly thank him.

[3] And thus able to take part in such specious feminist activities, as the Danube is well-known as a hotbed of radical thought and shoddy workmanship—even popularly referred to as "The Berkeley of Eastern Europe."

[4] University of Darvulia Press, 1987.

[5] Black Feminism, a movement which centralizes the role of the female Vampire, the succubus, in Sanguinary History, is somewhat tainted in the view of most historians due to its roots in human scholarship. In the mortal world, second-wave feminism resulted in a great deal of literature—much of which was written by women like Anna who would later be Converted, bringing this rather specialized interest into their Vampiric studies. In addition, many find it ridiculous, in light of the great Vampires of literature being predominantly male, to privilege the role of the female—in essence, placing the role of the Three Sisters over that of Dracula. However, Black Feminists trace their lineage through such actual Vampire personages as Elizabeth Bathory, Clara Geisslerin, Augusta Gordon, and Emily Draper, scoffing at any attempt to drag Dracula into serious discussions of gender in the Community. This remains a controversy which finds Anna and her colleagues at its center, however, it has been suggested that since Anna herself was Converted by a male Vampire, she ought to be more grateful to the masculine animus, and confine herself to more traditional histories.

[6] The 2005 Conference will take place July 25-29 in Lodz, Poland, hosted by Plogojiwitz University. Hotels fill up quickly, so reservations are suggested.

[7] Much as it was once considered beneath mortal nobility to engage in mercantile activities, it is widely asserted that for Vampires to produce their own quasi-fictional texts is vulgar in the highest degree. To speak for ourselves threatens the exposure of our entire Community, and most agree that the formulation of ridiculous and outlandish stories of bloodletting and cannibalism ought to be left to those mortal authors who find it titillating.

[8] Predictably, this has caused a number of rumors to arise as to the orientation of Dr. Petrescu. While the editors of this site feel that such a subject is merely salacious and has no place in a professional biography, or in the parlor rooms of certain aged male Faculty members, they will note, without commentary, that Dr. Petrescu has co-habited with the Italian Edenite scholar Genevra Verzini in Budapest since 1995.

University of Csejthe Press

14 dr. Razvan Zeklos str., bl. 12C, 1st floor, 1st district, 011035 Bucharest | Phone: +4021.3316688 | Fax: 4021.3316689

CONTACT: Andrei Bogoescu, publicity@csejthepress.com

EXSANGUINATIONS
A Handbook For The Educated Vampire

by Anna S. Oppenhagen-Petrescu
translated from the Romanian by Catherynne M. Valente

AN OCTOBER 2009 RELEASE

In October 2009, the prestigious University of Csejthe Press will release Anna S. Oppenhagen-Petrescu's long-awaited work, *Exsanguinations: A Handbook for the Educated Vampire.* This much-discussed volume will contain a distillation of 25 years of research into the Origins, Customs, History, and Literature of the Vampire Community. It will serve both as a primer for the Newly Converted and a convenient desk reference for the experienced Dark Academic. Never before has such a variety of scholarly work been brought together in one place, and readers can look forward to a truly definitive delineation of the Vampire Culture in Dr. Petrescu's trademark simple, elegant prose.

Look for *Exsanguinations* at fine purveyors of Demonic Texts throughout Europe and America in October 2009.

ADVANCE PRAISE FOR EXSANGUINATIONS

"Petrescu has done it! This text will stand for many cycles of Conversion hence. There can be no finer manual for the Vampiric existence than this lovely volume, no more concise and sensitive expression of the postmodern fiend."
—Genevra Verzini

"Dare I call this the Vampiric Bible? I think I must, for no more inclusive and profound a book has yet been produced in the Community."
—Adrian Maru

To interview Anna S. Oppenhagen-Petrescu, or to request more information about *Exsanguinations* or any other Csejthe Press titles, contact Csejthe Press publicity director Andrei Bogoescu at publicity@csejthepress.com.

EXSANGUINATIONS
by Anna S. Oppenhagen-Petrescu
(Non-Fiction / 978-1-59780-156-0 / $15.95 / 400 pages)
a Csejthe Press trade paperback / October 2009
to learn more visit www.csejthepress.com

LUCY, IN HER SPLENDOR

by Charles Coleman Finlay

Charles Coleman Finlay is the author of the novel *The Prodigal Troll*. Writing as C. C. Finlay, he has a historical fantasy trilogy called *Traitor to the Crown* just out from Del Rey, consisting of *The Patriot Witch, A Spell for the Revolution,* and *The Demon Redcoat*. Finlay's short fiction has appeared in several magazines and anthologies, and has been collected in *Wild Things*. His novella, "The Political Prisoner," is a finalist for the 2009 Hugo and Nebula awards.

Finlay says that the appeal of the vampire is about the seduction of easy, self-gratifying choices, and the prices we pay for our pleasures. "It's about the contradiction that happens when we peer at the darkness within ourselves only to find a light," he said. "I suspect that vampires are a kind of literary Rorschach test, revealing the suppressed secrets of our individual personalities and emotional states. That's why they're such a source of endless fascination."

"Lucy, In Her Splendor" is about a couple that owns a bed and breakfast on an island. What happens on the island stays on the island, even when you'd rather have it go away.

When they were done, they sat in the plastic lawn chairs by the lake and listened in the dark to waves lapping the sharp white boulders mounded along the shore.

The first moth came fluttering from the direction of the pumphouse. It slapped into Lucy's cheek almost accidentally and startled them both. She raised her hand against it and the moth settled on one white-tipped nail. As she flicked her fingertip, it lifted into the air and hurtled back at her face.

A second and a third moth followed seconds later, followed in time by others until a tiny halo of insects swirled around her short, platinum blonde hair.

"Could be worse," Martin said, trying to wave them off. "Could be mosquitoes."

She smiled at him, shifted her chair closer, and leaned against his shoulder.

"God, Lucy, you're hot," he said.

She laughed, a little sadly, making a warm vibration that resonated in his chest. "I'm glad you still think so."

"No," he said. "Are you sure you haven't turned into a bug lamp. I swear you're hot enough to zap those bugs to ashes."

"You—"

She lifted her hand to slap him, but he caught it and folded her fingers within his own. Her skin was dry, caked with grit. He gave it a little squeeze and looked around, but rows of trees blocked the view of their neighbors. More bugs flew at Lucy's head.

Her voice trembled. "I'm really sick, aren't I?"

"It's just a fever. That's all it is." He placed her hand in his lap, and tried to wave the bugs away. One of the moth's wings buzzed harshly while the stones tapped against each other in the susurration of the waves. "Let's go inside."

"I don't know what I'd do without you," she whispered.

Without saying anything to reassure her, he helped her to her feet, propping her up as they strolled back to the house. When they passed the hand-carved sign that read "Crow's Nest Bed & Breakfast, Little Limestone Island," he flipped the board. *Sorry, No Vacancy.*

Her fever burned all night. Martin sat on the edge of the bed, feeding her tablets of aspirin and ice chips.

A single moth had followed them inside the house, tickling Lucy out of her rest until Martin turned on the lamp and the tiny creature flew to rest, panting, on the white shade. He smashed it, leaving a smear of gray dust and wings.

Walking over to the gable window, he gazed out of their attic apartment at the lake. All their life's savings were encompassed by these few acres of land, bounded on one end by the stone jetty covered with zebra-mussel shells and on the other by the apple tree with the bench swing. When insects began collecting at the screen, he stepped away.

Lucy shuddered in her sleep, sucking air through her mouth. Martin bent over and slipped his tongue—briefly—between her teeth. He expected the soursweet taste of sickness, but it wasn't there.

That only made it worse.

In the morning, Martin puttered in the kitchen even though they had no guests, making himself a cappuccino and sitting at the dining room table beside the double-hung windows facing the lake. An ore carrier moved sluggishly away from the island, heading past Put-in-Bay for the Ohio shore.

A tall, silver-haired man in gold pants and shirt—their neighbor, Bill—walked along the shore with a little girl about four or five years old. Martin's heart began to skip. He set his cup down so fast it splashed and ran through the screened-in porch, the door clapping shut behind him.

Sunrise glinted off the water. He shielded his eyes with his hand as he walked barefoot over the dew-damp grass. "Hey, neighbor!"

"Good morning, Marty," Bill replied. He gestured at the little girl. "This here's our granddaughter, Kelsey. Say hi, darling."

The little girl looked up at Martin. Panic flashed across her eyes, and she spun away from him to look at the lake.

"Hi, Kelsey," Martin said. He noticed the cappuccino running down his arm, and absent-mindedly lifted his wrist to his mouth to lick it off.

Bill shrugged. "Kids, huh. Folks don't teach 'em any manners these days." He pointed to the pumphouse, a squat block of concrete that sat on the edge of the lake. "When did you block that up?"

"Oh." The farmhouse was over a hundred years old. Before the island built its water supply, the farmers pumped it in directly from the lake. "A couple days ago."

"I thought you were going to turn it into a sauna."

"That's still the plan. But one of our guests was poking around in it after he came back from the winery. Fell and cut his head. Pretty big gash. He didn't need stitches, but we figured—"

"Liability?"

"Yeah."

"That's a shame, people not being responsible." Bill looked up to the porch. "Say, where are your guests? Isn't it about breakfast time?"

"We had to cancel all our reservations," Martin said. He watched Kelsey closely. She poked around the rocks, searching for a way into the pumphouse. "Lucy's been sick."

"Gosh, I'm sorry to hear that. What's wrong?"

"She came down with this fever—"

"Hey, there she is."

Martin turned. Lucy stood outlined in the attic window. The glass caught the sun, casting it in such a way that she was surrounded by a corona of jagged, golden light.

Bill waved to the attic window and cupped his hands to his mouth. "Get well soon, Lucy!"

She returned the greeting.

"You have an awful pretty wife there," Bill said.

Martin frowned. "Some days she's more awful than—"

Kelsey pounded on the side of the pumphouse with a rock. Martin hurried toward her, hand outstretched, stepping carefully in his bare feet across the stones. "Hey, Kelsey, come here. I want to show you something neat."

The little girl looked to her grandfather, who nodded permission.

"Shhh." Martin pressed his forefinger to his lips. With exaggerated tiptoeing, he led her onto their other neighbor's property. It was a small cabin, seldom used. Its lake pump had been more modern, an eight-foot square of concrete that jutted out from the shore like a single tooth in a child's mouth. Algae-slick boulders, driftwood branches, and other debris heaped around it.

The two inched slowly out on the slab until they reached the edge and saw the snakes—a dozen or more of them ranging in length from one to three feet. Their scales glistened black as they sunned themselves on the rocks.

Kelsey gasped and clung to Martin's leg, pressing her face against his thigh and peeking out. Martin wrapped his hand around the top of her head and pointed out to the water, where a new snake sinuated across the rippled surface toward the shore. It lifted its nose, turning it like a submarine periscope.

Bill crept up behind them and stomped his foot on the concrete, chuckling as they jumped. The snakes immediately disappeared among the rocks and driftbrush. The snake in the water dived beneath the surface.

Kelsey lifted her head. "Grampa!"

Martin straightened, letting her go. "They're harmless," he said. "Lake Erie water snakes. Endangered."

Bill wrapped his arms around his granddaughter. "Just 'cause they're endangered don't mean they're not dangerous. Tigers are endangered too, but they're still dangerous."

Martin smiled and stepped off the slab. "You come back any time you want to see my snakes now, Kelsey."

They said goodbye to one another. Martin watched until they were off the property, then went inside and watched out the window to be sure they didn't come back.

The setting sun sheened off the windshield, causing Martin to slow the car as he passed the black-clad teenagers strolling down the road, trading cigarettes. A pink-haired boy sneered at Martin and Lucy, shaping his hand into a claw and gouging at them. The other kids laughed.

"Are you sure you feel well enough to do this?" Martin asked Lucy.

She ran her fingertips over her face to smooth the skin. "It's been long enough. We have to get back to normal some time. And I do feel better."

"Good." Martin pulled into the lot of the Limestone Island Winery, tires crunching on the gravel. He jumped out and opened the door for her.

They walked up the steps. The winery sat on the waterfront, within walking distance of the docks. The terrace faced the lake so that's where the tourists gathered. A Jimmy Buffet song started over the speakers, an impromptu singalong shaking the walls as Lucy and Martin went into the pub.

Martin traded nods with a few locals watching the TVs and waved to the fortyish woman behind the bar. She wore a tight T-shirt, logoed with a bottle of Two Worms Tequila, a picture of a lemon, and the slogan "Suck this."

She waved back as Lucy and Martin took their usual booth in the corner. Then she yelled something into the kitchen, threw the towel over her shoulder, and came to join them.

"God, Lucy," she said, sliding in across the booth. "You're *radiant*. You look wonderful. You sure you've been sick?"

An enthusiastic chorus of "wasting away again" came through the wall from the terrace outside.

"Hi, Kate," Martin said above the singing.

"I don't look nearly as wonderful as you," Lucy answered, smiling. "Is that a new perm?"

She struck a pose, vamping the hairdo for them. "What do you think, Marty?"

"Looks terrific."

Kate's daughter, Maya, a high school senior, stepped to the kitchen door, looked around, and then carried over a bottle of red wine and three glasses. "Thanks, honey," Kate said. "Now don't serve anyone else. Make Mike do it."

"He hates coming out of the kitchen, Mom."

Kate wagged her finger. "I'm not kidding." As Maya stepped away, Kate snapped the towel at her butt. She twisted around, frowning. Martin winked at her.

"Now don't go making eyes at my daughter, Mr. Marty Van Wyk," Kate said, threatening him with the towel.

"Here, give me the bottle," he said. "I'll open it."

"What happened to Christie and Boyko?" Lucy asked, looking around. All summer long, Christie had waited tables while Boyko worked the kitchen.

Kate curled her lip dramatically. "The Vulgarians?"

"Bulgarians," Martin corrected.

"You ever notice the way they pawed each other all the time?" Kate asked.

Lucy leaned her head on Martin's shoulder. "They're in love with each other. It's very sweet."

"It was out of control."

The cork popped out of the bottle. Martin poured the dark red liquid into their three glasses. He slid the first one over to Kate. "Why are you talking about them in the past tense?"

"Didn't you hear? Hristina"—Kate pronounced it with the accent—"and Boyko disappeared two weeks ago. Not a word—we were worried! But then someone saw them over at Sandusky Pointe, running the roller coasters at the park. They said the pay was better over there, and they had some other job at night. They're trying to make as much as they can before their green cards expire and they have to go home."

Lucy sipped her wine.

"Everybody disappeared at once," Kate said. "First it was those two, then you, then Pitr. We all suspected—" She dropped her voice and lifted her eyebrows. "—foul play."

Martin swallowed his wine the wrong way and coughed. Pitr was Czech, from some small town with a castle south of Brno; he came over through the same agency that hired the other foreign workers. "Pitr?" he rasped. "He go over to the mainland too?"

"Probably." Kate leaned forward, elbows on the table, eyes glittering. "Say, did he ever come out to your place to fill that hole of yours?"

Lucy pressed her leg against Martin's. "He wasn't interested in doing any yardwork."

"Who's talking about yardwork?" Kate laughed. "Pitr's not interested in *any* work, but he's still good for business. God, he's gorgeous! Every woman who came in here wanted him."

Lucy put a hand against her throat. "He has such a lovely, full mouth," she said, just above a whisper.

"Uh-huh," added Kate, who overheard. "And what was his mouth full of? I bet Marty knows." She glanced down at his crotch and winked at him.

"If I did," Martin said, "I certainly wouldn't tell you."

"Oh, pooh! You two are no fun tonight."

Martin dipped his finger in his wine and pressed it against Lucy's forehead. The droplets sizzled. "We're just tired," he said. "And Lucy's not quite as well as we thought."

They left the winery, sitting at the island's only traffic light just outside the parking lot. A tiny beetle of some sort, attracted to Lucy, buzzed around the inside of the dark car.

"Oh, that was so awful," she said, trying to chase it away.

Martin reached up and flicked the overhead light on. The beetle flew to it, rested a second, then buzzed back at Lucy. "We've got a little money left. Enough to get away somewhere."

"No, we can't."

"Let's go over to the mainland then. See if we can find a doctor—"

"No! I'll get better."

Martin could see the light getting ready to change, but he waited while a couple trucks full of quarry workers sped through the intersection and parked across the street in front of the Ice Cellar, a rougher bar where locals hung out.

"I suppose it has to get better," he said, turning onto the road that led to the other side of the island and their house.

Lucy swatted at the beetle. "It can't get worse."

The next morning she was too weak from the fever to rise from bed. Martin sat in the easy chair by the bed and popped the tape into the VCR. He turned the sound off so he wouldn't disturb her, and hit the play button.

Despite what Kate thought, Martin only liked to watch. He had been hiding in the closet under the stairs the day Lucy invited Pitr over to do the yardwork.

The peephole made the picture hazy around the edges. Lucy stepped into the room—the "special" guest bedroom, next to the closet stairs—shook off her robe, and turned around right in front of the camera. Performing for it. Underneath she wore only a black corset, black stockings, high heels. She had rings on her thumbs and fingers, bracelets on her arms.

She looked as gorgeous as Martin had ever seen her, ten years younger than her actual age, timelessly beautiful.

The second figure stepped into view from the left. Pitr. Prettier than Kate's description. Scrumptious. "To die for," Lucy had said. And Martin had agreed. Dark skin, all muscle, pale blond hair, and lips so full they looked as though they would burst like bubbles if you touched them.

Lucy touched Pitr's lips. First with her fingernails. Then with her mouth, as her hands began to undress him. Still performing.

Martin hit pause on the tape. When he closed his eyes, he could still hear their sounds come through the walls. He could still smell the candles that Lucy had burned.

Blankets rustled, a foot bumped against the wall. Lucy tossed, mumbling in her delirium. He stroked her leg once.

Scooting forward to the edge of his seat, he hit the forward button. On the tape, Lucy straddled Pitr, her favorite position, but he grabbed her arms and flipped her over, forcing himself on top of her, roaring as he bulled away between her legs. Neither she nor Martin minded the roughness. Martin had parted his bathrobe and taken his cock in hand by then, watching everything on the little camcorder screen—it was an old camera, one they had used for years.

Lucy, still performing, bit into Pitr's dark, hairless chest.

Martin liked to see her hurt the other men. But this time something went beyond the normal rough play. Grabbing her arms and pinning them above her head, Pitr slammed into her so hard that she clamped her teeth down, twisting her head as if possessed, until the skin tore. Martin, so intent on his own desire, realized it only when he saw the blood trickling from her mouth.

He had sat there, then, in the closet, still holding himself loosely, frozen with the thought of viruses; they'd been exposed before and escaped okay—

Pitr pounded away until he groaned and pulled away. Lucy rolled over on her side, spitting out the blood, scrubbing her mouth with the sheets. Pitr stepped back from the bed, out of view of the camera, and spoke to her in some language that didn't sound like Czech to Martin, but something far older, harsher. He slammed the closet door.

Martin snatched up the remote and hit pause.

A full-length mirror hung on the closet door. When Pitr stepped in front of it, there was no sign of his bare flesh, only a vague, indefinite mist.

Rewind, play, pause. Again. Martin watched it over and over, frame by frame, but there was never anything there but the mist. Finally he clicked forward.

Pitr stepped away from the mirror. Lucy leaned back, bare-breasted chest heaving like a B-movie diva. Pitr grew to the height of the room, cackling at her, wiping blood from the wound on his chest with clawed fingers and anointing her like a priest at a baptism. She screamed.

Blankets rustled. "What are you doing?" Lucy asked in a weak, sleepy voice.

"Nothing," Martin said. He hit the eject button. Yanking the tape out of the cassette, he piled it at his feet until the reels were empty. Then he carried it downstairs and burned it all in the fireplace.

Martin stood at the kitchen counter, making soup for Lucy when he saw the rat outside on the rocks. It crawled all around the pumphouse, trying to scale the sides. Martin went out to the screened-in porch to watch it.

Finally the rat fell exhausted, lethargic.

Martin went out and picked up a large, flat rock from the herb garden beside the foundation. He crept slowly out to the pumphouse, expecting the rat to bolt away at any minute. But it crouched there, on the concrete base, facing the blank wall.

Martin slammed down the rock.

There was a wet crunch as it connected with the concrete pad; blood squirted out one side.

A ferocious tapping, faint but unmistakable, came from inside the pumphouse. Martin cupped his hands to the stone.

"Shut up, Pitr!" he shouted.

Then he went back inside.

It was late afternoon before Martin gathered the courage to find a pair of gloves and a shovel. He went back to the pumphouse, and tossed the bloody stone among the other boulders piled up where the waves licked the shore. Then he buried the rat. He covered the bloodstain on the concrete with dirt, and scuffed it in as well as he could with his deck shoes.

When he was done, he cupped his hands to the stone. "How do I make her well again, Pitr?" He leaned his ear to the concrete to hear the answer.

"Let me to come out and I will tell you," the voice croaked, so faint Martin could barely make it out. "She is burning, with the fire. Only I can help her."

"Fuck you, Pitr."

"I am come out and you can do that do." Laughter. Or choking. Martin rather hoped it was choking. "You want young again, Martin?" the voice cracked through the stone. "I can give you the young again."

"Yeah, you and Viagra. Go to hell, Pitr."

Something hard pounded on the inside wall. "You cannot keep me here. You cannot run far enough. When I—"

Martin lifted his ear from the concrete and heard nothing except the sound of the waves and the cries of a few gulls.

The sky was the color of faded jeans. Jet contrails seamed the blue, taking other people to some point far away. Martin walked wearily back to the house.

Lucy sat up in bed. The blankets were shoved against the footboard, but she was wrapped in a kimono. The glow inside her lit it up like a Japanese lantern.

"You upset him," she said, her voice cold.

He grabbed his wallet from the dresser, and started changing his clothes. "You know, he was already pissed. Something about being hit on the head while you were su—"

"No, I mean it." Her cold voice shattered with panic like ice in the sun. "He's going to hurt me, Martin. You promised you wouldn't let him hurt me."

"He's not going to hurt you." He pulled on clean pants.

"Where are you going?"

"Into town for a drink."

She grabbed the lamp on the bedside table and shoved it onto the floor. The base cracked. "Are you going to go see Kate? Are you going to go *fuck* Kate? Is that it, Martin?"

"I don't even like Kate," he said softly. He leaned over and kissed her forehead, then pushed her gently onto the bed. "If it makes you any happier, I'll go to the IceHouse. Won't even see her."

"I'm sorry, Martin. I didn't mean that. It's just—"

"I know." Rising, he took their bank deposit bag from its hiding place and emptied the cash into his pocket. Then he took the rest of their bills and did the same.

She clutched at his sleeve. "You're running away! Omigod, Martin. You're going to catch the ferry and leave me. You can't do that."

"I just need time to think," he said.

He pried her fingers loose and left the house before he lost his nerve.

It was after midnight before he returned, driving down the long dirt driveway through the woods to their house. He was drunk. Two other trucks followed his.

Lucy waited for him on the porch, in the papa-san chair, sitting directly under the one bright light.

The trucks pulled up and parked beside him. Martin lifted the case of beer off the front seat and carried it over to the picnic table. "I'm going to go get some ice to keep this cold, guys," he shouted over his shoulder, staggering to the porch.

Doors slammed in the dark. "Ain't gonna last that long," a harsh voice said. A can popped open. The others laughed.

Lucy rose and pressed herself against the screen. Insects pinged against it, trying to reach her. Bats screeched through the air, feasting.

"Is that really you, Martin? Who are those men?"

"Just some guys who work, from the quarry," he said, his tongue thick in his mouth. "I ran into down at the Ice Cellar. They're good guys. We had a few, a few beers."

"What are they doing, Martin?"

"Shhh." His forefinger smashed his lips. "They're doing us a l'il favor."

Her nostrils flared. Her mouth flattened out in a ruby O against the screen as she strained to see what they were doing. She took a step toward the door and sank to her knees, too weak to go any further.

A stocky, bearded man walked stiffly over to the porch. "Howdy, Missus Van Wyk," he said, sounding a little more sober than Martin. "Your husband told us 'bout the problem with the water stagnating in the pumphouse, making you sick and all'a that. Well, this ought to take care of it."

"Can' tell you how much I 'preciate this," Martin said.

He grinned and patted a wad of bills in his shirt pocket. "You already did. Just remember, it wasn't us who did it."

As he turned and walked away, Lucy whispered, "What are—"

"It's self the fence," Martin slurred.

The bats veered suddenly from their random feeding and began to swoop and shriek at the quarry men. Martin stepped over, blocked Lucy's view. The bats flew with less purpose. The men finished their work and ran back towards their trucks a hundred and fifty feet away. One of them grabbed the beer.

Lucy scraped at the screen, making it sing, her face a mixture of anguish and hope. "He said we couldn't kill him. He said he could turn into—"

One man shouted something as she spoke, then a second, then the explosion, a sharp blast that was mostly dark, not at all like the movies, followed by the pebbled drum of debris pattering on the lake.

Someone whistled, a note of appreciation.

"That ought about do it," someone said, and the others laughed. They climbed back into their trucks and drove off into the night with their headlights off.

Martin and Lucy leaned against each other, not touching, the screen between them.

Nursing a hangover, having hardly slept at all, Martin walked up and down the shore at the first hint of dawn, searching for bones or other pieces of Pitr. He thought the gulls might come for them, the way they sometimes came for dead fish. But the gulls stayed way offshore and he found nothing.

Bill came over at sunrise. The island's sheriff and his only deputy arrived shortly after. Martin, prepared to confess everything, instead heard himself repeating the story about some guest injuring himself, with Bill corroborating. Telling them how they bricked in the pumphouse to be safe. Speculating that maybe there was some kind of gas build-up or something.

The sheriff and his deputy seemed pretty skeptical about that last part. They climbed all over the rocks, examining the pieces. The deputy waded down into the water's edge. The flat rock from the garden stood out among all the water-smoothed boulders. The deputy grabbed it, flipped it over. The rat's blood made a dark stain on the bottom.

Martin's heart stuck in his throat.

"Say, is Lucy feeling any better yet?" Bill asked.

"Her fever broke last night, after almost a week," Martin answered, his voice squeaking.

The deputy let go of the rock. It splashed into the water. "What's that? Mrs. Van Wyk's been sick?"

Martin explained how sick she'd been, what a strain it had been on him, with no guests, not able to get out of the house. The sheriff and the deputy both liked Mrs. Van Wyk, appreciated the volunteer work she did for the island's Chamber of Commerce.

The sheriff's radio squawked. Some tourist had woken up on his yacht this morning missing his wallet and wanted to report it stolen. The two men left their regards for Lucy and headed back into town.

The deputy's eyes stared at Martin from the rearview mirror as the car pulled away.

Lucy stood by the window, wearing a long dress, a sweater on top of that, with a blanket around her shoulders. A slight breeze ruffled the lace curtains, slowly twisting them. Martin pressed his hand to her forehead. Her temperature felt normal; the glow had dissipated.

"I destroyed the camera," he told her. "And all the other tapes. I patched up the hole beneath the stairs."

"I'll never be warm again, Martin."

"I'll keep you warm." He wrapped his arms around her.

She turned her back against his touch. "I'll never be beautiful again," she whispered.

"You're lovely." He fastened his lips on the rim of her ear. "You're perfect."

She jerked her head away from his mouth. Outside, a remnant of oily mist layered the surface of the lake, tiny wisps that coalesced, refusing to burn away in the morning sun.

THE WIDE, CARNIVOROUS SKY

by John Langan

John Langan is the author of the novel *House of Windows* and several stories, including "Episode Seven: Last Stand Against the Pack in the Kingdom of the Purple Flowers," which appeared in my anthology *Wastelands: Stories of the Apocalypse*, and "How the Day Runs Down," which appeared in *The Living Dead*. Both of those stories also appeared in *The Magazine of Fantasy & Science Fiction*, as has most of his other fiction. A collection of most of Langan's work to date, *Mr. Gaunt and Other Uneasy Encounters*, appeared in late 2008 and was named a finalist for this year's Stoker Award.

This story, which is original to this anthology, is the tale of a quartet of Iraq war veterans who were the only survivors of an encounter with a monstrous, blood-drinking creature during the 2004 Battle of Fallujah. "The story began with its title," Langan said. "A couple of months later, I was watching an interview with an Iraq war veteran who was discussing having been in a Hummer that had been struck by an IED. He described being pinned by the Hummer's flipping over so that he was lying on his back, staring up at the sky. That told me what the story was going to be."

I
9:13PM

From the other side of the campfire, Lee said, "So it's a vampire."

"I did not say vampire," Davis said. "Did you hear me say vampire?"

It was exactly the kind of thing Lee would say, the gross generalization that obscured more than it clarified. Not for the first time since they'd set out up the mountain, Davis wondered at their decision to include Lee in their plans.

Lee held up his right hand, index finger extended. "It has the fangs."

"A mouthful of them."

Lee raised his middle finger. "It turns into a bat."

"No—its wings are like a bat's."

"Does it walk around with them?"

"They—it extrudes them from its arms and sides."

"'Extrudes'?" Lee said.

Han chimed in: "College."

Not this shit again, Davis thought. He rolled his eyes to the sky, dark blue studded by early stars. Although the sun's last light had drained from the air, his stomach clenched. He dropped his gaze to the fire.

The lieutenant spoke. "He means the thing extends them out of its body."

"Oh," Lee said. "Sounds like it turns into a bat to me."

"Uh-huh," Han said.

"Whatever," Davis said. "It doesn't—"

Lee extended his ring finger and spoke over him. "It sleeps in a coffin."

"Not a coffin—"

"I know, a flying coffin."

"It isn't—it's in low-Earth orbit, like a satellite."

"What was it you said it looked like?" the lieutenant asked. "A cocoon?"

"A chrysalis," Davis said.

"Same thing," the lieutenant said.

"More or less," Davis said, unwilling to insist on the distinction because, even a year and three-quarters removed from Iraq, the lieutenant was still the lieutenant and you did not argue the small shit with him.

"Coffin, cocoon, chrysalis," Lee said, "it has to be in it before sunset or it's in trouble."

"Wait," Han said. "Sunset."

"Yes," Davis began.

"The principle's the same," the lieutenant said. "There's a place it has to be and a time it has to be there by."

"Thank you, sir," Lee said. He raised his pinky. "And, it drinks blood."

"Yeah," Davis said, "it does."

"Lots," Han said.

"Yeah," the lieutenant said.

For a moment, the only sounds were the fire popping and, somewhere out in the woods, an owl prolonging its question. Davis thought of Fallujah.

"Okay," Lee said, "how do we kill it?"

II
2004

There had been rumors, stories, legends of the things you might see in combat. Talk to any of the older guys, the ones who'd done tours in Vietnam, and you heard about a jungle in which you might meet the ghosts of Chinese invaders from five centuries before; or serve beside a grunt whose heart had been shot out a week earlier but who wouldn't die; or find yourself stalked by what you thought was a tiger but had a tail like a snake and a woman's voice. The guys who'd been part of the first war in Iraq—"The good one," a sailor Davis knew called it—told their own tales about the desert, about coming across a raised tomb, its black stone worn free of markings, and listening to someone laughing inside it all the time it took you to walk around it; about the dark shapes you might see stalking through a sandstorm, their arms and legs a child's stick-figures; about the sergeant who swore his reflection had been killed so that, when he looked in a mirror now, a corpse stared back at him. Even the soldiers who'd returned from Afghanistan talked about vast forms they'd seen hunched at the crests of mountains; the street in Kabul that usually ended in a blank wall, except when it didn't; the pale shapes you might glimpse darting into the mouth of the cave you were about to search. A lot of what you heard was bullshit, of course, the plot of a familiar movie or TV show adapted to a new location and cast of characters, and a lot of it started off sounding as if it were headed somewhere interesting then ran out of gas halfway through. But there were some stories about which, even if he couldn't quite credit their having happened, some quality in the teller's voice, or phrasing, caused him to suspend judgment.

During the course of his Associate's Degree, Davis had taken a number of courses in psychology—preparation for a possible career as a psychologist—and in one of these, he had learned that, after several hours of uninterrupted combat (he couldn't remember how many, had never been any good with numbers), you would hallucinate. You couldn't help it; it was your brain's response to continuous unbearable stress. He supposed that at least some of the stories he'd listened to in barracks and bars might owe themselves to such cause, although he was unwilling to categorize them all as symptoms. This was not due to any overriding belief in either organized religion or disorganized superstition; it derived more from principle, specifically, a conclusion that an open mind was the best way to meet what continually impressed him as an enormous world packed full of many things.

By Fallujah, Davis had had no experiences of the strange, the bizarre, no stories to compare with those he'd accumulated over the course of basic and his deployment. He hadn't been thinking about that much as they took up their positions south of the city; all of his available attention had been directed at the coming engagement. Davis had walked patrol, had felt the crawl of the skin at the back of your neck as you made your way down streets crowded with men and women who'd been happy enough to see Saddam pulled down from his pedestal but had long since lost their patience with those who'd operated the crane. He'd ridden in convoys, his head light, his heart throbbing at the base of his throat as they passed potential danger after potential danger, a metal can on the right shoulder, what might be a shell on the left, and while they'd done their best to reinforce their Hummers with whatever junk they could scavenge, Davis was acutely aware that it wasn't enough, a consequence of galloping across the Kuwaiti desert with The Army You Had. Davis had stood checkpoint, his mouth dry as he sighted his M-16 on an approaching car that appeared full of women in black burkas who weren't responding to the signs to slow down, and he'd wondered if they were suicide bombers, or just afraid, and how much closer he could allow them before squeezing the trigger. However much danger he'd imagined himself in, inevitably, he'd arrived after the sniper had opened fire and fled, or passed the exact spot an IED would erupt two hours later, or been on the verge of aiming for the car's engine when it screeched to a halt. It wasn't that Davis hadn't discharged his weapon; he'd served support for several nighttime raids on suspected insurgent strongholds, and he'd sent his own bullets in pursuit of the tracers that scored the darkness. But support wasn't the same thing as kicking in doors, trying to kill the guy down the hall who was trying to kill you. It was not the same as being part of the Anvil.

That was how the lieutenant had described their role. "Our friends in the United States Marine Corps are going to play the Hammer," he had said the day before. "They will sweep into Fallujah from east and west and they will drive what hostiles they do not kill outright south, where we will be waiting to act as the Anvil. The poet Goethe said that you must be either hammer or anvil. We will be both, and we are going to crush the hostiles between us."

After the lieutenant's presentation, Han had said, "Great—so the jarheads have all the fun," with what Davis judged a passable imitation of regret, a false sentiment fairly widely held. Davis had been sure, however, the certainty a ball of lead weighting his gut, that this time was going to be different. Part of it was that the lieutenant had known one of the contractors who'd been killed, incinerated, and strung up at the Saddam Bridge last April. Davis wasn't clear exactly how the men had been acquainted, or how well, but the lieutenant had made no secret of his displeasure at not being part of the first effort to (re)take the city in the weeks following the men's deaths. He had been—you couldn't say happy, exactly, at the failure of that campaign—but he was eager for what was shaping up to be a larger-scale operation. Though seven months gone, the deaths and dishonorings of his acquaintances had left the lieutenant an appetite for this mission. Enough to cause him to disobey his orders and charge into Fallujah's southern section? Davis didn't think so, but there was a reason the man still held the rank of lieutenant when his classmates and colleagues were well into their Captaincies.

The other reason for Davis's conviction that, this time, something was on its way to him was a simple matter of odds. It wasn't possible—it was not possible that you could rack up this much good luck and not have a shitload of the bad bearing down on you like a SCUD on an anthill. A former altar boy, he was surprised at the variety of prayers he remembered—not just the Our Father and the Hail Mary, but the Apostles' Creed, the Memorare, and the Hail, Holy Queen. As he disembarked the Bradley and ran for the shelter of a desert-colored house, the sky an enormous, pale blue dome above him, Davis mumbled his way through his prayers with a fervency that would have pleased his mother and father no end. But even as his lips shaped the words, he had the strong sense that this was out of God's hands, under the control of one of those medieval demigoddesses, Dame Fortune or something.

Later, recovering first in Germany, then at Walter Reed, Davis had thought that walking patrol, riding convoy, standing checkpoint, he must have been saved from something truly awful each and every time, for the balance to be this steep.

III
10:01PM

"I take it stakes are out," the lieutenant said.

"Sir," Lee said, "I unloaded half a clip easy into that sonovabitch, and I was as close to him as I am to you."

"Closer," Han said.

"The point is, he took a half-step backwards—maybe—before he tore my weapon out of my hands and fractured my skull with it."

"That's what I'm saying," the lieutenant said. "I figure it has to be…what? Did you get your hands on some kind of major ordnance, Davis? An RPG? A Stinger? I'll love you like a son—hell, I'll adopt you as my own if you tell me you have a case of Stingers concealed under a bush somewhere. Those'll give the fucker a welcome he won't soon forget."

"Fucking-A," Han said.

"Nah," Lee said. "A crate of Willy Pete oughta just about do it. Serve his ass crispy-fried!"

Davis shook his head. "No Stingers and no white phosphorous. Fire isn't going to do us any good."

"How come?" Lee said.

"Yeah," Han said.

"If I'm right about this thing spending its nights in low-Earth orbit—in its 'coffin'—and then leaving that refuge to descend into the atmosphere so it can hunt, its skin has to be able to withstand considerable extremes of temperature."

"Like the Space Shuttle," the lieutenant said. "Huh. For all intents and purposes, it's fireproof."

"Oh," Lee said.

"Given that it spends some of its time in the upper atmosphere, as well as actual outer space, I'm guessing substantial cold wouldn't have much effect, either."

"We can't shoot it, can't burn it, can't freeze it," Lee said. "Tell me why we're here, again?" He waved at the trees fringing the clearing. "Aside from the scenery, of course."

"Pipe down," the lieutenant said.

"When we shot at it," Davis said, "I'm betting half our fire missed it." He held up his hand to the beginning of Lee's protest. "That's no reflection on anyone. The thing was fast, cheetah-taking-down-a-gazelle fast. Not to mention, it's so Goddamned *thin*… Anyway, of the shots that connected with it, most of them were flesh wounds." He raised his hand to Lee, again. "Those who connected with it," a nod to Lee, "were so close their fire passed clean through it."

"Which is what I was saying," Lee said.

"There's a lot of crazy shit floating around space," Davis said, "little particles of sand, rock, ice, metal. Some of them get to moving pretty fast. If you're doing repairs to the Space Station and one of those things hits you, it could ruin your whole day. Anything that's going to survive up there is going to have to be able to deal with something that can punch a hole right through you."

"It's got a self-sealing mechanism," the lieutenant said. "When Lee fired into it, its body treated the bullets as so many dust-particles."

"And closed right up," Davis said. "Like some kind of super-clotting-factor. Maybe that's what it uses the blood for."

"You're saying it's bulletproof, too?" Lee said.

"Shit," Han said.

"Not—more like, bullet-resistant."

"Think of it as a mutant healing ability," the lieutenant said, "like Wolverine."

"Oh," Han said.

"Those claws it has," Lee said, "I guess Wolverine isn't too far off the mark."

"No," Han said. "Sabertooth."

"What?" Lee said. "The fuck're you going on about?"

"Sabertooth's claws." Han held up his right hand, fingers splayed. He curled his fingers into a fist. "Wolverine's claws."

"Man has a point," the lieutenant said.

"Whatever," Lee said.

"Here's the thing," Davis said, "it's bullet-resistant, but it can still feel pain. Think about how it reacted when Lee shot it. It didn't tear his throat open: it took the instrument that had hurt it and used that to hurt Lee. You see what I'm saying?"

"Kind of," Lee said.

"Think about what drove it off," Davis said. "Remember?"

"Of course," the lieutenant said. He nodded at Han. "It was Han sticking his bayonet in the thing's side."

For which it crushed his skull, Davis could not stop himself from thinking. He added his nod to the lieutenant's. "Yes he did."

"How is that different from shooting it?" Lee said.

"Your bullets went in one side and out the other," Davis said. "Han's bayonet stuck there. The thing's healing ability could deal with an in-and-out wound no problem; something like this, though: I think it panicked."

"Panicked?" Lee said. "It didn't look like it was panicking to me."

"Then why did it take off right away?" Davis said.

"It was full; it heard more backup on the way; it had an appointment in fucking Samara. How the fuck should I know?"

"What's your theory?" the lieutenant said.

"The type of injury Han gave it would be very bad if you're in a vacuum. Something opening you up like that and leaving you exposed…"

"You could vent some or even all of the blood you worked so hard to collect," the lieutenant said. "You'd want to get out of a situation like that with all due haste."

"Even if your healing factor could seal the wound's perimeter," Davis said, "there's still this piece of steel in you that has to come out and, when it does, will reopen the injury."

"Costing you still more blood," the lieutenant said.

"Most of the time," Davis said, "I mean, like, nine hundred and ninety-nine thousand, nine hundred and ninety-nine times out of a million, the thing would identify any such threats long before they came that close. You saw its ears, its eyes."

"Black on black," Lee said. "Or, no—black over black, like the corneas had some kind of heavy tint and what was underneath was all pupil."

"Han got lucky," Davis said. "The space we were in really wasn't that big. There was a lot of movement, a lot of noise—"

"Not to mention," Lee said, "all the shooting and screaming."

"The right set of circumstances," the lieutenant said.

"Saved our asses," Lee said, reaching over to pound Han's shoulder. Han ducked to the side, grinning his hideous smile.

"If I can cut to the chase," the lieutenant said. "You're saying we need to find a way to open up this fucker and keep him open so that we can wreak merry havoc on his insides."

Davis nodded. "To cut to the chase, yes, exactly."

"How do you propose we do this?"

"With these." Davis reached into the duffel bag to his left and withdrew what appeared to be a three-foot piece of white wood, tapered to a point sharp enough to prick your eye looking at it. He passed the first one to the lieutenant, brought out one for Lee and one for Han.

"A baseball bat?" Lee said, gripping near the point and swinging his like a Louisville Slugger. "We gonna club it to death?"

Neither Davis nor the lieutenant replied; they were busy watching Han, who'd located the grips at the other end of his and was jabbing it, first underhand, then overhand.

"The people you meet working at Home Depot," Davis said. "They're made out of an industrial resin, inch-for-inch, stronger than steel. Each one has a high-explosive core."

"Whoa," Lee said, setting his on the ground with exaggerated care.

"The detonators are linked to this," Davis said, fishing a cell phone from his shirt pocket. "Turn it on." Pointing to the lieutenant, Han, Lee, and himself, he counted, "One-two-three-four. Send. That's it."

"I was mistaken," the lieutenant said. "It appears we will be using stakes, after all."

IV
2004

At Landstuhl, briefly, and then at Walter Reed, at length, an impressive array of doctors, nurses, chaplains, and other soldiers whose job it was encouraged Davis to discuss Fallujah. He was reasonably sure that, while under the influence of one of the meds that kept his body at a safe distance, he had let slip some detail, maybe more. How else to account for the change in his nurse's demeanor? Likely, she judged he was a psych case, a diagnosis he half-inclined to accept. Even when the lieutenant forced his way into Davis's room, banging around in the wheelchair he claimed he could use well enough, Goddamnit, Davis was reluctant to speak of anything except the conditions of the other survivors. Of whom he had been shocked—truly shocked, profoundly shocked, almost more so than by what had torn through them—to learn there were only two, Lee and Han, Manfred bled out on the way to be evac'd, everyone else long gone by the time the reinforcements had stormed into the courtyard. According to the lieutenant, Han was clinging to life by a thread so fine you couldn't see it. He'd lost his helmet in the fracas, and the bones in his skull had been crushed like an eggshell. Davis, who had witnessed that crushing, nodded. Lee had suffered his own head trauma, although, compared to Han's, it wasn't anything a steel plate couldn't fix. The real problem with Lee was that, if he wasn't flooded with some heavy-duty happy pills, he went fetal, thumb in his mouth, the works.

"What about you?" the lieutenant said, indicating the armature of casts, wires, weights, and counterweights that kept Davis suspended like some overly ambitious kid's science project.

"Believe it or not, sir," Davis said, "it really is worse than it looks. My pack and my helmet absorbed most of the impact. Still left me with a broken back, scapula, and ribs—but my spinal cord's basically intact. Not that it doesn't hurt like a motherfucker, sir. Yourself?"

"The taxpayers of the United States of America have seen fit to gift me with a new right leg, since I so carelessly misplaced the original." He knocked on his pajama leg, which gave a hollow, plastic sound.

"Sir, I am so sorry—"

"Shut it," the lieutenant said. "It's a paper cut." Using his left foot, he rolled himself back to the door, which he eased almost shut. Through the gap, he surveilled the hallway outside long enough for Davis to start counting, *One Mississippi, Two Mississippi*, then wheeled himself to Davis's head. He leaned close and said, "Davis."

"Sir?"

"Let's leave out the rank thing for five minutes, okay? Can we do that?"

"Sir—yes, yes we can."

"Because ever since the docs have reduced my drugs to the point I could string one sentence after another, I've been having these memories—dreams—I don't know what the fuck to call them. Nightmares. And I can't decide if I'm losing it, or if this is why Lee needs a palmful of M&Ms to leave his bed. So I need you to talk to me straight, no bullshit, no telling the officer what you think he wants to hear. I would genuinely fucking appreciate it if we could do that."

Davis looked away when he saw the lieutenant's eyes shimmering. Keeping his own focused on the ceiling, he said, "It came out of the sky. That's where it went, after Han stuck it, so I figure it must have dropped out of there, too. It explains why, one minute we're across the courtyard from a bunch of hostiles, the next, that thing's standing between us."

"Did you see it take off?"

"I did. After it had stepped on Han's head, it spread its arms—it kind of staggered back from Han, caught itself, then opened its arms and these huge wings snapped open. They were like a bat's, skin stretched over bone—they appeared so fast I'm not sure, but they shot out of its body. It tilted its head, jumped up, high, ten feet easy, flapped the wings, which raised it another ten feet, and turned—the way a swimmer turns in the water, you know? Another flap, two, and it was gone."

"Huh."

Davis glanced at the lieutenant, whose face was smooth, his eyes gazing across some interior distance. He said, "Do you—"

"Back up," the lieutenant said. "The ten of us are in the courtyard. How big's the place?"

"I'm not very good with—"

"At a guess."

"Twenty-five feet wide, maybe fifty long. With all of those jars in the way—what were they?"

"Planters."

"Three-foot-tall stone planters?"

"For trees. They were full of dirt. Haven't you ever seen those little decorative trees inside office buildings?"

"Oh. All right. What I was going to say was, with the row of planters at either end, the place might have been larger."

"Noted. How tall were the walls?"

"Taller than any of us—eight feet, easy. They were thick, too, a foot and a half, two feet." Davis said, "It really was a good spot to attack from. Open fire from the walls, then drop behind them when they can't maintain that position. The tall buildings are behind it, and we don't hold any of them, so they don't have to worry about anyone firing down on them. I'm guessing they figured we didn't know where we were well enough to call in any artillery on them. No, if we want them, we have to run a hundred feet of open space to a doorway that's an easy trap. They've got the planters for cover near and far, not to mention the doorway in the opposite wall as an exit."

"Agreed."

"To be honest, now that we're talking about it, I can't imagine how we made it into the place without losing anyone. By all rights, they should have tagged a couple of us crossing from our position to theirs. And that doorway: they should have massacred us."

"We were lucky. When we returned fire, they must have panicked. Could be they didn't see all of us behind the wall, thought they were ambushing three or four targets, instead of ten. Charging them may have given the impression there were even more of us. It took them until they were across the courtyard to get a grip and regroup."

"By which time we were at the doorway."

"So it was Lee all the way on the left—"

"With Han beside him."

"Right, and Bay and Remsnyder. Then you and Petit—"

"No—it was me and Lugo, then Petit, then you."

"Yes, yes. Manfred was to my right, and Weymouth was all the way on the other end."

"I'm not sure how many—"

"Six. There may have been a seventh in the opposite doorway, but he wasn't around very long. Either he went down, or he decided to season his valor with a little discretion."

"It was loud—everybody firing in a confined space. I had powder all over me from their shots hitting the wall behind us. I want to say we traded bullets for about five minutes, but it was what? Half that?"

"Less. A minute."

"And…"

"Our guest arrived."

"At first—at first it was like, I couldn't figure out what I was seeing. I'm trying to line up the guy who's directly across from me—all I need is for him to stick up his head again—and all of a sudden, there's a shadow in the way. That was my first thought: *It's a shadow.* Only, who's casting it? And why is it hanging in the air like that? And why is it fucking eight feet tall?"

"None of us understood what was in front of us. I thought it was a woman in a burka, someone I'd missed when we'd entered the courtyard. As you say, though, you don't meet a lot of eight-foot-tall women, in or out of Iraq."

"Next thing…no, that isn't what happened."

"What?"

"I was going to say the thing—the Shadow—was in among the hostiles, which is true, it went for them first, but before it did, there was a moment…"

"You saw something—something else."

"Yeah," Davis said. "This pain shot straight through my head. We're talking instant migraine, so intense I practically puked. That wasn't all: this chill…I was freezing, colder than I've ever been, like you read about in polar expeditions. I couldn't—the courtyard—"

"What?"

"The courtyard wasn't—I was somewhere high, like, a hundred miles high, so far up I could see the curve of the Earth below me. Clouds, continents, the ocean: what you see in the pictures they take from orbit. Stars, space, all around me. Directly, overhead, a little farther away than you are from me, there was this thing. I don't know what the fuck it was. Big—long, maybe long as a house. It bulged in the middle, tapered at the ends. The surface was dark, shiny—does that make any sense? The thing was covered in—it looked like some kind of lacquer. Maybe it was made out of the lacquer.

"Anyway, one moment, my head's about to crack open, my teeth are chattering and my skin's blue, and I'm in outer space. The next, all of that's gone, I'm back in the courtyard, and the Shadow—the thing is ripping the hostiles to shreds."

"And then," the lieutenant said, "it was our turn."

V
NOVEMBER 11, 2004, 11:13AM

In the six hundred twenty-five days since that afternoon in the hospital, how many times had Davis recited the order of events in the courtyard, whether with the lieutenant, or with Lee once his meds had been stabilized, or with Han once he'd regained the ability to speak (though not especially well)? At some point a couple of months on, he'd realized he'd been keeping count—*That's the thirty-eighth time; that's the forty-third*—and then, a couple of months after that, he'd realized that he'd lost track. The narrative of their encounter with what Davis continued to think of as the Shadow had become daily catechism, to be reviewed morning, noon, and night, and whenever else he happened to think of it.

None of them had even tried to run, which there were times Davis judged a sign of courage, and times he deemed an index of their collective shock at the speed and ferocity of the thing's assault on the insurgents. Heads, arms, legs were separated from bodies as if by a pair of razor blades, and wherever a wound opened red, there was the thing's splintered maw, drinking the blood like a kid stooping to a water fountain. The smells of blood, piss, and shit mixed with those of gunpowder and hot metal. While Davis knew they had been the next course on the Shadow's menu, he found it difficult not to wonder how the situation might have played out had Lee—followed immediately by Lugo and Weymouth—not opened up on the thing. Of course, the instant that narrow head with its spotlight eyes, its scarlet mouth, turned in their direction, everyone else's guns erupted, and the scene concluded the way it had to. But if Lee had been able to restrain himself...

Lugo was first to die. In a single leap, the Shadow closed the distance between them and drove one of its sharpened hands into his throat, venting his carotid over Davis, whom it caught with its other hand and flung into one of the side walls with such force his spine and ribs lit up like the Fourth of July. As he was dropping onto his back, turtling on his pack, the thing was raising its head from Lugo's neck, spearing Petit through his armor and hauling him towards it. Remsnyder ran at it from behind; the thing's hand lashed out and struck his head from his shoulders. It was done with Petit in time to catch Remsnyder's body on the fall and jam its mouth onto the bubbling neck. It had shoved Petit's body against the lieutenant, whose feet tangled with Petit's and sent the pair of them down. This put him out of the way of Manfred and Weymouth, who screamed for everyone to get clear and fired full automatic. Impossible as it seemed, they missed, and for their troubles, the Shadow lopped Manfred's right arm off at the elbow and opened Weymouth like a Christmas present. From the ground, the lieutenant shot at it; the thing sliced through his weapon and the leg underneath it. Now Bay, Han, and Lee tried full auto, which brought the thing to Bay, whose face it bit off. It swatted Han to the ground, but Lee somehow ducked the swipe it aimed at him and tagged it at close range. The Shadow threw Bay's body across the courtyard, yanked Lee's rifle from his hands, and swung it against his head like a ballplayer aiming for the stands. He crumpled, the thing reaching out for him, and Han leapt up, his bayonet ridiculously small in his hand. He drove it into the thing's side—what would be the floating ribs on a man—to the hilt. The Shadow, whose only sound thus far had been its feeding, opened its jaws and shrieked, a high scream more like the cry of a bat, or a hawk, than anything human. It caught Han with an elbow to the temple that tumbled him to the dirt, set its foot on his head, and pressed down. Han's scream competed with the sound of his skull cracking in multiple spots. Davis was certain the thing meant to grind Han's head to paste, but it staggered off him, one claw reaching for the weapon buried in its skin. Blood so dark it was purple was oozing around the hilt. The Shadow spread its arms, its wings cracked open, and it was gone, fled into the blue sky that Davis would spend the next quarter-hour staring at, as the lieutenant called for help and tried to tourniquet first his leg then Manfred's arm.

Davis had stared at the sky before—who has not?—but, helpless on his back, his spine a length of molten steel, his ears full of Manfred whimpering that he was gonna die, oh sweet Jesus, he was gonna fucking die, the lieutenant talking over him, insisting no he wasn't, he was gonna be fine, it was just a little paper cut, the washed blue bowl overhead seemed less sheltering canopy and more endless depth, a gullet over which he had the sickening sensation of dangling. As Manfred's cries diminished and the lieutenant told—ordered him to stay with him, Davis flailed his arms at the ground to either side of him in an effort to grip onto an anchor, something that would keep him from hurtling into that blue abyss.

The weeks and months to come would bring the inevitable nightmares, the majority of them the Shadow's attack replayed at half-, full-, or double-speed, with a gruesome fate for himself edited in. Sometimes repeating the events on his own or with a combination of the others led to a less-disturbed sleep; sometimes it did not. There was one dream, though, that no amount of discussion could help, and that was the one in which Davis was plummeting through the sky, lost in an appetite that would never be sated.

VI
12:26 AM

Once he was done setting the next log on the fire, Davis leaned back and said, "I figure it's some kind of stun effect."

"How so?" Lee said.

"The thing lands in between two groups of heavily armed men: it has to do something to even the odds. It hits us with a psychic blast, shorts out our brains so that we're easier prey."

"Didn't seem to do much to Lee," the lieutenant said.

"No brain!" Han shouted.

"Ha-fucking-ha," Lee said.

"Maybe there were too many of us," Davis said. "Maybe it miscalculated. Maybe Lee's a mutant and this is his special gift. Had the thing zigged instead of zagged, gone for us instead of the insurgents, I don't think any of us would be sitting here, regardless of our super powers."

"Speak for yourself," Lee said.

"For a theory," the lieutenant said, "it's not bad. But there's a sizable hole in it. You," he pointed at Davis, "saw the thing's coffin or whatever. Lee," a nod to him, "was privy to a bat's-eye view of the thing's approach to one of its hunts in—did we ever decide if it was Laos or Cambodia?"

"No sir," Lee said. "It looked an awful lot like some of the scenery from the first *Tomb Raider* movie, which I'm pretty sure was filmed in Cambodia, but I'm not positive."

"You didn't see Angelina Jolie running around?" Davis said.

"If only," Lee said.

"So with Lee, we're in Southeast Asia," the lieutenant said, "with or without the lovely Ms. Jolie. From what Han's been able to tell me, he was standing on the moon or someplace very similar to it. I don't believe he could see the Earth from where he was, but I'm not enough of an astronomer to know what that means.

"As for myself, I had a confused glimpse of the thing tearing its way through the interior of an airplane—what I'm reasonably certain was a B-17, probably during the Second World War.

"You see what I mean? None of us witnessed the same scene—none of us witnessed the same time, which you would imagine we would have if we'd been subject to a deliberate attack. You would expect the thing to hit us all with the same image. It's more efficient."

"Maybe that isn't how this works," Davis said. "Suppose what it does is more like a cluster bomb, a host of memories it packs around a psychic charge? If each of us thinks he's someplace different from everybody else, doesn't that maximize confusion, create optimal conditions for an attack?"

The lieutenant frowned. Lee said, "What's your theory, sir?"

"I don't have one," the lieutenant said. "Regardless of its intent, the thing got in our heads."

"And stayed there," Lee said.

"Stuck," Han said, tapping his right temple.

"Yes," the lieutenant said. "Whatever their precise function, our exposure to the thing's memories appears to have established a link between us and it."

Davis said, "Which is what's going to bring it right here."

VII
2004-2005

When Davis was on board the plane to Germany, he could permit himself to hope that he was, however temporarily, out of immediate danger of death—not from the injury to his back, which, though painful in the extreme, he had known from the start would not claim his life, but from the reappearance of the Shadow. Until

their backup arrived in a hurry of bootsteps and rattle of armor, he had been waiting for the sky to vomit the figure it had swallowed minutes (moments?) prior, for
his blood to leap into the thing's jagged mouth. The mature course of action had
seemed to prepare for his imminent end, which he had attempted, only to find
the effort beyond him. Whenever word of some acquaintance's failure to return
from the latest patrol had prompted Davis to picture his final seconds, he had
envisioned his face growing calm, even peaceful, his lips shaping the syllables of a
heartfelt Act of Contrition. However, between the channel of fire that had replaced
his spine and the vertiginous sensation that he might plunge into the sky—not
to mention, the lieutenant's continuing monologue to Manfred, the pungence
of gunpowder mixed with the bloody reek of meat, the low moans coming from
Han—Davis was unable to concentrate. Rather than any gesture of reconciliation
towards the God with Whom he had not been concerned since his discovery of
what lay beneath his prom date's panties junior year, Davis's attention had been
snarled in the sound of the Shadow's claws puncturing Lugo's neck, the fountain
of Weymouth's blood over its arm and chest, the wet slap of his entrails hitting
the ground, the stretch of the thing's mouth as it released its scream. Despite his
back, which had drawn his vocal chords taut, once the reinforcements had arrived
and a red-faced medic peppered him with questions while performing a quick
assessment of him, Davis had strained to warn them of their danger. But all his
insistence that they had to watch the sky had brought him was a sedative that
pulled him into a vague, gray place.

Nor had his time at the Battalion Aid Station, then some larger facility (Camp
Victory? with whatever they gave him, most of the details a variety of medical staff
poured into his ears sluiced right back out again) caused him to feel any more
secure. As the gray place loosened its hold on him and he stared up at the canvas
roof of the BAS, Davis had wanted to demand what the fuck everyone was thinking.
Didn't they know the Shadow could slice through this material like it was cling
film? Didn't they understand it was waiting to descend on them right now, this
very fucking minute? It would rip them to shreds; it would drink their fucking
blood. At the presence of a corpsman beside him, he'd realized he was shouting—or
as close to shouting as his voice could manage—but he'd been unable to restrain
himself, which had led to calming banalities and more vague grayness. He had
returned to something like consciousness inside a larger space in the CSH, where
the sight of the nearest wall trembling from the wind had drawn his stomach tight
and sped a fresh round of protests from his mouth. When he struggled up out of
the shot that outburst occasioned, Davis had found himself in a dim cavern whose
curving sides rang with the din of enormous engines. His momentary impression
that he was dead and this some unexpected, bare-bones afterlife was replaced by
the recognition that he was on a transport out of Iraq—who knew to where? It
didn't matter. A flood of tears had rolled from his eyes as the dread coiling his
guts had, if not fled, at least calmed.

At Landstuhl, in a solidly built hospital with drab but sturdy walls and a firm
ceiling, Davis was calmer. (As long as he did not dwell on the way the Shadow's

claws had split Petit's armor, sliced the lieutenant's rifle in two.) That, and the surgeries required to relieve the pressure on his spine left him, to quote a song he'd never liked that much, comfortably numb.

Not until he was back in America, though, reclining in the late-medieval luxury of Walter Reed, the width of an ocean and a continent separating him from Fallujah, did Davis feel anything like a sense of security. Even after his first round of conversations with the lieutenant had offered him the dubious reassurance that, if he were delusional, he was in good company, a cold comfort made chillier still by Lee, his meds approaching the proper levels, corroborating their narrative, Davis found it less difficult than he would have anticipated to persuade himself that Remsnyder's head leaping from his body on a jet of blood was seven thousand miles away. And while his pulse still quickened whenever his vision strayed to the rectangle of sky framed by the room's lone window, he could almost pretend that this was a different sky. After all, hadn't that been the subtext of all the stories he'd heard from other vets about earlier wars? Weird shit happened, yes—sometimes, very bad weird shit happened—but it took place over there, In Country, in another place where things didn't work the same way they did in the good old U.S. of A. If you could keep that in mind, Davis judged, front-and-center in your consciousness, you might be able to live with the impossible.

Everything went—you couldn't call it swimmingly—it went, anyway, until Davis began his rehabilitation, which consisted of: a) learning how to walk again and b) strength training for his newly (re)educated legs. Of course, he had been in pain after the initial injury—though shock and fear had kept the hurt from overwhelming him—and his nerves had flared throughout his hospital stay—especially following his surgery—though a pharmacopeia had damped those sensations down to smoldering. Rehab was different. Rehab was a long, low-ceilinged room that smelled of sweat and industrial antiseptic, one end of which grazed a small herd of the kind of exercise machines you saw faded celebrities hawking on late-night TV, the center of which held a trio of parallel bars set too low, and the near end of which was home to a series of overlapping blue mats whose extensive cracks suggested an aerial view of a river basin. Rehab was slow stretches on the mats, then gripping onto the parallel bars while you tried to coax your right leg into moving forward; once you could lurch along the bars and back, rehab was time on one of the exercise machines, flat on your back, your legs bent, your feet pressed against a pair of pedals connected to a series of weights you raised by extending your legs. Rehab was about confronting pain, inviting it in, asking it to sit down and have a beer so the two of you could talk for a while. Rehab was not leaning on the heavy-duty opiates and their synthetic friends; it was remaining content with the over-the-counter options and ice-packs. It was the promise of a walk outside—an enticement that made Davis's palms sweat and his mouth go dry.

When the surgeon had told Davis the operation had been a success, there appeared to be no permanent damage to his spinal cord, Davis had imagined himself, freed of his cast and its coterie of pulleys and counterweights, sitting up on his own and strolling out the front door. Actually, he'd been running in his fantasy. The reality, he quickly discovered, was that merely raising himself to a sitting position was an enterprise far more involved than he ever had appreciated, as was a range of action so automatic it existed below his being able to admit he'd never given it much thought. He supposed the therapists here were as good as you were going to find, but that didn't make the routines they subjected him to—he subjected himself to—any easier or less painful.

It was during one of these sessions, his back feeling as if it had been scraped raw and the exposed tissue generously salted, that Davis had his first inkling that Fallujah was not a self-contained narrative, a short, grisly tale; rather, it was the opening chapter of a novel, one of those eight-hundred-page, Stephen King specials. Lucy, Davis's primary therapist, had him on what he had christened the Rack. His target was twenty leg presses; in a fit of bravado, he had promised her thirty. No doubt, Davis had known instances of greater pain, but those had been spikes on the graph. Though set at a lower level, this hurt was constant, and while Lucy had assured him that he would become used to it, so far, he hadn't. The pain glared like the sun flaring off a window; it flooded his mind white, made focusing on anything else impossible. That Lucy was encouraging him, he knew from the tone of her voice, but he could not distinguish individual words. Already, his vision was blurred from the sweat streaming out of him, so when the blur fractured, became a kaleidoscope-jumble of color and geometry, he thought little of it, and raised his fingers to clear his eyes.

According to Lucy, Davis removed his hand from his face, paused, then fell off the machine on his right side, trembling and jerking. For what she called his seizure's duration, which she clocked at three minutes, fifteen seconds, Davis uttered no sound except for a gulping noise that made his therapist fear he was about to swallow his tongue.

To the lieutenant, then to Lee and eventually Han, Davis would compare what he saw when the rehab room went far away to a wide-screen movie, one of those panoramic deals that was supposed to impart the sensation of flying over the Rockies, or holding on for dear life as a roller coaster whipped up and down its course. A surplus of detail crowded his vision. He was in the middle of a sandy street bordered by short buildings whose walls appeared to consist of sheets of long, dried grass framed with slender sticks. A dozen, two dozen women and children dressed in pastel robes and turbans ran frantically from one side of the street to the other as men wearing dark brown shirts and pants aimed Kalashnikovs at them. Some of the men were riding brown and white horses; some were stalking the street; some were emerging from alleys between the buildings, several of whose walls were releasing thick smoke. Davis estimated ten men. The sounds—it was as if the soundtrack to this film had been set to record the slightest vibration of air, which it played back at twice the normal level. Screams raked his eardrums. Sandals scraped the ground. Guns cracked; bullets thudded into skin. Horses whickered. Fire snapped. An immense thirst, worse than any he had known, possessed him. His throat was not dry; it was arid, as if it—as if he were composed of dust from which the last eyedropper of moisture had long been squeezed.

One of the men—not the nearest, who was walking the opposite direction from Davis's position, but the next closest, whose horse had shied from the flames sprouting from a grass wall and so turned its rider in Davis's direction—caught sight of Davis, his face contracting in confusion at what he saw. The man, who might have been in his early twenties, started to raise his rifle, and everything sped up, the movie fast-forwarded. There was—his vision wavered, and the man's gun dipped, his eyes widening. Davis was next to him—he had half-scaled the horse and speared the hollow of the man's throat with his right hand, whose fingers, he saw, were twice as long as they had been, tapered to a set of blades. He felt the man's tissue part, the ends of his fingers (talons?) scrape bone. Blood washed over his palm, his wrist, and the sensation jolted him. His talons flicked to the left, and the man's head tipped back like a tree falling away from its base. Blood misted the air, and before he realized what was happening, his mouth was clamped to the wound, full of hot, copper liquid. The taste was rain falling in the desert; in three mighty gulps, he had emptied the corpse and was springing over its fellows, into the midst of the brightly robed women and children.

The immediate result of Davis's three-minute hallucination was the suspension of his physical therapy and an MRI of his brain. Asked by Lucy what he recalled of the experience, Davis had shaken his head and answered, "Nothing." It was the same response he gave to the new doctor who stopped into his room a week later and, without identifying himself as a psychiatrist, told Davis he was interested in the nightmares that had brought him screaming out of sleep six of the last seven nights. This was a rather substantial change in his nightly routine; taken together with his recent seizure, it seemed like cause for concern. Perhaps Davis could relate what he remembered of his nightmares?

How to tell this doctor that closing his eyes—an act he resisted for as long as he could each night—brought him to that yellow-brown street; the lime, saffron, and orange cloth stretching as mothers hauled their children behind them; the dull muzzles of the Kalashnikovs coughing fire? How to describe the sensations that still lived in his skin, his muscles: the tearing of skin for his too-long fingers; the bounce of a heart in his hand the instant before he tore it from its setting; the eggshell crunch of bone between his jaws? Most of all, how to convey to this doctor, this shrink, who was either an unskilled actor or not trying very hard, the concentrate of pleasure that was the rush of blood into his mouth, down his throat, the satisfaction of his terrific thirst so momentary it made the thirst that much worse? Although Davis had repeated his earlier disavowal and maintained it in the face of the doctor's extended—and, to be fair, sympathetic—questions until the man left, a week's worth of poor sleep made the wisdom of his decision appear less a foregone conclusion. What he had seen—what he had been part of the other week was too similar to the vision he'd had in the courtyard not to be related; the question was, how? Were Davis to summarize his personal horror ride to the psychiatrist—he would have to tell him about Fallujah first, of course—might the doctor have more success at understanding the connections between his driver's-seat views of the Shadow's activities?

Sure, Davis thought, *right after he's had you fitted for your straightjacket.* The ironic thing was, how often had he argued the benefits of the Army's psychiatric care with Lugo? It had been their running gag. Lugo would return from reading his e-mail with news of some guy stateside who'd lost it, shot his wife, himself, which would prompt Davis to say that it was a shame the guy hadn't gotten help before it came to that. Help, Lugo would say, from who? The Army? Man, you must be joking. The Army don't want nothing to do with no grunt can't keep his shit together. No, no, Davis would say, sure, they still had a ways to go, but the Army was changing. The kinds of combat-induced pathologies it used to pretend didn't exist were much more likely to be treated early and effectively. (If Lee and Han were present, and/or Remsnyder, they'd ooh and aah over Davis's vocabulary.) Oh yeah, Lugo would reply, if they don't discharge your ass right outta here, they'll stick you at some bullshit post where you won't hurt anyone. No, no, Davis would say, that was a rumor. Oh yeah, Lugo would say, like the rumor about the guys who went to the doctor for help with their PTSD and were told they were suffering from a fucking pre-existing condition, so it wasn't the Army's problem? No, no, Davis would say, that was a few bad guys. Oh yeah, Lugo would say.

Before he and the lieutenant—who had been abducted by a platoon of siblings, their spouses, and their kids for ten days in Florida—discussed the matter, Davis passed his nightly struggles to stay awake wondering if the psychiatric ward was the worst place he might wind up. His only images of such places came from films like *One Flew Over the Cuckoo's Nest*, *Awakenings*, and *K-PAX*, but based on those examples, he could expect to spend his days robed and slippered, possibly medicated, free to read what he wanted except during individual and group therapy sessions. If it wasn't quite the career as a psychologist he'd envisioned, he'd at least be in some kind of proximity to the mental health field. Sure, it would be a scam, but didn't the taxpayers of the U.S. of A. owe him recompense for shipping him to a place where the Shadow could just drop in and shred his life? The windows would be barred or meshed, the doors reinforced—you could almost fool yourself such a location would be safe.

However, with his second episode, it became clear that safe was one of those words that had been bayoneted, its meaning spilled on the floor. Davis had been approved to resume therapy with Lucy, who had been honestly happy to see him again. It was late in the day; what with the complete breakdown in his sleeping patterns, he wasn't in optimal condition for another go-around on the Rack, but after so much time stuck in his head, terrified at what was in there with him, the prospect of a vigorous workout was something he was actually looking forward to. As before, gentle stretching preceded the main event, which Lucy told Davis he didn't have to do but for which he had cavalierly assured her he was, if not completely able, at least ready and willing. With the second push of his feet against the pedals, pain ignited up his back, and his lack of sleep did not aid in his tolerating it. Each subsequent retraction and extension of his legs ratcheted the hurt up one more degree, until he was lying on a bed of fire.

This time

VIII
2:15AM

"my vision didn't blur—it cracked, as if my knees levering up and down were an image on a TV screen and something smacked the glass. Everything spiderwebbed and fell away. What replaced it was movement—I was moving up, my arms beating down; there was this feeling that they were bigger, much bigger, that when I swept them down, they were gathering the air and piling it beneath them. I looked below me, and there were bodies—parts of bodies, organs—all over the place. There was less blood than there should have been. Seeing them scattered across the ground—it was like having a bird's-eye view of some kind of bizarre design. Most of them were men, twenties and thirties; although there were two women and a couple, three kids. Almost everybody was wearing jeans and workboots, sweatshirts, baseball caps, except for a pair of guys dressed in khaki and I'm pretty sure cowboy hats."

"What the fuck?" Lee said.

"Cowboys," Han said.

"Texas Border Patrol," the lieutenant said.

"So those other people were like, illegal immigrants?" Lee said.

The lieutenant nodded.

Davis said, "I've never been to Texas, but the spot looked like what you see on TV. Sandy, full of rocks, some scrub brush and short trees. There was a muddy stream—you might call it a river, I guess, if that was what you were used to—in the near distance, and a group of hills further off. The sun was perched on top of the hills, setting, and that red ball made me beat my arms again and again, shrinking the scene below, raising me higher into the sky. There was—I felt full—more than full, gorged, but thirsty, still thirsty, that same, overpowering dryness I'd experienced the previous…time. The thirst was so strong, so compelling, I was a little surprised when I kept climbing. My flight was connected to the sun balanced on that hill, a kind of—not panic, exactly: it was more like urgency. I was moving, now. The air was thinning; my arms stretched even larger to scoop enough of it to keep me moving. The temperature had dropped—was dropping, plunging down. Something happened—my mouth was already closed, but it was as if it sealed somehow. Same thing with my nostrils; I mean, they closed themselves off. My eyes misted, then cleared. I pumped my arms harder than I had before. This time, I didn't lose speed; I kept moving forward.

"Ahead, I saw the thing I'd seen in the courtyard—a huge shape, big as a house. Pointed at the ends, fat in the middle. Dark—maybe dark purple, maybe not—and shiny. The moment it came into view, this surge of…I don't know what to call it. Honestly, I want to say it was a cross between the way you feel when you put your bag down on your old bed and, 'Mommy,' that little kid feeling, except that neither of those is completely right. My arms were condensing, growing substantial. I was heading towards the middle. As I drew closer, its surface rippled, like water moving out from where a stone strikes it. At the center of the ripple, a kind of pucker opened into the thing. That was my destination."

"And?" Lee said.

"Lucy emptied her Gatorade on me and brought me out of it."

"You have got to be fucking kidding me," Lee said.

"Afraid not," Davis said.

"How long was this one?" the lieutenant asked.

"Almost five minutes."

"It took her that long to toss her Gatorade on you?" Lee said.

"There was some kind of commotion at the same time, a couple of guys got into a fight. She tried to find help; when she couldn't, she doused me."

Lee shook his head.

"And you have since confirmed the existence of this object," the lieutenant said.

"Yes, sir," Davis said. "It took some doing. The thing's damned near impossible to see, and while no one would come out and say so to me, I'm pretty sure it doesn't show up on radar, either. The couple of pictures we got were more dumb luck than anything."

"'We'?" Lee said.

"I—"

The lieutenant said, "I put Mr. Davis in touch with a friend of mine in Intelligence."

"Oh," Lee said. "Wait—shit: you mean the CIA's involved?"

"Relax," Davis said.

"Because I swear to God," Lee said, "those stupid motherfuckers would fuck up getting toast out of the toaster and blame us for their burned fingers."

"It's under control," the lieutenant said. "This is our party. No one else has been invited."

"Doesn't mean they won't show up," Lee said. "Stupid assholes with their fucking sunglasses and their, 'We're so scary.' Oooh." He turned his head and spat.

Davis stole a look at the sky. Stars were winking out and in as something passed in front of them. His heart jumped, his hand was on his stake before he identified the shape as some kind of bird. The lieutenant had noticed his movement; his hand over his stake, he said, "Everything all right, Davis?"

"Fine," Davis said. "Bird."

"What?" Lee said.

"Bird," Han said.

"Oh," Lee said. "So. I have a question."

"Go ahead," the lieutenant said.

"The whole daylight thing," Lee said, "the having to be back in its coffin before sunset—what's up with that?"

"It does seem…atypical, doesn't it?" the lieutenant said. "Vampires are traditionally creatures of the night."

"Actually, sir," Lee said, "that's not exactly true. The original Dracula—you know, in the book—he could go out in daylight; he just lost his powers."

"Lee," the lieutenant said, "you are a font of information. Is this what our monster is trying to avoid?"

"I don't know," Lee said. "Could be."

"I don't think so," Davis said. "It's not as if daylight makes its teeth any sharper."

"Then what is it?" Lee said.

"Beats me," Davis said. "Don't we need daylight to make Vitamin D? Maybe it's the same, uses the sun to manufacture some kind of vital substance."

"Not bad," the lieutenant said.

"For something you pulled out of your ass," Lee said.

"Hey—you asked," Davis said.

"Perhaps it's time for some review," the lieutenant said. "Can we agree on that? Good.

"We have this thing—this vampire," holding up a hand to Davis, "that spends its nights in an orbiting coffin. At dawn or thereabouts, it departs said refuge in search of blood, which it apparently obtains from a single source."

"Us," Han said.

"Us," the lieutenant said. "It glides down into the atmosphere on the lookout for likely victims—of likely groups of victims, since it prefers to feed on large numbers of people at the same time. Possibly, it burns through its food quickly."

"It's always thirsty," Davis said. "No matter how much it drinks, it's never enough."

"Yeah," Lee said, "I felt it, too."

"So did we all," the lieutenant said. "It looks to satisfy its thirst at locations where its actions will draw little to no attention. These include remote areas such as the U.S.-Mexico border, the Sahara and Gobi, and the Andes. It also likes conflict zones, whether Iraq, Darfur, or the Congo. How it locates these sites is unknown. We estimate that it visits between four and seven of them per day. That we have been able to determine, there does not appear to be an underlying pattern to its selection of either target areas or individuals within those areas. The vampire's exact level of intelligence is another unknown. It possesses considerable abilities as a predator, not least of them its speed, reaction time, and strength. Nor should we forget its teeth and," a rap of the artificial leg, "claws."

"Not to mention that mind thing," Lee said.

"Yes," the lieutenant said. "Whether by accident or design, the vampire's appearance is accompanied by a telepathic jolt that momentarily disorients its intended victims, rendering them easier prey. For those who survive the meeting," a nod at them, "a link remains that may be activated by persistent, pronounced stress, whether physical or mental. The result of this activation is a period of clairvoyance, during which the lucky individual rides along for the vampire's current activities. Whether the vampire usually has equal access to our perceptions during this time is unclear; our combined accounts suggest it does not.

"However, there are exceptions."

IX

2005

"I know how we can kill it," Davis said. "At least, I think I do—how we can get it to come to a place where we can kill it."

Lee put his Big Mac on his tray and looked out the restaurant window. The lieutenant paused in the act of dipping his fries into a tub of barbecue sauce. Han continued chewing his McNugget but nodded twice.

"The other day—two days ago, Wednesday—I got to it."

"What do you mean?" the lieutenant said.

"It was coming in for a landing, and I made it mess up."

"Bullshit," Lee said. He did not shift his gaze from the window. His face was flushed.

"How?" the lieutenant said.

"I was having a bad day, worse than the usual bad day. Things at Home Depot—the manager's okay, but the assistant manager's a raging asshole. Anyway, I decided a workout might help. I'd bought these Kung Fu DVDs—"

"Kung Fu," the lieutenant said.

Davis shrugged. "Seemed more interesting than running a treadmill."

Through a mouthful of McNugget, Han said, "Bruce Lee."

"Yeah," Davis said. "I put the first disc on. To start with, everything's fine. I'm taking it easy, staying well below the danger level. My back's starting to ache, the way it always does, but that's okay, I can live with it. As long as I keep the situation in low gear, I can continue with my tiger style."

"Did it help?" the lieutenant asked.

"My worse-than-bad day? Not really. But it was something to do, you know?"

The lieutenant nodded. Lee stared at the traffic edging up the road in front of the McDonald's. Han bit another McNugget.

"This time, there was no warning. My back's feeling like someone's stitching it with a hot needle, then I'm dropping out of heavy cloud cover. Below, a squat hill pushes up from dense jungle. A group of men are sitting around the top of the hill. They're wearing fatigues, carrying Kalashnikovs. I think I'm somewhere in South America: maybe these guys are FARQ; maybe they're some of Chavez's boys.

"I've been through the drill enough to know what's on the way: a ringside seat for blood and carnage. It's reached the point, when one of these incidents overtakes me, I don't freak out. The emotion that grips me is dread, sickness at what's coming. But this happens so fast, there isn't time for any of that. Instead, anger—the anger that usually shows up a couple of hours later, when I'm still trying to get the taste of blood out of my mouth, still trying to convince myself that I'm not the one who's so thirsty—for once, that anger arrives on time and loaded for bear. It's like the fire that's crackling on my back finds its way into my veins and ignites me.

"What's funny is, the anger makes my connection to the thing even more intense. The wind is pressing my face, rushing over my arms—my wings—I'm aware of currents in the air, places where it's thicker, thinner, and I twitch my nerves to adjust for it. There's one guy standing off from the rest, closer to the treeline, though not so much I—the thing won't be able to take him. I can practically see the route to him, a steep dive with a sharp turn at the very end that'll let the thing knife through him. He's sporting a bush hat, which he's pushed back on his head. His shirt's open, t-shirt dark with sweat. He's holding his weapon self-consciously, trying to look like a badass, and it's this, more than the smoothness of his skin, the couple of whiskers on his chin, that makes it clear he isn't even eighteen. It—I—we jackknife into the dive, and thirsty, Christ, thirsty isn't the word: this is dryness that reaches right through to your fucking soul. I've never understood what makes the thing tick—what *drives* it—so well.

"At the same time, the anger's still there. The closer we draw to the kid, the hotter it burns. We've reached the bottom of the dive and pulled up; we're streaking over the underbrush. The kid's completely oblivious to the fact that his bloody dismemberment is fifty feet away and closing fast. I'm so close to the thing, I can feel the way its fangs push against one another as they jut from its mouth. We're on top of the kid; the thing's preparing to retract its wings, slice him open, and drive its face into him. The kid is dead; he's dead and he just doesn't know it, yet.

"Only, it's like—I'm like—I don't even think, *No*, or, *Stop*, or *Pull up*. It's more…I push; I shove against the thing I'm inside and its arms move. Its fucking arms jerk up as if someone's passed a current through them. Someone has—I have. I'm the current. The motion throws off the thing's strike, sends it wide. It flails at the kid as it flies past him, but he's out of reach. I can sense—the thing's completely confused. There's a clump of bushes straight ahead—*wham*."

The lieutenant had adopted his best you'd-better-not-be-bullshitting-me stare. He said, "I take it that severed the connection."

Davis shook his head. "No, sir. You would expect that—it's what would have happened in the past—but this time, it was like, I was so close to the thing, it was going to take something more to shake me loose."

"And?" the lieutenant said.

Lee shoved his tray back, toppling his super-sized Dr. Pepper, whose lid popped off, splashing a wave of soda and ice cubes across the table. While Davis and the lieutenant grabbed napkins, Lee stood and said, "What the fuck, Davis?"

"What?" Davis said.

"I said, 'What the fuck, asshole,'" Lee said. Several diners at nearby tables turned their heads toward him.

"Inside voices," the lieutenant said. "Sit down."

"I don't think so," Lee said. "I don't have to listen to this shit." With that, he stalked away from the table, through the men and women swiftly returning their attentions to the meals in front of them, and out the side door.

"What the fuck?" Davis said, dropping his wad of soggy napkins on Lee's tray.

"That seems to be the question of the moment," the lieutenant said.

"Sir—"

"Our friend and fellow is not having the best of months," the lieutenant said.

"In fact, he is not having the best of years. You remember the snafus with his disability checks."

"I thought that was taken care of."

"It was, but it was accompanied by the departure of Lee's wife and their two-year-old. Compared to what he was, Lee is vastly improved. In terms of the nuances of his emotional health, however, he has miles to go. The shit with his disability did not help; nor did spending all day home with a toddler who didn't recognize his father."

"He didn't—"

"No, but I gather it was a close thing. A generous percentage of the wedding flatware paid the price for Lee's inability to manage himself. In short order, the situation became too much for Shari, who called her father to come for her and Douglas."

"Bitch," Han said.

"Since then," the lieutenant said, "Lee's situation has not improved. A visit to the local bar for a night of drinking alone ended with him in the drunk tank. Shari's been talking separation, possibly divorce, and while Lee tends to be a bit paranoid about the matter, there may be someone else involved, an old boyfriend. Those members of Lee's family who've visited him, called him, he has rebuffed in a fairly direct way. To top it all off, he's been subject to the same, intermittent feast of blood as the rest of us."

"Oh," Davis said. "I had no—Lee doesn't talk to me—"

"Never mind. Finish your story."

"It's not a story."

"Sorry. Poor choice of words. Go on, please."

"All right," Davis said. "Okay. You have to understand, I was as surprised by all of this as—well, as anyone. I couldn't believe I'd affected the thing. If it hadn't been so real, so like all the other times, I would have thought I was hallucinating, on some kind of wish-fulfillment trip. As it was, there I was as the thing picked itself up from the jungle floor. The anger—my anger—I guess it was still there, but…on hold.

"The second the thing was upright, someone shouted and the air was hot with bullets. Most of them shredded leaves, chipped bark, but a few of them tagged the thing's arm, its shoulder. Something was wrong—mixing in with its confusion, there was another emotion, something down the block from fear. I wasn't doing anything: I was still stunned by what I'd made happen. The thing jumped, and someone—maybe a couple of guys—tracked it, headed it off, hit it in I can't tell you how many places—it felt as if the thing had been punched a dozen times at once. It spun off course, slapped a tree, and went down, snapping branches on its way.

"Now it was pissed. Even before it picked itself up, the place it landed was being subject to intensive defoliation. A shot tore its ear. Its anger—if what I felt was fire, this was lava, thicker, slower-moving, hotter. It retreated, scuttled half a dozen trees deeper into the jungle. Whoever those guys were, they were professionals.

They advanced on the spot where the thing fell and, when they saw it wasn't there anymore, they didn't rush in after it. Instead, they fell back to a defensive posture while one of them put in a call—for air support, I'm guessing."

"The thing was angry and hurt and the thirst—" Davis shook his head. He sipped his Coke. "What came next—I'm not sure I can describe it. There was this surge in my head—not the thing's head, this was my brain I'm talking about—and the thing was looking out of my eyes."

"It turned the tables on you," the lieutenant said.

"Not exactly," Davis said. "I continued watching the soldiers maybe seventy-five feet in front of me, but I was...aware of the thing staring at the DVD still playing on the TV. It was as if the scene was on a screen just out of view." He shook his head. "I'm not describing it right.

"Anyway, that was when the connection broke."

Davis watched the lieutenant evade an immediate response by taking a generous bite of his Double Quarter-Pounder with Cheese and chewing it with great care. Han swallowed and said, "Soldiers."

"What?"

"Soldiers," Han said.

Through his mouthful of burger, the lieutenant said, "He wants to know what happened to the soldiers. Right?"

Han nodded.

"Beats the shit out of me," Davis said. "Maybe their air support showed up and bombed the fucker to hell. Maybe they evac'd out of there."

"But that isn't what you think," the lieutenant said. "You think it got them."

"Yes sir," Davis said. "The minute it was free of me, I think it had those poor bastards for lunch."

"It seems a bit much to hope otherwise, doesn't it?"

"Yes sir, it does."

When the lieutenant opted for another bite of his sandwich, Davis said, "Well?"

The lieutenant answered by lifting his eyebrows. Han switched from McNuggets to fries.

"As I see it," Davis began. He stopped, paused, started again. "We know that the thing fucked with us in Fallujah, linked up with us. So far, this situation has only worked to our disadvantage: whenever one of us is in sufficient discomfort, the connection activates and dumps us behind the thing's eyes for somewhere in the vicinity of three to five minutes. With all due respect to Lee, this has not been beneficial to anyone's mental health.

"But what if—suppose we could duplicate what happened to me? Not just once, but over and over—even if only for ten or fifteen seconds at a time—interfere with whatever it's doing, seriously fuck with it."

"Then what?" the lieutenant said. "We're a thorn in its side. So?"

"Sir," Davis said, "those soldiers hit it. Okay, yes, their fire wasn't any more effective than ours was, but I'm willing to bet their percentages were significantly higher. That's what me being on board in an—enhanced way did to the thing. We wouldn't be a thorn—we'd be the Goddamned bayonet Han jammed in its ribs.

"Not that we should wait for someone else to take it down. I'm proposing something more ambitious."

"All right."

"If we can disrupt the thing's routine—especially if we cut into its feeding—it won't take very long for it to want to find us. Assuming the second part of my experience—the thing has a look through our eyes—if that happens again, we can arrange it so that we let it know where we're going to be. We pick a location with a clearing where the thing can land and surrounding tree cover where we can wait to ambush it. Before any of us goes to ruin the thing's day, he puts pictures, maps, satellite photos of the spot on display, so that when the thing's staring out of his eyes, that's what it sees. If the same images keep showing up in front of it, it should get the point."

The lieutenant took the rest of his meal to reply. Han offered no comment. When the lieutenant had settled into his chair after tilting his tray into the garbage and stacking it on top of the can, he said, "I don't know, Davis. There are an awful lot more ifs than I prefer to hear in a plan. *If* we can access the thing the same way you did; *if* that wasn't a fluke. *If* the thing does the reverse-vision stuff; *if* it understands what we're showing it. *If* we can find a way to kill it." He shook his head.

"Granted," Davis said, "there's a lot we'd have to figure out, not least how to put it down and keep it down. I have some ideas about that, but nothing developed. It would be nice if we could control our connection to the thing, too. I'm wondering if what activates the jump is some chemical our bodies are releasing when we're under stress—maybe adrenaline. If we had access to a supply of adrenaline, we could experiment with doses—"

"You're really serious about this."

"What's the alternative?" Davis said. "Lee isn't the only one whose life is fucked, is he? How many more operations are you scheduled for, Han? Four? Five?"

"Four," Han said.

"And how're things in the meantime?"

Han did not answer.

"What about you, sir?" Davis said. "Oh sure, your wife and kids stuck around, but how do they act after you've had one of your fits, or spells, or whatever the fuck you call them? Do they rush right up to give Daddy a hug, or do they keep away from you, in case you might do something even worse? Weren't you coaching your son's soccer team? How's that working out for you? I bet it's a lot of fun every time the ref makes a lousy call."

"Enough, Davis."

"It isn't as if I'm in any better shape. I have to make sure I remember to swallow a couple of tranquilizers before I go to work so I don't collapse in the middle of trying to help some customer load his fertilizer into his car. Okay, Rochelle had dumped me while I was away, but let me tell you how the dating scene is for a vet who's prone to seizures should things get a little too exciting. As for returning to college, earning my BS—maybe if I could have stopped worrying about how Goddamned exposed I was walking from building to building, I could've focused on some of what the professors were saying and not fucking had to withdraw.

"This isn't the magic bullet," Davis said. "It isn't going to make all the bad things go away. It's…it is what it fucking is."

"All right," the lieutenant said. "I'm listening. Han—you listening?"

"Listening," Han said.

X
4:11AM

"So where do you think it came from?" Lee said.

"What do you mean?" Davis said. "We know where it comes from."

"No," Lee said, "I mean, before."

"Its secret origin," the lieutenant said.

"Yeah," Lee said.

"How should I know?" Davis said.

"You're the man with the plan," Lee said. "Mr. Idea."

The lieutenant said, "I take it you have a theory, Lee."

Lee glanced at the heap of coals that had been the fire. "Nah, not really."

"That sounds like a yes to me," the lieutenant said.

"Yeah," Han said.

"Come on," Davis said. "What do you think?"

"Well," Lee said, then broke off, laughing. "No, no."

"Talk!" Davis said.

"You tell us your theory," the lieutenant said, "I'll tell you mine."

"Okay, okay," Lee said, laughing. "All right. The way I see it, this vampire is like, the advance for an invasion. It flies around in its pod, looking for suitable planets, and when it finds one, it parks itself above the surface, calls its buddies, and waits for them to arrive."

"Not bad," the lieutenant said.

"Hang on," Davis said. "What does it do for blood while it's Boldly Going Where No Vampire Has Gone Before?"

"I don't know," Lee said. "Maybe it has some stored in its coffin."

"That's an awful lot of blood," Davis said.

"Even in MRE form," the lieutenant said.

"Maybe it has something in the coffin that makes blood for it."

"Then why would it leave to go hunting?" Davis said.

"It's in suspended animation," Lee said. "That's it. It doesn't wake up till it's arrived at a habitable planet."

"How does it know it's located one?" Davis said.

"Obviously," the lieutenant said, "the coffin's equipped with some sophisticated tech."

"Thank you, sir," Lee said.

"Not at all," the lieutenant said.

"I don't know," Davis said.

"What do you know?" Lee said.

"I told you—"

"Be real," Lee said. "You're telling me you haven't given five minutes to wondering how the vampire got to where it is?"

"I—"

"Yeah," Han said.

"I'm more concerned with the thing's future than I am with its past," Davis said, "but yes, I have wondered about where it came from. There's a lot of science I don't know, but I'm not sure about an alien being able to survive on human blood—about an alien needing human blood. It could be, I guess; it just seems a bit of a stretch."

"You're saying it came from here," the lieutenant said.

"That's bullshit," Lee said.

"Why shouldn't it?" Davis said. "There's been life on Earth for something like three point seven *billion* years. Are you telling me this couldn't have developed?"

"Your logic's shaky," the lieutenant said. "Just because something hasn't been disproved doesn't mean it's true."

"All I'm saying is, we don't know everything that's ever been alive on the planet."

"Point taken," the lieutenant said, "but this thing lives above—well above the surface of the planet. How do you explain that?"

"Some kind of escape pod," Davis said. "I mean, you guys know about the asteroid, right? The one that's supposed to have wiped out the dinosaurs? Suppose this guy and his friends—suppose their city was directly in this asteroid's path? Maybe our thing was the only one who made it to the rockets on time? Or maybe it built this itself."

"Like Superman," Lee said, "only, he's a vampire, and he doesn't leave Krypton, he just floats around it so he can snack on the other survivors."

"Sun," Han said.

"What?" Lee said.

"Yellow sun," Han said.

Davis said, "He means Superman needs a yellow sun for his powers. Krypton had a red sun, so he wouldn't have been able to do much snacking."

"Yeah, well, we have a yellow sun," Lee said, "so what's the problem?"

"Never mind."

"Or maybe you've figured out the real reason the dinosaurs went extinct," Lee said. "Vampires got them all."

"That's clever," Davis said. "You're very clever, Lee."

"What about you, sir?" Lee said.

"Me?" the lieutenant said. "I'm afraid the scenario I've invented is much more lurid than either of yours. I incline to the view that the vampire is here as a punishment."

"For what?" Davis said.

"I haven't the faintest clue," the lieutenant said. "What kind of crime does a monster commit? Maybe it stole someone else's victims. Maybe it killed another vampire. Whatever it did, it was placed in that coffin and sent out into space. Whether its fellows intended us as its final destination, or planned for it to drift endlessly, I can't say. But I wonder if its blood-drinking—that craving—might not be part of its punishment."

"How?" Lee said.

"Say the vampire's used to feeding on a substance like blood, only better, more nutritious, more satisfying. Part of the reason for sending it here is that all that will be available to it is this poor substitute that leaves it perpetually thirsty. Not only does it have to cross significant distances, expose itself to potential harm to feed, the best it can do will never be good enough."

"That," Lee said, "is fucked up."

"There's a reason they made me an officer," the lieutenant said. He turned to Han. "What about you, Han? Any thoughts concerning the nature of our imminent guest?"

"Devil," Han said.

"Ah," the lieutenant said.

"Which?" Lee asked. "A devil, or the Devil?"

Han shrugged.

XI
2005-2006

To start with, the lieutenant called once a week, on a Saturday night. Davis could not help reflecting on what this said about the state of the man's life, his marriage, that he spent the peak hours of his weekend in a long-distance conversation with a former subordinate—as well as the commentary their calls offered on his own state of affairs, that not only was he always in his apartment for the lieutenant's call, but that starting late Thursday, up to a day earlier if his week was especially shitty, he looked forward to it.

There was a rhythm, almost a ritual, to each call. The lieutenant asked Davis how he'd been; he answered, "Fine, sir," and offered a précis of the last seven days at Home Depot, which tended to consist of a summary of his assistant manager's most egregious offences. If he'd steered clear of Adams, he might list the titles of whatever movies he'd rented, along with one- or two-sentence reviews of each. Occasionally, he would narrate his latest failed date, recasting stilted frustration as comic misadventure. At the conclusion of his recitation, Davis would swat the lieutenant's question back to him. The lieutenant would answer, "Can't complain," and follow with a distillation of his week that focused on his dissatisfaction with his position at Stillwater, a defense contractor who had promised him a career as exciting as the one he'd left but delivered little more than lunches, dinners, and cocktail parties at which the lieutenant was trotted out, he said, so everyone could admire his Goddamned plastic leg and congratulate his employers on hiring him.

At least the money was decent, and Barbara enjoyed the opportunity to dress up and go out to nicer places than he'd ever been able to afford. The lieutenant did not speak about his children; although if asked, he would say that they were hanging in there. From time to time, he shared news of Lee, whom he called on Sunday and whose situation never seemed to improve that much, and Han, whose sister he e-mailed every Monday and who reported that her brother was making progress with his injuries; in fact, Han was starting to e-mail the lieutenant, himself.

This portion of their conversation, which Davis thought of as the Prelude, over, the real reason for the call—what Davis thought of as the SITREP—ensued. The lieutenant, whose sentences hitherto had been loose, lazy, tightened his syntax as he quizzed Davis about the status of the Plan. In response, Davis kept his replies short, to the point. Have we settled on a location? the lieutenant would ask. Yes sir, Davis would say, Thompson's Grove. That was the spot in the Catskills, the lieutenant would say, south slope of Winger Mountain, about a half mile east of the principle trail to the summit. Exactly, sir, Davis would say. Research indicates the mountain itself is among the least visited in the Catskill Preserve, and Thompson's Grove about the most obscure spot on it. The location is sufficiently removed from civilian populations not to place them in immediate jeopardy, yet still readily accessible by us. Good, good, the lieutenant would say. I'll notify Lee and Han.

The SITREP finished, Davis and the lieutenant would move to Coming Attractions: review their priorities for the week ahead, wish one another well, and hang up. As the months slid by and the Plan's more elaborate elements came into play—especially once Davis commenced his experiments dosing himself with adrenaline—the lieutenant began adding the odd Wednesday night to his call schedule. After Davis had determined the proper amount for inducing a look through the Shadow's eyes—and after he'd succeeded in affecting the thing a second time, causing it to release its hold on a man Davis was reasonably sure was a Somali pirate—the Wednesday exchanges became part of their routine. Certainly, they helped Davis and the lieutenant to coordinate their experiences interrupting the Shadow's routine with the reports coming in from Lee and Han, which arrived with increasing frequency once Lee and Han had found their adrenaline doses and were mastering the trick of interfering with the Shadow. However, in the moment immediately preceding their setting their respective phones down, Davis would be struck by the impression that the lieutenant and he were on the verge of saying something else, something more—he couldn't say what, exactly, only that it would be significant in a way—in a different way from their usual conversation. It was how he'd felt in the days leading up to Fallujah, as if, with such momentous events roiling on the horizon, he should be speaking about important matters, meaningful things.

Twice, they came close to such an exchange. The first time followed a discussion of the armaments the lieutenant had purchased at a recent gun show across the border in Pennsylvania. "God love the NRA," he'd said and listed the four Glock 21SF's, sixteen extra clips, ten boxes of .45 ammunition, four AR-15's, sixteen extra high-capacity magazines for them, thirty boxes of 223 Remington ammo, and four USGI M7 bayonets.

"Jesus, sir," Davis had said when the lieutenant was done. "That's a shitload of ordnance."

"I stopped at the grenade launcher," the lieutenant said. "It seemed excessive."

"You do remember how much effect our guns had on the thing the last time…"

"Think of this as a supplement to the Plan. Even with one of us on board, once the thing shows up, it's going to be a threat. We know it's easier to hit when someone's messing with its controls, so let's exploit that. The more we can tag it, the more we can slow it down, improve our chances of using your secret weapon on it."

"Fair enough."

"Good. I'm glad you agree."

Davis was opening his mouth to suggest possible positions the four of them might take around the clearing when the lieutenant said, "Davis."

"Sir?"

"Would you say you've had a good life? Scratch that—would you say you've had a satisfactory life?"

"I…I don't know. I guess so."

"I've been thinking about my father these past few days. It's the anniversary of his death, twenty-one years ago this Monday. He came here from Mexico City when he was sixteen, worked as a fruit picker for a couple of years, then fell into a job at a diner. He started busing tables, talked his way into the kitchen, and became the principle cook for the night shift. That was how he met my mother: she was a waitress there. She was from Mexico, too, although the country—apparently, she thought my old man was some kind of city-slicker, not to be trusted by a virtuous girl. I guess she was right, because my older brother was born seven months after their wedding. But I came along two years after that, so I don't think that was the only reason for them tying the knot.

"He died when I was five, my father. An embolism burst in his brain. He was at work, just getting into the swing of things. The coroner said he was dead before he reached the floor. He was twenty-seven. What I wonder is, when he looked at his life, at everything he'd done, was it what he wanted? Even if it was different, was it enough?

"How many people do you suppose exit this world satisfied with what they've managed to accomplish in it, Davis? How many of our fellows slipped their mortal coils content with what their eighteen or twenty-one or twenty-seven years had meant?"

"There was the Mission," Davis said. "Ask them in public, and they'd laugh, offer some smartass remark, but talk to them one-on-one, and they'd tell you they believed in what we were doing, even if things could get pretty fucked-up. I'm not sure if that would've been enough for Lugo, or Manfred—for anyone—but it would've counted for something."

"True," the lieutenant said. "The question is, will something do?"

"I guess it has to."

Their second such conversation came two weeks before the weekend the four of them were scheduled to travel to Upstate New York. They were reviewing the final draft of the Plan, which Davis thought must be something like the Plan version 22.0—although little had changed in the way of the principles since they'd finalized them a month earlier. Ten minutes before dawn, they would take up their positions in the trees around the clearing. If north was twelve o'clock, then Lee and Han would be at twelve—necessary because Han would be injecting himself at t-minus one minute and would require protection—the lieutenant would take two, and Davis three. The woods were reasonably thick: if they positioned themselves about ten feet in, then the Shadow would be unable to come in on top of them. If it wanted them, it would have to land, shift to foot, and that would be the cue for the three of them aiming their AR-15's to fire. In the meantime, Han would have snuck on board the Shadow and be preparing to jam it. As soon as he saw the opportunity, he would do his utmost to take the thing's legs out from under it, a maneuver he had been rehearsing for several weeks and become reasonably proficient at. The average time Han guesstimated he'd been able to knock the Shadow's legs out was fifteen seconds, though he had reached the vicinity of thirty once. This would be their window: the instant the thing's legs crumpled, two of them had to be up and on it, probably Davis and Lee since the lieutenant wasn't placing any bets on his sprinter's start. One of them would draw the Shadow's notice, the other hit it with the secret weapon. If for any reason the first attacker failed, the second could engage if he saw the opportunity; otherwise, he would have to return to the woods, because Han's hold on the thing would be wearing off. Once the lieutenant observed this, he would inject himself and they would begin round two. Round two was the same as round one except for the presumed lack of one man, just as round three counted on two of them being gone. Round four, the lieutenant said, was him eating a bullet. By that point, there might not be anything he could do to stop the ugly son of a bitch drinking his blood, but that didn't mean he had to stay around for the event.

Davis knew they would recite the Plan again on Saturday, and then next Wednesday, and then the Saturday after that, and then the Wednesday two weeks from now. At the Quality Inn in Kingston, they would recite the Plan, and again as they drove into the Catskills, and yet again as they hiked up Winger Mountain. "Preparation" the lieutenant had said in Iraq, "is what ensures you will fuck up only eighty percent of what you are trying to do." If the exact numbers sounded overly optimistic to Davis, he agreed with the general sentiment.

Without preamble, the lieutenant said, "You know, Davis, when my older brother was twenty-four, he left his girlfriend for a married Russian émigré six years his senior—whom he had met, ironically enough, through his ex, who had been tutoring Margarita, her husband, Sergei, and their four-year-old, Stasu, in English."

"No sir," Davis said, "I'm pretty sure you never told me this."

"You have to understand," the lieutenant went on, "until this point, my brother, Alberto, had led a reasonably sedate and unimpressive life. Prior to this, the most daring thing he'd done was go out with Alexandra, the tutor, who was Jewish, which made our very Catholic mother very nervous. Yet here he was, packing his clothes and his books, emptying his meager bank account, and driving out of town with Margarita in the passenger's seat and Stasu in the back with all the stuff they couldn't squeeze in the trunk. They headed west, first to St. Louis for a couple of months, next to New Mexico for three years, and finally to Portland—actually, it's just outside Portland, but I can never remember the name of the town.

"She was a veterinarian, Margarita. With Alberto's help, she succeeded in having her credentials transferred over here. Has her own practice, these days, treats horses, cows, farm animals. Alberto helps her; he's her assistant and office manager. Sergei gave them custody of Stasu; they have two more kids, girls, Helena and Catherine. Beautiful kids, my nieces.

"You have any brothers or sisters, Davis?"

"A younger brother, sir. He wants to be a priest."

"Really?"

"Yes, sir."

"Isn't that funny."

XII
5:53 AM

Lying on the ground he'd swept clear of rocks and branches, his rifle propped on a small log, the sky a red bowl overhead, Davis experienced a moment of complete and utter doubt. Not only did the course of action on which they had set out appear wildly implausible, but everything from the courtyard in Fallujah on acquired the sheen of the unreal, the delusional. An eight-foot-tall space vampire? Visions of soaring through the sky, of savaging scores of men, women, and children around the globe? Injecting himself with adrenaline, for Christ's sake? What was any of this but the world's biggest symptom, a massive phantasy his mind had conjured to escape a reality it couldn't bear? What had happened—what scene was the Shadow substituting for? Had they in fact found a trap in the courtyard, an IED that had shredded them in its fiery teeth? Was he lying in a hospital bed somewhere, his body ruined, his mind hopelessly crippled?

When the Shadow was standing in the clearing, swinging its narrow head from side to side, Davis felt something like relief. If this dark thing and its depravities were a hallucination, he could be true to it. The Shadow parted its fangs as if tasting the dawn. Davis tensed, prepared to find himself someplace else, subject to a clip from the thing's history, but the worst he felt was a sudden buzzing in his skull that reminded him of nothing so much as the old fuse box in his parents' basement. He adjusted his rifle and squeezed the trigger.

The air rang with gunfire. Davis thought his first burst caught the thing in the belly: he saw it step back, though that might have been due to either Lee or the lieutenant, who had fired along with him. Almost too fast to follow, the Shadow jumped, a black scribble against the sky, but someone anticipated its leap and aimed ahead of it. At least one of the bullets connected; Davis saw the Shadow's right eye pucker. Stick-arms jerking, it fell at the edge of the treeline, ten feet in front of him. He shot at its head, its shoulders. Geysers of dirt marked his misses. The Shadow threw itself backwards, but collapsed where it landed.

"NOW!" the lieutenant screamed.

Davis grabbed for his stake with his left hand as he dropped the rifle from his right. Almost before his fingers had closed on the weapon, he was on his feet and rushing into the clearing. To the right, Lee burst out of the trees, his stake held overhead in both hands, his mouth open in a bellow. In front of them, the Shadow was thrashing from side to side like the world's largest insect pinned through the middle. Its claws scythed grass, bushes. Davis saw that its right eye had indeed been hit, and partially collapsed. Lee was not slowing his charge. Davis sprinted to reach the Shadow at the same time.

Although the thing's legs were motionless, its claws were fast as ever. As Davis came abreast of it, jabbing at its head, its arm snapped in his direction. Pain razored up his left arm. Blood spattered the grass, the Shadow's head jerked towards him, and the momentary distraction this offered was, perhaps, what allowed Lee to tumble into a forward roll that dropped him under the Shadow's other claw and up again to drive his stake down into the base of its throat. Reaching for the cell phone in his shirt pocket, Davis backpedaled. The thing's maw gaped as Lee held on to shove the weapon as far as it would go. The Shadow twisted and thrust its claws into Lee's collarbone and ribs. His eyes bulged and he released the stake. Davis had the cell phone in his hand. The Shadow tore its claw from Lee's chest and ripped him open. Davis pressed the three and hit SEND.

In the woods, there was a white flash and the CRUMP of explosives detonating. A cloud of debris rushed between the trunks. The Shadow jolted as if a bolt of lightning had speared it.

"SHIT!" the lieutenant was screaming. "SHIT!"

The Shadow was on its feet, Lee dangling from its left claw like a child's bedraggled plaything. Davis backpedaled. With its right claw, the Shadow reached for the stake jutting from its throat. Davis pressed the two and SEND.

He was knocked from his feet by the force of the blast, which shoved the air from his lungs and pushed sight and sound away from him. He was aware of the ground pressing against his back, a fine rain of particles pattering his skin, but his body was contracted around his chest, which could not bring in any air. Suffocating, he was suffocating. He tried to move his hands, his feet, but his extremities did not appear to be receiving his brain's instructions. Perhaps his hand-crafted bomb had accomplished what the Shadow could not.

What he could feel of the world was bleeding away.

XIII
2006

Although Lee wanted to wait for sunset, if not total darkness, a preference Davis shared, the lieutenant insisted they shoulder their packs and start the trail up Winger Mountain while the sun would be broadcasting its light for another couple of hours. At the expressions on Lee and Davis's faces, he said, "Relax. The thing sweeps the Grove first thing in the morning. It's long gone, off feeding someplace."

The trail was not unpleasant. Had they been so inclined, its lower reaches were wide enough that they could have walked them two abreast. (They opted for single file, Lee taking point, Han next, the lieutenant third, and Davis bringing up the rear. It spread the targets out.) The ground was matted with the leaves of the trees that flanked the trail and stationed the gradual slopes to either side. (While he had never been any good at keeping the names of such things straight, Davis had an idea the trees were a mix of maple and oak, the occasional white one a birch.) With their crowns full of leaves, the trees almost obscured the sky's blue emptiness. (All the same, Davis didn't look up any more than he could help.)

They reached the path to Thompson's Grove sooner than Davis had anticipated. A piece of wood weathered gray and nailed to a tree chest-high pointed right, to a narrower route that appeared overgrown a hundred yards or so in the distance. Lee withdrew the machete he had sheathed on his belt and struck the sign once, twice, until it flew off the tree into the forest.

"Hey," Davis said, "that's vandalism."

"Sue me," Lee said.

Once they were well into the greenery, the mosquitoes, which had ventured only the occasional scout so long as they kept to the trail, descended in clouds. "Damnit!" the lieutenant said, slapping his cheek. "I used bug spray."

"Probably tastes like dessert topping to them, sir," Lee called. "Although, damn! at this rate, there won't be any blood left in us for Count Dracula."

Thompson's Grove was an irregular circle, forty feet across. Grass stood thigh-high. A few bushes punctuated the terrain. Davis could feel the sky hungry above them. Lee and Han walked the perimeter while he and the lieutenant stayed near the trees. All of their rifles were out. Lee and Han declared the area secure, but the four of them waited until the sun was finally down to clear the center of the Grove and build their fire.

Lee had been, Davis supposed the word was *off*, since they'd met in Kingston that morning. His eyes shone in his face, whose flesh seemed drawn around the bones. When Davis embraced him in the lobby of the Quality Inn, it had been like putting his arms around one of the support cables on a suspension bridge, something bracing an enormous weight. It might be the prospect of their upcoming encounter, although Davis suspected there was more to it. The lieutenant's most recent report had been that Lee was continuing to struggle: Shari had won custody of Douglas, with whom Lee was permitted supervised visits every other Saturday. He'd enrolled at his local community college, but stopped attending classes after the first week. The lieutenant wasn't sure he'd go so far as to call Lee an alcoholic, but there was no doubt the man liked his beer a good deal more than was healthy. After the wood was gathered and stacked, the fire kindled, the sandwiches Davis had prepared distributed, Lee cleared his throat and said, "I know the lieutenant has an order he wants us to follow, but there's something I need to know about."

"All right," the lieutenant said through a mouthful of turkey on rye, "ask away."

"It's the connection we have to the thing," Lee said. "Okay, so: we've got a direct line into its central nervous system. The right amount of adrenaline, and we can hijack it. Problem is, the link works both ways. At least, we know that, when the thing's angry, it can look out of our eyes. What if it can do more? What if it can do to us what we've done to it, take us over?"

"There's been no evidence of that," Davis said. "Don't you think, if it could do that, it would have by now?"

"Not necessarily," Lee said.

"Oh? Why not?"

"Why would it need to? We're trying to get its attention; it doesn't need to do anything to get ours."

"It's an unknown," the lieutenant said. "It's conceivable the thing could assume control of whoever's hooked up to it and try to use him for support. I have to say, though, that even if it could possess one of us, I have a hard time imagining it doing so while the rest of us are trying to shorten its lifespan. To tell you the truth, should we succeed in killing it, I'd be more worried about it using the connection as a means of escape."

"Escape?" Davis said.

Lee said, "The lieutenant means it leaves its body behind for one of ours."

"Could it do that?"

"I don't know," the lieutenant said, "I only mention it as a worst-case scenario. Our ability to share its perceptions, to affect its actions, seems to suggest some degree of congruity between the thing and us. On the other hand, it is a considerable leap from there to its being able to inhabit us."

"Maybe that's how it makes more of itself," Lee said. "One dies, one's born."

"Phoenix," Han said.

"This is all pretty speculative," Davis said.

"Yes it is," the lieutenant said. "Should the thing seize any of us, however, it will have been speculation well-spent."

"What do you propose, then, sir?" Davis said.

"Assuming any of us survives the morning," the lieutenant said, "we will have to proceed with great caution." He held up his pistol.

XIV
6:42AM

Davis opened his eyes to a hole in the sky. Round, black—for a moment, he had the impression the Earth had gained a strange new satellite, or that some unimaginable catastrophe had blown an opening in the atmosphere, and then his vision adjusted and he realized that he was looking up into the barrel of the lieutenant's Glock. The man himself half-crouched beside Davis, his eyes narrowed. His lips moved, and Davis struggled to pick his words out of the white noise ringing in his ears.

"Davis," he said. "You there?"

"Yeah," Davis said. Something was burning; a charcoal reek stung his nostrils. His mouth tasted like ashes. He pushed himself up on his elbows. "Is it—"

"Whoa," the lieutenant said, holding his free hand up like a traffic cop. "Take it easy, soldier. That was some blast."

"Did we—"

"We did."

"Yeah?"

"We blew it to Kingdom Come," the lieutenant said. "No doubt, there are pieces of it scattered here and there, but the majority of it is so much dust."

"Lee—"

"You saw what the thing did to him—although, stupid motherfucker, it serves him right, grabbing the wrong Goddamned stake. Of all the stupid fucking..."

Davis swallowed. "Han?"

The lieutenant shook his head.

Davis lay back. "Fuck."

"Never mind," the lieutenant said. His pistol had not moved. "Shit happens. The question before us now is, did it work? Are we well and truly rid of that thing, that fucking blood-drinking monster, or are we fooling ourselves? What do you say, Davis?"

"I..." His throat was dry. "Lee grabbed the wrong one?"

"He did."

"How is that possible?"

"I don't know," the lieutenant said. "I do not fucking know."

"I specifically gave each of us—"

"I know; I watched you. In the excitement of the moment, Lee and Han must have mixed them up."

"Mixed..." Davis raised his hands to his forehead. Behind the lieutenant, the sky was a blue chasm.

"Or could be, the confusion was deliberate."

"What?"

"Maybe they switched stakes on purpose."

"No."

"I don't think so, either, but we all know it wasn't much of a life for Han."

"That doesn't mean—"

"It doesn't."

"Jesus." Davis sat up.

The lieutenant steadied his gun. "So?"

"I take it you're fine."

"As far as I've been able to determine, yes."

"Could the thing have had something to do with it?"

"The mix-up?"

"Made Han switch the stakes or something?"

"That presumes it knew what they were, which supposes it had been spying on us through Han's eyes for not a few hours, which assumes it comprehended us—our language, our technology—in excess of prior evidence."

"Yeah," Davis said. "Still."

"It was an accident," the lieutenant said. "Let it go."

"What makes you so sure you're all right?"

"I've had no indications to the contrary. I appear in control of my own thoughts and actions. I'm aware of no alien presence crowding my mind. While I am thirsty, I have to desire to quench that thirst from one of your arteries."

"Would you be, though? Aware of the thing hiding in you?"

The lieutenant shrugged. "Possibly not. You're taking a long time to answer my question; you know that."

"I don't know how I am," Davis said. "No, I can't feel the thing either, and no, I don't want to drink your blood. Is that enough?"

"Davis," the lieutenant said, "I will do this. You need to understand that. You are as close to me as anyone, these days, and I will shoot you in the head if I deem it necessary. If I believed the thing were in me, I would turn this gun on myself without a second thought. Am I making myself clear? Let me know it's over, or let me finish it."

The lieutenant's face was flushed. "All right," Davis said. He closed his eyes. "All right." He took a deep breath. Another.

When he opened his eyes, he said, "It's gone."

"You're positive."

"Yes, sir."

"You cannot be lying to me."

"I know. I'm not."

The end of the pistol wavered, and for a moment, Davis was certain that the lieutenant was unconvinced, that he was going to squeeze the trigger, anyway. He wondered if he'd see the muzzle flash.

Then the pistol lowered and the lieutenant said, "Good man." He holstered the gun and extended his hand. "Come on. There's a lot we have to do."

Davis caught the lieutenant's hand and hauled himself to his feet. Behind the lieutenant, he saw the charred place that had been the Shadow, Lee's torn and blackened form to one side of it. Further back, smoke continued to drift out of the spot in the trees where Han had lain. The lieutenant turned and started walking towards the trees. He did not ask, and Davis did not tell him, what he had seen with his eyes closed. He wasn't sure how he could have said that the image behind his eyelids was the same as the image in front of them: the unending sky, blue, ravenous.

For Fiona, and with thanks to John Joseph Adams

ONE FOR THE ROAD

by Stephen King

Stephen King is the bestselling, award-winning author of many classics, such as *The Shining, The Dark Tower, The Stand,* and *The Dead Zone.* His novel *'Salem's Lot* is one of the classics of the vampire genre. His latest novel, *Duma Key,* was published in early 2008, and a new short fiction collection, *Just After Sunset,* was released last fall. A new book collecting several stories and novellas of King's that have been adapted for film, along with commentary by King—*Stephen King Goes to the Movies*—came out earlier this year. Other projects include editing *Best American Short Stories 2007,* and writing a pop culture column for *Entertainment Weekly.*

In his landmark study of horror literature, *Danse Macabre,* King argued that, in order to be effective, fictional, supernatural monsters must tap into and express in powerful metaphorical terms our actual fears about the real world.

For residents of Maine, one very real worry is that your vehicle will fail you in the snow and you will freeze to death before help arrives. Classic folklore imagined the brooding mists of Transylvania as malignant, corporeal beings. Here King does the same for the whiteouts of Cumberland.

These vampires are avatars of winter, chilling in every respect.

It was quarter past ten and Herb Tooklander was thinking of closing for the night when the man in the fancy overcoat and the white, staring face burst into Tookey's Bar, which lies in the northern part of Falmouth. It was the tenth of January, just about the time most folks are learning to live comfortably with all the New Year's resolutions they broke, and there was one hell of a northeaster blowing outside. Six inches had come down before dark and it had been going hard and heavy since then. Twice we had seen Billy Larribee go by high in the cab of the town plow, and the second time Tookey ran him out a beer—an act of pure charity my mother would have called it, and my God knows she put down enough of Tookey's beer in her time. Billy told him they were keeping ahead of it on the main road, but the side ones were closed and apt to stay that way until next morning. The radio in Portland was forecasting another foot and a forty-mile-an-hour wind to pile up the drifts.

There was just Tookey and me in the bar, listening to the wind howl around the eaves and watching it dance the fire around on the hearth. "Have one for the road, Booth," Tookey says, "I'm gonna shut her down."

He poured me one and himself one and that's when the door cracked open and this stranger staggered in, snow up to his shoulders and in his hair, like he had rolled around in confectioner's sugar. The wind billowed a sand-fine sheet of snow in after him.

"Close the door!" Tookey roars at him. "Was you born in a barn?"

I've never seen a man who looked that scared. He was like a horse that's spent an afternoon eating fire nettles. His eyes rolled toward Tookey and he said, "My wife—my daughter—" and he collapsed on the floor in a dead faint.

"Holy Joe," Tookey says. "Close the door, Booth, would you?"

I went and shut it, and pushing it against the wind was something of a chore. Tookey was down on one knee holding the fellow's head up and patting his cheeks. I got over to him and saw right off that it was nasty. His face was fiery red, but there were gray blotches here and there, and when you've lived through winters in Maine since the time Woodrow Wilson was President, as I have, you know those gray blotches mean frostbite.

"Fainted," Tookey said. "Get the brandy off the backbar, will you?"

I got it and came back. Tookey had opened the fellow's coat. He had come around a little; his eyes were half open and he was muttering something too low to catch.

"Pour a capful," Tookey says.

"Just a cap?" I asks him.

"That stuff's dynamite," Tookey says. "No sense overloading his carb."

I poured out a capful and looked at Tookey. He nodded. "Straight down the hatch."

I poured it down. It was a remarkable thing to watch. The man trembled all over and began to cough. His face got redder. His eyelids, which had been at half-mast, flew up like window shades. I was a bit alarmed, but Tookey only sat him up like a big baby and clapped him on the back.

The man started to retch, and Tookey clapped him again.

"Hold onto it," he says, "that brandy comes dear."

The man coughed some more, but it was diminishing now. I got my first good look at him. City fellow, all right, and from somewhere south of Boston, at a guess. He was wearing kid gloves, expensive but thin. There were probably some more of those grayish-white patches on his hands, and he would be lucky not to lose a finger or two. His coat was fancy, all right; a three-hundred-dollar job if ever I'd seen one. He was wearing tiny little boots that hardly came up over his ankles, and I began to wonder about his toes.

"Better," he said.

"All right," Tookey said. "Can you come over to the fire?"

"My wife and my daughter," he said. "They're out there... in the storm."

"From the way you came in, I didn't figure they were at home watching the TV," Tookey said. "You can tell us by the fire as easy as here on the floor. Hook on, Booth."

He got to his feet, but a little groan came out of him and his mouth twisted down in pain. I wondered about his toes again, and I wondered why God felt he had to make fools from New York City who would try driving around in southern Maine at the height of a northeast blizzard. And I wondered if his wife and his little girl were dressed any warmer than him.

We hiked him across to the fireplace and got him sat down in a rocker that used to be Missus Tookey's favorite until she passed on in '74. It was Missus Tookey that was responsible for most of the place, which had been written up in *Down East* and the *Sunday Telegram* and even once in the Sunday supplement of the Boston *Globe*. It's really more of a public house than a bar, with its big wooden floor, pegged together rather than nailed, the maple bar, the old barn-raftered ceiling, and the monstrous big fieldstone hearth. Missus Tookey started to get some ideas in her head after the *Down East* article came out, wanted to start calling the place Tookey's Inn or Tookey's Rest, and I admit it has sort of a Colonial ring to it, but I prefer plain old Tookey's Bar. It's one thing to get uppish in the summer, when the state's full of tourists, another thing altogether in the winter, when you and your neighbors have to trade together. And there had been plenty of winter nights, like this one, that Tookey and I had spent all alone together, drinking scotch and water or just a few beers. My own Victoria passed on in '73, and Tookey's was a place to go where there were enough voices to mute the steady ticking of the deathwatch beetle—even if there was just Tookey and me, it was enough. I wouldn't have felt the same about it if the place had been Tookey's Rest. It's crazy but it's true.

We got this fellow in front of the fire and he got the shakes harder than ever. He hugged onto his knees and his teeth clattered together and a few drops of clear mucus spilled off the end of his nose. I think he was starting to realize that another fifteen minutes out there might have been enough to kill him. It's not the snow, it's the wind-chill factor. It steals your heat.

"Where did you go off the road?" Tookey asked him.

"S-six miles s-s-south of h-here," he said.

Tookey and I stared at each other, and all of a sudden I felt cold. Cold all over.

"You sure?" Tookey demanded. "You came six miles through the snow?"

He nodded. "I checked the odometer when we came through t-town. I was following directions... going to see my wife's s-sister... in Cumberland... never been there before... we're from New Jersey..."

New Jersey. If there's anyone more purely foolish than a New Yorker it's a fellow from New Jersey.

"Six miles, you're sure?" Tookey demanded.

"Pretty sure, yeah. I found the turnoff but it was drifted in... it was..."

Tookey grabbed him. In the shifting glow of the fire his face looked pale and strained, older than his sixty-six years by ten. "You made a right turn?"

"Right turn, yeah. My wife—"

"Did you see a sign?"

"Sign?" He looked up at Tookey blankly and wiped the end of his nose. "Of course I did. It was on my instructions. Take Jointner Avenue through Jerusalem's Lot to the 295 entrance ramp." He looked from Tookey to me and back to Tookey again. Outside, the wind whistled and howled and moaned through the eaves. "Wasn't that right, mister?"

"The Lot," Tookey said, almost too soft to hear. "Oh my God."

"What's wrong?" the man said. His voice was rising. "Wasn't that right? I mean, the road looked drifted in, but I thought… if there's a town there, the plows will be out and… and then I…"

He just sort of tailed off.

"Booth," Tookey said to me, low. "Get on the phone. Call the sheriff."

"Sure," this fool from New Jersey says, "that's right. What's wrong with you guys, anyway? You look like you saw a ghost."

Tookey said, "No ghosts in the Lot, mister. Did you tell them to stay in the car?"

"Sure I did," he said, sounding injured. "I'm not crazy."

Well, you couldn't have proved it by me.

"What's your name?" I asked him. "For the sheriff."

"Lumley," he says. "Gerard Lumley."

He started in with Tookey again, and I went across to the telephone. I picked it up and heard nothing but dead silence. I hit the cutoff buttons a couple of times. Still nothing.

I came back. Tookey had poured Gerard Lumley another tot of brandy, and this one was going down him a lot smoother.

"Was he out?" Tookey asked.

"Phone's dead."

"Hot damn," Tookey says, and we look at each other. Outside the wind gusted up, throwing snow against the windows.

Lumley looked from Tookey to me and back again.

"Well, haven't either of you got a car?" he asked. The anxiety was back in his voice. "They've got to run the engine to run the heater. I only had about a quarter of a tank of gas, and it took me an hour and a half to… Look, will you *answer* me?" He stood up and grabbed Tookey's shirt.

"Mister," Tookey says, "I think your hand just ran away from your brains, there."

Lumley looked at his hand, at Tookey, then dropped it. "Maine," he hissed. He made it sound like a dirty word about somebody's mother. "All right," he said. "Where's the nearest gas station? They must have a tow truck—"

"Nearest gas station is in Falmouth Center," I said. "That's three miles down the road from here."

"Thanks," he said, a bit sarcastic, and headed for the door, buttoning his coat.

"Won't be open, though," I added.

He turned back slowly and looked at us.

"What are you talking about, old man?"

"He's trying to tell you that the station in the Center belongs to Billy Larribee and Billy's out driving the plow, you damn fool," Tookey says patiently. "Now why don't you come back here and sit down, before you bust a gut?"

He came back, looking dazed and frightened. "Are you telling me you can't... that there isn't... ?"

"I ain't telling you nothing," Tookey says. "You're doing all the telling, and if you stopped for a minute, we could think this over."

"What's this town, Jerusalem's Lot?" he asked. "Why was the road drifted in? And no lights on anywhere?"

I said, "Jerusalem's Lot burned out two years back."

"And they never rebuilt?" He looked like he didn't believe it.

"It appears that way," I said, and looked at Tookey. "What are we going to do about this?"

"Can't leave them out there," he said.

I got closer to him. Lumley had wandered away to look out the window into the snowy night.

"What if they've been got at?" I asked.

"That may be," he said. "But we don't know it for sure. I've got my Bible on the shelf. You still wear your Pope's medal?"

I pulled the crucifix out of my shirt and showed him. I was born and raised Congregational, but most folks who live around the Lot wear something—crucifix, St. Christopher's medal, rosary, something. Because two years ago, in the span of one dark October month, the Lot went bad. Sometimes, late at night, when there were just a few regulars drawn up around Tookey's fire, people would talk it over. Talk around it is more like the truth. You see, people in the Lot started to disappear. First a few, then a few more, than a whole slew. The schools closed. The town stood empty for most of a year. Oh, a few people moved in—mostly damn fools from out of state like this fine specimen here—drawn by the low property values, I suppose. But they didn't last. A lot of them moved out a month or two after they'd moved in. The others... well, they disappeared. Then the town burned flat. It was at the end of a long dry fall. They figure it started up by the Marsten House on the hill that overlooked Jointner Avenue, but no one knows how it started, not to this day. It burned out of control for three days. After that, for a time, things were better. And then they started again.

I only heard the word "vampires" mentioned once. A crazy pulp truck driver named Richie Messina from over Freeport way was in Tookey's that night, pretty well liquored up. "Jesus Christ," this stampeder roars, standing up about nine feet tall in his wool pants and his plaid shirt and his leather-topped boots. "Are you all so damn afraid to say it out? Vampires! That's what you're all thinking, ain't it? Jesus-jumped-up-Christ in a chariot-driven sidecar! Just like a bunch of kids scared of the movies! You know what there is down there in 'Salem's Lot? Want me to tell you? Want me to tell you?"

"Do tell, Richie," Tookey says. It had got real quiet in the bar. You could hear the fire popping, and outside the soft drift of November rain coming down in the dark. "You got the floor."

"What you got over there is your basic wild dog pack," Richie Messina tells us. "That's what you got. That and a lot of old women who love a good spook story. Why, for eighty bucks I'd go up there and spend the night in what's left of that haunted house you're all so worried about. Well, what about it? Anyone want to put it up?"

But nobody would. Richie was a loudmouth and a mean drunk and no one was going to shed any tears at his wake, but none of us were willing to see him go into 'Salem's Lot after dark.

"Be screwed to the bunch of you," Richie says. "I got my four-ten in the trunk of my Chevy, and that'll stop anything in Falmouth, Cumberland, *or* Jerusalem's Lot. And that's where I'm goin'."

He slammed out of the bar and no one said a word for a while. Then Lamont Henry says, real quiet, "That's the last time anyone's gonna see Richie Messina. Holy God." And Lamont, raised to be a Methodist from his mother's knee, crossed himself.

"He'll sober off and change his mind," Tookey said, but he sounded uneasy. "He'll be back by closin' time, makin' out it was all a joke."

But Lamont had the right of that one, because no one ever saw Richie again. His wife told the state cops she thought he'd gone to Florida to beat a collection agency, but you could see the truth of the thing in her eyes—sick, scared eyes. Not long after, she moved away to Rhode Island. Maybe she thought Richie was going to come after her some dark night. And I'm not the man to say he might not have done.

Now Tookey was looking at me and I was looking at Tookey as I stuffed my crucifix back into my shirt. I never felt so old or so scared in my life.

Tookey said again, "We can't just leave them out there, Booth."

"Yeah. I know."

We looked at each other for a moment longer, and then he reached out and gripped my shoulder. "You're a good man, Booth." That was enough to buck me up some. It seems like when you pass seventy, people start forgetting that you are a man, or that you ever were.

Tookey walked over to Lumley and said, "I've got a four-wheel-drive Scout. I'll get it out."

"For God's sake, man, why didn't you say so before?" He had whirled around from the window and was staring angrily at Tookey. "Why'd you have to spend ten minutes beating around the bush?"

Tookey said, very softly, "Mister, you shut your jaw. And if you get the urge to open it, you remember who made that turn onto an unplowed road in the middle of a goddamned blizzard."

He started to say something, and then shut his mouth. Thick color had risen up in his cheeks. Tookey went out to get his Scout out of the garage. I felt around under the bar for his chrome flask and filled it full of brandy. Figured we might need it before this night was over.

Maine blizzard—ever been out in one?

The snow comes flying so thick and fine that it looks like sand and sounds like that, beating on the sides of your car or pickup. You don't want to use your high beams because they reflect off the snow and you can't see ten feet in front of you. With the low beams on, you can see maybe fifteen feet. But I can live with the snow. It's the wind I don't like, when it picks up and begins to howl, driving the snow into a hundred weird flying shapes and sounding like all the hate and pain and fear in the world. There's death in the throat of a snowstorm wind, white death—and maybe something beyond death. That's no sound to hear when you're tucked up all cozy in your own bed with the shutters bolted and the doors locked. It's that much worse if you're driving. And we were driving smack into 'Salem's Lot.

"Hurry up a little, can't you?" Lumley asked.

I said, "For a man who came in half frozen, you're in one hell of a hurry to end up walking again."

He gave me a resentful, baffled look and didn't say anything else. We were moving up the highway at a steady twenty-five miles an hour. It was hard to believe that Billy Larribee had just plowed this stretch an hour ago; another two inches had covered it, and it was drifting in. The strongest gusts of wind rocked the Scout on her springs. The headlights showed a swirling white nothing up ahead of us. We hadn't met a single car.

About ten minutes later Lumley gasps: "Hey! What's that?"

He was pointing out my side of the car; I'd been looking dead ahead. I turned, but was a shade too late. I thought I could see some sort of slumped form fading back from the car, back into the snow, but that could have been imagination.

"What was it? A deer?" I asked.

"I guess so," he says, sounding shaky. "But its eyes—they looked red." He looked at me. "Is that how a deer's eyes look at night?" He sounded almost as if he were pleading.

"They can look like anything," I says, thinking that might be true, but I've seen a lot of deer at night from a lot of cars, and never saw any set of eyes reflect back red.

Tookey didn't say anything.

About fifteen minutes later, we came to a place where the snowbank on the right of the road wasn't so high because the plows are supposed to raise their blades a little when they go through an intersection.

"This looks like where we turned," Lumley said, not sounding too sure about it. "I don't see the sign—"

"This is it," Tookey answered. He didn't sound like himself at all. "You can just see the top of the signpost."

"Oh. Sure." Lumley sounded relieved. "Listen, Mr. Tooklander, I'm sorry about being so short back there. I was cold and worried and calling myself two hundred kinds of fool. And I want to thank you both—"

"Don't thank Booth and me until we've got them in this car," Tookey said. He put the Scout in four-wheel drive and slammed his way through the snowbank and onto Jointner Avenue, which goes through the Lot and out to 295. Snow flew up from the mudguards. The rear end tried to break a little bit, but Tookey's been driving through snow since Hector was a pup. He jockeyed it a bit, talked to it, and on we went. The headlights picked out the bare indication of other tire tracks from time to time, the ones made by Lumley's car, and then they would disappear again. Lumley was leaning forward, looking for his car. And all at once Tookey said, "Mr. Lumley."

"What?" He looked around at Tookey.

"People around these parts are kind of superstitious about 'Salem's Lot," Tookey says, sounding easy enough—but I could see the deep lines of strain around his mouth, and the way his eyes kept moving from side to side. "If your people are in the car, why, that's fine. We'll pack them up, go back to my place, and tomorrow, when the storm's over, Billy will be glad to yank your car out of the snowbank. But if they're not in the car—"

"Not in the car?" Lumley broke in sharply. "Why wouldn't they be in the car?"

"If they're not in the car," Tookey goes on, not answering, "we're going to turn around and drive back to Falmouth Center and whistle for the sheriff. Makes no sense to go wallowing around at night in a snowstorm anyway, does it?"

"They'll be in the car. Where else would they be?"

I said, "One other thing, Mr. Lumley. If we should see anybody, we're not going to talk to them. Not even if they talk to us. You understand that?"

Very slow, Lumley says, "Just what are these superstitions?"

Before I could say anything—God alone knows what I would have said—Tookey broke in. "We're there."

We were coming up on the back end of a big Mercedes. The whole hood of the thing was buried in a snowdrift, and another drift had socked in the whole left side of the car. But the taillights were on and we could see exhaust drifting out of the tailpipe.

"They didn't run out of gas, anyway," Lumley said.

Tookey pulled up and pulled on the Scout's emergency brake. "You remember what Booth told you, Lumley."

"Sure, sure." But he wasn't thinking of anything but his wife and daughter. I don't see how anybody could blame him, either.

"Ready, Booth?" Tookey asked me. His eyes held on mine, grim and gray in the dashboard lights.

"I guess I am," I said.

We all got out and the wind grabbed us, throwing snow in our faces. Lumley was first, bending into the wind, his fancy topcoat billowing out behind him like a sail. He cast two shadows, one from Tookey's headlights, the other from his own taillights. I was behind him, and Tookey was a step behind me. When I got to the trunk of the Mercedes, Tookey grabbed me.

"Let him go," he said.

"Janey! Francie!" Lumley yelled. "Everything okay?" He pulled open the driver's-side door and leaned in. "Everything—"

He froze to a dead stop. The wind ripped the heavy door right out of his hand and pushed it all the way open.

"Holy God, Booth," Tookey said, just below the scream of the wind. "I think it's happened again."

Lumley turned back toward us. His face was scared and bewildered, his eyes wide. All of a sudden he lunged toward us through the snow, slipping and almost falling. He brushed me away like I was nothing and grabbed Tookey.

"How did you know?" he roared. "Where are they? What the hell is going on here?"

Tookey broke his grip and shoved past him. He and I looked into the Mercedes together. Warm as toast it was, but it wasn't going to be for much longer. The little amber low-fuel light was glowing. The big car was empty. There was a child's Barbie doll on the passenger's floormat. And a child's ski parka was crumpled over the seatback.

Tookey put his hands over his face... and then he was gone. Lumley had grabbed him and shoved him right back into the snowbank. His face was pale and wild. His mouth was working as if he had chewed down on some bitter stuff he couldn't yet unpucker enough to spit out. He reached in and grabbed the parka.

"Francie's coat?" he kind of whispered. And then loud, bellowing: *"Francie's coat!"* He turned around, holding it in front of him by the little fur-trimmed hood. He looked at me, blank and unbelieving. "She can't be out without her coat on, Mr. Booth. Why... why... she'll freeze to death."

"Mr. Lumley—"

He blundered past me, still holding the parka, shouting: *"Francie! Janey! Where are you? Where are youuu?"*

I gave Tookey my hand and pulled him onto his feet. "Are you all—"

"Never mind me," he says. "We've got to get hold of him, Booth."

We went after him as fast as we could, which wasn't very fast with the snow hip-deep in some places. But then he stopped and we caught up to him.

"Mr. Lumley—" Tookey started, laying a hand on his shoulder.

"This way," Lumley said. "This is the way they went. Look!"

We looked down. We were in a kind of dip here, and most of the wind went right over our heads. And you could see two sets of tracks, one large and one small, just filling up with snow. If we had been five minutes later, they would have been gone.

He started to walk away, his head down, and Tookey grabbed him back. "No! No, Lumley!"

Lumley turned his wild face up to Tookey's and made a fist. He drew it back... but something in Tookey's face made him falter. He looked from Tookey to me and then back again.

"She'll freeze," he said, as if we were a couple of stupid kids. "Don't you get it? She doesn't have her jacket on and she's only seven years old—"

"They could be anywhere," Tookey said. "You can't follow those tracks. They'll be gone in the next drift."

"What do you suggest?" Lumley yells, his voice high and hysterical. "If we go back to get the police, she'll freeze to death! Francie *and* my wife!"

"They may be frozen already," Tookey said. His eyes caught Lumley's. "Frozen, or something worse."

"What do you mean?" Lumley whispered. "Get it straight, goddamn it! Tell me!"

"Mr. Lumley," Tookey says, "there's something in the Lot—"

But I was the one who came out with it finally, said the word I never expected to say. "Vampires, Mr. Lumley. Jerusalem's Lot is full of vampires. I expect that's hard for you to swallow—"

He was staring at me as if I'd gone green. "Loonies," he whispers. "You're a couple of loonies." Then he turned away, cupped his hands around his mouth, and bellowed, *"FRANCIE! JANEY!"* He started floundering off again. The snow was up to the hem of his fancy coat.

I looked at Tookey. "What do we do now?"

"Follow him," Tookey says. His hair was plastered with snow, and he *did* look a little bit loony. "I can't just leave him out here. Booth. Can you?"

"No," I says. "Guess not."

So we started to wade through the snow after Lumley as best we could. But he kept getting further and further ahead. He had his youth to spend, you see. He was breaking the trail, going through that snow like a bull. My arthritis began to bother me something terrible, and I started to look down at my legs, telling myself: A little further, just a little further, keep goin', damn it, keep goin'…

I piled right into Tookey, who was standing spread-legged in a drift. His head was hanging and both of his hands were pressed to his chest.

"Tookey," I says, "you okay?"

"I'm all right," he said, taking his hands away. "We'll stick with him, Booth, and when he fags out he'll see reason."

We topped a rise and there was Lumley at the bottom, looking desperately for more tracks. Poor man, there wasn't a chance he was going to find them. The wind blew straight across down there where he was, and any tracks would have been rubbed out three minutes after they was made, let alone a couple of hours.

He raised his head and screamed into the night: *"FRANCIE! JANEY! FOR GOD'S SAKE!"* And you could hear the desperation in his voice, the terror, and pity him for it. The only answer he got was the freight-train wail of the wind. It almost seemed to be laughin' at him, saying: *I took them Mister New Jersey with your fancy car and camel's-hair topcoat. I took them and I rubbed out their tracks and by morning I'll have them just as neat and frozen as two strawberries in a deepfreeze…*

"Lumley!" Tookey bawled over the wind. "Listen, you never mind vampires or boogies or nothing like that, but you mind this! You're just making it worse for them! We got to get the—"

And then there *was* an answer, a voice coming out of the dark like little tinkling silver bells, and my heart turned cold as ice in a cistern.

"Jerry... Jerry, is that you?"

Lumley wheeled at the sound. And then *she* came, drifting out of the dark shadows of a little copse of trees like a ghost.

She was a city woman, all right, and right then she seemed like the most beautiful woman I had ever seen. I felt like I wanted to go to her and tell her how glad I was she was safe after all. She was wearing a heavy green pullover sort of thing, a poncho, I believe they're called. It floated all around her, and her dark hair streamed out in the wild wind like water in a December creek, just before the winter freeze stills it and locks it in.

Maybe I did take a step toward her, because I felt Tookey's hand on my shoulder, rough and warm. And still—how can I say it?—I *yearned* after her, so dark and beautiful with that green poncho floating around her neck and shoulders, as exotic and strange as to make you think of some beautiful woman from a Walter de la Mare poem.

"Janey!" Lumley cried. *"Janey!"* He began to struggle through the snow toward her, his arms outstretched.

"No!" Tookey cried. *"No, Lumley!"*

He never even looked... but she did. She looked up at us and grinned. And when she did, I felt my longing, my yearning turn to horror as cold as the grave, as white and silent as bones in a shroud. Even from the rise we could see the sullen red glare in those eyes. They were less human than a wolf's eyes. And when she grinned you could see how long her teeth had become. She wasn't human anymore. She was a dead thing somehow come back to life in this black howling storm.

Tookey made the sign of the cross at her. She flinched back... and then grinned at us again. We were too far away, and maybe too scared.

"Stop it!" I whispered. "Can't we stop it?"

"Too late, Booth!" Tookey says grimly.

Lumley had reached her. He looked like a ghost himself, coated in snow like he was. He reached for her... and then he began to scream. I'll hear that sound in my dreams, that man screaming like a child in a nightmare. He tried to back away from her, but her arms, long and bare and as white as the snow, snaked out and pulled him to her. I could see her cock her head and then thrust it forward—

"Booth!" Tookey said hoarsely. "We've got to get out of here!"

And so we ran. Ran like rats, I suppose some would say, but those who would weren't there that night. We fled back down along our own backtrail, falling down, getting up again, slipping and sliding. I kept looking back over my shoulder to see if that woman was coming after us, grinning that grin and watching us with those red eyes.

We got back to the Scout and Tookey doubled over, holding his chest. "Tookey!" I said, badly scared. "What—"

"Ticker," he said. "Been bad for five years or more. Get me around in the shotgun seat, Booth, and then get us the hell out of here."

I hooked an arm under his coat and dragged him around and somehow boosted him up and in. He leaned his head back and shut his eyes. His skin was waxy-looking and yellow.

I went back around the hood of the truck at a trot, and I damned near ran into the little girl. She was just standing there beside the driver's-side door, her hair in pigtails, wearing nothing but a little bit of a yellow dress.

"Mister," she said in a high, clear voice, as sweet as morning mist, "won't you help me find my mother? She's gone and I'm so cold—"

"Honey," I said, "honey, you better get in the truck. Your mother's—"

I broke off, and if there was ever a time in my life I was close to swooning, that was the moment. She was standing there, you see, but she was standing *on top* of the snow and there were no tracks, not in any direction.

She looked up at me then, Lumley's daughter Francie. She was no more than seven years old, and she was going to be seven for an eternity of nights. Her little face was a ghastly corpse white, her eyes a red and silver that you could fall into. And below her jaw I could see two small punctures like pinpricks, their edges horribly mangled.

She held out her arms at me and smiled. "Pick me up, mister," she said softly. "I want to give you a kiss. Then you can take me to my mommy."

I didn't want to, but there was nothing I could do. I was leaning forward, my arms outstretched. I could see her mouth opening, I could see the little fangs inside the pink ring of her lips. Something slipped down her chin, bright and silvery, and with a dim, distant, faraway horror, I realized she was drooling.

Her small hands clasped themselves around my neck and I was thinking: Well, maybe it won't be so bad, not so bad, maybe it won't be so awful after a while—when something black flew out of the Scout and struck her on the chest. There was a puff of strange-smelling smoke, a flashing glow that was gone an instant later, and then she was backing away, hissing. Her face was twisted into a vulpine mask of rage, hate, and pain. She turned sideways and then... and then she was gone. One moment she was there, and the next there was a twisting knot of snow that looked a little bit like a human shape. Then the wind tattered it away across the fields.

"Booth!" Tookey whispered. "Be quick, now!" And I was. But not so quick that I didn't have time to pick up what he had thrown at that little girl from hell. His mother's Douay Bible.

That was some time ago. I'm a sight older now, and I was no chicken then. Herb Tooklander passed on two years ago. He went peaceful, in the night. The bar is still there, some man and his wife from Waterville bought it, nice people, and they've kept it pretty much the same. But I don't go by much. It's different somehow with Tookey gone.

Things in the Lot go on pretty much as they always have. The sheriff found that fellow Lumley's car the next day, out of gas, the battery dead. Neither Tookey nor I said anything about it. What would have been the point? And every now and then a hitchhiker or a camper will disappear around there someplace, up on Schoolyard Hill or out near the Harmony Hill cemetery. They'll turn up the fellow's packsack or a paperback book all swollen and bleached out by the rain or snow, or some such. But never the people.

I still have bad dreams about that stormy night we went out there. Not about the woman so much as the little girl, and the way she smiled when she held her arms up so I could pick her up. So she could give me a kiss. But I'm an old man and the time comes soon when dreams are done.

You may have an occasion to be traveling in southern Maine yourself one of these days. Pretty part of the countryside. You may even stop by Tookey's Bar for a drink. Nice place. They kept the name just the same. So have your drink, and then my advice to you is to keep right on moving north. Whatever you do, don't go up that road to Jerusalem's Lot.

Especially not after dark.

There's a little girl somewhere out there. And I think she's still waiting for her good-night kiss.

FOR FURTHER READING

compiled by Ross E. Lockhart

What follows is a selected bibliography of vampire fiction. This list focuses primarily on vampires in fantasy, science fiction, and horror novels published within the last thirty years or so, and largely ignores young adult, tie-in (*Buffy, Angel*, etc.), romance, and erotica titles, although some crossover is inevitable. This list also looks beyond the obvious origins of the vampire genre; if you're not already intimately familiar with John William Polidori's Lord Ruthven (*The Vampyre*, 1819), Sheridan Le Fanu's Carmilla (*Carmilla*, 1872), or Bram Stoker's Dracula (*Dracula*, 1897), then start there. Titles noteworthy for their high literary value are marked with an asterisk.

To learn more about the stories in *By Blood We Live*, visit the anthology's website at johnjosephadams.com/by-blood-we-live.

Acevedo, Mario
—*The Nymphos of Rocky Flats* (et seq.)
Aldiss, Brian W.
—*Dracula Unbound*
Altman, Steven Elliot
—*Zen in the Art of Slaying Vampires*
Andersson, C. Dean
—*I Am Dracula*
Armstrong, F. W.
—*Devouring*
Armstrong, Kelley
—*Bitten* (Women of the Otherworld) (et seq.)
Arthur, Keri
—*Full Moon Rising* (et seq.)
Aycliffe, Jonathan
—*The Lost*
Baker, Scott
—*Ancestral Hungers*
—*Dhampire*

Banks, L. A.
—*Minion* (The Vampire Huntress Legend) (et seq.)
Barbeau, Adrienne and Michael Scott
—*Vampyres of Hollywood*
Bellamy, Dodie
—*The Letters of Mina Harker*
Bennett, Nigel and P. N. Elrod
—*His Father's Son*
Bergstrom, Elaine
—*Shattered Glass* (et seq.)
—*Mina* (as Marie Kiraly)
—*Blood to Blood: The Dracula Story* (as Marie Kiraly)
Bishop, David
—*Operation Vampyr* (et seq.)
Bledsoe, Alex
—*Blood Groove*
Bodner, Hal
—*Bite Club*

ACKNOWLEDGMENTS

Many thanks to the following:

Jeremy Lassen and Jason Williams at Night Shade Books, for letting me edit all these anthologies and for doing such a kick-ass job publishing them. Also, to Ross Lockhart at Night Shade for all that he does behind-the-scenes, and to Marty Halpern for catching all my tyops.

David Palumbo, for another amazing cover. I fear I'm being spoiled.

Gordon Van Gelder: he gave me my start in the business, so if we were vampires, I guess that would make him my sire or master. Or something. Too bad this editing gig doesn't come with eternal life. On the plus side, it hasn't turned me into a living corpse.

My agent Jenny Rappaport, who exsanguinates me of 15% of my earnings but helps grant me (literary) immortality.

Rebecca McNulty, for helping me sort through tome after tome of vampire fiction and for providing me a highly valuable second opinion when needed.

David Barr Kirtley for helping me kill those header note demons. Visit his website at www.davidbarrkirtley.com and read some of his fabulous stories, why don't you.

Kris Dikeman, Jordan Hamessley, and Jeremiah Tolbert for various kinds of behind-the-scenes assistance.

My mom, for keeping me away from bloodsuckers when I was young.

All of the other kindly folks who assisted me in some way during the editorial process: Manie Barron, Deborah Beale, Blake Charlton, Mickey Choate, Douglas E. Cohen, Ellen Datlow, Gary A. Emenitove, Jennifer Escott, Amelia Greene, Elizabeth Harding, Merrilee Heifetz, Del Howison, Jay Lake, Paul Lucas, Gail Martin, Henry Morrison, James Morrow, Allison Rich, Irina Roberts, Betty Russo, Bill Schafer, Darrell Schweitzer, Steven Silver, Kevin Standlee, Jonathan Strahan, Charles A. Tan, everyone who dropped suggestions into my vampire fiction database, and to everyone else who helped out in some way that I neglected to mention (and to you folks, I apologize!).

The NYC Geek Posse—consisting of Robert Bland, Christopher M. Cevasco, (Doug Cohen and Jordan Hamessley belong here too, but I thanked them above, and once is enough, isn't it?), Andrea Kail, David Barr Kirtley, and Matt London, among others (i.e., the NYCGP Auxiliary)—for giving me an excuse to come out of my editorial cave once in a while.

The readers and reviewers who loved my other anthologies, making it possible for me to do more.

And last, but certainly not least: a big thanks to all of the authors who appear in this anthology.

ACKNOWLEDGMENT IS MADE FOR PERMISSION TO PRINT THE FOLLOWING MATERIAL:

"Much at Stake" by Kevin J. Anderson. © 1991 Kevin J. Anderson. Originally published in *The Ultimate Dracula*. Reprinted by permission of the author.

"Twilight" by Kelley Armstrong. ©2007 Kelly Armstrong. Originally published in *Many Bloody Returns*. Reprinted by permission of the author.

"Finders Keepers" by L. A. Banks. © 2008 L. A. Banks. Originally published as an e-book from Red Rose Publishing. Reprinted by permission of the author.

"House of the Rising Sun" by Elizabeth Bear. © 2005 Elizabeth Bear. Originally published in *The Third Alternative*. Reprinted by permission of the author.

"Lifeblood" by Michael A. Burstein. © 2003 Michael A. Burstein. Originally published in *New Voices in Science Fiction*. Reprinted by permission of the author.

"Lucy, in Her Splendor" by Charles Coleman Finlay. © 2003 Charles Coleman Finlay. Originally published in *Mars Dust*. Reprinted by permission of the author.

"Snow, Glass, Apples" by Neil Gaiman. © 1994 Neil Gaiman. Originally published as a chapbook from DreamHaven Press. Reprinted by permission of the author.

"Sunrise on Running Water" by Barbara Hambly. © 2007 Barbara Hambly. Originally published in *Dark Delicacies II*. Reprinted by permission of the author.

"Abraham's Boys" by Joe Hill. © 2004 Joe Hill. Originally published in *The Many Faces of Van Helsing*, and also in *20th Century Ghosts*, copyright © 2005, 2007 by Joe Hill, published by William Morrow, an imprint of HarperCollins Publishers. Reprinted by permission of the author.

"Blood Gothic" by Nancy Holder. © 1985 Nancy Holder. Originally published in *Shadows 8*. Reprinted by permission of the author.

"Ode to Edvard Munch" by Caitlín R. Kiernan. © 2006 Caitlín R. Kiernan. Originally published in *Sirenia Digest*. Reprinted by permission of the author.

"The Vechi Barbat" by Nancy Kilpatrick. © 2007 Nancy Kilpatrick. Originally published in *Travellers in Darkness*. Reprinted by permission of the author.

"One for the Road" by Stephen King. © 1977 Stephen King. Originally published in *Maine magazine*, March/April 1977. Reprinted by permission of the author.

Night Shade Books Is an Independent Publisher of Quality SF, Fantasy and Horror

FEATURING STORIES BY
JOAN AIKEN
PAOLO BACIGALUPI
STEPHEN BAXTER
PETER S. BEAGLE
ELIZABETH BEAR
HOLLY BLACK
TED CHIANG
GREG EGAN
KIJ JOHNSON
STEPHEN KING
MARGO LANAGAN
KELLY LINK
MICHAEL SWANWICK
AND MANY OTHERS

THE BEST
SCIENCE FICTION
AND FANTASY
OF THE YEAR
VOLUME THREE

EDITED BY JONATHAN STRAHAN

ISBN 978-1-59780-149-2, Trade Paperback; $19.95

An alien world with an argon atmosphere serves as the stage for the ultimate self-examination; an African-American scientist dissects a Lovecraftian slave race while fascism rears its head on the other side of the world; an elderly Jewish artist attracts a celestial muse; a doomed village of scavengers discovers the scattered pieces of a metal man; a stalwart reporter gambles on an interview with the power to alter the world; a steel monkey defends a young girl from a rival family's assassins; two girls discover that the cruel social rituals of adolescence apply differently in fact than fiction...

The depth and breadth of science fiction and fantasy fiction continues to change with every passing year. The twenty-eight stories chosen for this book by award-winning anthologist Jonathan Strahan carefully map this evolution, giving readers a captivating and always-entertaining look at the very best the genre has to offer.

Night Shade Books Is an Independent Publisher of Quality SF, Fantasy and Horror

THE IMPROBABLE ADVENTURES OF

SHERLOCK HOLMES

FEATURING STORIES BY

STEPHEN BAXTER	TANITH LEE
ANTHONY BURGESS	SHARYN MCCRUMB
NEIL GAIMAN	MICHAEL MOORCOCK
STEPHEN KING	NAOMI NOVIK
LAURIE R. KING	ANNE PERRY

AND MANY OTHERS

Edited by John Joseph Adams

ISBN 978-1-59780-160-7, Trade Paperback; $15.95

Sherlock Holmes is back! These are the improbable adventures of Sherlock Holmes, where nothing is impossible, and nothing can be ruled out. In these cases, Holmes investigates ghosts, curses, aliens, dinosaurs, shapeshifters, and evil gods. But is it the supernatural, or is there a perfectly rational explanation?

In these pages you'll also find our heroes crossing paths with H. G. Wells, Lewis Carroll, and even Arthur Conan Doyle himself, and you'll be astounded to learn the truth behind cases previously alluded to by Watson but never before documented until now. Here are some of the best Holmes pastiches of the last 30 years, twenty-eight tales of mystery and the imagination detailing Holmes's further exploits, as told by many of today's greatest storytellers, including Stephen King, Anne Perry, Anthony Burgess, Neil Gaiman, Stephen Baxter, Tanith Lee, Michael Moorcock, and many more. The game is afoot!

Night Shade Books Is an Independent Publisher of Quality SF, Fantasy and Horror

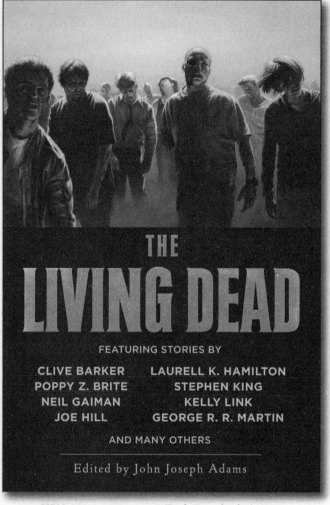

THE LIVING DEAD

FEATURING STORIES BY

CLIVE BARKER   LAURELL K. HAMILTON
POPPY Z. BRITE   STEPHEN KING
NEIL GAIMAN   KELLY LINK
JOE HILL   GEORGE R. R. MARTIN

AND MANY OTHERS

Edited by John Joseph Adams

ISBN 978-1-59780-143-0, Trade Paperback; $15.95

From *White Zombie* to *Dawn of the Dead*; from *Resident Evil* to *World War Z*, zombies have invaded popular culture, becoming the monsters that best express the fears and anxieties of the modern west.

Gathering together the best zombie literature of the last three decades from many of today's most renowned authors of fantasy, speculative fiction, and horror, *The Living Dead* covers the broad spectrum of zombie fiction; from Romero-style zombies to reanimated corpses to voodoo zombies and beyond.

"When there's no more room in hell, the dead will walk the earth."

Night Shade Books Is an Independent Publisher of Quality SF, Fantasy and Horror

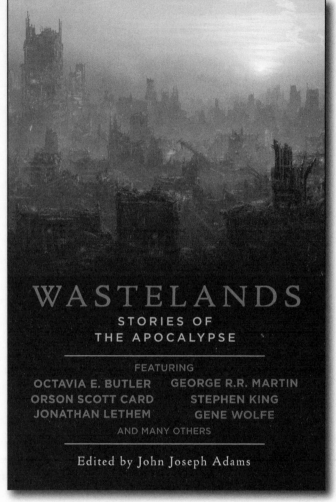

WASTELANDS

STORIES OF
THE APOCALYPSE

FEATURING

OCTAVIA E. BUTLER   GEORGE R.R. MARTIN
ORSON SCOTT CARD   STEPHEN KING
JONATHAN LETHEM   GENE WOLFE

AND MANY OTHERS

Edited by John Joseph Adams

ISBN 978-1-59780-105-8, Trade Paperback; $15.95

Famine, Death, War, and Pestilence: The Four Horsemen of the Apocalypse, the harbingers of Armageddon - these are our guides through the Wastelands.

Gathering together the best post-apocalyptic literature of the last two decades from many of today's most renowned authors of speculative fiction, including George R.R. Martin, Gene Wolfe, Orson Scott Card, Carol Emshwiller, Jonathan Lethem, Octavia E. Butler, and Stephen King, Wastelands explores the scientific, psychological, and philosophical questions of what it means to remain human in the wake of Armageddon. Whether the end of the world comes through nuclear war, ecological disaster, or cosmological cataclysm, these are tales of survivors, in some cases struggling to rebuild the society that was, in others, merely surviving, scrounging for food in depopulated ruins and defending themselves against monsters, mutants, and marauders.

John Joseph Adams is the editor of the anthologies *By Blood We Live, Federations, The Living Dead, Seeds of Change,* and *Wastelands: Stories of the Apocalypse.* Forthcoming work includes the anthologies *Brave New Worlds, The Improbable Adventures of Sherlock Holmes, The Living Dead 2, The Mad Scientist's Guide to World Domination,* and *The Way of the Wizard.* He is also the assistant editor at *The Magazine of Fantasy & Science Fiction.*

He is a columnist for *Tor.com* and has written reviews for *Kirkus Reviews, Publishers Weekly,* and *Orson Scott Card's Intergalactic Medicine Show.* His non-fiction has also appeared in: *Amazing Stories, The Internet Review of Science Fiction, Locus Magazine, Novel & Short Story Writers Market, Science Fiction Weekly, SCI FI Wire, Shimmer, Strange Horizons, Subterranean Magazine,* and *Writer's Digest.*

He received his Bachelor of Arts degree in English from The University of Central Florida in December 2000. He currently lives in New Jersey. For more information, visit his website at www.johnjosephadams.com.